Praise for William Trotter's Civil War novels, *The Sands of Pride* and *The Fires of Pride:*

"A grand triumph of the American imagination."

—Fred Chappell, Poet Laureate of North Carolina

"A spellbinding historical novel and a compelling work of serious literary fiction."

—Howard Frank Mosher, author of *Disappearances*

"A grand, opulent epic."

—Carolyn Kizer, Pulitzer Prize–winning poet

"Infinitely more readable than and interesting than . . . *Cold Mountain.*"

—*Civil War News*

"A masterful epic . . . [A] combination of superb research, compelling characters, and dry wit [will] enthrall readers."

—*Publishers Weekly* (starred review)

"A magnificent Civil War novel, epic in proportion and sweeping in its treatment. . . . Enchanting and hard to put down."

—*BookPage*

"A compelling and spellbinding work of historical fiction. . . . A great book."

—Barry Johnson of Books at Stonehenge,
designating *Sands of Pride* a Book Sense pick

"A sequel as splendid as its predecessor. . . . The same combination of superb research, compelling characters and dry wit that enthralled readers of previous installments will do so again."

—*Publishers Weekly* (starred review)

Warrener's Beastie

William R. Trotter

CARROLL & GRAF PUBLISHERS
NEW YORK

WARRENER'S BEASTIE

Carroll & Graf Publishers
An Imprint of Avalon Publishing Group, Inc.
245 West 17th Street
11th Floor
New York, NY 10011

AVALON
publishing group incorporated

Copyright © 2006 by William R. Trotter

First Carroll & Graf edition 2006

Library of Congress Cataloging-in-Publication Data is available.

ISBN-13: 978-0-78671-328-8
ISBN-10: 0-78671-328-3

9 8 7 6 5 4 3 2 1

Book design by Susan Canavan

Printed in the United States of America
Distributed by Publishers Group West

To my beloved son
Michael Scott Trotter
On the occasion of
His 18th birthday

CONTENTS

BOOK III: VOYAGES

Book IV: Petroglyphs

Warrener's Beastie

Book I:

INTIMATIONS

We know we are supposed to believe in it, but still we doubt. Can there really be a 60-foot-long creature with unblinking dinner-plate eyes in the unknown vastness of the icy depths? The existence of *Architeuthis* only confirms our fears and inadequacies; despite our puny efforts to capture or understand it, the monster perdures. What will happen if someone finds it and takes its picture? It will lose some of its mystery, and, in a sense, we will be poorer for having been deprived of the anticipation of finding it. Often the realization of a long-held goal proves less fulfilling than the hungry waiting. . . . We need to find the giant squid, but we also need not to find it.

—Richard Ellis, *The Search for the Giant Squid*

1.

The Wonders of *Earth, Sea, and Sky*

"Grandma, what's a 'floozy'?"

Mrs. Warrener's hand froze on the wad of dough she was shaping for biscuits, her parchment-fine complexion taking on a pink color that reminded Allen Warrener of mimosa blossoms.

"Where did you hear that word?"

"My friend Johnny Johnson's mom was talking on the phone, and she said my mother was one. She didn't know I was listening, I guess. *Was* my mother a floozy, Grandma, and how bad is that?"

Mrs. Warrener dusted the flour from her hands, poured Allen a glass of lemonade, and asked him to sit down at the kitchen table for a Serious Conversation.

"I can't ask you to forget or forgive your mother, Allen; but I can try to help you understand her. She was one of those women who can cast a spell over any man she sets her sights on, cause him to see 'qualities' in her that aren't really a part of her true nature. But she was also raised very strictly, to be a pious, God-fearing woman, and I'm certain to this day that your father was the first man she ever . . . um, *knew*."

Allen thought that was a puzzling remark—surely his mother had "known" lots of guys when she was growing up. She'd been a cheerleader, after all, and won a local beauty pageant when she and Bill Warrener were "courting," as Grandma called it—a slightly archaic term that Allen vaguely associated with medieval knights. But he kept silent, knowing his grandmother was about to tell him something important.

"Try to understand: when someone you love dies before his time, something inside you dies too: your future. Everything your mom planned and dreamed about, those things were all based on her belief that your dad would come home soon. Being a very religious woman, she had prayed hard, every day, for him to survive the war and come back to her. Unfortunately, like so many deeply religious persons, she made the mistake of thinking that, just because she was always praying to God, that God was always listening.

"Your mother didn't receive the telegram about Bill's death until three days after the war in Europe ended. She'd assumed he was fine, and would be coming home soon, and together they could get started on that rosy, comfortable future she had all planned out in her head. Then the doorbell rang one day, and that future just crumbled into dust. Your mother's faith was intense, but it was also very brittle. All that had supported her, while Bill was overseas, was her certainty that *her* prayers were special; that God wouldn't let any harm come to *her* man, and that the other women she knew whose husbands and boyfriends had been killed, well, that was because their prayers just weren't strong enough. That's a silly, rather pathetic notion—it makes you weak and vulnerable. She became angry at God—and that's even sillier and more pointless.

"After she learned of Bill's death, her future was just a dark, lonely, scary place, a place she didn't want to go. So she . . . ran away from it. I think she really wanted to start a new life, find something or someone else to fill that emptiness; but like so many people who put *everything* 'in God's hands,' she didn't have what your grandfather would call a 'fallback position,' another strategy for getting on with her life. She went out West to try and start over, try to find something that would take the place of her lost faith, but it's not so easy to do that. I guess, after a while, she stopped trying. I think she still loves you, Allen—you're her only child, and no mother can just turn off her love as though it were a light switch. But she's become . . . someone she doesn't want you to know. We've heard things . . . well, let that pass. The General and I will do our best to raise you right, the way your father would have done if he'd come home."

Allen sipped his lemonade, a precociously thoughtful expression on his five-year-old face.

"Does Johnny's mother hate my mom?"

"Don't you pay any mind to Marva Johnson when she badmouths your mom! Mrs. Johnson is one of those women who have to feel superior to somebody else, because it gives her an excuse not to examine her own shortcomings." Grandma Warrener sniffed disdainfully. "Which are considerable, I might add. . . ."

From that day forward, whenever Allen Warrener sensed that any of his friends' parents were looking at him with pity, or perhaps examining him for any character taint he might have inherited from his discredited mother, he reacted by squaring his shoulders and walking a little taller in their presence.

In 1944, at the age of thirteen months, Allen Warrener saw his father for the first and only time. The acquaintance lasted for the three weeks of his father's furlough; and in later years, when gazing intently at the surviving snapshots, Allen could not summon even the faintest residual memory of the experience. His father was killed by a mortar round in the fighting around Koblenz, in the last spring of the war, when the Reich was falling apart and his mother had already started anticipating his return. The timing of his death opened a wound in her that never healed.

Three months after Allen's third birthday, she took him to live with his grandparents in the postwar-booming town of Charlotte, North Carolina. Her story was that she had a "line" on a very good job in Los Angeles. She promised that she would send for the boy as soon as she was "established." She never did. Her last postcard came on his fourth birthday and mentioned nothing about "sending for him." One year later, his grandfather, retired Major General Norman Warrener, took down all of her photographs and moved them permanently into the attic. He left on the mantel one carefully selected photograph of Allen's father, Captain William Warrener: a ruggedly handsome brown-eyed man with curly hair, looking very relaxed yet soldierly in his Eisenhower jacket, binoculars draped around his neck and an M-1 carbine slung over his right shoulder.

Around that image, above the mantel and on both sides of it, like a constellation of bright and varied stars, were the historical images of the ancestors who had answered the call of duty and served in America's wars. General Warrener referred to that display, quite seriously, as "The Wall of Honor," and by the time he was old enough to read about the campaigns in which they had fought, Allen knew each of those men well and could recite, like a catechism, the roster of their deeds: one had fought with Gates at Camden and later with Nathaniel Greene at Guilford Court House; that man's son, represented by a rather anonymous woodcut, had served on General Scott's staff at the Battles of Chippewa and Lundy's Lane; next, in chronological order, came a veritable phalanx of Confederate stalwarts, ranging in rank from corporal to colonel—fierce-eyed men with biblical beards, brandishing for the camera a bloodthirsty assortment of sabers, horse-pistols, and muskets; half of them never returned.

But Allen's favorite image was a faded sepia-toned photo of his grandfather, Norman Warrener, with the shiny bars of a newly minted second lieutenant on his shoulder-straps and a dashing, broad-brimmed campaign hat pulled down at a rakish angle over his broad, intelligent forehead. He was riding in column just behind Black Jack Pershing, during the Pancho Villa Expedition, and his eyes were hard-set against the scorch and vastness of the Sierra Madre Mountains. Young Lieutenant Warrener looked comfortable in the saddle, with a big Springfield in a leather boot at his side and a piratical bandolier of bullets across his chest.

Not until Allen was seven, and judged old enough to comprehend the significance of the story, did The General invite the boy into his study, to tell him, formally, about Bill Warrener's deeds:

"Your father was a master sergeant in the quartermaster corps, so he rarely got close to the front lines. He wanted to see some action—he often spoke of that, in his letters to me—but he knew your mother would be very upset if he put in for transfer to a line unit. Except for some random German shelling, he was never really under fire until December of 'forty-four, when Hitler launched his surprise offensive through the Ardennes Forest. At that time, your dad was commanding a supply depot in a small Belgian market town. It was a pretty insignificant place, except for the fact that two paved roads intersected in the middle of town—and the Germans needed those roads in order to keep up the momentum of their attack. They assigned one of their best units, the Ninth SS Panzer Division, to seize that village, and their timetable called for it to be securely in German hands by the end of December seventeenth, the second day of the offensive.

"Bill knew there was a crisis brewing when he saw hundreds of American infantry streaming to the rear at twilight on the sixteenth—scared young replacements who'd been sent to the Ardennes sector because it was considered a 'quiet' sector, where they could get used to soldiering without too much risk. Those young men had never faced tanks before, never even been trained how to fight 'em; when they suddenly faced a tidal wave of panzers, it was terrifying; most of them panicked and ran away, not because they were cowards but because their leaders hadn't prepared them for the shock of a panzer attack.

"Bill Warrener hadn't been trained to fight panzers either; he'd barely been taught how to shoot his M-1, and he hadn't fired it since boot camp. But he could read a map, and it was clear as daylight to him why the Germans wanted his village, and why it was critical to stop them from taking it. Bill took command because no one else had the guts or the foresight to do it.

"He collared some of the men who were retreating and shamed them into staying and helping to defend the town. And he rounded up a ragtag battle group of 340 GIs: supply clerks and typists, radio repairmen, mechanics, medics, even a squad of veterinarians, and he broke into the supply stocks and passed out rifles and grenades to every man who didn't have a weapon; he uncrated a half-dozen bazookas and asked for volunteers to teach themselves how to fire the weapons. And all the vehicles that came through town mounting a machine gun or towing a trailer with ammo and spare parts, he stopped them too, and had the weapons dismounted and dug in around the defensive perimeter his men were throwing up. He cajoled some panicky engineers into planting minefields and burying barbed wire under the snow in the surrounding woods, so the German infantry couldn't outflank his position. By the time the enemy tanks appeared, at dawn on the seventeenth, Bill Warrener had turned that little Belgian town into a fortress.

"The Germans came right at the place, not expecting any resistance, and ran into a buzz saw; the after-action report said Bill's 'Battling Bastards' killed sixty SS troopers, destroyed two Mark IV tanks and three armored cars, and stopped that first attack cold. So the Germans fell back and regrouped, now aware that they'd lost the chance to seize that crossroads without a serious fight. When they attacked the second time, they led off with two Panther tanks—but Bill stopped one of them by sneaking around behind it, where the armor wasn't so thick, and slamming six bazooka rockets into the engine and the back of the turret.

"By the end of the day, the Germans had lost eight armored vehicles and suffered 130 casualties trying to overrun the town. The unexpected resistance had already ruined their timetable, so their high command decided to bypass the village altogether, surround it, and lay siege to it with artillery and a whole battalion of veteran SS infantry. Well, Bill's men *became veterans* very fast, either that or they died early in the battle. More than four thousand rounds of artillery and mortar fire landed inside his lines, pretty much leveling the village. And after every barrage, the Krauts sent their infantry in to finish the job. But for four days and nights, Bill's little battle group threw back every attack.

"When the forward elements of Patton's Third Army broke the siege, on the afternoon of December twenty-fourth, Bill had seventy-three men still standing, but there were more than six hundred dead SS troopers lying in the snow all around his lines. George Patton himself drove into town on Christmas Day, to congratulate your father on his 'magnificent stand,' to write him up for the Distinguished Service Cross, and to give him a battle-field promotion, to first lieutenant, on the spot.

"Bill never got the damned medal—the paperwork got lost, or Patton, the crazy bastard, forgot to sign the commendation, who knows? The important thing is that your dad discovered, at a moment when hundreds of other officers and noncoms were running away from the enemy, that he had a rare and powerful gift for leading men in battle. Regardless of your mother's anxiety, he transferred to a line outfit, led an infantry platoon with great skill and courage, and had just been promoted to captain the week before he was killed. Last letter I got from him, he'd decided to make the Army his career. Needless to say, I was, and still am, very proud of him.

"And you should always be proud of him, too."

Allen Warrener stared at the photo of his father with new understanding and no small sense of awe.

"My dad was a real hero?"

"Yes, he was. Even George Patton thought he was a hero, and that psychotic loon didn't toss the word 'hero' around lightly."

"Then I want to be a hero too, when I grow up."

"First things first, boy. If you want to join one of the services, that's fine; you know I'll support you. But not many men get the chance to be heroes; and, really, not many heroes are needed. You'd be wise not to set out to become one—in my experience, the men who start their careers with that goal in mind . . . well, they usually don't live long enough to reach it. And they usually irritate the hell out of the other men they serve with."

"Then I'll be like you, Grandfather!"

"Instead of being a hero? Thanks, kid!" But the old soldier was laughing, not scowling. "I'd be honored to serve as your role model. Meanwhile, I'll try my damnedest to be a decent father to you. And believe me, that's as hard a job as leading a battalion into combat!"

The General tried to be there for Allen, but it was difficult sometimes, because at the age of sixty-one, Norman Warrener had begun a new career, investing heavily in a new technology called "television." This proved to be the shrewdest non-military move he ever made. In 1948, he opened Charlotte's first commercial station, and five years later he owned a chain of broadcasting outlets that covered the southeast, from Raleigh all the way to his home town of Savannah. He became a very wealthy man, and when Allen was six, the family moved into a large, white-columned residence on Selwyn Avenue. The half-acre lot included a rambling back yard which seemed to Allen as vast as a prairie. The General constructed a sandbox big enough to become a major attraction for all the neighborhood kids; and it was there that Allen deployed his army of toy soldiers, building fortified lines and bridges and elaborate pillboxes, mostly from the construction medium of choice: Popsicle sticks. Sometimes the General came into the back yard and very earnestly suggested ways to improve the front line or refuse a flank, and Allen soaked up this knowledge like a sponge. The General's advice was always sound and professional: "Why is your supply dump way over there, Allen?"

"So I'll have room to dig in my artillery closer to my headquarters."

"Yet by doing so, you've made it easier for enemy armor to punch a hole in your left and attack your source of supply."

"Aw, Grandpa, it's just supplies! They're no fun to play with!"

"Try fighting a battle without 'em and see how long your brave lads can hold out! You've got a sense of tactics that's downright spooky for a kid; but, like too many commanders, you've neglected to protect your source of supply. Try to remember what Napoleon once said: 'Amateurs talk about tactics, but professionals talk about logistics!' "

"Yessir!"

From this pervasive but casually martial environment Allen Warrener absorbed the simplistic, unquestioning patriotism of the early fifties. He was one of the few students in his elementary school who took seriously the weekly "duck and cover" air raid drills, which General Warrener declared "would be as effective a measure of protection against a nuclear blast as a piece of Kleenex!" Communism was evil, and America was noble and good; stark certainties, but the evidence seemed irrefutable to him.

Like many an only child, Allen became a precocious reader, and the General's extensive library was his for the browsing. "Intellectual curiosity," the General averred, "is one of the qualities that marks a great commander. If you do go into the Army, Allen, you will find many men who have ignored that aspect of their training, and they may be prejudiced against you. Don't antagonize them, but don't listen to them, either. They will forever remain mediocre officers, and in some part of their minds, they know it. So never show off your intellectual attainments around them, because it'll bring out the 'nasty' in their personalities."

At the age of eight, Allen began to suffer from chronic asthma and was forced to spend many days at home, closeted in a dust-free room with a sputtering glass-kettle vaporizer. On doctor's orders, he was allowed out of his medicated cell only for meals and for brief forays into the library for more reading matter. He worked his way methodically through the General's collection of military classics, finding von Clausewitz to be a stuffy German pedant, Julius Caesar a master of coy self-glorification, and Sun Tzu to be a master of the obvious—vastly overrated, he thought, and if he hadn't been an ancient Chinese "sage," nobody would make such a fuss over his platitudes!

By age twelve, his respiratory attacks became less frequent, thanks in part to the hormonal onslaught of puberty. But the affliction didn't vanish overnight, and, as it happened, his last severe attack was a real punisher. He awoke one bright spring morning with a tight chest and a reverberant wheeze. His grandmother dutifully filled the vaporizer with its noxious elixirs, admonished him to stay within the ambit of its vapors, and then left to do the weekly shopping. Allen had endured this routine for so many years, patiently, stoically, that at first he complied meekly. But outside his window, the yard was frothy with blooming crepe myrtle and the sandbox looked mighty inviting. Worst of all, he had read everything in the library that interested him. In so vast a house, he reasoned, there must be *one* bookcase he had not yet explored. As soon as he heard Grandma drive away, he sprang out of bed and went on a methodical search for Something To Read. And in an old glassed-in bookcase in a dark corner of his grandfather's study, he found it.

On the bottom shelf were a number of very old-looking oversize volumes,

which, because of their unusual size, had been stacked flat rather than vertically, with their spines turned inward and their titles consequently not visible. He had never been curious about these volumes before, but he was
desperate for something new to read. The first volume he pulled out was not
encouraging: a history of the Georgia Presbyterian Church printed in dense,
eye-repellent type and illustrated with portraits of grim-faced men in funereal clothes. This was not the kind of book he was seeking.

Beneath it, however, was a massive volume bound in oxblood leather.
When he examined the spine and saw the bold, gilt-edged title, *Earth, Sea,
and Sky: A Compendium of Nature's Wonders*, he knew this was the book he'd
been seeking. He lifted it into full view and marveled at the craftsmanship
that had been lavished on its production: its endpapers were marbled in rippling whorls of umber, cream, and blue, and even though it had been published eighty-one years earlier, its pages were still supple and unfrayed.
When he carried it carefully into the sunlight, he felt as though the volume
had been waiting patiently for his discovery; he fancied that the book was
vibrating slightly in his hands, almost urging him to delve into its contents.

The moment Allen Warrener opened the pages of *Earth, Sea, and Sky*, he
fell under a spell that was every bit as compelling as his dreams of martial
glory. His sense of wonder, already ripe and poised on the cusp of adolescence, was enflamed by the list of captions for the lavish full-page engrav-
ings: *"Droll Antics of the Orang-Outang"* . . . *"Warrior Chieftains of New
Zealand Dressed in the Skins of the Apteryx"* . . . *"The Crocodile, Man-Eating
Terror of the Tropic Seas"* . . . *"Mountains of Fire and Caves of Ice."* . . . He
eagerly began reading the first chapter, "Early History of the Earth," and was
instantly captivated by the picture of a fearsome prehistoric reptile identified
as a *"Labyrinthodon."* He rolled the name over and over on his tongue,
savoring it.

Two hours later, his grandmother found him where he was not supposed
to be, and he jumped when she broke the spell by calling his name.

"Allen, those old books are full of dust—you shouldn't be handling them
in your condition."

"But Grandma, I'm not wheezing any more!"

Skeptical, she bent close to his chest. It was clear as a bell.

"Lord be praised, I guess that book must be good medicine! Come have
some lunch; then you can get back to it if you like."

"It's the most wonderful book I've ever read. I'm going to spend all day with it."

—*Monstrous Reptiles of the Equatorial Jungle . . . The Perils of Walrus Hunting . . . Encounters with Stupendous Whales . . . In the Jaws of the Hammerhead Shark*—

Twilight was gathering, and Allen's eyes ached from focusing on so much dense type. *One more chapter*, he thought. *I'll save the rest for another day.*

He turned the page . . .

—*"Monsters of the Great Deep"*—

. . . and plunged into a realm of dark and terrible wonders indeed. Waterspouts and tidal waves, narwhals and medusae—like living, drifting orchids whose casual touch could drive men mad with pain. And finally, the full-page engraving that changed his life:

"A Dreadful Encounter with the Giant Kraken!"

The artist had surpassed himself, conjuring the very essence of atavistic terror.

In the center of the illustration, a three-masted schooner in direst peril; forked lightning stabbed the black and churning horizon; waves rose in snarling, fanged peaks. The ship hung on a pedestal of seething foam, its sails torn to rags, helpless in the grip of tentacles a hundred feet long and thick as redwood trunks. They tapered from enormous muscular roots into serpentine, paddle-shaped tips, and the tips were tearing down the ship's rigging and spars and flinging terrified tars into the sea. Beneath the schooner's straining, creaking hull: an immense bulbous mass, sinewy and solid as tar. The artist had cunningly known that a menace half-glimpsed is more frightening than one that is fully seen, so he had only *suggested* the loathsome submerged body of the giant cuttlefish, blurring it under an eruption of foam. He had filled in just enough detail to evoke an apparition from the ultimate caverns of human nightmare—a great glistening malevolence heaving up from eternal night, big as a cruiser, alien as a thing that drifted between the stars, its enormous lidless nacreous eye contemplating the broken ship with a gaze as cold as a drowning moon.

Allen could not pull away from this terrifying image; it gripped him with fright, yet it also stimulated a delicious shudder of awe: he could almost *hear* the thunder, the howl of the wind, the awful snapping of spars and masts, the rubbery slopping sounds of tentacles tightening their grip on bulkhead and cabin, the puny and inconsequential shrieks of the doomed mariners. When Grandmother came to fetch him for supper, he showed her the illustration. She glanced at it briefly, then turned away in distaste.

"You'll get nightmares from looking at *that book*."

"No, I won't! I want to know if there really are monsters like this!"

"Ask your grandfather," she sniffed.

When Allen showed the picture to General Warrener after dinner, his grandfather smiled knowingly.

"Been wondering when you'd discover that book. It was my favorite—maybe still is. For His own inscrutable purposes, the Lord made many creatures that appear strange and terrible to us, but fortunately He had the good sense to place most of them in the hidden depths of the sea, so we and they would rarely meet. Isn't it marvelous to think that, even now, with all our sci ence, we've only explored a thousandth of the seas that cover so much of this planet?

"When I was not much older than you, I began pursuing a hobby: the study of elusive, mysterious creatures which may or may not exist . . . the fancy name is cryptozoology, which means, more or less, the study of critters that may-but-probably-don't-exist. The Loch Ness Monster, Bigfoot, the Abominable Snowman, the Jersey Devil . . . there are many more, but those are the perennials. Proper scientists scoff at the mavericks who actually research these things seriously, but then 'proper scientists' also used to laugh at colleagues who believed in the germ theory. Every year, we learn that the universe is vaster and stranger than we ever imagined. This planet of ours is still big enough to hide a few secrets . . . maybe a lot of secrets."

General Warrener tapped his finger on the engraving. "Now, you take this fellow, for instance, the giant squid—'kraken' is the Norwegian name for these things, I think, or maybe it's Danish; have to look that up. Anyway, we know it certainly exists. Every now and then, big pieces of dead ones wash ashore, but that evidence tends to rot pretty fast. There's never an ice truck around when you need one! More evidence? We've found the sucker marks from their tentacles on the skin of the great sperm whales, one of the few creatures that can dive down to where these monsters actually live. And if you extrapolate the size of the whole squid just from the size of those sucker marks, then we can say absolutely that there are krakens down there that measure eighty feet long. An eighty-foot-long squid is a monster in my book! And there's no inherent reason why they can't grow even bigger than that—a hundred feet, a hundred and fifty! We don't know how big they can get! They live at such extreme depths that we can't explore their habitat, at least not with the technology we have today. And thankfully, they seem rarely inclined to explore ours.

"Another interesting thing, Allen, is that these cephalopods—that's the fancy scientific name for the species—may be highly intelligent, although it's a kind of intelligence we would find very strange, like aliens from another planet. Their behavior seems to be almost rational. They're cold-blooded, of course, but that doesn't mean they don't feel rage, or fear, or other emotions more complex than blind hunger. Formidable creatures!"

The General hesitated a moment, then made a decision.

"Since you're so keenly interested, I'll show you some of the files and clippings I've collected over the years. Your grandmother calls it my 'Monster Collection' and thinks I'm a little dotty on the subject. Out of habit, I keep all that stuff in a locked case beside my reading desk. It's not the kind of thing you want to have lying out in plain sight when your commanding officer and his wife come over for dinner. . . ."

Inside the case were the books of Heuvelmans and de Camp, Willy Ley and Ivan Sanderson; Margaret Murray's controversial "crypto-anthropological" essays about gnomes, trolls, and other diminutive humanoids; and file folders containing hundreds of clippings about Nessie, the Yeti, the Sasquatch, the serpent of Lake Champlain, the Jersey Devil, the Beast of Bladenboro, the giant Black Dogs of Yorkshire, and dozens of more obscure, cultish phenomena. Allen's eyes bulged.

"Grandpa, I never would have suspected. . . ."

"I wasn't sure if I should tell you about this stuff. I mean, I wanted you to think of me as a stalwart old soldier, not as the reckless adventurer who actually tried to put together an expedition to Lake Tele in Africa, where the natives fear and worship a dinosaur-like creature that may well have survived since the Late Cetacean age. I was on extended leave from the Army, and I sank thousands into it; hired native guides and a big-game hunter, stockpiled the tents and food and mosquito netting, chartered a steamboat. . . . Oh, it would have been a grand adventure, Allen, even if I didn't find the monster I was looking for."

"Then why didn't you go, Grandpa?"

"The damn Japs bombed Pearl Harbor! How's that for cosmic irony? I used to kid myself about going back, after the war was over, but . . . well, I think your grandmother would have divorced me if I'd tried. I was getting a bit old for that sort of thing by nineteen forty-five, too, I guess."

General Warrener got a far-away look in his eyes.

"When I was a kid, Allen, I dreamed of the day when I would be free to 'do what I wanted'; but if that day ever came, I missed it because I no longer 'wanted' the same things as I did before I became a husband and a father. Then came that one window of opportunity, when the Army didn't need me and my kids were old enough to fend for themselves, and what happens? World War Two! Of all my undoubted virtues, good timing is conspicuously absent. . . .

"Even so, after forty-four years of collecting all this information, I would hate to think it'll all just be thrown into the garbage when I'm gone. So I'll tell you what, young man—tomorrow, I'll have a duplicate key made, and you can have this part of your inheritance early. Maybe there's a 'monster-hunting gene' or something like that, and I seem to have passed it along to you. So from now on, we'll be colleagues in the search for real-life mysteries!

"A word of caution, though: if you do choose the Army as your career, for God's sake keep this weirdness to yourself—word gets around about your strange 'hobby' and you'll be treated like a flying saucer nut. A reputation like that is a real career-killer. But the service isn't as rigid as it used to be. Who knows: you may find time to mount your own expedition to Lake Tele, or Tibet, or Loch Ness, and perhaps you'll make the kind of discovery I used to dream of making. That would please me very much."

Allen Warrener hugged his grandfather, who seemed at that moment to be the wisest and most interesting man in the world.

"I guess I better not tell Grandma about our arrangement. . . ."

"Smart lad."

2.

Funny Valentine

When Allen Warrener discovered science fiction, during the summer between the seventh and eighth grades, the genre was flourishing as never before. He skipped lunches so that he could scarf up each new issue of his favorite magazines; by spring of the eighth grade, he'd become immersed in Fandom, subscribing to dozens of mimeographed publications filled with reviews, amateur stories, and polemical screeds fueled by the throttled-in hormones of nerdy adolescent fantasists.

Quite the most ambitious and entertaining of the lot was a 'zine out of Miami entitled *The Vulture of Hyperspace*, edited by a boy one year older than Allen named Preston Valentine. Something about Valentine's acerbic, old-beyond-his-years style struck a sympathetic chord, and the two initiated a manic correspondence that revealed them to one another as true soulmates. A face-to-face meeting was inevitable, and it took place in 1959, over Easter vacation during Allen's tenth-grade year, when he hopped a Greyhound to attend Miami's famously flaky GatorCon. Preston had somehow wrangled the job of Official Photographer, and managed to anoint Warrener with a free pass and the thrill of seeing his name immortalized as a "Guest of the Con."

When Allen stepped off the air-conditioned bus into the blinding glare of south Florida, he couldn't *see* Preston, but he knew exactly where his friend was by the nagging *clak-clak-clak* of Preston's omnipresent Nikon. At his first glimpse of Valentine-in-the-flesh, Warrener could only mumble: "Gawd, you look like a shit salesman with a mouth full of samples!"

Valentine cackled, and the two teenagers embraced like long-separated twins encountering each other in the middle of the Gobi Desert.

Preston looked exactly as Allen had pictured him from his letters, only more so: he wore a starchy white Panama hat, intentionally sinister sunglasses, Madras-plaid Bermuda shorts, a lime-green tropical shirt open to the navel, and sky-blue socks. A Marlboro dangled rakishly from his thin, sardonic lips. He was one of those rail-thin naturally speedy people who seem to have been born with the metabolism of a hummingbird. Preston didn't walk—he *loped*, with the tense fixated stride of a stork. He was a star at the Con, both because of his wildly doctrinaire opinions and because he delivered them with comedic riffs that evoked wails of laughter even from the fans who disagreed with him. His sense of the scatological was profound, and his put-downs could draw blood; to the adolescent attendees, his vindictive soliloquies were red meat. Yet he could be remarkably compassionate; he was never too busy to rap with the geekiest, most tongue-tied neophyte from Podunk, who often went away as bedazzled as he would have been following a one-on-one with Isaac Asimov (whom Preston dismissed haughtily with the observation that "No grown man who appears in public wearing a *bolo tie* can be taken altogether seriously!").

The boys' friendship deepened through continued correspondence, even as Preston began to outgrow Fandom. Before he euthanised *The Vulture*, he put out one final collectors'-item issue crammed with brilliant but pitiless parodies of authors he disliked and the rival fanzine editors who'd pissed him off for one reason or another. Allen entered his senior year still enamored of sci-fi, but much distracted by an unrequited crush on a cheerleader, while Preston enrolled in the university at Gainesville. It was soon apparent from his letters that his interest in science fiction had been eclipsed by his obsession with sexual conquests. *"I walk through the Quad and there they are, on their blankets, in their bikinis, glistening in sun-tan oil, each riper and more succulent than the next: The Little Sizzlers! I want them all!"*

Evidently he worked his way through a fairly high percentage of them, at any rate. His letters, filled with enough sand-on-the-bedsheets detail to rival Henry Miller at his raunchiest, were minor epics. But in January of Preston's freshman year, the Conqueror was himself ambushed by Cupid. In a thirteen-page epistle, he told Allen that he had found his Guinevere, his Isolde, his Daisy. Her name was Sylvia, and he wanted Allen to know that she was the most beautiful girl in central Florida; many photos were dispatched to prove this contention. By April, however, Preston's letters had taken on a tormented, neurotic tone, filled with nothing but hyperthyroid accounts of Sylvia's ecstasies and tantrums, in about equal measure. The spoiled only child of old-money parents, she was in full rebellion against her Roman Catholic upbringing, and the whack of the nuns' rulers had inculcated a taste for S & M byplay that roused Preston to a priapic frenzy, even as her mood swings and flightiness derailed his academic performance.

Spring break of his senior high-school year, Allen got to meet this goddess. He journeyed to Daytona Beach, where Preston had rented a pair of motel rooms. When Allen first saw her, Sylvia was sunning herself beside a turquoise swimming pool, languid and stunning, an essence-of-blonde daydream, with a *café-au-lait* complexion, jade eyes, and a natural hauteur that bordered on arrogance. When she rolled over to greet him, he knew that the image of her molten thighs, dramatically highlighted by an electric-white bikini, would become the dominant *leitmotif* for his masturbatory fantasies.

"Well, what do you think?" Preston asked, the moment they were alone.

"She's devastating, all right."

"I know, I know," sighed Preston, puffing nervously on a Marlboro. "She's also seeing *two* shrinks and if she forgets to take her pills, she can suddenly turn into the Bride of Godzilla. Drives me nuts, keeps me on edge every minute . . . except, of course, when we're making the two-backed beast. For one of those blowjobs, I'd crawl a mile on broken Schlitz bottles."

"That good, huh?"

"You have no idea. . . . She is to oral sex what Horowitz is to the keyboard."

"Horowitz is queer."

"So is Sylvia, when she's in the mood—Catholic girls'-school kind of thing, I guess. Man, we had a threesome last weekend with this redhead from Tallahatchie. . . ."

Throughout the first semester of Allen's freshman year in college, Preston's letters became more hysterical and his grades plummeted. Sylvia was serially and flagrantly unfaithful, but "she does love me and she always comes back." Allen watched his fiercely independent friend deteriorate into a twitching marionette, dancing to the tune of his mercurial and increasingly unstable lover. One night just before final exams, Allen penned the first stern advice he'd ever given Valentine: "I don't care if she can suck the chrome off a trailer-hitch and has an IQ of three hundred, Sylvia's crazy as a shit-house rat, and if you don't get away from her, you will be too!"

When Allen moved back home after exams, and had heard nothing from his pal for an unprecedented two weeks, he became worried. He called the communal phone number of Preston's dorm, on the off-chance that he might actually be there, studying for exams. Preston's roommate eventually came on the line and reported a dire new development.

"Preston's dropped out, man. It was either that or flunk out. His grades were in the shitter. It was that bitch-on-wheels girlfriend of his that did it to him. She up and left him, just called him up one night and said she was leaving. Said she had gotten a modeling job in New York. What a crock!"

"Any idea where he is now? Back home with his folks?"

"Doubt it. They wanted to send him to a shrink, angry words were exchanged, and he fled into the night, God knows where. Sorry I can't tell you more, Allen, but I hardly saw the guy for the past three months. Too bad—I liked his company, in small doses of course. I mean, it was sort of like living with a very entertaining lunatic, y'know?"

"Yeah, I sure do. Well, I guess he'll get in touch when the bleeding stops."

In fact, Preston's next letter arrived three days later. It was uncharacteristically terse and contained no mention of Sylvia, but Preston did assure Allen that "something new has opened up, and it looks just right for me."

On the strength of his portfolio, Preston had landed a job as a stringer for the *Miami Herald*. He was, he declared, through with women and from now on would devote himself to the craft of photojournalism.

Preston's dedication to his new job was total; he pursued the Great Picture with the same frenetic zeal he formerly displayed in the pursuit of co-ed poontang. He worked the graveyard shift, by choice, which was the time when Miami's myriad urban horrors tended to boil over. He took all the calls that were too flaky, too stomach-turning, or too outré for his colleagues: Mafia massacres, ten-car pileups on the freeways, chain-saw dismemberments by Panamanian drug gangs. He moved quite happily into the city's steamy underbelly and his eye flinched from nothing. He went on full salary after four months and enjoyed a somewhat scandalous hour of fame when a trendy Key West gallery held an exhibition of his photos that had been deemed too macabre or too gruesome for the newspaper to print.

Allen was not altogether surprised, in the spring of 1964, when Preston suddenly announced a change of assignments: he was going to Vietnam, to cover the smoldering guerrilla war there as a fully accredited war correspondent.

Warrener merely wrote back: "I suppose I'll be joining you there after I get my ROTC commission. Keep me informed about what's *really* going on."

Allen had kept to his chosen course. When he entered Davidson College, he raised faculty eyebrows by opting to pursue a double major in History and Political Science, the two disciplines that seemed essential to a military career. And he actually took the ROTC curriculum seriously—an attitude so novel that the instructors made him squad leader at the end of his freshman year and platoon leader midway through his sophomore season. During the annual field exercises, he'd led a squad of gung-ho volunteers, theatrically swathed in tiger-striped camos, on a daring raid that captured the Blue Force's headquarters tent. After congratulating him for this feat, the department commandant, a somewhat long-in-grade major who was feverishly trying to get his ticket punched for Southeast Asia, took Allen aside and said, "You've got a flair for tactics, Mr. Warrener. After you receive your commission, I hope you'll consider the infantry. It's a foot soldiers' war over there in Southeast Asia, and a good platoon leader can jump the promotion ladder pretty fast."

Allen Warrener braced proudly to attention and replied, "I have a family tradition to live up to, sir. I'm ready to serve."

But the conflict in Asia was still a sputtering brush-fire war at that time; there seemed no urgency. When one of his faculty advisers mentioned a vacancy in a junior-year-abroad program affiliated with the University of Tampere, in Finland, Allen quickly applied. He'd been a fan of Sibelius since tenth grade, and every photo he'd ever seen of the Finnish countryside seemed to mirror the great composer's music so perfectly that the forests and lakes simply *beckoned*. For a Russian History seminar, he had written a paper on the Winter War of 1939–1940, which had earned him a nice fat "A." Since he'd been taking heavy class-loads all along and maintaining a good average in everything except algebra, he was granted permission to submit a dual thesis, provided he could find a suitable topic relevant to both of his majors.

After some reflection, he did. The working title was "Lion of the Baltic: Gustav Mannerheim and Finland's Strategy of the Tight-rope in the Second World War." It was enthusiastically approved, one week before he was accepted in the junior-year-abroad program.

The subject matter, after all, was hardly overexplored.

3.

LAPLAND FEVER

He started in June.

Tampere was a clean, pleasant city and its university was highly regarded throughout Scandinavia. The main obstacle to Allen's research was language. He'd tried to cram some Finnish vocabulary before arriving, but found the grammar impenetrable. His faculty adviser had seen other foreign scholars slam into the same brick wall, so he partnered Allen with some Finnish students who were eager to perfect their English, and they in turn advised him to forget the grammatical rules and learn the language by ear; this method worked well and after he adopted it he made respectable progress.

He went into his most monkish, ascetic mode, and after twelve weeks—the entire summer—of grinding, he started to feel the need for a break. His adviser sensed that and suggested—as one Sibelius fan to another—that now would be an ideal time to take a couple of weeks off and see the countryside. Winter, he reminded the American pilgrim, came early here, and during those long dark months there would be little chance to explore. "Why not go all the way up to Lapland? It's like another world up there, a somewhat magical one, and it's a part of the Northland that few Americans have ever visited. Here's the address of a friend, Colonel Eino Kekkonen, an old Army comrade who runs a hunting lodge way above the Arctic Circle. Gruff but good-hearted. I telephoned him, and he says he won't have any clients until October, so you're welcome to make the lodge your headquarters."

Well, why not?

Allen packed a knapsack, filled a notebook with the addresses of people who would be glad to shelter him for a night, and on the light-flooded crest of a blue and crystal morning, with the first turned birch leaves toppling like gold coins on the gunmetal surface of Tampere's many lakes, he began his odyssey to the far north.

For three days, he zig-zagged across central Finland, always bearing north. On the morning of the fourth day, he crossed the Arctic Circle, and within hours he experienced an eerie feeling of being drawn toward . . . *something*. Two hundred fifty miles farther north, he arrived at Col. Kekkonen's hunting lodge, a rough-hewn log building overlooking a large placid lake, on the shore of which stood a sauna hut surrounded by graceful birches. Kekkonen, a tall thin man with strong gray eyes, bade him welcome, in remarkably idiomatic English, and showed him around. The lodge was austere and entirely masculine, decorated with hunting trophies, Lapp carvings, and deep-piled wall rugs dyed in autumnal colors.

Kekkonen shouted for someone to carry Warrener's travel bag up to his room, and Allen caught a fleeting glimpse of a short, dark-skinned, thick-shouldered man scuttling by. He was just tired enough to think: *And there goes Igor.* . . . Ten minutes later, while he was sharing a drink with the Finnish colonel, the short man returned and grunted perfunctorily at Allen's extended hand as though it were an animal's paw.

"Pentti! Shake hands! Don't pretend you can't understand." The Lapp barely touched skin, his face averted, then accepted a glass of vodka the size of a soup can and slouched out of the room, evidently to prepare supper.

"Is he always that, um, reserved?"

Kekkonen snorted and clinked glasses. "Some of the guests, you see, expect a full-blooded Lapp to be silent, remote, and vaguely savage—Pentti obliges, indeed he relishes . . . what's that American phrase? 'Having you on?' "

" 'Putting you on.' I fully understand. Does Pentti have a last name?"

"Not that he's ever revealed to me, and he's worked for me twelve years."

After a simple dinner of potatoes, porridge, and sausage soup, all washed down with stout Finnish beer, the host, guest, and silent retainer all moved into the log-beamed den. Pentti took a newspaper and reclined in a patch of twilight, squinting fiercely and chain-smoking murderously pungent Russian cigarettes.

Allen estimated that the dark and saturnine Lapp could have been any age between thirty and fifty. The anthropological evidence was ambiguous, but Allen knew that the empire of the Khans had probably washed over this rump of Scandinavia before the knights of Novgorod and Rus expelled the Mongols for good. Pentti's pie-round face hinted strongly at the Asian tribesmen from whom he was descended. His features were blunt, his nose almost splayed, his mouth thick and sullen in repose but quick to smile when something amused him. His skin was dark adobe, gleaming as though rubbed with oil. His heavy-lidded obsidian eyes were deeply pouched from a lifetime of harsh weather and peering into great distances.

Even now, Allen thought, even disheveled, unshaven, and somewhat drunk, Pentti retained a faint air of steppe-ferocity. Mount him on a sturdy horse, dress him in leather armor, stick a murderous compound bow in his hands, and he could have ridden in the armies of Genghis Khan.

Observing Allen's scrutiny, Pentti growled something in a thick guttural dialect. Kekkonen translated: "Pentti asks, what is your . . . appraisal of him?"

"I didn't mean to be rude, but I'm fascinated. The blood-line back to the Mongols is so obvious. If he would not find it offensive, please tell him that he reminds me of a warrior from the court of the Khans."

Kekkonen uttered a string of syllables that sounded like someone trying to clear a knot of stubborn phlegm. Pentti mulled over the remark, then, to Allen's astonishment, raised his eyes and gave a big, sly wink. "He says to tell you this: 'The young American has the Eye-of-Lapland.' A bit oblique, but I assure you it's a compliment."

After his second vodka, Warrener's tiredness overcame him, and he palmed back an enormous yawn.

"I'm sorry, but I should get to bed soon. I rode all day with a logger from Ivalo who didn't speak or understand a word of English, but chattered at me for eight straight hours. I guess he just wanted to talk to somebody."

"It's a lonely road—I suspect he would have chattered that way if you had been a dead reindeer."

After sending Pentti upstairs with a basin of water and a chamber pot, Kekkonen bade his guest good night and wished him a pleasant sleep. In the morning, he promised, he would provide maps, directions, and a fueled-up Vespa, so that his American guest could get "a deep taste of Lapland."

Kekkonen's lodge was located on the western side of the one and only all-weather road running from Rovaniemi to the Norwegian border. On that side of the "highway" were the vast and rolling fells, tundra interrupted only by scraggly patches of brush and impassable bogs; to the eastern side of the road, dense and seemingly impenetrable, rose the primal forest of blue-shadowed spruce, tall arctic pine, and chalk-white birches. By this time, autumn's encroach had fired whole ridges with burnt orange, and the myriad lakes spotted the landscape with dark blue, their surfaces stirred to creamy swirls by the wind and spattered with golden birch leaves. Thanks to Kekkonen's sketch-map and his knowledge of the region, Allen was able to explore deeply, shouldering the knobby-tired scooter over old logging tracks and game-paths. He fished, with surprising success, in a torrential arctic river, swift and icy, so pure that when he got thirsty; he simply put his face into it and drank. Kekkonen even loaned him a sleek Finnish army carbine loaded with soft-nosed hunting rounds and told him what kind of game was in season and how to look for it. On his second morning, Allen stalked and cleanly killed a large arctic fox. Elated with his prowess, he aborted his plans for the afternoon and motored back to the lodge. After being duly congratulated by Kekkonen, who estimated the pelt would sell for two hundred Finnish marks, Allen impulsively offered the trophy to Pentti. The Lapp momentarily lost his composure and actually stammered in surprise. He weighed the fox thoughtfully in his hands, then slung it over his shoulder and clasped Allen in a somewhat fragrant hug. After Pentti went off to skin the animal, Kekkonen smiled at Warrener with something very much like admiration.

"You've made a friend for life. After he treats the skin, he can sell it at the nearest village for the equivalent of a month's wages. His family will be delighted. He had promised to buy them a radio, and your gift has made that possible."

Pentti returned a half hour later and with great solemnity presented Allen with a necklace adorned with runic symbols carved into hollowed-out pieces of reindeer bone. The Lapp also made a brief speech about the ornament, then went outside, muttering something about the sauna.

"Mr. Warrener, you are indeed favored! That necklace, Pentti claims, has been blessed by one of the most powerful shamans of his tribe. No harm will come to you in Lapland while you wear it, and should you lose your way— a contingency which I strongly urge you to avoid—any Lapp you meet will offer you shelter, food, and guidance, the instant he sees what you're wearing around your neck."

"The workmanship is wonderful," Allen said. "What do these runes mean?"

Kekkonen extracted a pair of spectacles and examined the necklace more closely. "They are . . . invocations, charms, symbols to ward off misfortune.

Oh, you can find trinkets like this in the ski resorts, advertised as 'Lapp folk art,' but this is the real thing! If Pentti swears they were blessed by a shaman, you can believe him absolutely—*if* you believe in shamans."

"In Lapland, why not?"

Just then, Pentti stuck his head back inside and startled Allen by saying in gnarled English: "Young hunter, my friend, come have long, hot sauna. You smell bad."

Allen lingered in the sauna for ninety luxurious minutes, until he reached the ideal "sauna-state," an exquisite balance between total relaxation and the feeling that every synapse in his body was electrified. After he finished the steam-bath ritual, he simply stood for a while at the end of the dock on the lake, buck-naked under the sky, steam rising from his body, savoring the sensation of slow honey-gold sunlight laving his flesh like a courtesan's tongue dipped in scented oil. A quickening breeze brought a scent of burly simmering stew; his appetite thundered and drove him back into his clothes and up the hill to the lodge.

In the den, Pentti was laying a big pyramid of firewood; the fresh-cut birch gave off a rich cidery smell. Colonel Kekkonen was nowhere in sight, so it was up to Allen to start a conversation. Pointing at the log pile, he said: "*Onko kylma tama illa?*—Is this evening cold?"

Grimacing at Allen's Finnish, the Lapp solemnly intoned: "No, but good night for a fire any-bloody-how."

"Yes, it is indeed."

They were enjoying preprandial drinks when they heard the front porch creak under solemn boots. Colonel Kekkonen entered and peeled off an autumn-pattern camouflage cape to reveal a crisp army tunic and sharp-creased woolen trousers fluffed around the top of all-weather boots that looked as though they'd been cobbled together from dinosaur hides. From his neck hung a pair of Zeiss field glasses, and in the crook of his right arm sloped a customized Mannlicher with a telescopic sight the size of a drain-pipe. This man was a *serious* hunter.

Impressed, Warrener tried out his conversational Finnish. "What the Herr Colonel today's afternoon-has-been-hunting?"

Kekkonen winced at the mangled syntax and tossed Allen a bit of drama in change: "*Korhut*—bears!"

"No shi . . . I mean, are there really some still around here?"

"Enough to make for a few good hunts each season, yes. Not like it used to be, before the paved roads and the ski-trekkers, of course. I saw signs that there may be more than usual—could be the weather's changed. I've seen the aurora lately, much brighter than usual for this time of year. Animals sense changes in the Earth's magnetic field, you know. And last winter, we saw some wolves—first time I've seen whole families of them up here since the war. I wonder what's making them cross over."

"Cross over? From where?"

"Across the border from Russia, of course. No wolves living in Finland since a long time!"

Allen thought that comment sounded both chauvinistic and dubious: unless Khrushchev had fortified 1200 miles of wilderness on a scale roughly equal to the Berlin Wall, he didn't think there was much you could do to prevent a pack of wolves from going wherever the hell they wanted to go.

After a robust meal, Allen retired to a leather easy chair and updated his travel diary; Pentti and his boss played cards, drank, and conversed, sparingly, in low voices. With darkness came a perceptible drop in temperature and a rise in the wind, which sighed and whistled through chinks in the log walls. Kekkonen lit a few oil lamps, and Pentti stoked the savory birch-log fire to renewed vigor.

When Allen finished his journal entry, he joined the two men in front of the fire.

"So, Allen-from-North-Carolina, have you fallen under the Lapland Spell yet?"

Warrener studied the Finn carefully, trying to detect irony, some trace of tourist-baiting. There was none; the question was utterly straightforward.

"It's like a land out of time."

Kekkonen grunted. "Out of *our* time, certainly." He leaned over and tipped another three fingers of vodka into Allen's glass. "Don't let it influence you *too* deeply. Some men, they end up giving themselves over to that feeling—the wilderness gets in their blood and eventually they aren't fit for city living again. By then it's too late—they don't *want* to go back to the cities, ever again. We have a word for that state of mind: *Lappiin Kuumi* . . . it means 'Lapland Fever.' "

"What kind of men are these hermits?" asked Allen.

Kekkonen elaborated: They were trappers and prospectors, reindeer herders and itinerant tinkers, crackpot herbalists, metaphysical poets who carried incomprehensible manifestos in their backpacks; they lived in army-surplus tents, abandoned huts, and lean-tos. When they needed cash, they guarded reindeer herds for the Lapps or did odd jobs for the scattered Finnish farms and factories. Once or twice a year, when even they could no longer stand the solitude, they wandered into the nearest hamlet and drank themselves into a stupor, or perhaps a berserk frenzy, depending on their mood.

"Most are harmless eccentrics who've chosen to inhabitant their own inner world. They're very careful not to steal or give offense, since their very survival might depend on the goodwill of their Lapp neighbors. And in turn, the Lapps hold these lonely men in particular esteem. If the Lapp religion—which is a crazy-quilt of folk superstitions and shamanistic magic, with an ancient hint of Buddhism thrown in for good measure—has any cardinal tenet, it's pantheism. Not only do animals and birds and fish have souls, but so do trees and rocks and rivers. The men gripped by Lapland Fever are thought to be especially sensitive to this invisible web of emanations. The Lapps think of them as a tribe of roving demi-shamans; anyone who spurns them or refuses them shelter is letting himself in for bad luck, if not something worse."

"Have you met any of these guys, talked to them?"

"I've taken in a few," mused Kekkonen. "Not here in the lodge, of course—bathing, after all, isn't one of their highest priorities. But I let them sleep in the woodshed or in the barn, and they always pay for their room and board by entertaining the paying guests with tall tales of things they've seen out on the fells or deep in the forest. Some of them are excellent storytellers, in fact. I've been toying with the idea of compiling an anthology of the most colorful stories I've heard over the years."

"What kinds of stories? UFOs landing under the aurora borealis, mastodons still roaming the ice?"

"Nothing of that kind—the guests want to hear Lapland stories! And most of those tales are quiet, enigmatic: glimpses-through-the-veil, so to speak. They're the sort of tales that could only be hatched in the mind of a man half-crazed from the very solitude he came here to seek. The commonest theme running through them is what I call The Encounter."

Allen leaned forward and with a slight catch in his voice, urged the Colonel for more details. "Exactly what kinds of *encounters?*"

"If they could be described in every particular, they wouldn't be mysterious, would they now? Pentti, hand me my notebook from the mantelpiece—that's where I jot down the outlines while they're fresh. Ah, here are a few examples: a giant albino bear whose constant companion is a gray raven . . . the King of Stags, who gives endless speeches in an unknown tongue to his own reflection . . . a quicksand bog near the Norwegian mountains where blind sluglike creatures emerge only on nights when the aurora burns brightest, to writhe in some kind of silent ecstasy—are those bizarre enough for you? And then, there are the most common stories, about enigmatic 'encounters' with the Little People."

Allen's hand shot up—*pick me, teacher!* "I know about those myths! I've read *God of the Witches!*" He didn't go so far as to tell Kekkonen that the maverick anthropologist Margaret Murray had also been one of his grandfather's favorite writers. Murray had collected thousands of references and quotes, from the dark ages to modern times, from all over Scandinavia and the British Isles, and from those threads had woven a tapestry of circumstantial "evidence" attesting to the literal existence of a separate humanoid species— elusive, diminutive, and inscrutably influential on century after century of folklore, religion, and poetry, they were the root-cause of every fairy tale about leprechauns, trolls-beneath-bridges, Puck and Rumpelstiltskin, and Tolkien's Gimli. *And let us not forget about Sleepy, Grumpy, and Doc!* Humanity's fascination with them was ancient and very deep.

And under this roof, Colonel Kekkonen had sheltered men who claimed actually to have *seen* them!

"Colonel, you've made Lapland your home for many years. You must be attuned to this world far more acutely than most who were not born here. Obviously you have a keen interest in these matters, or you wouldn't have taken the trouble to keep such detailed notes. Let me ask you straight out: could such beings exist?"

"Well, when you leave the handful of roads and the tiny Finnish towns, you *are* in a land 'outside of time'; a world of animism, pagan to its soul. Those men who've succumbed to *Lappiin Kuumi*, they have gone deeper still, perhaps crossed on to another plane altogether. Pentti's people understand those men. That's why they treat the wanderers with compassion and even a bit of reverence.

"I'm a rational man—mystics make poor soldiers, although there are exceptions like Lawrence and Wingate—but when Pentti told me that he, too, had had an encounter, it never occurred to me to scoff at him. Do I know *what* he encountered? Of course not. I'm perhaps too much of a twentieth-century man ever to win the trust of such beings; most likely, they will never reveal themselves to me. They sense who belongs here and who is just passing through, so to speak. But I hope that one day, by sheer chance, I will catch a glimpse. Sometimes, when I'm out hunting very deep in the forest, I feel a sudden prickling sensation that makes my hair stand on end, as though I had stepped inside a field of powerful invisible current, and although, even with all my skill in forest craft and all my trained senses I cannot see or hear anything out of the ordinary, nevertheless I *know* I am being observed, perhaps evaluated. So, Mr. Warrener, all I can say with absolute conviction is that Lapland is vast enough, mysterious enough, to hide, well, anything."

A few silent moments passed, while the men replenished their drinks and Pentti lit another of his gaspers. Allen decided it was time to press his luck. He leaned forward, right to the edge of Pentti's smokescreen, and spoke to the Lapp earnestly.

"Pentti . . . my friend . . . would you tell your story to me?" Kekkonen started to translate, but the Lapp cut him off with a curt chop of his hand.

"Pentti does not speak of it to tourists. . . ."

Allen was crestfallen.

The Lapp suddenly flashed a gold-toothed grin. "But Pentti *will* tell his young friend!" Then he began to narrate in a calm, almost analytical voice. While Kekkonen struggled for an idiomatic paraphrase, Allen took notes, which he revised later into a coherent account, so that he could send it to his grandfather.

Four years ago, Pentti left the lodge in the early spring, as was his custom, to help his clan with the annual reindeer roundup and tagging, and to participate in their . . . festival? . . . get-together? . . . reunion? A big annual pow-wow, at any rate. One day, it was discovered that a venerable stag—a giant of a fellow who had fathered dozens of offspring, a very valuable asset indeed—had simply wandered off. Custom dictated an immediate search and retrieval. Four pairs of men were selected, men deemed to be the most experienced and tenacious trackers. They set forth in pairs, each team following, as custom dictated, one of the four cardinal directions of the wind.

Pentti and his partner went north. For two days, they searched, until they finally found a spoor and some tufts of fur on a tree branch that matched the missing animal's coat. Pentti's partner, as it happened, was a very traditional Lapp and a true believer in the legends of the Small Race. As the sun went down at the end of that second day, he suddenly stood stock-still and announced: "They are near; watching us." Pentti was a skeptic; he thought the legends were bedtime stories for children. So just to pass the time, he engaged his partner in a debate.

"If they are all around us, why do we never find their dwelling places? Why have we never come across a diminutive skeleton? Are they not flesh and blood?"

"Is the aurora real?"

"Of course."

"Is it flesh and blood?"

Pentti saw the point; a protracted metaphysical debate would only tire and exasperate the two men, so he and his companion slogged on, their search growing ever more urgent. When they found partly melted tracks of the stag a half hour later, Pentti's friend threw him an I-told-you-so look and the two men hastened on, following the fragmentary signs out on to open tundra, heading west, the sky growing darker as the day progressed. It was unusual for a missing reindeer to head into the open. "Maybe he's in heat," suggested the other Lapp.

"Then his girlfriend must live in fucking Norway," Pentti said. He did not like the look of the sky and suggested they find shelter. But the tracks were now fresher-looking, so they pressed on.

They soon regretted it. As sometimes happens in the Far North in early spring, a sudden blizzard swept in from the White Sea, pouring down immense white flakes that piled up alarmingly fast. Even for two experienced Lapp trackers, the sudden whiteout was disturbing, and the stag's trail was obliterated within moments. They could only try to follow the bearing they had been on when the storm hit. Pentti was about to suggest that they turn back when his companion suddenly pointed to the left and shouted: "This way! There's an abandoned hut nearby! I told you—they are guiding us!"

Pentti remained dubious—how did his companion know that this still-invisible "hut" was "abandoned"?—but he followed: what choice did he have? Twenty minutes later, they entered a copse of trees and found it: a ramshackle fisherman's hut on the bank of a turbulent river. It was drafty and cramped, but it was still well stocked with firewood. Once they had a blaze kindled, they ate some dried reindeer meat and split a pack of powdered soup, and then, while daylight lasted, they went out and gathered more wood. Just before dark, while Pentti was taking a leak in the woods, he spotted a plump hare darting out of its burrow; he unlimbered his rifle and killed it with a snap shot. The butchered rabbit, when mixed with the remaining packaged soup, would sustain them for a couple of days. Surely the storm would blow itself out by then.

That first night in the hut passed comfortably enough. The other Lapp made no more comments about being under the protection of mystical dwarves. They split their one bottle of vodka, then fell asleep after assuring each other that the sun would be shining in the morning.

But at daybreak the snow was still coming down as hard as ever. A two-day blizzard, so late in the season, was rare, but not unheard of; they would wait it out. At that point, their main problem looked to be boredom. The light inside the hut was gray and depressing, and they were tired of each other's company. They rationed out the remaining rabbit stew, which had become greasy and barely edible. When the snowfall abated somewhat in the late afternoon, they foraged. Pentti dug up a handful of frozen but edible berries, and his friend uncovered some mushrooms under a fallen log, which he said were entirely safe to eat. Pentti did not recognize the species and waved off his portion—even with hunger gnawing keenly at his belly, he thought it unwise to partake of questionable fungi. After eating his meager rations, Pentti dozed off.

He was awakened by the sound of violent retching. He ran over to his companion, but it was too late to help him. The mushrooms had already been digested; their unknown but potently hallucinogenic toxins were flooding the man's bloodstream. Eyes pinwheeling, the Lapp babbled about how the Little People would save them. "They are near! They need shelter, too! If we leave food at the threshold, they will know they're welcome to share our fire!"

"You're crazy," Pentti told him. "We have one day's worth of food left, and you want to leave part of it outside where it'll be eaten by an animal?"

By nightfall, the other man was incoherent and clammy with sweat; his pulse raced like a charging horse and his body shook and quivered. Finally, he curled up near the fire and seemed to lose consciousness. Pentti did not know—and at this point did not much care—whether the man was dead or alive. Weak from hunger, he too fell asleep.

On the third morning, the snowfall had diminished but not stopped, and the temperature had fallen, glazing the trees and clearings with slick pearly ice. Without skis, they could not travel, even now. It was not until Pentti finished *rekindling the fire that he noticed that his companion was gone. And that he had left the hut without his fur-lined cloak, gloves, or scarf. Cursing, Pentti dressed and went outside to find the madman before he froze to death. As he struggled through high drifts around the door, following the man's tracks, he noticed that the fugitive had left an "offering" of stewed berries, cold bouillon, and a few sugar cubes, neatly arrayed on a piece of newspaper. Pentti almost took the time to retrieve the food, but decided that his first priority must be to rescue his delusional friend.*

He did not expect the fellow to get very far, and he was right, although it took him three hours of following the man's senseless zig-zag course until he found the stone-hard corpse. He marked the body's location for later retrieval, and struggled back to the cabin.

To his dismay, he discovered that the "offerings" were gone. By that time, the site was snowed over, and the scattered tracks around the spot were . . . ambiguous. He had water, a handful of berries, a couple of packets of instant coffee, and some sugar cubes; he would be all right for another day. No spring blizzard in memory had lasted longer than this one already had; surely by tomorrow conditions would be better.

But when he woke and saw that the snow now covered the bottom part of the window, he began to feel the first touch of despair. He read and re-read old newspapers in the dim, watery light that seeped through the window, and when his hunger became unbearable, at twilight, he heated and ate the rancid remains of the hare's leg and a handful of berries, mixed into a grisly stew by adding a handful of snow to the cooking pot. Within an hour, he was nauseous and sweating: he realized that in his distracted state, he had prepared his last meal in the same pot his friend had used to boil the lethal mushrooms. He had not ingested more than a trace of residue, but it was enough to rack his body with chills and convulsions, enough to disorder his mind.

Eventually, he passed out, but his sleep was troubled by disturbing dreams. He thought he was still dreaming when he awoke, in the dark heart of the night, and saw that the fire had been nursed to full flaring warmth and that two small humanoid figures were squatting in obvious comfort near the hearth. He was too weak to rise, could only see their outlines, which were the size of children yet with the musculature and proportion of mature adults. He fantasized that the two beings were conversing, in a faint, piping language that sounded as though it came from the throats of large squirrels.

Well, I am truly crazy now, *he thought, and sank, exhausted, back onto his sweat-fouled pallet. Before he passed out again, he muttered:* "I know you are not real, and that I will probably not wake from this dream, but you are welcome to share my fire and my company . . . I would not turn away a bear on such an awful night!"

In the morning, he woke to the touch of sunlight and the steady patter of melting snow on the roof. The thaw was as sudden and violent as the blizzard had been. By eleven o'clock, the window was half-uncovered. At this rate, the land would be navigable by the next morning, although it would be wet, slow going. But he was now very weak indeed; he did not know if he would even be able to rise in the morning, much less travel the thirty kilometers back to his village.

Then he remembered the two figures he had seen curled up by his fire, and he struggled up on to one elbow, staring intently at every part of the hut. There was no sign of them, yet something was different. Shakily, he got out of bed and limped toward the fireplace. Someone or something had torn up part of the floor, and in doing so had uncovered an emergency cache of canned goods stored there by whoever had once owned this dismal habitation. Several of the cans had been opened and cleaned out, but neatly piled before the hearth he found two cans of beans, a tin of crackers still sealed in cellophane, a jar of mixed fruit, a bar of Swiss chocolate—and, most welcome of all, a full bottle of excellent Swedish vodka. His spirits instantly revived. He ate cautiously but more or less constantly all day, watching the snow melt outside, and by the following morning he felt vigorous and filled with determination.

Pentti concluded his tale with a brief epilogue and an expressive shrug, then flashed Warrener another of his rare smiles.

"He says that what happened to him has made him a believer," translated Kekkonen. "The small beings, whatever they are, accepted the offering his mad companion had laid out for them, and with it the implied invitation to share the fire within. They had made themselves comfortable for the night, and, in return for that hospitality, they had left a bounteous—indeed life-saving—banquet for their host. Moreover, when Pentti did leave the hut, he found the missing stag—tethered to a birch tree only a few yards from the front door. There were strange runes daubed on the beast's muzzle and haunches, and it was so utterly docile that Pentti was able to ride it, like a trained pony, over the worst patches of standing water. When he returned to his village, there was rejoicing and wonder, for when his kinsmen saw the mysterious runes, they felt compelled to summon a reputable shaman. The wizard exclaimed that he had heard of such marks of favor being bestowed by small beings, but had never before met a Lapp who had actually been blessed by them as Pentti had been. Pentti did not understand, until the shaman held a mirror to his face and he saw that there was an amulet, finely carved with mysterious but clearly powerful symbols, which had been placed around his neck. 'Never worry about getting lost or starving again!' cried the shaman."

Kekkonen refilled their glasses. The tale, apparently, had ended.

"Has Pentti ever seen them again?"

"No," answered the Lapp, affably drunk by now. "But Pentti knows when they are near!" He cackled, coughed, and lit another cigarette.

"Do you still have the necklace they gave you? Can I see it?"

Pentti frowned, his dark brows wrinkling in puzzlement. "Pentti no have any more. Gave to young American hunter—*you wear it now!*"

For his last full day at the lodge, Kekkonen suggested that Allen make a long trek to an overlook, one that had been too covered with foliage to afford a good view earlier; now that many leaves had fallen, it should provide what the colonel described as "one of Lapland's most dramatic panoramas." It was a ridge, some seven kilometers northeast of the lodge, and it was called *"Ruskea Tunturri"*—"The Ridge-of-Autumn-Time." The Major would drive him as close as possible, then he would have to hike to the top. "It's worth the effort—you'll see."

The colonel was right, even though the hike was arduous and Warrener was too pooped by the time he arrived at the overlook to do anything more than pant and swig canteen water. Between the ridgetop and the road was a thickly wooded valley; the road itself, a pencil line of gravel, unrolled due north, ruler-straight, until it vanished in the glare of an intersecting river. From this height, the tundra had a Sahara-like grandeur not noticeable from the road—it just went on and on until it faded against a scribble of burnt-plum hills rising toward across the Norwegian border. Farther still, the horizon blurred into an indistinctive range of peaks and crags: troll country, for sure. So many tarns and bogs and intricately swirling creeks fragmented the tundra that it was impossible to trace their configurations without being blinded by the dance of sunlight from the crystal bell of the afternoon sky. Allen consulted his watch—there was plenty of daylight left. The vastness of the tundra beckoned! It was as strange a landscape as one could find on the planet, and he longed to see it more closely: this was, after all, his final day in Lapland. He descended once more through the cathedral stillness of the forest.

Up close, he discovered that the tundra comprised a patchwork of mossy hummocks, interspersed with patches of flat, grainy mud, spotted leprously with seepage from the shallow water table beneath. Tentatively at first, then joyously, he capered from hummock to hummock, leaping fearlessly, heedless of the distance he was putting between himself and the solidity of the roadbed.

Inevitably, his concentration wandered, and on one especially long leap he lost his footing and tumbled completely across the hummock he'd been aiming for, coming to rest directly from its western verge, his slightly bruised face ending up directly above one of those featureless gray patches of apparently stagnant muck. But his nostrils now detected a definite exhalation of menace. Colonel Kekkonen had mentioned, without undue concern, that the tundra was liberally sprinkled with extensive areas of quicksand. This nearly shapeless patch of mud looked harmless enough—inert, dull, and unruffled by the wind—but what did he know of *real* quicksand? He'd only seen it in Tarzan movies, where the stuff *looked* treacherous and gruelly, like really undercooked oatmeal.

Curious now, he backtracked to the roadbed and searched until he found a tree branch as long as he was tall. He went back out on the tundra and found a firm, relatively large hummock and carefully took a balanced stance before gingerly pushing the tip of his branch into the smooth, featureless mire. He encountered neither resistance nor suction. Vaguely disappointed, he pushed much harder, puncturing the membranous outer skin. And was shocked when unseen hands grasped the wood and greedily sucked it under until his hands made contact with an incongruously warm, mealy substance whose depths seemed determined to swallow his entire arm. He jerked his hands away as though he'd touched fire, and the quivering tree limb steadily continued to sink until the thickest part of the wood vanished with a sinister *ploop!*

"Holy shit!" he exclaimed. "Just like in the movies!"

Had he not been gripped by his own spell of Lapland Fever, he would have sensibly turned back. But the realization that, yes indeed, he was surrounded by a bizarre and nightmarish form of *predatory earth* only seemed to fire his determination to see more, to learn more. The tundra had issued a challenge, and he was energized enough to take its wager. Taunting the quicksand patches aloud, he resumed his balletic leaps and pirouettes, judging the distances of his jumps perfectly, defying the glue-of-death. He suddenly envisioned a new chapter heading on the contents page of *The Wonders of Earth, Sea, and Sky:*

"Perils of the Open Tundra—Exploring the Land that the Esquimaux Fear to Tread!"

He ran out of energy about a thousand yards from the road, found a seat on a large and reassuringly solid hummock, intending to take some photos. First, however, he lit a cigarette and took a mighty swig from the pint of vodka he'd stashed in his pack. He had become as oblivious to the passage of time as he had become foolishly contemptuous of the danger surrounding him. Oh, yes, he was definitely seized by "Lapland Fever," all right. Having passed some private rite of initiation, he reverted to a calm, contemplative frame of mind and took a cross-legged seat from which to savor the afternoon's beauty. The slow, subarctic sunset painted the sky and clarified the distant hills of Norway with colors for which he had no name. His mental state became trancelike. Nothing stirred except the wind and the peaceful cycle of his own breath. Spellbound by the melodramatic colors washing the sky, he hardly noticed when the sun finally winked out behind the purple hills of Norway, abruptly lowering the temperature of the ambient air. Still he did not move. When the sky modulated into a royal purple, the first wisps of the Northern Lights began to pulsate, first within the darkest quadrant of the sky; and then, as full night descended, the aurora seemed to spread itself—for the benefit of this solitary pilgrim—across the whole immensity of Heaven, *performing* for him like a living entity, stoking the rapture that consumed not only his senses, but his better judgment.

When at length he wrenched his attention away from the heavens back to his own terrestrial situation, he was stunned by the depth of darkness around him. Reflected from the tundra's numberless tarns, the shimmering sky conjured eerie and distorted shadows. When he stood, after having sat in a meditative position for three hours, his legs were rubbery and vertigo clutched him; he fell back to his knees, grasping the wiry sod-grass to restore his equilibrium. "Deep shit, Warrener. You're in deep shit now."

The time for him to make safe, easy passage back to the road was long past. He was now so far out that he could not even see the edge of the forest, never mind the road embankment. He sighted on the nearest eastward hummock and cautiously stepped across. The distance to the next one, however, now seemed too great for a safe jump—even though he was sure he had done so earlier. Or was that in fact a different hummock? It was hard to judge distances on this shimmering plain. The danger of losing his balance, or of twisting an ankle, was very real. Get a grip, he thought: one jump at a time, and sooner or later you'll reach the roadbed. He tensed, calculated the distance as best he could, and leaped into space.

His upper body landed on target, but while one leg scrabbled desperately for purchase, the other poked down into the quicksand. He cried out in panic as he felt the listless but insistent pull of it on his foot, uniform at all points of contact—a big, patient, jellied mouth that sought to draw him under. He tugged free and scrambled to the middle of the hummock, panting and trembling. Now he truly *was* alarmed, for he saw no other hump of dry ground within safe jumping distance. The realization pumped through him that he might have to spend the night right there, poorly dressed against the growing cold, with no materials from which he could build a fire. He pulled a lightweight plastic rain cape from his pack, but it did little to augment his body heat. How low did the temperature get out here in early autumn? The question was almost academic anyhow, for he was already so drenched in sweat that a five-degree drop in temperature would bring the danger of hypothermia. His watch informed him that it was only ten o'clock, but already he could see the steam of his breath. If he stayed put, hunkered down in a fetal knot on his tiny island, he might die from exposure; but the alternative—just leaping blindly from one dark mound to another—put him at serious risk of falling into quicksand. At the moment, he could think of no more hideous way to die, nor one more pointlessly absurd.

As he huddled beneath the flimsy plastic cape, befuddled by indecision and mentally berating himself for a fool, he noticed that the auroral glow was increasing all around him. He could now see well enough to trace the gnarled weave of the mossy vegetation around his feet. This, he thought, was decidedly odd: why should the Northland sky decide to throw a spotlight on his particular patch of ground? Then he realized: the glow was not coming from the aurora at all.

"Oh, Jesus, I'm not seeing this. . . ."

The radiance was coming instead from the deep-cut runes incised in the amulet Pentti had given him. While the amount of light was not sufficient to guide him, it was certainly adequate to serve as . . . a beacon. He stared at the bright, indecipherable symbols, seemingly lit from within, like miniature jack-o'-lanterns. If his sense of things was accurate, if the ornament *was* a beacon, a distress signal, was anyone or anything out there to see it, to respond to its silent plea for succor?

My God, there! In the direction of the road! He saw a small, wavering, indistinct shadow, and it was coming in his direction, navigating from one dry mound to the next with unerring aplomb. Its movements were traceable as its shape broke the shimmering green reflections from the sky. Someone was approaching him. As it approached, a commingled wave of fear and wonder surged through his nerves.

I'm probably hallucinating, but just in case I'm not. . . .

He stood and held the necklace out, waving it, beckoning the squat, shadowy figure.

"Pentti? That you, Pentti?"

The sky and tundra froze in silence. The figure, however, stopped moving. Allen saw a short, burly arm moving in an arc, and a small yellow-glowing object sailed across the intervening space and landed in the exact center of the hummock nearest to Warrener's. It glowed brightly, unmistakably marking the aiming point for his next jump. Although the dark stranger made no beckoning gesture, it fidgeted and tapped its foot, as though impatiently waiting for Allen to grasp the obvious.

All right, my enigmatic little guide; now that I can see it, that jump looks do-able.

Summoning not courage so much as faith, Allen backed up for a running start and leaped. He landed more or less in the vicinity of the glowing object, which promptly went dark. Allen peered eastward and was relieved to see that the next leap was shorter and less perilous. He jumped, landed safely, and repeated the process, making steady, if erratic, progress.

Each time he did so, the small creature seemingly teleported ahead of him to another safe location. He was taking a circuitous route back to the road, but the Benefactor, as Allen now thought of him, was so intimately familiar with the terrain that he unerringly chose points of aim that posed minimal risk. The figure bobbed like a liquid shadow, evanescent as mercury, sure-footed as a mountain goat. At times the creature vanished briefly, only to reappear as if by magic in an unexpected location. Allen's former panic was replaced by a feeling of confidence. Whatever it was, this silent nocturnal being was leading him, slowly but surely, to safety.

For an hour, Warrener played follow-the-leader, until finally the road embankment loomed ahead: solid and reliably climbable. He made the final leap and fell against solid ground, knotting his fists in its weeds and branches, limp with relief. When he looked up at the road, he caught one final glimpse of the Benefactor, and then the entity vanished, as silent as ever, into the forest. Warrener scrabbled up to the road and peered in all directions. He saw no sign of his savior, but there was a faintly "charged" quality lingering in the air, like the ozone tang before a thunderstorm.

His hike back to the hunting lodge was climactic in its beauty, for the aurora had become incandescent, like the grand finale of a fireworks show. It flared in vivid streaks of flame-yellow and electric blue, forming vast solar-flare streamers, whirlpools, sinuous pulsing ribbons of light, a Bach fugue painted across the vaulted sky. On this final episode of his Lapland odyssey, he sensed the full majesty and sweep of this land. To the west, the mottled sinister fells and the cut-glass mountains of Norway; to the east, the great mass of primeval forest that stretched all the way to the Urals; to the north, beyond the handful of coastal villages where Norway and Finland came together, the unimaginable frigid wastes of the Arctic Ocean. His senses had expanded to encompass the very shape of the Northland, and the vastness of his vision was both exalted and humbling. He had been loaned, for a brief moment of grace, the perspective of God. And he had been granted safe passage, on the wilderness's terms. His senses were so heightened that he smelled the fire-smoke from the lodge a full thirty minutes before its light came into view.

Kekkonen and Pentti looked up in amazement when he strode breathlessly into the den, his boots covered with dried muck and his eyes burning with Old Testament fervor. Colonel Kekkonen immediately handed him a large glass of vodka.

"I was about to launch a search for you, but . . . Pentti stopped me. He said you would be all right, even though you had foolishly blundered into dangerous ground."

Warrener didn't even try to speak until he had downed several gulps of the colonel's firewater. When he found his voice, he asked: "Did Pentti go out looking for me alone?" He had to ask, even though he could already see that the Lapp's boots were perfectly dry. Pentti understood every word, and began to chuckle quietly.

"No. He's been waiting there by the fire since nightfall."

"Were there any travelers on the road tonight? Other hikers, maybe, or hunters?"

"A lorry passed in late afternoon, a farm wagon just before sunset . . . otherwise, nothing."

Without asking permission, Allen squatted beside the Lapp, apparently welcome to share his personal space. When he turned around to face the old Mongol, Pentti nodded at him solemnly and croaked: "You saw."

Allen nodded.

"Then you had 'en-cown-turr,' just like me."

Allen held up the runic amulet. "This necklace glowed, like a beacon, and someone came out on to the tundra and led me to safety. I owe you my life."

"No, no. Not Pentti. Both you and I owe lives to *them*."

Nothing could be proved, of course, but Allen Warrener knew he had glimpsed a Secret, something rare, ancient, hidden from the sight of those whose spirits were not attuned to its wavelengths.

Grandfather, I can't wait to tell you about this!

Back in Tampere, Allen worked on his thesis throughout the long, dark winter. When spring vacation arrived in late April 1964, his first thought was to seek a destination as different from Lapland as possible. Enticed by the stories of other students, he chose Copenhagen. He found the city charming; but a chance occurrence, on the afternoon of his third day there, changed both his itinerary and his life. He'd made a pilgrimage to see the Little Mermaid in the harbor and dutifully took her picture, thinking: *Well, that's very nice . . . now what?* On the way back, he passed by a small travel bureau, and his attention was suddenly captured by a pair of posters in the window. One depicted a Wagnerian landscape: stupendous cliffs rising sheer from the pounding North Atlantic; the other showed a lush valley carpeted with emerald heather, veined with silver cascades, near a tiny, gaily painted fishing village where boats were drawn up on black sand, and on their bowsprits skilled artisans had carved the image of the Great Orms, the sea-dragons forever identified with the Viking marauders. Where in all of modern Europe, he wondered, was there a place so connected to its Viking heritage that its denizens had continued to adorn their ships with so pagan a symbol?

The answer was printed on the bottom of the posters:

SEE THE FAEROE ISLANDS, THE LAST OUTPOST OF VIKING CULTURE!

"THE WINDY EDGE OF NOWHERE"—UNSPOILED AND INEXPENSIVE!

Bargain cruises every week from Copenhagen to Torshavn.

Allen pondered the opportunity: The scenery was breathtaking, the fares were indeed cheap, and any place named "Thor's Harbor" simply *had* to be worth a visit.

He'd seen about as much of Copenhagen as he cared to, and so far he had *not* encountered any of the wild, wanton Danish goddesses his Finnish friends had touted with such extravagant hyperbole. The longer he stared at the images, the more he wanted to see this place, even though he knew nothing about it. This impulse amounted to a serious commitment, but his internal debate lasted as long as it took to count his travelers' checks. The excursion was more than affordable—the travel agency must not be over-whelmed with customers. He opened the door and went inside, convinced, beyond all logic and practicality, that he was doing the right thing at pre-cisely the right time.

4.

PIPE DREAMS

Karen Hambly was a Townie. She was born in a white frame bungalow on a potholed road about a mile from the soccer field that marked the demarcation between the college campus and the Land of the Lint-Heads (or, as the more callous students mockingly called it, "Wheezerville"). The Hambly house was identical to every other house in the neighborhood, except that Karen's mother, May, had installed a cement birdbath and made heroic efforts to coax some seasonal beauty out of a scraggly flowerbed about the size of a cemetery plot—until she became too busy raising young 'uns to tend her flowers. The pint-sized garden quickly reverted to crabgrass and ragweed; she barely noticed.

By the time Karen entered elementary school, the Hamblys' front yard had acquired the same scruffy-looking, rutted, junkyard neglect as the rest of the yards on her street. A derelict Big Wheel toy lay against the birdbath, and the grass had been worn down to bald red clay by the herds of semi-feral children who stomped the life out of one family's yard and then migrated to another, leaving in their wake a desolation worthy of Mongol horsemen. A few thin strips of grass still fought for life along the margins of the ruts Earl Hambly and his buddies had plowed across the front yard with their pickup trucks and clapped-out Studebakers.

Back in 1946, the White Oak Textile Corporation had built Karen's house and the 234 identical units surrounding it, as part of its strategy to convince young workmen, fresh out of wartime service, that it was better to work for them than any unionized employer. Indeed, at the time it was built, the Project was considered a remarkably progressive example of low-income "Company" housing—and, relative to the traditional corporate ethics of North Carolina's textile mills, it was. The bungalows were monotonous-looking and the yards were tiny, but the rents were affordable. In truth, the drab little saltboxes were better than the Depression-era shacks many of their occupants had grown up in—at least until the roofs began to leak, the cheap plywood siding started to warp, and the lowest-bidder plumbing ceased to function.

Year after year, the Project grew a little seedier, and its inhabitants became less and less concerned about leaks, cracks, and fallen drain spouts: why worry about it if you couldn't afford to pay for fixing it? In less than a decade, therefore, the Project went from being a corporate showcase to being a civic embarrassment—a neighborhood that fell into a category somewhere between "eyesore" and "Third-World slum."

At the time he was discharged from the Army, Earl Hambly—the fourth of seven children begat by a perpetually indebted cotton farmer—was a lanky, wavy-haired, smooth-talking charmer. He'd never seen any combat, but he did experience "action" of a different kind while serving with the occupation forces on the island of Hokkaido, Japan. Maybe ol' Earl had never learned to read beyond sixth-grade level, but he was Hell-and-Jesus when he sat down to play serious poker. And unlike most of his friends, Earl didn't fritter away his winnings on *sake* and geisha girls; he shrewdly invested in the thriving black-market deals feverishly being put together by supply sergeants who knew they'd never see a more lucrative setup than the one in which the Army had placed them. When Earl boarded the transport to sail home in 1947, he was burdened with a money belt containing approximately 400 times more than Uncle Sam had paid for his services.

Earl's intentions were certainly noble: he planned to pay off his daddy's debts, refurbish the old farm, plow under the barely profitable cotton fields, and resurrect the place as a modern tobacco farm—that was the Money Weed, thanks to the smoking addictions acquired by millions of recently discharged young men. But when his troop ship landed in San Francisco in the autumn of 1947, he learned that his father had passed away and the family farm had been repossessed by his creditors before the screws were tight in his coffin. Well, *shit*, he'd *meant well*, but God obviously had other plans for Earl Hambly and his cardsharp's grubstake.

So the first thing Earl did was a blow a good-sized chunk of that money on a shiny new convertible and some sharp-looking civilian threads to match. While most of the other local veterans were dutifully signing on for minimum-wage jobs at the Plant, Earl just tooled around for a year, flashing greenbacks, getting his car waxed twice a week, and serially seducing every good-looking bobbysoxer he'd ever had a yen for. He had one hell of a good time, too, until he lost his heart to a saucy, gum-popping strawberry blonde named May.

For her part, May thought Earl was a much better catch than any of the other drugstore cowboys who were putting the moves on her. He was good-looking, in a slicked-back, showoff kind of way; more importantly, he was always flashing a wad of cash big enough to choke a boa constrictor. He seemed to replenish that bankroll, in some mysterious but presumably honest way, in between one of their dates and the next. What May couldn't see, but Earl certainly could, was how steadily his financial resources were dwindling. But every time he peeled off another ten-spot to tip the waiter in some swank restaurant, he considered it an investment—the whole rationale for this profligacy was to get May to peel off her pedal pushers as wantonly as Earl peeled off greenbacks. It took longer and cost more than he'd bargained for, but eventually he was successful; everybody thought they were the hottest couple in town.

So hot was their courtship, in fact, that they got married only two weeks after May's test came back positive.

Earl figured, what the hell? May was a pistol in the sack, and he still had enough of his Japanese bankroll left to support them for four or five months—surely, in that time, he would find some new source of easy money, just as he'd done in Japan. But the thing he was best at—playing high-stakes poker—wasn't an option. In a post-war North Carolina mill town, the rubes played for quarters and Chesterfields.

The acquisition of a wife proved to be a surprisingly expensive proposition. He could still kick ass at a poker table, but the spare-change winnings didn't begin to compensate for the slow, inexorable hemorrhage of his basic capital. And the birth of their first child, to his even greater astonishment, seemed to transform May from sexy jitterbug queen to rawhide-tongued scold. Eventually, just to shut her up and get her back under the sheets with a smile on her kisser, he did the expected and responsible thing: he squared his shoulders and walked through the only door of opportunity open to him: a minimum-wage job at the Plant.

Surprisingly, he didn't find the life so bad. Textiles were booming, and a guy who worked hard, showed up sober, and sucked up to management whenever possible stood a good chance of promotion to a supervisory job. Up until the mid-fifties, Earl's periodic fifteen-cent-an-hour raises more or less kept pace with the cost of living. Alas, about the only time May would fuck him any more—at least, with any degree of her old spirit—was when she was good and drunk. Unfortunately, that was precisely the time when she was most likely to forget about putting in her diaphragm.

After the birth of their fourth child, they began losing ground. Like his sharecropper dad, Earl Hambly began to drag a ball-and-chain of financial woe behind his every step, even as he continued slowly to gain promotions and seniority. By the mid-fifties, the ownership of White Oak Mills had passed from third-generation local families into the hands of remote corporate entities who were no longer committed to promoting-from-within; the new owners' policies seemed to favor bright young college graduates who had used their G.I. Bill privileges to obtain the kind of specialized education that was quite beyond the means of men like Earl Hambly—and many of those ambitious young executives made little effort to hide their disdain for the way guys like Earl elongated their vowels, relied on redneck colloquialisms to enliven their limited conversational repertoires, and habitually tucked their Chesterfield packs inside the rolled-up sleeves of their tee-shirts. When one of those coveted management slots opened up, it was just as likely to be filled by some college boy's fraternity brother as it was by a hardworking guy with Earl's seniority, who'd slogged his way up through dogged perseverance. If a man was promoted to management from the ranks of the clock-punchers, he might never rise any higher, but at least he would enjoy a salary instead of an hourly wage; a better retirement deal down the road; and a clean, sit-down office with a nameplate on his desk—tangible rewards for his years of loyalty and competence.

The life of a textile worker wasn't supposed to be easy, but neither was it supposed to be indentured servitude. Time was when a man with Earl Hambly's unblemished record could reasonably expect *some* improvement in his lot; nowadays, the College Boys, with those mysterious letters after their names, seemed always to be at the head of the line, leapfrogging over the downcast heads of long-timers like Earl. After Earl had been passed over twice for low-level management slots he was amply qualified to fill, his sense of future possibilities became stiflingly narrow. He was not alone in feeling shortchanged. As more and more new technology came online, new job titles were created, to be sure, but those jobs all required the costly expertise of more and more College Boys who'd been trained to understand the intricacies of high-capacity looms, the long-range benefits that could be anticipated from "automation," or the chemical formulae for "optimizing the wear-ability" of polyester fabrics. A new and potentially ugly fault line of class antagonism began to undermine the easygoing traditions of working for White Oak Mills, Inc.

By the time Karen Hambly was potty-trained, the Mill was no longer as tolerable a place to work as it had seemed in 1948.

Karen was the fifth and last of Earl and May's kids, and she was definitely not on either parent's agenda. She was in fact the byproduct of a boozy Saturday night when her parents knocked off a quickie for auld lang syne. What little remained of May's good looks seeped away in her final upwelling of breast milk. Karen sometimes stared at the old snapshots of May as a gum-popping jitterbug temptress, and wondered how such a sparkling young beauty had become a sullen, stoop-shouldered matron whose heavy hips and bitter expression suggested a person who was both overfed and perpetually starving.

By the time Karen was old enough to tell the difference between Earl sober and Earl-after-he-had-a-load-on, it was plain that her father drank too much, especially when he thought he'd been passed over for another promotion. But sometimes, she noticed, Earl was much more sociable after he'd imbibed a few. On Friday nights, when Earl and his cronies sat around the kitchen table playing poker and swilling beer, Karen liked to eavesdrop when they started letting off steam. Their complaints were a ritual litany, but a therapeutic one:

"Hey, Earl, ain't that new guy at the Plant ol' Seth Blackwelder's son?"

"The fuckin' same, and ol' Seth'd be spinnin' in his grave to see that boy actin' all high and mighty. Johnny Blackwelder's family is as redneck as they come, but he's tryin' to cover it up by wearin' them prissy white shirts and skinny little ties."

"Not to mention them spectacles he wears—what're they called? Horny-toads?"

" 'Horn-rimmed, you idjit! Guess he thinks they make him look, I don't know, scientific or somethin'."

"Still puts his pants on one leg atta time, don't he?"

"Naw—in business school, they taught him how to put both legs on in one push. It's one of them new labor-savin' techniques!"

"Yeah? Well, I'll bet his shit smells like gardenias, too."

Karen always brought out the best in her father. There was never any hint of judgment in her wide brown eyes, and her solemnity set her apart from her squabbling and not-very-lovable siblings. Earl believed that *this* child was special; he desperately wanted her to understand that he was not a bad man; that once upon a time, he had been reckoned a success, a fellow who was going places. There weren't many chances for daughter and father to spend time alone together, so every Friday night, before the poker buddies arrived, Earl would take Karen with him on a beer-and-cigarettes run to the A & P. In Karen's company, Earl seemed to grow much younger in spirit. He joked, he sang, he teased, anything he could think of to elicit the benediction of her laughter. And in the checkout line, Earl always made a big fuss about letting her pick out a candy bar that she would not have to share with her greedy siblings.

One Friday evening in April, when Karen was five, she was sitting atop five cases of Schlitz, her legs dangling over the grocery cart's rim, earnestly debating the merits of a Three Musketeers over those of a Baby Ruth, when she felt a sudden tension in the air. At first, she was excited—maybe the store was being robbed! But no, there was nobody in front except old Mr. Ferguson, the retired millhand who only had one lung, cheerfully bagging groceries for the two elderly ladies in line ahead of them. The only other person nearby, and the obvious source of Earl's wariness, was the guy behind them, and he didn't look very menacing: just a dapper young businessman with a crewcut and horn-rimmed glasses, dressed in an expensive-looking sport coat. Karen thought the man was a bit pompous-looking, but she couldn't see any reason why his presence was causing Earl such distress. Her father looked strained, indecisive, and embarrassed all at once. Finally, after several preliminary throat-clearings, Earl hesitantly stuck out his hand, which the stranger affected not to notice. Undeterred, Earl spoke directly to him:

"Say, 'scuse me, but aren't you Johnny Blackwelder?"

Unable to ignore the question or the outthrust hand, the stuffy-looking man finally deigned to look at Earl Hambly—and at the cargo of beer in his cart. Karen's existence, he acknowledged with a brief nod and an utterly insincere smile.

"I'm John Blackwelder, yes, and you are . . . ?"

"Earl Hambly! I knew your pappy, Seth, and me and your older brother Woody used to play cowboys together, before he was . . . well, before the war and all. I ain't seen you since you was a kid, I reckon, but I recognized you right away when I saw you over t' the Mill. Looks like they made you an important executive. Well, your pappy'd be mighty proud, Johnny. Wasn't for that suit and tie, you'd be the spittin' image of him . . . I mean, when he was a young fella, of course."

Karen couldn't quite understand why the young Mr. Blackwelder looked so uncomfortable at being associated with his own father. Why, he had actually cringed when Earl said "spittin' image," and everybody knew that was supposed to be a compliment! Blackwelder disengaged from Earl's handshake and managed to avoid looking Earl in the eye even as he struggled to come up with another one of those phony smiles.

"My dad's in a retirement home now, Mr. Hambly; his mind's not too sharp these days—hardening of the arteries, they tell me. I'll pass along your best wishes, though I doubt he'll even know I'm in the room. So . . . ah, you work at the Mill, I take it?"

"Yessir! Almost twelve years now. I'm Chief Mechanic on the day shift, over in the hosiery wing."

"Ah. Yes. Well, I seldom get to that part of the Plant. I was hired to help set up the new Research and Development lab . . . on account of my having an M.B.A. in Textile Science . . . from M.I.T., you see. That's a big school up in New England."

"Yes, I believe we've heard of it in these parts, too."

"Yes, of course that stands to reason. Why right over here at the College, they're doing some cutting-edge research right now. There are so many exciting new developments in the field of synthetic fibers, you know!"

Earl just stared at the man in disbelief. Blackwelder's blustering manner and his obviously intense desire to flee the company of this intrusive linthead—with his cart full of beer and his mute or possibly retarded ragamuffin of a daughter—were both so absurd and so offensive that Earl went into some kind of momentary seizure. He drew himself to his full height and mockingly imitated Blackwelder's archly proper pronunciation in a voice so hectoring that it caused heads to turn all the way back in the dairy section.

"Why, *hell yes, son!* Everybody knows there's a shit-load of pro-FOWNDLY innarestin' things happenin' in the field of *synthetic-damn-fibers!*"

Mr. Blackwelder was not so full of himself as to be unaware that he was being baited by a disturbed and possibly violent bumpkin.

"Well, I . . . that is, I seem to have forgotten something my wife insisted that I pick up from the frozen food section, so if you'll excuse me, I'll . . . just . . . be. . . ."

Gone.

"Okay, Johnny! You tell your daddy ol' Earl said 'Hi'! I'll see ya at the Mill, I reckon, if you ain't too busy RE-searchin' and DEE-velopin'!" Under his breath, Earl added: "You stuck-up, tight-assed son of a bitch. . . ."

Karen could feel her father's anger knotted in his arms when he lifted her into the passenger seat. Even his driving was angry, for when he left the parking lot he scratched off so hard, the tires left smoking black streaks on the pavement. She was a little bit scared. The conversation in the checkout line hadn't *seemed* like an argument, exactly, but Earl was in a foul, simmering mood, grumbling cuss words under his breath. Instead of driving straight back to the Project, he headed toward the College and parked across the street from the big marbled archway that marked the main entrance to the campus. He hoisted Karen out of her seat and gently deposited her on top of the cab. Then he paced back and forth for a few minutes, gathering his thoughts. When he finally spoke, his voice was cold and constricted. Karen knew what that tone of voice signified: listen-to-me, kid, and listen good!

"See that place over there, Princess? They call it a 'campus,' but what it really is, well, it's like a castle—you know, a fortress with walls to keep the riff-raff out. If you've got the money, they'll open the gate for you, give you an I.D. badge, and you'll suddenly turn into a more exalted class of humanity than the scum outside the walls. They'll stuff your head with proper-gander for four years and if you spit up the right answers on the tests, you get . . . what do you get, really, besides the right to jump ahead of guys like me for every damn management slot that comes open at the Mill? Tell me, Princess, what do you get for four years and thousands of dollars?"

"I don't know, Daddy. . . ."

"You get a piece of paper that says: 'I'm a big shot, 'cause I spent four years readin' books and learnin' how to talk proper, so nobody will ever suspect my daddy was common as dirt.' One piece of paper and Junior Blackwelder can make more money on his first week at the job than a dumb lint-head like Earl Hambly makes in a year of punchin' the time clock! Didn't you see it, Karen-baby? How Blackwelder couldn't stand even bein' *next to us* in the checkout line!"

"But what does he do, Daddy, that's so important?"

"He sits around and dictates memos and stuff, I guess. But it's men like me who keep the Mill running! Johnny B. may know a lot about *SYN-thetic FI-bers,* but he couldn't fix a broke-down loom to save his soul from Hell.

"Y'know, back when I started workin' at White Oak, the owners treated their employees like human beings, but them days and those men are gone. And I could see it in Johnny's eyes: I'll never get no big promotion, not if he has anything to say about it . . . and he does. Tomorrow mornin', he'll tell the front office that 'Earl Hambly was drunk and insulting towards my precious self last night at the A and P!' You see, if there's one thing that drives a bad rich man crazy, it's for a decent poor man to look him in the eye and call his bluff.

"So you take a good look at that College, Princess, because that's where they take a good ol' boy, like Johnny used to be, and teach him to think there's something shameful about having honest dirt under your fingernails! Hell, book learnin' never greased a man's way into Heaven or made him a better friend or a better father." Earl paused and shook his head ruefully, finally compelled to mutter: "All the same, if I had the money to send you there. . . ."

Karen leaped into Earl's arms and hugged him fiercely, but her mind was aswirl with confusion. That had been quite the longest and most impassioned speech she'd ever heard from her father's taciturn lips, but Karen just didn't see any connection between the College and the misfortunes of Earl Hambly. The College was just a collection of rather pretty buildings, not the focus of an evil plot that had apparently been devised for the sole purpose of keeping Earl Hambly poor and frustrated for the rest of his life.

And as for *books,* well, Earl and May didn't own any (except the Bible), but Karen had looked through rather a lot of them at her friends' houses, and she thought they were kind of neat, especially the ones with lots of colorful pictures.

And the campus, on this soft April evening, was positively serene. Its tree-lined walkways were dotted with passing students, whose barely audible greetings sounded lighthearted and good-humored, not sinister and conspiratorial. If the College was such a bad place, why did those young people seem so happy to be there? Of course, Karen didn't ask that question out loud, nor did she reveal how reluctant she was to leave the soothing atmosphere that radiated out from the imposing gateway.

Earl touched her arm and said: "We'd better get home now, honey—the beer's gettin' warm!"

One day not long after her seventh birthday, while she was helping May hang up clothes in the back yard, Karen decided to tell her mother, as best she could, the whole story of that night at the A & P.

"Why does Daddy think the College is an evil place?"

May's reply was unexpectedly curt: "Because he was too dumb to take all that money he brought home from the Army and buy himself a good education with it, that's why."

"You think if he had gone to college, he could have been a manager at the Plant?"

"Sweetie, in them days Earl had a smile that could melt an iceberg. He had charm, and he wasn't stupid. He still isn't, but he sometimes says stupid things. . . . He has this weird attitude: that real men don't need to get their education out of books in order to make their fortunes. Fact is, Earl can read as good as anybody else with a sixth-grade education, and he could have learned any trade he chose to take up. Lord, I must have told him a thousand times, 'Earl Hambly, you take what's left of that money and buy yourself a good education! I'll go back to waitressing, if that's what it takes to put food on the table!' But his pride . . . well, you know. So you take heed from his example, Karen: you set your sights on a college education and never let anything distract you from that goal. We probably won't have the money for tuition, so you'll have to become such an outstanding student that when the time comes, the College will come courting *you!*

"I'll do what I can to help—somehow, I'm going to arrange for you to have a tutor, 'cause you're ready to jump way far ahead of the other kids in public school and you know it. You could be reading grown-up books inside a year, if you had some guidance. But if I do figure out a way to get a tutor, you mustn't ever let on to your father that I'm helping you that way. He's bitter enough as it is, and he'll pitch a fit if he finds out you and me are in cahoots behind his back. Shake hands on it?"

"You bet, Mom! You're the greatest!"

When Karen's sixteen-year-old sister eloped with a stock car driver, there was suddenly more space in the house and fewer demands on May's time. She began taking in piecework as a seamstress, and by the time Karen was eight, May had saved enough money to engage a young graduate student from the College to tutor Karen in English six hours a week.

Already withdrawn from the shabby world around her, and for the most part just as indifferent to her remaining siblings as they were to her, Karen found that books were both more interesting and more reliable than most human companions. By age ten, she was reading on an eleventh-grade level—although she took pains to keep her book addiction hidden from Earl, especially when Earl was "down in the dumps," as her mother euphemistically referred to his drunken stupors.

Having observed how well hypocrisy worked for others, Earl swallowed his pride and mended his relations with John Blackwelder, largely by pretending he was intensely interested in the MIT graduate's work. J.B. *was* flattered—his snot-nosed attitude hadn't won him any friends in the ranks of management, so after a brief period of wariness, he responded to overtures from an enlightened member of the proletariat. Earl subtly flattered the young executive's ego by allowing him to become an Honorary Good Ol' Boy, too. He taught Blackwelder how to play poker (making certain that J.B. won a hand now and then), and even took him hunting with a few co-workers who were willing to help Earl out of his career doldrums. The brown-nosing paid off: before too long, young Johnny had taken a genuine liking to Earl—as he did to anyone who reinforced his high opinion of himself. He arranged for Earl to be transferred to the new Research and Development wing, where Blackwelder pursued his private agenda with the same deadpan earnestness Earl showed when pursuing *his*.

Under pressure from the federal government, and as part of its ongoing strategy to lock out the dreaded union, White Oak Textiles was vigorously experimenting with different types of filtered masks that were supposed to keep fiber dust out of the employees' lungs. Of course, one of Johnny's prime mandates was to come up with the cheapest possible design that would satisfy the government inspectors, and in his eagerness to curry favor, Earl always volunteered to test each new design. Some of the early prototypes didn't work very well; but, for his willingness to serve as a guinea pig, Blackwelder rewarded Earl with the sonorous but meaningless title of "Research

Associate," along with an honest-to-God salary. These perquisites were the least White Oak could do for a man who was voluntarily, if unwittingly, inhaling ten times more particulate matter in six months than the average employee absorbed in six years.

The effects, however, showed up after only fourteen months, when Earl's customary bout of early-morning smoker's cough brought up the first flakes of blood from his lungs, like a telegram from the Grim Reaper. Earl knew at once what this signified; the symptom was an entrenched part of lint-head lore. His first reaction was denial—impossible to sustain for very long under the circumstances—and that was followed by pure dread, which was so unpleasant to live with that it was succeeded, in due time, by acceptance. He'd heard the old-timers talk about Brown Lung so often that he'd become an expert; he figured he had anywhere from three years to five, before the disease reached its final ghastly stages. He vowed before his Baptist God that he would use every day of the time left to him for redeeming his soul and bettering the lot of his family.

Having reconciled himself to the inevitable, Earl Hambly made peace with his fate and was seemingly rewarded for his courage. One fair sunny morning in June, he awoke without a trace of fear or anxiety. He'd been granted that state of clarity and grace that sometimes comes to a man when he knows for a fact what the worst possible thing is that can befall him, and roughly how much time he has before his life would cease to have any quality. He thought that three good, relatively pain-free years was time enough to mend both his ways and his fences. He wouldn't even tell May until his symptoms became too obvious to hide.

Earl wouldn't or couldn't explain his persistent cheerfulness, but everybody in the house knew that *something* odd and much-appreciated had "gotten into him." When Karen brought home a report card that fairly crackled with hand-written superlatives from her teachers, Earl-who-disliked-book-learning gave her a tremendous hug and excused himself long enough to retrieve a mysterious package from his closet.

"Such fine work should be rewarded, Princess," he said, impishly grinning, when he handed her the package. Inside it were two books: *Gulliver's Travels* and *The Yearling*. When Karen recovered from the shock, she stammered: "How did you know I wanted to read *these* two books in particular?"

"Well, that was easy enough, darlin'—I just went over and had a chat with that nice tutor-lady who's been helping you—you know, the graduate student your mother thinks I don't know about!"

Now that she could read openly, wherever and whenever she liked, Karen's appetite for the written word increased tenfold. But in a milieu like the Project, intellectual pursuits didn't win her any new friends. That didn't bother her much—the pastimes she'd formerly shared with the neighborhood kids now seemed shallow and childish. And her former peers, for their part, began to regard Karen as aloof, possibly strange, and certainly not much fun to spend time with.

But her oldest friend, a girl named Wanda June who lived two houses down, remained attached to her, out of habit and inertia, Karen suspected, more than anything else. Their favorite pastime was pretending that they were both the queens of exotic kingdoms whose worshipful inhabitants were dolls: large and small, rubber, plastic, rag, and one porcelain beauty dating from 1897 that May had picked up for her at a flea market. This exquisitely crafted doll was Karen's personal lady-in-waiting; she'd named the doll "Emily Montrose," after the shipwrecked English girl in *The Swiss Family Robinson.* "Miss Emily" went everywhere Karen went and, by the middle of the fifth grade, could most often be found in Karen's lap, listening with infinite patience to Karen's rambling commentaries on plots and characters.

Wanda June thought that forcing a doll to listen to amateur literary criticism was, at the very least, *peculiar.* You didn't *read books* with your dolls; you dressed them up or restyled their hair or poured imaginary cups of tea for them. By the start of their last year in elementary school, a certain wariness had begun to fray the girls' friendship as their interests diverged and their priorities shifted along the fault lines that always precede adolescence. To Wanda June, Karen's love of books was not merely incomprehensible, it was threatening—Wanda June didn't have too many other friends left. She'd become boastful and moody and prone to fits of irritability that caused her to become hugely unpopular in the space of one semester. Karen thought it had something to do with the sudden and prominent appearance on her chest of two precociously large "bumps."

This whole "puberty" thing was a rather ludicrous puzzle to Karen. Six months ago, boys barely said "hello" to Wanda June; now they were following her every move (and jiggle) with their tongues hanging out like the Big Bad

Wolf in a Disney cartoon. Maybe Karen would have enlightenment, or at least more empathy, when she developed her own set of bumps, but there was no sign of them yet. And while she might indeed be a little envious of Wanda June's accelerated "development," Karen had a strong suspicion that puberty wasn't going to be nearly as much fun as Wanda June expected it to be.

Karen had started avoiding her old friend, which of course only caused Wanda June to intrude on Karen's privacy every time she saw her and Miss Emily reading quietly outside of the house. On this soon-to-be-memorable afternoon, Karen had just gotten absorbed in her book when Wanda June's gangling shadow fell across the page like a harbinger of woe.

"Hi, Karen. Nice day, ain't it?"

"Sure is. That's why I came outside to sit in this chair and *read my book.* . . ."

Wanda June was oblivious to suggestion; *she* was far more worthy of Karen's time than any book could be!

"Hey, why don't you and me go down by the creek and see if we can catch some frogs? Big rainstorm last night, so there ought to be some whoppers jumpin' around. Come on, girl, get your nose out of that damn book and have some *fun!*"

"Wanda June, wading around in Pissin' Creek not only isn't fun, it might cut years off your life. God knows what kind of chemicals they pump into the water from the Plant. Might make your hair fall out just to touch the water." Pissin' Creek was a turgid, trash-clogged stream that got its name from the frequency with which the neighborhood boys relieved themselves behind the tall weeds lining its banks.

"God-a-mighty, Karen, you are such a stick in the mud!"

Quick as a cobra, Wanda June lashed out and snatched the book from Karen's lap.

"Hey!"

"Hey, yourself! You want to go play down by the creek with me, or you want to sit there like a bump on a log all afternoon?"

"Just give it back long enough for me to finish my chapter, and then we can go play by the creek. Okay?"

"No, it ain't okay, Karen! I'm a flesh-and-blood friend and this is just cardboard and paper! I got half a mind to throw your damn book into the creek!"

Karen knew she would, too, if a gesture of appeasement were not made right away. Sighing, she stood up and made a placating bow.

"Let me go put on my sneakers. Now please put my book down," and silently she added: *Or I'll punch you right in the nose, you low-rent little tramp!*

Karen had dreamed about the Island for as long as she could remember having dreams. Like a vast mosaic, it took form and detail bit by incremental bit. For the first two years, the Island appeared as a large geometrical abstraction: a pleasing shape made from pieces of heavy construction paper—it resembled an island as one might be drawn by a four-year-old who'd never seen a real one.

And the dreams persisted, growing more refined as the dreamer grew older and becoming noticeably more focused as her twelfth birthday approached. For one thing, the Island was no soft tropical paradise, but a gaunt, grand, flinty place of crags and mists and waterfalls that smoked like torches in the wind. There was only one town, inhabited by stoic fishermen and their families, and there was something about their shadowiness that suggested a population of ghosts. But they were stalwart, hardworking ghosts whose ships came back with their holds full of flapping silvery catch. And at some point during the third year of Island dreams, the inhabitants seemed to become aware of her. Sometimes she heard them hailing her in an archaic oddly stirring language: *Will you be the one to tell our story, Princess Karen? It's a tale well worth a listener's time, of that you may be sure!* And sometimes she heard compelling music in the background, music that sounded both very old and very vibrantly alive. The sound of it made her want to dance.

One of the oddest aspects of the phenomenon was her growing conviction that the fisherfolk were sometimes not addressing her directly, but were struggling to form words put upon their tongues by a third, invisible party who wished to communicate with her but for some reason could not make the necessary sounds. Instead, he or she seemed to manipulate the incorporeal villagers like human semaphore flags. Karen had a growing sense that the dreams were a strained attempt at some larger form of communication; that there might be *another*, more powerful, dreamer who was broadcasting these visions; that there might be a kind of formal structure to them— dreams-within-dreams. At times, she felt the very mountains vibrating, as though *they* were straining to speak directly into her mind, but those impressions always faded into a muted confusion as she made the transition from dreaming to wakefulness. She always awoke from the Island dreams feeling charged with a keen, but unfocused, energy—a knight-errant waiting for the right quest to come along. *Something* unusual was going on, that much was clear. One day, impulsively, she described the recurring dreams to her mother and asked what May could make of them.

After a long thoughtful pause, during which she continued to hoist dirty clothes into the washing machine's maw, May took a stab at it:

"Well, I see more'n one possibility here. May be that your mind's created this island out of, well, *spare parts*—left-over stuff from your daytime thoughts, maybe. It might signify that this is the place you'd be happiest living in . . . if you could find it. If that's what it means, then the nature of it will change as *you* change. You might say the island is one of them things-that-stand-for-another-thing. You know, a . . . what's the word, sweetie?"

"A symbol?"

"Bingo! Of course, there's another possibility; maybe it's a *real* place, and God has a plan for you that involves going to this place. Maybe God's sending you the same kinds of pictures over and over again, so there won't be any mistaking the right place when you *do* see it. Let's see now, you've got visions *and* voices *and* music . . . I'd say that was a powerful set of ingredients. Somebody—let's leave 'God' out of it for now—is sending you more than one symbol. Maybe your task is to figure out what it all stands for; and when you do, then you'll have some notion of what you're supposed to do with your life."

Karen had rarely seen so thoughtful a look on her mother's face, and never before heard her speak in such philosophical terms.

"Momma, you're so much smarter than. . . ."

"Than what, honey?" May smiled wryly, observing how hard her daughter was struggling to complete the sentence without hurting her feelings. "Smarter than I usually have a chance to show?"

"Something like that."

"Lord's sake, Karen, that's true of most everybody! Just 'cause we live where we live don't mean me and your daddy didn't have some mighty ambitious dreams of our own, once. But somehow they all got chucked out along the way, from gettin' married to gettin' old. Earl and me, we ran out of dreams a long time ago, and so we just don't talk that way to each other any more. It's nice I can talk to you, though, since all my other children appear to have maybe one good brain to share amongst the lot of 'em."

May started to pick up a basket of wet laundry, then suddenly plopped it down again and gripped Karen fiercely by the shoulders.

"Listen to me, now: If you find a man who dreams about islands, too, you'd better grab him and hold on to him, because there might not be two such men in the whole world! You find such a man, and I swear that you *will* fall in love with him and you both *will* sail off together to find your island, because that's the destiny your dreams are telling you not to ignore! 'Course, findin' that man could be a lot harder than findin' your island. . . ."

One month after her twelfth birthday and three weeks after her sixth-grade classes had begun, Karen was enjoying the late-summer weather in the company of Miss Emily, for whom May had just stitched together a Cinderella-type ball gown, using scraps of cloth too small to have any other useful purpose. Karen knew the time was soon coming when she'd lose interest in dolls, but on this hot afternoon, she could think of nothing she'd rather do than sit under the back yard's only decent shade tree and dress Miss Emily in her new finery.

"Now Miss Emily, when you are introduced to the Prince, you must curtsy like I showed you, extend your hand like this when he bows, so that he may kiss it if he wishes to. And you'll be able to tell, just from the way his lips touch your hand, whether or not he is truly interested."

"Whether or not *who's* interested?"

Wanda June's grating little voice snapped Karen back into the reality of a hot, dull Sunday afternoon in the Project. She had more or less expected the visit; lately, Wanda June had been making an aggressive attempt to repair their friendship. Both girls were entering their final year of elementary school, but Wanda June's precociously ripe body and brassy habit of making herself the center of attention had finally made her a pariah to all the girls whose hormones hadn't kicked in so formidably. More and more, she intruded on Karen's privacy; they had been best friends for so long that Karen at least was more tolerant of Wanda June's incessant monologues about her own burgeoning sexuality. And Karen was "in training" for the onslaught of her own "womanhood"—she figured that, buried inside Wanda June's blather, there might actually be some useful information: about what to expect, and about how *not* to behave.

Today, Wanda June had squeezed herself into a tube top that was at least two sizes too small, and she'd "forgotten" to put her bra on first—short of parading through the neighborhood half-naked, there wasn't much more she could have done to call attention to the glorious motility of her upper torso. Karen could tell, from the size of the smirk on Wanda June's face, that her old pal was bursting to impart some titillating new discovery about boy–girl relationships. So Karen prepared herself, mentally, to take notes.

She parked Miss Emily across her lap, murmuring: *Forget about the Prince, Miss Em. This ought to be a lot more interesting!*

"What's up, kiddo? Oh, I see. You and Miss Emily are going to another grand ball at 'The Prince's Palace.'"

There was so much condescension in Wanda June's voice that Karen couldn't help blushing and covering part of the doll's face with her hand. Miss Emily's eyes rolled up beseechingly.

"No, of course not. I'm too old for that kind of pretend-stuff now! I was just going through Miss Em's winter wardrobe. . . ."

Wanda June cocked one hip and thrust out her jaw. "Well, I put all of *my* dolls in the attic last weekend. I've got more important things on my mind these days. And you will, too, pretty soon. That's why you need to start *practicin'!*"

Miss Emily's glassy stare seemed to widen: *Don't put me in a shoebox and stuff me in the attic! What about my waltz with the Prince? What happens after he kisses my hand?*

Karen had no idea; she hadn't gotten that far in planning the scenario.

"So just what is it I should be 'practicing' for?"

"How to get a gorgeous hunky guy to go steady with you. The captain of the football team, for instance."

"Bobby Sudberry? He's a gorilla with zits on the back of his neck, and he only has one eyebrow; why would I even give him the time of day, never mind going steady?"

"That's just an example, you ree-tard! What I mean is, you need to start thinking seriously about *boys.*"

"What about them?"

"Oh, what makes 'em happy; what keeps 'em interested in you; that kind of stuff. I can tell you some things, but only if you promise not to spread any gossip."

"Okay," sighed Karen, "I promise." *This had better be good. . . .*

Wanda June leaned over like a conspirator and whispered: "Last Saturday, I 'Frenched' Tommy Herlocker!"

Karen blinked several times and wrinkled her nose. "Why in the world would you want to talk to Tommy Herlocker in French? You can't even read French. And he just barely manages with English."

"God-a-mighty, Karen, you *are* clueless! That means I stuck my tongue in his mouth when I kissed him!"

Wanda June obviously expected Karen's jaw to drop in amazement, but Karen merely shuddered. "Why would you do that? Tommy's always got little bits of food stuck in his braces. That's just gross."

Wanda June was dumbstruck by Karen's naïveté. Worse, Wanda June's overwhelming need to boast about *important* stuff had just sailed into a void, wasted on this *kid* who still *played with dolls*. Such a rebuke could not be tolerated; even the implication of mockery had to be punished. Wanda June flared angrily, and Karen shrank from her knotted fists, her hard, murderous glare.

"You're nothin' but a chickenshit bookworm! Except for that stupid doll, I'm the only friend you've got in the world!"

Karen suddenly knew what Wanda June was going to do, but the violation of trust was so monstrous she was too slow to evade the grasping hands that yanked Miss Emily from her grip with such fury that the doll's new dress was torn to rags.

"Why don't you grow up, Karen? Why don't you get your nose out of them God-damned books? Why don't you ever talk to me like I was a *real person?* Well, maybe if I got rid of little Miss Emily here, you'd pay some attention to *me!*"

Wanda June shook the doll like a rattle and scampered away when Karen came shambling toward her, moving like a bug on flypaper. "Don't! Don't you dare!" she shouted, but her reaction only increased the sadistic glee in her tormenter's eyes.

"Come on, Miss Emily, I think I'll take you for a nice swim in Pissin' Creek!"

Wanda June ran ahead, much too fleet for Karen to catch her. She was indeed making a beeline for the weedy thickets around the creek. If Karen couldn't take back Miss Emily before Wanda June chucked the doll into the water, the current would sweep Miss Em far, far away.

"I swear to God, if you don't bring Miss Emily back to me right this minute, I'm going to tell everybody at school that you're pregnant!"

"Go ahead, bookworm! I'll take a test and then everybody'll know you're a liar!"

Karen, picking up speed as she plunged into the briars and weeds along the creek, was fresh out of bluffs. Smugly satisfied with the way she had deflected Karen's shot, Wanda June turned back just long enough to flash a malicious, taunting smile, and then she vanished down the embankment. Karen couldn't believe Wanda June was actually wading across Pissin' Creek—not even the toughest-talking boys would put their bare feet into that vile morass. But when Karen, panting and dripping sweat, reached the shore, she saw that Wanda June had been able to skip dry-footed to the opposite side, by hopping over a natural isthmus of cinder blocks, old logs, and mounds of petrified garbage. When Karen reached the lip of the gully, she almost gagged from the combined smells of rancid chemicals and the ripe decay wafting off the distended corpse of a large dead possum. Wanda June was sauntering along the far side now, twirling Miss Emily by one leg and singing loudly to mask Karen's shrieks and pleas, clearly trying to decide what would be the most hateful, wounding thing she could do to Miss Emily. Karen only hoped she would stop short of simply smashing the doll to bits against the nearest drainpipe.

Wanda June came up with an inspired alternative—after all, if Karen ran sobbing to her house and showed Wanda June's mother the shattered pieces of an antique doll, Wanda June's daddy, who was already wondering aloud whether he had sired a daughter or a predatory delinquent, would take out his old razor strop and prove to her that she was not, in fact, too old for a sizzler of a spanking. So Wanda June decided not to break Miss Emily, but merely to dispose of her in a way that was guaranteed to prolong Karen's suffering to the maximum. She stopped in front of the largest, oldest drainpipe leading from the Plant, a dry cracked gaping mouth set high in the embankment. Her face ablaze with malice, she lifted the doll high above her head, made sure Karen was in position to see what came next, and pointed inside that dark orifice.

"Don't," whimpered Karen. "Please, Wanda June, don't to that!"

"Maybe I won't . . . if you promise to be my friend always."

"I promise."

"And you promise to always sit with me at lunch and not pretend you don't see me when I'm walkin' by myself in the halls."

"I promise, damn it! Now give me back my doll!"

"One more thing: you gotta promise that whenever I come over to your house, you'll put down whatever book you're readin' and *talk to me!*"

Karen had reached the limit of appeasement.

"No, I will *not* promise that, you boring, ignorant redneck *skank!* I'd rather read the phone directory than listen to you brag about your tits or hear about how you stuck your tongue into some guy's mouth! You know what, Wanda June? You'll get yourself knocked up before you turn fifteen! And when your daddy finds out, he'll kick your fat ass out onto the street!"

"If that's the way you want this to end, Bookworm, that's fine with me. So fuck you, and fuck your stupid doll too!"

Wanda June brought her pitching arm around in a powerful softball curve, and Miss Emily sailed deep into the black throat of the big spider-webbed pipe. "Strike three! Miss Emily's out!" Cackling like a witch, she gave Karen the finger, climbed back up the embankment, and vanished into the weeds.

Karen didn't bother with the cinder blocks; she splashed through the hot, reeking water and scrambled up to the pipe on her hands and knees. Afternoon sunlight poured over her shoulders and illuminated the first four or five feet of the interior. Retrieving Miss Em would be a creepy chore, but at least the doll was intact . . . somewhere down there in the darkness. Karen wiggled into the pipe, waited until her eyes adjusted to the gloom, and started to crawl carefully toward the doll's presumed location.

But when she got all the way inside, she saw no trace of it. There was just enough light to see that decades of erosion had loosened one section of pipe, angling it down and to the right, forming a blind curve about seven feet from the entrance. Miss Emily had apparently bounced off the wall and rolled down the seam between the shifted sections of pipe. Karen didn't particularly relish the thought of crawling deeper into that dark, confining tunnel, but it wasn't *that* narrow and she was a slender girl. She took a couple of deep breaths—how humid, how close was the air!—and began inching forward. She'd only traveled a couple of feet before she was blinded by the sweat from her brow. Instinctively, she tried to reach for the hem of her blouse, so she could wipe her eyes, but found no clearance for her elbows. She was increasingly sensitive to the harsh, abrasive concrete—which rubbed her skin like a cold cat's tongue—and to the narrowness of the passage. She'd already rubbed the skin off her right elbow, and it stung something fierce when sweat ran into the wound.

Well, she reasoned, she would only have to put up with it for another couple of minutes.

The entrance behind her seemed to shrink as she resumed her forward motion. As she moved, her own body blocked the light from outside, so that when she finally reached the bend, she had to grope blindly around it and try to locate Miss Emily by touch—after carefully purging from her imagination the menacing images of cool, sleeping copperheads and pissed-off black widows. She felt dry powdery mud, some blobs of unidentifiable debris, a scrap of rusted metal, and a muck-encrusted Coke bottle . . . but no doll. Wanda June really had a good throwing arm. Karen shuddered at the prospect of trying to bend her body through the out-of-plumb section, but there was no other way: she would not leave Miss Emily alone, in the dark, forlorn and abandoned, just because she was discovering the terrors of claustrophobia!

Karen was gasping like a landed fish by the time her fingers finally closed around the doll's left foot. "I swear, that bitch is gonna pay for doing this to you, baby!" she crooned. Perhaps she was getting too old to play with Miss Emily, but that didn't mean she wasn't going to cherish her . . . or that she was going to chicken out with the job half-done and leave her in this culvert for a raccoon to nibble on.

But when Karen tried to back out of the bend, her lower body encountered a steely-hard obstruction that she didn't remember passing. Her scrabbling feet could gain no purchase on the concrete, and since she couldn't turn her head to see what was wrong, she had to stop and try to visualize the geometry of the situation. *Don't panic! Panic uses up the air! Where did I read that? Poe, maybe, in "The Premature Burial." Right, just the story I need to be thinking about right now. . . .*

She figured it out, though the conclusion brought no relief: what had trapped her was a big split-off slab of concrete, angled in such a way that she could easily crawl over the beveled edges on her way *in;* but without any space to maneuver her knees and feet, she could not quite summon the same leverage when she tried to back *out.* And she certainly wasn't able to push away a three-hundred-pound chunk of concrete rooted in several cubic feet of packed red clay.

For the first time, she gave way to panic: churning uselessly in place, shouting, screaming, blinded by sweat, she convulsed and thrashed until her skin was scraped raw and she felt in real danger of suffocating. Shouting for help wouldn't do much good, either; her own body acted as a plug to trap whatever sounds she made. There were probably a dozen kids playing around Pissin' Creek on any weekend afternoon, but unless they just happened to be passing right by the entrance to this pipe, they would not hear her, no matter if she screamed herself hoarse.

Slowly, methodically, she imposed her will upon her wild, bucking nervous system, forcing her body to be still, to relax, to stop hurting itself. To reassure herself, she pretended to comfort Miss Emily. "It's okay, sweetie, it's all going to be fine. Wanda June knew I was going to crawl inside this thing—she'll be scared now, because I haven't come back out, and when she gets *really* scared, as in 'Child Suffocates in Old Drain Pipe,' she'll tell somebody. And the rescue squad will come and pull us out of here, easy as pie. You'll see. I'll tell you stories to pass the time." But Karen didn't, because her voice was quavering, and when she tried "Once upon a time," she began whimpering like a hurt puppy. The sound of her own terror frightened her so badly that she became silent. There was no point in screaming for help unless she actually heard voices. Maybe if she unplugged parts of her mind, too, the way she'd just unplugged her vocal cords, she would calm down.

That trick worked, too, because eventually, for a couple of merciful hours, she passed out. But her fear redoubled when she woke and felt cool night air against her legs and realized that nobody would be playing by the creek now. She and Miss Emily were alone in the dark. She had entered the culvert around three-thirty, and that was at least five—maybe six—hours ago, and no one had come searching for her. Wanda June might well be scared shitless about Karen, but she might also be too frightened to tell anybody where Karen was. Faintly, she heard the carillon sound nine o'clock from the far-off College bell tower.

All right, then, she would have to spend the night here and she'd better get used to the idea. She would be hungry and thirsty and afraid, but the sun *would* come up, and when Wanda June realized she was not at school tomorrow morning, then surely she would alert the grown-ups. Who *did* you alert in such cases? Every kid knew the answer to that: you alerted The Authorities! She could hear them now, their voices so reassuring and . . . *authoritative*: "Hello in there, Miss Hambly? Miss Emily? We're the

Authorities and we've come to pull you out!" What a relief it would be to hear those words!

Shortly after the distant chimes tolled ten o'clock, Karen couldn't hold her pee any longer. When the hot, urgent flood scalded the tender insides of her thighs, she wept with shame.

Just before eleven o'clock, the mosquitoes found her; she couldn't do anything to repel them except blow futile puffs of air at them. The insects landed on her flesh and began to feed at their leisure. When one especially large mosquito began to hum close to her left ear, she thought she would go mad. Its whine was like a drill-bit grinding into her skull. She bucked and thrashed, not caring how much skin she lost as long as she mashed some of the blood-suckers, and in doing so, she lost so much oxygen that she passed into the sweet oblivion of unnatural sleep. And she saw the Island again.

Only this time, she saw it from a strange new perspective. In some ways, her viewpoint was like that of a swimmer floating on his back. But she wasn't floating in a human body; instead, she had an amorphous, protoplasmic *shape* that molded itself to the warm billows of the sea. She may have had "eyes," but they were not human eyes, and they perceived wavelengths and colors that were outside of the human spectrum. The Island seemed to vibrate under ultraviolet rays. And far off to the west, under a flawless azure sky, an active volcano threw a ten-mile shadow across the ocean. She saw no sign of the fishermen from the village; indeed, she saw no boats, no airplanes, not one sign of human life! That wasn't so incredible, though, because from the temporal perspective of the entity whose consciousness she seemed to have borrowed, human beings hadn't evolved yet. This was *her* world; and to her overlapping senses, the solitude and tranquility were thoroughly agreeable.

Well, how about that? There *were* other critters, in the water, at least, because now and then she felt a disturbance from their passing. One of them, some sort of huge shadowy predator, tried to push her around, or maybe eat her—but she wasn't alarmed. In an automatic, lackadaisical manner, she felt a pulse of . . . energy? plasma? poisoned stingers? . . . ripple outward and make contact with the predator. To her senses, that brief interaction registered as a pleasant, drowsy tingle. To the other creature, it must have been dire agony, for she could feel its frenzied thrashing. When it was still, she sent more pulsations into it and, in return, she felt the even-more-pleasing intake of nutrition, as the creature's flesh and bones and muscle tissues slowly dissolved and were absorbed into her mass.

Karen would have been content to float like that forever, sentient enough to relish the fact of existence, dangerous enough to be left alone, her consciousness vast but elemental. If a cloud could have rudimentary awareness, it would feel something like this. How pleasant it was just to drift upon the sea's infinite breast.

But something intruded on that mood. A troubling vibration ruffled the water around her. Whatever its source, it signified danger. The alien consciousness she shared was stunned by a new and terrible emotion: fear.

Then the world exploded, or at least that segment of it that comprised the distant smoldering volcano. A stupendous blast seared her outer surface; a pillar of molten rock and vaporized seawater, wreathed in vile smoke, surged into the air, darkening the sky. And then the sea burst like a broken blister, rolling into a wave so high that it blotted out the sun. A surging crust of fire glazed the wave's summit; and as it bore down on her from one direction, the peaceful island—her Dream Island, she had no doubt about it now—heaved up and split, bleeding lava in arterial jets. The very crust of the Earth was rearranging itself far below, and its savage vibrations stunned and terrified her. The Island exploded just seconds before the tsunami engulfed her.

Darkness. Silence. For a long, long, time.

When consciousness returned—a dream nested inside another dream—she no longer "saw" the sky, nor did she float free and untroubled on that warm, soupy primordial sea. She had only one sensation now: a commingling of weight and density that completely immobilized her.

It was too much to bear. Karen fled from the dream in horror, only to remember who and where she was: like that ancient, strange, yet kindred entity, she too was immobilized beneath unyielding rock. *I see daylight, though! Pretty soon, we'll be rescued. Any minute now. And if I keep my eyes closed and do not look at the walls of this round gray tomb, I can keep my sanity until they find me.*

But already she was trembling and gasping for air. She felt the warmth of day creep up the pipe and the first wisp of sunlight against her scabbed and aching legs was so intense that she gasped, and repeated her new mantra: *Do not open your eyes! Madness will come roaring in and never leave!*

Slowly, her body began to relax. Except for her forehead, which for some reason was twitching uncontrollably. It was really annoying, this infernal twitching above her determinedly closed eyes, but she also felt *another* localized sensation in the same region of her body. In the center of her forehead, a drop of warm oil spread, from a pinpoint to the diameter of a half-dollar. And the nearby itching suddenly turned into sharp, tearing pain. What struck her as most curious was the fact that neither of these sensations was *internal.* Something was hurting her eyebrow and something else was conveying a sensation of well-being, like a salve, that penetrated her pores and seemed to refresh both mind and body. The juxtaposition of sensations was bizarre: one so painful, the other so mysteriously benign.

Is there an angel soothing me in one place and a demon stabbing me in another?

Her hold on sanity was already precarious; if she opened her eyes and saw nothing, then she was merely hallucinating. That was okay; she could handle that. But what if she couldn't tell hallucinations from reality any more? Would that even make a difference? Or would it kick her over the edge into madness?

Brace yourself, girl. What you're about to see may not even be real.

So surreal was the dichotomy, so extreme and schizoid was her reaction, that it took several seconds before her brain processed the information sent to it by the optic nerves.

The gently probing warm-oil sensation was apparently being caused by the flattened tip of a long, thin filament of organic matter, gray on its surface, mottled inside with tiny blue mica-flecks of iridescence. This baffling *connection* extended from the muddy surface of Pissin' Creek, arched upward through the entrance, and twined around the ledges of broken pipe that had immobilized her. She had never seen anything remotely like this softly vibrating column; she concluded it was living matter only from its texture, its slightly motile warmth against her skin, and its seemingly purposeful, even "guided," behavior.

The twitching, tearing sensation, on the other hand, was caused by the big, shit-caked sewer rat that was about to take its second experimental bite out of her right eyebrow.

Shock and madness roared in her brain, and the effect was as though a gate had been blown open deep within her consciousness; something akin to a bolt of lightning arced through that long tentacle-like extrusion, and her adrenal gland went nova. She'd heard stories about elderly grandmothers who suddenly found the strength to lift a wrecked car off a small child, but those feats were small change compared to what she intended to do next. What a fool she had been! Why, this seemingly unmovable concrete pipe was old, brittle, and had lost its tensile strength years ago! It was a husk, a bluff; its power-to-confine was only an illusion! All Karen needed to do was give one mighty heave, and it would crack like an eggshell.

She bellowed like a kung fu master and savored the surging strength that was being loaned to her, suffusing through her body from that warm-oil spot on her forehead. Her bones were burly piston rods; her sinews, cables of steel; her skull and shoulders were encased in armor plate . . . and her will power could have toppled empires!

First, she took care of the rat. Or *something* did. She hawked a gob of saliva into its face—spittle that was oddly streaked with the same shade of blue she'd seen inside the organic extrusion—and was savagely gratified to see its eyeballs melting in their sockets. The rodent shrieked in agony and fell to the bottom of the pipe, whirling frenziedly, chomping through its tail and convulsing in spasms so violent that its bones snapped like toothpicks.

You want a piece of me, Mickey? How did that *taste?*

The pipe cracked at the same time she fractured her left clavicle in two places. Surrounded by a flurry of shattered concrete, she clawed up through the matted roots of the creek-bank's vegetation; the mysterious organic connector, its mission evidently accomplished, recoiled slowly into the creek and, just as her head emerged from the soil, she caught a glimpse of it vanishing into the contaminated water, smooth and fast as a cable being rewound by a powerful winch. Aside from a few root-beer-colored bubbles, it left no trace.

Looking like a zombie from a B-grade horror movie, Karen Hambly surged out of the earth, shouting triumphantly. *I wish there was a paramedic around right now, not because I need rescuing but so that he could take a blood sample. There's something more than adrenaline flooding through my veins, because I just broke through an inch-thick concrete pipe with my* shoulder.

But it was ordinary human-grade adrenaline that kept her pain at bay while she crossed the creek and scaled the opposite side. In a nearby house, someone was frying bacon—the aroma made her drool. At the top of the embankment, she paused to get her bearings. It was about seven-fifteen, Monday morning. With any luck, the school bus hadn't picked up Wanda

June yet. Clutching the bedraggled Miss Emily by one foot, Karen strode between a pair of houses, the sight of her eliciting a scream from a toddler who happened to glance out his kitchen window when she lurched past, fierce and cadaverous and streaked with filth and blood.

All was as she had expected: the neighborhood kids gathering at the bus stop, moms in tatty bathrobes, many of them lighting the day's first cigarette, and a police car in the driveway of the Hambly residence.

And there was Wanda June, waiting at the bus stop, not as talkative this morning as usual, who kept glancing nervously at the squad car.

Bitch hasn't even told anybody!

One of the other kids spotted Karen, did a horrified double-take, and shrieked as though he had seen a ghost—which, in a sense, he had done. Holding Miss Emily in both knotted fists, Karen covered the distance to Wanda June too fast for her target to do more than stare in open-mouthed amazement at the sight of her, and with a maniacal sweeping chop worthy of a lumberjack, Karen brought the doll down on Wanda June's scalp, opening a five-inch gash that severed the top of her right ear and pretty much ruined her plans for winning the Miss America contest.

5.

THE WAR MEMORIAL IN TORSHAVN

It was Eiden Poulsen's custom, on days of good weather, to walk the uphill mile from his shipyard to a quiet arboreal corner of the War Memorial Garden and there spend a peaceful hour eating his lunch and skimming the newspapers flown in every morning from London, Copenhagen, and New York.

Eiden felt a proprietary interest in the War Memorial Garden; he'd chaired the committee in charge of selecting the site, commissioning the statue, and plotting the locations of the 200-odd trees that had to be imported individually and nursed like premature babies until they found ways to survive in the dank climate and thin topsoil of the Faeroe Islands. Every tree on the islands had begun its life somewhere else, and each was registered as a "national resource."

This particular spring day was so fair and beguiling that he adjourned the weekly management meeting long before half of the dull agenda had been discussed. "I hereby declare a two-hour lunch break," he announced rather airily. "The rest of this stuff can wait, gentlemen. 'Tis a sin to be indoors on such a day!" Then, following his own advice, he retrieved from his secretary's cubicle his thirty-year-old lunch box, his Royal Navy windbreaker, and the morning papers, which he stuffed into his briefcase. He sauntered forth in a fine mood, whistling a Rossini overture as passed through the main gate and commenced the daily ritual, which his fellow Torshavners had taken to calling "Poulsen's Passing."

Men doffed their caps as he strode by, greeting him with varying measures of respect and familiarity ("G'day to you, Cap'n Poulsen!," "Have a nice lunch, Skipper!"). As for the female pedestrians, Eiden responded to their greetings in a more circumspect manner. As the wealthiest man in Torshavn, he was by definition the town's most eligible bachelor. He looked (and usually

felt) younger than he was. He still had the broad, strong shoulders of a
trawlerman, the ruddy complexion of a vigorous outdoorsman, and the startling arctic-blue eyes of his Viking forebears. He would have been a splendid
"catch" for any female, and was often approached by precocious adolescents
as well as hopeful widows. He tried to spare a kind word for all the ladies,
but he could be curt when ambitious mothers thrust her comely young
daughters in front of him. Eiden found these attempts to engage his libid-
inal interest rather grotesque. Perhaps neither mother nor daughter really
cared about the age difference, but he certainly did.

By unspoken custom, nobody was supposed to pester herre Poulsen after
he passed the second of Torshavn's five traffic lights, so he was allowed to
finish the steeper half of his journey unmolested. He didn't really mind running the daily gauntlet of glad-handers and would-be sycophants he
encountered on the first half-mile; Torshavn was a small city, after all, and
everybody knew everybody else's business; interacting with the populace
provided amusement, stimulation, and the odd bit of useful gossip or commercial intelligence. As long as he *could* make these daily hegiras, he would.
This was his town, and the people who called out to him were his neighbors—
but not one of them would ever think of telephoning him or knocking, unin-
vited, on the door of his townhouse.

On this particular day, Eiden was somewhat bedraggled by the time he
located his favorite bench in the War Memorial Garden—the heavy
morning rain had left deep puddles in the cobblestones, and the fierce sunshine that followed had filled many of the uphill lanes with steam.

At least the fickle weather had discouraged any other pedestrians from
following Eiden's example: he apparently had the War Memorial Garden to
himself. The privacy was delightful, almost sensual. After all, he'd brought
this park into being, after two years of settling the ego clashes of every land-
scaper, botanist, sculptor, and meddling bureaucrat who had tried to dominate the project. Eiden thought it was not unreasonable for him to be
granted *some* perquisites in return for all the *pro bono* hours he'd invested. . . .

In savory solitude, therefore, Eiden Poulsen ate his lunch and drank his
coffee laced with Irish whiskey from his thermos bottle. As he had foretold,
the afternoon was waxing fair, almost balmy, and the clear, flower-scented air
was a tonic. He might just choose to linger here all through the afternoon.

He *was* The Boss, after all. He settled back and lit his ritual after-lunch cigarette. That's when he noticed that he was not, in fact, the only person who was enjoying the park.

The newcomer was a young man whose dress and general demeanor suggested that he was a Yank or a Brit. That this young pilgrim had fallen under the garden's spell was obvious from the thoughtfulness on his face and the diffidence with which he approached each flower bed and stand of trees, bending over carefully to read the informational placards.

He had the look of a Romantic, this lad: broad shoulders and curly windblown hair; that notebook in his hip pocket would almost certainly be filled with passionate but mawkish poetry. Eiden occasionally saw such wanderers in the streets of Torshavn, and they all came here for the same reason: they had encountered a travel poster or read a magazine article about the Faeroes, and the islands' wild beauty just drew them hither like an undertow.

But few of those wandering spirits ever came to this park. Generally speaking, they avoided anything that their guidebooks identified as being a "war memorial." Europe was filled with bombastic or bathetic "war memorials," and really, if you'd seen one, you'd seen 'em all. Somehow, this young man had responded differently. For Eiden, the litmus test would come when the traveler turned around that next copse of trees and came face to face with the memorial statue itself. Eiden decided to follow; he was curious to learn how this young foreigner, who most likely didn't even know of the sculpture's existence, would spontaneously react when he encountered it.

Eiden cut stealthily through a flower bed, locating a spot from which he could observe the statue, and the curious young man about to discover it, from close range. He expected to see the American stroll once around the pedestal or reach out to thump the bronze with his finger, and then move on to another scenic spot, uninterested in the sculpture or the story behind it. Instead, he saw the young man kneeling and bending to examine the statue from various angles, all the while speaking quite audibly into a small dictation recorder. Eiden felt like an eavesdropper, but anyone who dictated his poetry aloud was just asking for it. But then he realized with a start that, whatever the young man was saying into the microphone, it certainly didn't sound like *poetry*. Intrigued, Eiden cupped hand to ear and listened:

In the bleak, rain-soaked hills encircling Torshavn, I've discovered a public park of modest size but imaginative design. It is everything such a park ought to be, an oasis of peace, a place where flowers are cherished and groves of imported trees are immaculately tended—as though by Druids.

The official designation of this place is the "War Memorial Garden," and my guidebook states that it is: quote, "dedicated to the memory of all the Faeroese who sacrificed their lives in World War Two." This is news to me—I didn't know the Faeroese fought in that war. Moreover, the author of this guidebook states that, again quote, "while the view of Torshavn and the surrounding hills is worth the uphill trek, the statue itself is a disappointingly homely affair, executed in the kind of faux primitive style intended to be 'strong and simple' but which strikes most observers as merely banal. . . ."

Well, I beg strenuously to differ! I've seen a lot of war statues and war memorials in my time, everything from the ubiquitous Confederate soldier in the town square of Bumfuck, Georgia, to those hideous examples of Stalinist Baroque that clutter up the streets of Leningrad, and I think this Faeroese example may be the most touchingly honest monument I've ever seen. And it doesn't even have a military theme. In rough, simple bronze, it merely depicts the life-sized figure of a fisherman, clad in boots and a slicker, nets gripped in gnarled hardworking hands, gazing eternally out over Thor's Harbor—gazing at his home. And on the man's face is an expression of unutterable longing.

On to less contentious observations! This seems to be a typical spring afternoon in Torshavn: this morning, a furious rain squall swept the city, but now that's just a memory. Azure skies, flocked with innocent puffs of cloud, a generous flood of almost pagan sunlight—here in the garden, the foliage gleams as though each leaf and twig had been dipped in warm green paraffin. The air is cool and the scent of flowers is piercing. Fresh-scrubbed sunlight pours like a benediction over the hills and their terraced rows of brightly colored cottages. This park, the blunt casual power of the bronze fisherman, the ever-changing collage of sun and cloud-shadow—I've only been here two days, and have no earthly idea where to go from Torshavn or what to look for when I do, but I think I have fallen in love with these islands.

Here, the young chronicler seemed to run out of steam. He searched his notes for inspiration but finally shook his head. "Lost the riff, I guess," Eiden heard him grumble as he stuffed the recorder into his pack and fumbled in his shirt pocket for a cigarette. But the lighter-wheel only rasped mockingly as he snapped the ball of his thumb against it repeatedly. Eiden could *feel* how badly the American wanted a smoke, so he emerged from hiding with his own lighter extended, saying: "Pardon me, but I couldn't help seeing your frustration; so please 'grab some fire,' as we Faeroese like to say, from my lighter. My name is Eiden Poulsen, by the way."

The stranger nodded thanks and stood up to offer his hand and name, not seeming in the least embarrassed at the idea that Eiden had been listening to his soliloquy.

"My name is Allen Warrener, and I'm sure it's blindingly obvious that I'm an American . . . worse yet, a Southerner. Even worse than both those things, I'm also a writer, which is why I take notes on this thing . . . but only when I think there's nobody watching me."

"I assure you, Mr. Warrener, I didn't mean to be rude, but after I heard the first few lines, I simply had to keep eavesdropping. I'm very happy to hear that you approve of our 'banal' statue! You see, I was on the committee that had to judge all the artists' submissions, and I can tell you that it was not an easy job. Most of my colleagues wanted something big and pompous—a giant codfish waving a sword or something. As you so accurately said, Europe is already stuffed with bombastic memorials. I wanted this one to evoke a genuine, human experience."

"Please, call me Allen, and yes, I *do* like your statue. There's nothing phony about it—just a man, performing the most important work a man can do: putting food on the nation's tables. So what if he isn't bearing arms? Nothing will sap an army's will to fight more quickly than the knowledge that the soldiers' wives and children are starving behind the lines. That was one of the main reasons the South lost our Civil War, you know. Men won't fight for a government that can't or won't protect their loved ones from going hungry."

"Do you also write history, Allen? If not, you bloody well should!"

Allen was encouraged enough to permit Eiden a glimpse of his pride. He described the thesis he was researching, delivering a mini-lecture about the tortuous political and strategic course Finland had been compelled to follow in the name of national survival. The narrative had many twists, and Poulsen had trouble keeping up with some of them, but he *was* carried along by the sheer gusto of Allen's storytelling.

". . . and that, I think, is why Finland never became a Soviet satellite, as did all her Baltic neighbors. But now that I've talked your ear off, why don't you tell me about how the Faeroese experienced World War Two? I always thought you were neutral, like Switzerland or Monte Carlo or some other postage-stamp country. Obviously that's not the case, and obviously you know a lot about the subject. . . ."

"As it happens, I do. But why don't we sit down first—there's a bench just on the other side of those shrubs that offers a tremendous view of the harbor and the islands beyond. That way, if my middle-aged ramblings get too tiresome, you can always enjoy the scenery. . . ."

Eiden's father was a prosperous dry goods merchant, but when Eiden announced his desire to pursue the traditional calling of the sea, his father did not oppose, for the fisherman's trade was both honorable and necessary. One week after his fourteenth birthday, Eiden signed the papers of an Apprentice Seaman on the good ship *Hvildara* ("Still Waters"), commanded by his uncle, Anders Poulsen.

It was during a shore leave, midway through that crucial first year, that Eiden heard all the complexities of Faeroese life distilled by Anders Poulsen into one memorable phrase. Eiden had tagged along with his uncle and two shipmates to a Rotterdam tavern, where the first mate arranged for Eiden to lose his virginity after lunch and then to celebrate by getting just a bit plastered with the adults. As the bar got crowded, the Faeroese invited a trio of convivial Dutch merchant-mariners to join them. The Dutchmen were jolly companions, who stood their share of drinks and treated the young apprentice to a lot of ribald congratulations as soon as they learned how momentous his afternoon had been. At one point in the blurry evening, one of the Dutch bluejackets politely inquired: "Why is it that whenever we run into Faeroese sailors, they're always fishermen? None of you, it seems, ever chooses a career in the merchant fleet or the Navy! I've been told that ninety-five percent of all registered Faeroese mariners are employed in the fishing industry, and I've often wondered why, given the fact that the Faeroese are such natural-born seamen, they all choose to follow the same course."

Uncle Anders signaled a passing waitress for a fresh pitcher, and then turned back toward the Dutchman and calmly said: "Well, my friend, it's really a very simple matter. If you are born on our islands, you have two choices in life: you can fish, or you can starve. Therefore, we fish!"

Eiden matured rapidly under the tutelage of an experienced skipper who valued fairness but refused to coddle any boy who had chosen the hard life of a seaman. When the boy seemed ready, Uncle Anders began sharing with him the secrets and intuitions of the seamanship that had made him known and respected throughout northern Europe.

Before he was seventeen, Eiden Poulsen had: survived a murderous gale that sank three other ships; become a veritable shark at the billiards tables in a score of ports; acquired four dramatically different "fiancées" (in Reykjavik, Antwerp, Aberdeen, and Bergen); endured rough surgery on the wardroom table at the hands of the first mate (sixteen stitches in his left side, from a broken hook, and with only a pint of aquavit for anesthetic); weathered five cases of the crabs; fathered at least one illegitimate child; obtained his certi-fications in wireless telegraphy and navigation; served a memorable week in a Latvian jail (for demolishing the "Laughing Seal" tavern in Vilnius); acquired his first and last tattoo (in a place where few would see it); and killed his first man (a drunken Filipino stoker who tried to rob Eiden at revolver-point; the pistol misfired, but Eiden's sword-cane did not; he'd gutted the thug like a codfish and left him in an alley, stupidly trying to stuff his tripe back into his sundered abdomen).

All in all, Uncle Anders thought Eiden had the makings of a first-rate seaman and the potential to be an outstanding skipper. Eiden was tough, honest, capable, and always eager to learn more. After seven seasons of loyal diligence, Eiden Poulsen moved up to the responsibilities of first mate, when the gentleman who had held that that rating for many years elected to retire.

Anders was thinking of retirement too. A Scottish doctor, in the course of treating the old salt for pneumonia, had discovered a cluster of "pre-tuber-cular" spots on his lungs and advised him to do two things: one, stop spending two-thirds of every year standing on the bridge of a small vessel in the rough, cold waters of the North Atlantic; and two, find somewhere else to live during the other third besides the damp, gloomy highlands of tiny Nolsoy Island. Ever a pragmatist, Anders declared that *now* he could move his family to a sunny island in the Aegean, which was his idea of paradise, and devote his remaining years to learning how to read the *Odyssey* in Homer's own language. Papers were drawn up stating that: at the start of his ninth season aboard the *Hvildara*, Eiden Poulsen would become her legal captain, with a 15 percent ownership and 20 percent share of the gross profits from every load of fish sold at market price. For Eiden, it was the opportunity of a lifetime, and for Uncle Anders . . . well, he had no trouble at all persuading his wife to leave behind the cold, storm-flogged island of Nolsoy in favor of a Mediterranean villa.

Eiden spent the winter of 1939–40 making plans for his first voyage as captain. In January 1940, the ship went into drydock, to have its hull scraped, its paintwork refurbished, and a new long-range wireless installed. On the morning of April 9, Eiden and Anders conducted a bow-to-stern inspection, pronounced the overhaul complete, and headed from the dock-yard to the telegraph office to summon the crew to assemble.

They were both sauntering down one of the main streets, in search of a good restaurant, when Anders pointed and said: "What's that crowd doing over by the radio shop?"

" 'Milling,' I believe they call it." Eiden was about to walk past when he heard a young woman burst into tears, sobbing something about her fiancée being "trapped in Copenhagen by the fighting,"

"By the what?" cried Anders, suddenly spinning around and striding through the crowd that had gathered to hear a special bulletin from the BBC, piped into the street through a loudspeaker the shop owner had rigged over his door.

The news was grim: all telephone and radio communications between Denmark and the outside world had ceased at approximately 8:37 that morning. Ham radio transmissions, however, confirmed the worst— Germany had invaded neutral Denmark while the ineffectual Danish army was still in a state of massive denial. Resistance had been feeble and quickly crushed. The Danish government officially capitulated thirty-six hours after the first Wehrmacht tanks smashed through the candy-cane barricades on the border. In Torshavn, the provincial government pleaded for calm and hinted that this was *one* part of Denmark that would not yield to Hitler with such contemptible haste. As for the disposition of the Faeroese fishing fleet, the ships were required to stay in port until the situation was clarified.

As the Battle of the Atlantic entered a new and deadlier phase, the strategic importance of the Faeroe Islands was plain to anyone capable of reading a map. Torshavn lay athwart one of the main convoy routes, smack in the middle of a vast area that was beyond the range of Allied air patrols. While it was a provincial port by any standard and could never have been expanded into a support base for capital ships, it was perfectly adequate for escorts and submarines. Until a lot of work had been done by engineers, not one of the islands could support an air base, but many of them were ideal for seaplanes, and the Luftwaffe had rather a lot of those. It seemed obvious to both Eiden and Anders that if Great Britain did not garrison the islands first, the Germans certainly would. There were no naval units defending the capital except for two antediluvian gunboats assigned as "fishery protection vessels," armed with obsolete twelve-pounders and a handful of short-ranged Madsen machine guns.

Two weeks after Denmark surrendered, Winston Churchill announced that the Faeroes were now a British "protectorate." To back up that declaration, a battalion of Royal Marines landed, from the decks of four destroyers, before the sun went down. Reinforcements poured in, and Torshavn became a fortress, with pillboxes and barbed wire entanglements belting the landward approaches and a battery of hulking six-inch coastal defense rifles emplaced on concrete pedestals atop a ridge overlooking the seaward approaches to the harbor.

Such activity did not go unobserved by the Germans. On May 3, eighteen JU-88s caught the defenders by surprise and came in low out of the west, making two highly effective bomb runs across the waterfront. A British corvette was sunk, a *Tribal*-class destroyer was badly damaged, and supply dumps and cargo-handling equipment were set ablaze. In exchange for two aircraft shot down, the Luftwaffe left half the port a shambles and killed twenty-two Faeroese civilians, one of whom was a two-month-old child blown out of its mother's arms by German machine-gun fire.

The people of Torshavn boiled over with rage, and during the next twenty-four hours every able-bodied man between sixteen and sixty-five lined up at the office of the British garrison's commander and tried to volunteer for military service. Had they all been accepted, of course, the city's economy would have slammed to a halt. When the British colonel begged these bellicose would-be avengers to go back home and wait for a directive from London, some three hundred Faeroese men signed an emergency telegram to Winston Churchill saying, in effect: We are few, but we are brave; tell us how we can best contribute to crushing the Hun, and we will do it with all our might.

Two days later, at a crowded public assembly, the Prime Minister's reply was read aloud:

The people of Great Britain join me in expressing our gratitude for your noble gesture of solidarity, and we offer our deepest condolence for the loss of your friends and loved ones in the recent dastardly aerial assault on fair Torshavn.

But it is obviously not practical to form an all-Faeroese combat unit. In the aggregate, the total male population of your islands cannot furnish enough able-bodied recruits to constitute a small infantry battalion.

But there is a signal, nay a vital service which you can begin to perform now, without any delay, and by doing so, aid materially in our chances for victory.

As you know, our shipping losses have been severe, and they will only grow worse until we have sufficient escorts to turn the tide permanently against the U-boats. The loss of so many merchant vessels has created a crisis. England can no longer feed her people from her own resources. Every foot of cargo space taken up by imported food is that much less space that can be loaded with arms and munitions, with spare parts and lubricants, with all the myriad hard, durable things required to wage modern war.

You have asked me what the Faeroese people can do that will help to win the Battle of the Atlantic, and I reply: do what you have always done so courageously and skillfully—fish! And bring your catches to us, to feed our people! To meet the U-boat menace, we have been forced to convert hundreds of trawlers, sloops, drifters, and other commercial craft into armed escorts. With the diminished civilian ships left, we cannot possibly bring in sufficient seafood. If we cannot grow it, or catch it, or import it from abroad, we will soon be forced to cut civilian rations in half. Morale will plummet and the sick, the very young, and the elderly will all suffer accordingly. Hitler knows this; we know it too. And now we have told you, our new Faeroese allies.

I ask you, therefore, to return to the sea and direct your courage and skill to the vital task of feeding Great Britain. There is no more vital service you can render in this struggle, and it is a hard service, too, one that will require as much courage and determination in every particular as that required of a frontline soldier.

I send you greetings from the grateful people of England, and from His Majesty, King George VI.

Winston S. Churchill, Prime Minister

And so, in May 1941, the Faeroese fishing fleet sailed forth again. The crews set to their task with a will, working longer and harder, and with a greater sense of urgency, than ever before.

Thus it came about that Anders Poulsen never made it to his Aegean paradise. Eiden knew it would be awkward for the old man to ask for command of his ship back, so he visited his uncle and tore up the contract certifying his promotion to captain. Eiden volunteered to serve as first mate, unless the time came when Anders's health declined to the point where he *must* relinquish command.

It took the Germans some time to turn their attention to the nuisance of the Faeroese; but when they did, they first tried to intimidate the fishermen back into port by broadcasting a proclamation: henceforth, any Faeroese ship "suspected" of carrying food to England would be considered a legitimate naval target and as such would be subject to attack without warning.

At first, men such as Anders scoffed at this "Nazi bluster"—most Faeroese fishing ships could outrun a surfaced U-boat, and no submarine captain in his right mind was going to waste an expensive torpedo on a wooden fishing schooner. In the first two weeks of renewed activity, several Faeroese captains actually *had* outrun surfaced U-boats, or gave them the slip by hiding inside passing rain squalls.

Those tricks only worked briefly, of course. Soon, the U-boats began to pop up so close to the fishing boats that there wasn't time for them to haul out of range before the deck guns scored hits. In June, two Faeroese boats were sunk, and three were damaged so badly that they barely made it back to port. Anders said no more about "Nazi bluster."

Beginning in August, moreover, the Faeroese fleet faced a new and deadlier foe, one that simply could not be outrun. The Luftwaffe began operating long-range Condor patrol bombers out of newly enlarged bases in Norway. The Condors' primary mission was convoy reconnaissance, of course, but they also carried a powerful bomb load and mounted a pair of 20-mm cannon, which could chew a wooden vessel to splinters with a few accurate bursts. And since it was too dangerous to land the bombers with ordnance still on board, the Condor pilots began dropping their left-over bombs at any hapless fishing boat they happened upon—a more cost-effective option than simply jettisoning them into the sea.

When two Faeroese vessels were sunk by Condors in late August and another three badly strafed, even the bravest fisherman balked at going up against those airborne monsters without even a token means of self-defense. In London, the Admiralty was hard pressed to find enough deck guns to arm its merchant ships, but provision was made to equip each Faeroese boat with a pair of World War I Lewis guns. As each fishing boat returned to Torshavn for replenishment, shipfitters swarmed aboard and welded crude metal pedestal-mounts to each bridge wing. A team of instructors came up from Scapa Flow to teach the Faeroese crews the rudiments of anti-aircraft gunnery.

Realists knew that these light-caliber relics had more value as morale-boosters than as a serious deterrent, but they were better than shaking a fist at the sky.

"Anders's Luck" was with the *Hvildara* at the start of the year's last voyage, on September 10. Just four days out of Torshavn, the ship chanced upon a mighty school of cod, and the crew worked from sunrise to dusk to fill their nets and empty them in the age-old rhythm of their profession: the buzz-saw rasp of taut hemp lines cutting grooves in the stout oak of the gunwales; the rippling smack of heavy cod landing on the deck and the chaotic tap-dance of their fins and tails flapping on the slippery planks; the shouts and curses of the fishermen. It was all part of an ancient and elemental ritual, and the crew worked cheerfully to exhaustion, thankful for the sea's generosity. By twilight, they had caught all the fish the ship could carry, so Anders ordered the gear stowed and the remaining fish quickly processed, and sent Eiden to the navigator's station to plot a course for the nearest British port. Eiden gratefully stripped off his filthy work clothes and bent over the navigational charts, daydreaming of beer and hot showers.

Even if he and all the other crewmen hadn't been so distracted, they probably wouldn't have seen the periscope. Not in time.

When Eiden first saw the conning tower emerge, he thought at first that it might be the dorsal hump of a sea monster, a mythical beast from the days of the Vikings. Then he realized what it really was and shouted a warning to Anders.

"I see the bastard, Eiden."

They had no time to run; no place to hide; and only the feeblest power of resistance.

"Shall I order the Lewis guns manned, Uncle?"

"No point. We're a sitting duck if ever there was one. I've sent a man below, to bring up a white sheet from one of the bunks."

"Will they accept our surrender, do you think?"

Anders didn't bother to reply. He just lit a cigarette and watched the submarine's gun crew file calmly out on deck. When the improvised white flag went aloft, it was caught by the wind and spread out to its full length. There was no way the Germans didn't see it. But Eiden doubted that the enemy would accept their surrender; Berlin had defined wooden fishing craft as "valid naval targets," and the traditional chivalry between naval combatants had ended as the Battle of the Atlantic waxed in savagery. Not once had a German sub accepted the surrender of a Faeroese vessel. Why should this captain be any more humane than his predecessors?

Time slowed for Eiden Poulsen; the passing seconds seemed to roll over him like separate waves. He looked at the deck, at its powerful hieroglyphs of toil, at the nets still twitching with stubborn fish, at the open holds, so profitably filled. . . . Such a fine day's catch! So much hopeful toil, only to lose it all now. What a shabby, stupid, bad-luck end to a good ship and a first-rate crew! All pride, as sailors and as men, was soon to be negated by the cruelty of circumstance. . . .

The 105-mm deck gun flared and a jet of water reared up directly in front of Anders Poulsen, who did not flinch. The *Hvildara* shuddered under a cascade of icy water. Now he registered the bored, methodical pok-pok-pok of the U-boat's flak guns, unleashing a swarm of deceptively slow-looking yellow-green tracers, which brilliantly illuminated the sea as they skimmed across it and punched holes in the hull, blew out the portholes, gouged dense clouds of splinters from the superstructure, gnawing the ship to bits. The bullet-swarm sliced the second mate in half, spilling the fluid parts of him on to a deck already littered with fish tripe.

The German gunners put their second 105-mm round smack into the wheelhouse behind Anders. He died shaking his fist at them. When the searing flash subsided, there was nothing left of him but a few crimson scraps.

Eiden knew it was his turn next, but he'd be damned if he was going to stand there and only shake his fist. Chased by exploding 20-mm rounds, he raced up the ladder to the starboard bridge wing, tore the canvas tarp off the Lewis gun, slapped his cheek against the stock, and emptied the whole 41-round ammo drum in one long roaring burst. His small red tracers intersected halfway across with the fat wobbling tracers from the submarine's more powerful automatics, and two bullets actually collided like meteors in midair, creating a wild fireworks display. By sheer instinct, he'd placed his rounds spot-on, and he had the satisfaction of watching small red flares dance all over the conning tower, shattering the head of an officer on the bridge and stitching diagonally across the torso of the portside lookout on the periscope mount.

They weren't expecting that, he thought, and then braced himself for the inevitable, which was not long in coming. Enveloped by a blinding flash, deafened by a stupendous crash, he felt himself thrown headlong into the air and, for a short time, he lost consciousness.

He was awakened by the ocean's chill and the sting of brine in his wounds. The U-boat was still in the area. A kapok life ring, miraculously blown clear of the *Hvildara,* floated within reach and he grabbed it. Around him, the sea was filmed with oil, with mutilated cod, with planking and paper, and with a big piece of wooden railing with a human hand attached. All was quiet now except for the chug of the submarine's diesels. Smoke and a drifting twilight fog settled over the area, a fog that would have saved them had it appeared half an hour earlier. The U-boat slid away into the shadowy haze: dark, sinister, a smasher-of-boats, a drowner-of-men, a cruel and invulnerable foe.

He floated through the night, and, at dawn, just as he felt his brain shutting down for good, he saw the outline of a ship, a nimble Canadian corvette, hastening to catch up to a west-bound convoy from which it had become separated during the night. A sharp-eyed lookout spotted him by virtue of the enormous whirlwind of seagulls that had gathered to feast on the dead. He was treated kindly by the crew, and even though this class of warship was not much bigger than the *Hvildara,* there was a pharmacist's mate on board, a quiet fellow from Vancouver, who did a remarkable and almost painless job of patching him up until he could be admitted to a proper hospital in Halifax, Nova Scotia.

As soon as Eiden was discharged, he took his rage, his mastery of practical seamanship, and his proficient knowledge of English to the appropriate government office and there enlisted in the Royal Navy.

Five months later, Ensign Eiden Poulsen, fresh from officer training, reported for duty on the armed escort trawler HMS *Laertes,* a vessel of the *Shakespearian* class, fresh off the ways and preparing for its first combat cruise. Two of the officers and eighteen of the ratings were former sailors in the Royal Danish Navy, men who had fled the Nazi occupation and who still burned with shame at how unprepared their country had been to resist. It was a *very* motivated crew.

When the war ended, Lieutenant Commander Eiden Poulsen had risen to command of the *Laertes*. Stenciled on the bridge were the outlines of two conning towers crossed out with big black Xs, signifying the two U-boats the trawler had sunk; a further half-tower signified shared credit with another warship. There were also the silhouettes of four Axis planes brought down by the trawler's guns. For such a small ship, the *Laertes* had inflicted a lot of loss on the enemy, and that was fine with Eiden Poulsen.

Twelve ships were built in the *Shakespearian* class. Two were lost in action, but the surviving vessels were converted back to their civilian configurations relatively easily. Borrowing heavily against his reputation, Eiden purchased three of the surviving trawlers, refitted them with the newest technology available to the fishing industry, and virtually single-handedly caused the modernization of the whole Faeroese fishing industry. In 1949, his shipyard opened and he was soon constructing safe, efficient, state-of-the-maritime-art commercial vessels for clients on three continents. He had expanded into processing and canning; over time, he had branched out with lucrative investments in tourism, television broadcasting, and hydroelectric power. Had he desired the job, he could easily have been elected prime minister of the newly independent Faeroese nation; but it was more cost-effective, he realized, to befriend politicians than to be one.

But for all his wealth and prestige, he remained the same kind of man as his uncle Anders: an optimistic pragmatist. He despised ideologues of every stripe, but was adroit at manipulating them, and he continued to enjoy hugely the perks and privileges of being the richest man in Torshavn.

". . . and that's all there is to it," he said.

"*'All?'*" chuckled Allen Warrener. "But, Eiden, what are you going to do for the *next* forty or fifty years?"

Eiden laughed and offered his new American friend another cigarette. They smoked in meditative silence and enjoyed the view. After a while, Eiden spoke again, summarizing: "If there's any one thing I'd like you to remember, out of all that I've told you this afternoon, it is just this: relative to our total population, the Faeroese lost a higher percentage of men to

enemy action than England and America. And the fish we brought to England provided thirty percent of all the seafood consumed by the British
people from 1940 to 1945. When you get home and people ask you about
this place, you might want to work those statistics into the conversation. I
think that would please him."

"Please who?"

Eiden pointed up at the bronze fisherman. "Uncle Anders, of course! The
artist used photos of him as the model for that statue."

Eiden smoothed his hair and picked up his lunch box. "Did I hear you
correctly when you said that you have no specific plans?"

"Yes. I'm more or less just winging it from one day to the next."

"In that case, how about 'winging it' to my family home, up north in the
village of Tjornuvik? Some archaeologists from Denmark have been digging
nearby recently, and they've turned up some unusual Viking artifacts. You
might find that to be of interest, and even if you don't, the scenery is very
nice. Well, to be frank about it, it's also a long drive and a lonesome one—
I'd appreciate your company."

"I consider myself complimented."

"Yes, you should. I'll pick you up at your hotel at eight and take you to
breakfast."

6.

VIKING GRAVES

Seventy kilometers out of Torshavn, the road to Tjornuvik narrowed into a funnel, squeezed by massive shoulders of wet basalt, still bearing the marks of the drills used to bore the holes for the dynamite. Ahead was the arch of a rough iron bridge spanning an unseen crevasse. Eiden stopped the car at a tight pull-off next to a big pile of heavy rocks.

"Come take a look. It's quite a sight!"

Surging through a cleft in the rocks, then plunging violently down a hundred-foot cliff, the river hissed and spat, flinging icy droplets on Allen's face from twenty feet below. Its primal roar drowned conversation. The two travelers paused for cigarettes at an iron-fenced overlook; Allen took a dozen pictures, although he doubted that his camera had enough depth of field to capture the full spectacle. Eiden waited until Allen had put his camera away, then shouted in his ear: "Let's get this over with! I need you to help me load the trunk with rocks! Two hundred fifty kilos ought to do it, three hundred if you're feeling nervous."

"You've got to be joking!"

"Not in the least! A man driving one of those flimsy little Renaults got flipped into the river two years ago when a sudden updraft caught the underside of the car! By the time they fished out the wreckage, there wasn't much left of him. Ever since then, the Transportation Bureau has maintained these cairns of rocks to use as ballast. Load 'em up on this side, unload 'em on the other, so the next southbound vehicle can enjoy a safe passage. We use only the latest technology here, you see!"

The second half of the trip wasn't nearly so dramatic, for the island's northern part was a huge plateau spotted with leprous-looking tarns and isolated giant boulders, dropped randomly by retreating glaciers during the last ice age.

Unlikely companions though they were, Allen and Eiden Poulsen were becoming friends; after they crossed the waterfall–bridge, their conversation became more casual.

Allen answered the predictable questions about home and family, then reciprocated by asking "Mr. Poulsen" about his.

" 'Mr. Poulsen' was my father—to you, I'm 'Eiden,' okay? We are already good enough friends to throw formalities overboard."

"I feel that way too."

"Good. Well, to start with, as you may have guessed, I'm a widower—three years now. No condolences, please! We had a good, long marriage, and my wife died quite suddenly, without suffering, so I have that much to be thankful for—that and a lifetime of good memories. And two splendid children! The youngest is my son, Kristofur, who recently signed on a fishing sloop as an apprentice seaman; like his old man, he's got salt water in his veins, and he has no idea that Dad owns the ship and pulled a few strings to get him a berth with a reliable skipper, one who seldom flogs his crew. Kristofur just celebrated his sixteenth birthday. He's a fine lad—I'm sorry he won't be here so you can meet him.

"But you will get to meet my other child, Elsuba, who is eighteen and furiously determined to be a doctor. She plans to open a clinic in Tjornuvik one day—at the moment, all we have is a dispensary managed by a retired pharmacist. I've told her she won't make any money way up here—half the patients will pay her with baskets of puffin eggs or a pound of dried *klip-fisk*—but she's an idealist; what can I say? Elsuba's home on spring vacation, and, yes, she is very pretty, so take your best shot while you can! By God, you're blushing!"

"Yes, Eiden, I am. So change the subject and tell me about the village, instead of your daughter!"

"Well, it's one of those places where the sheep outnumber the people. It's isolated, but in the good meaning of the word: *snug*. But withal, rather cheerful. We've always painted our houses and barns in bright primary colors, to defy the elements—especially in the autumn and winter, when the landscape tends to look very forlorn. It's the home port for a few dozen small and medium fishing boats, and there's a small factory that exports woolen yarn, and our air-dried *klip-fisk* is considered a delicacy, although it's definitely an acquired taste. I suspect you'll find the mutton chops more to your liking. We've a small library, a primary school, and they show three-year-old movies in the town hall once a week. A real 'swinging place,' as you Americans would say."

"Sounds like all the 'swinging' I could handle, frankly."

"Ah, here's the turnoff; we're only five kilometers from town now. I always feel my spirits lift when I turn off the main road. Don't think me a sentimentalist, Allen—I enjoy running a prosperous corporation, I love to travel, and I'd damned sure rather be a rich man than a poor one; but when I come back to Tjornuvik, I'm just Eiden Poulsen, everybody's neighbor and most peoples' friend. I live in the same house I grew up in, I tend a small garden overlooking the sea, I bend elbows in the pub with the local fishermen and farmers, and weather permitting I waste hours just lounging on the terrace with a book in my hand. And for me, that as close to Heaven as you can get."

"Don't you have business to transact with the outside world?"

"Sure, but I do most of that by radio. Damn few people know the phone number out here, or ever will. I regard the telephone as Satan's own instrument. I always tense up when it rings, knowing that my real life will be 'on hold' until I can get rid of whoever it is on the line. Elsuba always tries to answer for me, tries to screen the really important calls from the crap that can wait. If she didn't, she claims, I'd become the worst grouch in Tjornuvik—and in a village full of old sailors, that's no mean distinction!"

Eiden tossed a pack of cigarettes into Allen's lap—a costly and mellow brand of English oval. "Now, Allen, when you enter my house, I want you to think of it as your home too. Do what I plan to do: kick off your shoes, settle into a comfortable chair, and read a good book. Or stare out the windows and daydream. Anything but work! We sleep late, eat whenever we feel like it, and the bar is open twenty-four hours a day."

At the top of a broad ridge, Eiden stopped the car and made a sweeping gesture: "Behold, fair Tjornuvik!"

In charmingly irregular concentric rows, plotted by Nature's whim, not by an architect's desire to impose order, the steeply sloping grid of Tjornuvik fanned upward from a half-moon harbor where gaily decorated boats bobbed restlessly on the tide. Stentorian reds, dazzling yellows, harsh imperial blues made the dwellings seem to leap out from the dun colors of the shore, the lead-blue of the harbor, and the flagstone-gray slab of the breakwater. The Poulsen house was set slightly apart, on a plateau high enough to provide an unobstructed panorama. It was painted an almost manic canary yellow, trimmed in tangerine-cream, its many over-large windows angled to the northeast so inhabitants and guests could enjoy the ebony crescent of black-pebbled beach as well as the two towering monoliths of free-standing granite—common geological vestiges known as *dranger*—which Eiden and his neighbors had long ago christened the Giant and the Hag.

Eiden batted the horn twice as he swung into a graveled parking circle on the westward side of his house. In response to the signal, a girl's face appeared at an upstairs window. As soon as he exited the car, Allen could hear her clomp-clomping as she ran downstairs. Allen might have been expecting a gangling adolescent, but the sight of Elsuba Poulsen rooted his feet to the ground. She moved, spoke, and carried herself with the poise of a mature, self-confident woman. Her handshake was firm and cordial; her welcoming gaze, unabashedly appraising. The twenty-one-year-old scholar and the eighteen-year-old pre-med student were already wondering if each had something distinctive to give to the other. Allen was reluctant to terminate the handshake; the graceful articulation of her grasp suggested a cool deep sensuality.

"Well, I see he's smitten already. . . . Watch out, Allen—she's already spinning her web around you!"

"In that case, I'm a willing victim."

The two young people laughed a lot at first, keeping things light, but the attraction between them was already strong enough to throw out a magnetic field.

Eiden, you rogue! You saw this coming.

At the dinner table, Allen's focus was diverted from Elsuba only by one other object in his field of view: over her shoulder, through the open passageway to the parlor, he saw a large wall-rug tapestry that riveted his attention. The weaver had made bold use of traditional Norse motifs: runic swirls in somber earth tones framed a large, stylized representation of a Great Orm, the sea-dragon whose ferocious visage was commonly hewn into the prows of the Viking longships. In this wall-rug, texture, color, and thematic treatment had all contributed to an aura of barbaric force.

"Allen, what *are* you staring at so hard?" asked Elsuba. "Is someone creeping up on me from behind?"

"She's annoyed because you took your eyes off her for even an instant," Eiden winked at Elsuba, then innocently returned to stabbing his lamb chop.

"Ignore him, Allen. Senility is encroaching faster and faster. Still, you cannot evade my question! What are you staring at so intently?"

"The Orm tapestry in the other room; I think it's very powerful. Is it Faeroese?"

"Quite Faeroese," said Eiden, a little stiffly. "It's my wife's work, actually. She was well known, at least regionally—the national museum owns two pieces. She employed a lot of Dark Ages motifs. She used to say that the Vikings were the most perfectly adapted culture for their times, especially in the way they created sublime myth and poetry from a brutal quotidian reality."

Eager to show off his expertise, Allen pointed over Elsuba's shoulder and blurted: "That's a representation of the Great Orm, isn't it? The Vikings spread that mythical beastie all over Europe in just two centuries."

"Well,"—Elsuba's tone grew serious—"I suppose if you looked up and saw a ship full of wild, hairy men bearing down on your village, waving their swords and chanting to Odin—and with the Orm figurehead pointed straight at you—you'd not be likely to forget it soon."

"These kinds of things have always been a special interest of mine," said Allen, trying once more to display expertise without sounding like a braggart. "I don't mean tapestries, but sea serpents and the like. I'm a True Believer—I believe the Orms exist. Or did, a thousand years ago."

"Keep your eyes open, then," Elsuba teased, "because they usually come out to feed at dawn and at sunset! The village children throw table scraps at them from the breakwater." Elsuba waved her hands in a gesture of apology. "I'm sorry, I just can't help teasing you. Your expression, when you said 'sea serpents,' was priceless."

"But surely you get my point, Elsuba! If there's one place left in the world where you might see a giant Orm splashing around on a sunny day, it would be here, in the Faeroes."

"Right out there between the Giant and the Hag," muttered Eiden from behind that day's edition of the *London Times*. Now he peered around the paper with a mischievous expression, to do some teasing of his own. "Daughter, you're evading a direct answer to Allen's question."

"Er, I don't recall asking her a direct question. . . ."

"Hush! Yes, you did . . . by implication. Come on, Elsuba, are you a True Believer too?"

Elsuba tilted her head in thought and pursed her lips before responding— a trait that Allen found charming . . . like everything else about her. "It isn't so cut and dried, Poppa. For one thing, we know the climate was much different a thousand years ago. These islands were teeming with big, ferocious bunnies—where are they now? The summers were longer, and trees grew here naturally—all gone now, all different. So, why shouldn't there have been fairly large life forms in these waters back in the ninth century, that are gone now? Allen, you did say that the Orm symbol spread throughout Europe over the course of two hundred years?"

"Give or take, yes."

"Then isn't it possible that other factors contributed to that spread? Other than Viking brigands, I mean. Perhaps the creatures spread *themselves* widely, because their environment was drastically threatened."

"By marauding Vikings?" piped Eiden.

"Be quiet, Poppa—you're enjoying yourself entirely too much! My point—if my father ever lets me make it—is that if a symbol spreads widely and quickly, across many different cultures, one reason could be that the symbol has some basis in *reality*. It may be a thousand-year-old reality; nevertheless, the tales persist to this day."

"Exactly my point. You'd be amazed at how many sober, God-fearing mariners have seen mysterious creatures in their travels. And for every sailor who tells such a tale, there must be five or six more who could but *won't* for fear of being ridiculed. I've collected hundreds of such tales. . . ."

"Where did you get your interest in such things, Allen?"

"From my grandfather, oddly enough."

"Was he a sailor?" asked Eiden.

"No, he was a soldier; career army. Ever since I arrived in Scandinavia, I've been collecting Orm souvenirs for him—also trolls, goblins, and a set of *Kikimora* dolls I found in Leningrad. I don't want him to think I've lost interest."

"And your parents, Allen," said Eiden. "You haven't yet mentioned them. . . ."

"I was raised by my grandparents. My dad was killed in the war, and my mother never quite recovered from the shock. I haven't heard from her since I was a child."

"I'm very sorry," said Elsuba.

"Please don't be," Allen shrugged. "I never really knew my father, and from what I've heard about my mother, I was better off not living with her. The General did a good job of raising me. Now, about those sea monsters. . . ."

"I didn't mention any," said Eiden.

"That's my point! If there's any place in Europe where you'd expect to hear sea-monster tales, it's right here, and yet you tell me you've never heard any! For the first time, the Faeroese disappoint me!"

"Now that you mention it, Allen, it does seem a bit odd that we Faeroese don't have a whole cupboard full of ghosts and beasties . . . mind you, I've seen strange things at sea, but 'strange' isn't the same as uncanny. Elsuba, can you think of an indigenous beastie of any kind?"

"I can't think of anything except those old fishwife tales about Vardinoy. . . ."

Allen leaned forward, instinct kicking in, at the sound of that word, with its trio of hard-edged Nordic consonants.

"What's 'Vardinoy'?"

Silence swallowed his question. Father and daughter exchanged glances, each seemingly waiting for the other to pick up the dangling end of the conversational thread. Finally Eiden cleared his throat—a bit disingenuously, Allen thought—and said: "You're the logical one to answer that, Elsuba. Your mother made the mistake of telling you the story when you were a child, and you pestered her unmercifully to tell it over and over again, and to make up a new ending to the mystery every time she did so. Finally, as I recall, she told you that aliens from outer space were responsible, and that seemed to satisfy you."

"A-*hem!*" interrupted Allen. "Would one of you tell me, please, if this 'Vardinoy' is a place, a person, or the name of some minor Viking deity?"

Elsuba slugged back her drink with enough practiced insouciance to elicit a stare from her father that was both proud and reproachful.

"It's the Faeroese equivalent of a haunted house, I suppose you could say: our version of the Bermuda Triangle. Vardinoy is a very rugged, mountainous island, far to the north, one of the last in the archipelago. Since a long time ago, there have been accounts of 'mysterious disappearances' in that area, people and boats that have vanished suddenly and without a trace—the most recent one was four or five years ago, I think—a fishing sloop that simply vanished one night. Father, didn't you have something to do with the investigation of that incident?"

Eiden nodded glumly over his drink. "Yes, I did. The Coast Guard office in Torshavn had tape-recorded the crew's last radio message—a distress call of a very unusual sort. The authorities asked me to listen to it, to see what I could make of it. Well, there was no mistaking the terror in the voices you could hear. One sailor was shouting something like, 'Don't touch that black jelly!' but the rest was too garbled to understand."

Allen interrupted, excited as a boy: "You actually heard somebody describe this Vardinoy creature as a giant jellyfish?"

"Don't go jumping to assumptions! The man shouted something about 'don't touch that black jelly,' yes, but that could describe any number of phenomena. These were experienced seamen, Allen, and if they had seen a giant jellyfish, they would've said so! But whatever happened, there were no survivors. The ship piled up on a big clump of *dranger* the next day—a total loss to everyone except the insurance company! As I said, a real 'Bermuda Triangle' story."

"Has *anybody* gotten a good look at this Vardinoy Monster and lived long enough to give a description of it?"

"Oh, yes, but the problem is that no two descriptions are alike, and all of them are pretty vague. In one story, it is seen rising out of a big lake on *top* of Vardinoy, but in another story it's spotted off the western coast, where the cliffs are very high. How it manages to move around like that, no one can say. The discrepancies add to the mystery, but they also take away the credibility of the witnesses."

Elsuba nodded solemnly. "It's very far from any shipping lanes up on that end of the chain, and the water is very deep. There's a submarine trench down there the size of the Grand Canyon—a whole city of Giant Orms could be down there and nobody would ever discover it."

Allen was scribbling notes furiously. "Eiden, you did say that, except for that shipwreck a few years ago, most of the Vardinoy stories are old. . . ."

"Most of them, yes, and most of them would have been forgotten long ago if it hadn't been for something strange that happened on Vardinoy in the late nineteenth century. That incident caused the journalists to dig through the archives and re-tell some of the older yarns. Y'see, there was only one village on Vardinoy, and during the ten-day interval between one mail boat and the next, the entire population of that village simply vanished. The houses and shops looked like they'd been abandoned in great haste, but there were no human remains, no sign of violence or pestilence. Just to be on the safe side, the government quarantined Vardinoy for twenty years. Since that ban was lifted, as far as I know, the only people who've set foot on the island are a few eccentric Scottish fishermen."

"There were no messages scrawled on the village walls? No clues of any kind?"

"Nothing. Just empty buildings and cold cooking pots. Of course, there was a lot of speculation, and some of it was pretty wild. Even to this day, the people of Vesturoy, the closest neighboring island, never set foot on Vardinoy."

Allen's eyes were bright as he did some personal speculation. "Is there any possibility of my going up there and digging around on my own?"

"You'd have to charter a boat, Allen," said Elsuba. "And it might take a while to find some skipper who was going in that direction. If you were going to stay in the Faeroes for another two or three weeks. . . ."

"Well, at least you can go 'digging around' in the Torshavn library," said Eiden. "I'll make a couple of calls on your behalf, so you can gain access to the historical records as well as a translator."

"Don't forget, Poppa, that Kristofur's ship is sailing past Vardinoy on its way to the fishing grounds—when he gets back, you should ask him if he saw anything unusual in those waters. I'll write you, Allen, if there's anything to report."

But Allen was distracted now. He was surprised at the surge of regret he felt from remembering how brief his Faeroese visit would be. This was only his third day in the Faeroes, and already he felt such a deep affinity for the islands that he didn't want to leave. More specifically, he did not want to leave this house, or to cut short by so much as one hour the time he could spend in Elsuba's company.

That there was already a mutual flow of chemistry between them was undeniable. He tried to avoid staring, but every aspect of her was so compelling that he would have been content to do nothing *but* stare at her. She was the distilled essence of Scandinavian Blonde, that was certain: long, thick, hair the color of polished brass, high cheekbones, sparkling eyes that shaded from cornflower blue to muted violet, and that ripe, sensual mouth, which he longed to kiss. He'd already idealized Elsuba Poulsen; he had in fact enshrined her as the paradigm of everything he looked for in a female companion—and, to top it off, her formidable father was already treating them as a couple.

Hey, God? It's me, Allen! Just wanted to say "thanks" for setting this up!

Allen Warrener, in fact, had found his paradise, and, in it, his Isolde. He had entered—he was certain of it—a unique time and place, and he wanted never to be anywhere else. An intoxicating vividness quickened his senses.

I will remember everything about this place and every detail of everything that happens to me here.

Shouldn't I be just a little bit afraid of such intensity?

Their first morning together, they breakfasted in a sunny alcove overlooking the bay; the Giant and the Hag assumed an almost jolly appearance in the full morning light, and the sea was benevolently calm, decorating the bases of the two monoliths with collars of creamy lace. Allen fueled himself for the day's activity by eating big portions, washing them down with cup after cup of strong coffee, and by chattering gaily . . . until he realized that Elsuba was just barely managing an occasional monosyllable in response. Allen thereupon clammed up, stiffly self-conscious, tormented by Elsuba's apparent sullenness. Finally, Eiden peered around the spread-eagled pages of the morning paper from Torshavn and threw a block in Allen's favor, so both young people could take a deep breath and try again; they would find their rhythm together, soon enough.

"Elsuba, you're tormenting poor Allen. He's in a strange place, a long way from home, and I think perhaps he's a little bewildered, because last night you two couldn't stop babbling to each other, and during breakfast you've been about as warm and friendly as the Sphinx. It's not Allen's fault that you're rather disagreeable for the first hour or so of *every* morning. . . ."

"Honestly, Poppa, you'd think he had never eaten breakfast with a girl before."

"Don't tease, daughter. I'm sure Mr. Warrener has eaten many morning-after breakfasts with other girls, and most of them were surely more civil to him than you're being. I'll bet that, in Finland, he probably has to beat them away with a stick—he's an exotic foreigner with dark poetic eyes, and all that."

"I *have* noticed his eyes, Poppa."

Allen got his second wind and surged ahead, nodding a fleet *thank you* toward Eiden: "Ahem! Elsuba, I'm over here on *this* side of the table, and if you insist on discussing me in the third person, I'll not only remain shy, I'll *turn mute!* Now, as a matter of fact, I do not have a Finnish girlfriend. Most of the Finnish girls I know treat me like a monk—and that's because I bloody well live like one!"

His vehemence took her by surprise; but when he stopped, she smiled and took his hand. "You're cute when you bristle."

The day awaited their pleasure. Over cigarettes and a second pot of coffee, they discussed itineraries. A morning cruise in Eiden's motorboat . . . a picnic lunch near a cave complex where fearless seals turned cheap tricks in exchange for a handout of fish heads . . . and then, from mid-afternoon on, if the weather held fair, they'd hike over the southerly massif and investigate the archaeological dig. Allen nodded eagerly as each possible activity was discussed; everything sounded marvelous to him.

"And what are your plans for the day, Eiden?" he asked, politely but somewhat distractedly.

"I'm going to sit here in the sunshine with my feet propped up and skim through that stack of magazines, then perhaps go down to the breakwater and do a little fishing. A very strenuous schedule!"

In the parlor, the telephone jangled.

"Oh, bloody hell! Not on my first morning here!" Throwing the newspaper down, Eiden stomped off to answer.

"God, he hates to get phone calls when he's here," Elsuba confided.

"I know. He told me. I thought he was exaggerating."

"Oh, no, he never exaggerates. . . ."

Without really intending to, they strained to overhear the one-sided conversation. But Eiden's monosyllabic replies gave no hint as to the nature of the discussion. When he returned, his face was a businesslike mask, devoid of emotion.

"Father, what's wrong? And don't tell me 'nothing,' because whenever you get that Chairman-of-the-Board expression, it means something *is*."

"Can't fool you, can I? Yes, there's a problem at the shipyard. An accident —a couple of men hurt. I don't know the details, but I need to be there personally to assess the situation. You know, before having to deal with the insurance people and so forth." He strode over and shook Allen's hand, then hugged his daughter. "Allen, I apologize for having to run off like this, but at least I leave you in good hands. If I'm not back before you have to leave, Elsuba will make the necessary arrangements to get you to your ship in time." Then he disappeared into his bedroom for ten minutes, emerging with one piece of luggage and his briefcase. He was so preoccupied that he left without another word.

"I wonder what all *that* was about!" Elsuba looked concerned, but not really worried. In minutes, there had been a dramatic shift in ambience. They'd been left alone together for an indefinite time. Uninhibited now by a parental presence—even a parent as obviously broad-minded as Eiden— they talked nonstop for the next two hours, forgetting all about the panhandling seals, completely comfortable in the sunlit breakfast nook, avid for knowledge of each other. Her hard-edged air of adult sophistication melted away, her voice became softer and her manner more youthful. Allen saw that beneath her confident façade, she was just as apprehensive of the future as anyone her age would be, on the verge of a career that would require her to forgo the carefree pleasures of university life. But she knew what she wanted from life and was determined to go after it.

"As a doctor, I can make a difference in many peoples' lives. And you, Allen, if you do choose a military career, what do you expect to gain from such a hard and dangerous life?"

"It's hard to answer without resorting to macho clichés, but sometimes clichés are true. I want to find out if I have what it takes to lead men in battle. I want to continue my family's tradition, to live up to the examples of my father and grandfather. And I feel it would somehow be an act of moral cowardice if I turned away from experiencing something that's fascinated me since I was a child. All of that sounds too simplistic, I know, but part of what appeals to me is the stark simplicity of war. I don't 'love' it, or anything idiotic like that, but I feel compelled to look on its face and see how I react. That's better than being cautious and never knowing for sure, isn't it?"

"Like my father, I don't think we were meant to live 'cautiously.' But having said that, I think we must now change the subject! On a bright, beautiful morning, I refuse to think about you crouching in a foxhole with bullets flying around your head!"

"I vote we change the subject too. So . . . what shall we talk about instead?"

She had apparently come to her decision suddenly, to judge from the decisive *"clink!"* of her coffee cup and the abrupt change in her manner.

"Would you be terribly disappointed if we postponed our picnic until tomorrow?"

"Won't the seals feel insulted?"

"Let them catch their own fish. And, my God, their *breath* . . . !"

She was still talking as she leaned across the table, grabbed his head, and clamped a kiss on him that sent a jolt of arousal through his spine.

"This is *our* morning, Allen, and if it's going to be as good as we both want it to be, then we would be fools not to let the tide carry us where it will."

"I hope you mean what I think you mean."

In reply, she methodically unfolded his fingers, isolated the longest digit, and slowly sucked it into the pulpy heat of her mouth, using her lips ands tongue to send little rings of exquisite sensation down its length. As she slowly withdrew his finger, she delivered a parting vortex of suction so concentrated that the fingertip made an audible *"pop!"* when it came out.

"My bedroom is on the right, at the top of the stairs. Wait there for me, while I lock up and take the cursed telephone off the hook. And don't you dare take off any clothes before I arrive. Whenever I'm with someone new, I love the ritual of disrobing each other! It's like unwrapping a mysterious birthday present!"

"And just how many times have you been 'with someone new'?"

Her eyes went hard for an instant and then she shook her head in wonder. "My God, you really *haven't* had much experience, have you? All right. I was going to slap you silly, but instead I'll just offer you a lifelong piece of advice: *Never ask a girl that question.*"

Elsuba with her clothes off was not quite as openly aggressive as Elsuba leaning-over-the-breakfast-table had been, but she wanted satisfaction from her impulsive commitment and wasn't shy about making practical instruction a delightful part of the preliminaries. For Allen, it was a day of revelations: *Oh, so* that's *where it is!* Elsuba wasn't gruff and commanding—mostly she was quite gentle and patient—but she was by-God not going to settle for a mediocre performance. Whatever kind of lover she wanted at that stage of her life, she was going to remake Allen Warrener into that man. Allen was a willing, earnest, and enraptured student. His diligence was eventually rewarded with the wild crescendos pouring from her throat and the exquisite tremors coursing through her long-limbed body. After a certain point in that first four-hour marathon, Allen began to trust his intuition, and his skill at interpreting her feedback grew exponentially. He gained a sense of nuance about pressure, angle, tempo, and the cadenzas of technique, which caused her to become hotter, more abandoned, and more lavish with the bounties she paid back to him. All in all, it turned into one hell of an afternoon.

They shared a playful shower and a quick lunch, and because a chill, misty drizzle had begun to fall, Elsuba averred that it would be dangerously slick on the overland track; then she radioed the archaeologists' camp and requested transportation. Twenty minutes later, a heavy-duty inflatable boat, crewed by a pair of high-spirited Danish grad students, pulled alongside the concrete quay and picked them up. At 2:35 P.M., they cast off and began their voyage.

After twenty minutes of bucking a choppy sea, they arrived at a veritable forest of *dranger,* which the Danes negotiated at very low speed. As the boat emerged in front of a shallow black-pebbled beach, one of them pointed melo-dramatically to the west and announced: "Behold! The Valley of the Vikings!"

Without sunlight, its sheer basalt walls wreathed in curls of fog, the valley loomed as an immense purple-gray void, although Elsuba said that its true dimensions were eight hundred meters deep and four hundred wide. Allen could barely discern a cluster of tents and awnings, staked down in east–west rows wherever there was room between the myriad foaming creeks that carried runoff from the surrounding cliffs into the welcoming sea. As they helped the two Danes haul the boat ashore, they heard a cheerful booming voice, and then, rather surrealistically, they saw the bearded face of a barrel-chested middle-aged man emerge from the mist, wreathed in a pungent cloud of pipe smoke that was two shades darker than the rain clouds.

"Good afternoon, Miss Poulsen! And you, too, Mr. Allen—I think that's what she calls you, anyway; I'm Professor Knudsen, the fellow who gains the fame if this dig turns out to be important, and who goes back to teaching high school in Greenland if it doesn't!" After shaking hands with Allen, who was perfectly content to be known as "Mr. Allen," Dr. Knudsen smacked the ashes out of his pipe, his movements curiously edgy, as though he had revelations to share and could barely wait to start revealing.

"Things have changed a bit here in Niflheim, since your last visit—oh, Mr. Allen, I should enlighten you: 'Niflheim' is the Hades of Norse mythology, and . . ."

Elsuba interrupted, very smoothly Allen thought. "Professor Knudsen, I think you'll find that our American guest has done his homework; he knows more about the sagas than I do."

Knudsen beamed at the news. "Excellent; then I won't have to make all those tedious introductory remarks about the people and the period—which I have to do every time some idiot flies up here with a television news crew!"

Wasting no time, Knudsen pivoted on his heels and strode vigorously into the fog, leaving Allen and Elsuba to follow as best they could.

The site, Professor Knudsen told Allen, was uncovered, as the most surprising sites often are, by sheer happenstance. Some climbers had come up from Torshavn for a weekend, planning to descend the valley's western wall, camp out overnight, and climb out the following day. While looking for a suitable campsite, they noticed that a combination avalanche and mudslide had carried away part of the cliffs near the shore. Exploring, they found some pottery shards. Fortunately for science, the climbing party didn't just help themselves to souvenirs and depart, but used their radio-phone to call in a description of their finds to the resident antiquarian at the Torshavn library. He immediately took a boat up the coast, examined their findings, and was sufficiently excited to notify the University of Copenhagen.

"When I showed the department heads the photos he wired to us," said Knudsen, "they agreed that a full-scale expedition was warranted. We've been digging, sifting, measuring, and taking notes for seven weeks now. As more fragments were uncovered and catalogued, we began to get a good idea of who—and what—these mysterious settlers were. More important, however, is the 'when.'

"I'd always subscribed to the accepted notion that the first Viking settlements on the Faeroes dated from the ninth century. But during the fourth week of the dig, we found a *Byzantine* coin bearing the likeness of the emperor Constantine IV, who ruled from 668 to 685 A.D.! So, obviously, there was at least one Viking settlement in the Faeroes approximately two hundred years earlier than anyone had previously thought.

"Strictly speaking, of course, they were not 'settlers,' but castaways—driven ashore and unable to leave, they made the best of things. From the evidence we've gathered so far, however, they seem to have built a fairly comfortable little community in this valley. They fashioned crude wooden huts from the wreckage of their ships, and later on replaced them with sturdy, fairly large, stone dwellings. For cooking and heat, they would have utilized peat—there's enough of it scattered around all these streams—and supplemented it with driftwood. Because the valley's deep, narrow, and set back from the open sea, they would have been protected from high winds and storm surges. Of course, their diet was monotonous—fish, birds, and seal meat—but at least it was rich in protein."

"Were there enough of them to last more than a generation?" asked Elsuba.

"Well, that depends on how many ships were in their convoy, how many were in those ships, and what their ages were at the time they were stranded. After we found the King and Queen, we began to think in terms of more than one ship, or, if there was only one, a very large craft—"

"The who?" asked Elsuba.

"Ah, yes, you haven't met them yet! I'll introduce you in a moment, Miss Poulsen. That's what we call the two intact bodies we found, and if they weren't royalty, they were certainly nobles of some distinction. Their personal effects prove that much. They were exiles, perhaps, or the losing faction in a civil war—anything is possible. My point is that, given their obvious status, they would have been accompanied by an assortment of retainers, soldiers, slaves, et cetera—including some strong young men and women of prime childbearing age. A shallow gene pool, to be sure, but a viable one. If they didn't lose too many through attrition, it's just possible they might have lasted indefinitely."

The three were walking toward a roped-off area halfway to the foot of the western cliffs. Plastic awnings and sheets protected the site from the elements. The peat bog was small, one of several they'd passed, but two dead Vikings didn't take up much room. Knudsen halted them at the entrance, preferring to build the suspense. "Behold, the Royal Chamber! I'm sorry if I seem theatrical, but how often do archaeologists get to show off anything more exciting than a chunk of pottery? Let me go inside first and light the lamps, so you can enjoy the full impact of meeting His and Her Majesties!"

Knudsen had the right idea, thought Allen: if these people weren't royalty, it would be very surprising. Even in musty death, the peat-pickled bodies gave off a palpable aura of dignity. On their faces were expressions of somber, stoic acceptance. The lady had been beautiful, and the mate she cradled in one arm must have been a virile figure indeed when he bestrode the deck of his longship. One of "the King's" arms was beneath the woman's waist and the other still held against his chest the haft of a mighty axe.

"Did they die together, do you think?" asked Elsuba, almost as though she were asking the bodies to speak.

Knudsen seemed to ponder his answer carefully. "It certainly looks that way, doesn't it? Both of them have severed carotid arteries . . . and our tissue samples show traces of ingestion just before death—perhaps an herbal sedative. Exactly what kind, we don't know yet, but I'm hoping for a lab report soon."

"A suicide pact?" Allen ventured.

"That's my 'gut instinct,' so to speak. But before I comment further about that, let me show you the most recent find. . . ."

He led them back toward the sea, then veered to the right about a hundred feet from the high-tide line. At this point, they were at the bottom of the valley's thousand-foot-high southern wall, which sloped down into a wild tumble of scree and disorderly *dranger*. Knudsen produced a flashlight and led them carefully through the gloom toward a glowing oval, obviously a cave mouth with work lights glowing inside. Knudsen paused to get his breath just below a ledge that masked the cave's interior. Fragments of conversation indicated that some members of the team were working inside.

"We found them quite by chance," puffed the professor. "It's a labyrinth up here: caves, crevasses, stretches of tunnel that end at blank walls, and other stretches that just keep going into the mountains, God knows how far. Frankly, no one's felt up to exploring *them*, not after the ossuary we found up here."

He called out in Danish to whoever was working inside the cave. "I've asked Hans and Frieda to turn on all the floodlights so you can see as much as possible. You two go first, so I can see your reaction! Just climb up and over—the cave floor's quite level for a few meters, before it drops off to form a charnal pit. . . ."

"Jesus," Elsuba whispered. Allen would have said it if she hadn't. Automatically, they reached for each other's hands.

The assistant archaeologists had uncovered and pieced together two nearly intact skeletons. Knudsen asked the woman named Frieda if she had found "the missing foot" yet, and she replied: "No, but we've found portions of three other feet."

"Before you even ask me, Mr. Allen, the answer is no, I have no idea what happened here. The skeletons are all broken up, obviously, but there's no sign of a battle or any other kind of violence. Human violence, that is."

"What's that supposed to mean?"

"Here, I'll show you."

Knudsen led them to the closest reassembled skeleton and knelt beside the left hip. After drawing on a pair of surgical gloves, he lifted the femur and held it under the light, taking a monocular out of his pocket.

"Look just there, on the area near the joint."

Allen could already see that the bone, which had been carefully cleaned of dirt and sand, looked strangely porous; when he looked with magnification, he saw that it was pitted with tiny holes and shallow, carved-out-looking striations. Where the cartilage normally was, the ancient tissue had a fused, slick appearance, almost like melted plastic.

"Elsuba, you're the pre-med student—have a look and tell me what you think."

Elsuba bent over the monocular and studied the abnormality intently before saying: "I have no idea what I'm looking at."

"Nor do any of us, but most of the bones in this cave show similar markings. The only things I can think of that might cause such an effect on human bone would be some kind of extremely powerful acid or a massive dose of radiation—and it strikes me as unlikely that some eighth-century Norsemen came into contact with either. Frankly, we're mystified."

A large pottery fragment, lying near the skeleton's cranium, attracted Allen's attention. When he asked if he could examine it, Knudsen nodded and peeled off another pair of gloves. The paint or glaze had faded to a muddy brown, but the image was clear enough.

"Another Great Orm. . . . Those things really got around. But what's this other symbol beside it, sir? The one that looks like a tangle of vines or branches?"

"Your guess is as good as mine. Whatever it is, the artist seems to have partnered it with the Orm symbol on purpose, almost as if one mythical beast were attending to another, although whether those lines are supposed to be antennae or tree branches or tentacles, I have no idea. I can tell you, though, that this, along with everything else in this cave, is rather disturbing. I mean, on an atavistic level. Are these merely decorative designs, or are they representations of living things?"

Elsuba carefully replaced the femur and handed the magnifying glass back to the archaeologist. "Professor, back in the tent you indicated that there might be some connection between the King and Queen and these remains."

"It's only my personal reconstruction of things, but it goes like this: suppose those two individuals had gone off somewhere, when this massacre or epidemic took place. And they came back to their settlement and discovered that everyone else had simply vanished. What would they have done? How long would they have survived? How long before an accident, or illness, took one away from the other? Imagine them staring into the future and seeing nothing but a pointless, slow, lonely death! If I were one of those people, I would have thought it over and concluded that the best option might indeed be a mutual suicide—going to Valhalla hand in hand. They might have enjoyed a last meal together, a final night of making love perhaps, and then they prepared their own gravesites in the softest ground they could find, embraced, and died together quietly in each other's arms."

"Makes sense to me," said Allen.

"Can we go now?" said Elsuba. "This place gives me the creeps."

"I have an excellent cure for that, Miss Poulsen. It's called aquavit, and I have a bottle chilling in my tent. Would the two of you care to join me for a few drinks?"

Dr. Knudsen, weary from the demands of a long, physically demanding day, was determined to get drunk and made sure his guests' glasses were never empty for long. By the time Allen and Elsuba started back to Tjornuvik, they were both tipsy; and because the weather had turned fair, they decided to walk back along the beach, hand in hand, deep in thought. The sun's final rays smote the Giant and the Hag full force, causing the two *dranger* to smolder a hematite red and staining the sea a rich, winy purple. High tide was at spate; the inrushing waves were boisterous as they tumbled through gleaming black stones along the shore, conjuring a hushed, murmuring sound, as though ancient ballads, awakened by the twilight's blaze, stirred, reverberant, in the tenebrous air.

"They must have been devoted to each other," Elsuba mused. "To see them lying together, in an embrace that's lasted a thousand years . . . I feel . . . *honored*, somehow."

"I do, too. I wish I were a poet."

They had reached the cove below Eiden's house. Elsuba tugged on his hand and turned him around, for he had been so lost in mood that he was about to continue walking past the steep whitewashed wooden stairs leading to the back door.

"Hello, hello, this is the twentieth century calling Mr. Warrener! This is where you live, mate, so it's time to climb back to reality!"

Allen heaved an exaggerated sigh: "Oh, must we?"

"Not entirely," said Elsuba. She suddenly spun around, leaned down, and drove a molten tongue into his surprised mouth, corkscrewing it in a way that seemed anatomically impossible. Despite the prolonged intensity of their earlier lovemaking, Allen was as ready for another round as she.

On the afternoon of his last night in Tjornuvik, Allen Warrener's emotions came flooding out. They had done some traveling together during the week—she'd taken him to three other nearby islands in her father's runabout, in fact—but wherever they went together, they continued to follow their simple agenda of food, sleep, and sex interspersed with long, earnest conversations. Inevitably, as the date of his departure drew near, they had tried to cram each day with as much intimacy as possible. Even though some kind of summing-up was in order before their final night together, Elsuba was nevertheless startled by the vehemence of his soliloquy.

He declared passionately that he had never loved another girl as much as he loved her, nor ever would, and if she loved him in return even half as much, then this was his plan for eternal bliss: he would finish his formal education, obtain the minimal necessary graduate degree, and then he would move back to Torshavn and teach English . . . while she finished medical school, internship, whatever; once they were reunited in the Faeroes, he would write great novels in his spare time; she could open her clinic; they would be together always, sharing long and gloriously fulfilled lives; they would be famous and respected in their professions; and finally, they would be buried side by side, like the two Viking castaways, and a thousand years from now, his books would still be read and her contributions to medical science would still be venerated, and their biographer would write: "Theirs was truly one of the great unions! Each brought out the finest qualities in the other; each found the other endlessly fascinating and ever-desirable, and those who knew them well would insist that they remained passionately devoted until the day they died."

After he ran out of momentum, Elsuba just stared at him for a time, flabbergasted. Her first comment sounded rather stunned: "Wow . . . you really have planned everything out, haven't you?"

"Yes," he said sheepishly. "That's my fantasy, anyhow."

"Nothing wrong with a bit of fantasy, but let's not spoil things on our last night together by daydreaming about the future. I love you madly, and I know you feel the same about me, and believe me, Allen, *that's enough for now!* If you want a fantasy, how about this one? For tonight, I am your slave girl."

"That's a real good start," he said, already thickening with lust.

When the alarm clock woke him at seven on the morning that his ship was scheduled to leave Torshavn, he found his suitcase already packed and a letter from Elsuba taped to the mirror:

> My dearest—
>
> I've arranged for the town's only taxi to drive you to Torshavn in plenty of time to board the ship for Copenhagen. The driver is Mr. Pedersson and his English isn't so hot, but he'll get you there OK. The fare, and the tip, are already taken care of.
>
> Well, so much for the easy part of this letter; now to the important part—
>
> We have a saying in Faeroese: *Gud man rada, hvar drekkum onnur Jul,* which translates into: "God alone will decide where we take our drinks next Christmas."
>
> My dearest, beloved Allen—Perhaps it's monstrous of me to say good-bye in this manner, but in truth, the thought of waving good-bye from the dock, then watching your ship grow smaller and smaller, makes my stomach churn. I should not be able to bear it. The days and nights we have shared, they were very special, and if God were merciful, he would allow us the kind of life you described last night: eternal loyalty, eternal joy in companionship; eternal arousals and magical climaxes as numerous as the stars in heaven.
>
> But as we both know, God *isn't* very merciful. One day, three

or five or ten years from now, one or both of us would wake up, look at the other one sleeping beside us, and think: *Christ, what did I ever see in this person???* No matter how passionately you deny it, Allen, you're too smart not to know that day would come, sooner or later.

Wouldn't you rather remember our dreamlike interlude as it has been since you came to Tjornuvik, than to endure the erosions of Time? I would. That's the decision I've struggled to reach, and that's why you're reading this letter instead of listening to the speech I had all prepared!

I know I am hurting you—by leaving now, in the hour before dawn, so that I won't have to listen to your pleas and promises— and that you may never forgive me, but this is the easiest way for us both to part. For 99% of the human race, there is no happy-ever-after; why should we be exempted? So I am packing up my memories and taking them somewhere safe—so they, at least, will never tarnish or become corrupted.

Farewell, my dearest love.

Thank you for this treasury of great memories; I will guard it all my life. In time, I hope you'll understand why you woke up alone.

Allen Warrener stayed to the fantail of the ship as it steamed slowly away from Torshavn, but, as her note had intimated, she never appeared on the dock to wave good-bye. When at length the Faeroe Islands vanished into the clouds above them, he went down to the ship's saloon and methodically drank himself into a stupor.

When he got back to his dorm room in Tampere, Allen wrote Eiden Poulsen a fulsome letter of thanks. A few weeks later, Eiden sent him a clipping from the English-language newspaper in Copenhagen, attaching the handwritten comment: "I'll write to you when all this is not so raw. Elsuba sends love, as do I."

According to the newspaper:

The only son of Faeroese millionaire Eiden Poulsen has suc-cumbed to injuries sustained when his sloop was sunk, with no other survivors, by a fierce, unseasonable gale that struck the northern part of the archipelago.

Kristofur Poulsen, age 16, was serving his first year of apprenticeship aboard the *Sildberin*, a 560-tonne fishing sloop owned by his father, Eiden Poulsen, the man credited, shortly after World War II, with modernizing the Faeroese fishing industry.

On the night of May 18, while the sloop was heading north through the straits between Vesturoy Island and the uninhabited island of Vardinoy, it was overwhelmed by an unseasonable and violent gale that came and went before the Faeroese weather service could radio a warning.

The younger Poulsen was seriously injured when rescuers brought him to the clinic on Vesturoy, where the attending physician, Dr. Rasmus Mikelssen, decided that his injuries were too severe to permit his being transported to the capital city's better-equipped hospital. The young man passed away soon after his father arrived from Torshavn; he never regained consciousness.

A spokesman for the Poulsen corporation stated: "Here in the Faeroes, we have always lived by the sufferance of the sea, and Kristofur had already showed great ability as a seaman when the sea claimed him. He will be greatly missed by all who knew him."

Funeral arrangements were said to be incomplete at the time this story was filed, but a burial-at-sea, said the same spokesman, "would have been Kristofur's wish."

Book II:

NOSTALGIA AIN'T WHAT IT USED TO BE

The highest treetops

are still visible

on the farthest roads.

Only the path

that broke off there

knows the gorge.

—Eila Kivikkaho

7.

GLORY DENIED

Warrener's grandmother had died of pancreatic cancer in the autumn of 1960, his senior year in high school. General Warrener weathered the loss stoically, ordering a simple cremation and refusing to hold a large family reunion afterward. "She was a modest woman who hated fuss," he said. "In this family, we rend our hearts, not our garments."

During his college years, Allen spent as much time with the General as possible. The old soldier sometimes seemed bewildered by the size of his own house, now that he was its only permanent resident, but he always perked up when Allen showed him a new clipping or a transcribed anecdote about the "Vardinoy Monster." Eiden Poulsen sent fresh information whenever he chanced upon it, and he had turned up a goodly amount of it buried in the Torshavn archives. Nothing, so far, provided more than vague, contradictory descriptions; but Eiden dug up archived clippings occasionally, and he questioned the sailors who traveled past the island on a regular basis. It was clear that Eiden pursued this activity as a distraction from his grief, even as the General did from his. After a while, Eiden and the General even struck up a cordial correspondence, which evidently had little to do with Allen, but confirmed the General's initial opinion that "this man Poulsen is okay. You were lucky to run into him." The subject of Poulsen's *daughter* never came up. The General knew, and presumably so did Elsuba's father, that Allen still "carried a torch" for the young woman, now in her second year of medical school, but that was the young peoples' business and the older men stayed out of it.

In the spring of 1965, his senior year, Allen Warrener was duly commissioned a second lieutenant in the Army Reserve, and officially notified that he could expect a callup to active duty some time within the next six months. The conflict in Vietnam was seriously heating up by then, and cannon-fodder second lieutenants were being shoveled into the battlefield as fast as they completed their training. As to which part of the Army he would serve in, Allen's outstanding ROTC record, plus his grandfather's connections, assured a certain freedom of choice unavailable to the average officer candidate. He'd made that choice not long after he returned from Finland; and on the night following his commissioning ceremony, he broached the subject, rather hesitantly.

"Why Special Forces?" General Warrener asked, genuinely perplexed by his grandson's decision. "Surely you know that the highest rank you can expect to reach there is bird colonel. The Pentagon elite still thinks the Green Beret guys are showoffs and glory hounds."

"What's wrong with a little glory, Grandpa?"

"Nothing at all, but you can find it just as easily in the Rangers, or one of those new airmobile outfits. I'm not trying to give you a hard time, boy, I just want to make sure you're clear about your motives."

Allen loosened his tie, then stared for a moment into the swirls of his drink, gathering his thoughts before proceeding.

"It has to do with history, Grandpa. This is a new kind of war, but we have to assume it won't be the only one of its kind. It's the pattern of future warfare, not just an aberration caused by Ho Chi Minh's stubbornness. It's a matter of *political will!* The Communists have it, and our electorate doesn't. And it seems to me that, out of all the American units over there, the Green Berets are the only ones who've taken the trouble to study *why* the enemy fights the way he does, *why* Ho Chi Minh really thinks history is on his side. Americans always go to war with the idea of getting it over with as fast as possible and then resuming their normal way of life. I don't think the enemy's just boasting when he says he'll fight a hundred years if necessary. I think he means that literally. Which means he has a perspective about this war that we, as a nation, find baffling and unsustainable. And that's why Westmoreland measures 'victory' by something as crude as 'body counts.' To be honest about it, sir, if I had my druthers, I'd rather have fought in *your war,* where the cause was clear and simple; but this is the war history's dealt us, and if I must fight in this one, I want the risks I take, and the hardships I might have to endure, to *make a difference.* I'll have a better chance of doing that in Special Forces, because they're trained to fight in the political dimension as well as the tactical."

General Warrener nodded thoughtfully. "I just wanted to make sure your motives were clear in your own mind. And I also agree with you about

Westmoreland—he's spent his entire career preparing for a big, conventional showdown between the Warsaw Pact and NATO, and it's made him set in his ways, narrowed his imagination. If our officers think they'll advance their careers by producing bigger 'body counts,' then you can take it to the bank that they'll pad those statistics with every dead civilian, squirrel, or mongrel dog left on the ground. It's an idea that rewards dishonesty and guarantees lousy intelligence. All of which translates into bad tactics and worse strategy."

"My feelings exactly, Grandpa."

The General looked at his grandson somberly. "You know the training's going to be brutal, don't you?"

"Yes, of course. I think I can hack it, as long as my head's in the right place."

"It'll have to be. Promise me that if you wash out—and a lot of strong, motivated young men do, I understand—you won't give up on the service. You owe Uncle Sam a tour of duty for those bars on your shoulders, oo any task the Army gives you, even if it's not an assignment you want, even if it's not one you *believe in*, hold your head high and perform your duty honorably."

"I won't let you down, sir."

"I know that, Allen. Just don't let pride get in the way of good sense, and you'll do all right."

The first three weeks of Special Forces training almost killed him; but that was the point, after all, and candidates who were still standing upright after four weeks usually got their second wind—the attrition curve leveled off for a couple of weeks. Then, just when those who'd let their guard down were starting to think they'd Made The Green, the regimen ratcheted up again cruelly. Allen was more prepared than some, because that's how he would design a training program for men who'd volunteered for high-intensity combat roles. He took everything the cadre threw at him, sucked up the pain and shut out the exhaustion; learned how to think analytically and calmly, by creating a tiny spiritual chamber—in his mind it was about the size of a coffin—where he could withdraw for a few seconds in the midst of chaos and observe the situation in self-imposed slow motion. He grew physically tough, mentally resilient, and tactically savvy. His fitness reports were uniformly sound, and his prospects seemed unlimited.

Two weeks before graduation, the bottom fell out of his world. During the final field exercises in the wood around Fort Bragg, he slipped on a pile of wet leaves and fell face-first into a big slimy patch of tree fungus. Whatever was inside that mass of organic rot, it triggered an immediate, massive allergic reaction. Twenty-four hours after breathing the spores, he was inside an oxygen tent. Thirty-six hours after the accident, he was fighting for his life against double pneumonia.

When the antibiotics finally turned the tide, he resembled a man just liberated from a World War II Japanese P.O.W. camp, not a fit young warrior who'd been on the verge of a Special Forces commission. His case was remarkable enough to warrant a full-scale study by no fewer than three physicians.

It's very rare, they told him, but not unheard of, for an adult male who'd suffered from, and then seemingly outgrown, severe childhood allergies and/or asthma, to suffer a sudden, life-threatening relapse years or even decades later. These episodes were usually triggered by a chance encounter with some microbe that just happened to hit the wrong spot. If random contact with a pile of Carolina tree mold could send him to the hospital, there were hundreds of chemically similar organisms in the Vietnamese jungles, any one of which might trigger cardiac arrest. The bottom line: a man with his medical condition had no business leading combat troops in a tropical environment. There were many excellent career opportunities in Today's Army for a man with his outstanding qualifications, but leading a Green Beret team in South Vietnam was not one of them.

There was no dishonor in this, the doctors assured him, just bad luck. If Lieutenant Warrener was hell-bent on a combat command or nothing, perhaps he ought to consider the Army's alternative offer: an honorable discharge with half-pay for a disability incurred in the line of duty.

"I'm not disabled!" shouted Allen, at which point the doctors had him tranquilized and returned to bed.

A few days later, Allen received a distinguished visitor: a three-star Pentagon general who'd served under his grandfather in World War II.

"I didn't ask the General to intervene on my behalf," Allen insisted.

"I know you didn't, Lieutenant. You weren't even going to tell him you'd been hospitalized. But somebody connected your name with his and told him what was going on. He called me at the Pentagon, and out of respect for him, I agreed to see what could be done in your case."

The Pentagon general reached into his briefcase and pulled out a copy of

Allen's service record. "You have an outstanding record, so far, Lieutenant: top grades in ROTC, top twenty percent of your class in S.F. training, and you come from a family with a distinguished military heritage. No doubt about it: you're just the kind of young officer the Army would like to groom for high command some day."

"Sir, I—"

"At ease, Warrener! I'm more sympathetic to your situation than you may believe: I wanted to be a fighter pilot, more than anything in the world, when I was your age. But I washed out. Want to know why? Never mind, I'll tell you anyway. I got airsick, Lieutenant. I puked all over the cockpit each and every time I went aloft. Which is why I ended up in the Field Artillery, where I discovered that it was better to be an outstanding gunner than a mediocre pilot.

"Getting sick like that, after all you went through to win your Green Beanie, that's a tough break. But you seem to think that just because you volunteered for an elite outfit and had the back luck to fall into some toadstools or whatever they were, that the Army owes you some form of recompense. Maybe in a just and perfect world, you would have gone on to become the greatest American soldier since Bobbie Lee, but right now, Warrener, you're just another wet-behind-the-ears shavetail who's never heard an angry shot.

"You've already turned down one fair offer from Uncle Sam, and usually one chance like that is all you get. There's a war on, son, and your personal bad luck doesn't mean squat in the Big Picture. But because of your grandfather's intervention, I'm going to make you one last proposition, and if you want any kind of decent career in the Army, I advise you to take it."

"Yes, sir," Allen glumly replied.

"The Army needs good historians as well as good riflemen, just a lot fewer of them. As it happens, there's an opening for such a specialist in the Fourth Infantry Division, headquartered at Pleiku, Vietnam. The posting comes with a promotion to first lieutenant, and your chief responsibility would be to compile regimental histories with regard to certain campaigns and battles in South Vietnam. While you are not authorized to take part in combat operations *as such,* you will of course need to conduct interviews with men who have. This will sometimes necessitate traveling to, um, quiet sectors in areas that are sometimes not very quiet. Should the outfit you're visiting happen to come under enemy attack while you are present, then of course you're entitled to act in self-defense. And anyone traveling to a front-line location over there is supposed to bring along his M-16; nobody will think twice about that. Is this getting through to you, Lieutenant Warrener?"

"Yes, sir; it's getting through loud and clear. Thank you very much, sir."

He arrived at Pleiku just as Preston Valentine was packing to go home. During his years in-country, Preston had four times come close to winning a Pulitzer for his combat photographs. He'd fearlessly gone "looking for the shit" and usually managed to find it. He was one of the two photojournal-ists who hitched a chopper ride into the Ia Drang Valley cauldron on the last night of the battle, when the Air Cav's shrinking perimeter was almost overrun by fanatically brave North Vietnamese. That was where Preston snapped a once-in-a-lifetime photo of a Communist sapper rising up under flarelight to hurl a satchel charge at an American machine-gun position. The shot made the cover of *Newsweek* and some commentators compared it favorably to Capra's immortal *Death of a Spanish Loyalist*. Valentine had faithfully written to Warrener at least once a week, and his gallows-humor observations did much to correct any idealistic notions Allen might have had about the conduct of the war:

"The generals running things in Saigon have all the charisma of shoe salesmen—they're the kind of men who probably have cement deer in their gardens at home. . . . But if there's one thing more contemptible than Westmoreland's cretinous "body-count" strategy, it's a scruffy antiwar activist yelling 'Baby-killer!' at some poor kid who's getting off the airplane after surviving a year's tour. . . ."

During the interval between Special Forces training and his arrival in Pleiku, Allen had outrun Preston's letters, but he was certain Preston would find *him*. And two weeks after Allen settled in as the new assistant director of the 4th Division's Historical Section, Preston did. He'd just come in from the bush, dressed in grungy, sweat-soaked camo fatigues and draped with battered Nikons and Minoltas. Allen offered to take him to the officers' hooch for drinks, but Preston insisted on taking Allen to a bar in town, a garish dive named *The Vegas Strip*, where the upstairs brothel did a booming business at night but was as peaceful as a nunnery during the early after-noon. They were effusively greeted by a moon-faced Vietnamese woman with a mouthful of gold teeth who offered to arrange blow jobs "on the house," should her guests be so inclined.

Afterward, Preston bought the first pair of watered-down drinks and gave Allen the lowdown on their matronly hostess: "Mrs. Tuang's been the madam of this pig-farm since the days when Pleiku was home base for the Foreign Legion's *Groupe Mobile Trois*. She's also V.C., by the way."

Instinctively, Allen dropped his hand down on his holstered .45.

"Cool it, man! We're safer in here than most anywhere else in this fucking province. Me and Mrs. Tuang have been buddies for close to three years, I reckon. I take family portraits, wedding pictures, christenings, funerals, whatever she needs souvenirs of, and in return she's put the word out that I'm not to be murdered. I think that's a pretty square deal. Now, tell me about the deal *you* made—usually, if you wash out of Green Beanie training, they throw you into a frontline rifle company to atone for your sins."

Warrener haltingly explained his situation; Preston was sympathetic, but only up to a point.

"I understand your frustration, Allen, and you're right—there was a time, even a year ago, when I thought maybe the Green Berets had the answer to fighting, maybe even winning, this fucking war. Maybe they did, once. But it's become so much bigger and messier now that good intentions can't make a dent in the situation. I've stayed as long as I can—longer than I should have, really, given the places I've been to and the shit I've photographed. Frankly, I just can't get it up any more—metaphorically speaking. So I'm going home before I get killed."

"No one can blame you. So, what's next for you?"

"I'm heading for New York, my friend. Have you read about the Underground Cinema movement that's sprung up there?"

"Umm . . . you mean, like Andy Warhol?"

"Warhol's a one-trick pony who's conning every pretentious intellectual film critic in town. No, Allen, there's a *lot* more to it than that; there's a whole cauldron of creative activity bubbling and seething—people who are seriously trying to reinvent the cinema! Right now, Manhattan is to the movies what Paris in the Twenties was to literature and painting! It's the long-needed alternative to Hollywood, man! I'll write you all about it, and if you decide the Army isn't your bag after all, come join me and we'll make movies together!"

They drank the afternoon away, and at around three-thirty Madam Tuang joined them. She proved to be a jolly old lady and a rollicking storyteller.

Eventually, however, it was time for Preston to catch his flight for Da Nang, the first stage of his journey back to the Real World. After a weepy, hug-filled farewell, Madam Tuang took Preston aside and spoke to him in a mixture of Vietnamese and English, then smiled rather mysteriously at Allen and bade them both good luck.

"What was that all about?"

"It seems Madam Tuang has taken a shine to you, buster. I *think* she was passing along a friendly warning, too. You know the biggest holiday on the Vietnamese calendar is coming up soon—Tet."

"Yeah, I know, it's their version of New Year's Eve or Saint Crispen's Day or some damn thing. And supposedly both sides are going to observe a truce that weekend."

"Yeah, well, don't bet the farm on it. Mrs. Tuang's exact words were: 'Tell your good friend that he should be careful on the first night of Tet. Tell him "a wise man would sleep deep in a bunker that night.' " So there it is, straight from the enemy's lips—I suspect there might not be as much of a truce as Saigon thinks there will be. Try not to get assigned to guard duty that night."

"I'm not allowed to pull guard duty."

"Then just hunker-in-your-bunker, brother. If Mrs. Tuang says you're in danger, then your ass *is* in danger!"

Allen was still a very conscientious soldier, so he reported the incident to his commanding officer—carefully avoiding any mention of Madam Tuang—and was laughed at for his trouble.

On the night of January 30–31, 1968, the first night of Tet, he and the two other guys who had taken his warning seriously moved their weapons, flak jackets, flares, and hand grenades into their sleeping quarters. The base was not on heightened alert, so when the first salvo of 122-mm rockets went scorching through the sky at 12:46 A.M., many of the Americans who spotted them thought they were New Year's fireworks. When the warheads impacted, seconds later, on a line of parked helicopters 300 yards from Allen's lightly fortified sleeping quarters, they sounded like the veritable crack of doom.

After that first salvo, things escalated very fast. Right behind the big rockets came the swish of mortar rounds and the wail of warning sirens. Allen had barely donned his flak jacket when he heard the blood-curdling cry: "Gooks in the wire!"

While his companions were still groggily groping for their boots and helmets, Allen was in already in full combat gear and slapping a magazine into his M-16. At the last instant, he decided to strap on a .45 as well.

At least, he was *trying* to buckle on the pistol, which proved to be not such a hot idea because he was so excited that his hands were shaking. It required a critical ninety seconds, and a volcanic stream of obscenities, to get the sidearm secured around his hip.

Had it not been for that delay, it was entirely probable that he would have made it across the shell-pocked tarmac and into a foxhole. But just as he ran out of the hooch, bellowing wildly, another 122-mm missile struck seven feet in front of him. His life was saved because someone had parked an APC in the wrong place and its armor plate deflected the shrapnel that otherwise would have torn him to shreds. Even so, it was bad enough. He suffered twenty-two lacerations and contusions, and sustained a skull fracture that exposed, but didn't penetrate, a half-inch segment of his forebrain.

He regained consciousness in the Da Nang hospital, with a purple heart pinned to his pillow and a headache like the wrath of God. He remained there for three months, suffering from trauma-induced muscle spasms and auditory hallucinations. He refused to speak to anyone—including his grandfather—for five weeks, and five minutes into his first private-room psychiatric interview, he vomited all over his personnel file.

When the Army deemed him whole enough and sane enough to be sent home, he was simply handed an honorable discharge and told to pack up.

He was never officially diagnosed with post-traumatic stress disorder—the tremors went away and his hearing slowly returned—but his bitterness was slow to fade.

All his life he had prepared himself, mentally and physically, to lead men into battle. When he was forced out of Special Forces, he had prayed for God to arrange just one test of combat, just one chance to face that challenge and prevail.

And God, with His legendary sense of irony, had granted that wish ... sort of.

For the next three years, at least once a day, Allen would berate himself silently: *I should never have stopped to buckle on that stupid forty-five!*

But in time, he stopped torturing himself. If it hadn't been a recalcitrant belt buckle, it would have been something else. That's how the Lord works, when He deems it appropriate to humble an overly proud man.

8.

"Well, I *Could* Have Gone to Woodstock. . . ."

When Allen returned to his grandfather's house, General Warrener let him settle back into civilian life at his own pace, maintaining a courteous distance until he sensed that Allen was ready to talk about what had happened in 'Nam. He figured Allen was ready when he walked into his study and found his grandson methodically demolishing a lonesome-looking bottle of Wild Turkey. The venue was significant—here they had shared their daydreams about monsters when Allen was a boy, and now here was Allen the adult male, clogged with bitterness because he'd been massively stoked to go fifteen rounds with the greatest monster of all, Death, and he'd unwittingly forfeited the contest because of a T.K.O.; General Warrener knew a lot of men who'd gone the distance in that arena and suffered grave spiritual wounds because of it, even though they had technically "won" on points. Like the guys with post-traumatic stress, Allen was now required to walk a lonely path indeed, on his journey back from a realm that could not be comprehended by those who'd never dwelt there.

When he found Allen waiting for him, a third of the bottle already down the hatch, he didn't lecture the young veteran on the evils of drink; he just walked to the bar, fixed himself a potent martini, and joined him. For the first time in their long relationship, the retired general and the young would-be general got plastered together. When he judged the mood loose enough, the General quietly brought up the topic that had been squatting over the attempted conversation like a slab of ferroconcrete. "Allen, I really think this is the time for you to tell me what happened to you—if you don't get it off your chest, you're going to start visiting that bottle more and more, and while it may be a very good listener, in the short term at least, it's never going to say anything intelligent back to you. And don't tell me it's none of my business, because I raised you like my son and when the Army told me how seriously you'd been wounded, I broke down and wept—so yes, it damned well *is* my business. So start talking, Lieutenant, and that's an order."

Hesitantly at first, and then in a pent-up emotional deluge, Allen told the General everything. And at the end of his narrative, he pulled the Purple Heart from his blouse pocket and flung it disdainfully to the floor. The General bent over with creaking joints and retrieved the medal, and when he spoke there was a trace of anger in his voice.

"If you don't value that decoration, at least treat it with respect for the sake of all the other brave men who've earned it!"

"I'm sorry, Grandfather. It's just. . . ."

"I know what it is, Allen. And I tell you now, as an officer who's served in two world wars and given orders that sent hundreds of young men to their deaths, that you have *absolutely nothing* to be ashamed of. When the moment of ultimate testing came, you didn't flinch, you didn't hesitate; you just picked up your weapon and went forth bravely to join the fight—and according to the witnesses, if you *had* hesitated, you'd have been killed for sure. I have known many a brave young man who had the qualities to become a great leader, but who was cut down before he had a chance to prove himself. So out of respect for *them*, I'm taking this Purple Heart you just threw on the floor and having it framed, and then placed on the mantelpiece next to your father's picture. Because you were every bit as brave as he, and he would have been as proud of you as I am. The most important thing is that the enemy did his best to kill you, yet here you are, getting plastered with a superior officer, with your full inventory of body parts, with an outstanding military service record, and with ninety percent of your life still ahead of you! I'd say that was no small victory, so pull it together and stop acting like you did something shameful."

"All right, General, but when does this feeling of being a worthless shit go away?"

"As soon as you start living a decent, productive life! You know, every huge verbose book on psychoanalysis can, in my opinion, be reduced to one simple equation: If you *think* you're a shit, then you'll *act* like a shit. Look, Allen, it's not as though every man only gets one chance in his life to be brave! In fact, because of the adrenaline rush and the passionate desire not to let down your buddies, it's sometimes easier to be brave in combat than it is in the dull, tiresome context of everyday life. You'll face a thousand choices and challenges where it would be so much easier *not* to do the morally or intellectually brave thing, and the sum total of all those everyday acts and choices, well, that's what other people come to see as your 'character.' I'd rather have men admire your character than this piece of ribbon-and-metal pinned to your jacket."

Allen was grateful to the old man; for the first time since he'd been wounded, he felt some of the rigidity relax its chokehold on his spine.

"On one level, I know you're right, Grandpa, but what about—?" And the conversation rolled down the runway, gaining momentum and continuing in this Socratic vein until both men more or less passed out in the leather chairs. Allen thought it was the longest, widest-ranging, most revelatory dialogue he'd ever shared with his grandfather; and at some point in the long evening, Allen realized that the General was no longer speaking "in rank" as the formidable *paterfamilias*, but simply as one man to another; and that change in status did more to heal him than all the self-righteous bromides he'd been spoon-fed by the VA shrinks who'd interviewed him before.

They never shared another such moment. General Warrener died of a stroke two weeks later, and Allen suddenly inherited a large house on a prime corner lot and enough financial resources to permit total self-indulgent excess for five extravagant years—or twice that long if he kept his more gluttonous appetites in check and opted for a parsimonious lifestyle. He spent many brooding nights pacing through the house he'd grown up in, pondering which of the many branching paths he ought to follow. The "correct" thing to do would have been to enroll in grad school and pursue a master's degree, maybe shoot for a doctorate. But when he reflected on his life, the primary image he saw was that of a monkish ascetic young man who was always preoccupied with Serious Matters, and who—until his abortive stab at martial glory—had lived his adventures vicariously, in the pages of books. The only time he remembered actually living in a state of transcendent glory was during his sojourn on the Faeroe Islands, an interlude that now seemed almost mythical, and even that idyll had been dependent on the near-miraculous happenstance of meeting Elsuba Poulsen.

No, he would not return to the academic grind. What he wanted, in fact, was to go some place totally new and different, and if Preston Valentine's letters were halfway credible, the demimonde of New York's "Underground Cinema" was the place to be. A new and vibrant art form was exploding, Preston insisted, and it would revolutionize the cinema as nothing had since the invention of talking pictures. And by the way, the dope was great, the chicks were compliant, and every one of them was on the Pill! "What in God's name are you waiting for, Allen? *This is where it's at!*"

Well, that certainly proved to be the case for many youngsters, but so deeply was Allen indoctrinated with middle-class values that he had to have *some* purpose for moving to Manhattan that was larger and more meaningful than partying and getting laid. He had no experience in, and relatively little passion for, filmmaking; still, there must be *some* project he could turn his energies to.

Inspiration came from his encounter with a former high school girlfriend, now a full-fledged hippie down to the flaring of her bellbottoms, who called him one night, out of the proverbial blue. She'd heard that he had been wounded and had lost his grandfather, and she wanted to "turn him on to the healing power of LSD."

Why not? Time to learn what all the fuss is about!

This chick made an elaborate, grandiose, and somewhat silly ritual out of the simple act of getting zonked with her date: black lights shimmered on her wall posters; Janis Joplin and the Airplane wailed on her stereo; and on the mattress between their naked bodies she'd placed a basket full of touchy-feely fabrics and patches of fur; in the fridge was a jug of cold orange juice; on a bookcase within easy reach were incense, body lotions, fluorescent beads, and an assortment of vibrators arrayed by length and diameter like the socket wrenches in a mechanic's tool kit. She took the role of Spiritual Guide a little too seriously for Allen's taste, but thanks to the genius of Designer Chemicals, he was entirely malleable. He listened to a lot of music that sounded better than it ever had before, explored the female body like a conquistador mapping an Aztec gold mine, and discovered that—hey!—Tantric sex wasn't as goofy as it sounded. His partner finally passed out about two hours before dawn, and Allen was still having Visuals and Flashes when he drove, ever so carefully, back to the General's house, which was now, of course, his.

Until that night, he had just about become resigned to the notion of graduate school. But his mind was changed, and his whole life somewhat altered, by the apparition he encountered on the back-porch steps. After parking the car, he'd staggered from the garage and headed for the kitchen entrance through the familiar backyard night, made extra-savory by the scents of mimosa, magnolia, and roses—and then, *ZAP!*, one last molecule of Sandoz's Finest kicked in and compelled him to hold colloquy with the Little Professor on the steps. Wee Faculty Feller was a very solid-looking hallucination: a round-bellied, half-bald man, sporting a ridiculous pair of horn-rimmed glasses and a bow tie that Bozo the Clown would have donated to Goodwill. As Allen approached, the specter wagged his finger reproachfully, fogging the air with . . . with *chalk dust?* Allen couldn't be sure, thanks to the blobs of day-glow color that were chasing around his optic nerves like playful kittens.

"WhothefuckareYOU?"

"I'm the future Professor Allen Warrener, and I offer you the greatest of all gifts: tenure! All you have to do is *not* write a novel about your trip to the Faeroes! Above all, you must *not* write about your ecstatic love affair with Elsuba Poulsen!"

"Oh, yeah? Well, maybe that's what I *really WANT* to do!"

"You haven't got the talent, you haven't got the technique. Oh, you've got energy and 'passion' enough to write some hot stuff about that Faeroese broad, but after you come all over the typewriter putting that on paper, you'll be forever trapped in the hideous intellectual wasteland of the Mediocre *Bildungsroman!*"

(At the sound of that term, a dreadful wild beast roared, and then began to whimper, in the depths of the garage: the Bandersnatch for sure!)

"I can too write a great novel, so you just fuck off to whatever dimension you came from. To quote Mr. Dickens, you're nothing but an ill-digested piece of cheese!"

"Well, smart-ass, that's *gouda-nuff for me! See ya in the Big Apple, sport!*"

The dumpy little pedagogue poofed out in a flurry of pixie dust, and Allen Warrener promptly upchucked all over his grandfather's prize-winning azaleas.

He put all of the family effects in deep storage and leased the General's house to a wealthy executive with Burlington Industries, thus assuring a monthly income more than sufficient to guarantee the basic comforts of life, even in Manhattan. He apprised Preston of his plans and sent him enough money to cover a year's lease on a two-bedroom apartment "somewhere close to the action." The place Preston signed for was a dingy old tenement on East

Twenty-seventh, on the top floor of a six-story walk-up that probably dated back to the days of Boss Tweed. It was frowsy and roach-infested, but it had room enough for all their books and records, and Allen's bedroom, at the rear of the layout, facing the fire escape, had a U-shaped bay window nook just big enough to hold his writing desk and typewriter and a small filing cabinet.

All he had to do was unload the U-Haul van, and *voila!*, he was a Young Writer in New York! Just to be a part of that tradition was intoxicating, and he set to work with great naïve enthusiasm. When Preston dragged himself out of bed at 7:45 to go to work at the Film-Makers Co-Op on Lexington Avenue, he often heard Allen already hard at work, the keystrokes of his old upright manual alternating with his morning bout of smokers' cough: *Tap-tap-tap! Harrumph! Tap-tap-tap! Hack! Hack!*

Allen had no idea how to *plot* his opus; he just knew what he wanted to evoke—and after three cups of coffee and a couple of Yellow Jackets he sat down and evoked his ass off. His method, such as it was, primarily consisted of turning on an emotional faucet and letting the words gush forth in torrents. It certainly seemed to him that he was writing something uniquely vivid, a conviction aided immeasurably by the fact that he could afford to write when the mood was on him, without having to worry about the exigencies of a nine-to-five job.

And when "the mood" wasn't on him, he followed Preston through the swirling Underground Film scene, which he found both less and more than Valentine had described it to be. Warhol, he thought, was transparently a charlatan (but the parties at The Factory were memorable, and he did count coup by getting a blow-job from Nico, although she was so wasted on smack at the time that she might have thought she was going down on King Kong), while the more serious artists, people steeped in cinema aesthetics such as Gordon Ball and Stan Brakhage and Ed Emshwiller, were creating powerful and pathbreaking works of visual art. As for the guttering counterculture milieu as a whole, Allen discovered that he was already too grown up, too worldly, too inherently cynical, to groove witlessly along with The Scene. He envied those who could, for to them New York was one huge traveling block party; but he was disturbed by their allegiance to clichés and deeply offended by their ignorance of and contempt for History. Given a choice between hearing Moby Grape down in the Village and suiting up to hear Stokowski conduct at Carnegie Hall, he generally opted for the latter.

He and Preston, however, made ideal roommates; each kept to his personal agenda, and each enjoyed hearing the other's after-action reports of the day's adventures. When their free time overlapped, they ventured forth together and cruised the East Village streets, tirelessly searching for a good time or a quick piece and usually finding both. Allen reconciled himself to the notion that unbridled hedonism could not be counted on to foster an abiding concern for High Culture.

Six months and 300 pages of wordy preliminaries behind him, Allen plunged into the burning heart of the narrative, his account of the affair with Elsuba. Writing those chapters was the most intense creative high he'd ever experienced, but after the scene in which his fictional doppelganger read the Farewell Epistle, he suddenly ran into God's Own Wrath of a writer's block. He had absolutely no idea what his fictional alter-ego was going to do after he sailed away from Torshavn. His own biography certainly provided no roadmap. Too late, he saw the trap he'd fallen into: for the past thirteen months he'd been writing himself into a cul-de-sac, and now, just at the moment he needed to slam the engine into reverse, he was totally out of gas.

While Warrener was pounding out his epic paean to Elsuba, Preston was still keeping all channels open for some current news about *his* First Love, the erotically charged and elusive Sylvia. The years he'd spent in Vietnam had cauterized that old heart-wound like a branding iron, so he now talked about that turbulent episode as though it had been nothing more than a naïve dalliance. The suffering Sylvia had put him through, which Warrener remembered as being very real indeed, Preston now characterized as a self-flagellating rite of passage, something he had to go through in order to validate his credentials as a Sensitive Artist.

"Don't get me wrong, man," he said to Allen one night after they'd taken in a Fugs concert at the Fillmore East. They were now passing the bong in commiseration for their mutual failure to find female companionship afterward. "I would still love to fuck her, but mostly I'm just curious. Is she still in New York? Did she become a model after all? Marry a rich Wall Street tycoon, or become a junkie? Inquiring minds want to know!"

"You've updated your address whenever you moved, right? I mean, if she really wants to contact you, she can do it with two or three phone calls."

"One, actually; we're in the fucking *phone book*, you know!"

"What I think is that she saw your *Newsweek* cover and has been kicking herself in that incomparable ass for dumping a Pulitzer Prize nominee."

"And I'd have won it, too, if it hadn't been for those damned My Lai pictures! Nobody could top those! That little prick Calley should have been fragged before he ran amok in that village."

"Well, Sylvia doesn't know you didn't *win* the Pulitzer—she probably figures, 'Hey, he landed on the cover of *Newsweek*, so he must be rolling in bucks.' If for no other reason, she'll get in touch when she needs to borrow some money. My point is that'll you'll hear from Sylvia when it suits Sylvia to be heard from. Mark my words, Preston, one night we'll be sitting here, just like this, and suddenly, without any warning, the door buzzer will go *Squawk!*"

Squawk! Squawk!!

"You mean . . . like that?" said Preston.

"Yep. Just like that."

Sylvia waltzed into the apartment as though her last encounter with Preston had been four days ago, over bagels and coffee, instead of four years ago, in an operatic mad-scene. She sniffed the air haughtily, looked askance at the thrift-shop furniture, lit a cigarette with exaggerated *film noir* insouciance, took one drag . . . and began mawkishly to sob. Allen was startled. This was the first time he had seen her stripped of all pretense—vulnerable, sad, and soft-centered beneath the armor of her lacquered makeup. The effect was both wrenching and beguiling—she'd probably rehearsed it for days.

Well, he thought, here we go again. . . .

Time, at least, had been kind to her: even in the heyday of the miniskirt, she was still a traffic-stopper. But her eyes had gone hard at the corners, her mouth was a little tighter, and her voice had picked up a vaguely ethnic grate that was, Allen supposed, a South Florida take on the classic New York brogue. Her moves still had that old bone-deep *hauteur* that seemed to demand genuflection. Once she got over that Method-Actor burst of tears, she put up a terrific front, but there was a brittleness behind the façade, which both men sensed immediately. From abject tears, she turned brassy and sassy, but she was obviously not a happy woman, never mind the fact that the outfit she'd chosen for her grand entrance was probably worth two months of their rent.

Preston, for once in his life, was speechless. When the big group-hug finally ended, Sylvia dab-dabbed with a hankie and raised her armored shields again, pivoting sharply on one high heel and drawling: "Who do you have to blow to get a drink around here?"

"*Me!*" they shouted in unison; the serve-and-volley of repartee was so nicely timed that all three giggled inanely. Allen decided that there was still some mighty funky chemistry at work whenever this trio got together in the same room.

After a round of drinks and the ritual Passing of The Joint, some of the guy wires began to loosen around Sylvia's personality. For the moment, anyway, they adopted an agreeable masquerade: that they were three old college chums holding an unexpected reunion.

Sylvia grabbed the mike first, filling them in, rather sketchily, on what she'd been doing since she left Miami. Her "modeling career," assuming it was ever anything more than a fantasy, had not panned out. It was *such* a vicious, cut-throat racket, she confided. This was hardly Headline News to a couple of guys who routinely partied with Andy Warhol's crew, but they nodded soberly, as though she were revealing the identity of the men who ordered the JFK hit. Naturally, she had nothing good to say about the modeling profession, although in all honesty she thought she deserved some credit for simply refusing to play the disgusting power games a girl had to master in order to land the Big Runway Jobs, and she had walked away from a promising future with her integrity unsullied. (Mighty indeed were the gentlemen's efforts to suppress their guffaws!) Many were the minimum-wage jobs she had been forced to take just to keep body and soul together *and* to save up enough money to take a shot at her *other* lifelong fantasy career, that of singing soprano roles at the Met—but, alas, she couldn't afford a good voice coach. She'd ended up working in the box office . . . but at least she'd gotten Leontyne Price's autograph!

Abruptly jump-cutting to the present, Sylvia admitted that she was now a Kept Woman. As gilded cages went, hers was admittedly luxurious ("Preston, this blouse is a Blomberg *original,* I'll have you know!"—the statement followed by a big pause which was intended to cue either Allen or Preston to ask "How much?" and when neither gentleman, obtusely or perversely, rose to the bait, she scowled peevishly).

But in truth, both of the guys were now just grooving on a prime Sylvia Performance, a virtuosic blend of arrogance, self-pity, and bathos, all heated to a low but constant boil. She was spellbindingly good at it, just as long as the spectators had no emotional stake in her charades. Of whom was she the mistress? Preston finally inquired. If she'd claimed it was Nelson Rockefeller or Norman Mailer, Preston wouldn't have batted an eye.

"Sorry. But I can't tell you that—he's very jealous and very powerful."

That sounded plausible; if Sylvia had been shagging a celebrity, she would have dropped his name like a bowler lofting a gutter ball. Even if the sex was mediocre (neither Allen nor Preston wanted to know *that* much), the compensations were not bad: luxurious digs, oodles of leisure time, and a weekly shopping allowance roughly equivalent to the Gross National Product of Samoa.

She proceeded to demonstrate one of the perks of being Mystery Man's concubine by laying out three generous lines of Peruvian flake on the coffee table and rolling a one-hundred-dollar bill into a cylinder. The drug loosened Preston's libido to such a degree that after a while, under the pretense of rough-housing, he began pawing at her shamelessly. At first Sylvia was amused, maybe even interested, but when Preston became irritatingly persistent, her ebullient mood snapped off like a light switch.

"It's been real, guys, but I have to split now. He'll be home soon, and if I'm not there . . ."—she let the implications of domestic cruelty throb in the air, details left to their imaginations. Then, at the moment of leave-taking, another mood swing. She sighed pathetically and turned upon them the imploring gaze of an orphaned puppy.

"I don't want to cramp your style, but would it be okay if I just sort of *dropped in* occasionally? Your pad's as skuzzy as a gorilla's armpit, but it's a comfortable place to kick back in . . . and I need an oasis *somewhere* in this city."

"Dearest lady, " Warrener spoke up gallantly indeed, bending to kiss her languid hand, "you may consider this your *sanctuary*. . . ."

"Why . . . thank you, Allen! That's very gracious of you. Maybe some of it will rub off on your roommate!"

Exit stage left, those matchless ass-cheeks as roundly as mutant succulent pomegranates.

Sylvia did start dropping by, at unpredictable intervals, and an interesting triangular relationship evolved. The more relaxed she became, the more genuinely attractive she was. When she wasn't putting on airs, a habit that came to her as naturally as breathing, she became witty and charming. Warrener had never before had occasion to realize how well-read she was, or how entertaining was her repartee.

On her fifth visit, Warrener and Valentine got off on one of their dream-project riffs: a proposed filmic rhapsody about the Faeroe Islands, sparked by Allen bringing out a scrapbook full of spectacular photos. "We won't use any narration, man, just those wonderful barbaric folk dances! A pure melding of music and imagery! Turn me loose up there with a Bolex and half a ton of Super Agfachrome, and we'll have an Oscar on our kitchen table!"

While Preston continued in this overheated vein, oblivious to everything except his sudden vision, Sylvia suddenly bent over the photo album, having spotted Allen hastily covering one image with an ashtray and trying surreptitiously to turn the page. Sylvia mimed a slap on his hand.

"Uh-uh! Momma says no! Show me what you're hiding!"

Sheepishly, he moved his hand away from an image of Elsuba, reclining on a field of wildflowers, voluptuous and regal, her superb mouth softly parted and her wild Viking hair spread like an angel's wings.

"So that's her."

"What?"

"Your Nordic goddess, Elsie, or whatever her name is. I've often wondered what sort of woman would motivate you to write five hundred pages. . . ."

"And now that you've seen her?"

Sylvia rested her hand atop his, and her voice dropped to a rare timbre of sincerity.

"Now I understand."

And then, for the first time in all the years he'd known her, Sylvia turned upon him the full emerald death-ray of her sexiest gaze. Warrener felt as though a meteor had just dropped on his head from outer space, and while Preston continued obliviously to rant and rhapsodize, Sylvia slowly stroked Allen's hand with cool elegant fingers that left invisible furrows in his skin and an impact crater on his libido. She was one perilous flirt, all right, and his dormant adolescent lust for her came rampantly alive. When she rose to go to the bathroom, she casually dropped one arm and lightly grazed the tip of his ill-concealed erection, sending about five thousand volts through the base of his spine.

Allen did not, of course, reveal this sudden sea change to his roommate. He had already sensed that Preston and Sylvia were on the verge of renewing their carnal relationship, and if he did anything to frustrate Preston's designs, he might seriously jeopardize their friendship. For this simple act of loyalty, he was forced to endure sleepless torments, listening to the groans and cries that rattled the thin wall between bedrooms. The sword-stroke of lust he felt whenever Sylvia winked or bent over to reveal the buttercream tops of her breasts caused him to silently bay at the moon. She was *interested*—she'd made that perfectly clear—but as long as the arrangement in the apartment had her cast in the role of "Preston's Paramour," Allen felt honor-bound to hide his feelings. A further irritant was Preston's casual take-it-or-leave-it attitude toward the renewed affair, but again Allen kept his mouth shut.

Matters were made worse by the fact that Allen was spinning his wheels with the novel. He had poured his hottest inspiration into the Elsuba chapters, and this writer's block definitely had him stymied. He'd never given much thought to *plot*, assuming that enthusiasm, energy, and inchoate talent would more or less solve any piddling structural problems, if and when they intruded. But now that "inspiration" had carried him beyond the Elsuba epiphany, he faced the literary equivalent of the Maginot Line. Over and over, he began wildly typing . . . anything—hoping some form of salvation would descend on wings of grace. It never did.

In all the months he'd been working the material, his subconscious hadn't even drawn a sketch map of what might come after his protagonist had sailed away from Torshavn. For two months he flailed about desperately, experimenting with all the literary tricks he could think of, but the results were forced and pretentious, even to his own eye. My God, for more than a year he had been writing like a dervish, and now he couldn't summon one paragraph that didn't read like a Hemingway parody.

Allen kept bouncing ideas off Preston, and Preston finally got tired of returning the lobs. "I'm not a fucking writer," he finally shouted in desperation, "I'm a photographer! If you want my honest opinion, just put this manuscript away for a couple of years and work on something completely different. A play, a sci-fi adventure, a cookbook! Have some fun with your talent for a change! But whatever you decide to do, for God's sake stop moping around the apartment all day, acting out the Sorrows of Young Werther, okay? Because it's become a fucking *drag!*"

After living together in fairly tight quarters for two years, they were finally starting to get on each other's nerves. Preston several times let it be known that so much breast-beating was unseemly in a man who'd survived a near-miss from the biggest warhead in the North Vietnamese arsenal, not to mention a guy who still had lots of money in the bank from his grandfather's estate. Allen thought that last remark was a low blow—like most people living on unearned wealth, he was acutely conscious of the difference between his self-indulgent lifestyle and Preston's nine-to-five drudgery. But until that one remark slipped out, Preston had never before mentioned the discrepancy. Allen, to his surprise, resented being made to feel defensive about his situation.

But the malaise that made both men cranky wasn't solely caused by the creative impasse that robbed Allen of his primary reason for getting up in the morning; nor was it a function of Preston's growing conviction that he was just spinning his wheels as a film custodian, carefully preserving and repairing an enormous archive of "underground movies," at least 90 percent of which were self-indulgent crap.

The fundamental problem was that, while nobody was really looking, the sixties ended; just as Allen Warrener had finally gotten into the groove, the decade sneaked out the back door so quietly that most people didn't know it was gone until the day after John Lennon got waxed by a hapless little nerd who was just like two or three people *everybody* knew. Allen and Preston had noticed the changes: gone now were the happy-go-lucky potheads who gave you flowers on the street, replaced by menacing hollow-eyed speed freaks whose requests for "spare change" sounded more like threats and sometimes were; the anti-war movement had turned bitter and increasingly violent— just a week ago, a gang of terminally inept Weathermen had dropped a smoldering roach into their hidden stash of C-4 and demolished a marvelous old brownstone, taking with them two-thirds of the "Aquarian Liberation Brigade." For all their exuberant noise and glitter, the hippies had ultimately brought about neither the enlightenment of a New Age nor the expansion of the American consciousness as a whole. As for the Underground Cinema movement, which, for a few gloriously yeasty seasons, had actually seemed to be forging a new cultural paradigm, it too was clearly running out of steam. A handful of the earlier and more accomplished auteurs had been lucky enough to find berths in academia or had sold out totally and gone to

Hollywood, but the cinema-anarchists who used to roam the streets with battered old eight-millimeter cameras glued to their eyeballs were nowhere to be seen. Once it dawned on them that creating a watchable film required some amount of *work,* most of them pawned their Bolexes so they could buy a bus ticket back to Duluth.

It had been one hell of a good time while it lasted; but little by little, the sour reality percolated into the mind of all but the most oblivious stoner: *The Party Was Over.*

Inertia kept Preston going through the motions for about six months after Sylvia came back into his life, but Allen was not surprised when Valentine came home one evening and announced that he had resigned from the Co-Op.

"So . . . another fork in the road. Whither goest thou, my friend?"

"Fortune and fun, Allen! Pornography has become socially acceptable, and there's a fortune to be made in it by the man who knows how to work a camera. There's a new gold rush on, and I've staked my claim!"

"Staked it where?"

"The bustling new Sodom of the South, Atlanta. I got a call from a guy who used to work at the Co-Op, see, and he told me about this new porno production company that's setting up shop right now. Very deep pockets, good distribution, no Mafia connections, all the cops' palms are greased in advance, and the production costs are one third of what they would be in California. I'll get a starting salary of five hundred a week, plus all the pussy I can eat! Does that sound like utopia, or what?"

"Do they need a scriptwriter?"

" 'Script'? Allen, these movies don't even *have* scripts! But come on down anyway, man, the city's exploding and I can always wrangle you some kind of job—towel boy, gaffer-in-charge-of-lubricants, Dildo Master, whatever! If anything in the world can recharge your, ahem, creative juices, this is the gig that'll do it!"

"I'll think about it, Press. Right now . . . too much unfinished business. Besides, I'm probably still too uptight and middle-class to swing with it. But for you, it sounds like the perfect gig."

When Preston moved out, he left in Allen's care a long exculpatory letter for Sylvia. She next showed up on a cheerless, rainy March afternoon. Warrener handed the letter to her, mumbling a needlessly apologetic explanation. He watched her read it, then ball it up in a trembling fist, muttering: "You sleazy mother-fucking *traitor!*"

She turned to him and added: "Not you, Allen. You're sweet and kind and I hope you find the success you're so starved for. It's been a slice, baby." She blew him a very formal kiss, turned sharply, and walked—as he then believed—permanently out of his life.

Alone now in an apartment that suddenly seemed too big, he was totally at loose ends. His spasmodic attempts to concoct a second half for his novel foundered on the reefs of inexperience. He fiddled with the idea of seeking employment, but there was absolutely nothing he wanted to pursue in terms of an alternate career. He'd been charging ahead on the assumption that he was, at least potentially, a very talented writer. But if he was, why couldn't he even finish his first goddamned book?

One muggy night in June, he was glumly watching an old war movie on television and methodically wasting a case of beer when the door buzzer blasted him to his feet in surprise. No one had visited him in weeks. He buzzed back and spoke tremulously into the intercom grill by the door: "Yeah? Who is it?" and a very small, very tired female voice replied:

"Sanctuary, Allen, for the love of God. . . ."

Sylvia looked like a drowned rat. She'd shrunk to ninety-eight pounds and there were bruises on her face; everything she owned, she said, was in these two small suitcases. Mr. Big-Shot had started dating an anchorwoman with CBS News and had summarily kicked Sylvia out to make room for her celebrity replacement. Bye-bye, luxury condo!

There'd been no warning. He just brought her a Tom Collins and told her that if she polished it off in one gulp, he'd give her a special gift. Naturally, she tossed off the drink like a trouper. His "special gift" turned out to be her suitcases, already packed, and a "going-away" present of two fifty-dollar bills, paper-clipped together. There was, to put it mildly, an "altercation," involving the destruction of much crockery and glassware. By prearrangement, however, a burly doorman soon arrived to manhandle Sylvia into the street. She didn't realize the depths of her ex-lover's cruelty until she read the note he'd sandwiched between the fifty-dollar bills.

In order to "get even"—Sylvia didn't explain "for what"—he had slipped a massive hit of notoriously bad-trip LSD into her cocktail. *"No use sticking a finger down that talented little throat, baby—by the time you're reading this, that acid's already in your system. Happy trails!"* Anyway, that's what Sylvia claimed he'd written; truth or not, it made her story into a saga much more operatic than a routine kiss-off from a bored lover.

She claimed to have no idea where she'd been or who she'd been with over the past twenty-four hours, and when Allen took a close look at her pupils, it was obvious that she'd been whacked-out on *something*.

He toweled her off, fixed her a sandwich, and put clean sheets on what used to be Preston's bed. Sylvia was so exhausted, she was half asleep by the time he tucked her in, gave her a chaste little peck on the cheek, and told her not to worry: she was safe here, and he would never hurt her. "I believe you," she whispered, and then began gently to snore.

Bewildered by this sudden turn of events, but feeling mighty virtuous, Allen became painfully conscious of his own body odor—no shower in three days—and decided that he would at least be clean and shaven when he fixed breakfast in the morning. After his shower, he tiptoed into his bedroom, took pajamas out of his underwear drawer, and was hobbling, storklike, on one leg, when he was jolted by a throaty female voice softly intoning:

"No need to bother with those jammies, baby. . . ."

There she was, wide-awake and naked, curled up enticingly on his bed, portions of a sheet strategically draped so as not to reveal all the goodies at once.

"Look, Sylvia, there's really no need. . . ."

She turned off the bedside lamp. New York City thoughtfully provided just enough ambient light for a glimpse of Heaven.

"Once you offered me sanctuary; and when I needed it, you did not turn me away. For thy courtesies, Sir Knight, come and claim thy reward."

"Sir Knight" didn't need a second invitation. He dropped the pajama bottoms and climbed in.

Whereupon she proved to him, several times in the ensuing six hours, that she was every bit as spectacular in the sack as Preston had always boasted she was.

For the next two weeks, they clung to each other like two survivors on a raft. Nothing remained of the dreams that had drawn them to New York, and, after years of excess, now soured by frustration, they both found the idea of peaceful domesticity suddenly very alluring. Allen solicited advice and letters of endorsement from two of his former professors, and was accepted in a well-regarded Master's program.

"You mean I'll be living with a full-fledged professor?" Sylvia chirped when he told her the news.

He cleared his throat nervously and then, because he knew the gesture would impress her, he actually got on his knees and grasped her hands.

"You can be married to one, if you think you can put up with my moods."

"If you can put up with *mine,* I think that sounds like a really nice proposition. Is it also an actual proposal?"

Suddenly flooded with resolve, he answered: "You bet it is. I'm determined to make an honest woman out of you."

"No church wedding, please. There are limits to my hypocrisy."

Three weeks later, he made the down payment on a two-bedroom bungalow six blocks from the campus.

9.

Becalmed in the Boondocks

By Christmas of Karen's senior year in high school, Earl Hambly's Brown Lung symptoms appeared to be in remission; and so far, he'd managed to keep his condition a secret from the bosses. If Earl could just stay on his feet and look reasonably healthy for another two years, he could come clean about the ailment and still qualify for early retirement on disability. Earl was sure he would make it—he hadn't smoked a Chesterfield for a year and a half.

In smashing through the concrete drainpipe, Karen had sustained injuries severe enough to keep her upper right torso immobilized in a cast for three months. Before he removed the cast, her doctor warned Karen that she might never regain complete freedom of movement in the injured shoulder—that even fully clothed, she would always resemble someone "on the verge of making a very emphatic shrug." Unsure as to whether that condition would prove to be a trifling annoyance or a gross disfigurement, Karen spent an inordinate amount of time fretfully scrutinizing her body in May's full-length mirror, practicing ways to avoid looking lop-sided.

May kept assuring her that the asymmetry was barely noticeable, promising her that boys would soon be "too preoccupied lookin' at your pretty face to pay attention to nothin' else."

She needn't have worried; once her "bumps" finally appeared, between her eighth- and ninth-grade years, they rapidly matured into perfectly proportioned apple-sized breasts. Suddenly, she was being asked out on dates, as her mother had predicted, by male classmates who were attracted to her large, solemn eyes, her lithesome dancer's legs, and her sensuous mouth. The irony was that she seldom found any of *them* equally attractive, so she voluntarily maintained a low social profile. The graduate student who'd been

her reading tutor went to Europe during the summer between Karen's sixth-
and seventh-grade years and got married to a Spanish gentleman, but she
thoughtfully arranged for Karen to inherit her library study carrel, an irreg-
ularity that the College allowed only because Karen had already tried to pre-
enroll and was known to some of the faculty as being a student of
exceptional potential. Most evenings and weekends, she was in that carrel,
reading as voraciously as ever. When she wasn't sequestered with books, she
spent her time just hanging out, studying the older students, observing their
patterns of behavior, imitating their taste in clothes, and soaking up whatever conversations she managed to overhear or, sometimes, participate in.

Change was in the air, palpable and fervent. Karen understood—from
magazines, TV programs, and student bull sessions—that this was a nation-
wide phenomenon. She was no more immune to the ferment than any other
impressionable, well-read adolescent. Once a week, spare change jingling in
her pocket, she went to the student bookstore and bought the new issue of
Rolling Stone, which she then devoured cover to cover. Thus did she learn the
true scope of What Was Happening in the late 1960s. The vast, unexplored
(to her, at any rate) distances of America were full of young people who were
Tuning In, Turning On, and Dropping Out—and they all seemed to be
having one hell of a good time!

In her wanderings around the campus, Karen saw the rallies and heard
the jeremiads of the resident political activists, a handful of extremely hip
students (mostly from out-of-state home towns) who seemed determined to
drag this somnolent rural institution into the turbulent national maelstrom,
whether most of the other kids wanted to be there or not. Until Karen was
a high-school junior, the College adhered to standards of dress and decorum
that had congealed during the Eisenhower administration. But when the
winds of change belatedly reached central North Carolina, they swept
through Dormitory Row like a hurricane. In the space of a single summer,
the students' clothing turned exotic, their taste in music louder, the tone and
subject matter of their bull sessions stridently political; and the acrid-sweet
aroma of marijuana began to waft provocatively through the scent of honeysuckle and magnolia. In her state of omnivorous innocence, Karen soaked up
everything like a sponge; her senses quickened and her intellect stretched as
she tried to figure out what *her* place might be in this unprecedented crazy
quilt. Much of it was beyond her comprehension and some of it defied her

notion of common sense, but campus life now seemed charged with so much electricity that she simply couldn't remain a spectator for long.

When the first rather tepid anti-war rallies were organized, they ignited from Earl Hambly loud fulminations against "long-haired Commie agitators." Naturally, he forbade Karen from associating with any "hippie scum," so Karen of course took every opportunity to do just that. She learned much—some of it even accurate—about right-wing fascism and the riots in Chicago; My Lai and the Civil Rights movement; the slayings at Kent State and the philosophy of Timothy Leary . . . and she saw the movie *Woodstock* fourteen times. She inevitably gravitated to the groups who followed the more charismatic male activists and developed a sizable crush on at least three of them. She even bought some hippie outfits at the local head shops, stashed them in her library carrel, and faithfully changed into them before reporting for duty at one factional headquarters or another. A growing number of male students began paying attention to the new groupie, and Karen, in response to their overtures, grew much less concerned about her "deformity"—a belated growth-spurt, in fact, blessed her with quite a shapely figure; the leggy brown-eyed girl who stared back at her from the mirror was not without demonstrable allure. Her last two years of high school passed in a mostly pleasant blur of activity, some of it sexual, and some of the sex pretty damned good; on *both* sides of the bed, if her partners' comments could be taken at face value.

In the spring of 1972, with high-school graduation just two months away, Karen laid plans to escape the Project and its dreary conservatism. She'd saved enough money for a one-way bus ticket to San Francisco. Her sense of things was that, if she didn't break away now, she was doomed to miss what was left of the sixties—like most of her hippie-esque friends, she'd barely noticed when the calendar flipped over into 1970, but by the spring of '72, under the shadow of Richard Nixon's jowls, whatever remained of the sixties' spirit was fading into historical irrelevance.

The Class of Seventy-Two graduated at 3:00 P.M. on June 3. Because Karen had already been accepted by the College—on full scholarship, no less—her plans seemed comfortably settled. No one suspected her intention to flee from the very middle-class future she had always pursued. She had packed a suitcase in secret and hidden it in the back of her closet. The night before the Great Escape, she wrote a long, painful, rather disjointed letter to her mother, explaining her motives and promising to keep in touch. She had the addresses of lots of run-away shelters, safe houses, and crash pads in the Bay area, so she wouldn't just hit the sidewalk aimlessly when she got off the Greyhound. Even in rebellion, she was still careful, still trying to act responsibly.

On the night after graduation, at the parent–student "banquet" that followed the ceremony, Earl Hambly accepted a flask from one of his co-workers, a man who also had a child in the graduating class and who was just as bored by the interminable speeches as Earl was. They took turns sneaking off to the men's room to get their nips, and Earl got just tight enough to lose his inhibitions. He bummed a Chesterfield from his buddy and slid outside the auditorium to smoke it, rationalizing his relapse in the classic manner: *Today's special—one little cigarette ain't gonna matter, and tomorrow I'll go back on the wagon.*

The third time he inhaled, savoring the once-familiar rush of nicotine into cells that had missed the stuff badly, Earl felt something lurch inside his chest, with an unpleasant "shoveling" sensation. All at once he began to wheeze desperately for air, and when he finally worked up enough breath to launch a really good cough, what came up was a monstrous wad of bloody mucus. When the emergency-room X-rays came back, they confirmed the worst: Earl's long-dormant symptoms had sneakily evolved into Stage Two cancer. His condition was too advanced for the hospital to do anything for him, so the doctors basically just sent him home to die in whatever comfort he might find there.

The timing of Earl's mandatory retirement left the family in financial trouble; for one thing, there were still thirty mortgage payments outstanding. Without complaint, May applied for a job as a clerk at the local Kmart. To Karen—the only offspring still in residence—fell the scut-work of nursing. She fed Earl and cleaned up his mishaps, and tried to distract him from morbid thoughts. Of course, she didn't get on that bus for San Francisco, nor did she ever tell May that she had been planning to. But her enforced intimacy with her father wasn't all drudgery. When Earl was lucid and floating on his painkillers, father and daughter talked, really talked, as they never had before, and each came to love and understand the other as they never would have done otherwise.

Earl lapsed into a permanent coma, fourteen months to the day after he'd bummed his last Chesterfield. How or why his body continued to live, no one could guess, but live it did, week after doleful week, filling the Hamby residence with leaden gloom and turning Karen's life into a round-the-clock bad dream. The very air smelled of mortality too long denied. Karen sealed off the tiny back porch with plastic sheeting and slept outside, just to escape the suffocating atmosphere, until the temperature fell below freezing three nights in a row in late November. Christmas was a grim mockery, and by the start of the new year, May Hambly was taking sleeping pills for the first time in her life. Karen cadged one from her now and then.

Without any warning or sudden crisis, Earl Hamby died on the night of February 3, 1974. Karen never came right out and asked May if the oxygen line had come off the tank by accident or by intent, but May certainly didn't sound surprised when Karen phoned to tell her that Earl was gone. And there was some ambiguity in May's voice when she responded to the news: "God's will be done."

Earl's company-administered insurance wasn't worth much, but it did enable May to liquidate the mortgage; on the night they burned the contract, she and Karen both got looped on champagne.

Karen had no trouble renegotiating her scholarship arrangement with the College; all she had to do was sign a contract stipulating that the first five years of her teaching career would be within the borders of North Carolina, and she was home free. When May drove her to the campus in Earl's decrepit old car, the two women sang Beatles tunes all the way from the Project to the Admissions Office.

From that morning in late August, until the afternoon of December 4, Karen enjoyed the happiest time of her life. Perhaps that happiness would have continued if there hadn't been an ice storm that day. By noon, the streets were impassable for any car not equipped with chains or snow tires. When the Kmart manager saw the noon weather report, he decided to close early; there hadn't been a customer in the place since 11:15. He was kind enough to offer May a ride home in his four-wheel-drive truck, too, and she was waiting for him in front of the store when a UPS van—whose driver was also in a hurry to get off the roads—went into an uncontrollable skid and slammed into May Hambly before traveling on through a plate-glass display window.

May's spinal injuries left her with limited use of her right arm and some mobility in her neck, but that was all. She would never walk, or be able to speak intelligibly, again. UPS offered to settle promptly, out of court, for much less than May could have gotten if she'd allowed Karen to hire a good lawyer. But as of January 24, 1975, when May rang her little hand bell to summon Karen, the check still hadn't arrived. May had already scrawled her first remark on the newsprint pad she used in place of her voice:

Steel box bottom Earl's closet Pls fetch.

Karen did as her mother asked, then she placed the fireproof document box in May's lap.

"Shall I open it for you, Momma?"

No—just wanted you to see it. Deed to house is inside. Call lawyer tomorrow— name on deed. Want to remake my will—

"Damn it, Momma, don't even talk like that!"

You heard what Dr. said: blood clots, strokes, any ol' time. Honey, this aint Life it's Shit & Im TIRED of it—DON'T SHUSH ME!!

"All right, Mother, calm down. What shall I say to the lawyer?"

Change will—YOU GET HOUSE, not worthless bros and sisters!!!

"I don't think they're going to like that very much—"

Screw em, I don't see THEM helping out around here! You get house so you finish grad school & not have to worry about paying rent!

But Karen was worried. She'd fallen so far behind, she might not graduate with her class; and she couldn't even think about re-entering school until the UPS settlement came through and she could afford to hire a good professional caregiver for May. But, somehow, UPS's attorneys managed to jiggle the terms of the settlement so they didn't have to pay in one huge lump sum, but by escalating yearly installments. The first check, for a piddly ten thousand, wasn't enough for two grown women to live on—not with May's medical bills. But in order to take a job, Karen would have been forced to commit May to a poor-folks' nursing home that was a notorious snake-pit of neglect; meantime, May couldn't be left alone for more than ten minutes. Karen began to suffer from both depression and insomnia, although she tried mighty hard to keep May from seeing how worn-down she was.

But May knew, of course. And in her ever-resourceful way, she managed to solve their dilemma.

How May managed to get 48 econal, without being able to either walk or speak on the phone, would forever remain a mystery. Her death, in any case, was peaceful and private, and her final note to Karen was *some* comfort, as she'd meant it to be:

Better like this and you KNOW it! Live here or sell it and go to grade school with the money, i don't much care no more—this place is a rat hole anyhow and always was.

YOU'R BEST THING OLD EARL & ME EVER DID!

See you in Heaven, sweety. P.S. call those shit-pokes at UPS and thretten to take em to court if they don't get that check to you P.D.Q.

Love always—

Karen had missed so much of her freshman year that her advisers thought it best for her to start all over again, come September. In July, she sold the Project house and moved into a three-room apartment within walking distance of the campus. As the first days of the fall semester drew near, she felt as though she'd been in a stupor ever since high-school graduation, and was only now starting to regain consciousness. Once settled in her new abode, she counted the days until classes began. And when they did, she thrived.

She was so comfortable with her choice of careers that she taped a sign to her library carrel: "Born to Teach English!" Without meaning to, she became one of those industrious, undemonstrative grinds who remain half-invisible to their classmates. Her social life was mostly confined to lukewarm political activism. She drifted in and out of a few tepid affairs, all of which she terminated either when her partner became inconveniently serious or mistook her quiet demeanor for submissiveness.

But she couldn't escape one nagging discontent, one aching frustration that haunted her moments of loneliness: what if she *had* made it to San Francisco? Some nights, she would light a stick of incense, fire up her bong, and play the old iconic records, just to reconfirm how fucking *great* the music still sounded. Those piercing vocal arabesques from Gracie Slick! *Après vous le Disco!*

She was still playing the same music three years later, but not so often. She'd come far; a half-dozen graduate schools were already courting her. May would be mighty proud of her. But she wasn't as eager to crack the books this year as she had been previously.

Here she was, just starting her senior year of college, for God's sake, and she realized that something important was missing from her life: fun. She hadn't experienced much of it so far. That old road-not-taken itch returned with a vengeance. Just once, before she had to immure herself in the cloisters of graduate school, she wanted to spread her wings in rarefied air; dance to outlaw music; take a few walks on the Wild Side. And she definitely, yes *definitely*, wanted to meet a handsome, obscure genius and cast such a spell over him that he would be inspired to write a great novel or discover the cure for cancer, the secret of faster-than-light travel . . . *something!* And she wasn't likely to find him *here*.

Two weeks after her senior-year classes started, Karen paused on her way into the library to read a bright orange flier on the bulletin board, one that hadn't been posted on her last visit:

Woodstock Ten Years After!
Were The sixties a Crock, or what?
A SYMPOSIUM FEATURING EIGHT FACULTY EXPERTS
REPRESENTING A CAREFULLY-CHOSEN
CROSS-SECTION OF DISCIPLINES, GENDERS,
RACES, AND THE "DIFFERENTLY AGED"
THE SYMPOSIUM WILL BE FOLLOWED BY EXTENDED Q & A!

Well, it was free, open to all, and it was scheduled for Thursday night, a date that just happened to be free on Karen's engagement calendar. Just like Wednesday . . . and Tuesday . . . and . . .

What the hell? Maybe I'll learn something.

Evidently, the topic had only limited box-office appeal—out of the two hundred-plus seats in the auditorium, only about sixty were occupied. Karen had no trouble finding a vacancy down front, and also on the aisle; she wanted to observe the speakers' facial expressions, but she also wanted the option of slipping out unobtrusively, should boredom set in early.

According to the female moderator, the faculty members here assembled were both "well qualified" to address the topic, and "extremely keen to generate a lively interchange of ideas with the audience." Each speaker had twelve minutes to say his or her piece, then the free-for-all would start. Since all the people on stage wore an identical expression that fairly shouted "Dear-God-how-did-I-ever-get-conned-into-doing-this?" Karen didn't expect a rousing debate.

A forty-ish brillo-haired Poly-Sci professor, a woman in serious need of facial electrolysis and sporting the torso of a Bulgarian shot-putter, grasped the microphone like it was a coiling rattlesnake. As soon as Karen heard the phrase: "The defining period in the struggle against phallo-centric sociopolitical patterns of gender oppression," she tuned it out and palmed back a yawn. Perhaps the next speaker would provoke a livelier response from the listeners.

It was not to be, for the next "expert" was a black man from the Music Department who launched into a needlessly antagonistic and, Karen thought, intellectually dubious case for the inclusion of "World Musics" (a shorthand euphemism for be-bop, soul, disco, and jazz) into the departmental curriculum, to offset the "unjustified" emphasis on music composed by "D.W.E.G.S." It took Karen almost until the end of his diatribe to realize that this was an acronym for "Dead White European Guys." Sure, she liked to throw a Miles Davis LP on the turntable when the mood was right, but she wasn't quite convinced he belonged on Olympus next to Beethoven.

Next came an economist, a neo-Hobbesian whose lengthy reign as department head was reportedly due to his murderous skill at political infighting. He didn't even try to lay out a formal argument. He just spat invective at the whole decade and everything associated with it, apparently because it had unleashed the scourge of "One-World Relativism," whatever the hell that was. What began as an arch-conservative statement-of-principle deteriorated into an incomprehensible ideological screed shrill enough to drive a dozen auditors from the room.

I've heard enough of this codswallop! Karen gathered her books in preparation for making an anonymous lunge for the nearest exit. But derisive hoots forced the economist to halt in mid-diatribe and sit down in an icy sulk, and when the moderator hurriedly began citing the credentials of the next speaker, Karen decided to stay a while longer. Three speakers in a row had either condemned the sixties or tried to bend the decade to fit their current agendas. But she'd heard enough about this next guy to think that he might present a more sympathetic point of view. Or so campus scuttlebutt would indicate.

Professor Allen Warrener, History Department; had published a monograph and several articles on political and cultural affairs in post-1918

Scandinavia (not exactly an overcrowded field); never wore a necktie unless the occasion made it mandatory; chummy with some students, scathing with others; had allies and enemies in roughly equal numbers. "A renowned expert on the major artistic, political, and military leaders of Scandinavia and the Baltic States," droned the moderator.

Right, thought Karen. *Name two.*

The Word On The Quad about this guy was generally enthusiastic. Warrener was so fiercely opposed to *all* ideologues that his stance, in a manner of speaking, had *become* an ideology unto itself. He was a passionate writer-of-letters-to-editors, and a maverick whose contempt for intra-departmental politics was so proverbial that it was reportedly jeopardizing his chances of gaining tenure—the scholastic equivalent, in other words, of a kamikaze pilot.

And he wasn't bad-looking, either, especially those smoldering Byronic eyes. Female students had tried flirting with him, but were always gently and regretfully rebuffed. The guy wanted to mess around in the worst way, but always seemed to be straining on the end of an invisible choke collar. If the campus gossip was true, the poor bastard was brutally pussy-whipped by his wife, a brassy blonde who thought nothing of publicly ordering him around like a waiter, and who was reported to be serially unfaithful, although no one would admit to screwing her. Most of it was probably bullshit, Karen supposed; any youngish, good-looking professor who had the balls to steer an independent course was bound to be the object of scorn, envy, and malice from at least half of his peers.

Therefore, he might actually have something interesting to say. . . .

The moderator evidently thought so, too, for she was introducing Warrener more fulsomely than the three speakers who'd gone before. Here, she declared, was a man who had lived at the heart of The Scene, who'd been closely involved in the fabled Underground Cinema movement, and who had routinely hung out with the likes of Warhol, Burroughs, Mailer, and Ginsberg. *Now* Karen was definitely interested; and so, evidently, was a large contingent of the audience, who greeted the speaker with cheers of "Right on, Allen!," in stark contrast to the apathetic patter of palms that had greeted the earlier speakers. Warrener seemed unsure of how to respond to this demonstration.

"Thank you—thank you for making me feel more interesting than I probably am!" He shuffled some note cards awkwardly before continuing.

"To be honest with you, I do not have any prepared remarks, because it is my belief than ten years isn't nearly enough time for Americans to reach any consensus about one of the most turbulent periods in our history. I was right there, at the heart of things, for more than three years, but even now I still have conflicting emotions and shifting perceptions. I mean, did the Flower Children leave a genuine legacy, or just a lot of trash for other people to clean up? It would be admirable if I could get through this talk without once quoting Mr. Dickens, but I can't, because he said it so perfectly: *It was the best of times, it was the worst of times.* Maybe the most valuable contribution I can make to this symposium is to provide you with some illuminating examples of both. The decade is already so encrusted with myths that some of the people whom I knew as conflicted, conscientious individuals have been turned into frozen icons.

"If I'm interpreting my students' comments correctly, there are a lot of young people today who would love to have time machines, so they could go back and take LSD with Timothy Leary, or experience the risk and excitement of the heroic years of the Civil Rights movement, or listen to the great bands of the period before they became burned out self-parodies; or, more commonly, just wallow in a glut of guilt-free consensual sex. . . . And I hope one of you science majors does invent that time machine . . . because I'd like to do that too!

"Those are all major components of the gestalt, for sure, and some of them were indeed memorable. But, like every idealized period in history, the sixties were also messy and full of ambiguities that made those experiences, at various times and in various contexts, a lot less glamorous than Nostalgia makes them seem from the perspective of a decade kater. I think the wisest contribution I can make to this discussion is simply to show you some 'snapshots' and read you some brief—I assure you, *very* brief—journal entries written at the time.

"Yes, it's true, as our moderator pointed out, that I did know Allen Ginsberg, and I believe him to be one of America's great maverick poets. But the reason why I remember him is not because we sat around and discussed his theories of poetry; it's actually because every time we ran into each other, and even though he knew I was straight as an arrow, Allen used to reach around and give me the sweetest little pat on my ass. As for Bill Burroughs, my most enduring recollection of him comes from the time he dropped a big glass of vodka-and-tonic in my lap, because he hadn't had a shot of smack that day and his hands were shaking so badly he couldn't hang on to his drink. Mailer I knew because we sometimes got invited to the same parties, and if you caught him in a good mood, he *would* pontificate, with drunken brilliance, about the art of writing. And yet, the only thing he ever said to me that I remember with absolutely clarity was: 'Why don't you go fuck yourself, Warrener?'

"So yes, ladies and gentlemen, I think it's permissibly accurate to say that we had a pretty good time, but certainly not *all* of the time. And the social pressures to conform, to fall in line with all the other face-painted lemmings, were so unrelenting that you were well advised to keep your negative opinions to yourself if you wanted to avoid being ostracized.

"I could go on dropping names, like a turtle lays eggs, for the next half hour. Instead, I thought you might find it illuminating to hear a partial list of the opinions I felt socially coerced into never speaking aloud. I could only write down my true feelings, never utter them. I hope you're all taking notes, kids, because I'm about to serve up the giblet gravy of History."

Karen, in fact, *was* taking notes, diligently.

"Here's what I had to say about two of the decade's Top Ten media celebrities. These are spontaneous observations I jotted down in my journal, right after I had the ineffable pleasure of meeting these people:

"Many years ago, on a playground far, far away, a gang of 12-year-old WASP bullies decided to torment a bookish, bespectacled, socially ostracized 10-year-old Jewish kid whose tendency to burst into hysterical tears from an unkind word had brightened many a dull lunch period. They surrounded him, snatched away his glasses, tromped on his yarmulke, rabbit-punched him to his knees, rubbed a pail full of sand into his frizzy hair, and shouted to the other kids that his sister blew Puerto Rican gang members for a dollar and always got change. The torture stopped only when a wrathful teacher heard the victim's wails, but the gang leader had enough time to land one more kick to the kid's ribs and snarl: 'We'll finish you off later, you creepy little kike.'

"Guess what? Even though he's taller today, much more articulate, and able to mobilize enough naïve followers to paralyze the traffic in a major city, Abbie Hoffman is still *a creepy little Jewish kid. Growin' that silly Afro don't change* nothin', *man."*

Warrener shuffled his note cards; Karen, tight-lipped, readied her pencil.

"Here's an entry about an artist we all know and love: *'Bob Dylan swaggered into the party about 2 A.M.,* a pair of long-haired nymphets clinging to his arms and a phalanx of PR flacks from Columbia Records trailing in his wake. I was not impressed. He's a scruffy, sullen little gnome who mumbles worse than Marlon Brando with a mouthful of hot oatmeal. A filmmaker of my acquaintance, a member of the In Crowd, asked if I'd like to meet him. I declined. Dylan's arch mannerisms, the willful obscurantism of his lyrics, and the shameless arrogance with which he rips off better, braver men like Woody Guthrie and Pete Seeger, undermine the image he tries to cultivate. And, Christ almighty, that VOICE! That rusty-nail adenoidal whine—it melts the fillings in my teeth!

"On the other hand, as my In Crowd friend acidly pointed out, 'Yeah, well, all that may be true, but Bob's gonna get laid tonight and you and I probably aren't.' " Warrener ignored the irritated glances of his colleagues and doggedly plowed ahead: "My misanthropy knew no bounds in those days. I quickly concluded that: Andy Warhol was a vicious and gossipy little faggot without a molecule of real talent in his whole boneless body; I thought the only Beatle who looked like he'd be fun to go out with on a pub-crawl in Liverpool was Ringo, the group half-wit; I thought John Lennon forfeited all respect by joining forces with Yoko Ono, one of the most vapidly pretentious 'artists' of that or any other decade, and a woman so unbelievably ugly that she always put me in mind of the towel-girl in a cheap Yokohama whorehouse."

Karen scribbled frantically: *Oh my God, see the Feminist writhe! If this guy Warrener wasn't on her Shit List before, he surely is now. "Ugly"? Just for a male teacher to use that word is like throwing down the gauntlet! If only he'd said "differently beautiful"!*

Warrener grinned disingenuously. "Have I left anything out? Oh, yeah: I also thought that 'I Am the Walrus' was the *dumbest* damn song since 'How Much Is That Doggie in the Window.' "

He shuffled his notes again, glanced at his watch: "I have just enough time left to tell you a story, a parable that summarizes my most enduring memories of the sixties. It concerns a young man we'll call 'Tony,' who'd been my close friend in high school and who moved to New York a few years before I did. Tony had fallen hopelessly in love with a very sexy but essentially bubble-brained girl named Hannah, who led the poor bastard around with a ring through his nose. Hannah really and truly swallowed the whole

Age of Aquarius Party Line. She leaped giddily and unquestioning from one fad to the next. I mean, if Donovan sang about 'electrical bananas' on Monday, I would drop by their apartment on Thursday and find them laboriously roasting the gunk they'd scraped from the insides of a dozen banana peels. After they dried this shit in their oven, they smoked every bit of it. Hannah claimed she got off. 'It's like mild MDA,' she promised. Tony agreed it was 'promising' because he never wanted to rain on her parade. I naturally gave the stuff a test drive, and I can vouch for the fact that the one and only effect it produced was a sore throat and a mild attack of asthma.

"Next, Hannah fell under the sway of an 'organic guru,' who preached such an extreme form of dietary self-denial that Hannah refused to consume any more honey, claiming that by doing so, you were, quote, 'ripping off the bees.' What *did* they eat? I never wanted to know, but their refrigerator was stocked with Tupperware containers filled with some kind of lumpy gray paste, which smelled faintly like toadstools and which they consumed, rather joylessly I thought, every single day for two weeks—until Hannah found something newer and even more bizarre to obsess on.

"But she did love her drugs, and they tripped incessantly, on LSD, on MDA, on mescaline, on pot, on Hawaiian wood rose, on horse tranquilizers, whatever was the substance de jour . . . and that is the subject of the verbal snapshot I want to show you of Tony and Hannah . . ."

"My last contact with them, before I fled New York for good, was on the night Hannah gave birth to her first child. No doctors allowed, of course, just a self-declared 'organic midwife,' whatever the hell that was, who was dressed like a gypsy fortune teller and chanted in some made-up language while Hannah struggled through her contractions. They *had* gotten a gender test, though, so they knew the child was going to be a girl, and they'd decided to name her 'Wood Rose.' In between contractions, Hannah boasted she'd dropped a monster hit of acid just after her water broke, so that, quote, 'Wood Rose can have her first trip while she's coming into the world!' I thought that was the most insanely irresponsible thing I had ever heard this young woman say—what kind of mother was she going to be? Tony didn't look too thrilled about it either, but he dutifully went along, and when the baby slid out, he was waiting with sterilized gloves and a sanitized kitchen knife to cut the cord. The whole scene had become medieval—I couldn't watch it anymore. I left, pretending the spurt of blood had made me nauseous.

"I was so disturbed by Tony's complicity in his wife's delusional behavior that I didn't even call him on the phone for two, maybe three, months, and when I did finally work up the resolve to call and ask how little Wood Rose was doing, Tony sounded utterly desolate. Hannah had abruptly decided that marriage was a male-chauvinist, middle-class 'plot' designed to oppress women, and that pure communal living was the only alternative. She wanted to join a hardcore Vegan community somewhere in rural Pennsylvania. Tony assumed she was talking about all three of them, so he started packing up their stuff.

"But that's not what Hannah meant at all. The day after she announced her intentions, she said she was going out to score a lid of grass—and she never came back. She just left the baby behind like a toy she'd grown tired of playing with. Ten days later, Tony got a postcard from her—not a phone call, because the guru who ran the commune didn't approve of telephones—or of electricity, or indoor plumbing, for that matter and on that card Hannah had written: 'At last I've found a place where I can live as the Goddess intended,' or some such rot. Not a word, mind you, about their child.

"Tony was a decent, conscientious man; he was willing to sacrifice whatever it took to raise Wood Rose properly. Which would have been all right, except two years later, the doctors discovered that little Wood Rose had been born with severe, irreversible brain damage, and would probably never develop mentally beyond the age of two. So for the past seven years, Tony's been living alone, on a carpenter's wages, with a daughter who does nothing but sit and stare all day at the TV set. She cannot feed or clothe or clean herself . . . and she wears a big apron fastened around her neck to soak up the drool. Tony's one remaining hope is that one day his daughter will actually look at him with just one flicker of cognizance and say the word 'da-da.' But she never has; she has the vocabulary of barnyard animals . . ."

"Because his wife fell for every bullshit fad that wafted through the air, my friend Tony's entire life has been, and will continue to be, dedicated to cleaning up after an eleven-year-old girl who has the IQ of a cocker spaniel.

"So forgive me if I cannot honestly tell you how groovy I thought the sixties were. Every time I flash back on the period, the most enduring vision that comes to mind is the image of Wood Rose, sitting in front of her television set, staring vacantly at soap operas, drooling all over herself, and making sounds like a very large chipmunk.

"Thank you for your kind attention. If it's all right with my fellow panelists, I'm going to skip the rest of this symposium, because I can see from their expressions that I've already pissed off too many worthy colleagues. If anyone wants to discuss the points I've raised, I'll be drinking coffee in the Student Union, brooding over my misspent youth. Feel free to join me."

Karen watched from a distance while six students, four of them openly flirtatious females, peppered Professor Warrener with questions. He was obviously trying to pay attention to them and give honest, thoughtful answers, but he kept glancing at his watch until they finally took the hint and began to depart. But when all the students had gone and Warrener still remained at his table, Karen realized that all those watch-glances were just an act, a polite way to clear the room of pestiferous students. Now he was just sitting quietly and alone, at a corner table in the snack bar, flipping idly through a newspaper and getting wired with his third cup of coffee. Karen sidled slowly into his peripheral vision, so as not to startle him.

"Excuse me, Professor Warrener. . . ."

His appraisal was wary, but he strove to be cordial.

"Guilty as charged, Miss . . . Miss . . . ?"

"Karen Hambly. I'm not in any of your classes. . . ."

"I would have noticed if you were," he grinned.

"But I *am* keenly interested in the sixties, and I was wondering if you'd mind discussing a few of your points."

Karen was amazed at the challenging tone she heard in her voice; Warrener, on the other hand, reacted with bemused curiosity.

"Please sit down, then, Miss Hambly, and take your shots."

In fact, Allen was a bit slow coming up from the flashback-reverie he had been sinking into. Miss Hambly's sudden appearance was startling, if only because she looked as though she had just stepped out of a time machine from 1968: long straight hair, minimal makeup except for a very dark Theda Bara eyeliner, which augmented her attractive brown eyes with a certain witchy allure. She wore a loose cottony shift that might as well have had "Product of Third World Peasants" stamped all over it, and big cloppy sandals, a wardrobe that made it difficult for him to see if her ankles were as shapely as the outline of her legs suggested they might be.

"So, then, may I assume from your tone of voice, Miss Hambly, that you took exception to some of the things I said earlier this evening?"

Warrener had her pegged, now: she was one of those kids who'd been born just a few years too late to take part in the revels, and who still got all goose-bumpy thinking about the fun stuff they never quite had a chance to do. Her first shot was a doozy.

"I'm just curious to know why you're *still* so bitter."

"You mean my scintillating presentation actually struck you as 'bitter'?" He raised mocking eyebrows. "Please forgive me—I never meant to reveal so much of my inner torment—"

"And I'll thank you not to fucking patronize me!" she snapped.

"Hey, lighten up, kid. I just felt like puncturing some balloons, that's all. I promise not to be 'bitter' if you promise not to be so belligerent . . . deal?"

"Fair enough. I apologize for being rude."

"You weren't being rude, just refreshingly disrespectful. I admire that in a student, especially if she's not one of *my* students. Please, go ahead and say what you want to say."

"I think you made some good points, Professor, but maybe you were too close to things to see the positive accomplishments of your peers. And there *were* some. . . ."

"Give me a for-instance, please."

"You stopped a war, for God's sake!"

"By 'you,' I take it you mean my generation collectively, because I assure you that part of my 'bitterness' stems from the fact that I *wanted* to fight in that war, but due to circumstances beyond my control I wasn't allowed to."

"Why on earth did someone as intelligent as you *want* to go over there and fight for a bunch of corrupt, lying politicians?"

"Strange as it may sound, Miss Hambly, I once had my heart set on a career in the professional military. It's a long family tradition, you see, and I'd been preparing myself to be a soldier, physically and mentally, since I was five or six years old. I didn't approve of the Vietnam War either—but career soldiers don't have the luxury of choosing their fights. Uncle Sam says 'go,' you go. He did and I went. But I wasn't over there very long. I was wounded before I saw any real action and discharged because of my injuries. You seem like a person who appreciates irony, so here's a prime example of it. I might have been the only so-called hippie in New York who would *rather* have

been fighting in Southeast Asia. I'm sure that colored my attitude somewhat, but not enough to distort my perceptions. Everything that struck me
as being bullshit, really *was* bullshit; ten years of reflecting on it hasn't
changed my basic feelings one iota."

"So you were one of those guys who felt compelled to prove your manhood?"

Allen shrugged. "That's an oversimplification, but basically, yes, I was.
I've also never met a good professional soldier who didn't hate war, but
combat is the ultimate test life has to offer. I wanted to take that test and
pass it. Don't look for psychological nuances—a twenty-three-year-old second
lieutenant, going into battle for the first time, doesn't cloud his mind with
subtleties. He can't afford to, or he might hesitate at the wrong moment and
get himself or the men under his command killed."

"But aren't there plenty of 'tests' in everyday life?"

"Of course there are. But for some men, that's just irrelevant. If you have
to ask why, I'm afraid I can't give you a more convincing explanation. Trust
me when I tell you that men like me never outgrow the need to play soldier;
it may be a primitive drive, but that's the way evolution has wired my brain."

Say this for her, Allen thought, she's really listening, not just dismissing
me as a right-wing wacko. He wondered where this conversation was going
next. She might not turn heads *en masse* when she walked down the street,
but she was definitely worth a second look. Beneath the anachronistic hippie
duds and the slightly gothic makeup, there was something compelling about
Karen Hambly. For a wandering, careless moment, he wished she *was* in one
of his classes; she was good scenery at least.

"I wish you'd been able to have more fun." She seemed—almost—on the
verge of taking his hand. "When you were in New York, I mean."

"That's very kind of you."

"I'm not being flippant. Don't you honestly think, if you could go back in
a time machine and live through those years again, you'd be able to relax and
let your guard down a little more? Be less cynical. . . ."

"I *did* have fun, some of the time. And it wasn't just because of what I'd
done, or not done, in the war—I was definitely not a monk. I guess, no
matter what had gone before, I was just a little bit too old, and little bit too
judgmental, to 'go with the flow,' as they used to say. Beyond a certain point,
I find that if you have to embrace hypocrisy in order to join in the revels, it
taints the entertainment a bit too much for my personal comfort level.

"What spoiled the 'fun' for me more than anything else was how totalitarian the mood became in sixty-eight, sixty-nine. You see, there just weren't any comfortable positions in the middle—which is philosophically where most people prefer to be, even if they won't admit it. If you wanted to be accepted, be allowed to play all the games, you had to check your intellect at the door, and that I refused to do."

Karen tilted her head, one side to the other, scrutinizing him, genuinely bewildered at meeting someone who had been at the heart of the milieu that she found so enticing, even now, yet who had rejected it for reasons that sounded oddly Calvinistic. "It's just hard for me to believe that, in all the time you lived in New York, you didn't find any one aspect of things that you could . . . I don't know, just relax and completely *groove with!*" She mouthed the catch-phrase with a charming little smile.

God, she was cute when she was bewildered! Allen could have steered the dialogue in several very different directions at that point, but his resident imp of perversity had a hankering to zap her with a cattle prod instead of teasing her out with a handful of verbal sugar.

"Well, now that you mention it, there was one kind of ritualistic event that I never had any problem 'grooving with. . . .' "

"The Human Be-Ins? Joe Namath winning the Super Bowl? Sunday afternoons at the museums?"

"No, Miss Hambly, I'm referring to the orgies. The only time I truly got a glimpse of universal peace and harmony was on the mornings after an erotic marathon with fifteen or twenty people, most of them strangers, who asked nothing from each other except physical pleasure and lots of it. There was this one time when—"

A hard transparent shell came down over her eyes like the nictitating membranes on a lizard.

Oh shit, she thinks I'm hitting on her! Wait! Wait! I only beat my chest this way when I'm with someone who makes me comfortable!

Too late.

"Professor Warrener, you really have an uncanny knack for undercutting your own sincerity. I'm sorry I took up so much of your time."

She rose, turned, and walked out of the building, her stride brittle and her shoulders hunched belligerently. Allen knew he'd just made an ass of himself, and with one of the few young women on campus he might conceivably want to spend more time with in the future. He considered pursuit and an apology, but his "sincerity" was already a debased currency, so why make things worse? Even if she did have terrific legs and, for such a slender girl, an ass to die for.

And then he glanced at his watch and shuddered inwardly. He had promised to be home early enough to take Sylvia to a late-night screening of *Last Year at Marienbad,* a film he considered insufferably pretentious. But somebody, somewhere, had once told Sylvia that she sort of looked like Monica Vitti, the film's frigid but stunning female lead. If he'd showed up on time and been appropriately flattering, Sylvia might have thrown him a quick fuck before bedtime.

But the screening had started five minutes ago; no chance now. She wouldn't be standing at the door, furiously tapping her foot and smacking her palm with a rolling pin, but she *would* punish him, for a period of time commensurate with her pique at missing the movie, with offhand remarks sharpened to a scalpel's edge. Or she might pretend to shrug it off, thus lulling him, and simply disappear for the entire weekend to shack up with one of her current lovers. Who *were* those guys, anyway? They could all be buff, well-hung, working-class morons, for all he knew, but the statistical odds favored at least one of them being a faculty member. How would he know which one? She didn't always choose her extracurricular partners on the basis of physique alone, so he couldn't narrow it down to the young athletic studs. And what slow, cumulative damage was being charged against his career?

He began to sweat, hating the sour crescents of anxiety he could feel thickening under his arms. His only chance of moderating her wrath was to change into The Mode of Abject Apology—like putting on a clown suit he carried around in the trunk of his car. He would despise himself for it in the morning, but he simply didn't have the spunk tonight for a knock-down, drag-out argument.

Feeling ten years older than he was, Allen Warrener picked up his briefcase and shuffled wretchedly out of the Student Union building.

By the time he reached the faculty parking lot, he'd forgotten about Karen Hambly.

10.

BETTER LATE THAN NEVER

Allen Warrener had just finished spending two crowded Christmas-vacation weeks with his son, Brian. He had learned that a single parent's sense of Time, and especially of its passing, could be a very pragmatic example of Relativity: if things went well, two weeks flashed by like a weekend; if they did not. . . . On previous visitations, he'd made the mistake of over-programming in advance, trying to wring Quality Time out of every minute; that hadn't worked very well—both father and son ended up being frazzled, irritable, and feeling somehow cheated. This Christmas, Allen had resolved to take things easy, to permit one hour to flow into the next as it would, and to put his trust in spontaneity. The results were gratifying. By not working so hard to prove what a terrific part-time dad he was, he managed to be a perfectly adequate one; both father and son had enjoyed their time together.

As though to reward Allen for improving his strategy, Nature offered the gift of a long, downy snowstorm on December 26—the first time they'd watched snow come down together since Brian was three. They'd gone sledding, rolled a big funky snowman in the front yard, and joined the other neighborhood families in waging epic snowball battles. That day was as near to perfect as it gets, and Allen had stored every memory in the most inviolate chamber of his heart, a trust fund he could draw from during the inevitably strained years of adolescence.

Brian stayed until January 2, and every day had been good—the best succession of days they had spent together since the divorce. But the time came, all too soon, for Allen to drive Brian to the airport and put him on his flight back to Miami, back to the luxurious house Brian lived in with Sylvia and her second husband. The sky was low and dark, the roads foul with slush, the wait until boarding time strained and seemingly interminable; the farewell hugs both overwrought and utterly inadequate; and on his way home from the airport, Allen had to pull off onto the shoulder because he was crying too hard to see the road.

Classes resumed in two days, and he chose to spend that afternoon in his campus office, cleaning out files, answering correspondence . . . just puttering, really. He just wasn't ready to face the house yet. It would be too silent, too empty, and too booby-trapped with memories for him to cope with just now. By late afternoon, he'd shuffled enough papers and grown restless. He decided to head over to the Student Union to catch up on his magazine browsing or perhaps run into some not-altogether-clueless student who was worth a conversation.

But not many students had returned yet, and the only ones he found in the egalitarian lounge were gathered around the big TV set in the rec room, watching a Giants–Packers game in which he had no interest whatever. He ordered a large coffee from the snack bar and wandered over to the newspaper rack, intent on losing himself in last Sunday's *New York Times*. As he hefted the bulky newspaper, he noticed that there *was* one other solitary reader in the lounge area: a young woman with dark hair, sprawled on one of the Naugahyde sofas, cigarette smoke curling lazily from her hand, intently scanning a recent issue of *Time*. As Warrener hung his overcoat on the rack behind this person, he could not help but notice that she was studying the reproductions of the controversial underwater strobe-pictures brought back by the latest Loch Ness expedition. He'd caught a glimpse of them on the evening news last week, but he hadn't been very impressed. The images resembled nothing more than a floating cloud of algae; one would *really* have to be a True Believer, he thought, to see anything monster-like in the murk. But *Time*'s reproductions had obviously been computer-enhanced, and even from a distance, they looked much more tantalizing and suggestive. He made a mental note to grab the magazine as soon as the young woman was finished. Without being conscious of doing so, however, he drifted closer and squinted to get a better look, a stealthy motion, but one that caused his shadow to fall over the pages.

"Just let me finish this article," she said without turning around, "and you're welcome to the magazine. In the meantime, you're blocking my light."

"I'm sorry," he stammered. "I didn't mean to disturb you. I was just hanging up my coat and those pictures happened to catch my eye." She turned, as though the sound of his voice signified something, and regarded him with a quizzical tilt of her head.

"My, but you *do* look interested! Here, be my guest—I hate to see a grown man fidget."

He took the proffered magazine, nodded his thanks, and sat at the opposite end of the sofa, immediately sucked into the article. He naturally expected the girl to get up and find another magazine, but she didn't; she just smoked her Marlboro, with the attentiveness of a serious nicotine fancier, and appeared to be studying Warrener's reaction as intently as he was studying the article. Her continued presence was both annoying and intriguing. Had he met her before? He couldn't be certain without staring, and that probably *would* make her get up and leave. He would much prefer to strike up a conversation—almost any legal-age female was worth making a pass at on so dismal an afternoon as this. If she was still there when he finished the article, maybe he would say something to her. What luck if she turned out to be a fellow monster-enthusiast!

"Do you think it's real?" she suddenly asked, leaning forward to stub out her cigarette and revealing long-fingered graceful hands.

By God, he had seen this girl before . . . but where? Without meaning to, he was staring intently at her.

"I said: do you think it's real?"

"Um, which do you mean—these photographs, or the Loch Ness Monster?"

"Either. Both."

"Yes, to both. There's *something* in Loch Ness, all right. There are stories about it going back to the eleventh century, and now that I've seen these images digitally enhanced, I'm not as skeptical as I was when I saw them on TV. Look—this might really be a giant flipper, and this curved shape could be either the traditional long neck of a Great Orm—that was the name the Vikings gave to these creatures—or possibly the big hump of its back as it dives away from the strobe-flash."

"Hey, you *have* studied this stuff, haven't you?" she returned his conversational serve with a solid backhand, for he detected no hint of mockery, only an invitation to extend the dialogue, which was fine with him.

"Or, more than that! I'm probably the only person you'll ever meet who's a card-carrying member of the International Cryptozoological Society . . . I collect clippings and magazine articles and subscribe to some oddball newsletters. It's an eccentric hobby, I admit, but utterly harmless."

"The range of your interests continues to surprise me, Professor Warrener."

He started at the sound of his name and her tone of familiarity.

"You have the advantage, my dear. You know my name, but if I ever knew yours, I've long forgotten it. Give an old history professor a break and help me out. . . ."

" 'Old professor,' my ass. Don't you remember the orgy we went to in New York, back in, oh, nineteen sixty-eight, I think it was?"

The memory-zap jarred him. Her "got-cha!" grin was charmingly mischievous.

"Oh my God, you're the girl who jumped all over me the night I took part in that stupid symposium about the sixties! 'Woodstock for Dummies' or something like that! And your name is . . . wait a second, it will come to me—your name's Katie, or Kathy, right?"

"Close enough!" She extended her hand behind a genuinely friendly smile. "Karen. Karen Hambly, and please don't call me 'Miss Hambly' this time, because I'm not an undergrad any more. Well, that's not strictly true, but I am old enough to be spoken to as an adult."

"Well, obviously you are. At least this means I can finally clear the books of an apology I've owed you for an awful long time. I herewith beg your forgiveness. I acted like a real jerk that night—usually, I'm just quietly obnoxious. Should I grovel on the floor, or just slink away in disgrace? Whatever penance you prefer, as long as you don't jump up and walk out like you did before. Not that I blame you. . . ."

She waved her hands in mock absolution, and mumbled some clever pig-Latin to go along with the gesture. She had a good, rich, grown-up laugh, not the nervy teeny-bopper snigger he remembered. And she no longer dressed like a left-over Flower Child, but rather like a young professional of some kind—albeit a young professional on a tight budget. He pegged her for a recent graduate who'd stayed on to work as a receptionist or a keypunch operator in one of the rabbit-warrens of cubicles that filled the basement of the Administration Building.

"No need to apologize, Professor Warrener; the statute of limitations on dumb sexist pick-up lines runs out after three years; and, besides, I was pretty snotty to you, too. Let's call it even and start over again, shall we? Are you in the mood for a beer?"

"Yes, I am; more or less perpetually."

"Then I suggest we take the rest of this conversation down to the Pickwick, where we won't feel like we're in a fishbowl. That *was* your favorite watering hole, wasn't it? I mean, when your wife let you off the leash for a few hours?"

"Yes, as a matter of fact—yes to both questions. Only, the tavern's still around and Sylvia isn't."

They retrieved their coats, and she took the lead with a brisk no-nonsense walk. More details of their first encounter were now coming into focus, and he was pleased to note, as she bent over to adjust a shoe-heel that had come loose on the steps, that his recollection of long, coltish legs was entirely vindicated.

The Pickwick Tavern had just opened for afternoon business, and the number of elbow-benders was low as yet. They found a highly desirable booth—far enough from the television to permit unforced conversation, yet close enough to the bartender to facilitate quick refills. Warrener ordered a pitcher and a wicker basket of tortillas and dip. Their mugs were frosted, and the beer was so cold it was flecked with ice. Karen immediately lit a cigarette and offered him the opened pack.

"I'd love to, but I had to quit about four years ago. Lung infection—the X-rays showed a tiny lesion. Nothing bad in the pathology reports, but it was God's way of firing a shot across my bow. I'd been feeding a two-pack-a-day habit since the tenth grade, so for someone with a predilection for asthma, it was death on the installment plan."

"I admire your willpower; do you ever miss it?"

"Every damn day! But don't feel obligated to not smoke, just because we're sitting together."

"I don't," she said smugly. "And if you asked me to put mine out, I'd probably tell you to go fuck yourself. How's that?"

"I'm glad we could come to an amicable understanding, Miss . . . oh, shit, I'm supposed to call you 'Karen,' aren't I?" She nodded emphatically. "Well, Karen, I looked high and low for you during the weeks after our tête-à-tête, to apologize for all the heavy Attitude I laid on you, but you seemed to have vanished. . . ."

"I didn't just 'seem to,' Allen. I did. I dropped out of school two weeks after the night we met."

"Mind telling me why? You struck me as being a very serious student."

"I was, actually, except for those silly Sonny-and-Cher outfits I always used to wear. And that was my downfall, in point of fact. Either I finally caught up with the sixties, or the sixties decided to ambush me and teach me a lesson, I'll never know which."

" 'Be careful what you wish for,' that kind of thing?"

"Exactly. I thought I'd hit the jackpot because everything I'd fantasized about just suddenly fell into my lap, and when it did, I put graduation, graduate school, my plans for a teaching career, all of it, on indefinite hold. It all started with . . . well, do you remember a band named The Sensible Shoes?"

"Yeah, I sure do. I saw them open one night for Iron Butterfly at the Fill-more East. I can't say as how they left an indelible memory, but I seem to recall they had at least one big hit . . . 'Leopard-Skin Boots' or something like that?"

"Boy, you are getting senile! The song was called 'Laughing-Gas Lady,' and it reached the number-three spot on the *Billboard* charts for eight weeks, back in sixty-eight."

"Now I remember! It had really gushy, romantic lyrics—not exactly something you could dance to, but a terrific makeout song, sort of the Kmart version of 'Nights in White Satin.' "

"Bingo! I used to play the single in my room when I was feeling lonely and undesirable, and it always made me hunger for the glories of True Love—you know: the wind in your hair, hand in hand with the perfect guy, strolling on a golden beach, you embrace and the surf comes crashing in behind you—like a shampoo commercial on TV."

"I didn't quite have the same reaction, but I know what you mean."

"Well, two weeks after you and I met, I learned that the Shoes were playing a gig over in Chapel Hill, and I went. I even went early enough to get a front-row seat and drop a tab of acid. I was totally primed by the time the show started, and about halfway through the first set, I realized that Freddy Bravermann was making eyes at me!"

"Sorry, but who the hell is Freddy Bravermann?"

"Vocals and lead guitar. He's the guy who wrote that song. Now get this: here I am, dressed up in my sexiest hippie outfit, tripping my ovaries out, and during intermission, Freddy sent one of his roadies out to buy me a dozen fucking roses! And when he came out after intermission, with the spotlight on him, he came over to the stage apron, knelt down on one knee, and one by one, peeled off each rose and handed it to me. Mind you, there were a hundred other chicks crowded down front, most of them a lot sexier than I was, and all of 'em trying to get Freddy's attention, but I was the girl he wanted that night. Man, what a rush to see all those other chicks glaring daggers at me!"

"I can well imagine. I think I can also imagine what happened after the concert. . . ."

She nodded rueful confirmation. "You don't have to be a psychic. A phalanx of roadies came out after the last encore and formed a flying wedge to escort me backstage and into the Great Man's dressing room. Freddy was dazzling and charming and so ridiculously seductive that how could I help but jump into the limo with him, smoke some dynamite weed, and shout 'Thank you, Jesus!' when he tore my clothes off back in his hotel room. I kept saying to myself, over and over again, *I'm with the band! I'm with the band! At long-fucking-last, I am inside the sixties, and there's still enough of it here for me to have the time of my life!*"

"Was he that great in the sack?' Allen asked, unsure of whether or not he wanted to know.

"Considering where my head was at the time, it seemed that way. Freddy must not have been disappointed, either, because the next morning he asked me to go on the rest of the tour with him. I didn't hesitate. Called the school and made up some bullshit story about having to drop out for a while due to a family emergency. They bought it. Freddy gave me a roll of cash, told me to go out and buy some sexy clothes and a new toothbrush, and just like that, I was no longer just a 'friend of the band,' I was the lead singer's Main Squeeze! Imagine if you had jumped from being an inexperienced lieutenant to being Napoleon—the transition was that cosmic."

"And was it everything you'd dreamed it would be? The tour, the gigs, the parties, the hobnobbing with celebrities . . . ?"

"Oh, yes; for a while. And for a long while after that, I kept pretending it was, and that worked okay, until the glamour wore off. Freddy and the guys used to jabber a lot about updating their act, writing some new material, getting another tune on the charts, so they wouldn't be forever known as One-Hit Wonders. But the band was on its way down, and I don't think anything could have stopped the decline. The concert dates were mostly nostalgia gigs, in second-rate venues, with almost as many cover songs as original material, and always finishing up with 'Laughing-Gas Lady.' They were all sick to death of that damn song, but if they tried a fresh interpretation, the crowds booed and hissed and wouldn't shut up until they played it straight, just like the original recording. If I'd been smarter, known more about the business, I would have spotted that as the classic sign of a band on the skids.

"But I didn't care. I was living the fantasy, and for a long time, that was all that mattered. And I was consuming the best drugs money could buy. So for a couple of years, I just floated inside a time-warp, where it was still 1968. You have to understand, Allen: it's easy to do that, if you're traveling in a bus painted psychedelic paisley and you live in motel rooms, and the audiences are just as reluctant to give up the illusion as you are. If you're in that kind of a space, you can switch off reality when it becomes annoying; well, you just take another hit of acid and turn the music up another notch, and you drift right back into the dream."

But the dream must have ended badly, because Karen was here, and drinking her beer in desperate gulps, and her hands were shaking when she lit her next cigarette. Allen touched her arm very gently. "If you want to end the story right there, it's okay with me."

"I do and I don't, you know? I need to tell *somebody*, and you came along at just the right moment—today, now, here. So you get to hear it, Professor, whether you want to or not!"

Suddenly, tears welled from her eyes. Taken by surprise, she fluttered her hands, muttered, "Excuse me for a minute," and darted into the ladies' room. Allen ordered another pitcher. Father confessor was a rare role for him—he usually avoided it like the plague—but today was different.

When Karen returned, she was dry-eyed, freshly made up, and surprisingly calm.

"Finish the story, Karen. I've got no place to go and no one I'd rather spend the afternoon with. . . ."

"I'm going to take a big chance and assume you mean that. Okay, it's the start of act two, and our heroine awakes in . . . Jesus, where were we?"

"Still on the road with the band, but going nowhere fast."

"Right, right. About halfway though my second year with Freddy, even the nostalgia gigs started drying up. We played birthday parties, frat houses, whatever we could get. By this time, Freddy was doing a lot of coke—'to keep his spirits up,' he said. He also needed to do it to keep something else up, which did wonders for my ego. We started missing concert dates; the road manager quit; the guy who replaced him was a moron—everybody knew this band was one step from oblivion.

"When we weren't touring, we lived in a ramshackle old ranch house in the middle of fucking nowhere, between Amarillo and Lubbock—place belonged to somebody's uncle's cousin or something, I never figured it out. I hated that part of Texas. Hot, dusty, no *green* like there is here, you know? Sometimes, when we were at the ranch for a long period, Freddy and his bass player would sit on the porch and start jammin', just for fun. That's the best they ever sounded. They claimed they were working on new material—a comeback album."

"But they never had a hit album, just a single."

"That's why Freddy claimed this new project would put them on the charts again, like it would amaze everybody who thought they only had one good song in them. When he was working on the new songs, he didn't do as much coke, he was kinder and easier to live with, so naturally I encouraged him. Told him the new songs sounded great. He sucked up to me, told me I was his life-saving muse, all kinds of horseshit. What he really wanted was twenty thousand dollars—to produce the album, he said. Like a fool, I contacted my bank here and had the money wired out to me. Gave it to him. He and the band took off for a couple of days, 'to set up the recording sessions in Dallas,' he claimed. He'd come back and get me when the project was ready to go.

"Well, he didn't come back for nine days and when he did, he didn't have the band with him, but he did have twenty thousand dollars' worth of coke under the cargo bed of his truck. A temporary problem, he assured me. The recording was going to be more expensive than he'd been told, so he was just going to unload this coke, triple his money, and then we'd be in Fat City again. Talk about denial—I actually bought the story!

"For the next six months, he would come and go, all hours, day or night; either that, or really mean-looking guys would pull up to the ranch, transact some business, and vanish. I once had the temerity to ask him how much of my money was left, and he beat the shit out of me for it. Oh, the next day he came crawling back, weepy and pitiful, begging forgiveness, swearing it would never happen again. And for a week, it didn't. He kept trying to get me hooked on the coke, too, so I could share his ever-shrinking, paranoid little world, I guess. I didn't have the metabolism for it, though. It never made me feel good; it just made me feel skanky and scared and jumpy as a June-bug.

"It really pissed him off that I stopped doing lines with him, so one night, when he said he was in a kinky-sex mood and he took out the handcuffs and the ankle-spreader—"

"Whoa, back up! You skipped that part."

"I'm going to keep right on skipping it, thank you. Anyway, once I was spread-eagled, Freddy went apeshit. He stuffed a huge ball gag into my mouth and started drizzling little streams of coke into my nostrils. Well, shit, I *had* to breathe, so a rain of that shit just poured down the back of my throat. I got so swacked, so fast, I didn't know where I was. I tried to beg him to stop, Allen, but all that came out through that damn gag were moans—which just flipped him even further over the edge. My heart was slamming like a triphammer, I was choking and spewing powder out my nostrils and bucking up and down like ten thousand volts were shooting through me . . . thought either my heart would explode, or my brain would. I mean, stroke or aneurism, you keep pumping a human body full of that much cocaine and something's going to pop!

"But, talk about saved by the bell, the fucker's cell phone buzzed right at the worst moment, and since the only people who had that number were either his suppliers or his richest customers, he *had* to answer it. Even as fucked up as I was, I could see that that phone call was big trouble for the One-Hit Wonder Boy. He was jabbering in pidgin-Spanish, so I knew it was Colombians on the other end; and from the way Freddy's face went white, I gathered they'd figured out, finally, how much of the goods he'd been skimming off for private deals. In the coke trade, you short your suppliers and you don't stay in business very long.

"Freddy dropped the phone like it was red-hot and grabbed this overnight bag he kept packed for emergencies. But as panicky as he was, he still took the time to leer at me and snarl, 'I'm gonna leave you just like that, princess! Who could resist the opportunity? When those goons show up, they'll have some fun with you, and that'll buy ol' Freddy some time! It's been real, baby!' And then he was gone. I heard the front door slam.

"But I also heard a car skidding on the gravel and some really angry shouts in Spanish. Freddy didn't get as far as the barn where he kept his truck. Whatever they did to him, they took their time about it—he screamed an awful lot, at least until the chainsaw started up, then it didn't last much longer."

Allen couldn't help blurting: "Are you shitting me? They really *do* that?"

"Yep; it's not just in the movies, Allen. It's the punishment reserved for only the most treacherous scumbags in the business, which gives you some metric to measure how low Freddy had fallen. When the *pistoleros* were finished, they just drove away and left the pieces for the flies. They never even came into the house, much less gang-raped me, like Freddy was hoping they'd do.

"Now, you have to remember what an overload of adrenaline can do for somebody who's terrified, and then factor in all that speed Freddy had force-fed me. I was Wonder Woman, buddy. I knew he kept a Beretta hidden in his sock drawer, and I knew he hadn't taken it with him, so I just humped and thumped the whole bed a couple of feet to the left, until I could get one hand on a knob, then opened the drawer, knocked the gun on to the bed, and somehow managed to shoot one handcuff off. The rest was easy, 'cause I'd become a damn good pistol shot by then. Wasn't much else to do in that shithole except hunt lizards and prairie dogs.

"Looking back on it, I was amazingly calm. Got dressed, reloaded the gun, packed a few things in a laundry bag, and went outside. Freddy was in, oh, eight or nine pieces and already black with big ol' Texas blow-flies. The buzz saw crew hadn't bothered with his pockets, so the, um, torso still had a wallet and the truck keys. I even remembered to use a handkerchief, so I wouldn't leave any fingerprints. Sumbitch had three grand in cash! I ditched the truck in Amarillo, walked into the bus station and bought a one-way ticket to Macon, where my older sister lives.

"We were never very close, but blood is thicker than, etc. Besides, when I offered her a thousand bucks to put me up until I could get my shit together, she suddenly got all loving and sisterly. I bought some nice clothes and a train ticket, and I got back here five weeks before Christmas vacation. I re-enrolled in school, to finish out my last semester. Got my old job back at the library. Picked up, essentially, at exactly the place where I'd dropped out. Of course, after almost two years, I'd voided the terms of my scholarship, so I'm investing like crazy with what's left of the money, so I can afford graduate school. I've still got my heart set on a teaching career, and I am definitely one-hundred-per-cent cured of any obsession I ever had with the sixties.

"I work in Periodicals, by the way, third cubicle to the left after you go through the door. Drop by some day at twelve-thirty and I'll buy you lunch."

"I . . . I don't know what to say! I mean, about—"

Karen placed a finger on his lips. "Shhh. There isn't any reason you should say anything. I went into it with my eyes open, got it out of my system, and lived through the bad stuff. No nightmares and surprisingly few regrets. The first ten or twelve months on the road were a gas, Allen. And, you know: you pay up front, or you pay later, but sooner or later, you do pay. The only thing I want to hear you say is, yes, I will have lunch with you, Miss Hambly."

"I have a counter-proposal: why don't you come over to my house, this Friday, and I'll treat you to my world-famous barbecued ribs and show you my collection of monster clippings?"

" 'Come up and see my etchings, huh?' Well, shit, Allen, how could any girl resist such an exciting invitation?"

"Oh. Well, for a while, there, you seemed interested. . . ."

She impulsively leaned across the table and gave him a perky little kiss.

"I'm teasing you, silly man. Actually, that sounds like fun. And maybe I *will* become interested. At the very least, I'm interested to know why *you're* so interested. Besides, I needed to spill my guts to somebody, and you were kind enough to listen. So now it's your turn. And by the way, how long ago were you and Dragon Lady divorced?"

"Oh, the bleeding stopped hours ago."

"Yeah? Well, I still see a few old bruises. I've unloaded on you today, so if you want to, you can unload on me while we grill the ribs."

"I promise I won't do that."

"I didn't expect you would; I just wanted you to know you *could*. Jesus, look at the time! I'm on duty tonight, so I'd better go home and shower off the beer smell. Thank you for letting me cry in your beer—I needed to tell *somebody,* and I feel better for it. You're actually kind of a nice guy."

"Nah, I'm still a cynical jerk. But I would like to walk you home."

"Another time, that would be great, but I rode my bike over this morning, and I'd better ride it back. I'm a little bit drunk, you see, and the cold air will do me good."

"Then I'll walk you over to your bike."

"That would be nice."

"And on the way, I'll tell you about the Faeroes. . . ."

"Well, okay, I'm as interested in ancient Egypt as the next person, I guess."

"No, no, I'm talking about some islands. The Faeroe Islands. Ever heard of them?"

"Nope, but I have a feeling I'm about to. . . ."

Halfway to their destination, Karen very casually took his hand. Her fingers were warm and strong inside her mittens, and he couldn't help but silently pray: *Please, God, just once, don't let me fuck things up!*

11.

WHY DON'T YOU COME UP
AND SEE MY MONSTERS?

Another helping?"

"Not unless you have a forklift to carry me home. Those were sublime ribs, Allen!"

"That's because I'm a specialist—all I can cook worth a damn is grilled meat. Thank God you're not a vegetarian."

"I don't have the willpower. The day somebody invents a way to make broccoli taste like filet mignon, that's the day I'll consider converting. And now, unless you have a problem with it, I'm going to indulge in a post-prandial cigarette."

"As long as you enjoyed the ribs, I don't have a problem with anything."

He gathered their plates and carried them into the kitchen.

"You know what the oddest thing about those photographs is?" Allen heard her say. At first he had no idea what she was talking about.

Allen poked his head out of the kitchen, wiping barbecue sauce from his hands with a paper towel.

"What pictures would those be? And how many sugars do you take in your coffee?"

"Two packs of something low-cal, if you've got any."

"I think my ex left some in the cupboard. . . . You were saying something about pictures?"

"Yeah, I was. I went to the library this afternoon and looked through some books about Loch Ness. It just seems strange that not only those recent pictures, but all of the older ones, too—well, it's amazing how this creature avoids being photographed. Like it knows when there's a lens pointed at it. I also read that, on any given day, there must be two hundred cameras of all kinds pointed at the water, all loaded and ready to shoot, and yet nobody's ever captured *the shot*—the one that's clearly in focus, with something else in the frame to establish distance and scale. You look at the images and think, yeah, well, *maybe* . . . and that's as far as you can go."

"I think the critter does know, and refuses to cooperate out of sheer contrariness. Here's your coffee."

"Thanks. I know it's a big deep lake, but it's got to be the most closely watched body of water since Niagara Falls, and still . . . zip. Whatever's under that water remains as much a mystery as it was a thousand years ago. And in a way, that's what makes it so cool!"

"So you weren't as impressed with the *Newsweek* photos as I was?"

"To you, they might be evidence, because you want them to be so badly. But to a skeptic, they're just a bunch of plankton and a soggy log."

"You know, one of the scientists on that expedition was quoted as saying: 'A lot of men have gone to the gallows on the strength of less evidence that we've accumulated about Nessie.'"

"He was missing the point. If a crime's been committed, the jury *knows* there's a criminal who did it. Criminals exist; no one disputes that. But not everybody believes that giant plesiosaurs still do, so the standard of proof has got to be utterly convincing. And in this case, the only 'judge' is Science, and scientists, in some ways, have even more power than judges, because we've come to rely on them to tell us what is or isn't 'real.' And the layman, intimidated by the scientists' credentials and expertise, doesn't want to challenge their verdicts. In a way, the debate hinges on power, Allen! The power to define what belongs in the real world and what doesn't. Thousands of people probably have seen sea serpents—but only a handful will admit to it publicly. They think it's equivalent to claiming the Earth is flat."

She was very bright; she'd picked up on subtle things, unlike the other visitors he'd shown his monster files to, all of whom had glanced uneasily at the material and muttered, "Yeah, gee, Allen, what a neat hobby you have!"

"Point well taken, Karen. But some of the most dramatic discoveries of modern science are based on 'evidence' that can't be seen, heard, photographed, or even manipulated—except with pure, abstract mathematics. Subatomic particles, for instance. What color is a gluon? How many mesons in a teaspoon? And if dark matter really *is* 'matter,' why can't we touch it?"

"Zoologists aren't theoretical physicists. They demand evidence, Allen.

Hard evidence. The only thing that'll make them admit there's a Loch Ness monster would be a prolonged sighting that takes place in broad daylight, in front of a hundred people, including a biologist, a mathematician, a priest, and Walter Cronkite!"

"You're really quite fetching when you play devil's advocate, you know."

"Oh, what a sweet, goofy, utterly lame thing to say!"

Was that a put-down, or was she just testing his ability to take a joke? He decided to be a good sport and responded by chuckling and making gestures of self-deprecation; but in truth, she had slipped in a tiny jab of the needle, even though her relaxed expression gave off no hint of belligerence.

She lit a cigarette and leaned back in her chair. Allen wondered if she had chosen to wear such a flattering, form-fitting sweater because it was cold outside, or because she wanted to show off her assets. Probably both. Whatever her motives, she was mighty easy on the eye tonight. And mighty easy just to *be* with. He already knew she was tough; but that inner toughness combined with such outer warmth: such a combination of traits was rare. Whatever it might be like to have sex with her, he felt certain that merely *sleeping* beside her would bring comfort, restoration, and gentle dreams. Sitting across the breakfast table from her on the morning after wouldn't be bad, either.

"More coffee?"

"No, thanks, Allen—too much caffeine, and I turn into a monster too."

An attenuating, soon-to-be-awkward silence suggested that they were both adrift on comparable speculations about each other. Such lulls could open the shutters for the stale wind that had spoiled many a promising date. Allen felt compelled to feed some conversational twigs on to the dying embers of their dialogue.

"I'll give you a classic example of how these things usually go—of the kind of blinkered attitudes that make us stalwarts of the Cryptozoology Society gnash our teeth."

Karen brightened at once. He'd read the situation correctly, and she seemed grateful to him for taking the initiative and, conceivably, salvaging their evening.

"I'd like to hear it, Allen."

"Okay, then! Well, there's a remote, isolated bay on the Irish coast, in County Connaught, where the local farmers have reported 'monster sightings' for generations. Well, back in the old days, nobody took them seriously—'Ah, Paddy's hitting the bottle again, lads, seein' his beasties!' But more recently, there have been backpackers hiking along that coast— well-educated, middle-class European people, not bog-hoppers, and many of them have seen the same things. Nine years ago, so did a visiting parish priest, who thought the matter was serious enough to perform an exorcism! Altogether, there's a pretty credible bunch of witnesses."

"Didn't anyone take pictures?"

"Sure. Or at least they tried to. But the best vantage point is a fifty-foot-high overlook, down into a shadowy cove roiled with surf and mist; plus the critters, whatever they are, move very fast when they're visible above the surface—which, of course, is all you can see in the pictures of them. Yet all the accounts seem to agree: these are large vertebrates, at least twenty feet long; they're carnivorous, strong as hell, and very aggressive—they've been known to thrust their heads out of the water and drag down full-grown seals. They look like 'giant eels,' according to some witnesses, or 'enormous water snakes,' according to others. Fast, elusive, dangerous, unknown mothers! But even though they're hard to photograph, too many people have glimpsed them, very clearly, for this to be a case of tourists or tipsy Irish farmers misidentifying a common species—there are indeed some very weird animals in that bay!

"Back in 1971, one of the London tabloids got wind of the story, collected a bunch of photos and written affidavits, submitted them to the British Museum, and offered five thousand pounds to the man who first produced a clear picture and a plausible identification for these things.

"Now: here's a pile of testimony from dozens of reliable, educated witnesses—you'd think some biologist would jump at the chance. But if you guessed that, you'd be wrong. The data was submitted to a senior biologist named Alistair Metcalf, if you can believe that, who purported to review the documentation 'extensively' and who identified the creatures as sea otters. And refused to speculate any further. Well, excuse me, but a twenty-five-foot-long, savagely predatory sea otter fits most people's idea of a 'monster'? The tabloid issued a challenge: if Dr. Metcalf truly believed they were otters, the newspaper was willing to fund a full-scale expedition to verify that fact. The British Museum haughtily declined, saying something to the effect that 'reputable scientists do not traipse around Ireland hunting "monsters."'" Case closed.

"Here's a neat paradox: unless a sighting is reported by a reputable scientist, it's not taken seriously by all the *other* reputable scientists.

"This Dr. Metcalf was just like the captain of the whaling ship *Hardranger*, which was sailing off the coast of Brazil back in 1887 when its crew spotted a sea serpent more than sixty feet long. The entire crew watched it for twenty minutes, and the first mate kept calling down the voice-pipe: '*Sir, you really must see this marvelous monster!*' And the captain hollered back: '*If I come up on the bridge, and actually witness this remarkable creature, I would never be able to refrain from telling people about it—and I do not relish the prospect of being called a liar for the rest of my life.*'"

Karen drained her coffee. "Hey, instead of listening to these tales, can I look at your collection now?"

"Oh, God, of course! I got carried away again. This way, please, m'lady."

"You have a comfortable house," she remarked as she followed him back through the living room and down the hallway. "It's definitely a professor's house."

"It's definitely a *divorced* professor's house, you mean. Just watch out for the dust bunnies under the furniture—at night they come out to feed."

No one had visited Allen Warrener's inner sanctum since he and Sylvia had divorced. Karen therefore entered a space that had been inviolate, except for its creator, for more than two years. To enter its doorway was to enter Allen Warrener's most private, most cherished realm. She felt that demarcation, like passing through a force-field, when she moved from the hallway and stood before the giant photomural Allen had set up on his walls, depicting Streymoy, the central of the Faeroe Islands, the site of Torshavn, the homeland of Eiden and Elsuba Poulsen.

Karen had of course heard his enthusiastic comments about the beautiful, unspoiled Faeroese landscape, but she wasn't prepared for its stark monumental power. The panorama swept from purple-black headlands, their edges upward-beveled cliff faces three thousand feet high, rearing sheer and sharp above the North Atlantic in a solid rampart; behind those natural battlements spread a vast bay that glittered in chill pure sunlight, its waters a cold, creamy jade; and in the distance to the west, serrated like a succession of stage-flats, rose island after island, cut-glass sharp, thrusting into the sea like battleships' prows, the farthest island, defining the horizon, steeped and angled like a Mayan temple. Only at the bottom, snuggled in a pocket of light encircled by hard, towering shadows, was there a sign of human habitation: a tiny fishing village at the deepest indent of a narrow fjord, its houses seeming to cling fiercely to the land, their rooftops whiskery with sod, their walls painted in defiant primary colors—their inhabitants were staking a claim upon the stark wilderness all around; a rough stone breakwater protected this tiny enclave, and a clutch of gaily colored fishing smacks, each one's bow carved into the Orm-shape of a Viking figurehead, bobbed joyously against their mooring lines. Above, gathering all these diverse elements and unifying them, its color distilled from the Gulf Stream into a luscious glazed azure, loomed a titanic cathedral-dome of sky, its emptiness refined and given architectural solidity by cloud formations so varied and dissimilar that one sky could barely contain them: arching groins of weathered iron held aloft the weight of a rain front drifting east, from whose trailing edge swept veils of luminous mist, and soaring minarets of hard-packed, intricately swirled snow-cream inserted an element of tropical luxuriance, an exquisite contrast to the prevailing Nordic character of the scene.

Karen was stopped in awe: nowhere else on Earth could there be such a symphonic contrast, such a paradox of balanced elements, and such a breathtaking display of geological music. What held her in rapture and stasis was the fact that she had seen this island before.

"My God, Allen . . . it's . . . it's so much like *my* island! I mean, an island I used to dream about. Where in the real world is this place?"

"It's the island of Streymoy, the largest of the Faeroese chain and the location of the capital city, Torshavn . . . 'Thor's Harbor.' Marvelous name, isn't it?"

"Not just marvelous . . . it's perfect. That village: it's also like one I used to dream about."

"Well, according to the Norse beliefs, if you dream so vividly about a strange place, then the gods are telling you that it's your fate to go there. I must say, nobody else who's ever seen this mural has had a *personal* reaction to it. . . ."

"My mother used to say things like that, and I doubt she'd ever heard of the Faeroe Islands. And until tonight, I never believed my dream island really existed, much less knew where it was. You can actually *visit* these islands? I mean, without a magic carpet? The land is firm under your feet and the sky is really that vast?"

"Yes, Karen. What you see in that poster is all real, all accessible, and the people who live there are strong, poetic, and brave. It's a land where the Vikings felt close to their gods, and when you're standing up on one of those incredible cliffs, you feel close to something ancient and magical. Now you understand why I became so obsessed with the Faeroes, and why I've always wanted to return there."

Karen turned away from the panorama and gestured to the file cabinets, the floor-to-ceiling bookcases, the statues and figurines of Nessie, Godzilla, Bigfoot, and many-tentacled Chthulhu. "Honestly, Allen, if there's any place on Earth where I wouldn't be surprised to see a giant Orm basking on the surface, it's *there*. Do the Faeroese ever claim to see the Orms? Are they part of the local culture?"

"Only in the sense of being a decorative motif. But, now that you mention it, there *is* a sort of resident monster in the Faeroes. And it's even more elusive and camera-shy than Nessie. Never been photographed at all, in fact, so far as I know."

"And what do the Faeroese call this creature?"

"It's generally referred to as the 'Vardinoy Phenomenon,' because the sightings of it are confined to the waters on or near the island of Vardinoy."

"Is it close to this place Streymoy?"

"Depends on what you mean by 'close.' Vardinoy is the northernmost island in the Faeroese chain, completely uninhabited, or so the story goes, and it's a whole day's sail from Torshavn. My friend Eiden Poulsen—he owns a shipyard in Torshavn and is one of the richest men in the country—he definitely has an obsession with the Vardinoy legends. He sends me every new piece of information he digs up: articles in Danish newspapers, old letters and scrapbooks, stuff like that. Unlike me, he has the leisure time to dig deep."

"Has it got giant claws, or mile-long tentacles, or does it breathe fire, or what?"

"None of the stories agree on the details. I must confess, even for a confirmed cryptozoologist, I find the Vardinoy creature to be infuriatingly ambiguous. Even *I* might be skeptical, if Eiden wasn't so convinced that there's something real beneath the legends. And he's a no-nonsense seaman, not an idle dreamer. He commanded an escort ship during the Battle of the North Atlantic and actually sank a couple of U-boats, so you can bet he's not given to idle fancies. The funny thing about it is that until recently, he pursued his research very casually, like an old gentleman collecting stamps—then, all of a sudden, only about four weeks ago, he began to sound very serious. Said he'd found a reference to the Vardinoy phenomenon in a book and recommended it to me urgently."

"Have you got the book?"

"Yep, right here; the library managed to find a copy for me." He handed her a large volume entitled *Fighting for Old Blighty: Recollections of a Soldier's Life, from the Burma Rifles to the Battle of the Ruhr Pocket*, by General Sir Alexander Teal, D.S.O., O.B.E., V.C.

"Obviously a distinguished soldier-of-the-queen, but what does he have to do with the Vardinoy Monster?"

"Indirectly, perhaps quite a lot. Because the Faeroes were situated on the northern flank of the convoy routes, they were quite a strategic prize. So the British occupied them, before the Germans could, and General Teal here was the first commander of the Allied garrison. He tells the story of a German pilot who was shot down near the Faeroes, and whose crew, when they tried to parachute to safety near Vardinoy, was supposedly devoured or absorbed or sucked under by . . . something . . . that came out of the sea, or maybe out of a big, deep lake on the island—the details are pretty fuzzy. Still, it's the most extensive modern account Eiden's discovered yet, and he thinks it's worth following up. He found out that General Teal's still alive and he's written to him. I can't wait to read the reply, if there is one."

"Can I borrow this long enough to read the part about Vardinoy?"

"Be my guest; there's not a long waiting list. And tell me what you think after you've read the story. No hurry bringing it back."

"Okay—but that'll give me an excuse to barge in on you."

"You don't need an excuse. And a visit from you would never be an imposition, only a joy."

Allen sat down and gazed at her somberly. They had arrived at a crossroads in the evening. One of them had to up the ante or fold.

"I don't want to interrupt your privacy," she said quietly.

" 'My privacy' is an affliction sometimes. I'm serious, Karen, you don't need an invitation to come back. Visit me you whenever care to, and stay as long as you like, whenever you do. As if it weren't laughably obvious by now, I enjoy your company very much."

"I enjoy your company too, Allen. For a couple of solitary people, we seem to make a pretty good pair."

"Well, then. . . ."

"Well, then, why don't you come over here and kiss me? I'm curious to see if that works."

It worked just fine. The initial contact was somewhat wary—she almost pulled back from it, as though having second thoughts. But when he hesitated, not wishing to seem too eager or too aggressive, she reached out and pulled his head closer, softening her lips until their mouths melted into one. The tongue contact was gentle, almost shy, and he did not violate that with any hard, lustful thrusts. For all of her worldly woes and disappointments, for all the brutality she had endured in her quest for an ideal that Warrener had turned his back on ten years before they met, this was still the yielding, ripening kiss of a young girl. He savored in turn the shifting textures and motions of uncertainty, desire, fear, playfulness—the timid girl inside the tough self-confident woman. And she had the skill to crown that titanic fervor with a sense of his good fortune. It was, hands down, the most complex and fascinating kiss he'd experienced since the first night he'd slept with Elsuba, and that alone was sufficient to kindle the beginnings of devotion.

They did not come up for air for a long time, mutually surprised to discover that they had migrated, during the course of that operatic kiss, from standing in the middle of the floor to lying entwined on the sofa bed where Allen sometimes napped.

"Are you certain you want this to go any further?" he asked.

"Stop being so conscientious and unbutton my damn blouse. I'm ready to see the monster now."

"I hope he won't disappoint you."

"Listen, Professor, if we make love as well as we kiss, nobody's going to be disappointed."

12.

VALENTINE'S DAY (IS SPOILED)

Preston Valentine began his career as a porn director at just the right moment. The Pill had worked its liberating magic on the middle class—hippie hedonism had spread into the suburbs, inspiring the tepidly married to explore new erotic territory, often with gratifying results. Dirty movies had emerged from their stag-party ghetto into the light of commercial acceptance and quasi-respectability. The big-city grind houses ran round-the-clock triple-X marathons, while the Cineplex at the mall in Hometown, U.S.A., showed James Bond films during the week and ran midnight showings of *The Devil in Miss Jones* on the weekends.

There was obviously a fortune to be made, for those shrewd enough to get into the industry on the ground floor. In bustling, ever-expanding Atlanta, two real-estate tycoons, the Sizemore brothers, heard the knock of opportunity and tapped into their real-estate fortune in order to build a new state-of-the-art production facility. They advertised for technicians and cameramen and cut-to-the-chase directors who would work for chump change up front in exchange for a few points of the gross. That was Preston's kind of deal, all right, and he parleyed a one-shot trial gig into a steady job with Sizemore Studios—his films came in on time, on-budget, and with sufficient professional glitz to impress even the mainstream critics.

Preston found the atmosphere congenial, his paychecks got larger, his name-recognition soared, and the Sizemore brothers allowed him the creative freedom to employ the techniques he'd absorbed during his tenure at the Film-Makers' Co-Op. His game plan was for a few years' work in this immensely profitable new industry, to amass a grubstake that would provide him with the financial resources to enable him, eventually, to realize his ambitions as a serious independent filmmaker. *His* dirty movies were distinguished by such comparatively elegant production values—including solid plots and believable contexts for the eroticism—that college boys could take their dates to see them under the guise of "art films." When the curmudgeonly Russ Meyer, one of Preston's idols, praised his work in a *Film Quarterly* interview, Preston's star rose to new heights, and his reputation went global. He created a trademark erotic gestalt that delivered the goods without insulting the intelligence or the taste of his widening audience. And he avoided the deadly seriousness of most porn directors. As Preston told one interviewer: "Look, there are few sights more fundamentally ridiculous than a naked butt humping up and down under ten thousand watts of Klieg lights. Sex without *fun* is like food without seasoning. I want my audiences to feel invigorated when they leave the theater; I want Mom and Pop to rush home, lock the bedroom door, and try out something new! When the Bible-thumpers accuse me of being anti-marriage, I have to laugh—couples who enjoy my movies probably have sounder, more honest relationships than the prudes who shun them."

Things were rolling along pleasantly and profitably until, midway through the studio's third season, one of the Sizemore brothers got hooked on a TV evangelist and Found Jesus. The resulting born-again fraternal schism, though not without its comedic aspects, wrought havoc on the studio's bottom line. Productions were suspended while the two brothers duked it out via their attorneys. Ultimately, the secular brother couldn't match the Christian Crusade's bottomless war chest and he folded, putting the studio up for auction and sullenly returning to the boring life of a real-estate speculator.

Preston Valentine found himself out of a job. But he'd been smart enough to sock away most of his earnings in blue-chip stocks; and because he was now a well-connected, bankable director, he had no trouble raising enough capital to buy the boarded-up Sizemore Studios and go into business for himself. Thus was born Valentine Films, Ltd. Preston designed the logo: a heart pierced through by a ridiculously long spike-heeled shoe, emblazoned with the motto: "We Give the Best Heart-Ons!"

His debut was an ambitious and loosely connected trilogy, a Southern Gothic takeoff on *Gone With The Wind* (*Miss Scarlett's Scarlet Thighs, Honeysuckle and Black Lace,* and a grand finale that parodied the entire genre, *Sex Life of the Confederate Dead).* The films' success was due in no small part to the first appearance of a sensational new actress named Norma Davenport, a statuesque ripely endowed woman with a stunning mass of auburn hair and the face of a pre-Raphaelite angel.

Preston had discovered her waitressing in a skuzzy titty-bar in one of Atlanta's redneck suburbs—a job she hated, but which enabled her to support her year-old illegitimate son, Nicolas. She had been initially skeptical when he made his pitch, less so when she saw his business card and press kit, and totally snowed when he showed up the next night in a stretch limo the likes of which nobody in that part of town had ever seen. She quit her job on the spot and happily allowed Preston to sweep her away to a new and glamorous life as the undisputed Queen of Quality Porn.

Preston and Norma got married one week after Norma's first film opened to enthusiastic reviews and boffo box-office. She always removed her wedding ring before a shoot, of course, and the sexual chemistry that looped from Preston's lens through Norma and into whomever she was partnered with in a given scene might have seemed perverse to an outsider, but to them it was simply a day at the office. Norma wondered, at times, if her occupation might some day be an embarrassment to her now two-year-old son, but for the time being, such concerns were remote and abstract.

Rather to his surprise, Preston quickly came to love his stepson. Nicky was a sunshine toddler whose smile brightened the rainiest day. As happy as they both were to have this child, neither wanted another. A pregnant Norma Davenport would have been box-office death, and they knew their porn-film gravy train wouldn't run forever—it was vital to make their fortune while the genre was at peak popularity.

Therein lay the cause of Valentine Studios' demise. There was so much money being made in the adult film industry that the Mob started muscling in aggressively, buying up regional studios or contriving to drive them out of business. Preston was vouchsafed a glimpse into the Syndicate's strategy during a surprisingly low-key and reasonable business conference with two well-dressed men from New Jersey. They explained that videotapes were the wave of the future, and while the installed base for Betamax units was small at the moment, in three years it would turn into a monster market. Mr. Valentine was obviously a savvy businessman, one of the mobsters said, and he could appreciate that the powerful gentleman they represented wanted to consolidate the profits from this new technology into the coffers of his own "family"; for that reason, he would not look favorably on regional competitors.

Then the other well-dressed gentleman pulled a contract from his briefcase, which contained a surprisingly generous offer to purchase Valentine Films outright, lock-stock-and-*now*. Preston was unfortunately fatigued and irritable after a long day of trying to shoot around a leading man who'd been consistently unable to "get wood" when it was time to perform. Preston's reaction was unwisely antagonistic.

"Go home and tell Don Giovanni, or whatever the fuck his name is, that if he sends even one goon onto my property, all I have to is make one phone call and there'll be a SWAT team formed up in front of my door in ten minutes."

"Not any more, they won't," said one of the New Jersey negotiators, showing Preston to the door.

Nevertheless, even though the incident struck him as ludicrous, Preston took the precaution of sending Norma and Nicky to a hotel fifty miles away, and settled down, as best he could in a state of inflated paranoia, to wait for another telephone call. But the Syndicate not only wanted Preston Valentine out of the market, they wanted to make an example of him in order to scare other independent film companies all over the Southeast. After a jumpy and sleepless thirty-six hours, Preston got an anonymous, terse, and very alarming phone call. He swung into the Valentine Studios parking lot just in time to see the roof of the main sound stage collapse in a flurry of sparks. The fire department's response was suspiciously dilatory—the Chief was a born-again Baptist who had no real motivation to save Valentine Studios and the satanic movies originating there. By morning, virtually nothing was left, including the master work-print of Preston's newest film. All of the company's financial records were likewise burned to ashes. The Fire Marshal confirmed that it was a professional torch job, but of course the investigation turned up no leads. And the local Evangelicals seized on the incident like sharks going after chum, proclaiming the fire to be proof of God's wrath turned against the smut peddlers who had too long polluted the community with their abominations.

Devastated by the sudden loss of his empire, Preston went into seclusion. Four days after the holocaust, he finally heard from one of the New Jersey go-betweens: it was most unfortunate, he said, that Mr. Valentine hadn't signed that contract, which was a very reasonable offer. But he wanted Preston to know the arson job was "strictly business," intentionally timed to minimize danger to his employees; indeed, "my boss asked me to pass along his condolences, and to tell you that your films are greatly admired by himself and certain of his associates." Furthermore, Preston had the solemn oath of this Capo Rigemo that no harm would come to him or his family, provided Preston gave his word never to make another erotic movie. Preston was given twenty-four hours to decide.

Preston's first act after this bizarre conversation was to call his oldest friend, Allen Warrener, and solicit Allen's advice, which turned out to be highly pragmatic:

Look at this as a sign, Allen advised: you've always said the porn movies were just a means to an end, a source to amass enough money to launch your career as an independent "mainstream" filmmaker. Maybe Preston didn't have enough in the bank to finance a remake of *Ben Hur,* but surely he had enough to shoot at least one full-length feature, one of those serious, artistic, *personal* films he'd always dreamed of making, and if the resultant movie was good enough, Preston would have an easier time rounding up financiers for his second film, etc. That was just the pep talk Preston needed to hear.

But he was accustomed to working within the budgetary constraints of a porn movie. He was unprepared for and rather stunned by the escalating costs of just one black-and-white mainstream feature. By the end of production, he'd sunk just about every liquid asset he had into the project.

Movie Man was an eccentric serio-comic romp, and it was set in the milieu of New York's underground movie scene in the late sixties. But because Preston's funding problems were so on-and-off, the final edit betrayed too much herky-jerky stress, and about half the gags fell flat on the screen, no matter how clever they looked on paper. Most viewers admitted that *Movie Man* had flashes of brilliance, but the director's hand was too heavy and he deployed his technical skills in a way that too often called attention to themselves, instead of serving the script. ("A virtue, perhaps, in Mr. Valentine's former line of work," sniffed John Simon in his *Village Voice* review, "but not in the sort of films he now aspires to make.") A few of the more iconoclastic film journals and fanzines—the kind with minuscule circulations—had more charitable things to say about the movie, but in the venues that counted for generating "buzz," the movie closed after a one-week run. The Valentines recouped roughly fourteen per cent of their investment.

Preston withdrew from public view, maintaining contact only with a handful of loyal former employees and with his best friend, Allen. His savings were dwindling fast and the only job offers he had were attached to bottom-drawer porn movies, some of them no doubt financed by his former acquaintances from New Jersey. That route was not an option; he would rather go back to photojournalism than work for the goons who'd torched Valentine Studios.

On his thirty-seventh birthday, Norma gave him a present that had taken her six months to track down: an *uncut* theatrical print of Sam Peckinpah's *The Wild Bunch*. Even Peckinpah no longer had an uncut print and was reportedly very angry when he learned that one existed, but it was locked away in a private collection; Norma had obtained it by means not entirely financial.

Preston was delighted, and immediately hustled Norma into their private screening room to watch this rarity in pristine form. Nostalgia-creep had not betrayed his recollections: the uncut version was magnificent in its sweep and riveting in its balletic slow-motion battle scenes.

"It's funny," Norma said afterwards, "that you can show every imaginable sex act on the screen, but because of the way they crucified poor Peckinpah, no director since then has dared to be so over-the-top when it comes to violence."

"Squeamishness over Vietnam, I reckon," was Preston's glib conclusion.

"Vietnam's been over for a while now, honey," Norma mused. "I'll bet the public would line up in big numbers to see a shoot-'em-up that didn't pull any punches. You know, a kind of violence-porn. . . ."

She gathered up the empty popcorn bowls and started for the kitchen.

That's when the light bulb popped on in Preston's head.

"Hey, Norma, what'd you just say? Repeat it, please."

She did. Preston ran to his editing desk and grabbed a clipboard and a hand-held calculator.

"Here, you take the calculator and I'll use tick-marks. I want to run the movie again, and get an exact count of the number of blood-squibs Sam deployed in this movie!"

"Even in the Mexican shoot-out at the end? I can't punch the 'add' key that fast."

"Do the best you can."

After the screening, they compared totals and found that their figures almost matched.

"Where are you going with this, Press?"

"Take this number and double it. And calculate thirty percent of that for non-lethal mutilations, car crashes, chainsaw amputations, whatever. And *that's* our target quota, sweetheart. Now all I have to do is come up with a plot line that can sustain so much carnage and still be plausible."

Galvanized by his new project, Preston immersed himself in research, culling from medical, historical, and psychoanalytical tomes a veritable *grand guignol* database of macabre and outré forms of death, including such exotica as death-by-swarming-piranha and the exceedingly rare but truly disgusting Exploding Bowel Syndrome, only eight authenticated cases of which were recorded in the annals of medical science.

They had to re-mortgage the house and sell off all the antiques Norma had collected during their salad days, but when PressFilm's first feature, *Massacre on Peachtree,* opened, it grossed six million in drive-in receipts during its first week alone.

Preston Valentine had found his true métier.

Their second feature, *Cycle-Trash on the Warpath,* was even more successful, and it only cost half a million to make because Preston hired the actual Atlanta chapter of the Hell's Angels to play the two rival gangs that gruesomely decimated each other throughout the course of that gut-churning epic. The climactic shootout was staged in a deserted part of the Okefenokee Swamp, and because Preston hadn't bothered to obtain permission from the Parks and Recreation Agency, it was imperative to leave the site as clean as possible. But the morning after the wrap revealed a boggy plain that looked like Genghis Khan's Mongols had passed through on a rampage. Preston couldn't afford a professional cleanup crew, so he pitched in a half-dozen technicians who'd agreed to do the work for time and a half. The chore proved to be immense, however, and Preston was both surprised and grateful when seven of the bikers returned and offered to help. Early in the morning, when most of them were too hung over to understand what they were volunteering for, they had been recruited and were now efficiently supervised by a burly giant with shoulder-length hair, a pronounced "Jaw-jah" drawl, and a "Harley Davidson Rules!" tattoo covering a bicep the size of Popeye's forearm. During the long day's labor, this particular Hell's Angel continually peppered the technicians with questions—about how they lit certain scenes in yesterday's fracas, about the different lenses they used to achieve various effects, and how long it took to rig up a convincing faux disembowelment. His name was Dewey Tucker, and he hailed from some flyspeck town near the Florida line. As it happened, he had also served in Vietnam, with an elite LURP detachment that Preston had spent some time humping the boonies with. After showing his gratitude to the biker volunteers by sending out for a truckload of beer, Preston invited Dewey home for supper, suggesting that it might be fun to get shitfaced together and swap old war stories. This they did, with so much macho-gusto that Norma excused herself after the first hour.

To cap the well-lubricated gabfest, Preston showed his priceless uncut print of *The Wild Bunch,* at the end of which Dewey Tucker unashamedly wept and vowed that he would even trade his beloved hog for the chance to be the head cameraman on Preston's next project.

"Are you serious, Harley-Man, or is that just the beer talking?"

"Serious as a fuckin' heart attack, Mr. Valentine."

"Call me Preston, and why don't you crash here for the night, so you don't injure yourself or, worse yet, smash up your Hog. In the morning, when we'll both be feeling like homemade shit, remind me that the last thing I did before passing out was to offer you a job. If you really want to learn the business after you sober up, that is. . . ."

Dewey looked stunned, and then he demonstrated just how serious he was by throwing his arms around Preston and squeezing the breath out of him.

Dewey proved to be a natural. He mastered the basics of cinematography in four weeks, and soon he was composing shots with a reckless élan that imparted vigor and freshness to Preston's blocking setups. When they weren't in production, Dewey served good-naturedly as a gofer, a gaffer, a set decorator, a bit actor, a dialogue coach, a chauffeur, and, on certain occasions, a bodyguard.

Preston transferred all the energy and creativity he had formerly put into his erotic films into his new slash-and-crash epics. He was enthusiastic, but under no illusions about the product. To interviewers, he often boasted that, unlike his porn films, the blood-and-guts sagas contained "absolutely no redeeming social value." He felt entitled to be defiantly pragmatic. After all, he'd *tried* to go "straight," and for his efforts, the Establishment critics had slapped him down hard. Sometimes, when he was intently editing an especially gruesome bit of mayhem, he could be heard muttering "Fuck you, Bosley Crowther!" or "Take that, Monsieur Godard, you pretentious, snail-sucking bore!"

Preston's "Gore Period" films became box-office phenomena, and for them he was loudly reviled from pulpits, in PTA meetings, and even from the floor of the U.S. Congress. He derived a mordant satisfaction from metaphorically flipping off his critics. At all of his public appearances, he sported a big lurid button that said: "Fuck Art, let's go kill people!"

He was on a roll now, making money by the truckload, but his previous experiences had taught him how quickly this gold mine could play out. Imitators were springing up, some of them so low-rent that they were shooting direct-to-videotape. Because Preston had started out at such a high pitch of virtuosity, it required considerable ingenuity to top his own last film, but by diligent research and sheer rococo imagination, he managed.

No matter how anatomically, pathologically, or medically accurate Preston's cinematic atrocities were, he always delivered the gore with tongue-in-cheek attitude. Innocent characters might die horribly in their dozens, but he always reserved some especially fiendish and baroque termination for his villains.

Nobody was prepared for his magnum opus, however; for in it he created an icon for his times. The eponymous protagonist, *Hammerhead,* is a mild-mannered Vietnam vet who's suffered a massive head injury and has lost six years of his life in an artificially induced coma. While the VA surgeons try to figure out how to fix him up with a prosthetic skull so he can return to his "normal" life, his faithful wife, Patty, visits his bedside every day and talks to him and holds his unresponsive hand, whispering words of endearment to a man so hideously mutilated that his face is always screened off by an opaque plastic curtain. Then, because of federal budget cuts, the surgeons have to rush their long-planned repair job, and the surgery is horribly botched, leaving the wretched veteran permanently attached to an enormous, misshapen, titanium-steel skull.

Revolting to his wife, so disfigured that his children run screaming from the room when he tries to approach them, the anonymous protagonist now becomes a victim of budget cuts as well. There's nothing more the VA doctors can do, and he's taking up bed space; the bureaucrats expel him from the hospital, the only refuge he knows. Shunned by society, forced to live alone in dark places, the exiled veteran adopts the name "Hammerhead" and, while under local anesthetics, welds to his steel cranium a macabre battery of weapons and high-tech gadgets (one of Preston's happier inspirations was to make these gizmos interchangeable, so that in every Hammerhead movie the protagonist's "Utility Skull" was configured with a different assortment of cool hardware). Hammerhead becomes an avenging anti-hero, dwelling in the dark underbelly of a nameless metropolis, a rarely glimpsed urban legend whose mission is to avenge the innocent. The battering-ram irony, of course, is that Hammerhead is the "innocent" here, and the scumbags to whom he metes out gruesomely poetic justice are in fact genuinely evil monsters.

Long and vociferous were the debates that followed the stunning success of the first Hammerhead opus. Particular attention was paid to the climactic scene, which Preston filmed from the point of view of a detached eyeball, still hanging from the villain's bloody socket by a long glistening thread of optic nerve . . . until Hammerhead spears it, just firmly enough to secure it but not to blind it, and slowly inserts it into his mouth like an olive from a martini. The screen fades to black as the audience hears a loud, squishy *plop!*

Just one week after the Atlanta premiere of *Hammerhead,* every punk-rock shop in town was selling miniature rubber-eyeball trinkets: buttons, earrings, T-shirts. At Norma's urging, Preston had long before copyrighted the eyeball logo, so the licensing fees alone brought in millions. By the time the second Hammerhead movie was rushed into release, the fad had gone global. There was a British band named The Hammerheads; there was a limited-edition comic book series; there were Halloween masks. . . . And there was a tsunami of outrage from concerned parents, Congressmen, and the same flock of religious zealots who had crossed swords with Preston before.

Nicolas, who had just turned fourteen when the first Hammerhead film came out, wasn't allowed to see the movie, not even at home, but he and his friends thought it was incredibly cool that Nick's dad was the guy who'd created the Hammerhead phenomenon, and Preston was delighted to provide Nick's buddies with free T-shirts, buttons, action figures, and other Hammerhead Collectibles.

Norma was now thankful she had been forced into early retirement from the porn industry. As the mobsters from New Jersey had predicted, home videotape had ripped the bottom from under the porn theaters' attendance numbers. Hundreds of seventies-era porn movies were being transferred to the new medium, but Norma was glad that hers would never be among them—no duplicable prints had survived the studio fire, and, as far as she knew, no bootleg prints existed.

But Norma was wrong. Although no suitable prints had survived the fire, Preston had never been averse to striking off a pristine new print for any collector who could pay the cost of doing so. And among well-heeled collectors, the Valentine films were highly regarded. Some of those collectors, or their heirs, or the burglars who'd heisted the films from the collectors' libraries, had made deals with the videotape distributors. There was a pent-up demand for Valentine films, and Nature abhors a vacuum. There were not many tape copies in circulation, and they always commanded a premium price, but unfortunately the parents of Nick's closest friend happened to be such collectors. They thought their erotica collection was safely hidden and inaccessible to their children, but of course that wasn't the case at all.

One Saturday night, not long after Nick's fifteenth birthday, those parents went out of town . . . and that friend organized a sleep-over party, the main attraction being his parents' porn tapes, which he had recently discovered, quite by chance, in the attic, sealed in boxes labeled "Xmas tree ornaments."

Norma was awakened at three A.M. by the sound of the back door being forcefully closed. It had to be Nicolas, of course, but why wasn't he staying at his friend's house with the other guys? Perhaps there had been an argument. Perhaps Nick and the boys had gotten into some mischief. After a few moments of indecision, Norma put on her robe. If the kids *had* gotten into trouble, she needed to know about it before either the cops arrived or she got an angry phone call from some other kid's parents.

She sensed tension as soon as she entered the boy's bedroom. Nicolas was lying stiffly on his sofa, still fully dressed in his skateboarding rags, staring at the ceiling.

"Hi, kiddo. Home kind of early, aren't you?"

Norma didn't detect any beer or pot fumes, for which she gave silent thanks, but there was definitely something alarming about the surly twist of her son's mouth. "Yeah, so what?"

"Don't use that snotty tone with me, young man. I'll tell you so what—your stepfather and I cut you a lot of slack by letting you spend the night out. We're not morons, you know—Charlie's parents *are* out of town, are they not? We trusted you to behave responsibly. Did they come back before you thought they were going to and catch you guys doing something you shouldn't have been doing?"

Nick gave her a slow, unsettling appraisal, as though seeing his mother for the first time.

"No, Mom, we didn't get into any trouble. How could we, when all we did was watch some videos?"

"Oh, that's right—Charlie's folks just bought a video deck, didn't they? I guess we'll break down and buy one, sooner or later. How was the picture quality?"

"Oh, it was clear enough, for *those kinds* of movies. You see, Charlie's folks have a big stash of porno tapes they think Charlie doesn't know about. But he does, and now we all know about them. Me and all my friends. . . ."

Norma felt an icy knot forming in her stomach.

Nicolas rose to a sitting position and spoke in a numb, matter-of-fact voice. "I was in the bathroom taking a leak, when all of a sudden I heard Charlie yelling 'Nick, come here quick! It's your *mother!*' And, boy, he was right. There was my mom, in living color."

Norma's hands made useless, placating gestures, her tongue a lump of wood.

And now her son's voice rose to the edge of hysteria: "Don't worry, Mom! All my friends were impressed by how *good* you were, and all the things you knew how to do! And by lunchtime Monday, everybody in school's going to know about what we saw and *who* we saw!"

Nick buried his face in the sofa pillow and began to sob. Norma marshaled the arguments she'd held in reserve against the day this might happen, praying she would never need to use them ("It was a very different time back then, Nick, and to me it was just another kind of acting job" . . . "Lots of moms did it back then!"). But none of her rationalizations was going to lessen the damage. If only this had happened two or three years later, Nick's friends would have envied him; but now they were going to tease him to death. The truth of the moment impaled her: there *was* nothing she could say, no rationalization she could offer, that was going to make things right again between them. Not for years. Maybe not ever.

She did try to hug him, and after a writhing spasm of confusion, he allowed her to. Now she could smell the beer and cigarettes on his breath, but she wasn't going to jump on him for those minor transgressions. After a while, he fell asleep in her arms, just as he used to. Norma wondered if waking Preston would serve any useful purpose. Nor was there anything else she could do, now that her disillusioned son was asleep. She poured a double gin and washed down three valiums, then crept into bed beside her husband.

She woke to an earthquake. No, it was Preston shaking her, very urgently. She turned her face away—her mouth tasted like the bottom of a parakeet's cage—and tried to clean the cobwebs out of her head.

"Nick's gone!" her husband was shouting. He had taken one suitcase and his skateboard, and he had not left a note. Instead, he had ripped his Hammerhead posters to shreds and smashed a framed picture of his parents. The police could find no trace of him, and he had not divulged his intentions to any of his friends. The ticket agent at the bus depot vaguely remembered a teenage boy buying a one-way to Nashville, which was as far as he could go on twenty-six bucks.

Norma collapsed after she heard the news, was admitted to the hospital, where she remained, under heavy sedation, for eighteen days. On the seventh of those days, Preston picked up the telephone and heard his stepson's voice.

"Just tell my mother I'm okay."

"Nick, where are you? Please tell me where you—"

"Someplace where nobody knows me. And I'm not going to talk long enough to trace the call, so don't even try it."

Preston heard muted traffic noises outside the presumed phone booth; his mind flashed back to New York, a montage of all the scary, dangerous dead-end places a distraught teenager might run to.

"Nick, we love you. Please come home and let's work this out together!"

"Fuck you! You're the one who made her do all that stuff!"

"Nick, I didn't *make* her do anything! Please, son, give us a chance to explain some things!"

Preston heard a horn blaring in the background before the line went dead.

When Preston told Norma about the phone call, he shaded it rather more optimistically than its cold brevity warranted. Norma grabbed hold of the news like a drowning woman clasping a life jacket. Nicky was alive; he was healthy; he had communicated—the bridge between parent and child had not been burned, only scorched. He'd call again, maybe not right away, but he would call. Preston, remembering the pitiless resolve in the boy's voice, did not think so, but he went along with Norma's "selective denial." Life would go on, albeit with a constant undercurrent of woe and a momentary jolt every time the phone rang. Norma rarely left the house; she had three extension phones jacked in, and she bought a new answering machine every time a more advanced model caught her attention.

Preston's own emotional train wreck was also intensifying, albeit in slow motion. It began one Tuesday morning about six months after Norma came home from the hospital. Preston returned to his office from an early-morning production meeting and found two detectives waiting in the reception nook. When they stood up and presented their badges, Preston almost fainted—something dreadful had happened to their runaway son. But the policemen hastened to assure him that they hadn't come here to discuss Nicolas's case. despite issuing an all-points bulletin, the police had found no trace of him, for good or ill, since that one phone call to his stepfather.

The matter they wanted to discuss, however, *was* tangentially connected with Mr. Valentine's films. Had Mr. Valentine read about the unsolved and exceptionally grisly murders of three teenaged boys, all within the last six months?

Of course he had; there was not a parent in the city who hadn't felt a chill when they read about those crimes.

What Mr. Valentine did not know, said one detective, was what had been kept *out* of the newspapers: all three victims had been slain ritualistically, in ways that mimicked some of the deaths in his *Hammerhead* movies. It had taken the crime lab some time to extrapolate a connection from the meager evidence. But two nights ago, there had been a fourth murder, and this time the killer had left a clear sign of his "source of inspiration."

"Excuse me?" stammered Preston.

"Those are the killer's words, sir, not mine. We're not here to start a witch-hunt about your films; it's not your fault that some psycho has latched on to this gimmick," the detective said, in a tone that implied he believed otherwise. "But now that we've established a causal link, we need to ask you a few questions."

"Anything. If it helps put a stop to this madman."

"We appreciate your attitude. Now, first of all, can you think of anyone who might have behaved oddly or secretively during one of your more recent productions, going back, say, two years? A disgruntled employee, perhaps? Or a hardcore fan who's been calling or writing letters in an obsessive way? Any connection at all that you can remember along those lines might be very helpful to us."

Preston came up blank to all their questions. His crew was loyal, tight-knit, a kind of family.

Apparently satisfied, the cops handed Preston their cards and left. He promised to interview each of his thirty-one employees separately and in private, just to make sure they would speak freely. It was an exhausting process that ate up his entire day and produced no information of value.

He called Norma at seven, told her what was going on, and suggested she not wait up for him. If he got out of the office quickly enough, he wanted to unwind in a titty bar somewhere, but in fact the employee interviews lasted until nine-thirty, leaving him too exhausted to go anywhere but home. A couple of stiff drinks from his office bar revived him enough to make the journey to his car, after leaving a note for the receptionist saying that he would be in late the next morning.

The night watchman let him out, but Preston declined the man's offer to escort him to his car. He'd been holding his feelings in check throughout this mercilessly long day, those belts of booze were making his stomach act up, and his hands were trembling badly. No, he did not want the night watchman to see him like this. Nor did he want any witnesses in case he suddenly threw up halfway to his parking place.

When the man hiding behind his car stepped into the dead-white pool of overhead lighting, Preston's instinctive reaction was to mutter: "Jesus Christ, what *now?*" He couldn't see the man's face, hidden by a workman's cap emblazoned with the logo of the Hog Heaven Bar-B-Cue Emporium, but there was menace in his posture.

Whoever this fucker is, I am NOT going to run from him.

When the man was about three feet away, he stopped and demanded: "Are you Preston Valentine?"

"No, I'm Martin Luther King, and you're trespassing, pal."

Instead of the expected surly comeback, Preston felt a piledriver slam into his kidneys and doubled over with shock and pain. Preston couldn't get enough wind to yell for help, and whoever this clown was, he'd done a proper job of casing the area before laying his ambush—the spot he'd chosen for the beating was in one of the garage's few "dead" areas not covered by the security cameras. Preston curled into a self-protecting knot, shielding his face effectively but sustaining one methodical kick after another to his legs, hips, and buttocks. In between the punctuating blows, the assailant gasped out his story:

"This is for my son [!!!] you piece of human shit! His name [!!!] was Matthew [!!!] and some maniac killed him last Sunday night. [!!!] He was nineteen years old [!!!] and he loved your goddamned movies! He was walking home [!!!] from a midnight show of *Hammerhead Takes Manhattan* [!!!] when that serial killer spotted him, forced him into a car, and took him somewhere private [!!!] so he could torture my son to death! [!!!] [!!!] When the cops found his body, they also [!!!] found *this* jammed into one of his eyeballs! I should [!!!] poke the pin into *your* eyeball, you soulless fucker, [!!!] but then you wouldn't have to live with your [!!!] conscience. If you still have one. [!!!] So you keep this to remind you of my [!!!] dead [!!!] son. [!!!] [!!!] [!!!]"

After delivering one final, exhausted kick to Preston's groin, the man pulled something shiny out of his shirt pocket and dropped it to the pavement in front of Preston's swelling face. A few minutes later, Preston heard the screech of tires. He struggled to his feet, his entire lower body a mass of swollen bruises and contusions, and reached for the object. It was a *Hammerhead* logo pin, one of the pricier models, an enameled eyeball attached to a long "optic nerve" wire intended to fasten the souvenir to clothing or rearview mirrors or key rings, wherever a fan wanted to display it.

Preston briefly considered filing a report with the police, but then, if he had been that boy's father, he would have felt the same way. In a sense, he might have *been* that man, for he did not know if Nicolas was alive or dead. If there was one Hammerhead copycat murderer on the loose, there would be others, in other cities, and sooner or later Preston Valentine would hear about *their* victims, too.

No bones were broken, so he could drive, and he did so aimlessly for a while. But when he passed a strip mall where an open multiplex advertised a "Special Limited Engagement: *Hammerhead Takes Manhattan!*" he turned around and drove into the parking lot. The Clearasil-dabbed girl in the ticket booth looked at him askance when he shoved a twenty through the cash slot.

"I'm sorry, sir, but the show's almost half over, and I'm getting ready to close up. The cash drawer locks automatically at eleven, so I couldn't even give you change."

"I don't give a damn about the change; in fact, here's another twenty, just for your trouble. And I assure you that the reason I look this way is that someone rear-ended my car a while ago. I'm not a street person or a robber, young lady, in fact, I happen to be the director of this movie."

Preston slipped his business card through the cash slit, then on impulse peeled off another ten. The cashier's eyes widened when she saw his name.

"Oh, wow, sure, come on in. If you'll autograph my time sheet!"

"With the greatest of pleasure."

Inside the crowded theater, the ambience was very different from what Preston had expected. The audience, comprised entirely of teenagers, was not responding at all to the numerous instances of black comedy and "insider" movie jokes and parodies. He had arrived in the middle of the second-goriest fight scene in the script, and the audience was *not* abuzz with excitement or yelps of enthusiasm, not even when the gory special effects were so gratuitously exaggerated that no rational person could take them seriously. And then it hit him: *These are not rational people; they're teenagers.* And all of them were leaning forward in their seats, as silent and rigidly attentive as Orthodox Jews at a Yom Kippur service. Their fixed, unwavering stares reminded him of the loners in trenchcoats he used to see in porn theaters. When the montage of on-screen carnage reached its totally off-the-wall climax, the rapt observers uttered a sigh of release, as though each one of them had experienced a very discreet simultaneous orgasm. The more avid Hammerhead fans—the ones decked out in eyeball medallions and lapel buttons—shuddered with unnatural pleasure.

The next sequence of shots and dialogue was intended as comic relief, a breather while the plot set things up for the next bloodbath. That was the formula that seemed to work best in these pictures, and Preston had taken a lot of care with this particular entr'acte, putting in some of his most outrageously inappropriate dialogue and some of his most inspired parodistic riffs on classic older films. But nobody laughed. Not once, not at the best lines or the cleverest visual puns. In fact, the crowd became restless and many of the viewers took this opportunity to go to the restroom, to replenish their popcorn supply, or, in a surprising number of cases, to make out with their dates.

Except for himself and, presumably, the unseen projectionist, not one of these people knew or cared about all the in-jokes, puns, and tomfoolery Preston had crafted with such care. They were looking at their watches, like commuters on a subway platform, counting the minutes until the next outburst of slaughter and sadism on the screen.

He slumped despairingly against the back wall, fighting down an urge to shout: *"Don't you cretins know a brilliant takeoff on* The Maltese Falcon *when you see one?"*

Preston felt as though his beaten-on bowels were swelling with gangrenous gas. It was not so long ago that his generation had fought for an end to hypocritical and stultifying censorship, and thought they had accomplished something profoundly liberating when the hoary old codes finally crumbled. How many times had he defended his movies on talk shows by insisting: "It's just a movie, folks! It's not meant to be taken seriously, and if you don't want your sixteen-year-old to see it, don't buy the tape or give 'em the money for a ticket!"

The exit door closest to him creaked open as one audience member sneakily admitted half a dozen underage kids. They filed in with hungry faces and glittering eyes, dispersing quickly into the crowd so their illegal entry could not be proven . . . if any other adult had even noticed.

On the screen, Hammerhead was now stalking another victim. With savage deliberation, he selected a barbed dart, a cluster missile of needle-thin poisoned wires, and a long thin rod hooked up to a massive battery pack, so he could administer shocks to the villain by jabbing his head like an enraged unicorn. Every time a new instrument of pain and death clicked loudly into one of the skull-mounts, the crowd roared.

Lions 15, Christians 0. . . .

As the audience heated up, Preston was assailed by the odor of greasy popcorn butter and cheap pizza sauce, not to mention the combined body odor of three hundred teenagers. He knew that if he stayed in the theater one more minute, he was going to throw up all over the kids in the nearby seats.

He got as far as the parking lot before retching violently all over his shoes.

He and Norma sold the Hammerhead franchise to a Japanese conglomerate for ten million and change. He sold the studio property, oddly enough, to one of the same New Jersey mobsters he had had to deal with almost a decade earlier. The reunion was surprisingly cordial. After Preston signed the bill of sale, the one named Mr. Santini came around the table and gave him a sincere *abbraccio*, congratulating him on both his comeback and his foresight in divesting himself of an "artistic property" that was too hot even for the Wise Guys to handle.

Lastly, they sold their posh Buckhead residence and moved into a secluded chalet on forty acres in the Great Smokies. Norma took up painting full-time, and became good enough at it to place some of her work in the sort of galleries that were patronized by people who collected Thomas Kincaid landscapes. Preston wrote essays about film history. After a while, they stopped jumping when the phone rang. Norma received one card from her son; it was mailed from Nepal and tersely informed her that Nicolas had found "my true spiritual guide and mentor" and was seriously considering a career as a Buddhist monk. They both laughed until they got dizzy. At least their son was safe, somewhere in the world.

Allen Warrener's letter came at precisely the right moment, informing Preston that Allen's wealthy Faeroese friend, Eiden Poulsen, was willing to foot the bill for an expedition to the mysterious island of Vardinoy, and that they would need a great cameraman to document the adventure. To Preston, Allen's letter seemed like absolution for all sin.

13.

KAREN READS THE MAIL OF HER MALE

Both Allen and Karen were basically solitary persons who needed their private sanctuaries as much as they needed each other's company. They briefly discussed cohabitation, but decided against it. As a gesture of trust and commitment, each had given the other a front-door key. They came and went from each other's residences as whim and circumstance dictated. They had been lovers for five months, and so far the arrangement was satisfactory.

Technically, Karen Hambly was still an undergraduate, although she was by now considerably older than the rest of the senior class. Student/teacher liaisons were not unheard of, and were tolerated as long as no vindictive spouses or outraged parents were involved, but Allen had made enough enemies among his colleagues to warrant discretion.

If Allen was out when Karen arrived unannounced, she usually chose a book from his library and curled up on his cozy but threadbare sofa until he returned. On this particular afternoon, however, she was distracted by the sight of a long letter, with several paper-clipped attachments, that he'd left in plain sight on the coffee table. Either he wanted her to read it, or he had been in a hurry and just dropped it there. In any case, Karen did not feel as though she were violating his privacy by peeking. These documents had been posted from Torshavn and the cover letter bore the elegant silver-trawler logo of Eiden Poulsen's corporation. Allen had shared some of Eiden's letters with her before, and the Faeroese millionaire generally scrawled them in a condensed, telegraphic longhand. This one, by contrast, was professionally dictated onto heavy watermarked paper. *Mighty high rag content*, Karen thought. *You draft international treaties on paper like this, not casual notes to old chums.* Intrigued, she brewed a fresh pot of coffee and settled back on the sofa, spreading the documents on Allen's lapboard.

Dear Allen:

It did not prove so difficult to track down General Teal as we speculated. Last summer's commemoration of the 40th anniversary of V-E Day brought a great many elderly warriors out of obscurity and briefly into the media spotlight. One employee of my London branch had some excellent contacts inside the gigantic bureaucracy that runs the BBC, and since General Teal had been interviewed several times, on various documentary programs, his current address was on file. I wrote him a letter and here is his reply—very illuminating it is, too, although— as always seems to be the case with Vardinoy—the details are very speculative. Our job is to bring speculation to an end and replace it with knowledge!

Well, I don't want to over-sell my proposition. Just read the General's account and see my attached comments and my initial plan of operations. Unless you've changed beyond all recognition in the twenty-three years since I first saw you, I think you'll be as excited as I am. This old sea dog is ready for one last adventure— what about the young rogue who won my daughter's heart as no man has been able to win it since?

Well, well, thought Karen—here's a tale we haven't heard before! She felt a prickle of curiosity that another young woman might have identified as long-distance jealousy; but of course, *she* had purged herself of that particular bourgeois emotion long ago. Hadn't she?

The next document was General Teal's reply:

Dear Mr. Poulsen:

It was a pleasure to hear from you, as your father extended numerous kindnesses to me when I arrived to take command of the British garrison at Torshavn many years ago. Your inquiry was most interesting, and it provoked a spate of memories that came back to me quite vividly, despite the passage of so much time.

The incident you refer to took place shortly before I was transferred to the North African theatre, where a great many dramatic events took place in a short period of time; if I had not located some mildewed files and a diary I kept during my assignment in the Faeroes, I would have been able to supply only the dimmest recollections, but those documents jarred my memory and I was soon able to recall a surprising number of details.

The German aviator's name was Ernst Bauer, a veteran Luftwaffe pilot with an excellent record. He was captured and brought to Torshavn by a young lieutenant

named *Robert Telford. Robbie had a commando-type personality, always looking
for some chance to strike out independently and do something heroic. The other
chaps jokingly named him "Lawrence of Torshavn." He was second-in-command
of the Faeroese Militia, an ad hoc Home-Guard-style unit of some 200 men and
boys, all volunteers, whose job it was to patrol the outer islands in the chain, thus
freeing up the professional soldiers to concentrate in and around Torshavn, which
was, of course, the only place in the whole region with any real strategic value.*

*The Militia had its own small fleet—fishing smacks, equipped with radios and
an antique Lewis Gun bolted to their bows—and Robbie Telford's "squadron" was
responsible for patrolling the northern islands. Their instructions were to check out
anything suspicious, report U-boat sightings, rescue survivors from torpedoed vessels, that sort of thing. It would have been idiotic for Jerry to land saboteurs way
up there (nothing for them to sabotage!); however, it was possible that they might
try to set up a clandestine weather-reporting station on some isolated coast, so the
patrols weren't utterly meaningless. But they were long, boring, and wet; it says
much for Telford's leadership that his Faeroese crews were devoted to him and
faithfully went out in all kinds of weather, undeterred by anything less than a full-
bore gale.*

*The chain of events began when some fishermen on Vesturoy radioed that they
had seen a German bomber trailing smoke and losing altitude on a course that
would take it over Vardinoy—or into it, if they didn't have enough engine power
to fly over those formidable cliffs on the island's west coast. Telford's bunch had just
returned from a patrol, but they refueled and headed back north as soon as they
heard about the enemy bomber. Thirty-six hours later, they were back in Torshavn
with a single German prisoner, our pilot, Kapitan Bauer, who had been seriously
injured and was alternately either unconscious or thrashing around in delirium,
raving incoherently and becoming on occasion so uncontrollably agitated that he
had to be sedated.*

*Since I was fluent in German, I drew the job of interrogating our prisoner. I was
willing to do what I could, of course, but the poor man's mental state bordered on
derangement, so I didn't expect to get any information from him of military value.*

*From the moment Telford came into my office to make his initial report about
the patrol, I sensed that he was uneasy. This in itself was peculiar, for Robbie was
a steadfast, clear-minded chap. But* something *had obviously gotten his wind up.
He seemed distracted and curiously reluctant to give me much detail about the circumstances under which he had captured the first and only Nazi combatant ever*

taken on Faeroese soil. This was a unique achievement, and I was startled when Robbie seemed quite uninterested in receiving praise for what he and his crew had achieved.

Well, of course he was exhausted, so I suggested he just go to his quarters for a long sleep; I would handle the prisoner interrogation personally. After Robbie left, I went to the makeshift holding cell and tried to have a soldierly conversation with Hauptmann Bauer.

When he was neither sedated nor having one of his spells of dementia, the pilot spoke lucidly, and over the next couple of days, by fits and starts, I learned a good deal about the man and his mission. Bauer's Focke-Wulf Condor had departed its Norwegian airfield at dawn on August 12th, 1942, on a routine sweep over the convoy lanes between the northern U.K. ports and Iceland. Remember that those enormous Condors were quite a menace at that stage of the Battle of the North Atlantic. They had simply enormous range, and they carried enough firepower to sink or shred any vessel smaller and less well-protected than a destroyer. The Germans used them to pick off damaged or straggling merchant ships and to relay timely convoy sightings to the wolfpacks lurking in that part of the ocean. The Condors flew well beyond the range of any land-based interceptors, and they could loiter over a convoy for hours, flying too high for the ships' armament to touch them.

But Bauer had the bad luck to encounter one of the first catapult-launched Hurricanes that had been outfitted on a few of the larger merchantmen, in lieu of escort carriers, the first of which would not be able to join the fray until early 1943. This innovation was a measure of how desperate Britain's situation was—sending a single Hurricane aloft, from a cumbersome steam catapult, simply to chase away any loitering Condors was a pretty extreme measure, because of course there was no flight deck on which the poor buggers flying the Hurricanes could land! Once their mission was complete, the pilots had only two rather risky choices: parachute out, as close to a friendly ship as possible, or try to pancake-land the aircraft, which was near-suicidal unless the sea was dead calm, which, as you well know, is not often the case in those latitudes! I saw many kinds of bravery during the war, Poulsen, but for sheer ice-cold guts, those Hurricane pilots were unsurpassed.

Bauer had the misfortune to encounter a very aggressive pilot. He stalked the big bomber and got the drop on it, came at the Jerry head-on, all guns blazing, and shot one of the port-side engines to pieces with his first pass—the Germans were so surprised, they didn't get off a single burst. Bauer also thought that Hurricane pilot was as stupid as he was brave, because he should have quit while he was ahead.

He'd doubtless burned up half his ammunition in that first pass, and he'd damaged the bomber so badly that Bauer would have to abort his mission and limp back to Norway.

But this young aviator wanted a "kill," so he foolishly circled around and attempted another attack, this time from behind. But the German gunners were waiting for him and the dorsal turret blew him to smithereens. The range was so close that Bauer's aircraft suffered serious damage from bits and pieces of exploding Hurricane; his co-pilot's head was blown off, the fuselage and wing surfaces were cut up badly, and the canopy over the cockpit was shattered before Bauer could reconnect his oxygen. He blacked out from the sudden change in air pressure and suffered a concussion when a big chunk of debris smashed into the canopy over his head. For a few minutes, nobody was flying that Condor. What woke Bauer again, just in time to pull back on the stick and recover from the spin, was a spray of blisteringly hot oil from one of his engines, which the slipstream had flung into the cockpit.

The Condor was yawing badly, and it kept trying to go into a nose-dive. The entire airframe was vibrating, rivets were popping loose, control cables had been shot away, the co-pilot was dead, and one fuel tank had been punctured. But Bauer stayed calm. He got on the intercom and assured the crew that he would get them back to Norway, or failing that, try to make an emergency landing on one of the Faeroes.

What only Bauer and his navigator knew, however, is that the Faeroe Islands are about as dodgy a place to attempt an emergency landing as the Swiss Alps. Their best bet was to follow a course to Torshavn, radio the British for help, and then bail out within range of a rescue launch.

But it was soon apparent that the Condor's airframe was breaking up. A sharp course correction toward Torshavn might tear the bomber in half. His only recourse was to maintain a slow straight-line heading, which would take them over one and only one remote part of the Faeroese chain: the island of Vardinoy. No member of the crew had ever heard of the place. A note on the chart said it was thought to be uninhabited, and Bauer noticed that it was depicted, on the usually precise Luftwaffe maps, with a curious vagueness of hand, like unexplored land whose shape was extrapolated by an Elizabethan cartographer.

If the contour lines on the map were even approximately accurate, the dominant terrain feature on the island was a large Alpine lake, several square miles of water, sheltered and made calm by the high surrounding ridges. Bauer's plan was to bring *the wounded Condor in slow and low and as level as possible, just high enough for his crew to parachute safely, and then he would attempt to pancake the bomber on to the surface of that lake.*

But when the Germans got a look at Vardinoy, they were not encouraged: titanic cliffs of black, gleaming, foam-washed basalt, deeply cut by crevasses that looked like tectonic plates stood upright. A mile or two ahead, he saw a bright gleam, which he took to be a reflection of ambient light on the surface of the lake.

But the Condor wasn't going to make it that far. Unable to withstand the drag of the big smashed BMW engine, the port wing began to buckle and the giant plane lost what little aerodynamic lift it still possessed. Bauer poured emergency power to the starboard engines, just to maintain some forward momentum, and ordered his crew to bail out instantly.

As I stated, Mr. Poulsen, when Bauer was lucid and calm—and the doctor was pumping enough morphine and tranquilizers into him to sedate a bull elephant— he talked to me freely, and in coherent sentences. He wanted someone to know *what* had happened, *and the fact that I was a fellow officer seemed to reassure him. But he could not give a clear account of what happened* after *he told his crew to bail out.*

It was as though his memory suddenly went off the rails, or ran into a barrier he could not will himself to go beyond. Invariably, at this point in his story, he began to shake like a man with ague—his words became jagged shards, "imagistic" might be the word for it. He screamed or babbled in metaphors, *shouting that something was "like" something else, but never coherently describing what the original "something" was! I jotted some of these outbursts down at the time, thinking that if he recovered, they might be valuable to the psychiatrists who would obviously be talking to him after the regular doctors had patched up his body:*

". . . like the caps of rotting mushrooms!"

". . . like the ocean had grown mouths, nests and garlands and clusters of mouths, all of them ravenous!"

". . . like cups of black jelly, sparkling with electric blue stars, it opened to receive the helpless airmen and enfolded them, carrying them under the waves while they still screamed for help!"

I never got a clear sense of what he was attempting to describe. Sometimes it sounded like a giant spider waiting inside its web—other times, like the writhing tentacles of a giant squid—all my attempts to visualize "it" led to something God- awful and, well, "monstrous." I've only quoted a few of the more vivid ones—much of what he said was mere gibberish. Whether this man actually saw something emerge from the sea and devour or smother or suck down his comrades, or whether he was just barking mad and resorting to the images of Hieronymus Bosch because he had a piece of metal lodged in his brain, I can't say. Of course, it must have been horrible to see your friends and comrades shatter against those savage rocks, or swept under by the waves, unable to move because of the weight of their wet parachutes—that horrific experience, compounded by traumatic injuries—well, my God, who among us would not be a little bit off his nut? If you ask me point-blank: did Bauer see a living, predatory creature or some portion thereof—God only knows. I didn't witness the event, and so I refuse to speculate on what really happened.

But I know genuine terror when I see it, and sheer terror was what broke the spirit of this brave man. I survived the Battle of the Somme, sir, and three campaigns in the Second War, so I've witnessed more than my share of fear and horror; ░░░░░ ░░░░░░ ░░░░░ ░░░░░░░░░ ░░░░ ░░░ ░░ ░░░ ░░░░░░░░ ░░░░░ ░░ ░░░░ ░░░░ ░░░░ ░░░░░░░░ *cally: Hauptmann Ernst Bauer had seen or experienced something that traumatized his very soul. I am absolutely certain of that. Imagine my astonishment when I read your letter, more than forty years later, with its descriptions of a legendary "monster" that lurks near the coast of Vardinoy!! My dear sir, I have never believed in such things; but neither have I ever seen a highly trained professional officer become hysterical at the recollection of something he cannot name or even adequately describe! So logic alone suggests that perhaps the cause of Bauer's distress was, if not "a monster," then at least something which was like unto a monster.*

We will never know, alas, because the night after my last conversation with him, during the worst hours of a ferocious gale, Bauer sneaked out of the hospital and made his way to a steep ledge overlooking the Torshavn breakwater. He threw himself into the storm-surge and drowned. He left no explanatory note, but there is no doubt that it was suicide, for he had carefully tied two full jerry-cans of petrol to his legs, each containing 3.5 gallons, and for good measure stuffed about thirty kilos of stones into the pockets of his robe. He was determined; the thoroughness of his preparations proved it.

We know the sea holds far more mysteries than Mankind has ever been allowed to glimpse; only God knows what might live in its abyssal depths, and (as I just learned from looking at a map) there is a submarine trench cutting a canyon below the north–south axis of the Faeroes, which some oceanographers estimate to be two miles deep. We cannot know what lies down there, in eternal darkness. If Ernst Bauer glimpsed something so terrifying that he preferred to kill himself rather than

endure the memory of what it had done to his crewmen, then the word "monster"
is no exaggeration. It may be simply a factual description.

I hope my recollections have shed some useful light on the matter, and I wish you
every success on your planned expedition.

Yours faithfully,

General Sir Alexander Teal, O.B.E., V.C.

"Fascinating shit," muttered Karen, putting aside the general's letter and
picking up Eiden's postscript. She scanned it for any further mention of the
daughter who had given her heart to the dashing young Allen Warrener, but
the note was curiously like a message from one macho adolescent to
another—and *that* she did find strange, given the difference in ages.

This account from General Teal is, for me, the keystone that caps our edifice of
speculations! It comes frightfully close to confirming the V.M.'s existence, and fur-
nishes corroborative evidence that the stories of its hostility toward human beings
are not folk tales intended to frighten unruly children! If this thing was big enough
and ferocious enough to annihilate the six-man crew of a Nazi Condor (all of
whom presumably were carrying side-arms when they bailed out, and thus were
not defenseless!), and it was "monstrous" enough to unhinge the mind of a tough,
battle-wise Luftwaffe officer, then it must be as formidable as it is elusive.

Now is the time for us to do this thing, Allen! No more daydreaming! Battle
stations and full speed ahead! On the assumption that you'll jump at this chance,
I've started planning our logistical requirements. My research assistants tell me
that there are some items that are easier and cheaper to acquire in the States, so I've
enclosed an international bank draft for $90,000 to get the ball rolling. On reflec-
tion, I agree with you that we ought to have a first-class documentary cameraman
along—if we succeed in finding something extraordinary, we must have the best
possible photographic evidence. If your old chum Mr. Valentine is available, why
not use some of this money to put him on retainer? As for the camping gear, etc.,
I've always believed that cheap stuff isn't good and good stuff isn't cheap, so do your
homework and invest in top-quality goods.

As you can probably tell, I am very excited by the prospects for our Vardinoy
Expedition. Haven't felt this young in . . . well, never mind how long! This
summer is not too soon, if we get cracking now!

I eagerly await your reaction, my old friend!

Eiden

P.S., Elsuba asks me to tell you she would have written you at Christmas, but she's doing her residency in the trauma ward, so she hasn't had much leisure time. Anyway, she is well and sends her love.

Oh she does, does she? Karen had of course heard the reverence in Allen's voice whenever he spoke the name "Elsuba Poulsen," and she knew that, in addition to being the first great love of Allen's life, Elsuba had been the "inspiration" for his aborted shaggy-dog of a novel . . . the one he had never been able to finish. According to Allen, that failure was almost equal in its consequences to the derailment of his long-planned military career.

Karen replaced Poulsen's letter where she had found it.

Whenever Allen called to say he would be late, his habit was to say "pick out a good book and read yourself to sleep." And one night, when Karen was feeling insecure about the future of their relationship, she'd followed that suggestion. She had gone into his study and rummaged around until she found the manuscript of that novel. Unsure of his reaction if he came home and found her reading it without express permission, she had walked to a nearby copy shop and had all 534 pages duplicated. That way, she could read it in the privacy of her apartment, in digestible bites and at her own pace. It was perhaps a sneaky thing to do, but Allen attached such iconic significance to his failed novel that she felt obliged to study it carefully, hoping to find insights into his passionate but often rather *unfocused* personality.

If anything, Allen had understated the book's deficiencies. It wasn't the work of a clumsy amateur, but it was painfully obvious that, however well-read he must have been at the time he started it, he didn't know how much he didn't know about structure, character, point of view, and most of all, When To Quit. His style was not without sporadic brilliance, and the energy he'd thrown into it must have been prodigious. But he never gained control over his material; he was one of those appallingly earnest would-be Prousts who think it's enough to open a vein over the typewriter and just let the juice pour forth. It was utterly monothematic: the first two hundred pages set the scene for his life-altering affair with Elsuba Poulsen; the next two hundred fifty pages described that affair, in lubricious ultra-purple prose; and the last hundred pages simply shot off in all directions, with the author desperately scrambling to find some unifying theme strong enough to pay the mortgage of his emotional investment. Hell, he couldn't even think of an *ending*. If

Karen had a dollar for every undergraduate composition she'd read that howled for recognition with the same shrill urgency—*Pay attention to my epiphanies; I am so sensitive to Nature, so full of milk!*—she could go downtown and buy a BMW with cash.

And yet . . . and yet, for all its windy rhetorical excesses, its overwrought intensity, its tendency to deploy ten lush similes when one would suffice . . . the Elsuba Codex, as Karen now thought of those chapters, contained extended passages of such scorching, tactile immediacy, such damn-the-torpedoes exuberance, that when she finished reading them she was both exhausted and envious. If the real affair had been half as intense as Allen's evocation of it, no wonder he'd enshrined that young woman in his memory. Could *any* subsequent lover take the place of the mythically radiant Elsuba?

Karen Hambly was wise enough to know how absurd, how futile, and how potentially destructive it was to be jealous of a rival who was forever frozen in twenty-year-old amber; who could not possibly still be so devastatingly beautiful as she had been at eighteen—if, indeed, she ever *had* been.

But if Karen knew these things, why had her stomach knotted at the mere sight of Elsuba's name in a letter?

She'd never confessed to Allen that she had read his would-be masterpiece. Maybe she never would. But if her subterfuge was driven by the need to gain insight into her companion's sometimes baffling ambiguities, well, "be careful what you wish for," because she'd gleaned more insight than she had been able, so far, to digest.

Allen's early-middle-aged persona, it seemed to Karen, had been shaped primarily by a triumvirate of signal failures: of his military career, of his marriage, and of his attempt to write the Great American Novel. Small wonder he had mythologized Poulsen's daughter: in Allen's memory, she was Helen of Troy and Alma Mahler combined into one soul, then packaged as a dynamite Scandinavian blonde who had dropped into his life in the middle of the grandest landscape he'd ever seen. After experiencing such splendor, it was no wonder that he came to believe himself a man of Destiny, smiled upon by fortune and surely destined for Greatness in all subsequent endeavors. That he had been compelled to settle for *adequacy*, on the faculty of a mediocre state college, might not have been the worst alternative fate, but it was more than enough to account for his moodiness and his acerbic sense of irony.

Karen's uncomfortable reverie was broken by the ringing phone. It was Allen, wearily informing her that the "routine" faculty conference scheduled for three-thirty had proven to be anything but, and he'd be home late and would she like Chinese takeout?

"What's the big deal?" asked Karen, somehow disturbed by how shaky his voice sounded.

"Apparently, sweetheart, *we* are. Actually it's just me, but the Lynch War-rener faction's dragged you into the muck with me. You'd be amazed at how grotesque some of the rumors are about what we did—and with whom—at the Playboy bash. The words 'statutory rape' were thrown about, until the Dean confirmed that Miss Hambly is, in fact, a legal adult and if these rumors about her alleged depravity didn't cease, she could hit the school with one hell of a lawsuit, for defamation of character and . . . well, a whole raft of feminist-type things. Unfortunately, there's still a regulation forbidding teachers from 'cohabiting' with students—"

"We do *not* 'cohabit,' and half the teachers at this school are screwing one or more of their students on any given day of the week!"

"I know—it's ludicrous. But whoever's behind this smear campaign has a lot of ammunition, and they've managed to convince even some of the more sym-pathetic of my colleagues that I just might be a corrupting influence on my stu-dents, or a closet Communist, or God knows what. Damn it, Karen, they bushwhacked me! I walked into that meeting thinking it would be just another boring routine gabfest, and all of a sudden I'm being grilled by Torquemada and the Ten Inquisitors! For the past two hours, I've been defending myself with a tapdance and a lot of chutzpah—but the arguments finally became so nasty and personal that the chairman called for a fifteen-minute break just so we could all cool our jets. Christ only knows when I'll get home tonight."

"Dear God, Allen, this is so unfair! Just hang tough! Whoever these pigs are, there's nothing they can do except harass you."

"Actually, that's not strictly true, Karen. My contract comes up for renewal in October, and I'm way overdue for tenure. I don't want to spend the rest of my career teaching Civics classes in some high school in Bum-Fuck, Alabama. Shit, they're waving at me to hang up. Just find a good book and try to lose yourself in it."

"Oh, I have found a very engrossing book, Allen. Can't wait to see how the story turns out."

Typically, he didn't ask for the title; just made a perfunctory kiss-kiss noise and hung up.

Anxious as well as moody now, Karen switched from coffee to vodka. If the anti-Warrener cabal was determined enough to bring up something as silly and irrelevant as their three-day vacation at the Playboy Mansion, they must really be out for Allen's scalp. And the whole zany escapade had been such a serendipitous lark!

Among his many other eccentric interests, it turned out that Hugh Hefner was *also* a dedicated member of the Cryptozoology Society; he'd even published a few articles in the organization's bi-monthly journal, under a pseudonym. And he'd been very impressed with Allen's well-researched essay on the legends of the Jersey Devil—so impressed that he'd phoned Allen in person and offered him a more-than-generous fee to write a three-part series about the "Ten Most Famous Monsters of Modern Times." Allen had enjoyed the gig, and the fat paycheck, enormously. The readers of *Playboy* apparently liked the series, too, which in turn made Mr. Hefner both richer and happier. Four months after the final article was published, Allen was flabbergasted when he received an engraved invitation ("for yourself and one special companion") to attend Hefner's legendary three-day-long New Year's Eve party.

Karen had been initially skeptical, but once they arrived, she found the whole surreal scene "utterly groovy." For three days, an obscure history professor from a cow college in North Carolina, together with his not-quite-but-almost-beautiful young companion, hobnobbed with the Rich and Glamorous. They'd even been accorded the signal honor of a private luncheon with Hefner himself, who turned out to be genuinely charming, surprisingly well read, and remarkably gracious. And Allen had enjoyed a nice private epiphany when he discovered, during their first dip in the heated Olympic-size swimming pool, that Karen Hambly, while not quite center-fold material, definitely looked terrific in a bikini.

They hadn't taken part in the numerous orgies, but in masquerade they'd been royally entertained by watching a room full of celebrity tits-and-asses combining and recombining in many permutations. It had all been great, goofy, harmless fun, and certainly nothing to be ashamed of. But somehow, Allen's professional enemies had inflated and distorted the episode into a moral catastrophe roughly comparable to the Sack of Byzantium. Whoever the ringleaders of this Lynch Warrener cabal might be, it was none of their goddamned business what two consenting adults did off-campus and on their own free time!

After a couple of drinks, Karen fired up a joint and wandered from room to room, until she burned her fingers on the yellow stub. The more she replayed Allen's phone call in her head, the more aware she became of just how anxious—even fearful—his voice had sounded. And that realization, coupled with the kick of smoking an entire joint on top of two—or was it three?—stiff vodkas, all on an empty stomach, flipped Karen into her own spasm of paranoia. She did some deep-breathing exercises, then drifted into Allen's study to stare at the Faeroe Islands mural. That, at least, always had a dependably calming effect on her.

But not this night. She remembered the startling lurch she'd felt in her stomach when she'd read Elsuba Poulsen's name in her father's letter. Well, here Karen was, overly stoned and anxious on several fronts, staring at a giant picture of Miss Poulsen's homeland, and whether from a desire to affect a homeopathic improvement in her mood, or a nasty sudden attack of masochism, Karen did something unprecedented: she started searching Allen's floor to ceiling bookcases for the album containing his collection of Elsuba photos. It didn't take long—Karen zoomed in on the right bookshelf like a water witch following her magic willow wand. In all the time she'd been Allen's lover, he'd never displayed a picture of the real Elsuba, and of course Karen had never asked to see one. She thought she didn't need to; she'd read The Book.

But now she opened an old, frayed album and confronted the reality behind the myth, and understood instantly that she'd made one hell of a mistake. All the fictionally wrought elements were there, all right: the mass of gold-and-bronze hair, those mysterious, riveting, unforgettable violet-and-gray eyes, that lush and oh-so-kissable mouth, those gravity-defying breasts. . . . If the literary construct had been powerful, the whole *gestalt*-y eighteen-year-old package was one devastatingly gorgeous young woman. Feeling plain as a dead twig, her cheeks flushed and her eyes welling hotly, Karen glared at the blurry old snapshots and heard herself snarl:

"Don't you fucking *dare* come to Vardinoy! Because if Allen thinks you're going to be there, he won't ask me to go with him, and *my island's* up there too! Neither of you has any right to keep me from finding it! So stay in

Copenhagen, you Nordic jerk-off fantasy, and give this poor-white-trash country girl her chance!" Then her voice dropped to a whisper: "If you were here, Elsuba, I would beg you . . . you and Allen had your Garden of Eden time together; let that be enough! Please, please, don't come to Vardinoy. . . ."

Karen was right on the edge of an uncontrollable crying jag when she heard Allen's car pull into the driveway. She jammed the Elsuba album back in its place, rinsed the tears from her face, did an emergency makeup application, and was reasonably composed when she heard the front door open and Allen's hoarse, weary voice calling out: "Sanctuary, for the love of God!"

Grateful for Karen's absolving hug and for the stiff drink she thrust into his hand, Allen dropped his briefcase and sank into the nearest chair, mumbling something about how he'd just lived through a Franz Kafka story.

"Did you ever get to the bottom of this crazy witch-hunt?"

"In a manner of speaking. . . . Do you know anything about Dr. Chadwick Merritt?"

"Heard the name, that's all. Some big shot in the Science Department, isn't he?"

"Head of the Biology Department, actually. Stuffy, pedantic little man. I doubt we've ever exchanged more than ten words. But it turns out that he's the guy behind this vendetta, and he's apparently willing to go to insane lengths to squeeze a public apology out of me."

"Apology? But you just said you hardly know the man!"

"Yeah . . . it's all very bizarre, but Merritt seems to think I've publicly impugned his 'professional integrity and reputation,' or words to that effect. Near as I could make out, this is how it went down: it seems that Dr. Merritt's hobby is the exact opposite of mine. I want to prove 'monsters' exist, and Merritt's made a fearsome reputation out of debunking UFO-cranks, charlatans who pretend they can melt spoons with telepathic force-fields, and 'monster-mongers,' to use Merritt's preferred term.

"It was all totally coincidental, but it just so happened that, five or six months before Hefner published the first of my articles, ol' Chadwick won a prize for an essay he'd written, for something called the *Journal of Scientific Skepticism*, utterly demolishing those alleged movies of Bigfoot."

"Jesus, Allen, you suspected those were faked, too! What's his problem?"

"His problem was that portion of my first article where I went into one of my typical screeds against narrow-minded academic drones whose brains slam shut the minute they get tenured—you've heard me rant about that dozens of times. Well, despite the fact that I didn't mention anyone by name, the timing of publication made some of Merritt's colleagues think I was unloading on his Bigfoot exposé; and, for whatever personal reasons, it chapped his ass to the point where he wants my head on a platter or some kind of groveling public apology. And the crazy thing about it is that Chadwick Merritt has the power to twist this whole college by the balls if he doesn't get his way—that's why so many of my formerly indifferent colleagues suddenly turned on me."

"I don't understand. This guy's just a biology professor."

"No, my dear, he's a biology professor who happens to be married to the daughter of the President of the Alumni Association, a deranged old coot whose politics are somewhere to the right of Attila the Hun's and who positively loathes liberal young professors. Here's the scenario: if Chadwick Merritt doesn't get satisfaction, he convinces his wife that Allen Warrener is the academic equivalent of the Anti-Christ; then wifey-poo goes to her father and tells Dad-ums that this depraved, child-molesting atheistic Warrener guy has started forcing all his students to read *Das Kapital,* lecturing them on the virtues of free love, and passing out dope in the lecture hall! The Chancellor gets a phone call from Dad-ums, demanding that this Warrener character be sacked immediately and threatening to cut off all donations from the Alumni Fund until he's run out of town in disgrace. For a colorless little dweeb, Chadwick Merritt has the murderous political instincts of a Borgia prince angling for the Papacy! The whole convoluted mess would boil down to this: either Allen Warrener gets the axe or the College suddenly loses one of its primary sources of income. Do you think the administration would hesitate for ten seconds before throwing me to the wolves?"

"Oh my God, Allen, what're you going to do?"

"Something about as pleasant as eating ground glass; something dishonest, dishonorable, and borderline contemptible—I'm going to save my ass by giving the little fuck-weasel what he wants: a public apology and a triumphant vindication. And so much for *my* fucking integrity."

Karen grasped his hand; she could feel the bitterness coursing through his very flesh.

"How will you handle it?"

"I thrashed out the plan with some people who know perfectly well I've been set up and who want to make the cup of hemlock as small as possible. I set up an interview with the editor of the campus paper, ostensibly so I can announce the formation of an expedition to the island of Vardinoy, but that's just the McGuffin. In the course of that interview, I make a big point of praising Dr. Merritt's Bigfoot exposé, lauding his intellectual acumen, just lay it on with a shovel. If I can manage to do that without puking—it has to sound ever-so-sincere, you see—then Professor Merritt's sense of umbrage will fade as quickly as it appeared, and. . . ."

"And what? Come on, Allen, let me hear the rest of it!"

"And I *will* be offered tenure next October. Oh, sure, all my colleagues will know I sold out, but at least I won't have to spend the rest of my life teaching at Podunk Agricultural College. So tomorrow morning, I call the editor—Sugarbowl, or something like that—and invite the kid over for dinner and drinks and give the interview."

Karen tried gamely to cheer him up. "Like you said, Allen, it's a small cup of hemlock. Two or three years, nobody will even remember this farce. Your students will still think the world of you, and I'll still be warming your bed— if you'll have me. And besides, I know Dick Sugarman. He's a fan of yours. He wrote a sharp, funny little piece about the Playboy Monsters. Said it should serve as an example for other faculty members, about the joys and rewards of publishing outside the academic-press ghetto. I think he said: 'At least Prof. Warrener's piece will be read by a wider audience than the usual two dozen colleagues, sycophants, and brown-nosers.' "

"Wow, that really helps my case. . . ."

Richard Sugarman arrived punctually, bearing a bottle of classy wine and some flowers for Karen, whom he at least had the good sense not refer to as "Mrs. Warrener."

"Richard, in order to avoid any misunderstandings, let's you and I decide how we're going to handle this interview before we even pop the wine cork. I suspect you're aware that there's a pretty bizarre subtext to this whole thing. . . ."

"You set the ground rules, sir; whatever makes you comfortable. Or, um, less uncomfortable. My cards are on the table: I tape-record everything on these two identical machines, and I give you a copy when I leave. That way, you're guaranteed accurate quotes. But the editorial slant and the interpretive stuff, that's my responsibility, and unless you think I've written something outrageously wrong or downright libelous, you have no grounds for complaint after the piece goes into print. Agreed?"

"Sounds fair to me. I'm not especially thin-skinned, you know."

Karen pretended to have a coughing fit.

The tape recorders were primed, and Karen was discreetly keeping the wine glasses topped off. Sugarman took out his notebook; Allen made an expansive gesture that could have meant anything or nothing.

"I hope you've got a killer leadoff question, because that usually warms me up faster than when somebody eases into the controversial stuff."

"I know—I mean, I know that's how you like to operate, sir. I've studied up on you, just as I would if I were assigned to write a feature about, oh, new frontiers in organic fertilizers."

"I am immensely flattered by the comparison. Take your best shot, Sunny Jim."

"Okay, then, how about this: if I read your *Playboy* essays correctly, you seem to be contending that 'monsters' play a necessary and surprisingly important role in the subconscious life of modern urban civilization. Please expand on that theme and then tell us how the so called 'Vardinoy Monster' fits into your thesis."

Warrener gulped and forced a thin smile of appreciation.

"You really don't fuck around, do you, Richard?"

"No, sir, not if I can help it."

"I'm going into the bedroom and become heavily medicated," sighed Karen, rolling her eyes.

For a journalist who'd only had a day and a half to prepare, Sugarman had force-fed himself enough essential monster lore to keep the dialogue pumping until 1:15 A.M. The editor and his subject traded volleys and witticisms with increasing zest as their initial wariness faded and something akin to comradeship percolated into the atmosphere.

Yes, Allen confided—with a degree of enthusiasm that surprised Karen, who had not heard him *make* the commitment yet—he *was* going to "lead" an expedition to the far-off island of Vardinoy, probably starting in late June, and it would be no amateur hike-in-the-woods, but a serious venture, equipped with all the latest technology, and documented by a veteran film-maker, Mr. Preston Valentine.

"No shit!" said Sugarman, momentarily losing his cool. "God, I adore his *Hammerhead* movies! Any chance he might be persuaded to make a new one?"

"Not for all the pot in Mexico. That's a part of his life he doesn't even talk about now—I pass that along in case you ever meet him. But he's a master cameraman, and he's committed to making a spectacular documentary about the quest."

"Okay with you if I use the 'quest' theme as the main hook in this piece? I mean, unless you think it sounds too pretentious?"

"Hell, yes, just so long as you avoid using four words: 'Holy Grail' and 'Don Quixote'!"

They were both pretty crocked by the time the last tape was full, and the mood was downright cordial. Sugarman said he'd gotten plenty of good material and he was inclined to portray Warrener and his cohorts as anachronistic idealists instead of over-the-hill eccentrics, trying to redeem their screwed-up lives by making one last lunge for fame and glory. Allen did notice that, during the last fifteen minutes of the interview, Karen kept making cryptic gestures and mouthing silent prompts, but he was on too much of a roll to be distracted. At the door, Sugarman thanked them profusely for their hospitality and Allen for his frankness.

"I swear I'll do justice to you, Allen! I know we were both set up for this, but nobody tells me what to write."

"I'm sure you'll do an honest job, Richard, and that's all I could ask for."

"Oh, one more question—a very, very urgent one."

"Yeah, okay, shoot—"

"Can I go, too?"

"You're serious, aren't you?"

"Why not? You've got an expert photographer, so why not have a hardworking journalist to write the commentary?"

"Let me think about it when I'm sober and get back to you."

After the editor drove away, Karen snapped off the porch light and grabbed Allen by the shoulders.

"What? What?" he protested. "Was my fly open or something?"

"Didn't you see those signals I was frantically trying to give you?"

"Yes, but I thought you were just telling me to wrap it up because you couldn't wait to jump my bones."

She shook her head, bemused but also a little pissed off. "No, Allen, that's not what I was signaling."

"I'm not telepathic, sweetheart. Spell it out for me, would you?"

"All right, Allen, I will. Here's something else for you to think about when you sober up: you went through that whole rap session, which was set up so you could make amends to Dr. Merritt in a non-humiliating, indirect, yet appropriately excessive manner. Your colleagues helped to set this up, all right, but they set it up to get you off the hook without having to eat a peck of shit in public."

"Yeah, sure, I know that. Pretty decent of them, considering how many of them dislike me. What's your point?"

"My point, you self-destructive asshole, is that not one time during the whole interview did you even *mention Dr. Chadwick Merritt and his Big Foot article!*"

"Christ on a pogo stick! I'm roadkill for sure. Bye-bye, tenure!"

"The next time I start 'frantically signaling' you in pantomime, maybe you'll pay some fucking attention! Now take this sleeping pill and come to bed—otherwise you'll stay up all night pissing and moaning about the Unfairness of Life and I don't want to hear it."

14.

The Scientific Establishment Refutes Heresy

Allen Warrener had not inhaled a cigarette for five years, but no matter how stoically he prepared for it in advance, he always had to struggle not to ask Karen for a drag when she reverted to post-coital habit and took that first delicious, almost smug, puff after they had successfully made love. He could almost feel the rippling pleasure of that nicotine hit as she reached behind the guttering candle and balanced an ashtray on the downy slope of her belly. Even the way she smoked could be sexy as hell.

"God, Allen, you were copious tonight."

"Yes, ma'am. That's just one of the wonderful effects you have on me. And by the way, how many times did *you* come tonight?"

"A true gentleman doesn't keep score."

"A true gentleman always wants to *improve* the score."

"That's the spirit! Oh, I guess eight or nine—the last two kind of blurred together. Nice effect, I must say. Have you been practicing behind my back?"

"No; I'm just learning how to listen to your body more attentively."

Karen stubbed out her cigarette, then snuggled against his shaggy chest, idly toying with one of his nipples. "You are an attentive lover, Allen. Our bodies just sort of *fit* together so well—you know, 'insert Tab A into Slot B....' "

" 'Slot B' is one of my favorites."

"This is turning into a Woody Allen dialogue. I mean, you really seem to get off on my multiples."

"Don't all guys?"

"No. Some don't care if a girl gets off or not. It's Neanderthals like them who generate legions of lesbians. I wish I could make you come six or seven times...."

"Jesus, so do I. But once is just fine, when it feels like Vesuvius erupting."

"Just wait a few weeks, mister. I'm working up to Krakatoa. Better buy some rubber sheets."

"Speaking of rubber sheets, I've got to pee like the proverbial racehorse."

"By all means do, but this time remember to put down the seat after you finish!"

Just before he closed the bathroom door, he said: "Sylvia used to make that same request . . . only she made it sound like a direct order from the Führer."

I'll bet she made the grocery list sound like that too. Karen plumped up the pillows and pulled on her nightgown. Normally, Allen would come back, bladder empty and every muscle purring with relaxation, then murmur a few endearments before sinking into a most voluptuous sleep. Karen had never made a big thing about post-coital conversations; she thought the sex manuals were full of crap for emphasizing how important those intimate dialogues were to a healthy relationship. No normal adult male could possibly sustain an interesting conversation after good sex—not voluntarily, anyhow, for longer than 6.5 minutes; trying to force them to exceed that limit was a waste of time. Poor things couldn't help it: the pattern was hard-wired into their endorphin mechanism. After-sex conversations, she believed, should be tender and intimate, of course, but they should also be brief. If a guy works hard enough to give you eight orgasms in approximately sixty-eight minutes before indulging in *one* for himself, he'd earned the right to conk out.

But not tonight.

She cut on the bedside lamp and tucked the new edition of the campus newspaper under her pillow. He must have had a hugely satisfying pee, because he was humming the "Peasant's Dance" from Beethoven's *Pastoral* Symphony—always a good sign. She hated to ruin his mood, but she had no choice. To withhold her advance knowledge would be dishonest, and would do nothing to lessen his shock when the student newspapers were distributed tomorrow at noon.

When he exited the bathroom, still humming, she patted the bed, and when he stretched out beside her, she melted into a hug that clung like Spandex.

"Uh-oh, something's amiss; I can feel the tension all the way down your back."

"Here. Read this. I heard a thud on the front porch while you were taking your shower, and when I opened the door I found the paper lying under the mailbox. It was literally warm from the press."

He unfolded the tabloid and knew right away that he'd been bush-whacked. If the garish sea-serpent cartoon wasn't enough, the big *National Inquirer*–style headline surely clinched it:

HISTORY PROF INHERITS CAP'N AHAB'S HARPOON!!

"What the fuck?"

"Deep breath, Allen. They really did a number on you."

" *'You can swim, but you can't hide!' warned Prof. Allen Warrener, addressing the legendary but never-photographed Vardinoy Monster. . . .*"

You had to hand it to Dick Sugarman. He not only knew how to conduct ambush–interviews, he was brilliant at selecting actual quotes, then arranging them out of context so that they flowed naturally, even as they grossly distorted the intent of the speaker. This was a hatchet job performed with a laser scalpel. Without misquoting a single phrase, the editor had done a cut-and-paste job that made Warrener sound not unlike a UFO zealot, preparing to lead his lobotomized flock into the desert to welcome the Mother Ship. Stripped of the dignity of context, the very notion of an expedition to Vardinoy sounded silly, vain, and self-indulgent. No hint survived of its serious intent, its high adventure, its possibility of risk.

Most of the quotes were extracted from the last forty-five minutes of the interview, when both participants had been drinking and Allen had long since let down his guard and begun to wax messianic about the monster legends, about his mysteriously motivated tycoon friend Poulsen, and about Preston Valentine's genius with a camera. (A helpful sidebar reminded students and colleagues of Preston's palmy days as a porn director; the man's mere resume had been made to seem prurient!) Any reader not personally acquainted with the principal characters would have little choice but to conclude that the whole notion of a "Vardinoy Expedition" was less nobly quixotic than it was just plain goofy—a madcap excursion by a boatful of Victorian eccentrics, complete with wicker baskets, frilly parasols to ward off the beastly sun, magnums of chilled champagne, and a retinue of turbaned wogs perpetually wielding rattan fans, fly-whisks, and croquet mallets. (*"Will Lord Bumbershoot be joining us for tea, Agatha?" "Alas, no, Sir Dudley—a cheetah made off with his dinner jacket!"*)

Reinforcing this general air of dottiness was the cartoon: a peg-legged

Allen Warrener, posing heroically on the bow of an absurd little rowboat, a Wagner-opera helmet precariously perched on his head, his arms cocked to hurl a rusty harpoon at an idiotic-looking sea serpent with goggle eyes and smoke-lines coming from its nostrils. Above the longhorn helmet was a dialogue balloon:

"A gold doubloon to the mate who spots the white Chimera!"

Karen put a comforting hand on his trembling arm. "They didn't miss a trick, baby. But mark my words, your students are going to love this!"

"My students are not the people who pay my salary or decide whether or not I get tenure at this institution. What hurts the most, really, is that I believed that goddamned puffed-up scribbler when he gave me that spiel about his high journalistic ethics."

"Allen, that's ugly. You don't know what kind of pressure they put on him. You've taken worse hits to your dignity than this one. It's just a political smear in a two-bit college paper. And when the students find out you're Preston's best friend—I mean, to them he's a living legend!"

"You know, just once, *I* would like to be the fucking legend instead of the sidekick who never got his fifteen minutes of fame."

"Save the bitterness until after you've read Chadwick Merritt's sidebar."

"I need a stiff drink before I tackle that one."

"How about sharing a joint?"

"Even better—especially since they've probably got hidden cameras in every corner of this house!"

After she pinched out the roach, she said: "Would you like me to read it to you? Might make the pill go down easier."

"Yes, if you don't mind."

"A-hem: THE 'SCIENTIFIC ESTABLISHMENT' IS NOT AMUSED, by Dr. Chadwick Merritt, Biology Department, blah, blah, blah. It starts:

> According to my atlas, the island of Vardinoy is so far from anything resembling civilization that a creature two hundred feet tall and wearing a Washington Redskins uniform could hide out there undetected for centuries. I should lay my cards on the table here and state that, contrary to Prof. Warrener's paranoid theories, I do not, as a trained scientist, automatically reject the possibility

that exotic, hitherto-unknown species might exist, especially in such out-of-the-way corners of the planet. Indeed, once in a while we come across living fossils, creatures thought to have been extinct for thousands of years. . . .

"Uh-huh," sighed Warrener. "Here comes the good old coelacanth again."

There is, for example, the well-known case of the coelacanth, a large and unusually repellent fish which was thought to be as dead as the dinosaurs until a Portuguese trawler caught a perfectly healthy specimen off the coast of Africa in 1938. Since then, dozens more have been caught.

But in the case of Prof. Warrener's beastie, we are dealing with a fish story of an altogether different kind; one might say, a textbook case of a supposed "monster" which has become a kind of ongoing factoid, without anyone having been able to present the slightest shred of evidence that it exists. Once we separate the references to this creature from the hyperbole and heavy-breathing enthusiasm with which Prof. Warrener surrounds them, we find a rather unimpressive list:

- A handful of ambiguous, rather generic, references embedded in obscure fragments of Norse literature, whose authors seem to have trouble distinguishing the Vardinoy what-cha-ma-call-it from the mythology surrounding Yggdrasill, the so-called Tree of Life whose massive branches support the surface of the world and whose gigantic roots go deep into Niflheim, the Norse version of Hades (one wonders how the writers managed to mix up a sea monster and a giant tree, but never mind; the Scientific Method was unknown to them!);
- A number of allegorical allusions in medieval church records and manuscripts, which are even more obtuse for modern scholars, because they could just as easily be interpreted as glosses on the Book of Revelations;
- The wildly apocalyptic ravings of an Edwardian theosophist (who was also a firm believer in the existence of unicorns, brownies, and trolls);

- A scattering of boogie-man-in-the-closet references in Faeroese folk tales, the sort of fables sadistic parents tell bad children at bedtime;
- And most recently, the distraught ravings of a half-dead Luftwaffe pilot as recounted, forty years later, third-hand, by an obscure British general.

"Shall I keep going, or is that enough?"

"That's enough. I think I can predict the rest of it, including the bit about how amateurs who are not trained in the techniques of scientific inquiry have no business bad-mouthing experts who've devoted their lives to etc., etc."

"That's more or less where he's going, yes, after three or four hundred additional words of sarcasm. And by the way, he thinks the German pilot was hallucinating about a herd of sea-lions,"

"Right. A trained Luftwaffe officer would surely confuse sea-lions with a giant, unknown blob that was gobbling up his crew like canapés. What makes this tirade so ridiculous is—well, do you know what Chadwick Merritt's special field of expertise is? I looked this up!"

"Not a clue."

"Fruit-fly entomology! So help me God! He's had a species named after him!"

Karen blithely tossed the newspaper aside and straddled Allen's lap. "My God, what must it do a man's psyche to realize that his greatest claim to immortality can usually be found buzzing around open garbage cans!"

Maybe it was the pot, or maybe just relief that they'd read most of the whole screed and still found something to laugh about, but they both started giggling, imagining the sharp-nosed Chadwick Merritt sitting smugly in his office, surrounded by display cases filled with microscopically differentiated *drosophilae*.

"Just lie back and finish your drink. I want to make sure you go to sleep with a smile on your face, confident that Chadwick Merritt is going to sleep horny as a toad."

His mood was, in fact, improving by the second, as she began a series of slow but expert manipulations. Her tongue was hot wet velvet.

"Karen?"

"Mmmph? Ca'd dalk wi'd mouf-full, dammit!"

"I guess this crazy expedition is really going down, huh?"

"Gezz zo. . . ."

"I mean, it's public knowledge now. No way to bluff my way out of this thing."

"No way to bluff *that* tent-pole, either. Be inside me, Allen. Quick!"

On the downhill side of forty, it was satisfying enough to reclaim an erection; to climax more than once in the space of an evening was a rare and life-affirming feat. But Karen surprised herself by arching into a quick, sharp climax after rocking back and forth on him for only a moment, and he caught the wave with her—a slow, tender turbulence that surged up from his spine and triggered another string of firecracker aftershocks deep within her. The hot fleshy squeeze of her contractions was exquisite. Usually, when they went at it this hard, Allen's response was to congratulate himself for having found such a skilled and compatible piece of ass, but tonight he stared hard into her luminous brown eyes and finally admitted that *some* credit for this erotic bounty was attributable to the fact that he had fallen in love with this young woman.

Sooner rather than later, Karen was going to turn those bear-rug eyes on him and ask him straight out: *Can I go to Vardinoy too?* He did not think being in love with her was compatible with an honest answer: *Well, that all depends.* Karen was not likely to accept that, and he didn't blame her.

Make up your mind, soldier. If you sail away without this lady, she won't be waiting meekly when you come back.

God, please let this be simple for us. Please make sure Elsuba stays in Copen-hagen. If it became an either/or situation, he might be compelled to act like a monster instead of hunting for one.

15.

WE'RE GETTING OUR ACT TOGETHER
AND TAKING IT TO SEA

Karen still hadn't asked if she could go to Vardinoy; Allen still didn't know if he really wanted her to. They had casually discussed the expedition, but only in the most general terms. Karen had asked some questions about the logistics and "strategy" but they had been the sort of inquiries a disengaged reporter might ask at a press conference. Allen rather hoped the decision would become moot—that she would let him off the hook by announcing she'd landed "a great summer job" (whatever that might be), or a professional opportunity she just couldn't pass up. But she didn't offer any such sacrificial alternatives. Nor could she comprehend his muted response to Eiden's proposal. After all, according to Allen himself, the notion of investigating the Vardinoy Phenomenon had been a pleasant, speculative fantasy for more than twenty years. Now, without much forewarning, Eiden Poulsen had written what amounted to a blank check and said: "Well, it's time to get on with it!" It was incredible—to have an old daydream suddenly start lurching toward realization; Allen should have felt a quickening of excitement, the anticipation of an *adventure*, at least—but instead he felt listless, unmotivated, and, worst of all, completely indecisive.

When he got home from work one day a few weeks later, he was surprised to find Karen enjoying a cigarette and a beer on his living room sofa, looking quietly sensational in what had to be a brand-new cocktail dress, provocatively slit on one side.

"Wow," he said, tossing his briefcase into the hall closet. "Are we having an audience with the Pope?"

"Does premature senility run in your family, or did you really forget that Preston and Norma flew in from Atlanta this afternoon?"

"Jesus H. Christ, I *did* forget! Weren't we supposed to have dinner with them tonight or something?"

"Or something. He asked me the name of the best restaurant within a thirty-mile radius, and he's made reservations for seven o'clock."

Allen looked at his watch. "Oh, shit!"

"Relax. I phoned the hotel and told them we'd be at least an hour late."

"Were they pissed?"

"Preston certainly wasn't; he just chortled and said 'What, only an hour? You must be a good influence on him!' "

When Allen knocked, the door was flung open before he could lower his fist, and Preston leaped forth like a kangaroo, his skinny arms, fluttering like twigs inside the sleeves of a pin-striped Cassini blazer, closing around Allen like vise-clamps.

"Come in, come in, you mad old hermit! And this stunning specimen of jailbait must be Karen, of whom I've heard extraordinary things."

"Not half as extraordinary as I've heard about you, Preston."

Valentine ushered them into a luxuriously appointed suite, poured drinks, and then brought forth a silver cigarette case filled with tightly rolled reefers. Karen whistled appreciatively when she beheld the diameter of the "fatty" Preston placed in her hand. "Usually, when somebody says 'let's smoke a joint,' it means all three of us would be sharing one of these—but Preston just passed out one apiece! I like this man already!"

From the presumed direction of the powder room, Norma's taffy-soft voice chimed in: "So do I, most of the time! Is one of you so-called gentlemen going to bring one of those in here for me, or do I have to smear my makeup by comin' out there to beg for one?" Karen quickly rose to the occasion and handed the lit cylinder through a crack in the bathroom door.

"Why, thank you, honey! You must be Karen, and I guess that makes me Norma. Or maybe Margaret Thatcher, I'm not sure. My Lord, look at you! Allen's been braggin' about you to Preston, telling him how much you'd helped him clean up his act and all, but he didn't tell us what a drop-dead looker you were!" Karen exhaled and turned long enough to shoot a venomous glare in Allen's direction.

"Same old Norma," chided Allen. "Subtle, nuanced conversation . . . gracious manners . . . and how many breast augmentations is it now?"

"Fuck you, Warrener! I've only had one. How many dick enlargements have *you* had?"

"None, sugar-tits—they had to trim three inches off mine 'cause I was hurtin' too many gorgeous co-eds with it!"

"You'll pay for that line when we get home, buster!" snickered Karen. Norma had evidently finished donning her warpaint, for she and Karen now emerged arm in arm, good pals already.

"Karen, sugar, do you like to dance?"

"Yes, ma'am, I do."

"And how often does the good professor take you out to dance?"

Allen felt his cheeks reddening. "Not once, I do confess it. I'm about as graceful on the dance floor as a gimpy octopus."

"In that case, why don't Karen and I go down to that tacky little disco on the mezzanine floor, while you two boys go over your lists of sampling toys and such, and see if we can't make all the early drinkers howl like horny tom-cats? You game for some sport, honey?"

Giddy with pot and obviously dazzled by Norma's Tiger-Tank sexuality, Karen agreed.

"Okay with you, Allen? It's been a long time since I shook my booty in public. . . ."

"I shall alert the media. By all means, go—have a ball. If you two are gone when Preston and I come looking for you, do we tell the cops to watch for a Rolls Royce, or a pickup truck with fuzzy dice hanging from the mirror?"

"Depends on who makes us the best offer," smirked Norma, blowing a kiss at both of "the boys" before steering Karen into the hall.

"My God," said Allen, "those two are loaded for bear. . . ."

"Norma's just loaded, period. But she holds it mighty well for an old broad."

"She's still a knockout, Press." Allen pinched out the stub of his reefer and took off his jacket, while Preston refilled their drinks. They took seats around the stack of notebooks and colored pens.

"Allen, man, I gotta thank you for giving me a chance to do this gig. It's absolutely the right project at the right time. I've been a recluse for more than two years, and Norma's spent so much time painting flowers and cottages-in-the-sunset that she's become convinced she's actually a serious artist! We needed to recharge our batteries, that's true, but I miss having a camera on my shoulder the way an amputee misses a limb."

"Well, I showed Eiden some of the landscape shots you took after you guys moved into the mountains, and he just nodded and said 'This man should most certainly be our official photographer. Have him work up an estimate for whatever he needs in the way of film and equipment. Tell him not to cut corners—good stuff isn't cheap and cheap stuff isn't good.'"

"Do you know how long I've waited to hear a producer say those words? But one thing still puzzles me, Allen; why did Poulsen get so cranked up about this expedition thing right now? I mean, you two have been fantasizing about it for years; now all of a sudden it's full speed ahead. You gotta admit, that's kind of peculiar. . . ."

"I sent you a copy of his letter—about finding the old sailor who was present when that German flier was fished out of the sea off Vardinoy."

"Yeah, that's an interesting development, but Eiden doesn't really tell you what it was about the old guy's story that tripped his trigger and caused him to start firing off checks for tens of thousands of dollars! Don't you get the feeling that Poulsen either knows or suspects something that he hasn't shared with you yet?"

"That thought had crossed my mind, but I'm not concerned about it. If there's one man in the whole of the Faeroese archipelago I would trust with my life, it's Eiden Poulsen."

"That's good enough for me. What about your *personal* conundrum?"

"Which one? I have so many. . . ."

"You know damn well which one. Are you going to bring Karen along, or are you going to mount one more desperate assault on reality and see if you can rekindle the flames with your Nordic goddess?"

"I'm fervently hoping the issue won't come up; that Elsuba will stay in Copenhagen."

"You know, from what you've told me—and from the twenty minutes I've actually spent in her company—I think Karen could handle it if Elsuba came along."

"I just don't want to drag Karen all the way to the ends of the Earth and suddenly feel irresistibly compelled to break her heart. I know myself too well, Press. It could happen. I wouldn't be able to help myself."

"In that vase, compadre, you are faced with what is technically known as A Decision. You know, that's what good generals have to come up with all the time, and you once had your heart set on being just that. Why don't you accept the fact that, sooner or later, you're going to have to decide what the middle-aged Allen Warrener's priorities really are—do you want to cling to those oldie-goldie memories for the rest of your life, or do you want to grow old with a chick like Karen warming your bed on a cold night? My point is that coming to terms with the flesh-and-blood Elsuba may not turn out to be as traumatic as you're expecting it to be—you *just don't know,* not before it happens. But you do know—or you damned well should—that if you just park Karen here for the summer and sail off on your private adventure, there's a really good chance she won't be here when you get back."

Preston realized he was edging into a sermon and saw that Allen's eyes were beginning to glaze over with impatience.

"Okay, okay," Preston held up his hands. "I'll keep my advice to myself. Now, let's take a look at some of these damn lists and shipping schedules."

They spent an hour going over paperwork and discussing Preston's professional needs in detail; the time passed quickly. Then Preston suddenly remembered the ladies.

"Oh, my God, look at the time! Will they ever be pissed at us!"

"They," however, were cavorting on the dance floor, without any male partners, but with plenty of lounge lizards ogling them and demonstratively showing their appreciation for the entertainment. Indeed, the two women were having so much fun that only the prompting of their pot-sharpened appetites caused them to end the frolic and partner off with their respective dates—who were loudly hissed and booed when they escorted the women from the disco room.

Dinner set Preston back two hundred dollars, and it was definitely not Alpo. They stayed in the restaurant until midnight, at which time they adopted Preston's suggestion that they all meet the next night at the Pickwick, Allen's favorite watering hole and a place Preston knew well from previous visits. Before Norma got into their rented Mercedes, she gave Karen a huggy-bear and warbled: "Allen, you lucky dog, you better take good care of this girl, or I'll stomp on you with my high-heeled boots!"

Once inside their own more modest vehicle, Karen clamped Allen's thigh and scorched his ear with her tongue.

"My place or yours, big boy?"

"Who's got to get up earlier in the morning?"

"I do. Eight o'clock class, remember?"

"How uncivilized! I vote for your place. It smells sexier."

"It smells cleaner, at any rate."

Karen was feeling unusually frisky—Norma's company could bring that out in men, women, and, for all Allen knew, a variety of animals. Once inside her apartment, she placed a drink in his hands, then danced prettily into her bedroom, saying "Don't go anywhere!"

"Wasn't planning to, lady fair."

Five minutes later, she came back out, smelling faintly of perfume and toothpaste, wearing slinky, easily shed underwear, including his favorite black bra and a set of elastic-topped stockings that would turn Gandhi into a leg fetishist.

But Allen missed her grand entrance, for he was still standing next to the stove, staring moodily into his drink. She came up behind him, wrapped her arms around him, and wantonly rubbed his back with the hard tips of her small, high breasts. He made appreciative sounds, but continued to gaze rather morosely at the floor.

"Hey, mister, pay attention to these!"

With startling force, she grasped his shoulder and spun him around. He finally looked at her, but his eyes showed minimal interest as yet—he'd been off somewhere, anticipating the future's mysteries or rummaging through the museum of his memories. Anger flared in Karen's eyes as she yanked the drink from his hands and tossed it, glass and contents, into the kitchen trashcan. Pulling his face to hers, she stripped off his shirt, heedless of popping buttons, and stabbed him with the sharpest, most insistent kiss she'd ever given him.

That did the trick, all right. He cupped her breasts greedily, thumbing and then pinching her swollen nipples; the deep, ululating moan this summoned from her throat inflamed him so intensely that they made it right there on the shag carpet, greedy for each other as two teenagers in the back seat of Daddy's car.

They'd put together some wild combinations; it was possible they'd rubbed a bald spot on the carpet. Afterward, they lay half-dazed until Karen noticed the oven clock hovering close to 3:00 A.M.

"Come on, stud; let's crawl into the real bed. We sleep naked out here on the rug, we're both going to feel really, really itchy in the morning."

"You have my permission to cut your eight o'clock class. I'll write you a note. . . ."

No question about it: bed was the place to be, and the clean sheets might as well have been costly silk, so luxurious was their welcome. Allen conked out almost instantly, but she'd expected that and he had certainly earned a good sleep tonight. Just as his breathing took on the sonority of profound slumber, she bent close to his ear and whispered: "Nine times. I was counting."

His only response—instinctively a perfect one—was a sweet little grin, just before his first rather quiet snore.

For Karen, there yet remained the ritual of the Final Cigarette, which she located by the light of a three-way bulb on its 40-watt setting. Just enough light, as it happened, to study her lover's face while she smoked.

They had been mighty hot for each other tonight. Chalk it up to "chemistry" or a ritzy dinner with good companions, whatever: they had steamed up the windows. Eighteen months, they had been together; in the beginning, Karen had thought they'd be lucky if it lasted three. He was not the coziest partner she could have chosen; nor was she the youngest, sexiest student he could be shacking up with. In all that time, she had studied the planes and proportions of his face many times, under just such post-coital conditions, and each time she thought she saw something new or glimpsed something that had been elusive before.

Too often, she sensed a twist of old, dark pain still inside him, and she'd learned enough about his life by now to know that there could be many possible causes. Was it from loss, or from resignation? Whatever the origin, it had symptoms she'd come to know all too well. What she hadn't figured out was why he was so unwilling to disengage from those discontents; it was almost as though he felt compelled to visit periodically a state of penitence so familiar that it had ceased to be a conscious burden. Karen thought that maybe part of him had just been *plugged in* too long; something was always slightly out of phase. His career, until he settled into the agreeable rut of the classroom, had been nothing special, a disappointment, really, after a precocious adolescence that had promised much. Sometimes, when Karen studied his face, she thought about an old boxer who only had one style throughout the whole arch of his career: even when he went up against younger, stronger opponents, he waded in throwing haymakers, and perhaps he still drew a crowd because of the picturesque way he got beaten up. He'd get off the canvas after every bloody-mouthed, head-cracking defeat, not wiser, not more sophisticated in his tactics, but determined to go into the next bout and throw longer, wilder, harder haymakers. *Yeah, I get the shit beat out of me a lot,* he might say to the sportswriters, *but one of these nights, I'm gonna* connect!

And grew old, wondering why he never did.

Aware of how close she was to nodding off, Karen rolled over and tried to make a spoon with Allen's backside. In doing so, she awakened him just enough to elicit a somnolent stroke of his hand on her hip, which she found very nice. But when he started muttering actual words, what few she was able to hear didn't sound so nice. He wasn't faking it: the man was ninety percent asleep; but it was entirely possible that his subconscious was talking-to-her-without-talking-to-her—so his conscious persona could wake up guiltless.

"Really like . . . take . . . Vardinoy . . . sweet Karen. . . ."

"I didn't quite catch all of that."

She waited for repetition, or a clarification, but when he said nothing further, she quietly prompted:

"Was that a 'yes,' or a 'no,' or a 'maybe'?"

His snoring grew louder and deeper in timbre. She listened intently for any words masked by his breathing, but hard none.

"You prick!" she whispered, pulling the sheet over both of them.

The next night, when Norma and Preston arrived at the Pickwick, they found Allen already half-drunk, with four tall empties stacked up in front of him and Karen on the other side of the booth, chain-smoking and doodling in the beer-rings with a wooden toothpick. "Not a good sign, when he starts pyramiding the beer cans like that," muttered Preston. Karen snapped out of her funk long enough to hug the newcomers, and then lapsed back into it; she could be a world-class sulk when she felt like it.

"Wow, Allen," said Norma, gesturing at the bar and hoping to spark some conversation, "this place really is a dive."

"Now, it may look somewhat decrepit, but I can assure you, the restrooms are absolutely vile."

Norma flagged down a waitress and ordered two pitchers for the booth.

For whatever symbolic reasons, the mood brightened a little when the waitress scooped up Allen's pyramid.

"Hey, I was planning to reach the ceiling with those!"

The waitress ignored him, much to Karen's visible relief. Norma redoubled her attempt to sound perky.

"Hey, Allen, Press tells me you got a telegram this morning from Mister Poulsen."

"Yep; first time I've ever had one delivered to my door. I was terrified for a moment that I was about to learn I'd been killed in action."

Only Preston managed a half-hearted chortle at this brittle witticism.

"Just a few last-minute logistical details. Everything's pretty much set to roll, at least on his end. We've set June 10 for the day we rendezvous in Torshavn. That'll give me time to grade the last exams, take care of some personal stuff, you know . . ."

Since Allen was apparently not going to do it, Preston poured a mug of beer for Karen, who accepted it from him with a nod and a brief resentful glance at Warrener, which was, of course, noticed by everyone.

Gamely, Norma kept plugging away: "So, uh, tell me some more about this Poulsen guy."

"Self-made millionaire; decorated war hero; designed the first modern diesel trawlers for the Faeroese fishing fleet; builds ships for clients in fourteen nations; import–export businesses of all kinds; owns a TV station—and is planning to build a chain of 'em in places like Greenland and Spitzbergen—the Esquimaux will be very grateful. And beneath all that, he's a generous, smart, kind-hearted old sea-dog."

"Allen, that's a jacket blurb, not a description of a real, live friend," said Karen.

"Like it? It's from my *new* novel." His testy answer was met with a tight-mouthed sulk and the extraction of yet another cigarette, only to discover that her butane lighter was out of fuel. Ignoring Preston's swiftly proffered lighter, she tugged an ancient-looking pack of book matches from her purse. But her hands were shaking and she dropped the striking side into a beer puddle.

"God *damn* it!"

Even Preston stopped trying to jolly the other two out of their mood. "Okay, okay, will somebody please tell us why you guys are so scratchy?"

Warrener attempted to throw up a not-too-plausible smokescreen: "Sorry, Press. Guess I'm still kind of paranoid about that newspaper smear."

Karen suddenly spoke up rather too loudly: "Allen, are you going to let me read that fucking telegram or not?"

"Later, baby, I didn't bring it with me."

Without missing a beat, she lunged over the table and jerked a folded yellow document from his shirt pocket.

"You lying bastard. I hope the goddamned monster *eats you!*"

"Well, I've never dabbled in bestiality before, but who knows? Like Norman Mailer used to say, 'Once a philosopher, twice a pervert'!"

Karen stood up and glared at him. "It was *Voltaire*, not Mailer! Thank God you don't teach philosophy!" She snatched up her purse and strode out of the bar.

"Naughty, naughty, Allen," chided Norma. "I'll go out and talk to her, but it would help if you told me why she's so upset."

"Ask her yourself. And then stand back before she spits venom at your eyeballs."

"Have it your way, but if I coax her back inside with a smile on her face, you owe me big time."

"Well," sighed Preston, "I hope the rest of the evening turns out to be somber and depressing, because all of this levity is making me giddy!"

"Hey, Allen, my Main Man!"

Warrener looked up and spotted Dewey Tucker parting the crowd by means of his sheer intimidating bulk. Allen stood up and took a deep breath before the ex-biker delivered his customary rib-cracking hug.

"Hey yourself, cycle-trash! You just blow into town?"

"Yep. Woulda been here earlier, except a highway patrolman pulled me over to 'inspect the cargo.' He was hugely annoyed to find nothing but film stock and camera equipment, but at least he got to tell somebody to 'Get-a-fuckin-hair-cut!' "

"Do people still *say* that?" asked Preston.

"In North Carolina they do," said Allen.

"Gimme some cash, boss, I'm in dire need of a cheeseburger and a six-pack."

Preston dealt him a twenty. "If that beer gut gets any bigger, you'll never catch sight of your own pecker again."

Dewey snapped up the cash and patted his massive beer belly. "I don't need to, boss—it glows in the dark!"

When Dewey lumbered off in search of nourishment, Preston refocused on Allen, pecking at his nerves with a stern glance and irritable gestures.

"You going to tell *me* what's in that telegram, buddy?"

Allen just handed it to him and resumed his joyless drinking. Preston tilted the document this way and that until he found enough light to read by:

"Good news, STOP. Elsuba applied early leave from hospital, STOP. Quasi-Socialist Danish Health Administration approved, STOP. I told you she wants to see you again, STOP. Besides, we should have doctor along and she's damn good one, STOP."

"Full-stop. Now I get the picture. That Big Decision I was talking about? It just snuck up and bit you in the ass."

"Aw, shit, Norma's dragging Karen back in, and I need to say something appropriate. Help me out, pal!"

"Sorry, man. Except for Norma, the only three things I've said to women in the past fifteen years are *Action!*, *Cut!*, and *Can't you fake a better orgasm than that, honey?*"

Norma looked wrung out, and Karen was utterly pokerfaced. The awkwardness would have frozen all tongues had not Dewey returned at that moment, bearing a sack of burgers and a huge pitcher of beer. Thankfully, he defused some of the tension by asking Preston where the men's room was, and Preston chicken-shitted out of the impending confrontation by offering to show Dewey the place where he and Allen had carved their initials in a toilet stall, back in the Late Jurassic.

After they'd gone, Norma gamely tried to make conversation: "I didn't know Preston went to school here."

"He didn't—he just visited me from time to time. His own college career ended the night Sylvia shafted him and he decided to become a great photographer instead of a great scholar."

"And went on to become a rich smut-peddler, instead. . . ." said Norma.

"He did a lot better than I did when I tried to write the Great American Novel."

Karen gave it one last shot by half-humorously saying: "Stop beating up on yourself, Allen. At least you *tried.* You had enough dedication to write five hundred pages. Most would-be novelists don't get beyond five paragraphs. Maybe you should use the expedition to explore the possibilities in non-fiction. Remember that biography of Field Marshall Mannerheim you told me you wanted to write? You did a lot of good research, way back when. . . ."

"You want to know why I'll never be able to do that? It's because twenty-three years ago I could read *Finnish!* But now, well, Jesus, there's no way I could teach a full course load and relearn the most difficult language in Europe. Get real, Karen!"

Too late, he realized what a smack in the face he'd just given her. She had really been trying to patch things up, and he'd just put her down like some snippy freshman asking what the Green Light stood for in *Gatsby*. A look of cold rage shattered the tentative smile she had worked so hard to summon. She flared to her feet again.

"You can really be a shitheel when you're drunk, Warrener. Which in your case is at least half the time! Thanks for trying, Norma, but I knew it was a bad idea to come back into this puke-hole."

She was opening the door when he caught up to her.

"Let go of my arm, Allen; you're hurting me."

"I just don't want to drag you off to some place where you'll be miserable! That's the long and short of it."

"You mean: drag me off to some place where *you* would be miserable if I were there to cramp your style! That's the 'long and short of it,' sweetheart. I don't think I'd be miserable at all, even if your precious glorious Elsuba *was* there! Christ, Allen, what gives you the right to make that assumption about me? And what happens if there is no monster, Allen? What happens if you go all the way to Vardinoy and find nothing except a lot of dried puffin shit? Do you think I'd laugh at you, like so many of your colleagues are doing? I honestly don't give a rat's ass if Elsuba or Princess Diana is coming with us. If all these other people won't get in the way of your fantasies"—she gestured wildly toward the booth and its occupants—"why the hell should *I?*"

"Karen, you're making a scene!"

"Not half as big a scene as I'm going to make *if you don't let go of my fucking arm!*"

Numbly, he did. And with a final snarl, she was through the door and gone. He heard her begin to sob as she ran down the street. He was about to run after her, when one of his students—the one in the second row, as it happened, who kept crossing her legs slowly while he was trying to give lectures—flounced up and touched his shoulder solicitously.

"Are you all right, Professor Warrener?"

"Nothing wrong with me that a good blow job wouldn't cure," he snapped back at her. She recoiled as though she'd touched a live wire.

That'll go down well with the Administration, if she files a sexual harassment complaint!

By the time he apologized and halfway mollified the girl, he was too late reaching the street. Karen had vanished. He sagged against the nearest wall and took deep breaths. The sudden throbbing of his bladder reminded him that it was time to pay the rent on those last four beers. There would be too long a line at the men's room, so he did what he used to do as a student and scurried into the alley behind the bar, where a large, grisly-smelling dumpster provided cover for those whose need to urinate would brook no delay. He was in luck—there was nobody in sight. He went into the shadows and unzipped. When he felt the first surge, he almost moaned with relief.

I'll patch things up somehow. I shouldn't have panicked when I saw that stupid telegram. Like Karen couldn't read my mind when I stammered: "I'd feel really bad if something happened to you on that island. I mean, it might be dangerous—ships get sunk in those waters every year by awful storms!"

"When was the last time a whole island got sunk?" she had replied, the pain of his rejection filling her eyes.

Next time I feel like being mean, I'll just go off somewhere and torture a kitten.

Suddenly, he felt a jolt of apprehension: a figure was braced in the alley, staring at him. Well, this was just perfect: now he was going to be mugged. And with his dick hanging out, no less.

He was trying to shake off the last drops and locate something more lethal than a Budweiser bottle to use as a weapon, when a car in the parking lot made a U-turn and flung a shaft of light into the alley, just long enough for him to recognize that his "assailant" was Richard Sugarman.

"Jesus wept, Sugarman, can't you even let me pee in peace?"

"I'm sorry about the circumstances, but I just have to talk to you about that newspaper article." Sugarman held out his hands, I-come-in-peace, and cautiously threaded his way through the garbage cans and stacks of empty beer kegs.

"You and I have had our conversation, Buster, and after what happened, I don't think I want another. I'm really drunk, plus I'm a lot older and slower than I was when I went through Special Forces training, but I can still take you apart with one hand!"

"Mother Teresa could take me apart with one hand, Professor. I'm the skinny Jewish kid with glasses, remember? Look, I know how you must feel, and you can take a poke at me if you want to, but please read this first!"

The editor was holding what appeared to be a newspaper layout sheet. Allen was really feeling those beers, now that the adrenaline rush was fading. He had to lean against a wall under a lamppost in order to bring the document into focus.

"This is the front page of the school paper, but I don't recognize any of the shit that's on it. . . ."

"That's because it hasn't come out yet. Just read it, please."

After a lot of blinking and squinting, the words jerked into paragraphs and began to make sense. The text was a front-page editorial. It started with Richard Sugarman announcing his resignation and explaining that an interview he had recorded, in good faith, with Prof. Allen Warrener, concerning his upcoming expedition to the island of Vardinoy, had been furtively and substantially re-edited, without his knowledge or permission and presumably at the behest of a Dump Warrener cabal; their purpose was to portray the popular history professor and his research into the Vardinoy legends in the most mocking and distorted manner possible. When he finished the piece, Allen looked at the former editor with new respect.

"They . . . whoever the fuck 'they' are . . . won't let you print this."

"It's already been printed. I made up a phony front page and left it on the layout table; nobody but me knows this is the version that's being printed as we speak, and that will be distributed before dawn by myself and some student volunteers who think you got a shitty deal. And by the way, I did some snooping and I found out why Chadwick Merritt hates your guts."

"Inquiring minds want to know . . . I'll bet this is going to be interesting."

"You have no idea, Professor. Long story short, back during the time you and your wife were starting to drift apart, ol' Chadwick and *his* spouse were having their own troubles. It seems Dr. Merritt has this fixation about, um, vaginas and such. He doesn't mind poking them with the authorized reproductive equipment, but when it came to oral gratification, he just couldn't bear to put his mouth anywhere near the hairy old thing. Unfortunately, Mrs. Merritt loved nothing better than a good spirited rug-munching."

"I see the cause of much marital friction. . . ."

"You better believe it. She saw it as a perfectly natural favor to ask of her husband, and her husband felt like he was putting his tongue into a Petri dish full of bacteria. One night, or so faculty legend has it, he made a maximum effort to overcome his hygienic phobia and, holding his nose all the while, he dived into the pit and manfully tried to do his duty. Her response was so enthusiastic that she clamped his head in a scissors grip, the poor man had a panic attack, and, well, not to put too fine a point on it . . . he threw up."

Allen leaned against the dumpster and laughed so hard, he almost did the same. "You mean to tell me he upchucked right into her snatch?"

"Wait, the best is yet to come. Mrs. Merritt, understandably, was both disgusted and humiliated. She threw him out of the bedroom, perhaps for good. That very weekend, at a big, free-floating faculty party, Mrs. Merritt ran into a very sexy, very talkative blonde lady who was also on the outs with her husband. . . ."

"Oh, God, I see where this is going. . . ."

"They both got plastered in some trustee's backyard gazebo, and one intimacy lead to another. Mrs. Merritt's new friend assured her that the only way to get a really satisfying cunnilinguistic experience was—wait for it, Allen! *From another woman!* I understand they ended up in a motel in Huntersville that night and the Gates of Heaven opened for Mrs. Merritt. They'd been having this hot Sapphic romp for two months before Chadwick hired a detective and learned what was really going on. I understand that when . . . what was her name?"

"Sylvia."

"When Sylvia left you and moved back to Miami, Mrs. Merritt was so distraught, she tried to overdose on sleeping pills. So that's why the man has such a pathological hatred for *you*—he thinks that if you'd only kept your wife on a tight leash, he wouldn't be known as the biggest cuckold on the faculty! That's why he spends his weekends jerking off to porn videos while Mrs. M. shacks up with a high school gym teacher down in Charlotte!"

"And all that time, I thought Sylvia was getting planked by some young faculty stud! Oh, this is priceless—absolutely the ultimate Sylvia escapade! Richard, I don't know how to thank you properly."

"Just say 'yes' when I ask you if I can go to the Faeroe Islands with you."

"Christ, there must be something in the air tonight. . . ."

"I'm sorry, I didn't catch that."

"Wasn't worth catching, really. Look, I deeply appreciate what you've done, and I'm sorry I almost bashed your head in with the beer bottle, but why in God's name would you want to go to that island with us? I'm not running a summer camp for bored M.B.A. students."

"It's pre-law, actually, and I can pay my own way, and I can help you write a better book about the adventure."

"How in the world are you going to do *that?*"

"By having a nice chat with my uncle Maury, who's Senior Acquisitions Editor for Powell and Croft Publishing, that's how."

"You realize you're already in deep shit for pulling this newspaper switcheroo? What if Chadwick tries to sabotage your graduate school career?"

"Fuck him. I've already been accepted at Yale and Columbia. Take your pick. I'm untouchable. And my dad contributed ten grand to the Alumni Fund last September. If push comes to shove, I can have Chadwick Merritt fired instead of you. *Now* can I go with you to Vardinoy, Professor?"

"Come on in to the bar and meet some strange but altogether wonderful people. If you pass muster with them, you're in."

"Is Mr. Valentine here? I'll really get to meet him?"

"Yeah, Preston's here. And so is his wife, better known as Norma Davenport."

"My God, I used to jerk off thinking about her!"

"Didn't we all, son. . . ."

Warrener closes the car door and almost turns his ankle by misjudging the height of the curb. He focuses on the front door and its overhead light, which seem far away, down a long, unstable catwalk. It's a straight line, but he manages a course deviation that propels him through a clump of gnarly, unkempt shrubbery, and he must paw his way through a whole rose-window of spider webs to recover his balance. Icky stuff, spider webs.

After considerable fumbling, he manages to get his front door unlocked. Before moving past the foyer, he carefully drops the keys into a ceramic bowl Brian had made in kindergarten. These days, there are so many holes in his short-term memory that he must be ritualistic about putting the keys in the same place every time, or sure as hell they won't be findable in the morning. Those little black holes in your brain . . . what was that marvelous term the astrophysicists had come up with? *Singularities!* Yes, his brain is being eaten by *singularities!*

Time for a nightcap, what ho? Drink in hand, he unlocks the back door and carefully follows a row of flagstones to the big tool shed attached to his carport. No tools inside now, of course, because he'd cleaned the place out a few weeks ago and turned it into the main supply depot for the North American brigade of the Vardinoy Expedition. Most of his personal effects are boxed up and ready to go: soap, razors, trash bags, blank cassettes, and an entire case of canary-yellow legal pads. How *did* Civilization evolve without them?

He walks through the narrow cleared space leading to a big sturdy work-table and switches on a fearsomely bright Tensor lamp. Centered between a pyramid of empty beer cans and a coffee cup containing two dead moths is the big ring binder containing Eiden's printout of the Master List, an amazingly detailed inventory of all the equipment and supplies Poulsen has already assembled in a dockside warehouse in Torshavn. Taped to the heavy-duty plastic cover is a supplementary list that's actually been stamped *CONFIDENTIAL*. For the hundredth time, and with undiminished puzzlement, he reads the covering note Eiden had paper-clipped to this file:

Allen—I've been thinking hard about something lately, and finally decided to act on the matter. Without wishing to seem melodramatic, there are certain aspects of our quest that concern me. While it's true that only a fraction of the references we've collected depict the V.M. as being HOSTILE to human beings, it clearly poses a danger to our kind. Like a shark, it may simply be a big eating machine, utterly driven by instinct, even if it's wholly without malign intent. But the fact that sharks don't intend to inflict pain does not make their bites any less dangerous. Once we land on Vardinoy, we cannot just pick up the telephone and call the local sheriff! We know, or at least we think we do, that this creature has killed humans before. In the case of the Condor crew, it committed mass murder! It's big, it's elusive, and under certain circumstances it's capable of killing people in batches. It only seems prudent that we have adequate means of self-defense; furthermore, the weapons we bring should combine maximum firepower with light weight and robust construction—the constant rains and rough terrain will be hard on almost any kind of infantry weapons.

Since I'm familiar only with World War II–era firearms, I sought the advice of a friendly NATO colonel who handles security at the radar station on Streymoy— he suggested the weapons on this list. Study up on the matter, please, and if you concur, check out the prices and availability (I know it's much easier to obtain such things in America than in pacifistic modern Denmark!), give me a "ballpark" estimate, and I'll send the money. Don't worry about the customs formalities—I have it on good authority that any shipments imported for the Vardinoy Expedition will receive only the most cursory examination!

General-Purpose Weapons
Hechler & Koch HK-33, 5.56 mm
Swiss STG-90, NATO 5.56 mm
Winchester "Street-sweeper" shotgun, pump action, 12-gauge
Grenades
Dutch V-40 (small; fragmentation)
UK L2A1 (general purpose)
Germany DM-5 (heavy frag.)
UK WP-80 (white phosphorus)
Germany DM-62 (stun, concussion, and flash)

Based on his own military expertise, rusty though it is, Allen thinks a balanced assortment of these weapons will cover most any contingency short of a surprise assault by an SS panzer battalion. Rereading the list once more, he whistles in admiration and frowns in bewilderment.

"Eiden, old buddy, you and I need to have a serious talk about this shit. . . ."

Having once more studied this curious new document, Allen forgets exactly why he came to the tool shed in the first place. So he cuts off the light, locks up again, and navigates his way back to the kitchen—very cautiously now, having just poured three ounces of 100-proof Wild Turkey on top of his previous load.

"My God. . . ." The light's on in his study. And he hasn't been in his study since yesterday! But clearly, somebody has.

"Karen?" He hopes to hear her answering voice, but doesn't. When he enters the room, however, he sees that she has been here earlier. Indeed, the Marlboro smell in the air indicates that she was here within the last hour. And she's left a note, taped to the lamp on his desk:

HEY, MISTER! PLAY MY TAPE!!

With an arrow pointing to his pocket-sized dictation recorder. Before he pushes the "Play" button, he refills his glass: maybe this is her "Fuck-you-and-good-bye" declaration.

Hi, Allen. Sorry to be having a one-way conversation like this, but that's the only kind I could have right now. Walking back into that bar, after our decorous farewell scene at the door—well, that was not an option. Unlike your ex-wife and

Norma, I never cared for exhibitionism. And I just don't have the energy to write a long letter. So I'm taping one instead.

I don't know if this expedition-thing will enable you to break out of the prison of old bad habits or not, and I'm too brain-dead now to go into the existential ramifications of that statement. You know what they are. Think about them a little deeper.

You see, I'm afraid you're about to do it to yourself again—setting yourself up for a fall, I mean. You're starting to conceive of the Vardinoy trip as some kind of magic portal to the mystical past, when you briefly visited—to hear and read you tell about it—the Garden of Eden. It's time to make a big Reality Check, dearest, because whatever this quest turns out to be, it surely won't be that. *God knows how you managed it, but somewhere along the way you got yourself into a loop you can't get out of. You're like a kid who still longs to set the world on fire, but you've been told too many times that it's dangerous to play with matches. Yes, it is. You bet it is.*

Well, shit, this tape is supposed to be about me, for a change, not you, so let me start over again. About Vardinoy and the Islands. . . . Remember when you first showed me of your Faeroes photos? Yes, I let on that I was impressed, but you don't know the half of it. Those images knocked my socks off; I had an incredible déjà vu *rush. I went yo-yoing between the past and some dim, vibrant state of precognition. It was almost an out-of-body sensation! The only time I'd ever felt that way before, with such intensity, was when I got trapped in that awful drainpipe, and at some point incipient madness broke down the defenses we all instinctively have against penetration by the ineffable. Okay, that sounds pretentious, but how else can I describe what it was like to feel* in contact *with some force, or some emanation that was located somewhere very far away, yet was powerful enough to send me a blast of energy, loan me a surge of superhuman strength powerful enough to blow me loose from that horrible tomb? It was not just an emergency flood of adrenaline, Allen; my own chemistry alone could never have juiced me up that much. That manic strength came from something Other, and it was a gift. Some sort of super-molecules went into my system and reorganized my metabolism for sheer survival.*

What does that have to do with the Faeroe Islands, you may well ask? If I knew the answer to that, I wouldn't need to go there. All I know is that it does! *As surely as I know the sun will rise tomorrow, I know there's a connection between that experience and the Faeroe Islands. Possibly, indeed probably, with Vardinoy itself.*

Maybe, like the classic UFO abductees, there's now a genetic marker in my blood that gets to vibrating under certain circumstances. Well, Mister, the night I first saw your wall poster of Streymoy, that vibration kicked in so hard that it damn near knocked me down. I knew that I was going to that place; destined to go—maybe had been since I drew my first breath.

What I'm awkwardly trying to tell you is that we might be going to the same place on the map, but we'll also be taking two distinct trips, and maybe not even sharing the same itinerary. We won't be looking for the same things; one of us might find it and one of us might not. . . . Or we both might get lucky—if "lucky" is the word for it.

You certainly never counted on this, Allen, but here it is: going up there has now become my dream, too.

Understand me well, Allen: whatever hit me when you showed me those photographs, it was so strong that I would eventually have made that connection, sooner or later, even if I'd never met you. I would have seen the islands somewhere, in a book, on TV, Jesus only knows, but the instant I saw them, that same electric arc would zap through me: connection made, circuit complete!

However, I did meet you, and you now have this unbelievable opportunity to go back, and, well, here's Karen, newly converted True Believer in the Vardinoy Whatever, and I've been hinting, for weeks, that perhaps we ought to clear the air by having an open and honest discussion about a certain Faeroese woman, because it's your hangup about Elsuba that's prevented you from asking me to go. But either you've got the world's worst case of tunnel-vision or you're in massive denial, because you never picked up on those hints, did you? And today, when your behavior was so wishy-washy, I wanted to shake you till your teeth rattled and scream: either say yes or say no, dammit, but don't turn mealy-mouthed and try to CONVEY "no" without having the guts to live with your guilt and my disappointment. I walked all the way from the bar to this house, not having any idea what I wanted to do, other than have a huge sappy cry, and then I ended up in your study and all of a sudden the truth crashed over me.

I knew you'd just learned that Elsuba was coming; and I'm charitable enough to allow as how that was the reason you were so damn mean to me tonight—that certainty just overloaded your circuits, melted your diodes. . . .

Remember when you told me, early in our relationship, that I should feel free to read anything in this house? Well, I took that more literally than you probably intended. I made a copy of your novel manuscript one day when you weren't home, and over a period of three weeks I read and re-read every word. Let me don my English teacher's hat and tell you that reading it was not always such a pleasure, because, as you know, it's lumpy, self-indulgent, and structurally incoherent. It could never be published as it is, and even you probably wouldn't want it to be.

But let me also tell you straight out: the chapters about you and Elsuba, and the magic you found in the Faeroes? They're not just good, they burn.

Allen, we both had *a transforming and possibly mystical experience, only yours happened to involve a rival female! I'm okay with that, and I understand how sacred the memory of that must be to you. Listen to how seriously I say this, please: if you get to the Faeroes, and you do find once again the same magic you found as a young man, well, I'll know I've been outclassed. I'll simply have to accept it and give you my blessing. What else could I do? Maybe this sounds illogical, but somehow I think it would be easier for me to cope with the contingency if I were actually* there, *not sitting in my apartment waiting for the "Dear Karen" letter. If Vardinoy turns out to be nothing more than the place where I'm destined to lose you, then so be it. That possibility does not lessen the undertow that's pulling me toward those shores.*

If you really choose to go without me, I'll pray for your success and eventually forgive you. But as much as I would rather explore the Faeroes with you, I can do it alone, if I must. And I will, if that's the only way left for me to do it. Maybe your personal obsession with the Faeroes has evoked some kind of harmonic echo within the souls of Preston, and Norma, and Richard, and even Dewey too! Maybe what we find there will be a collective gestalt, constructed from bits and pieces of all our souls. I've got to wonder, though: will you be able to accept that, or will it ruin things for you to realize that Vardinoy isn't reserved for Allen Warrener alone?

It is your right, of course, to leave me or take me along as you wish. But do not leave me if your only reason is because you think that by doing so, you'll improve your chances of recapturing the past in all its idyllic purity. I don't really think that is possible, for anyone, but let's say, for the sake of argument, that you do. *Then you'll be one of the luckiest mortals alive; you would have been able to freeze Time and thaw it out again, like a TV dinner. I'm basically a realist, Allen. I know that if such proves to be the case, there is nothing in the world I can offer you that will compare. Nothing. It will be an alchemy performed on Time. I could no more replicate what you had with Elsuba than I could grant you immortality!*

But I am real, Allen; and the Elsuba you wrote your book about, no longer is. And the love I offer you is real too. I'm vain enough to think I'm as real as it gets, and equally worthy of your consideration.

Just remember: it isn't me you need to be afraid of. Any way it goes down, I won't spoil your party. And now, while I still can, I'm going home, get stoned, and take my phone off the hook.

16.

GIGANTICUS, THE MANATEE

The morning after Karen had taped her message, she was too hung over and too despondent to get out of bed for her two morning classes; but what the fuck, she already knew she would ace the exams and so did her professors. When she finally did get vertical, she couldn't quite remember everything she'd said into that microphone. Her intent had been to tread a very fine line between an appeal and an ultimatum; if she'd shaded her words too far in the direction of the latter, then her relationship with Allen was in serious, possibly terminal trouble. Of course he'd behaved like a swine in the tavern, but like a wounded and bewildered one, snarling at anyone who tried to get close, because there was a confusion eating at his insides like a huge bubble of pain, and it must have seemed to him that even trying to be rational, even setting hypothetical priorities, would only make the hurt grow worse. Which still didn't excuse the bastard. But she'd given him, as her justification for going to the Faeroes on a voyage that was none of her devising, a vague tale about persistent childhood dreams.

And how bloody rational is that?, she asked herself, fumbling to load the coffee brewer.

Allen hadn't called during the morning, which might mean only that he'd stayed up later and gotten far drunker than she and had probably canceled his morning classes. She didn't remember having said, "Call me tomorrow and let's talk," so it wasn't surprising that he *hadn't* called. He disliked using telephones even on his best days, so if he felt half as wretched as she did. . . . He might be sulking; furiously angry; or just . . . confused.

As it turned out, he was on his way to Florida. Karen took a shower at 11:45 and missed his brief, almost furtive message: "I forgot to mention it, but I'm taking a plane to Miami at one-thirty, to see Brian one last time before we leave for the Faeroes, and to take care of some legal and financial

244

crap—updated insurance policies and such. I won't be gone long; if there's anything worse than spending a day in Miami, it's spending two. I'll spend the night in a motel tonight, so I'll be bright-eyed and bushy-tongued when I confront the ex, spend the day doing Absentee-Dad stuff with the kid, then fly back tomorrow night. I'm taking Flight 58 from Miami and I'll be home sometime around eleven-twenty. Take care of yourself and wish me luck."

She redialed immediately, but of course he'd just left for the airport. He'd probably timed the call so he could leave a message without having to speak directly to her—ordinarily, she would have been in class at that time, and he knew it.

But he had said "before *we* leave for the Faeroes." What a loaded pronoun! Who was included in "we"? Had her taped epistle finally pushed him into a decision? And if so, which way had he moved? He had not specifically asked her to meet him when he came home   but he *had* given her the flight number.

Karen decided to play things out a bit more subtly this time: she wouldn't be at the airport—that would signal too much obedience, too much eagerness to please Massa. But she would, very coolly and casually, be at his house when he pulled into the driveway, with a tall bourbon-and-soda iced down just the way he liked 'em. She had sensed that the time immediately preceding an encounter with his son was one of near-purgatorial emotions; and she'd seen for herself, on the occasion of their second meeting, how wretchedly lonesome and mentally disheveled he was *after* an encounter with his son. Striving for a "farewell" kind of closeness whilst on enemy turf—the fiefdom Sylvia's rich, buff, younger-than-she-was second husband had constructed, in one of Dade County's most exclusive and pricey developments—was going to make Allen feel like a pauper as well as a supplicant; a man who absolutely adored his son but who knew better than anyone that he had been and always would be a lousy full-time dad. If Sylvia was in the mood to be vengeful, she could turn him into a quivering plate of raw hamburger. And even if Sylvia was in a forgiving mood, Allen would still have to make polite small-talk with Hubby the Deuce, whom he knew virtually nothing about but whom he professed to despise anyway. However this last-minute impromptu visit turned out, Allen Warrener was going to be an emotional and psychological mess when he got back.

So Karen would be there for him, at least as far as a cold drink and a warm hug. Much would depend on what happened, or was said, after the hug and the drink.

And on who, exactly, was included in that "we" who were leaving for the Faeroes; would that party be limited to Allen, the Valentines, and Dewey Tucker, or would everybody slide over one seat to make room for one more pilgrim?

He came slowly up the walkway from the garage, listing to starboard as though his overnight bag weighed half a ton and he was a Method actor determined to earn the role of Willy Loman.

Karen waited until he mounted the front porch steps before opening the door and holding out the drink she'd prepared as soon as she heard his car enter the driveway.

"You look like you could use this, buddy."

"How about a hug first?"

So far, so good. . . .

The hug turned into a prolonged embrace. At least Karen knew she'd done the right thing by being here for him.

"I'll put the bag away—you kick off your shoes and enjoy your drink. And while you're enjoying it, you can tell me as much or as little about the trip as you want to."

Brian's carpool dropped him off only fifteen minutes after Allen arrived, which was about the maximum amount of time he and Sylvia could make polite conversation without the old tension starting to harden the air between them. When the boy came down the hall and saw his father, he dropped his book satchel and ran toward Allen with his arms wide.

Brian had grown a lot since Christmas, and, like his mother, he seemed to flourish in the pitiless sun of south Florida. Allen could smell that sunlight coiled in his hair and feel its energy pumping through the arms that hugged him, warming the damp blossom of a kiss the boy planted on his father's whiskery neck.

"Dad! You've got to come for a ride in my sailboat! There's something very special I want to show you! Did you bring a bathing suit?"

Sylvia solved that problem in her usual double-edged manner, saying: "You've lost some weight, Allen. I'll bet you could squeeze into a pair of Brad's gym shorts."

Now there's *a cozy thought.*

After changing into proper boating attire, Allen dutifully padded along behind his son, on very tender feet, down to the canalside dock. Sylvia waved from beside the pool as they passed, her drink in one hand and a Danielle Steele novel in the other. At least she was being more honest, these days, about her plebian taste in literature. When they reached the dock, Brian scampered around the hull of his kid-sized fiberglass sailboat, expertly casting off the mooring ropes. It was one hell of a cool little sailboat, just as Brian's house was one hell of a palace and Brian's private school was no doubt one of the best and most expensive in the state; and Brian's tennis instructor was probably a runner-up at Wimbledon. . . . Of course the kid was thriving here—what was not to like?

The canal behind Brad and Sylvia's hacienda was eight to ten feet wide, a regular river compared to most surviving waterways around here, the water was reasonably clear and pleasantly olive-colored. A hot breeze pushed them into midstream, and Allen enjoyed watching the careful way his son handled the boom and the rudder, the skill he showed in catching every particle of the lethargic wind. When the boat reached the spot where the current could do the work, Brian relaxed and tossed a lifejacket to his father.

"You have to wear one of those, Dad. Like me. Otherwise, it's not safe to take you out."

Allen nodded, respectful of the stern righteousness in the boy's tone and also glad his stepfather had impressed the basic rules of water safety on an eleven-year-old's mind. *Nice job, Brad; thanks.*

It was a weekday, so there wasn't much leisure traffic on the canal; having the waterway entirely to themselves was a treat for father and son. Once the boat began moving with the central current, Brian locked the rudder in place and settled back against his father's encircling arm, leaning his head close to be nuzzled, like a small blond bear. The ensuing half hour, spent drifting slowly through dappled shade and sunlight, both of them hot and drowsy and tender, was as good as any time they had ever spent together, right up there with the snowball fights at Christmas. They talked about everything and nothing: school, friends, movies, video games, and how much fun they planned to have *next* Christmas. Brian's concentration leaped, grasshopper-like, from one subject to the next, often without transition; sometimes in the past Allen hadn't been able to follow these jump-cuts and found himself growing irritated with the chatter. Not today; today father and son were on the very same wavelength.

At least, they were until Allen remembered that Brian was only a year or so away from the onslaught of adolescence; when that happened, he couldn't count on ever sharing another such moment with his son. Not one. Not ever. He shook that thought out of his head; plenty of time to brood about that later. Like, for the rest of his life.

"Hang on Dad, here comes our turn-off!"

Hard a-starboard! Abruptly, after ducking their heads to clear a screen of low-hanging branches, they entered a hidden side channel, one of those odd but striking splinters-of-wilderness, fringed with ferns and high sawgrass, that could sometimes still be found in the corners of otherwise tamed suburbs. The air suddenly grew thicker, more humid, more jungle-smelling; the silence more attenuated and darker. Allen enjoyed the pleasant sensation of being on a well-designed theme ride at Disney World. When they drifted into a surprisingly large oval-shaped lagoon, Brian collapsed the sail and backstroked with the return-trip oars to slow the boat until it made almost no headway. They were in the center of a strange, lush clearing, the banks fringed with lily pads and curious intricately woven reeds. No traffic noises disturbed the silence; nowhere could they see any ostentatious party boats moored alongside homes where the servants' quarters were worth more than Allen's life savings. For the moment, they might as well be drifting along the headwaters of the Amazon.

Urgently, the boy began whispering and pointing. "Dad, look over there and see my own special sea monster!"

Allen followed where the brown arm pointed, peering deep into the translucent grotto beneath the keel. Sunlight streamed down in shafts and flowed very thickly once it penetrated the quiet surface; he fancied he could trace the currents by watching the bend of light, granular and sinuous.

"There he is! At least, I think he's a male. . . ."

By following his son's proud, knowing gaze, Allen soon spotted it: a large, somnolent, mysterious shape barely moving, yet discernibly rising, as though in response to their arrival. "Here comes my monster, and I call him Giganticus!"

Whatever the gender, it was the biggest manatee he'd ever seen, big as an African hippo! And what a wonder to find one here! There weren't a whole lot of them left, and the state was moving out the ones who still survived. Landfills had deprived them of habitat, pollution had sickened them, outboard motor blades had mutilated them, and despite their size, they were the gentlest and most harmless creatures imaginable, utterly unequipped either for fight or flight. Manatees just drifted—that was their role in the scheme of things. What magic did his son possess that something so rare had revealed itself to the boy?

"He's . . . not exactly handsome, is he? But he's wonderful anyhow! Look at him peering up at us with those little-bitty eyes. . . ." Brian splashed the water in a syncopated pattern that was obviously his private greeting code for the sea-cow. Damned if the animal didn't turn its itty-bitty gaze upwards!

"Hi, boy! I can't stay long, but I wanted Dad to meet you. I'll come back soon with my goggles, so I can see you clearly."

"Brian, you haven't told anybody about Gigantious, have you? I mean to your Mom and your stepfather, I mean."

"Gee, Dad, I'm not *dumb!* I know they're *endangered* and all. My science teacher says there aren't but a few hundred of them still living. Don't you think that's sad?"

"I think that's one of the saddest things I've ever heard. Also, that's why you have to keep him a secret—maybe a girl manatee will come along and they'll get married and have baby manatees."

Brian cocked his head a little skeptically. "I don't think they mate very often, Dad. That's part of their problem."

"Right, right. Very good point."

". . . when I hugged him good night, I was amazed at how sinewy his body felt. That's when it really hit me, I think: he will never be a 'little boy' again. That part of it's over, Karen, and I may as well get used to it." He squeezed her hand a little more tightly. He was on his third drink now, and because both of them were so much more relaxed than they'd expected to be, after the confrontation in the tavern and the tape-recorded message, Allen had even joined her in consuming a joint, a pleasure he seldom indulged in these days. He was glad of it now, though, because otherwise he didn't think he could finish the tale without getting weepy. He did not, for instance, go into elaborate detail about how bittersweet was that last good-bye hug. Instead, he exhaled a mighty toke and said: "As I was reaching to turn out the bedside light, he suddenly sprang up again and said, 'Dad, I almost forgot! Here's something I made for you to take to Vardinoy. It's for good luck, and to keep the monster from hurting you!' It's in my overnight bag, so if you'll excuse me for just a second. . . ."

"Not until I give you a kiss—for being such a good story-teller."

"Am I really? Maybe I should write a book!"

"Maybe you should just kiss me and then go get Brian's present."

He did both, in the proper order. When she unrolled the big drawing, Karen gasped. This had obviously been a major project, undertaken with great care and dedication; and it was altogether wonderful. The monster Brian had depicted was an amalgam of every creature the boy had ever seen on television or in comic books; it came fully equipped with claws, tentacles, talons, enormous fangs, two heads, and multiple eyes. Two stylized mountain peaks loomed, one on either side of the struggling beast, and on top of each mountain stood a heroic figure, one labeled "Dad" and the other "Brian." Together, they were lowering a gigantic net over the monster's head and grinning hugely at their own bravado. The drawing was entitled *"How My Dad and I Capchured the Vardnoise Monster!!!"*

Karen studied the drawing for a long time, and when she spoke, her voice was trembling—it was a timbre he had never heard before, and the sound caused a great upsurge of feeling in his heart.

"Oh, Allen, this boy loves you so much! And he's so proud of you! Even after all that's happened, no matter how far apart you are, your son really loves you. That's a reason to be happy, isn't it?"

"Do you still love his father? That would be a reason to feel even happier."

Her face remained unreadable and she said nothing, but she nodded slowly, and one tear escaped down her cheek. He leaned forward and with all the gentleness he could summon, he touched the corner of his clean handkerchief against the tear, blotting it up, restoring her composure.

"You'll have to get a passport, you know."

"I already have one. I sent off for it the day after you got Eiden's letter. Just in case. . . ."

"Well then, I suppose you're already packed, too."

"No, not packed. I got superstitious about being packed. But everything is laid out and organized."

"That's my girl. Okay, the next thing is to make an appointment for your shots, and you'll need to go shopping for a good pair of hiking boots, and a good sturdy rucksack. . . ."

"I will, yes, all those things, yes."

Now they could hold each other, and he could surrender to the blessed sensation of her embrace drawing out some of his exhaustion and dulling the edge of his woe. He no longer felt old, nor tired beyond measure, and he was so grateful for the warmth and scent and closeness of her that he could have shouted a prayer of thanks. He had been a selfish prig even to consider making this trip without her; she believed in him as no other woman had; and, for reasons he hadn't fathomed yet, she *believed* in this quest—perhaps more than he did at this stage—but then, she had dreamed of the Faeroes, while he had merely been there; he suspected that her motives were at least as powerful as his, and surely more pure.

Allen Warrener drew resolve from the knowledge that this young woman would not cease to love him, even if all they found on Vardinoy was mist and rocks and the dust of old and broken dreams.

Book III:

VOYAGES

"A boatless man is a man in chains!"

—Old Faeroese Proverb

17.

THE EVENTFUL VOYAGE OF
THE *CROWN PRINCE FREDERICK*

From the journal of Richard Sugarman:

Our last night in Copenhagen . . . the one reliable recollection I have is centered on a pulsing red neon sign, blinking on and off: "Tuborg! Tuborg!" Warrener's passionate advocacy of Danish beer, and a wad of Finlen Pewbenk money, were the prime ingredients of a raucous "Bon voyage" night on the town. I am told I had a lot of fun, but the next time I perform "Singin' in the Rain" in Tivoli Park, I'd like to be able to remember doing it!

We embarked from Copenhagen at sunset and are now somewhere in the straits separating the northern tip of Denmark from the southern bulge of Norway. Our ship is named the Crown Prince Frederick*—a freighter of indeterminate age and a real working ship, not a cruise liner. There are accommodations for only two dozen passengers, and while the food is good, the only concession to the passengers' entertainment is this cozy, Joseph Conrad–style saloon, with dark wood paneling, fittings of polished brass, and big 19th-century nautical maps on the walls. There are a handful of other passengers, Faeroese returning from the mainland I assume, but apart from our group, the only other person in the saloon is the affable Danish steward named Nielsen who tends the bar.*

A little while ago, the intercom telephone buzzed, and Nielsen had a rather long conversation with whoever was on the other end. When he had finished, he clinked a glass with a spoon to get our attention and announced: "Ladies and gentlemen, that was the captain, calling from the bridge. He asks your indulgence, but wishes you to know that we're battening down the ship in preparation for a rather nasty storm. As a safety precaution, he requests that no one please go out on the open decks until we have sailed through the bad weather."

"What bad weather?" said Preston Valentine; "it's been smooth as glass ever since you weighed anchor."

"Yes, and that's because we haven't reached the open sea yet. I can assure you, however, that you will notice a difference as soon as we head into the North Atlantic proper. No worries, though; this old ship has come safely through worse storms."

Warrener, however, took this news with a frown. I saw Karen whisper something to him, and then he got up and led her to one of the maps and began pointing things out and showing off his nautical expertise. She nodded thoughtfully and began to look worried, too, as we all noticed. Pretty soon, the whole Expedition was gathered around the chart and A.W. was enlightening us.

I rather wish he hadn't. It seems the waters between the Straits of Denmark and Iceland are considered the most dangerous in the North Atlantic. Warrener explicated: "Say a tropical depression forms down here in the Caribbean, and the winds move it out to sea . . . it sits on top of the Gulf Stream and rides it all the way up to our latitude, sucks up power all the way from the warm currents. What started as good sailing weather around Bermuda can turn into a real ship-killer by the time it reaches these waters."

Indeed, even as he finished speaking, we could feel a new, deeper vibration in the deck under our feet, a combination of more power going to the engines and more resistance from the water. Definitely a bit ominous. Dewey, who's already told us he has "a thing" about drowning (like the rest of us don't?) asked A. W. the 64-dollar question:

"Just how bad can this shit really get?"

"Well, some of these storms are so memorable, the Faeroese write ballads about them. I met an old-timer once who could remember a gale they call 'The Great Beast,' back in nineteen-ought-nine. The top of the island of Hastoy—this little speck here—was completely submerged for about ten minutes, and all seventy-odd people who lived there were swept away—it's never been resettled, either, because the islanders figure if it happened once, it will happen again, sooner or later."

"Err, how high would a wave have to be in order to do that?" Dewey asked in a very small voice.

Allen peered closely at the contour lines on the chart. "Well, according to this map, the coastal cliffs on Hastoy are between ninety-six and one hundred eleven feet high."

Observing the color drain from Dewey's face, Nielsen lamely hastened to add: "Of course, you only get a storm like that once in a century, maybe. The kind of gale we're heading into, well, you might see a few waves as high as forty feet."

"That's a big fuckin' comfort, Nielsen, thanks." Dewey slumped into a big solid-looking chair and hung on tight.

*Valentine then had a wicked idea: he took a big brandy snifter and set it in the center of the bar, then dropped a ten-*kroner *banknote into the bowl. "This is now the official Vardinoy Expedition Seaksickness Pool, as it were. Everybody pony up a ten-spot, and the first one to blow his or her cookies gets the prize."*

As silly as it seems, we all dug money out of our pockets. As we dropped the bills into the snifter, the intercom phone buzzed behind the bar. Without understanding a word of Danish, I could hear the tension creep into Nielsen's voice. "That was the skipper again. Sorry to inform you, but the latest update now officially classifies this storm as a Force Ten gale on the Beaufort Scale. Which means it's just one notch below a full-fledged hurricane."

After delivering this cheery piece of news, the bartender began methodically collecting all the loose glassware and dishes and storing them in rough-weather cabinets, secured by rubber straps.

Although from a physiological point of view it may not be the wisest thing to do, everybody's getting drunk just as fast as they can manage. To aid us in our quest for serenity, Nielsen handed out three complimentary bottles of Hennessey's Five-Star brandy. Mighty smooth stuff! What the hell, if I'm going to end up in Davy Jones's Locker, I might as well go down with a stupid grin on my face!

Allen was bringing Karen a fresh drink when the *Crown Prince Frederick* plowed into the storm. He suddenly felt the deck shoving hard against his feet. The old ship rose steeply, and then seemed to hang, shuddering, on the edge of a watery cliff. He threw his other arm around a chair and waited for the ship to level out. It didn't. The moment stretched, became a taut bowstring of suspended time. Norma looked frightened for the first time and shouted: "Nielsen, make this goddamn ship *do* something!" and the bartender merely smiled and replied: "Oh, don't worry, madame—it *will.*"

For Karen, that moment of suspended motion, like the last creaking inches before the "screamer" descent of a roller-coaster, was a slice of time removed from the normal continuum. What the others endured for thirty seconds, expanded for her like the worst LSD trip imaginable.

The Sound came to her inner ears from far off in the night, a low, black-toned vibration, almost subsonic, passing as easily as cosmic rays through the vibrating steel plates that were the only thing shielding her from the cold black abyss below. Only she could hear it, and it muted the others' voices into a blur of dim static. Even though she could see their excitement, now tinged with apprehension, their movements were only the gesticulations of mimes. The Sound raked across the hull. She visualized it as a giant bone-white scimitar, flensing off the outer plates, one by one, powdering their rivets into ferric dust, snapping the bulkheads like chicken bones. And as the surrounding steel became insubstantial, she began to see *through* the floor, through the layered decks below, then through the keel itself, down into the sea, far far down, and The Sound grew vaster and heavier inside her head until she thought: if a mountain could scream in pain, this would be its cry!

The ship had melted into a transparent capsule, with Karen its only passenger. She was reminded of that concrete pipe, so long ago. . . .

No, please, don't take me back to that place!

But where was that hallucinatory Other, her savior, the rescuing entity that had loaned her some portion of its own immeasurable strength? She forced herself to be still, to breathe shallowly, trying to summon its help with the screams of her mind.

Yes! *Something* was approaching, trying to make contact with her! This feeling of encapsulation *was* somehow connected to her ordeal in the culvert, because she was able to recall sensory input she'd been too frightened to process at the time: a harsh, chill, oddly *mineral* scent—the salts and bitters of the planet's very crust; for that solitary critical instant, she had fused with something so deep inside the earth that she became, in effect, a hybrid of flesh and stone, an impossible amalgam, yes, she knew that, but no unalloyed little-girl's body could have rammed its way through so much cement and impacted earth. And now, too, she remembered the moment when she first inhaled sweet clean air: she had screamed in ecstasy and so, too, had a remote primordial throat, which seemed to echo her feeling of triumph in companionship and harmony. And she remembered now how, when she wiped the dirt and sweat from her eyes, she'd glimpsed what must have been her mind's conceptualization of some part of her rescuer's form: a shiny gray-brown cable sliding back into Pissin' Creek, its task accomplished.

But why did it seem so close *now*, in this terrible storm, four thousand miles from the site of their first encounter?

As quickly as it had manifested itself, the replay of her miraculous escape faded; in objective time, her vision of it had lasted only a few heartbeats; her companions were still freeze-framed in apprehension, waiting for the ship to move on or go down, and nothing external to Karen had occurred. Yet she perceived herself and the others as being surrounded by a pale, wafer-thin bubble, slowly descending, like a surrealist's idea of an elevator-into-Hell, through the abyssal depths of the North Atlantic.

How deep was that trench beneath Vardinoy? Miles, it was said, although no one really knew. But Karen Hambly was penetrating its secret darkness. A sudden insight blasted her mind: this was where "it" lived, in a place that had never known daylight, in pressures so titanic they could crush the freighter like a wad of foil. Whatever invisible colossal Awareness was drawing Karen's bubble-skin deeper into the ultimate depths, she knew she was close to its dwelling place.

Now there were lights ahead! Not stars and moons and comets, but snowflake patterns of cold ichorous radiance shimmering from clouds of microplankton; and bioluminescent nodules, polyps, predatory lures, by the light of which she glimpsed a hundred undiscovered species, from exquisite veils of living lace to grotesque, lantern-jawed gargoyles, peering at her with a brute curiosity equal to her own; in their thousands, colonies of green-white tube-worms, as long as her legs, writhed past, like living fields of wheat; and lastly, an enormous living shadow-mass, which crept along the bottom, slug-like, bearing a big light-flashing organ atop its dorsal hump, a moving lighthouse, calling for a mate or blinding a predator, whatever it was doing, its candle-power was sufficient to give her a thrilling glimpse of the trench itself: a stupendous silt-fogged canyon, a mile wide and unguessably deep, a Wonder of the World no human eyes but hers had ever seen.

But Karen's tour was ending. Whatever the empowering source had been, it was drained and fading; the illusions it conjured could no longer be sustained; the connection broke, and Karen's consciousness rocketed upward until the saloon and its occupants materialized around her again. She staggered and almost fainted.

Either gravity, or the force of its own sturdy engines, finally shifted the ship's equilibrium just enough to tilt the *Crown Prince Frederick* over the edge. Its bow chopped like a giant axe into a swollen ridge of ocean, sending thunder down the length of her hull, making her ribs groan.

Allen lunged for Karen just as her knees buckled. Her eyes were dilated, absolutely fixed on the starboard bulkhead. As she landed in his arms, he thought he heard her mumble: "It *is* coming, you fools . . . like a great black wall. . . ."

Nielsen examined her briefly, disappeared into a "crewmen only" area behind the bar, and returned with some smelling salts. That did the trick. Karen revived quickly and could not remember losing consciousness.

"You feel okay now?"

She worked up a thin smile and squeezed Allen's hand. "Not used to five-star brandy, is all. Or maybe it's the motion-of-the-ocean. Damn good thing I don't get seasick."

Until the moment Karen connected the words "five-star brandy" and "seasick," Dewey had been calming himself with manly pulls on the brandy bottle; the fact that this was some of the most expensive booze around made it work even better. But as soon as he heard Karen's speculative linkage of words, he began to stare at the half-empty bottle as though a live scorpion were swimming in the bottom. He was obviously steeling himself to do the manly thing and throw down another slug, but when he tried, the very smell of the stuff caused his body to rebel violently.

"Oh, Christ, Preston—Allen—somebody, gimme a hand, quick, if you know what's good for you. I gotta find the head really fast!"

"Why, you *pussy!*" sneered Preston. "Big bad biker can't handle a little brandy? Would-ums like a little Dramamine cocktail?"

Allen was still tending to Karen, so Richard and Preston went to Dewey's aid. Preston was met with a glare that could penetrate armor plate. "Show some compassion, boss—it ain't right to make fun of a sick colleague."

"You're not my 'colleague,' you're my fucking employee," Preston grunted, trying to give the big man some support.

"If you don't get me to the men's room in thirty seconds or less, I'm gonna be your goddamn *murderer.* . . ."

"Second door on the right, down that corridor," said Nielsen, pointing. "And do hurry, gentlemen, because from his color I'd say he's just about to reach critical mass."

A moment later, those remaining in the saloon heard Dewey's high-pitched shriek of "You motherfuckers think this is *FUNNY?*," followed by moans and bloodcurdling oaths. Another fifteen minutes passed before Preston and Richard staggered back into the saloon, where both of them studiously avoided the proximity of brandy.

By this time, the ship's motions weren't too alarming. The helmsman had put her bow into the wind, and the *Crown Prince Frederick* now felt more under control, less vulnerable.

"I do believe the skipper has her in the right groove," said Nielsen, after ten whole minutes had passed without another sickening lurch. As if on cue, the intercom buzzed again from the bridge. Nielsen smiled when he hung up.

"The captain's compliments to you all, and he would like to report that the worst seems to be over. In fact, the gale should be more exciting than dangerous from now until we sail out of it, so he's invited you all to come up to the bridge, so you can get a good look at the spectacle. Anybody who wants to go, follow me and I'll show you where the wet-weather gear is stowed."

In the watch-changing room, Nielsen led them to a row of lockers and demonstrated how to don the survival-yellow foul-weather suits and how to secure them to eyebolts and lifeline cleats. As they exchanged their civilian outfits for the heavy-duty slickers, the ship sounded much more alive than it had when they were three decks below, and the fire extinguishers, bolt cutters, suitcase-sized first-aid kits, and rack of flare pistols reminded them that they were sailing on a blue-collar ship that actually hauled *stuff* from one country to another; as passengers, they were just another kind of cargo. When they were weather-dressed, Nielsen inspected each person until he was satisfied, then he buzzed the bridge and told the captain they were coming up.

One short flight of metal stairs separated the changing room from the bridge's hatch. The only illumination came from a pair of red night-vision bulbs nested in wire cages. This far above the main deck, the roar and hiss of the elements was deafening; Nielsen had to shout his final instructions: "Once we go through that hatch, we'll be on the bridge! Don't talk to anyone unless someone asks you a direct question; keep your hands off the controls, and don't forget to hook up your safety lines! When we left Copenhagen, we had four Volvo trucks lashed down on the afterdeck—now there are only two! *That's* how fucking strong this storm is! Everybody ready?"

Nielsen undogged the hatch and stepped into the nerve center of the ship; the Vardinoy Expedition followed, a bit hesitant now that they could hear just how ferocious the wind truly was. A man with gold braid on his cap, obviously the captain, waved briskly at them as they filed through the hatch, his preoccupied features illuminated by the eerie green of instrumentation. Having acknowledged their arrival, neither he nor anyone else on the bridge took their eyes away from the awe-inspiring fury engulfing their ship.

Now that they were all inside the wheelhouse, there wasn't much room to spare, so Nielsen suggested half of them go to the port bridge wing and half to the starboard side. Allen and Karen were already standing close to the portside hatch, so they and Richard Sugarman took hold of the four handles that secured the watertight portal; and when they did, they could feel the gale's violence through a half inch of steel.

"Count to three, Karen, then we'll throw the last two handles. Ready, Richard?"

"I guess. You know, we Jews have never been intrepid seamen. . . . Salt-water immersion is not kosher!"

"Tell that to a pickle! One . . . two . . . *three!*"

Wind shear almost tore the hatch from their hands, and when they stepped through it, an angry wet flapping thing—the wind—hurled itself into their faces, clawing at their eyes and cheeks and furiously trying to rip the slickers from their bodies. Richard yelled, Allen cursed, and Karen screeched as they pushed forward, heads down, into the proverbial teeth of the gale; but their exclamations were barely audible, each syllable torn away the instant it left their mouths. The tempest attacked them, raked their faces, hissed against their bared teeth, and stabbed its tiny blade-points of rain against their eyelids. And the wind howled like a thousand maniacs, screaming through every rope and wire and halyard, every cleat and stan-chion, every ventilator and lifeboat davit: a high, demonic keening; a toothache made audible.

At first they could see nothing but chaotic eruptions of spray. Then, at a great distance, a sine-wave of lightning cracked from one side of the horizon to the other, and by its baleful stutter Karen beheld mountain ranges of ebonite marching in great serried ridges toward the ship, their steepening slopes as tight and sleek as tensing muscle fibers, their peaks boiling with phosphorescent broth. Wind gusts boosted the higher wavetops into seething crests; the engulfing roar sounded like an overweight jet struggling to gain airspeed. Her bow knifing into the waves at an angle as close to 90 degrees as the helmsman could manage, the ship struggled north by northwest, either flattening the swells with her mass or carving a furrow into their leading edge.

On the slope of one especially mountainous swell, the *Crown Prince* reached a point where its momentum and the ocean's force canceled each other out and caused the vessel to hang there for a long scary moment—like a lover verging on a climax whose intensity will carry some hint of extinction—and then she plunged down helplessly into a lightless canyon. She seemed to slide down for hours, the angle of the bridge wing growing impossibly steep . . . another few degrees and the freighter would not right herself at all, but just keep going down, straight to the bottom. At the moment of steepest incline, Karen heard a new and fearsome noise, a laborious grinding rhythmic chug. She grabbed Warrener's arm and shouted: "My God, what is *that?*"

"Our propellers are out of the water!" Allen said. "It's not as dangerous as it sounds—the thing to really worry about is if they stop!"

That made sense, as did the captain's handling of his vessel: as long as their bow was at right angles to the marching swells, the *Crown Prince* had enough steerageway to ride up, over, down . . . up, over, down the gigantic sea-hills, although each time the bow bit deep on the downward part of the cycle, the whole vessel shivered like a giant tam-tam, and darts of spray cut the air like icy shrapnel.

"We'll be all right, Karen, as long as we can hold her bow at right angles to the wind."

Karen remembered the blackout she'd had down in the saloon, heard the echo of her own semi-unconscious warning: *"It's coming! It's coming like a big black wall!"*

"Out there, Allen! You can't see it, but there's a rogue wave heading for us and it's going to hit us broadside!"

"There's nothing out there, love!"

Now she was pointing, her eyes wide and bright with fear. "Warn the captain!"

"I can't interrupt him now—besides, they've got radar, and—"

But she pushed him aside and went back inside the wheelhouse. "Sir! Sir! You must listen to me!"

"Young woman, please don't distract me!"

"God damn it, listen! Fifteen points off the starboard bow there's a rogue wave! It's a ship-killer! It's huge! You've only got a couple of minutes! For God's sake, order the bow to come right fifteen degrees or it'll broach us for sure!"

"Radar?"

"Radar, aye!"

"Anything on the scope off our starboard bow?"

"Don't think so, skipper—lots of storm-hash and rain reflections, though, so I can't be positive what's out there. . . ."

"Keep a sharp eye on that bearing and try a higher resolution setting."

"Aye."

"You see, Miss? We've got things under control. Now, please, if you don't step out of the way, I'm going to order you off the bridge!"

Allen had noted the rigidity of Karen's posture, the clenched fists, the innate reluctance she had overcome to approach the captain at all, never mind blurting out to an experienced professional sailor that his ship was about to be whacked on the beam by a wave as tall as a seven-story building . . . and now he also remembered those cryptic words she babbled when she was coming out of her trance in the saloon. "*It's coming.* . . ."

"Sweet Jesus! Nielsen, does that ladder go topside?"

"Yes, but. . . ."

"Hand me those binoculars, please! Waves don't always show up on radar, especially not with the kind of clutter we're picking up from the storm."

Somewhat dubiously, the steward took a big pair of glasses from a hook welded to the bulkhead. When the captain saw Warrener clomping up the ladder and working the dogs on the overhead hatch, he frowned and gestured authoritatively: "You! Sir, please get down! It's not safe up there!"

"If there is a rogue wave heading for us, captain, and it strikes us flush on the starboard side, this ship could capsize like a toy boat. Let me try for a visual confirmation, please! Nielsen will hang on to my legs!"

Nielsen blanched at the suggestion but he, too, had witnessed Karen's bizarre fugue-state in the saloon, and he was familiar with these storms, in these waters. "Let him take a look around, skipper—it couldn't hurt. Remember the S.S. *Gripsholm,* three years ago? Vanished during a gale just like this one, and in about the same place we are. No survivors, not even a piece of wreckage! Her crew didn't even have time to radio an S.O.S. The only thing that can sink a ship that fast is a monster rogue. . . ."

"Very well, then, Mr. Warrener, but hook your lifelines to the eyebolts on the railing; and if you're not back down in two minutes, I shall order the Master-at-Arms to haul you down by the balls, understood?" Allen nodded, grim-faced.

Beyond the hatchway was an old-fashioned signal-flag station, little more than a railing and some halyards, an emergency backup in case the ship ever lost all electrical power. Although the platform was surrounded by a waist-high steel railing, and there were lifeline hooks evenly spaced around the inside rail, it was open to the elements and never intended to be occupied in these conditions. The wind jabbed at him like a circling heavyweight. Despite the anti-skid patterns on the deck plates, the only way he could gain purchase enough to make an observation was by hooking both elbows over the top rail and covering the lenses with the rubberized neck-piece of his slicker.

At first, all he could see through the glasses were insanely foreshortened tartan patterns of white spume and the angry bobbins of racing squall lines. It was not sight that told him where to look, but a puzzling diminuendo in the storm's roar, a gradual muffling of the ocean's havoc off to the north-northeast . . . right off the starboard bow, where Karen had pointed. *My God, it's so high it's cutting off the sound-waves!* Focusing with numbed, shaking fingers, he caught sight of a featureless black band, bisecting his vision.

He yanked the life-line hooks free and thrust his sopping legs into Nielsen's waiting grip, drawing the hatch down as he fell, dogging the latches and shouting at the same time:

"She's right, captain: rogue wave off the starboard bow! I don't know how long we've got, but it's coming at us fast!"

"What exactly did you see, Mr. Warrener?"

"Damn it, there's a wall of black water so high it's cutting off the sound of the wind—can't you hear it?"

They all could, now, that eerie diminuendo. The captain shouted new orders: "Helmsman, come right twenty degrees! Engine Room, give me emergency power on the port engine for fifteen seconds, then emergency power on *both* shafts. Got that?"

"Aye-aye, sir!"

"Mother of God, help this old bastard come 'round," Nielsen said, wrapping his arms around the compass stand. Karen was staring fixedly at the bow, which began ponderously to turn to the right as one engine idled and the other raced at maximum power. Unable to say, much less do, anything else, Allen threw one arm around Karen and the other over the same steel pole Nielsen was hanging from.

Panic shivered in the helmsman's voice: "Cap'n, I don't think I can control the wheel. . . ."

"Executive officer, assist the helmsman!"

"Aye, sir."

Rated for 9550 tons displacement, even without cargo, the *Crown Prince Frederick* was not capable of turning on a dime; she opened the angle from 00 degrees by agonizing, ponderous increments, her hull groaning in protest at the strain, the bearings of her prop shafts overheating from the tremendous forces of torque. Even with two strong men putting all their muscle into it, the wheel was turning very slowly.

The bow began to angle upward, even as it continued inching to starboard. The starboard lookout's voice cracked when he too glimpsed the rogue: "Jesus, skipper, there it is! Look at that monster!"

Everyone looked; no one said anything—the sheer majestic size of the swell stopped their tongues and reduced all the hard-earned seamanship on that bridge into a matter of angles and pressures. The closer to a right angle they were when the wave reached them, the better their chances of riding over it or slicing through it. The ship's main deck was twenty-eight feet above her waterline and the bridge was thirty feet above the deck, and still the wave kept rising, until they were staring upwards at the flaring crest.

"Everyone brace for impact," ordered the captain, resigned and phlegmatic, now that he had done everything possible to avoid disaster. Implacable, relentless, big enough to swallow the *Crown Prince* whole, the wave towered over them like a smooth tectonic plate ripped loose from the planet's crust. Riding its stupendous shoulder, the ship angled up, up, forty-five degrees and rising, engines roaring, both props now at maximum R.P.M., the helm slowly steadying on the desired course.

"There's a notch in the top, sir!"

As the gleaming black wall reared over the forward cargo winch, they saw a narrow V-shaped opening between the wave's two primary masses.

"We're going to ride over it! Go, you rusty old scow, *go!*"

Lined up just right between two heaving cliffs of foam-streaked ocean, the freighter seemed to know what she had to do in order to survive, and they could feel her propellers digging deeper as she fought to stay on course. With a sound like tearing cloth, the freighter bucked over the narrow bottom of the notch and surged forward.

Allen Warrener watched the giant rogue—eighty feet high if it was an inch—reaching out for them, seeking to smash and devour. But the stout old ship fought for her life; it reared up, almost like a living, desperate creature. As they slid through the notch between its two mountainous shoulders, he heard a vast and dreadful *sucking* noise as the wave neared its breaking point—the snarl of a thwarted predator? As the crest surged past his vantage point, however, the shielding water mass unleashed the fury of all the wind it had been holding in abeyance. Cresting at eighty-three feet above sea level, the *Crown Prince Frederick* hung, propellers throbbing and hull shaking so hard it seemed impossible that her spine should not break when she made the inevitable plunge down the rogue wave's backside. Allen pulled Karen close and shouted: "Hold on, love, for just another minute, and then we'll be okay!"

"No!" she screamed, her mouth working furiously against the briny slickness of his rain gear. "Not okay! We're falling off the edge of the world!" She clutched at his upper arms as though he were the only thing between her and oblivion. "I had a *vision* of that wave, long before we entered the storm, and now here it is . . . don't you understand what that means, Allen?"

He had no time to respond, because at that instant the ship fell over the edge of a cliff and plunged straight down into that all-devouring roar of wind. Thanks to Karen's warning, Allen's sturdy sense of duty, and the quick reaction time of her crew, the *Crown Prince Frederick* had not taken the giant wave's full deadly power; but still, the rogue had lifted the ship five stories high, and now on the far side of the crest, they were about to ride nine thousand tons of uncontrollable iron down a ski-slope and maybe the ship would just keep on going down and down and down. . . .

All light, all sound, vanished; a cold, roaring vacuum engulfed the wheelhouse. In the penultimate second before the downward slalom began, he sucked in as much air as his lungs could hold, wondering if these gasps were, in fact, his final breaths. Then the *Crown Prince Frederick* slid into the valley on the rogue wave's backside and she went perilously deep, knifing into the sea from her thundering bow all the way back to the cargo boom below the bridge. Instinctively, as the surface rushed toward them, the people in the wheelhouse cringed and held their arms uselessly before their faces, as if windscreens, bones, and prayers could hold back that marrow-freezing darkness, and into their nostrils flowed a raw sea's-blood stink of iodine and ozone. Allen knew there was nothing any of them could do now but ride it out and pray that the shipwrights at the ship's home port of Odense had practiced their craft well. Too slowly for his liking, the ship stopped accelerating, one third of her turned into a temporary submarine, both her props out of water and banging furiously in midair. Port and starboard, outflanking the wheelhouse, two wings of burning black seawater tried to encircle the superstructure and pull them to their doom. This is what Oblivion tastes like, he thought, this is the red-meat stink of Creation itself—the odor of the sea back in the dawn of Time, when it boiled with meteor strikes and howled its anguish at the red and blistered Moon.

When the ship finally bottomed out, the impact knocked everyone sprawling, and the sea's final blows cracked the reinforced windscreens on both sides of the wheelhouse, but at last the churning props bit into water, and the helmsman reported the blessed return of steerage. Lightning and stars became visible once more, and although the up-and-down motions remained severe, that sickening sideways yaw diminished and within ten minutes the captain was able to announce: "We have resumed our original course for Torshavn!" The *Crown Prince Frederick* had taken the sea's most punishing blow and still sailed on.

"I shan't ask you how you knew about that rogue wave, Miss," said the captain, handing Karen a dry towel from his day locker. "Some things do happen at sea that cannot be explained to anyone who has not been a sailor. But on behalf of everyone on board, thank you for your intervention. And you, too, Mr. Warrener, for going aloft, in defiance of both my wishes and, no doubt, your own common sense—that took some courage."

"Amazing what adrenaline can do, sir. This is the lady who saved us, and I know her well enough to take her warnings seriously. But you didn't, and you had every right to throw us off your bridge. Thank you for trusting us."

The men shook hands, while Karen looked around in wide-eyed surprise, astonished to see that they were still afloat and to hear the storm's fury palpably diminishing around them.

"Admirable seamanship, Captain," she finally croaked, thrusting out her hand and then impulsively hugging the skipper, the helmsman, the Executive Officer, the navigator, three anonymous but clearly delighted seamen, and Nielsen, who seemed a bit dazed by what had just occurred.

"Now, Mister Nielsen, kindly escort these good people below and find some dry clothes for them. Also, the drinks are on the house!"

"Aye-aye, skipper!"

They had survived the worst the North Atlantic could throw at them, so the members of the Vardinoy Expedition swaggered back into the saloon with a powerful collective thirst—and very short memories about the potency of five-star brandy.

Richard was the first to call it quits, stumbling off to his cabin glassy-eyed and wondering how he was going to describe the night's events in his journal. Preston and Norma followed a half hour later, with Preston improvising a sea shanty as he lurched from one side of the corridor to the other:

> *Ohhhh, I must go down to the sea again,*
> *for some beans and a bottle of rum!*
> *Let's pick out a victim and he'll walk the plank,*
> *Then we'll grease up the cabin boy's bum!*

These departures left Allen, Karen, and Nielsen to close down the bar and drain the last open bottle of brandy. Allen was now feeling the effects of his exertions and his bruises, but in the wake of her own bizarre experience, Karen had become voluble and a bit manic. Allen thought it was best to let her get as sloshed as she wanted before he tucked her into her bunk. Nielsen obliged by poetically describing the pastoral beauty of his home island, Fyn, and by keeping their glasses filled. At 2:00 A.M. he said:

"Mr. and Mrs. Warrener, or however the arrangement goes, I'm obliged to close the bar now, but before I do, let me offer one last toast: to the two of you!"

They clinked glasses.

"May your love for each other bloom in the harsh and wind-swept Faeroes, may you find whatever you're seeking up there, and may your brandy always be as smooth as this!"

Still coming down from their adrenaline high, Allen and Karen tottered down the companionway, giggling and nipping each other playfully.

"Mmmm, you smell of brine and brandy, sailor."

"So do you, Cassandra! Wanna do something about it?"

"You got enough energy left for a quick roll in the hay?"

"My harpoon may not be sharp, but it's always handy!"

As Allen was unlocking their cabin, however, the ship took another moderate rise and fall—nothing like the undulations of an hour ago, but strong enough to fling open the door of the cabin next to theirs. From the darkness within came the sort of despairing moan usually associated with Third World dungeons.

"Oh, God, we forgot about poor Dewey!"

"I'll go see if he needs a drink of water or a new puke bucket or something. Go, wench, and prepare thyself to shiver my timber!"

"Tell him he missed all the excitement."

From the pitiful mewling sounds emanating from behind the cabin door, it didn't sound like Dewey was interested in excitement of any kind. Careful not to breathe the fumes, Allen opened the door a crack and called gently to the poor wretch inside.

"Hey, Dewey, can I fetch you a glass of nice cold water, or a clean towel, or maybe a priest?"

"Allen? That you, brother? Oh, Jesus, man, there's nothing anybody can do except put a merciful bullet in my brain. Don't come in here if you know what's good for you!"

"Now, now, it can't be that bad," clucked Allen as he strode manfully and with many good intentions into Dewey's cabin.

But when his forward foot landed in something lumpy and greasy, he lost his balance and had to grope for the door frame to keep from falling. Automatically, he also took a deep breath, and immediately realized what a prodigious mistake that was. A stench like that of newly disemboweled hogs clubbed him in the gut, and his gorge rose on a cloud of hot brandy fumes. He only had time to mutter: "Aw, shit . . ." before he doubled over and launched the first of many salvoes.

Karen came looking for him, after a while, and read the situation for what it was. "Sorry, boys, but I'm not setting foot inside that cabin until it's been purged with a flame-thrower. But I will fetch the cabin steward—he gets paid to deal with these situations. Anything I should ask him to bring for you?"

"A loaded pistol, please. . . ." moaned Dewey.

"Get a grip, macho-man. Remember, seasickness is all 'in your head. . . .' "

By ten o'clock the next morning, Allen was ambulatory again, though his color was still ghastly, and the only sustenance he could keep down was warm broth and dry crackers. Once he'd showered off the stink and changed into clean clothes, he felt strong enough to join Karen on deck.

The sea was calm, and large patches of hesitant sunlight kept breaking through the clouds and throwing lozenges of emerald-green across the otherwise lead-colored swells. Karen helped him walk to the bow and shared a cup of coffee with him.

"Watch our for your tongue, Captain Queeg; I still have plans for it."

"Ah, God, that tastes sublime! I swear to Odin that I will never, ever drink brandy again. Not tonight, not tomorrow, not in ten years."

"Don't worry," she patted his hand and knelt behind the railing to light a cigarette. "There's lots of other booze to choose from."

"I'm amazed you never even burped."

"I was too distracted by the chamber of horrors next door. Honest to God, the sounds you two were making. . . ." She tilted her face and gazed at him somberly. "You know what astonishes me the most about last night?"

"Aside from your unexplainable ability to predict the future?"

"Yes, aside from *that*. I'd rather not talk about that, until I can get it straight in my head. Please don't ask, not until I've figured out whether I'm precognitive or schizophrenic, or just made a lucky guess. Okay? Because any way you slice it, that was pretty fucking weird."

"And pretty lucky, for all of us. All right, then, what else do you find 'astonishing' about last night?"

"Well, it was the realization that once upon a time—what was it, ninth century? Yes, about a thousand years ago, entire families, men and women who were not much stronger or more intelligent than we are, sailed across this same ocean in open boats, with nothing to guide them but the stars and nothing to protect them except the capricious mercy of Odin. My God, what people they must have been!"

"Indeed they were. We tend to think of them as hairy barbarians, and picture them as always being murderously violent. Well, sometimes they were, but the world they lived in was a violent place, and a storm like the one we sailed through could snuff out their lives any time they sailed beyond the sight of land. And yet they cherished life, they valued honor, they idolized good poets, and they faced death with courage and a curious sort of acceptance. There's a lot that was admirable about them."

"Are there many remnants left of the early settlements?"

"Not much—some eroded old foundations, and indecipherable runes chiseled into the old stone breakwater outside of Torshavn's anchorage. My runic is pretty rusty, but they're worth seeing. We should stroll down there and take some pictures—they're not far from Eiden's townhouse."

"Well, we shouldn't have to wait too long—look there, about five points to port."

He shielded his eyes with both hands and squinted into a patch of clean white sky, just able to discern a thin scribble of land hunkered below a towering bluff of cumulus cloud.

He took her hand and squeezed. "That's Torshavn, baby. We're almost home now. Doesn't it feel that way to you, too?"

"Yes; amazingly enough, that's exactly what it feels like."

18.

WELCOME TO TORSHAVN!

From the journal of Richard Sugarman:

As ocean voyages go, the one from Copenhagen to Torshavn isn't all that long, but because of everything that happened to us, this passage had an epic (or would that be a "mock-epic"?) quality that transcends mere distance.

And now that we've arrived in "Thor's Harbor" (on the main island of Streymoy), we also have the sensation of journeying back in time. In this remote corner of Scandinavia, modern devices come and go—diesel trawlers, motor scooters, a few hundred compact cars scooting around on the island's grand total of 216 km of highway—but one's attention is held mostly by the envelope of sea and sky and mountains, which seem eternal and totally unimpressed with the twentieth century and its works. They shall abide, while the puny contraptions scuttling around them are precarious tenants at best.

Preston and I had just finished manhandling poor Dewey into a deck chair and force-feeding him some broth when we heard Warrener whooping at us from the bow. Dewey was instantly revived, and we all went forward to share the excitement. Karen was beside Fearless Leader, a big pair of binoculars jammed against her lovely brown eyes. Both she and Allen, I thought, looked to be on the verge of striking a pose—a pair of figureheads looking for a clipper ship to hang from.

Well, okay, I thought; this must be the fabled First Glimpse. If it turns out to look like Atlantic City, I'm going to be pissed.

I needn't have been so cynical. If even I could feel my spirit lift at so welcoming a sight—that garland of color, that splash of human warmth amid the vast gray wastes of the North Atlantic—how much more intense must a Faeroese sailor feel when he first sees this haven after a long, rough voyage?

The natural ambience, in fact, is as kaleidoscopic as it is stupendous! Here's the scene, as we slowly glide past the arms of the huge stone breakwaters that protect the harbor: everywhere the colors are perpetually changing, and the sky on the western horizon glows a porcelain white while the clear patches overhead have a delicate eggshell-blue made more vivid by the clotted-cream solidity of the clouds, the smaller clouds; the high, small clouds, propelled by the Gulf Stream air currents, are swift as prancing colts, while five or six miles ahead, the town's outlying ridges are swept by long thin scarves of misty rain. Ask "How's the weather today?" and a Faeroese might answer: "Oh, good, bad, and everything in between; we had winter this morning, summer at lunchtime, and spring in the afternoon—we skip autumn altogether up here—no trees, you know."

Torshavn is the smallest capital city in Europe—only about 8,000 souls, give or take, and from where I'm writing, I can see where all of them live. It's a glorified village, and therein lies its charm. They have bookshops and radios and a couple of cinemas; they have parks and soccer fields and dancing halls; but everything is on such a small scale! The houses are small, too, and snuggled together wherever there's enough flat land to build on, their only ostentation being the vivid primary colors of their exterior walls—as though their owners were seeking to impose a vibrancy upon the oppressively somber colors of the surrounding landscape. I like what I see, so far; beginning to understand how and why Allen Warrener left a piece of himself here, twenty-odd years ago.

More later—ship's about to dock!

LATER: No sooner had the mooring lines been cinched up than Allen began waving and pointing. I scanned the small crowd on the waterfront and quickly spotted the gent who turned out to be Eiden Poulsen: a broad-shouldered, blue-eyed man in maybe his early seventies, but ruddy and robust-looking, with a thick mane of white hair combed straight back and a rugged, weather-beaten face dominated by expressive, thatchy brows. He wore a business suit, but somehow, just looking at him, you got the feeling he'd have been happier in a fisherman's pullover and boots.

Standing beside Eiden (as he insisted we call him) was a young man dressed in fisherman's garb: a tall rangy fellow in his late twenties, with a long shock of yellow hair and big, articulate hands decorated by calluses and tiny scars—the hands of a trawler-man. This, I learned, was Birgir Jakobsen, one of Eiden's youngest skippers and a native of Vesturoy, the closest inhabited island to Vardinoy, our mysterious destination. He'll be our guide and facilitator, and he seems to be a most affable young man, both competent and likeable.

As enthusiastic as Warrener's reunion was with his old friend, I noticed that he kept glancing nervously from side to side, as though he were raising antennae to find out if the fabled Elsuba was anywhere nearby. Karen noticed this, too, and I saw her stiffen, then make an effort to relax again. But I saw no Nordic goddesses hanging about, so evidently she has not joined her father yet. Warrener drew the same conclusion and seemed enormously relieved.

Jakobsen peeled off to shepherd our baggage and equipment through customs, and Poulsen led us to his personal vehicle (one can hardly call it a "car")—a great hulking Land Rover with safari racks bolted to its roof. As Warrener was sliding into his seat, Poulsen turned and said: "By the way, Allen, Elsuba sends her greetings, but she'll have to join us later, I'm afraid. One of the women in Tjornuvik is in labor and Elsuba wants to see it through." Allen made no reply, his face a study in blankness.

Turning to the rest of us, Poulsen said there was a big smorgasbord lunch set up in the board room "but it's relatively light fare, as I understand that some of you— how can I put this delicately?"

"Puked our guts out?" suggested Preston.

"Just so, Mr. Valentine! And even those who did not, might not care for a heavy meal after last night's excitement."

"Ah, you heard about the gale, then?" said Warrener.

"Oh, yes! Two of my ships suffered some damage, and an Estonian tanker sent out an S.O.S. around midnight . . . and hasn't been heard from since. I fear the worst."

"Midnight?" echoed Allen. "That's about the time we spotted the rogue wave!"

"Nasty things, those. What'd your captain do?"

"Well, for one thing, he listened to Ka—" —and I saw Karen clamp her hand on his knee to shush him, then she smoothly picked up the sentence: "He listened to his intuition, I guess, because he suddenly changed course and put us bow-on to the wave. And not a minute too soon, either."

"Intuition, eh?" said Eiden. "Well, that's a fine quality in a skipper."

"Didn't you tell me once, Eiden, that only a fool would try to guess what the sea might do?"

"Yes, I did, Allen, but I must have forgotten to tell you the corollary maxim: only a bigger fool would stop trying."

And with that, Poulsen jammed the gearshift and hit the gas, driving more like a teenager than a tycoon, the cross-country tires humming over wet cobblestones. We didn't see much of downtown Torshavn, but followed the harbor's curve to the west, until we passed through a big gated entrance beneath a sign that read:

POULSEN'S SKIPAMIDJA

. . . which my dictionary renders as "Poulsen's Shipwrights." Sheds, warehouses, cranes, chugging little donkey engines, the carapaces of two steel trawlers a-building on the ways, sparks from welding torches cascading down from the scaffolding—a busy and prosperous-looking shipyard. Clearly, Eiden Poulsen has done all right for himself since he took a war-surplus trawler back in 1946 and used it as the foundation of the modern Faeroese fishing fleet.

In the board room, the Americans enjoyed an ample but not stultifying meal, along with a magnificent view of the harbor. After socializing for about forty-five minutes, Eiden clanked on an empty Tuborg bottle so he could announce: "If you've all finished eating, I would like very much to show you something . . . before I have to go back to work. There's a big, dreary agenda of things I must take care of before sailing off to Vardinoy. Birgir has rejoined us and reports that all your equipment is safely stored and your luggage has been taken to my townhouse, where I have room to put everybody up until we sail. Birgir is at your disposal this afternoon, for sightseeing and shopping, and will bring you all back to my place for drinks at six. After we're properly fortified, we shall have dinner at what passes for Torshavn's only decent restaurant—do not get your hopes up, as there are only so many ways one can cook halibut and cod!"

Eiden then led them downstairs and out into the clutter and bustle of the shipyard. The procession halted before a door in the side of a huge prefabricated shed. Inside, it was dark and redolent of fuel oil, paint, and spent welding rods. Eiden left the door open just a crack, so they could see to line up against the nearest wall.

"Birgir thinks I'm being whimsical, but I simply couldn't resist making a little drama out of this. Just stay put for a moment, while I go turn on the power." They heard him clomp up a short flight of metal stairs and flip a couple of switches. Allen whispered to Birgir: "What the hell is this all about?"

"Humor him—too much salt water on the brain!"

"Everybody ready?" Eiden's disembodied question elicited a chorus of affirmatives. There was a loud click as some kind of master switch was thrown. On came the lights. And down went the collective jaw of the Vardinoy Expedition.

Looming above them was the steeply raked bow of a deep-sea trawler: 545 tons displacement, 167 feet long, 28.5 feet wide, and 11.5 feet from the waterline to the main deck, a gleaming gull's-belly gray in her new coats of paint, and proudly identified by the crisp lettering below her starboard anchor-well:

H.M.S. *LAERTES*

"My God, Eiden, it's your ship! I mean, your *first* ship!"

She was an impressive sight, but only Allen immediately grasped the full significance of her being here.

"In 1951, an old comrade from the Battle of the North Atlantic days, recently promoted to rear admiral at the time, notified me that he had seen her name on a list of ships that were about to be broken up and sold for scrap. I flew to Scotland, bought her for cash, just like a used car, and had her towed back here and put out to pasture in this shed. Call me a sentimentalist, but I couldn't bear the thought of her having survived forty-two convoys and twenty-one attacks by U-boats and Nazi aircraft only to be turned into junk. I had her sheathed in weatherproof plastic and paid a maintenance crew to scrape the rust off once a year, and for ten years or so, she was carried on the list of the Danish government as an auxiliary fishery protection vessel, even though nobody seriously expected her to go to sea again; I used to come down here sometimes, just to be alone with the memories. . . . Then, when Allen and I started exchanging letters about the Vardinoy trip, it suddenly hit me that with some modernization and remodeling, she'd make a superb headquarters for us. I've had a cargo winch installed aft of the funnel, so we can load and unload the Land Rover and the tents and such, and partitioned the crew's quarters into individual sleeping compartments. She's still rather spartan, in terms of creature comforts, but she's got brand-new radar and wireless systems, her engines are still perfectly sound, and by God she *is* seaworthy! Does she meet with everyone's approval?"

A lusty cheer from all throats signaled confirmation. With a youthful spring in his step, Eiden led them up the gangway and turned everyone loose to claim a cubicle and explore the interior. Warrener and Karen followed

Eiden from one compartment to the next, up to the crow's nest and down to the bilge pumps. Old she might be, but the trawler-turned-submarine-killer still had a quality which, in the presence of the ship itself, could only be defined as "dignity."

When they followed Eiden onto the foredeck, Karen pointed out the empty steel gun tub that rose on a pedestal mount just abaft of the steep pugnacious bow.

"If you took her to sea as a working trawler, Eiden, how come she still has a gun mount?"

"Well, as I said, nobody expected her to be called up for active duty, but with that gun tub in place, she could be readied for service in a matter of days. That happened, briefly, during the Cuban Missile Crisis, when NATO was on full alert for a Soviet attack. I was called up along with her, and actually took her out on a single patrol—although what hostile force we were supposed to engage, I have no idea. She was only carrying a single Oerlikon in that bow position, and it certainly didn't have the range to engage a Russian bomber. Even so, for a little while there, she was a warship once more, and I was on the bridge in my old uniform, which still smelled of mothballs. . . ."

They were interrupted by Norma, shouting at Karen from the starboard bridge wing: "Hey, kiddo, come look at the Little Girl's Room they installed just for us! It's painted pink, for Chrissakes!"

"If you two naval enthusiasts will excuse me, I have to see this!"

When Karen was gone, Eiden climbed into the gun tub and sat on the steel ammo box welded to its floor. He lit a cigarette and congratulated Allen when he turned one down.

"Perhaps this is something we should keep to ourselves, Allen, but we will have access to that Oerlikon, should an emergency arise. In fact, it's stowed below already, in a big heavy crate labeled 'Emergency Rations' or some such bogus disguise."

Warrener glanced around rather nervously, making sure that they were, in fact, alone, and then said: "I don't know how the Faeroese Coast Guard, or whatever you have for a navy now that you're independent, likes to do things, but the American Navy takes a very dim view of privately owned ships that carry functional anti-aircraft cannon. If we're inspected, couldn't we get in trouble with the customs authorities, or somebody like that?"

"First off, I *am* the customs authority, or one of them. Whatever paperwork there might be concerning the status of that weapon, it's been filed away in some bureaucratic warehouse for more years than you and I have known each other. I doubt that anyone's given it a thought since the early sixties. Okay with you?"

"Well, it *would* be okay, if you could explain to me why you think it's desirable to be hauling a twenty-millimeter automatic cannon up to Vardinoy. . . . Do you know something about our supposed monster that I don't know?"

Eiden seemed to choose his words carefully before answering. "It's just as we discussed in some of our letters. We both agreed that it would only be prudent to bring some weapons along for self-defense, because what we are looking for—if it exists—is presumably large and known to be very dangerous. I know we already have enough small arms to start an insurrection, but as long as we've got this ship, I thought it wouldn't hurt to have something else up our sleeves, something with long range and a heavy punch. It's not that I'm being evasive, Allen, just cautious."

"And maybe a bit romantic?" ventured Allen.

"Mmmm, maybe. But it seems to me that *you've* been considering the Vardinoy Monster from a Loch Ness frame of reference, and nobody has ever told stories about Nessie suddenly ramming rowboats full of Scottish anglers. Admittedly, the Vardinoy literature is often vague and even contradictory, but when you consider that a veteran Luftwaffe pilot was terrified by the one glimpse he had of this thing, then I think we can conclude that it's not as benign as Nessie seems to be."

Allen shrugged. "Hey, don't get me wrong, man, I think it's great that we have an Oerlikon stowed below. Heck, if World War Three happens to break out while we're at sea, we won't even have to come back for a refit."

Eiden nodded, relieved but still somewhat secretive in manner. He said nothing more about the ship's armament, however; and when he stood up to discard his cigarette into the water, he glanced at his watch.

"Damn, I'm late for my appointment at the Economic Planning Commission! Allen, there's an intercom microphone on the bulkhead behind the captain's chair—could you go up there and summon everybody back to the front of the ship? If you lot want to go shopping or sightseeing, you ought to do it now, before the afternoon rain starts."

"How do you know. . . . Oh, wait, I remember the joke: if you're going out after two o'clock in Torshavn, always take an umbrella, because if it isn't raining then, just wait ten minutes and it *will.*"

After a well-lubricated meal, the members of the Vardinoy Expedition walked back to Eiden's residence in the Old Town. The townhouse would not have been out of place in modern Nantucket: the lamps in his living room were made from brass ship fittings, the walls from blocks of locally hewn basalt, warmly timbered with wooden beams salvaged from a Danish barque that had run aground near the house in 1927. Above the peat-burning fireplace hung a large, raw-hued painting of men battling pilot whales in shallow water, a rendering taut with savage energy, blood its brightest color.

"That's a very powerful painting," said Norma, walking close to admire the thick but precise brush-strokes.

"By one of our few native artists who enjoys an international reputation," said Eiden. "Chap named Andreas Dahl; I've purchased several of his works for my corporate offices. He's a bit eccentric, wanders around the islands making sketches during the warm months, then retreats to his studio to do the full renderings; nobody knows where that studio *is,* but when the national museum held a retrospective a few years ago, he actually showed up—the first time anyone had seen him in Torshavn—long enough to pick up his check, get roaring drunk, and make off with one of the trustees' wives! Well, that's a genius for you! Can't follow other people's rules, can you, or it would spoil the image!"

Eiden busied himself stoking the fire, and the Americans clustered around it, drying themselves externally by its flames, and internally with glasses of Eiden's high-octane aquavit. The others were midway through their second drink, and Allen was reaching the bottom of his third, when they heard a key rattling in the front door. When it opened, puffs of rain rushed in; after it closed, they heard a female voice mumbling curses in the foyer, followed by the "clomp" of rubber boots hitting the floor. Then a husky, tired-sounding tone: "Hello, Poppa! Bring me a towel, please, and a stiff drink, too!" At the sound of the answering voice, the color drained from Allen's face. Preston sidled over to him and whispered: "Is that the voice of fabled Brunnhilde?"

Allen nodded tightly and slugged down the rest of his drink.

"*Velkommen*, daughter!" Eiden rose and bustled first to the bar, then to a linen closet.

"I'm not ready for this," Allen muttered to Preston. "I needed another day or two at sea, just to get psyched up for it."

Preston patted him reassuringly on the shoulder. "Ain't that just like life, buddy?"

Into the living room strode Elsuba Poulsen, clad in a yellow parka slick with rain. She threw back the hood, tossing a corona of droplets from the emerging mane of her hair. That hair was as Allen remembered it: a vibrant bronze , streaked with Rapunzel gold. Preston looked from Allen to Norma to Richard Sugarman, and they all nodded simultaneously—when such a woman made her entrance, one *noticed.*

Allen was the slowest to rise in greeting, coming up from his chair like a man struggling through heavy surf. Elsuba greeted the room's occupants with a stiff, all-inclusive nod and a perfunctory "Hello, everyone."

Eiden handed her the requested drink. "I did not expect to see you until tomorrow evening."

"And I wish you were *not* seeing me now, Poppa. There were severe complications with the woman in labor—she needed better treatment than I could give her at the village dispensary. I radioed to Torshavn, to have the emergency team meet us on the road, but then the weather up in the mountains turned vile. The ambulance slid into a gully, so I had to cram everybody into my little car. One of the paramedics drove, the other worked with me in the back seat, trying to deliver that baby. We had to drive too damned slow because the rain was so heavy."

Elsuba's voice turned angry. "My patient went into labor twenty kilometers from town—I hadn't the instruments, the room to work, the driver was unnerved by this woman screaming in the back seat . . . the baby's head was purple when it emerged—the cord was strangling it, but I couldn't get a grip on it. . . ."

She refused to say more until Eiden put his arm around her and told her to go on, to let it out.

"The woman will be all right, physically at least. The child, I'm afraid, died five minutes before we reached the hospital. So: that's the cheerful situation that brings me here tonight. Thanks for the drink, Poppa."

She mimed a stoic shrug as the first swallow went down, then shook her head vehemently, as though purging her memory. Two more gulps of Eiden's firewater restored composure. She glanced around the room at the silent witnesses.

"And now, some introductions are in order. . . ." A thin suggestion of a smile made a brief, experimental showing, then faded quickly. While Eiden made the introductions, she went from person to person, shaking hands very formally, making sure she had the names. She acknowledged her past relationship with Allen by means of one light, dry peck on the cheek. "Allen," she said briskly, "It's good to see you again. You've aged well."

"Is that a compliment?" he responded, much more curtly than necessary.

"It is meant to be, yes. Should I have said: 'You really look decrepit?' "

She didn't wait for an answer, but turned away and retreated to a vacant armchair in a shadowy corner, leaving uneasy silence in her wake. The others tried to resume conversation, but the talk had become stilted and self-conscious.

Karen took a moment to study Elsuba Poulsen. Elsuba *for real*. The dream-woman suddenly made flesh.

Karen was wary, but for the moment she did not feel particularly threatened. She almost felt sorry for Allen, who was acutely uncomfortable at being suddenly confronted with the woman who embodied his private mythology.

She had, of course, seen snapshots of the young Elsuba, rather too many of them for her own good, but Karen's strongest image of Elsuba was not based on those rather generic Kodak portraits. It was instead defined by Allen's written descriptions, which Karen had studied more often and more intently than their author probably suspected. Her mental portrait of Elsuba Poulsen—until this moment—had been cloned from Allen's lush, overcooked recollections of Elsuba at eighteen.

Now a mature woman approaching her middle years, Elsuba-in-the-flesh presented a clashingly different reality. The long years of study and internship, the dreary procession of runny-nosed Copenhagen winters, had rubbed much of the luster from Elsuba-the-icon; the passing of time had done its work too, eroding the concupiscence of yore. She was certainly less willowy, more angular and meatier in the hips than Karen had been expecting, and her face was already reshaping itself for middle age. But when she shook hands, Karen had caught a rain-wet hint of Elsuba's natural scent, so warm and sensual that it was almost embarrassingly intimate. Hard-edged doctor or not, the woman was a walking cluster-bomb of pheromones, for she still projected a surge of erotic force. Karen did a quick inventory-check: yes, there were age and care lines deepening on her face; yes, her mouth was no longer ripe—it had thinned to the extent that it seemed more prim than generous. But her lips were still finely sculpted and expressive, and *those eyes!*

Elsuba's eyes defied Temporality itself. However much the rest of her body had changed, those eyes were startling. And they were still as Allen had rhapsodized: a dark, haunting, bewitching violet. What extraordinary genetic recipe had produced such an ineffable hue? Elsuba might otherwise have been plain as a stick, but a passionate communion with those eyes would have branded many a man's memory forever.

Karen's conclusion: Elsuba Poulsen was no longer—if indeed she ever had been—the Nordic goddess Warrener had enshrined in his opus. Yet her presence was still compelling, her pride and dignity palpable. No matter how many imperfections Karen might catalogue, there remained elemental qualities that made Elsuba still, and probably for the rest of her life, an uncommonly attractive woman. As she relaxed in her chair and the aquavit took effect, Elsuba's features steadied into a different archetype: poised and grave, remote and hieratic—the abbess of Guinevere's nunnery. Yet that same face, mobilized by passion, would be stirring indeed.

Despite a communal effort, the conversation never regained its spontaneity. When the mantelpiece clock chimed midnight, a general exodus took place, which left Allen, Karen, and Elsuba alone with the dying fire. Karen suddenly felt that, by default, it was she who had to make the next move. Would it be too heavy a gesture simply to say good night and leave the two ex-lovers alone? Experience as well as instinct told her that that might be unwise, especially since Allen had been drinking steadily for about six hours. Karen knew he had reached that stage of inebriation which offered him the greatest latitude for doing something foolish or nose-diving into mawkish sentimentality, mood-swings Dr. Elsuba Poulsen was most unlikely to tolerate.

Get a grip, Allen! If I leave you alone with this woman, there's liable to be some kind of emotional dog turd to clean up in the morning and I'm damned if I came on this trip just to clean up your mess!

Even as Karen tried to send him this telepathic admonition, Elsuba seemed to understand how tense and ambiguous was the mood engendered by her surprise appearance. She caught Karen's eye, and Karen saw compassion and intelligence in the tiny smile Elsuba had the grace to send her way. Elsuba stood up, walked over to her and bestowed a simple, sisterly embrace. The gesture was completely spontaneous, and it felt to Karen like a blessing.

"I am very glad to meet you, Karen," Elsuba said, just loudly enough for Allen to hear, but pitched so privately that it was an invitation to confidence between two women. "I want us to become friends. Allen is fortunate."

Then she moved over to Allen, who stood up, somewhat unsteadily, to accept a hug, given with precisely the same warmth she had displayed with Karen . . . and then she ruffled his disorderly hair playfully with her fingertips. When she spoke, her voice was again private in pitch, yet it reached out to include Karen as well. She seemed, for the first time, to be acknowledging their past intimacy, yet she was also clearly establishing a demarcation: their passion for each other was *historic,* not dormant.

"Forgive me, Allen, if I seemed distant when I came in. It was nothing personal. It's just that tonight was the first time I've lost a patient—even an unborn patient—and I'm taking it pretty hard. Intellectually, I know I did everything possible, but it still feels like failure. They warned us about this in medical school. They also said that, in time, we'd 'get used to it.' By God, I never want to 'get used to' losing a patient! I don't think any doctor should! But for now, I'm going to prescribe a sedative for myself and get some sleep. In the morning begins a new day, *ja?* So then, good night to both of you, my old flame *and* my new friend."

When she had gone, and the silence in the room had grown intolerably strained, Karen asked quietly: "Is it going to be all right, Allen?"

He could not answer that question, but it seemed to trigger a sudden manic burst of energy. He strode briskly, and without the slightest sign of inebriation, into the foyer, where he called back over his shoulder: "Get your rain gear on, darlin'! There's a place I want to show you, a short pilgrimage I want to share with you."

"Allen, you've had a lot to drink, and the streets are slippery and steep."

Already dressed for the weather, he poked his head back into the room and grinned at her in a manner simultaneously irritating, challenging, and somewhat impish.

"I know what you're thinking, Karen, and it isn't about slippery cobblestones.

You're worried that I'm going to lay one more thing on you than you're ready to handle tonight. Well, maybe so, maybe not. But it's a trip I've been meaning to take you on, and now, by God, is exactly the right time to do it. Come on—I checked outside, and it's barely drizzling. Warmer, too! So shake a leg, lady. It's not far, I promise!"

She really didn't want to leave the coziness of Eiden's house, but Allen was obviously determined to go through with . . . whatever. He threw her slicker across the hall and she recoiled from it as though it were a giant, rubbery bird, repulsively wet and chilly. Her expression went hard as she jammed her arms through the sleeves with a vehemence close to anger.

"So help me God, Allen, if you're planning to show me some pastoral hillside where you and Elsuba screwed each others' brains out twenty years ago, you'll make the rest of this expedition as a eunuch!"

"That particular hillside is a long, long way from here, lady. I'm going to show you Torshavn the way you'd never see it in the daylight, and believe me, it's worth seeing." He flung open the door. "Are you coming with me, or not?"

She bit back the urge to snarl: *I don't take orders from a drunk.* But there was something so genuinely childlike about his excitement that she was now almost as curious as she was pissed off, so she pulled up the hood and followed him into the night, grumbling: "Whither thou goest. . . ."

The night air *was* warmer now, and the gentle misty rain almost invigorating. There was a mood on the wind close to magical. It was as though the sea were blowing its breath through the streets of the Old Town. Funneled up from the foaming bowl of the harbor, amplified by the narrow lanes between the leaning, crooked buildings, came long rolling gusts as temperate and fragrant as the breath of sleeping lambs. Gone now was the cold, driving tempest that had chased them uphill from the restaurant; the wind danced on the cobblestones almost playfully. Glancing quickly at the harbor, she saw its waters roiled to a creamy froth, the fishing boats bobbing like corks: the diminutive fleet of a Viking king. Torshavn seemed deserted. Not a soul walked its streets, not a vehicle broke the spell with its headlights; nowhere did a neon sign compromise its timelessness. The harbor, occluded by spume, no longer seemed solid and laid out by engineers, a mariners' haven fortified by ferroconcrete and shaped by the sharp-edged requirements of commerce. With a feeling verging on awe, she beheld Torshavn, from its stout protective breakwaters up to the sensed-but-unseen loom of the encircling hills, as it might appear on an aerial map: a minute and vulnerable indentation in a mass of uninhabitable cliffs and gorges, a man-made artifice, serving only to define the scale of the blind, overwhelming emptiness that surrounded it.

For an instant, she was dazed by that now-familiar but never welcomed sense of being *in touch* with the fundamental realities of this place: she could sense the latent power of the North Atlantic, its capacity to reclaim in moments these scattered islands, so vast by human scale, yet so puny in comparison to what lay *beneath*. . . .

"This way!" called Allen, setting a brisk pace uphill. Now Karen, too, felt oddly energized, and she followed almost eagerly. As if to confirm her decision to follow, the wind shifted, rising from the harbor to push helpfully against her back.

Around them, the Old Town slept, boarded up tight against the elements. The street twisted up in a gradual slope, unevenly tilting from side to side, paved with rain-polished cobblestones. There were few streetlights here in Old Town's labyrinthine heart, and those too were old, for the glow of their low-wattage bulbs was not much brighter than the radiance of an oil-fired fixture. Had there been a suitable fog, Karen thought, this part of Torshavn could have served nicely as the setting for a Jack the Ripper movie. The buildings tilted and jutted almost whimsically, their foundations built up by palimpsests of generational stone, like the walls of an ancient city rebuilt on the rubble of its sacked and subjugated predecessors.

Karen was fascinated by the diapason of wind-sounds: the soft sizzle of rain gusts on glazed roof tiles, the dark flute-moan emanating from overhead wires and swaying signposts, the low fluttery piping that issued from the chinks in old stone walls. The downhill runoff, compressed into deep stone-lined gutters on both sides of the street, added a merry, chuckling counterpoint, as though the waters tumbling from the heights far above were eager to reach the sea at last.

Rather belatedly, Allen slowed down and took Karen's hand. He seemed delighted when he saw the grin on her face. "I think you like this, after all."

"Well, shit yeah; I mean, it's impossible to realize that we're in modern Europe! This is like walking through a village painted by Arthur Rackham—Hamelin on the night before the coming of the rats!"

Allen nodded agreement. "I think we can shorten the trip if we cut through some of these alleys. . . ." His tone of voice was slightly less confident than it had been back at Eiden's house. Second thoughts?

"Okay. You have my permission, if that's what you waiting for. You lead the way—it's too narrow for both of us. I'll follow, and I'll holler if I get lost."

"Just follow the breadcrumbs," he joked, before setting off briskly through a jumble of alleys and footpaths. Although Karen was only a few paces behind, Allen was soon a long psychic distance away—he seemed to belong to the wind, to be at one with the old dreaming houses and silent little shops.

Suddenly, out of what had seemed a cul-de-sac, they emerged onto a sidewalk in what must have been the main shopping district of Torshavn, and he led them north beside a modern paved street that must surely have been the only *autobahn* in all the Faeroe Islands. Sleek modern streetlights, precisely intervaled and antiseptically bright, burned any lingering atmosphere from the scene—they could have been in any small town on the mainland. Allen grimaced in distaste.

"All *this* shit is new! Pre-fab concrete shops, billboards—ugh."

"At least we haven't seen a McDonald's. . . . Are we lost?"

"Well, it has been a long time. . . . Let me get my bearings. You want to break for a cigarette? Once we get past these next few blocks, it isn't far."

"I'll reward myself with one when we get . . . to wherever it is we're going."

Once he picked a direction, it didn't take long to leave the streetlights and tacky little shops behind. Between one block and the next, Karen felt the air pressure change; from all around her came a sense of things *widening*, of the lift and nighted bulk of encircling ridges. They paused again at what surely had to be the last traffic light on all of Streymoy.

"Which way now?"

"Mmmm, to the right, I think."

The old one-and-a-half-lane street they now followed soon began to curve steeply uphill, past small trim cottages, snugly buttoned up, a few still showing lights behind brightly colored squares of curtain. In small rock-fenced yards, Karen saw sheep grazing on wet heather, their presence adding a sharp, pleasant barnyard tang to the air, redolent of wet wool and warm nuzzling breath. A large brown dog left its sentry post long enough to huff twice at them, darting up to lick Allen's hand before trotting back to its duty. Two more blocks brought them to a small park, where Allen touched Karen's shoulder and turned her around to show her the view to the south.

They were now in the hills high above Torshavn. Below, the lights of the town followed the roll of the land down to the harbor's black crescent. Low scrims of cloud passed by, like exhausted marathon runners. On the stout breakwaters enclosing the port, both navigation beacons burned brightly, defining the border between sheltered waters and the black immensity that spread beyond them.

"Are we there yet?" Karen puffed, more than ready to light that cigarette now and searching for a dry place to sit.

"Yes, ma'am, we are." In one of those unexpected Southern gentleman gestures that made his companionship a lot more tolerable than it would otherwise have been, he whisked out a clean handkerchief and wiped off a spot on a bench for her. They sat close together, but not touching.

Facing them was a two-story barracks-like structure, set in isolation on a landscaped plateau across the street. To one side of the entrance, a flagpole nested in the circle of whitewashed rocks, and a tri-lingual sign identified the building as a youth hostel. Taking a deep breath, Allen pointed to a corner room. Behind its curtains, they could see the shadows of a young couple, one of whom abruptly shed an enormous backpack. Footloose young students. . . . For a moment, Karen envied them and silently wished them well.

Warrener began without preamble: "When Sylvia and I made *our* trip to the Faeroes, it was during the summer after my first year as a teacher. I wasn't making much of a salary—we did it on a shoestring, figuring that we had enough for airfare and a week or ten days of cheap sightseeing. But when I went to the currency exchange booth in the airport, I was pleasantly surprised to get back about twice as many Danish *kroner* as I had expected. I figured we just got lucky with the exchange rate or something. But we had so much extra money, we changed our plans. Left the return reservation open, hopped on a boat, went for a tour of the southern islands. You know, that way, we would be exploring territory that was new to *both* of us, instead of me just dragging her around to places I'd already discovered."

"Sort of like you're doing now, with me?" Karen grumped, dragging tight-lipped on her Marlboro.

"Bear with me, okay? Anyhow, that turned out to be the best time we ever had together. Until we got back to Torshavn. . . .

"Waiting for us on the dock was an official from the national bank, accompanied by a very stern-looking customs agent. 'Oh, Mr. and Mrs.

Warrener, I'm so sorry to tell you this, but the clerk at the currency exchange made a serious mistake—she's just not used to handling American money, and, while it is most regrettable, I'm afraid you owe the national bank approximately four hundred dollars. If you can't settle things today, we'll have to impound your passports until you can wire someone in America to send you the money.' Well, I wasn't about to give this clown our passports, so I paid the difference, figuring we could wire Preston for the money. And not knowing Preston was on location and wouldn't get the telegram for eight more days. That left us with thirty-six dollars and no idea how long that would have to last. We asked at the Tourist Bureau, and they directed us here—three bucks a night, and until Preston wired us the airfare, we were stuck. We stayed in that room, on the second floor. I fully expected Sylvia to make me feel miserable the whole time, for screwing up with the currency exchange. Amazingly enough, she didn't. She thought it was a great adventure. And it turned out to be.

"What the hell? We were young and healthy, we could walk anywhere we wanted to go, and we lived just fine on bread and cheese and coffee. There was even a library—books either donated or left behind by other guests—so when it was raining, we could stay in our snug little room and read. Mostly, though, when it was too wet to go out, we stayed in bed and screwed like minks. The days blurred together, and I guess we kind of lost track of things like birth control pills and periods. . . ."

Oh, God, I know where this is leading. . . . Karen stubbed out her cigarette and snarled impatiently. "Allen, *no* woman loses track of her periods and her pills unless it's deliberate. You can spare me the punch line, 'cause I see it coming like an eighteen-wheeler. Your son was conceived up there in that corner room. A freebie blow job if I'm wrong!"

"Jesus, did I telegraph it *that* obviously? Well, yes, that's what happened. But there's more to it that that. And by the way, I long ago figured it out about the pills and the periods—I'm not entirely dim, you know, just a little naïve sometimes. When she told me she was knocked up, I went berserk. I accused her of *trapping* me, tried to make her agree to an abortion. This was one time she didn't choose to escalate the fight—just let me rant and throw things until I ran out of steam. And then she said: 'Are you willing to hear my explanation now?' Something about the way she was being so calm and reasonable . . . I just nodded and lit up a joint.

"Sylvia could be a harridan, and over the years she turned into a bitch from hell, but she knew me, lady, she knew me. She ticked off her points, and every one of them was like a bullet I couldn't dodge. First, because she'd already had a miscarriage, she was lucky to have conceived at all. And didn't I remember that night in the hostel room in Torshavn when she said to me: 'You were right, Allen; these islands are a magical place. I want to move here, and have a magical baby here,' and I said 'All right, we can move here and have a magical baby . . . some day.' But with me, she said, there was likely never to be a 'some day.' Having a child was always somewhere off in the nebulous future, but that future never seemed to get any closer. She knew, just *knew*, we would never go back there. So on our last night in Torshavn, she decided to throw the dice. If she came back pregnant, then we had a *magic baby*, and everything else that was wrong between us would somehow be set right. If she didn't, then we would just continue to drift from week to week the way we had been doing, until, one day, we wouldn't be able to stand each other. That was why we had to have *this* child. Did I now see the logic? Strangely enough, I did. A child conceived on the Faeroes, in the harbor of Thor: how could it fail to be so special, so wonderful, that it would fix everything that was wrong with our lives."

"That's a heavy burden to place on a goddamned fetus, Allen!"

"Yes, it was. We didn't feel any magic. We just had a baby, a child we weren't emotionally, financially, or in any other way prepared to bring up properly. Brian brought no peace, no closeness—just shitty diapers and sleepless nights and postpartum depression. Oh, the kid was adorable enough—the Lord makes 'em adorable, you know, so we won't automatically strangle half of every generation before it reaches the age of four. But having him didn't change our lives, and it sure as hell didn't strengthen our marriage. I hated the distractions, she hated the responsibilities. It was only later, when I knew I was in danger of losing my son, that I began to understand just how magical he really was! And how desolate my life was going to be without him. . . . Much too late, of course, but isn't it always?"

Karen turned on him not with the smile of compassion he seemed to expect, but with anger. She grabbed his shoulders and shook him.

"That's a real two-hankie monologue, Allen, but just what the *hell* does any of it have to do with *me*? You dragged me out into the rain, made me walk a mile or two uphill, suckered me into this huge emotional buildup, and then you point to a perfectly anonymous bedroom window and tell me, *'My child was conceived up there!'* I can't help but notice that the Faeroese government hasn't put up a commemorative plaque! Jesus, you could have just *told me* about all this while we were back at Eiden's, sitting around a cozy fire and getting quietly plastered!"

"I thought you would enjoy the walk," he said flatly.

That pulled Karen up short, and the edge crumbled from her rage. Truth to tell, she *had* enjoyed the walk. But the object of that rain-swept hegira had turned out to be such a commonplace, whiny little confession, that she still could not understand why he had framed it so elaborately. "Let's go for a walk in mysterious nocturnal Torshavn!" would have been enough—well, *probably*—to get her moving.

"I have a more important point to make, Karen, and it's already slipping out of focus, so kindly shut up long enough for me to get as far as the whole *exculpatory fucking bit!* Because this isn't simple to say and I've been gnawing on the words all the way up here, and if I don't just ad-lib the speech now, it'll be gone forever."

"You've got the mike, Allen. Read your damned poem, and let's get off this cold wet bench."

"What I'm leading up to . . . I mean, the first time I came here, when the affair with Elsuba happened, I *did* feel charged with 'magic' when I left. I was so cocksure, absolutely certain I was going to set the world on fire, that when the years went by and that lightning bolt never hit me, I felt . . . *cheated.* Like I was being deprived of something I was entitled to, just because I discovered the Faeroe Islands and as far as I was concerned, they were my own private Valhalla. After the second time I came here, I convinced myself we'd created a child so beautiful and fine that his mere existence would transform my train wreck of a marriage into something fulfilling and solid. Again, when that didn't happen, I felt *betrayed.* And yet, the moment I saw these mountains again, the minute I set foot on the docks of Torshavn, that same sense of wonder came flooding back. Jesus, Karen, you're feeling it too! There *is* something magical about this place!"

She nodded slowly, beginning to understand but still not sure she liked it, not one bit.

"Yeah, Allen, there is. But you *can't take it with you when you leave!*"

"This time, I'm wise enough to be content with the memories. This time,

I have to live every moment one hundred percent *while* I'm here, because whether we find our monster or not, my heart tells me this is my last visit. So I'm wide open to this place, to every particle of mood, and it's almost like those first two experiences have finally been washed out of me. I know, I just *know,* that the Faeroes are going to show us something special. *Us!* Because you *do* get off on this place as much as I ever did! There's a mystery to *that* every bit as weird as our Vardinoy Monster might be! Oh, Jesus, Karen, I know I'm on the verge of speaking in tongues or something, but I just know we are both going to find something here that will change us profoundly! Maybe it'll be the same thing for both of us, or maybe we'll find utterly different things! But from now on, I swear to you, the Faeroes have nothing to do with Elsuba, and nothing to do with Sylvia! From this night on, whatever we find here, it's every bit as much yours as it is mine."

Was there ever a man so intelligent who labored under such a curse of bad timing? Karen listened in amazement as Warrener finished his oration, halfway expecting some voice in the nearby bushes to sing out: *"Can I hear a loud 'A-men,' brothers and sisters?"* From the dark stony hills above, came back a mocking echo instead: ". . . it is mine . . . mine. . . ." If there was a third reverberation, it was masked by the return of cold, hard rain. Just to make a point, Karen waited until her hair was plastered and her cheeks were freezing before she deigned to lift the rain hood and stand up. She saw that Allen now looked embarrassed, confused, even a little dazed.

"Thank you, Allen," Karen said, "Thank you so very, very much for giving me permission to enjoy myself on the Faeroe Islands."

"Okay, fuck you, too," he snapped, turning his back on her.

She hadn't meant to sound so *bitter,* really, just disgruntled and familiar with the kinks he tied himself into when he tried to combine intimacy with rhetoric. It was time to make peace now. She put her arms around him, kissed the cold wet nape of his neck, and let some warmth creep back into her voice.

"I was just alarmed there, for a minute, that you were going to ask *me* to make a baby here. . . ."

He guffawed at the very notion. "Did the stormy sea make ye daft, woman? Ye have told me of'n enough that ye dislikes rug-rats!"

"Ah, Cap'n, I dunna like the wee vermin. In my neighborhood, they were regarded as a punishment for Original Sin. Now take my hand and let's get back to Eiden's before the first thing we share turns out to be galloping pneumonia!"

But as if on cue, the rain stopped when they joined hands, and the wind changed yet again, now southerly; and, as if for their private delectation, they watched in open-mouthed wonder as the North Atlantic breathed upon Torshavn harbor a low, rolling, luxuriously thick fog. It came toward them at a walking pace, heralded by warmer air, silently blacking out the bright highlights of the harbor, and then, in smooth succession, every block of town through which they had walked. They glanced at each other, nodded in agreement, and strode downhill, arm in arm, to meet it. And so they walked back through a Torshavn transformed anew, a ghostly, insubstantial dream of a place, through a warm and welcoming exhalation of the Gulf Stream, a private, shared wonder—as though the islands were confirming Allen Warrener's prophecy

By the time they were back in the heart of Old Town, the need had grown upon them to make love, although neither quite knew if the act would be one of consecration or of exorcism. But when they finally closed their guest-room door and got down to it, they were both so sensitive to the nearness of the other Americans that the coupling proved to be something of a lick-and-a-promise affair. Technically successful, though—like many a hardworking, veteran married couple who either get it on while all the kids are at the movies or not at all, they knew which buttons to push, even if they knew in advance that the Earth wasn't going to move on this occasion. Karen managed to come three times, sharp little whip-cracks with her vocalizations drowned in a pillow, and Allen spurted like a jackrabbit as soon as she whispered it was okay for him to let it go. It was an odd little fuck—surrounded by such a fierce silence that it seemed strangely, even penitently, appropriate for that evening. And when they were done, they spooned exhaustedly and passed swiftly into a shared and dreamless oblivion.

19.

OLD SALT

From the journal of Richard Sugarman:

After we passed the Torshavn breakwater, we steamed northeast for thirty minutes, then turned due north and entered the narrow strait that separates Streymoy from its neighbor, Eysturoy, the second-largest island in the archipelago. When we nosed into that channel, I got my first sight of the "real" Faeroese landscape. As quaintly old-fashioned and "Nordic" as Torshavn was, it didn't prepare me for the immensity of scale and the sheer wildness of the vista now unfolding on either side of the Laertes.

Eysturoy's headland came into view five minutes ago, looming up off our starboard bow: a massive wedge of terraced basalt a thousand feet high and shaped exactly like the prow of an old dreadnought. The headland came to a knife-sharp point, and the long throw of sunlight made the southern side of it glow like wet garnets but cast the northern side into deepest shadow. As we passed into the shadow of that huge formation, the ambient temperature fell ten degrees! The sudden chill, coupled with the abrupt descent of darkness all around, gave us the feeling that we were crossing an invisible line of demarcation, leaving behind modern civilization itself.

Here's what I see at this moment: the high barren spines of the two islands both define and restrict our horizons. On Eysturoy, to the right, a multitude of keen edges sculpted out of solid gloom—the sun will not touch their lower reaches until noon. But on my Streymoy-side, the strike of sunlight reveals in surgical detail each scar and ragged spill of eroded rock. Between each layer of exposed stone, the slopes are carpeted with malachite-green heather. The transverse ridges bulk up like a hundred Gibraltars, gathering mass and height as they near the sea, then breaking off to form sheer cliffs, some of them five or six hundred feet high at the water's edge. Some of these formations have been amputated from the mainland by storm and tide, transformed into those gaunt free-standing monoliths the Faeroese call "dranger"—sea-riven honeycombs of gleaming fuliginous basalt, the larger ones seeming to breathe as the water hisses and gurgles through their countless fissures. And periodically, we glide past the black staring eyes of caves. Inside some of them, I can see the currents bubbling and churning into a phosphorescent broth, ceaselessly tunneling—how deep do they go? No one knows; they're un-explorable. Even a total landlubber like me can see the folly of steering too close to them in a small boat—the riptides around them must be ferocious!

The central massif of both islands resembles a layer cake, with bands of basaltic rock alternating with layers of soft wet turf; in some places it looks as symmetrical and purposeful as the ramping stairs constructed up the sides of Aztec temples. And always, high above, the constant shift of Gulf Stream currents, clashing with southerly blasts from the Arctic, creates a weather system so dynamic that it amounts to meteorological combat. These wildly clashing fronts and troughs all generate chaotic skyscapes in total contrast to the brute silent mass of the islands. A few thousand feet above Streymoy's jagged spine, a fierce wind drives phalanxes of torpedo-shaped clouds to the west. We cannot feel its passing down here, yet we can see its power when a half dozen waterfalls suddenly get sucked upwards by it, turning their plunging torrents into plumes of streaming vapor, as though the entire crest were lined with gigantic smoking torches.

Because so much of this landscape is foreboding, glowering, even threatening, the odd splashes of color stand out all the more vividly. At the base of one especially grim and lunar plateau, the land suddenly forms a gentle, shallow bowl, where the sun conjures a green so outrageously bright it almost hurts your eyes, and bringing out in the gentler rock outcroppings surprisingly delicate shades of roseate pink and smoky orange.

What contrasts! Vibrancy and turbulence juxtaposed against monolithic stillness! If I walk to the starboard railing, I face the jagged towering escarpment of Eysturoy's western flank: foreboding, unclimbable, fanged with ship-crushing reefs and gouged with the sinister pits of caves. But if I walk to the port side, I behold a different world: the leeward slopes of Streymoy, awash with morning light—soft meadows of a moist earthy green so saturated with color that it seems to be on fire from within.

We angle to the right, to get around a jutting promontory, and there on the opposite side, on the coast of Streymoy, I see a tiny village clinging to the land—I count ten, no, eleven houses and a scattering of barns and sheds. They're all roofed over with whiskery green sod, and all are painted in defiant primary colors:

canary yellow, fire-engine red, Caribbean blue! Tying these people to the outside world is a single rather forlorn strand of electrical cable, which zigzags up the mountain on skinny steel pylons and disappears through a notch in the rocks. This village has probably been here for three hundred years, withstood uncounted tempests, yet it looks fragile, *as vulnerable as a candle flame inside a drafty cathedral. There are no cars, of course, just a few farm carts and some double-ended boats pulled up on the shaley beach in the shelter of a low breakwater of dripping stone, on top of which sits an old fisherman, mending his nets with gnarled hands. On the bridge wing, Norma looks up from her sketching and waves jauntily at him. He nods impassively, then gets a better look at her and flashes a lewd, almost toothless grin. How often does such glamour pass his way?*

What do these people do *when the sun goes down? Such a purity of isolation is both alluring and appalling.*

Observations of the Expeditioneers: To my surprise, the one who seems most outwardly affected by the scenic grandeur is Dewey! He's positively wired, *loping from one side of the boat to the other, afraid he might miss something special by turning his back at the wrong moment. Brawny in a new Faeroese sweater, his hair pulled back and fastened with a grungy rubber band, he's affecting a new Viking look, and it suits him well. As he lumbered past a moment ago, I sought to elicit from him some sort of Rousseau-esque comment about the puny-ness of Man in such a primal landscape. The exchange was classic Dewey.*

Inquisitive Jewish student: "So, Dewey, what does all this say to you?"

Pretend-redneck ex-biker: "Don't 'SAY' anything, Little Dick! What it does, is SING!"

"I can dig it."

"Yeah, man! It's just . . . just fuckin-GREAT, iddun it?"

I reckon it is, if you're into the Nordic Thing. And maybe I am getting into it. . . .

Up at the tip of the bow, Eiden and his daughter are talking, leaning close together against the rail. When the ship noses into a trough, they're outlined for an instant by a fine penumbra of crystalline mist. Uh-oh—Elsuba just undid her scarf and the wind caught her hair and pulled it out into golden wings, so that she looks for all the world like a valkyrie figurehead. Warrener's been surreptitiously glancing at her, pretending to polish his binocular lenses; Karen is studiously pretending to study the sheep on a distant hillside, but she senses it every time he sneaks a peek. Probably keeping count. What is the chemistry between her and Warrener? I'll bet even they don't have any idea.

Up on the bridge, Birgir just rang the ship's bell. Time for lunch, and the first Tuborg of the day!

Allen forced himself to study the landscape; it offered a safer reverie for him than the wind-blown glory of Elsuba's hair.

"Ah, there's the lunch bell! Can I bring you something from the galley?"

"Yes, thank you—one of those mutton sandwiches, a bag of chips, and the coldest Tuborg in the ice chest, thank you."

Allen caught the brittleness in her tone—damn it, she had seen him glancing at Elsuba! What a pisser if he had to avoid even glancing at Eiden's daughter for the rest of the trip!

But Karen's smile was real enough when he handed her the sandwich and twisted the bottle cap off of her Tuborg. Washing down the first bite, she gestured with the bottle's neck toward the shore.

"You were right, Allen, about how the light changes all the time! This place is a painter's paradise. Look at how wrapped up Norma is in her sketching! She has good technique, you know; it's just that her style is too sentimental. She needs to develop a bolder line, learn how to really bear down and carve a groove in the paper—don't you think so?"

"To be honest about it, except for a couple of still-lifes hanging in their house, I've never seen much of her work. I just knew she dabbled in painting now and then."

"*Dabbled?* Jesus, Allen, you don't really give a shit, do you?"

"Hey, lighten up, will you? She could be Picasso, Grandma Moses, and Salvador Dalí all rolled into one, and I wouldn't know about it unless she or Preston made a point of showing me her work! Which neither one of them ever did."

"Norma wouldn't have brought it up without Preston's okay—and I'm sure he wasn't interested in promoting her artwork."

Allen tried to turn the dialogue into banter. *The last thing I want to be distracted by on this gorgeous morning is an impromptu Feminist rant! And she thinks I have lousy timing. . . .*

"His most frequent description of Norma was 'multi-talented,' but I don't believe her painting and sketching was what he had in mind."

"Honest to God, Allen, wipe that smirk off your face!"

Oh, God, she was going into Escalation Mode—

Until that moment, his mood had been close to sublime, and he was ready to admit to the Flat-Earth Theory if that would shut her up. Instead, he tried a preemptive strike: "Listen, Karen, I've known those two people a long, long time, and I've never disparaged Norma's intelligence, not once made a bimbo joke about her, or felt anything for her other than respect and affection. As much as I hung around the porn-movie sets to get my jollies, I never once heard Norma say anything, even in private, about feeling *exploited.* She and Preston were having a damn good time and getting rich— an ideal combination if ever there was one. You can see that in her films, for God's sake! Compared to the skanks who were her competition, she was Marilyn Monroe, she was Garbo! And she could turn it on like a light bulb, the instant that clapper came down—she made love to the *lens* . . . no, *through the lens.* And that was a genuine Gift, Karen; her fans sensed that, and Norma worked really hard not to disappoint them."

"Never let the boys down, huh?"

"She never did. And the fortune from their dirty movies gave her the time and freedom in her private life to cultivate her painting, get her pilot's license, or to read Wittgenstein in the German, for all I know—whatever she wanted to do, she could. If that's 'being exploited,' where do I sign up? Oh, please, for Chrissakes, let's not argue—it's too gorgeous a day. I promise, now that you've brought it to my attention, I *will* show some interest in Norma's artwork from this day forth. Fair enough?"

Her smile softened. "Yeah, okay—that's all I wanted. But your mini-lecture was kind of interesting, too."

Allen relaxed . . . somewhat. Whatever had made Karen edgy (*Oh, come on, Warrener, you know it was those stolen glances at Elsuba! Okay, Jiminy Cricket, guilty as charged!*), she'd agreed to let it go, at least for now. They clinked Tuborg bottles and settled back in deck chairs to watch the scenery again.

And the Faeroes rewarded them for their good sense by soon revealing a vista grander than any they had yet beheld. Norma, from her perch atop the wheelhouse, spotted it first, and called it to everyone's attention, pointing excitedly. All the members of the Vardinoy Expedition swiftly mustered on the starboard rail to bear witness.

The island of Eysturoy, which had hitherto shown them nothing but high bleak stony ramparts and the pockmarks of mephitic caves, suddenly revealed a hidden splendor: a mile-long stretch of uninhabited valley, where the grim unbroken coastal cliffs curved sharply inward and converged at a hazy distance to form a colossal amphitheater whose walls were at least two thousand feet high. A hundred streams, from wire-thin silver threads to brawny pummeling cataracts, poured over the edge of that enclosure, urgent to reach the sea. Above the *Laertes* was a sun driven into the sky like a brass nailhead, its light so sharp that it saturated the huge natural arena with an almost violent luminescence, and the myriad waterfalls collided with that light; and the constant febrile wind from the North Atlantic combined the two elements, generating an impossibly complex fugue of rainbows, looped and intertwining, arching grandly, quivering like pastel serpents. The color-fugues enclosed a stupendous volume of space; so high were the mountains at the far end and the cliffs along the straits that it was entirely possible no human being had ever walked in that place. But, thanks to the Vardinoy Expedition, millions might at least be able to *see* its wonders. The rapid clacking of camera shutters sounded like popping corn in a hot skillet.

"Dewey, are you getting this on film?" shouted Preston.

"You bet I am, boss! I got three cameras rolling!"

For another hour the H.M.S. *Laertes* moved steadily north, but the scenery became monotonous again, and the passengers dozed, read, or cleaned the salt air off their cameras. Everyone flinched when Birgir's voice crackled over the loudspeaker. "Ladies and gentlemen, if you would direct your gaze toward the bow, you will soon see the charming and incomparably dull village of Tjornuvik!"

"Tjornuvik"—the name held no emotional resonance for the others, so only Allen and Karen moved to the bow to watch the place come into view.

From Allen's descriptions, Karen had expected a much smaller, almost primitive-looking village; but Tjornuvik was now the third-largest town on Streymoy. It boasted a cannery, a small boatyard, a school, a well-stocked library, a town hall, even a tiny cinema. Karen thought the place looked prosperous and hospitable.

"Does it look like you remember it, Allen?"

"Pretty much, except there weren't any TV antennas back then. I'm kind of sorry to see *those*."

Birgir rang "All stop!" and the trawler's engines fell silent. He spun the wheel expertly so that the *Laertes* drifted into her mooring space, making gentle contact with the rubber-tire bumpers lining the breakwater's side. Two young sailors leaped ashore, their mates hurled mooring lines to them, and soon the trawler was snug in her berth. Eiden climbed into the empty gun tub and motioned for Allen to follow.

"Welcome, one and all, to my home town of Tjornuvik! We shall be here for two days, loading the last of our supplies, and I've arranged for all of you to have lodgings at the sailors' inn, that picturesque barracks-like structure over by the warehouses. Don't worry—it's more comfortable than it looks, but be forewarned: they don't allow booze inside. So if you want to drink, you'll have to visit the two local pubs. I recommend neither of them, but you may feel differently. Now, Allen, isn't this the moment for *you* to make a speech?"

Somewhat taken aback, Allen mumbled into Eiden's ear: "Warn me, will you, the next time you put me on the spot like this!"

Eiden glared at him with mock severity and whispered: "You're the *leader* of this expedition, Mr. Warrener, not me, so it's bloody well time you started acting the part."

Allen realized what Eiden was doing and was somewhat startled by it. Until this moment, he had rather assumed Poulsen would take that role. But Eiden had just anointed him, before everyone and unambiguously, so there was nothing for it but to strike an appropriate pose and wing it.

"Okay, everybody! This is your last chance to pick up anything you forgot to pack: toothpaste, chewing gum, Preparation H, whatever. Behave yourselves and remember that we sail at dawn, the day after tomorrow, and we'll have a lot of work to do when we get to Vardinoy. Adjust your hangover schedule accordingly. Until then—enjoy the place but don't trash it. Any questions?"

Dewey waved a half-full Tuborg bottle. "What does a guy do for fun around here, bwana?"

"He behaves himself, for one thing. Shit, man, look around you! Write postcards, go fishing, climb a mountain, count the seagulls, read a good book. Just don't molest any of the local girls."

"Why not, Allen?" Elsuba was teasing him and everyone knew it. "Some of them might like it!"

General chuckling and a loud braying laugh from Preston. Elsuba, the hitherto silent enigma, had just charmed the whole bunch. Allen blushed to see the playfulness in her eyes, then realized it was kindly, not mocking. He forced himself to put on a good-sport grin and actually felt some of the brittleness fade in the air. The past seemed to relinquish its grip on him . . . just a little.

"Thank you for that contribution, Miss Poulsen. Okay, gang, that's my 'Fearless Leader' speech. Everybody have fun, and be back on board when you're supposed to!"

Warrener leaned back from the railing toward Eiden and said: "Was that okay, Commodore?"

"Not exactly Churchill, but good enough." After he ascertained that no one was in earshot, Eiden added: "Remember I told you that my people had tracked down an old sailor who was actually present when they fished that German pilot out of the drink? Well, you and I will be meeting him right after supper. And until we hear what he has to say, let's keep this just between you and me, all right?"

In honor of their arrival, Eiden had laid out a lavish buffet dinner in the dining room of the Poulsen family manse—the whole array of delicacies dominated by an immense glazed ham flown in from Copenhagen, then trucked up from Torshavn, that very day. On the whole, it was a relaxed celebration, although the mood changed when Eiden rather pointedly suggested that Elsuba take everyone except Allen on an orientation tour of the local nightlife, such as it was. He and Allen had "some business matters to discuss." When the others had left, Eiden poured two tumblers full of aquavit and handed one to Allen, who slugged it down in one long, burning gulp. When he could speak again, he lifted his briefcase from beneath the table.

"I've got a tape recorder and lots of spare batteries, a notebook, a camera, my basic collection of clippings about the Vardinoy Monster, and a copy of General Teal's letter. Can you think of anything else we should bring?"

"Yes—a bottle of good Scotch. He keeps asking visitors to smuggle some in for him, but you can't buy the good stuff up here, so I had some Glenlivet sent up from Copenhagen. Here, tuck these pints in your satchel—those'll be easier for him to smuggle back into the retirement home. It's time now—if we wait much longer, he'll start nodding out, or so my employee tells me."

Moments later, they were again down at the harbor; silhouetted against the long twilight of sub-arctic summer, the old *Laertes* once more resembled the tough little warship she had been. Beyond the harbor, the sea was quiet and slick as oil, and the only sound was the rasp of keels being hauled across the strand as tired fishermen finished their day's labor and prepared to go home.

"You're awfully quiet, Eiden."

"I generally am, when I have nothing to say."

"Haven't you already found out what this old salt's going to tell us?"

"I'm not interested in hearing tall tales second-hand, Allen. My sources say that he *does* have, as one man expressed it, 'a real whopper of a yarn,' but right there, that's an *interpretation*. I want to hear his story without any pre-views, and hear it in your company, both of us together. Better that way, don't you think?"

"Of course. I take it he speaks English?"

"Like a native—he worked with the Brits during their occupation, and many of his voyages were to the U.K."

"I don't know his name, yet, Eiden."

"Damn, I must be getting senile! It's Kollsoy, Petur Kollsoy, and it might win some points for you if you address him as 'Captain Kollsoy,' since he did own a ship toward the end of his career. His health isn't good, and all he has left is his pride."

They halted at a cinderblock warehouse fronted by some nondescript offices. A hand-painted sign above the front door stated simply *"POULSEN"*; in this town, that was enough. Eiden knocked. A burly man in fisherman's garb opened the door, pointed toward the end of a short corridor, then slipped discreetly outside. When they reached the lighted cubicle at the far end, Eiden pushed open the door and was greeted by a rough voice, speaking lightly accented English: "Ah, that must be you, Poulsen. And the other gen-tleman with you . . . ?"

"Captain Kollsoy, this is Mr. Allen Warrener, from America. Allen, shake hands with Petur Kollsoy, as fine a sailor as you will ever meet."

"As *old* a sailor as you'll ever meet," rumbled Kollsoy, extending his left hand and not rising from his chair. Allen observed that Killjoy's right arm was in a sling and mostly covered by a scruffy brown jacket. Kollsoy's eyes were embedded in deep pouches of pleated skin, and most of the color had washed out of their pupils. Over his unkempt thatch of white hair Kollsoy wore a traditional Faeroese cap, snug around the skull but loose and floppy to one side, like a beret woven by elves. The ashtray on the desk before him was filled with yellow filterless stubs, and the air in the room was oppressive with stale smoke and the screw-you smell of an old man who didn't take as many baths as he should and didn't give a damn if you weren't happy with it.

When Allen's tape recorder clinked against one of the Scotch bottles in his briefcase, there was nothing slow about Kollsoy's reaction. "That was the sound of a bottle, and no mistake. Did you bring me some Scotch, Poulsen, like your men promised you would?"

"Aye, Petur, two pints of the best! One for now, and one to sneak back with you into the retirement home." Eiden went to a water cooler and brought back a couple of paper cups. Allen poured two fingers of Scotch into one, but when he held it out for Kollsoy, the old man raised his left hand and groped unsuccessfully for it. "You'll have to stick the bloody drink into my hand, sir. Can't see anything but blurs these days, even in bright daylight. Me, who used to have the sharpest eyes in the fishing fleet!" Kollsoy smiled when Allen put the cup against his palm, and he drank from it avidly. Smacking his lips, he belched in appreciation.

"Damn fine stuff, Mr. Warrener. Single malt, and seven years if it's a day."

"You know your Scotch, Captain Kollsoy. I'll keep refilling the cup, if you'll tell us your story."

"Where do you want me to start? The day I was apprenticed?"

"Not quite that far back. Start with the war years. When you served in the Home Guard under a British officer named Telford. . . ."

"Aye, Lieutenant Robbie! Fine young soldier, he was."

"So you do remember him clearly?"

"Better than I remember yesterday's breakfast. We sailed on many a boring patrol together."

"That's what I want to learn about, sir, a particular patrol in the autumn of 1942, when you and your mates went out to search for the survivors of a German bomber that had crashed near the island of Vardinoy. Tell me everything you remember about that incident."

Kollsoy motioned impatiently for another drink. He sipped it ruminatively and with an expression that Allen thought was both shrewd and wary. After a moment of awkward silence, Kollsoy pointed the cup at Warrener and said: "Why don't *you* tell *me* what you've learned about it. That'll save us some time, and give me a minute to sort out my thoughts."

Allen nodded, then remembered that Kollsoy was blind, or nearly so. "Everything I know about the incident comes from an account written twenty years after the war, by General Teal—he was only a colonel, then, of course— who commanded the British defense battalion at Torshavn, Lieutenant Telford's commanding officer. According to him, Telford and several other men sailed north to Vardinoy to try and locate any survivors from a shot-down German Condor. Supposedly, they found no trace of the aircraft itself, but they did find a single survivor—the pilot, a man named Bauer. He was floating near the Vardinoy coast in his life vest, badly injured and delirious. When Telford hauled the man aboard, the German began raving about how, when his crew parachuted out of the falling aircraft, *something* emerged from the water and . . . well, the word he kept using was 'absorbed' them, one by one, and . . . that the men just *melted* while this . . . absorption took place. Bauer alone survived, because he landed on a solitary rock that jutted out of the sea, and he clung there until he lost strength and fell. By that time, this *thing*, whatever it was, had vanished beneath the surface, presumably carrying the other crew members with it. Telford and his men took the pilot back to Torshavn, where he had to be kept heavily sedated so he wouldn't start raving about . . . whatever happened to his men off the coast of Vardinoy. One night, Bauer managed to sneak out of the hospital—there was a bad storm blowing in the harbor, and he either became disoriented and fell into the surf, or he committed suicide. Telford's C.O. thought it was suicide, but he also thought there was something to it besides simple dementia."

"Weren't nothing 'simple' about that whole business," snorted Kollsoy. "He jumped, all right—because, whatever he'd seen, his mind couldn't handle it. Poor bugger probably thought the whole world had gone insane. . . ." Kollsoy paused while a heavy smokers' cough racked his frame. Then he patted his jacket and hauled out an empty cigarette pack. "God damn it, I'm fresh out! Either of you gents got a gasper?"

Eiden slid a half-pack into Kollsoy's hand and offered the sailor a light when he managed to extract a fresh cigarette. Kollsoy dragged hard on it, with exaggerated relish, and blew a fresh cloud of smoke into the general murk hanging over the table.

"Go easy on those things, Petur," Eiden chided. "You'll live longer."

"No, I fucking won't," Kollsoy laughed grimly. "I can smoke as many as I please and it won't make a bit of difference. But first things first, eh? Tell me, Mister American, why do you want to know about a strange thing that happened so long ago?"

Allen tried out his "cover story": "We—there's a small expedition involved—we're going to be doing some archeological research on Vardinoy. There used to be a thriving town there, back in the nineteenth century, but suddenly the population just abandoned it. No one knows why. I've been commissioned by a magazine to explore the place and write an article about the mystery, if there really *is* a mystery and not just a plague or something like that. So naturally, I've been collecting all the information I can about Vardinoy—and since no one apparently lives there, I've tracked down anyone I could who has visited the area."

Kollsoy seemed to weigh this explanation; from the way his eyebrows arched, he found it somewhat wanting. "If you say so, Mr. Warrener, if you say so. . . ."

Instead of dulling the old man's mind, the Scotch seemed to have acted as a stimulant. He leaned forward, trying hard to focus on Allen with his rheumy eyes.

"Let's start with Robbie Telford, shall we? A proper soldier; to him, the King's Regulations were the Word of God. My guess is that he wrote nothing in his official report that could not be explained in proper military terms. And a lot of what we saw and heard that day, well, he may have told his C.O. some of it privately, but he sure as hell wouldn't have put it down in his official report, not the way it really happened.

"We didn't often have cause to patrol way up in the northern islands. If the Krauts were going to land anywhere, they would've done it here, on Streymoy, within striking distance of Torshavn, which was the only place up here with any strategic value whatever. But on the day you're asking about, we actually had a mission of some importance, or so we liked to think. We'd been ordered to take a pair of boffins—"

"I'm sorry," Warrener interrupted. "A pair of *puffins?* What did the British use birds for?"

Kollsoy and Eiden both chuckled. "*Boffins*, Allen! That was a slang word for the scientists, the technical blokes, the guys who fixed broken radars and made the weather forecasts. Please go on, Captain Kollsoy."

"Our mission was to take those two boffins on a tour of the northernmost islands, to locate a suitable spot for a remote weather station—unmanned, basic instruments, radio link to Torshavn. The instruments would transmit data that might help the Allies make more accurate weather forecasts available for the convoys.

"We set out from Torshavn with five men: Telford and I, a radioman, and the two boffins. We planned a systematic survey of all the northern islands, including Vardinoy, looking for just the right spot to put that weather station. After three days of poking about, we were bored and cold and running low on supplies, so we were ready to pack it in. Fortunately, Vardinoy was the next-to-last place we had to check out."

"What was the other place?"

"Little Norduroy, the last and loneliest of all the Faeroes. I was for ignoring it, because the people who live there, well, they're very clannish, not friendly to outsiders: they might steal the weather equipment just to get back at us for violatin' their fuckin' privacy! Anyway, we set course for that abandoned village you spoke of, supposedly the only decent anchorage on the whole coast of Vardinoy, when all of a sudden this bloody huge German *Condor* comes roaring out of the clouds, trailing smoke! It passed over our heads, and it was clear the pilot was trying to gain altitude, so his mates could bail out. I saw one man's parachute open, but then we lost sight of the airplane in the fog, so we didn't know if the rest of 'em made it out. A minute later, we saw a dull flash and, a few seconds after that, heard the explosion. Naturally, Telford turned the patrol boat around and put on full speed. From the look and sound of it, there wasn't much hope of finding any Germans alive, but if there were survivors, we wanted to save them, and I think we also wanted to be the first Home Guard patrol to bag some Nazis!

"It was a foggy, drizzly, miserable day, and we were bucking a strong headwind, so we were good and soaked by the time we finally got near the crash site. We started a methodical search under the high cliffs, and it was slow going, because the currents there, below the cliffs, are bad, very bad. Nobody fishes on the west coast of Vardinoy—although there's plenty of fish in those waters. It ain't worth the risk. It's the caves, y'see. The coast of Vardinoy is riddled with 'em, and some of them are so big and so deep that when the tide and wind are just right, they're like giant storm drains. In the days before engine power, sailing ships had actually been sucked into caves under the surface, all hands lost . . . the boats never seen again. We stayed a respectful distance from the cliffs and just crept along. About halfway up the length of the island, we came to a place where there were a lot of big, solitary rocks, pieces of the cliffs that just haven't fallen into the sea yet. 'Dranger,' we call 'em in Faeroese. That's where we spotted the wreckage."

Warrener leaned forward, startled. "Wreckage? Telford told his C.O. there was no wreckage to be seen."

"Well, it wasn't much. Just a single big piece, really: a machine-gun blister of Plexiglas. It looked like the force of the explosion had popped it out of its mounting, more or less intact. It had fallen on to a cluster of rocks and gotten stuck there. Telford thought it would be a good idea if we fished it out and brought it back, to confirm that the Jerry plane had gone down. So we eased closer and got a boat hook into it, me and the radioman. And when we hoisted it into the launch, we could see there was something strange about it.

"That bomber must have slammed straight into the cliffs and been blown to bits. But this hunk of Plexiglas—it wasn't shattered or cracked, the edges weren't jagged, as you would expect after such a crash. Instead, they looked sort of *melted*, like candle wax, and they gave off a funny kind of shimmer, like an oil slick, when you look at one from certain angles. Telford said it first: 'That thing looks like it was dipped in some kind of acid.' I guess he was right, because both me and the other man who handled it got burned when we touched it. I ask you, how could a thing that's been drenched in cold seawater for an hour or more . . . how could such a thing burn your flesh? And it burned *cold*, colder than the sea, colder than any ice I ever touched. It burned, I imagine, the way atomic radiation burned those Japs at Hiroshima . . . you've seen the pictures. And even after we dropped the thing onto the deck, our skin tingled where we had touched it. After a while, that faded away, and I thought no more about it . . . until about ten years later, when that tingling came back. And this time it never went away. Very slowly, year by year, it got worse until . . . well, here, mate, see for yourself. . . ."

Kollsoy removed the sling from his right arm, and then the elaborate sheath of bandages. Carefully rolling up his sleeve, he placed his forearm on the table, under the light, then turned it over, palm upward. Allen's stomach lurched at the sight. But when Eiden Poulsen looked at the affliction, he sucked in his breath sharply, as though someone had punched him in the stomach, and his face twisted not only in revulsion but also, it seemed to Allen, in recognition.

From palm to elbow, the inside surface of Kollsoy's arm had fused into a blue glaze of seared tissue, corded with stark, angry-looking welts where muscles had cramped and veins had swollen. The discoloration and tissue damage were darkest and most ruinous on his palm, but tendrils of the same loathsome blue had enveloped his elbow and risen beyond the cuff of his sleeve.

"Goes all the way to my shoulder now. And that's just what you can see on the outside. Inside, it's gone deeper, a lot deeper. That's why they didn't just amputate the arm. It looks like a system of roots on the X-ray pictures, all these little threads just branching every which way. It grows very slowly, though, a millimeter a year maybe. And it doesn't hurt, oddly enough; the nerves are all dead under that blue crusty shit, whatever it is. But one day, in two or three years, it'll reach the spinal cord or the heart, and just shut me down like somebody flipping a light switch. So that's why I can smoke and drink as much as I like. . . .

"At least I'm luckier than that radioman—he grabbed the thing in his arms and cradled it, lifting it out of the water. I only put one hand on the shimmery part, to steady it for him. He died back in fifty-two, of skin cancer, so they said; but the first time I visited him in the hospital, I knew damned well it weren't no 'skin cancer.' The doctors knew it too, but they had to make up something, so they could keep poking him and sucking his blood, like he was a lab rat. He told me they'd tried antibiotics and radiation and skin grafts and experimental drugs that just made him sicker. Last time I went to see him, half his body looked like my arm—and when he asked me to bring him something to help him, you know, 'check out early,' I brought him arsenic. He was grateful; he might have lasted another four or five months otherwise.

"So when I saw the first blue spot on the inside of my wrist, I thought, well, hello Mr. Skin Cancer; let's you and me not even *go* to the doctor, so we won't end up like that poor sodding radioman. The medics would never figure out what it was. I already knew it would kill me, but not for a long while, I reckoned. So I just rolled down my sleeves a lot more and kept on working. I'm glad I handled it that way, because I earned enough to buy my own boat, and for five years I had the satisfaction of being a real sea captain. I'd've kept on enjoying life, too, if I hadn't lost all the use of this arm."

Allen refilled the cup, wondering if the Scotch supply would prove equal to Kollsoy's thirst.

"Anyway, to continue my story: we resumed our search after hauling the wreckage aboard, and about twenty minutes later we came upon the pilot, Bauer, dangling from a high solitary rock, his parachute snared on the top. He'd broken a leg when he landed—compound fracture, must have hurt like hell, to judge from the screams when we cut him down and hauled him on board. Now, Lieutenant Telford spoke a fair amount of Kraut and *he* told me the German wasn't only yelling because he was hurt, but also out of sheer bloody *terror!* He was ravin' and thrashin' around something fierce, at least until one of the boffins jabbed him in the thigh with a morphine syrette. This guy Bauer was so hysterical, though, that it took a long time before the dope stunned him. And he never really went under all the way—kept twitching, like he was trying to jump away from a bad dream. And every few minutes, he'd roll his eyes and moan something about '*eggs in the rain.*' "

Allen frowned and interrupted: "Beg pardon, but I didn't catch that."

"Neither did we, 'cause it didn't make no sense, but that's what the man was raving about: 'eggs in the drizzle,' it sounded like. And whenever he said it, he'd try to raise his arm and point toward Vardinoy, as though he was mortally afraid that something would pop up there and come after him. We were all relieved when Telford authorized a second shot of morphine. That one finally put him under.

"We got on the radio to Torshavn and requested they send a doctor to meet us halfway, on the fastest launch in port. Robbie Telford looked at the charts and saw that it would be faster to keep heading north, then swing east around the top of Vardinoy, than it would be to double back on our former course. So off we went, at maximum speed. We were only a mile or so from the northern tip of the island when we saw the Gray Boats. If we'd worked up to full speed, we might not have spotted them, 'cause they were the same color as the fog. There were four of them, with several men in each, and they were drawn up around the mouth of this enormous cave, one of the biggest I ever saw. Lieutenant Robbie ordered the engines set on idle and turned toward the boat-line using our momentum to move us closer—so we wouldn't be perceived as threatening, he explained. There was something damned odd going on, and he was concerned about the Gray-Boats maybe finding another German survivor."

"One moment, Captain Kollsoy: who or what were these 'Gray-Boats'?"

"That's what we call the fishermen from Norduroy, because they have this tradition of painting all their boats the same color, a kind of dark smoky gray; just like they have a tradition of always carving an Orm's head on the bowsprit of their boats. I guess it makes 'em feel like Vikings or something. To find a small fleet of those boats right up against Vardinoy—at the same time we were there—struck all of us as being pretty damned queer.

"As we drifted closer, Robbie and I both tried to see what was beyond the boat line, but it was so dark inside that cave that even binoculars wouldn't reveal anything. But then we spotted two more Gray Boats, riding at anchor just outside the cave's mouth—and with nobody in them. Obviously, a number of Norduroy men had gone inside that opening, which you could do if you didn't mind getting wet, 'cause it was low tide at the time—hell, at high tide, you could have sailed those two boats right inside, that's how fuckin' big it was!

"When we were close enough, the lieutenant took out his loud-hailer and very pleasantly said 'Good afternoon,' or some such nonsense. They didn't answer at first. So the lieutenant tried again, in a slightly chillier tone: 'Hallooo! We're Royal Navy, out of Torshavn, and we have a medical kit on board—do you require assistance or the use of our radio?' The Norduroy men spoke among themselves, and then one older man—a bearded, patriarchal-looking fellow who was obviously a leader of some kind—called back: 'We've been fishing here and one of our men fell overboard. But we've found him inside that cave, and we need no assistance. Just go about your business, and we'll finish ours and go home.'

" 'Might have said *Thank you kindly for the offer,* you old bugger,' muttered Telford. And then I spoke up: 'Lieutenant, there's something not right here. *Nobody* fishes in these waters—you've seen how dangerous the currents are. They're lying for some reason.' He agreed. All this time, the Norduroy men were looking more and more annoyed with our being there. It occurred to us that perhaps we'd somehow gotten ourselves into a potentially dangerous situation.

"The older Gray Boat man now started jabbering with Telford, and I got the feeling that he was trying to distract us. That's when I noticed that one of their boats, the one farthest away from us, was very slowly hauling around our port side and would soon be *behind us,* in a position to block our line of retreat. I was about to call the lieutenant's attention to this, but just then we heard the first scream from inside that damned cave. It was like those shouts the German pilot had made before we doped him up: not so much a scream of pain as a cry of pure terror. We froze. There was a second scream or at least part of one, and then the screamer's voice suddenly became muffled, as though someone had stuffed a gag into his mouth. Then, silence.

"Robbie Telford's hand went for the big Webley on his hip. The bearded Gray Boat raised his hand in warning. 'One of our men was injured when the current swept him inside that cave. It's none of your concern. We will tend to him.'

"Telford insisted: we had a good medical kit on board, including morphine, which that man obviously could have done with a shot of. But the old Gray Boat dropped any pretense of being friendly. He glared at us with real malice in his eyes and practically commanded us to leave.

"Naturally, with all this going on, nobody'd been paying attention to poor Bauer. But the sound of those screams had roused him, morphine or no, and he was now thrashing about, his face contorted, trying to shout a man's name. It was clear to us—*he recognized that voice!*

"By this time, Telford saw the boat working its way behind us, and I could see the conflicting emotions on his face. Nazi or not, a fellow warrior was trapped in that cave, and obviously in desperate need of help. How could we turn our backs on him? The honor of Great Britain was at stake! And those men blocking our way, why, they were nothing but a bunch of scruffy fishermen! But now we could see that they were also *well-armed* fishermen! Their leader, the old bloke with the beard, had picked up a double-barreled shotgun, and several of his mates in the other boats had produced old muskets and a few Enfields, along with a number of wicked-looking harpoons that could take your head off with one swing. In the launch, we had the Lieutenant's Webley, and two Enfields for the radioman and me, that was all. We had no choice but to back down.

" 'All right, Petur,' Telford whispered to me. 'Put her in reverse and back us out. Is your Enfield loaded? Good, because if that old bastard with the shotgun so much as spits in our direction, I'm going to drop him and run for the nearest fog bank.'

"And that's about all. Except that poor fucker Bauer kept moaning and thrashing around, because he sensed—as we all did by that time—that we were abandoning one of his crew. Not one of us believed it was a Norduroy man making those screams. What puzzled us the most, though, was their motive. For some reason, Norduroy had dispatched a veritable fleet to look for survivors, and we knew they'd found at least one. As to what their reasons were for keeping it secret, and what they planned to do with their prisoner, we couldn't even guess.

"And so we sailed back to meet the medical launch from Torshavn. When we reached port, of course Telford filed both a report and a protest. He sought permission to take a motor launch mounting a Bofors gun, along with a squad of infantry, to chastise those hostile buggers on Norduroy, and to demand extradition of their prisoner. It never happened, of course, because just hours after we returned, there was a sudden flareup of U-boat activity in that part of the Atlantic, so our punitive expedition to Norduroy was postponed. And when the U-boat flap subsided, Lieutenant Telford suddenly got transferred to the Eighth Army in North Africa, as he had long wanted to be. He left us on the next flight to Scotland. Two months later, we got a letter from him, with a snapshot of him standing beside a brewed-up Italian tank. After that, we never heard from him again."

Kollsoy was nodding off now, his voice thick with whiskey. The effort of telling his story had clearly drained most of his energy. "I think that's all he can tell us," said Eiden.

"I think so, too," said Allen. Eiden went back outside for a minute, to arrange for Kollsoy to be taken care of. Allen took the second bottle of Scotch from his briefcase, and pushed it across the table into the old sailor's good hand. Kollsoy woke up at the bottle's touch, and wrapped his clawlike hand around it possessively.

"That's for you to take back to the retirement home, Petur. Drink a toast to us when you open it."

"You're kind, sir." Kollsoy raised his head, his milky eyes now sharp and appraising. "And if I may say so, you're a very strange man indeed if you want to go to Vardinoy and live there."

"I have a feeling, Captain Kollsoy, that you haven't told us everything you know about Vardinoy. . . ."

"I grew up in the same neighborhood, sir, on the island of Vesturoy. The people there believe that if nobody's lived on Vardinoy for a hundred years, then it must be because Vardinoy isn't such a good place to live—an unlucky place, maybe a cursed place. As I told you, ships have sometimes vanished in those waters, and some of them were just sucked right into those big caves by a sudden riptide. Over the years, I reckon some of those stories got exaggerated in the telling; and, if you ask me, that's where the idea of a 'monster' came from—of something around Vardinoy big enough and malicious enough to drag down a ship and its whole crew. You may say, 'Yes, but it's still only winds and tides and rocks'; but our prisoner, Bauer, was an experienced Luftwaffe officer, and such men are not given to making up fantastic stories. I do believe that he saw *something* that scared him to the depths of his soul. But I can't even guess what alerted the Norduroy men and compelled them to send a whole squadron of their boats over to investigate, at the same time *we* arrived. What was their special interest in Vardinoy? Maybe you and herre Poulsen can find out, and if I'm still alive when you return, I'd like to hear what you discovered. Because I strongly suspect that you're all not going up there just to do some 'archaeological research.' Tell me the truth now: you're not going up there to poke around in the ruins of an old fishing village, are ya?"

"Well, actually, yes, that's a part of it. We honestly don't know what our plans will be until we get there and check things out for ourselves."

"Don't bullshit me, Mister Warrener. You're all going up there to look for the monster, aren't you?"

"Yes, Captain Kollsoy, we are."

"Then God be with you."

At that moment, Eiden and two of his employees came into the room and assisted the besotted Kollsoy into a wheelchair. As the employees rolled him down the corridor and out through the front door, he was singing a bawdy English sea shanty.

"Go on outside, Allen, while I shut off the lights and lock up. We'll talk about this in a moment."

Allen sucked in the cool night air, letting it wash the cigarette fumes from his chest and throat. A sweet glassy tranquility hung over Tjornuvik's anchorage. Despite the lateness of the hour, the western sky retained a touch of twilight purple; the Giant and the Hag looked especially gaunt and monolithic—like the last standing pillars of a drowned Atlantean Stonehenge. Eiden joined him and offered him a drink of aquavit from a flask. Allen downed one fiery slug and turned suddenly on the older man.

"God damn it, Eiden, I *knew* you had some ulterior motive for bankrolling this snark-hunt! Your face, when Kollsoy showed us his arm, it wasn't just the ugliness of it. Hell, you've seen wounded men before! But when you saw Kollsoy's arm, it was like somebody kicked you in the balls, like you'd *seen that kind of wound before!* So let's hear it, whatever it is you've been keeping from me, before this expedition goes another foot toward Vardinoy!"

Poulsen put his arm on Allen's shoulder and steered him to the concrete seawall that protected the harbor. They sat down and stared at a dark plum-colored sea and the two towering *dranger* that had probably looked the same on the day the Vikings first saw and named them.

"You remember how I was summoned away suddenly, the morning after you arrived in Tjornuvik? I wrote you about it—about how my son's fishing boat was sunk in a freak storm, all hands lost except for Kristofur, who lived just long enough for me to reach his bedside and watch him die. His boat went down in the straits between Vardinoy and Vesturoy, and the men who fished him out took him to the little clinic on Vesturoy, and made him as comfortable as they could. But when they contacted me, they warned me: there was nothing any doctor could do. Evidently, they told me, the propane tanks in the galley had exploded when Kristofur was on duty there. That's what blew him clear of the ship and saved him from drowning, but that's also what killed him. His burns, they told me, were just too extensive. All they could do was to pump him full of morphine and let him die without pain. . . ."

Eiden Poulsen sighed and flipped his cigarette into the water.

"Ships sink, ships blow up—nothing worse than a fire at sea. Every year, some Faeroese men leave on an ordinary fishing trip and simply don't come back. I'm a sailor, from a clan of sailors, and we *know* how easily the sea can kill a man. As long as I believed that my son was killed by an accident at sea, I could live with it, and honor his memory as a sailor who died a sailor's death.

"But over the years, as we corresponded and you developed your theory that there might really be something big, unknown, and maybe very dangerous, living on or near Vardinoy, I began to wonder if there was not something more to the circumstances of my son's death than just another accident-at-sea. You see, there were *aspects* to his death, his condition, that were most unusual. His ship went down in approximately the same area as that German bomber. And the behavior of its pilot, Bauer—such a man

314

would never rave about a 'thing' rising out of the sea and 'absorbing' his crewmen unless he had actually *seen it happen.* We now have two accounts by eyewitnesses that the German was delirious. Maybe so, but he was *not* hallucinating. He saw something that disordered his mind! Something that so challenged his ideas of Reality that he chose to commit suicide rather than try to deal with it! Perhaps Bauer's experience and my son's death *were* connected. As long as I remained convinced that it was the sea which killed Kristofur, I could reconcile myself to his death. If the North Atlantic decides to kill a man, it will—but it kills in a blind, impersonal way, and every man who chooses to earn his bread on the sea understands that. But what if something else sank his boat? What if some unknown, horrible *thing* rose out of the depths and deliberately smashed that vessel? That possibility, however remote, has tormented me for more than twenty years!

"At the very least, I need to explore Vardinoy for myself, and eliminate that possibility. I financed this expedition as a means of doing that. I've kept an open mind, though; and until tonight, I never really *believed* there was something up there monstrous enough to destroy a three-hundred-ton ship, and savage enough to drag down its entire crew!

"But now, Allen, I'm not so sure. You see, the injuries that killed my son— the doctors called them 'third-degree burns' because that's the closest approximation they had. True, in the war, I saw every kind of damage fires and explosions can do to human flesh. But the injuries to my son were *not* like anything I had ever seen. Until tonight. My son's face and upper body . . . they looked like *that!*"

"Jesus. . . . You mean he was covered with those same blue scabs or scars or whatever that stuff is?"

"Exactly the same. Parts of his face were melted down to the bones beneath. These things cannot be mere coincidences. Something *did that* to those two men. Something that lives up there, in the waters near Vardinoy."

"Eiden, if by some miracle we do discover something like that, a creature capable of pulling down a three-hundred-ton vessel . . . what are you going to do?"

"You can take your movies of it first, Allen, and then, if I can, I'm going to kill it."

Book IV:

PETROGLYPHS

But the danger was past – they had landed at last

With their boxes, portmanteaus and bags;

But at first the crew were not pleased with the view,

Which consisted of chasms and crags.

—Lewis Carroll, *The Hunting of the Snark*

20.

LANDFALL, VARDINOY

From the journal of Richard Sugarman:

    3:20 A.M. We're all too wired to sleep, so I'm updating this account while I can, as tomorrow—or rather, today—is liable to be, as Dewey creatively phrased it, "busier'n a one-legged Cajun at an ass-kickin' contest!"

    I've got the map of Vardinoy & surrounding waters spread out on the ward-room table, trying to get oriented. This is not only the sole extant map of Vardinoy we were able to find, it's also rather out of date, having been prepared for the British occupation force in 1940. About the lake, the R.A.F. cartographer made an intriguing notation: "sample sonar soundings indicate the bottom drops precipi-tously only 15–20 meters from the shore, and its average depth may be in excess of 500 meters." Jesus, how much 'in excess'??

    On the upper western shore, at least, the map indicates several acres of relatively flat, well-drained land that ought to be suitable for our campsite. The Brits were able to sketch the outer coast in great detail, since they could survey it at their leisure from boats, but the whole interior of the island, except for the general con-figuration of the lake, is rather nebulously drawn. I'm reminded of the Eliza-bethans' depiction of the terra incognita beyond the eastern coast of America, where vast regions were filled with puffing Neptunes, imaginary routes to Cathay, and spouting Leviathans ("Here be Grate and Parlous Beasties of Diverse Kinds . . ."). Allen's looked up the historical records, and the apparent reason for this topograph-ical vagueness is because the only survey of inland Vardinoy ever made was carried out by one perfunctory overflight by a photo-reconnaissance Spitfire. It was a cloudy day (when is it not?), and whatever areas of terrain were obscured when the pilot shot his film, the cartographers filled in with contour lines extrapolated from the terrain features that were visible.

    Vardinoy lies a full day's sail north-northwest of Torshavn. Its shape is pecu-liar, sort of upside-down looking: an elongated right triangle with the right angle forming the northwest corner, and the narrow tip pointing due south. The island's widest point, about two-thirds of the way up from the bottom, measures about eight miles across. The coastline's configuration is unusual, too. Whereas most of the Faeroes are mountainous only on their western sides, then taper off on their eastern halves into meadows and hillocks, Vardinoy's completely encircled by steep cliffs, almost like battlements, except at the very northern end, where a wide shallow fjord offered shelter to the boats that once anchored there. The western coast is the steeper and more foreboding—the chart shows a number of peaks and promontories in excess of 2,500 feet; the eastern coast is inaccessible to boats or people as well, comprising rank upon rank of wildly irregular formations ranging from 200 to 800 feet high. Not to make a big deal about it, but it's almost as though Nature had given this island a natural barrier against intruders—except on the northern end.

Another way to view the geological setup is to think of the shoreline as the jagged rim of an old volcano and the big central lake as the ancient crater. In any case, once you leave the abandoned village, there is only one dominating terrain feature: that big nameless lake, a place where there have been a couple of sightings of our equally nameless quarry.

Allen's decided that the lake on Vardinoy should be our first priority for exploration, rather than the seas around it. There is at least one fairly recent "eyewitness" account that mentions the monster coming out of the lake (but others that speak of it rising from the sea—maybe it travels back and forth through some of those conjectural big tunnels said to honeycomb the base of the island). This account is lurid and sensational, and worth quoting from. Its author was a Scottish sportfisherman named Frazier, who had been badly shell-shocked during the Battle of the Somme and who had come to Vardinoy in 1917, as Frazier described it himself, "to seek the quietest and most private location I could find." The account he gave to the Torshavn newspaper actually sounds a bit shell-shocked, too. He had enjoyed a good day's fishing, landing "a brace of majestic trout," and had retired early after making a hefty meal of them.

He was awakened near midnight by the "furious barking" of his canine companion, a 200-pound Irish wolfhound named Bismarck, who, he assures us, "was not the sort of dog to fear anything that walked on two legs or on four." Yet there was faithful old "Busy" yowling like a banshee from the edge of the lake, his ears erect, his fangs gleaming, and every hair on his body erect and quivering. Frazier took his trusty Weatherby elephant rifle and ran down to the shore to see what was causing this hubbub. It was difficult, he averred to the interviewer, to describe what he saw with any degree of precision.

"It was a large mass of dark, matte-black viscid substance, moving in a way that suggested the rolling wake of a large boat." Before Frazier could reach the dog, however, that upwelling mass of matter had encroached on dry land far enough to cover the paws and forelegs of the animal, and either the scent of it or the sensation of it had caused this normally fearless dog to become "paralyzed." Whatever it was, it seemed to well up more speedily after it made contact with Bismarck, and the substance was clearly drawing the dog deeper inside itself. Suddenly, the wolfhound's ferocious barks ceased, to be replaced "by a pitiable whimpering such as might be made by a terrified newborn puppy. The stuff then engulfed the animal's upper body until it surged over the dog's muzzle and head, muffling its cries, enveloping it with a smooth, purposeful *flow. Having completely absorbed the dog, the sinister material swiftly withdrew back into the depths whence it had risen, and my last sight of dear old Busy was a haunting image of his bulging eyes, growing dimmer and dimmer as predator and prey slipped beneath the surface. The outline of the wolfhound's body remained visible for another moment or two, but it was losing the distinctness of its form, eerily like softening wax, as though it were not being gnawed upon so much as being decomposed with a rapidity which suggested immersion in a vat of highly corrosive acid. Perhaps the oddest thing of all, however, was the way in which the sinking shape acquired a brightening bluish hue even as it became more granular and its shape became more diffuse. . . ."*

Frazier fired both barrels of his Weatherby at a range of twenty feet, scoring direct hits with bullets designed to stop a charging rhino. Yet upon impact, the projectiles cause no discernible damage, but simply careened around inside *the submerging substance in slow, lazy trajectories, "like flaring match-heads inside a bowl of aspic" . . . and that was the last he saw of his friend Bismarck or of the "Vardinoy Monster."*

No wonder Warrener got fired up for this expedition—Eiden discovered Frazier's lurid tale only a week after he got that letter from the retired British general, so after years of trying to make sense out of fragmentary allusions, folk tales, and ancient Church records which might not have been entirely objective information, POW!—two detailed accounts dating from 1917 and 1942, respectively. The "Beastie," it turned out, HAD left a modern trail!

I'm keeping a skeptical attitude, though, because, well, because somebody *on this Ship of Fools has to!*

Ooops, gotta go! Birgir just got on the PA system and announced that Vardinoy's now visible!

(4:58 A.M.) And there it was, by God! Looming up all sharp and black against the pre-dawn eastern sky exactly like King Kong's island in the movie! We were within a mile or two of the west coast before the sunrise exploded over the horizon and glared-out the details, so my impression right now is: My God, that's a BIG chunk of rock; even at this distance, it radiates a sense of bulk that's almost ominous.

Vardinoy broods as it waits to receive us. All of us felt it—the excited chatter died down as we got close enough to see the free-standing fangs of the "dranger" rocks, and the violent churn of the surf as it gnawed on the base of towering cliffs and spat wild foam where the waves were sucked into the mouths of ominously large caves.

It's a chilly morning on a desolate stretch of the North Atlantic: the sun looks as thin and pale as a lemon-flavored Necco wafer; the sea is sullen, with low ponderous dark gray swells; gulls and gannets berate us with bad-tempered squawks as they circle our wake, looking for a garbage-breakfast; the Expedition members are silent, hunched in their sweaters and pea jackets and caps. Our bow cuts the water with a dull slapping rhythm; the diesels rumble softly; Vardinoy projects a huge, hard Silence as though daring us to intrude upon its enigmas.

No city-slicker cynicism at this moment! I admit it: this is awfully exciting! A dark, legend-haunted island, a cold and windswept ocean—and the prospect of the greatest camping trip any kid ever dreamed of going on, complete with a library of movies, electric lights in all the tents, and all the Tuborg you care to drink! All this savage wilderness plus all the comforts of home (or at least a really classy RV park)—what a combination of hardships and luxuries. We seek a great Unknown, a mysterious, half-mythical thing that may well have killed people, but after each hard day of probing Nature's secrets and climbing those murderous-looking cliffs, we come home to charcoal-broiled steaks, cold beer, and a hot shower.

Which of the two possible outcomes disturbs me more: that we either find nothing at all, or that we find exactly the kind of phenomenon that the adjective "monstrous" was coined to describe?

A word on logistics: to give Allen his due, he and Birgir have worked out a sound logistical plan for setting up our base camp. The map shows a clear trace of old wagon track leading south from the deserted village, zig-zagging upgrade through a disorderly-looking range of hills, traversing their crest through a rocky defile, then plunging downhill rather steeply until it reaches the lake, whereupon it turns to the right (west) and follows the western shore down to a point where it just stops, abruptly, in front of what appears to be a wall of fallen rock from a huge landslide. And nearby the map shows a large meadow that ought to be perfect for the campsite.

There's not even any way of knowing if that old path is still usable, not until we try it, but it's our best bet for hauling our stuff from the dock to the presumed area of our campsite. Warrener "combat-loaded" the Laertes' *cargo holds, which means that the equipment we're likely to need first got loaded aboard last. First, the crew will winch down the Land Rover and the half-ton trailer, which we'll use to haul the initial necessities (sleeping bags and tents; the ice chests full of Tuborg—you know, the* essentials *of life!), and later on, the heavy gear, such as the generator and the prefab sections of the mess hall/laboratory/whatever room.*

Between them, Poulsen and A.W. seem to have thought of every contingency: one of their best ideas was to bring two large heavy-gauge inflatable boats, big enough for eight men and powered by electric motors—so we won't frighten away any shy creatures with motor noises. One of those boats is rigged up for a sonar unit that scans for moving objects and paints a sound-wave picture of the bottom contours.

Time to go to work, Seaman Sugarman! Oi vey!

The abandoned village might have once been home to four or five hundred souls. Of the few-score buildings that remained intact, most were in a state of advanced neglect, their sod roofs wildly overgrown, so that long curtains of rattailed grass fell in tangles over their sides. No sheep grazed their ragged pastures, no dogs barked. And of the fishing boats that once had lined the long storm-battered breakwater, only a single specimen remained: a petrified rind of a hull, bleached bone-white, driven into a nest of rocks by some long-ago tidal surge and held together now only by a handful of rusted nails.

About a quarter-mile beyond the village, the land began to rise. The once-pastoral fields, now covered with waist-high jungles of seagrass and gnarled shrubs, tapered off into a rolling sward of dew-bright grassy moorland, its refulgent wetness pricked here and there by spiky wildflowers, rising in a succession of increasingly steep contour lines, the encircling slopes converging on a narrow notch that marked the pass through which the old wagon track meandered toward the interior lake. The sight of that gloomy pass beckoned irresistibly to the bemused members of the Vardinoy Expedition. That faint suggestion of a road, untraveled for a hundred years—so fragile-looking that it resembled a trace of chalk dust, vulnerable to the next stiff breeze—was, by virtue of its very singularity upon the landscape, a tantalizing artifact.

The aft cargo hoist groaned under the strain as the crew tried to manipulate the ponderous Land Rover from deck to stone breakwater dock without damaging either the winch or the vehicle. Until the Rover was squared away and the trailer hitched to the back, there was nothing much for the Expedition members to do, so—in their eagerness to commence the having of Serious Adventures—they roamed the empty streets and poked into the tumbledown buildings, their voices as shrill and carefree as those of school children who'd just been turned loose for an unexpected holiday. After the crew had attached the trailer and packed it with the tents and other lightweight gear, Birgir batted the horn to summon the Expedition back to the day's mission.

Eiden got behind the wheel, Elsuba rode shotgun, and the Americans crammed into the double row of hard-sprung safari seats. Dewey volunteered to take the point, walking fifty feet ahead of the Rover—the track was severely eroded and no one wanted to risk a sprung axle or a flat tire. Dewey was wearing a "genuine" Viking helmet he'd bought in Tjornuvik and had unbound his hair so he could, as he put it, "get the feel of the Vardinoy wind." He took position, swung his right arm out dramatically, and shouted: "Forwaarrrd HO-OH!" Cheers from the Land Rover's passengers: they were off!

The village streets were easily navigable, but when Eiden reached the spot where the old wagon track began to climb toward the pass, he downshifted into one of the Rover's several hill-climbing gears and experimentally nosed its front bumper into the concealing weeds, keeping Dewey's back centered in the hood ornament. Almost immediately, the vehicle began to bump and shimmy on brutal potholes, and every time they hit wet ground, the wheel went buttery in Eiden's grip until the cross-country tires bit down and gave traction. Coming around one especially hairy switchback, they encountered Dewey, blocking their path and waving a day-glow caution flag.

"What's up, faithful scout?" said Allen.

"There's a miniature version of the Grand Canyon ahead, with a fuckin' waterfall gushing through it. I doubt you can get through it, man."

"Nothing stops Poulsen's Land Rover!" boasted Eiden.

"Unless you can make it fly, this mother will. However, I located a suitable fording spot about fifty yards east of the track, so if you'll kindly follow me. . . ."

Eiden did so, dead slow, and had to admit that Dewey's assessment was correct.

"Your hirsute cyclist is proving to be most useful, Preston," said Eiden.

"He always has been, Eiden; whether I needed somebody to run a camera-crane or to break some heads, Dewey's the man!"

Yawing through a slurry of mud and rain-soaked grass, the Land Rover banged and swayed back onto the main track. Eiden decided to send Birgir and some men up there to repair the break. "I brought along some half-inch aluminum runway mats just in case we ran into something like this."

"Eiden, you think of everything," said Norma admiringly.

"Thank you for your confidence, my dear, but we've only been on Vardinoy for ninety minutes!"

Eiden regained the wagon track about two hundred yards below the mountain pass, just as a typically Faeroese weather front moved in and covered the ridge with dark woolly clouds. Dewey guided them through the murk with signals from a powerful flashlight. The pass was narrow and boulder-strewn, and when the Land Rover crept between the steep rain-slicked walls, its occupants felt the temperature drop ten degrees. Dankness, chill, and gloom. . . .

"I think the mountains are trying to tell us something," ventured Norma.

"I never learned to speak Mountain," Karen muttered, suddenly oppressed by a sense of claustrophobia. "What're they saying?"

"*Turn back, you fools!*"

But when they reached the south end of the notch, their persistence was rewarded. Just at the point where the track began to descend again, there was a sudden roar of wind, and with a fine sense of dramatic timing, the weather obligingly swept away the clouds and switched on blinding sunlight, revealing a stunning panorama of the southerly three-fourths of Vardinoy.

"My God, *there it is!*" cried Allen.

Ever-alert, Preston threw open his door and leaped out, almost spraining an ankle, shoving a video camera into Norma's out-thrust hands and fumbling to pop a telephoto lens on the barrel of his Nikon—he had assumed, from the urgency in Warrener's voice, that Allen had just spotted a sea serpent basking on the lake.

"Where is it, Allen? Point me in the right direction, damn it!"

Allen made a placating, calm-down gesture and rather sheepishly qualified his previous outburst. "I was talking about *the lake*, Press! Just the lake."

Both disappointed and relieved that he hadn't blown the Shot of a Lifetime, Preston surveyed the panorama more calmly now, and agreed that they were not likely to get another shot that would convey so vividly the sheer vastness of Vardinoy's landscape.

Twenty minutes later, they located as fine a campsite as they were likely to find on the whole island—a level sward covered with soft heather and broad enough to contain all the tents and utility structures they required, and just elevated enough to give a panoramic view of the lake. Eiden radioed the ship and told Birgir to unload the heavy gear: the generator, the frozen-food locker, the prefab construction panels, the computer systems, the water-purification system—the list was a long one. Both he and Allen had agreed that, in view of how many weeks it might take to accomplish . . . *whatever* . . . there was no point in "roughing it" any more than necessary. They were going to set up a more-or-less self-contained village, complete with a wide-screen TV and two hundred VHS movie tapes.

Allen and Karen set up their tent with the entrance facing the lake, inflated their air mattresses, and attached a screened-in canopy to serve as a front porch, complete with folding beach chairs and a pair of TV tables. The other Expedition members busied themselves with similar chores, the Land Rover shuttled back and forth every half hour, and as soon as the bulky but powerful generator was uncrated, the ship's electrician—assisted by Allen, Dewey, and Preston—wired the camp for lights and small appliances. Karen and Allen both jumped in surprise when Eiden tested out the public address system at 4:47 in the afternoon. The initial shriek of feedback was answered by a chorus of: *"Turn it down a few notches!"*

"Is that better?"

"Yes!" "Much!" "Eiden found the volume knob!"

"Okay, okay—now that we know the bloody thing works, I'm pleased to announce that all the essential equipment and most of the food and so forth has been brought up from the ship, and in exactly ninety minutes, Birgir and the ship's cook are going to start broiling meat! Steak, chicken, lamb, whatever you desire! But the consumption of Tuborg and/or whiskey can begin any time now, for, as captain of the *Laertes*, I hereby order an end to all manual labor for today! Now, in about ten minutes, Birgir will be making one final round trip to the ship, so if anyone wants to bring up some additional baggage or retrieve something he's forgotten, now's the time."

Karen snapped her fingers. "Damn, I almost forgot! I'm sorry, baby, but I need to go back to the ship and fetch something important. Okay if I leave you to chill on our new 'sundeck' by yourself?"

His shrug was nonchalant, but Karen could tell he was slightly miffed—they'd just gotten settled in and Allen was still sweaty from the day's exertions. "Yeah, sure, go on. What'd you forget that's so critical?"

She leaned over and nibbled the slightly unsavory lobe of his ear. "My diaphragm, if you must know. Don't you want to christen the tent properly tonight?"

On this, his fourth trip, Eiden drove with confidence—the old wagon trace held no surprises for him now, especially since the weather had stayed remarkably clear and balmy. As they negotiated the first hairpin curve and Karen caught a glimpse of the toy village they had all constructed beside the lake, she couldn't help letting out a little cheer.

"Are you all right?" asked Eiden.

"Never better, Eiden. That was just a little yelp of joy, I think."

"Yes, I heard quite a few of those today. I suppose you're all very excited."

"Well, yeah, we are. But I guess all this scenic grandeur is old stuff to you, since you're a native Faeroese and all."

"It's not 'exotic' to me, if that's what you mean, but of course I'm excited. And very optimistic, for a guy who hasn't the faintest idea what we're looking for!"

"That's true, we don't, but that's one of the things that make it so cool!"

So cool. . . . Eiden understood the idiom, of course, but Karen was right, to a certain extent—he wasn't exactly jubilant. This morning, he'd gone through a bad period when the *Laertes* sailed over the spot where his son's ship lay on the bottom.

He intended, however, to abide by his private resolution: until he had reason to think or speak otherwise, he was not going to share with Karen or anyone else the darker emotions he'd revealed to Allen Warrener. To conjecture a connection between the Vardinoy Monster lore and the hideous death of his son was, he knew, an extraordinary leap of assumption. Perhaps it was nothing more than an old man's delusion—they had been roaring back and forth on northern Vardinoy all day and hadn't seen anything unusual. But at least Allen and his friends were in excellent spirits, and Eiden certainly didn't want to spoil anybody's fun.

Especially not Karen's. He'd already grown to like her, this dark slim quiet girl. She had an innate steadiness; she could enliven any sort of conversation when she felt like it, but mostly she chose a mode of quiet observation. And her perceptions were damned keen—there was not much, he suspected, that escaped Karen Hambly's notice. Another unusual trait he noticed about her was the ease with which this young woman blended in with the Faeroese ambience. Allen's love for the Islands had been like the onslaught of a fever, whereas Karen seemed to have taken one good look around, nodded to herself—Yep, it's what I was hoping it would be—and then gone on about the business of living. Allen had responded to the place with high poetic intoxication; Karen responded with the quieter but just-as-profound satisfaction of a foot-sore shopper slipping into a really comfortable pair of shoes.

From the moment she set foot on the Torshavn dock, she had seemed unsurprised by anything. With care and affection, Karen seemed to be weaving her own conception of the Faeroese *gestalt* into an intricate mosaic; as though she were composing a complex symphony from the tiniest particles of sensory data borne upon the wind. Her response to the islands was no less passionate than Allen's boyish, gushing enthusiasm, but—remarkably —it seemed quite detached from Allen's own private mythology. For Allen was so stuffed with sanctified memories, and the memories themselves so encrusted with the costumes and jewelry he'd lavished on them, that his past must seem like a series of still photos, not a dynamic recollection of continuous events in the midst of which he had actually moved and spoken. Whatever Karen's impressions of the Faeroes, they were unencumbered and singularly pure. You could trust her judgments, and you would be smart to trust her instincts as well. As the captain of a warship, Eiden had valued most highly that rare subordinate who combined these same attributes in one personality. Somehow, Eiden thought, it logically followed that Karen was also capable of displaying courage, if and when the need arose for it.

If he'd been twenty years younger, he'd have given Allen Warrener a run for his money with this young lady! But as matters stood, he just wanted to learn if they might become friends.

"So, Karen, now that you're here, what do you think of Vardinoy?"

"Pretty much like the other islands, isn't it? Spectacular, but bleak. And it feels as isolated as it looks on the map, way up here at the north end of the chain. Actually, it feels more than 'isolated,' Eiden. There's a *lonesomeness* to this place. . . ."

"Does it bother you, this lonesomeness?"

"Honestly, no, Eiden, it doesn't. It's like something inside *me* expands to fill up all that emptiness. Some people just thrive on solitude, you know, and I've always had a taste for it. I think Allen does, too; but the difference between us is that he feels *guilty* about enjoying it, for some reason. But now that he's actually here on Vardinoy, he's so much more at ease with himself that it's kind of like being with a different man! I mean, we really had *fun* putting together our little cottage-by-the-lake! Did you see his face up there on the ridge, when the clouds moved away and he saw the whole island spread out before him? He's like a kid on the first day of summer vacation."

She fell silent and tilted her head to gaze out the passenger-side window, speculatively scanning the ranks of sharp escarpments to the west. Their shadows were longer now, but because of the high latitude there would still be daylight over the camp when the Expedition gathered for supper. Hell, in the summer there would still be an afterglow at midnight, a prospect Karen found agreeable. On impulse, she turned around and asked: "Eiden, what was Allen really like when you first met him? A candid opinion, please, not one colored by nostalgia."

"I am largely immune to the charms of nostalgia, my dear. Let's see . . . what was he like? Well, I could see right away that he was a romantic young pilgrim badly in need of finding a quest. Outwardly, he seemed ready and eager to conquer the world. But he also struck me as curiously vulnerable *to* it—sometimes you could see that in his eyes. You can't set the world on fire if you've been told too many times not to play with matches."

"I know exactly what you mean, Eiden. He's always desperately wanted to do something *memorable*. His intentions were good, and his impulses can be noble, but every time he tried to get some momentum, he picked the wrong time, the wrong occupation, the wrong spouse . . . the wrong time to be living in."

"Well, when we are twenty, we all have a vision of where we'll be and what we will have accomplished by the time we're fifty. And when we *are* fifty, we look back at that twenty-year-old self and wonder: *how foolish I was to think Life would allow me to march forward in a straight line!* When I was twenty, I wanted to become a great dramatist! Yes, it's true! When I was that age, I had this radiant vision of becoming the Faeroese Ibsen, or Strindberg, or Shaw! Had you told me then that I would spend five years hunting Nazi submarines, and then go on to become what that *old self* would have regarded as a ruthless Capitalist, I would have driven you from my presence, shouting '*I am going to be a great playwright, you fool!*' And who knows? Maybe I could have done. But I don't think I would have had nearly as exciting a life, and I certainly wouldn't be a millionaire—which I rather enjoy, to be honest with you. So, not long after I envisioned myself as Ibsen, the war broke out and I found myself stalking U-boats, and eventually becoming rather skilled at it. The world at that time did not need another mediocre windbag of a play-wright, but it *did* need men who knew how to handle escort ships in combat. I believed then, and I still do, that the fate of the free world hung on that skill! What more exciting, more important thing could I have done with those five years? And now, looking back, I can't imagine my life working out differently. I am content with who I am, proud of what I've accomplished, and I'll be damned if I'll ever apologize for being happy!"

"That's just it, Eiden! Most people, as they grow up, find *equivalents* for their younger selves' vision of the future! All that energy you have when you're twenty—part of it comes from just *not knowing any better.* But Allen missed that turning point somehow. He just kept doggedly trying to go in that straight line you mentioned, bitterly resenting it every time he was forced to take a detour. Where you saw those course changes as new opportunities, Allen saw them as unacceptable compromises—as defeats, even. I'm trying to get him to just cut loose of all that and enjoy the life he still has left. You know: shit hap-pens, people change, the world doesn't stand still just so you can wait around to catch the perfect trolley! It all started, I think, when he sort of put himself in suspended animation so he could write that elephantine novel about— oops, I mean—oh, shit, we don't want to go *there*, do we?"

Eiden laughed, swinging the Land Rover into the last high switchback before the mountain pass. "You mean, 'ever since he fell madly in love with my daughter'? Well, why wouldn't he? She was quite a stunning beauty back then, so I wasn't in the least surprised. And one thing you must remember: to Elsuba, Allen was a very exotic figure! A handsome, dark-eyed dreamer from grand and distant America! And here he was, in tiny, insignificant Tjornuvik! I'd say the mutual attraction was pretty overwhelming for both of them. They, um, *got along* famously during the time they spent together. But was Elsuba 'in love' with him? Certainly not in the same way he was with her! Oh, yes, she was very fond of him, and very sad when he left, and for a while she thought it was very charming that that he carried such a raging torch for her."

" 'For a while,' you said. I take it the 'charm' wore off after a while?"

"He was still writing long, passionate love letters *three years* after they said good-bye! It reached the point that she dreaded opening her mailbox! Finally, just to free herself from the obligation of writing back to him, she tried to let things cool down, taper off. Very gently, at first, she tried to suggest that maybe it was time for him to get on with his life and to let her step down from the pedestal. But by that time, he just couldn't—he'd turned Elsuba into a symbol, or a fetish or something. Mind you, his letters to me were always charming and witty and intelligent. But his letters to Elsuba became ever more maudlin, pleading, desperate—and finally just a nuisance. She had a theory: since he could not break the pattern on his own, he was pushing *her* into writing an ultimatum. So that's what she had to do, for both their sakes, and she resented the hell out of being in that position. She showed it to me before mailing it, which was a bit of a surprise—more information than a parent really wants to have, you know?"

"Did she let him down easy, or give him both barrels?"

"She made it cold as ice and very straightforward. Look, she told him, I am *not* this idealized dream-girl you're still obsessed with, and I refuse to feed your obsessions any longer. If you want to write to me as a *grown-up* and as a friend, that's fine. But if he sent her any more moon-struck rhapsodies about their love-making. . . ."

"She actually *showed you that?*"

"You *are* in Scandinavia, Karen. As I said, that was a bit more than I cared to know, but I was touched that she would take me so much into her confidence. In any case—"

"Eiden, *WATCH OUT!*"

He reflexively stomped on the brake pedal and the Rover fishtailed to a stop, flinging a wave of gravel and mud over the astounded pedestrian who was staring goggle-eyed at the massive bumper that had halted just inches from his kneecaps. From his posture and state of partial undress, he'd just finishing answering Nature's call behind a nearby screen of boulders. The sight of his splayed belt buckle and unzipped fly struck Karen as one of the most incongruous things she'd ever seen. *Even on a totally uninhabited island, we slink behind the bushes to do our business!*

Now that he realized he was not going to knocked off the mountain by the only vehicle ever to be driven on Vardinoy, the man resumed zipping and re-buckling, a process made somewhat cumbersome by the amount of gear he was carrying, which included a rucksack the size of Santa's toy bag, a custom-made outdoor-artist's easel complete with clawed feet and pneumatic telescopic legs that would theoretically hold it stationary during an earthquake, and his hiking equipage resembled that of a Survivalist rather than a casual landscape painter—including a rain poncho made out of what Karen identified as "NASA stuff"; two canteens; a first-aid kit; a Swiss Army knife, dangling from a lanyard, of approximately the same size and heft as a Roman short sword; binoculars; and a cutting-edge Global Positioning Device, complete with telescoping antenna. Was he a wandering artist, or some kind of secret agent? Adding to the seeming paradoxes was a pair of St. Laurent sunglasses that must have cost more than the total amount shown on Karen's last three paychecks, *and* one of those goofy-looking floppy wool berets the Faeroese loved to wear, rain or shine. And propped up against a boulder was a big driftwood walking stick, elaborately carved in runic motifs. *If you spotted him tramping across the mountains in full regalia, he would resemble nothing so much as a young, beardless Gandalf!*

While Karen was sizing up the stranger, Eiden had switched off the ignition and leaped from the cab, babbling apologies in rapid-fire Faeroese, which Karen of course could not follow. But she did understand universal sign-language when both men pointed at themselves and declared their names. At the sound of Hiking Painter's name, Eiden's face lit up and he began talking eagerly, obviously familiar with the fellow's name and just as obviously impressed. Somewhat miffed at suddenly turning invisible, Karen opened the passenger door and joined the men, clearing her throat to remind them of her presence.

"Eiden, do you mind telling me just who the hell this person is?"

"Ah, forgive my rudeness," said the hiker, turning to shake hands with her and smoothly shifting into fluent, pleasantly accented English. " 'This person,' my dear young woman, is your humble servant, the itinerant painter named Andreas Dahl, who is every bit as surprised to encounter you as you are to find him in the path of your formidable vehicle." He doffed his floppy wool beret, revealing a shock of sun-bleached hair, fine-stranded, which was, to Karen's sensibilities, the same as a neon sign proclaiming: "*well-known European Intellectual.*"

Snapping back into English, too, Eiden hurriedly finished the introductions and to make sure Karen understood the stature of the man they had almost run over.

"Mr. Dahl is our most famous living artist, Karen! He's been exhibited all over Europe!"

"And he's quite astonished to meet one of his most generous patrons, out here in this Godforsaken wilderness. I must thank you, Poulsen, for brightening my summer."

"How, by not running you over in my car?"

"Oh, besides that! Your firm just bought two of my latest paintings—to hang in your new branch office in Aberdeen, I believe."

Now that he had removed his cap and turned an affable smile in her direction, Karen realized that Andreas Dahl was an uncommonly attractive man; had she run into this man at a gallery opening two years ago, she might well have made a pass at him. He was tall, rangy, and strong-jawed, with the powerful arms and shoulders of a rock climber combined with the long-fingered, articulate hands one expected of an artist. The rest of him wasn't bad, either: a high, aristocratic nose, sky-blue eyes, and a wide mouth made ample by its expressiveness. He moved, gestured, and spoke with a patrician grace—or was it *noblesse oblige,* beneath which lay an undertone of arrogance? Karen sensed a lot of latent energy coiled within him, too, as though he might suddenly produce a rapier and shout *"En garde!"*

For all that he looked completely at home in these mountains, schlepping what appeared to be at least sixty pounds of art supplies and hiking gear, Karen visualized him most clearly in the celebrity circle at a major gallery opening, stroking the press, ever-so-discreetly sucking up to potential patrons, a long-stemmed wine glass slowly rotating in those beautiful fingers, and a slinky up-and-coming Versace model clinging to his free arm like a diamond pendant.

She wasn't in the least surprised when Dahl ended their first flurry of conversation by kissing her hand, nor by the fact that his lips lingered on the satiny and erogenously charged—could he possibly have suspected as much?—declivity between her first and second knuckles. In fact, she was rather sorry when he stopped.

"I say, since we've already run into each other, so to speak, do you mind if I hitch a ride back to the village with you? I turned my ankle a bit on some loose rocks a while ago, and it's starting to be a bit of a bother."

Eiden flung open the rear door. "I'd say we owe you at least that much, considering how close we came to terminating your career!"

Dahl kept pulling out more and more equipment and accessories—Karen was reminded of the tiny circus car that somehow managed to disgorge fifteen contortionist clowns—until he'd nearly filled the cargo bay. Then, stretching and rubbing his shoulders with relief, he slid into the middle row of seats. Eiden lined the Rover up with the wagon track again, and they churned upward once more.

"I hate to be a nuisance, but would you mind awfully if I caught a ride back with you, too, assuming you are going back? I really only need to retrieve a couple of tubes of paint, and then I'd like to finish the color sketch I was doing when you came along."

Karen decided to tease him a bit and see what happened.

"Beg pardon, sir, but you weren't exactly 'sketching' when we came along."

Dahl didn't miss a beat in returning the lob: "How do you know? There's this new technique I'm trying to perfect, you see, which involves some novel ways of applying pigment—intended to foster a new kind of intimacy between the artist and his medium." His eyes were mischievous now, and the effect was charming and a little bit wicked.

"All right, all right—*touché!* You can spare me the details."

Coming around the first nerve-rasping switchback on the north side of the pass, they caught sight of the crumbling village and the battleship-gray shape of the trawler.

"Whereabouts do you live in the village, Andreas?" Eiden asked.

"Oh my, no, I don't actually live *in* the place! At night, it's much too creepy for me. I've set up housekeeping in what used to be the rectory for the village church—the building's situated in a pleasant little cove about a half-kilometer east of the breakwater. It's small but cozy."

"Where'd you set up your studio?" Karen asked. Dahl gestured all around them.

"*That's my studio!* The whole island! herre Poulsen, you remember the nature of my ongoing project, don't you?"

"I should: I was on the arts council committee that voted you a rather generous stipend so you could finish it! But explain it to Karen; I think she'll be interested."

"It's the most ambitious undertaking I've ever tried! Every year, from early April until October, I spend all of my time on one island and one only, a different island every year, getting to know the place and its inhabitants intimately, sketching and doing oil studies. Then when the autumn storms are imminent, I pack everything up, rent a local building that's suitable for a temporary studio, and work all that raw material into a single monumental panel, wherein I attempt to capture the essence of life on that single island. Last year, for instance, I lived and worked on Mykines; this year, I chose Vardinoy; next year, I'm planning on little Hastoy, where there's barely room on top for seven families. When the entire project is finished, I will have created a unified artistic vision of my entire homeland, rather like what the composer Smetana did, in music, for his native Bohemia, a kind of *Ma Vlast* in paint instead of musical tones. Are you familiar with that composition, Miss Hambly?"

Karen tried to stop herself, but couldn't: "The Ancerl and Kubelik versions are probably the best of the stereo era, but I still think nothing quite compares to the old monaural set by Vaclav Talich and the Czech Philharmonic, don't you?"

"I see you know the piece quite well," Dahl commented in an alum-dry tone, followed by a quick little smile, to let her know he appreciated the quickness of her put-down.

Karen gave him absolution with a smile and a reassuring pat on the arm. "I'm sorry, but I couldn't help myself. That's one of Allen's favorite pieces of music—he must have eight or nine different recordings of it."

"So which of the islands do you call home, Dahl?" said Eiden, negotiating the last steep section of track before the route leveled out for its final stretch into the village.

"I'm a South-Islands man, born on Suduroy, near the village of Tvoroyri. Maybe you've been there?"

"Once, many years ago. I remember it as a pleasant enough place. Tell me, how many more years before this magnum opus is finished?"

"Oh, another five or six. . . ." Dahl let the estimate trail off vaguely, then changed the subject. "Now that you know my story, how about telling me yours? May I ask what brings an entire shipload of people to this deserted island? For five weeks I've been wandering around Vardinoy and not a living soul did I encounter; then all of a sudden, the island's being colonized!"

Eiden slowed the Land Rover as they re-entered the narrow village lanes, and exchanged a questioning look with Karen. At no previous time since the Americans had arrived in Torshavn had anyone directly asked that question, and it would hardly do to blurt out: "Oh, we've come to look for the famous Vardinoy Monster!" Dahl knew the island well; he could be a useful ally, as long as he didn't dismiss them out of hand as a bunch of loonies. So Karen ruminated a moment before answering, trying to put the matter in the context of a respectable scientific enterprise. Over many centuries, she began, a sizable body of anecdotal evidence had accumulated, pointing to the possibility that Vardinoy or the waters contiguous to it might be the habitat of a large and previously unknown species of marine life, something remarkable enough that some of the witnesses had described it as "a monster." They had organized this expedition—under the auspices of the International Society of Cryptozoology, she added, just because that sounded good and because it was most unlikely that Dahl had ever heard of such a thing—in hopes of documenting the reality behind those legends.

Now that the cat—or the Great Orm—was out of the bag, she watched Dahl carefully. Her opinion of this oddly prepossessing man, she decided, was riding on the nature of his initial response. She consciously glared at him as though defying him to scoff. If Dahl burst into mocking laughter, she would resent the hell out of him—the day's mood had been superb, so far, and she wanted to keep it that way as long as possible.

But Dahl heard her out with no reaction at all, save the slow, thoughtful glide of his pipe from one side of his jaw to the other. When Karen was finished, he removed the pipe, batted ashes out the window with his palm, and carefully said: "I see. You're involved in something very much akin to the ongoing search for the Loch Ness Monster."

"We try to avoid using the word 'monster,' " she snapped, and then felt hypocritical, because they *did* use the word, amongst themselves, casually and often. Why it would bother her so much to hear Dahl say it, she didn't know, but bother her it surely would. "Just because a species hasn't been discovered and catalogued yet, doesn't make it 'monstrous'—just 'unknown.' "

"My apologies, please! I didn't mean to sound like a skeptic, much less give the impression that I was laughing at you." Now that the Land Rover had reached the waterfront, Dahl gestured toward the *Laertes,* where crewmen were bustling up and down the gangway, adding boxes and crates to the supplies already offloaded. "The seriousness of your intent speaks for itself. Someone obviously has gone to a lot of time and expense to organize your 'expedition.' And since many of those crates bear the logo of Mr. Poulsen's corporation, I can only assume that he's one of the major investors. I'm surely not foolish enough to make fun of a patron."

"What you see on the docks, Mr. Dahl, represents the life savings of the man who's leading the expedition, an American scholar named Allen Warrener; and, yes, it also represents a considerable investment not only of money, but of faith, on the part of Mr. Warrener's old friend, Eiden Poulsen, who will surely back me up when I tell you that we are very serious people."

Eiden seemed to be enjoying the exchange, for he chuckled as he turned his head to show Dahl a very stern expression. "I warn you, Dahl, not to get on the bad side of this young woman! The last man who made mock of her underwent a sudden sex-change operation! She's a Carolina Redneck, and never goes anywhere without her straight razor!"

"He's right, Dahl," growled Karen, menacingly reaching for the nonexistent weapon she supposedly carried inside her sweater. "I'm died-in-the-wool trailer-trash and I've got four sets of balls in a jar on my mantel to prove it."

Realizing he was being gulled, Dahl broke into appreciative laughter and waved his hands in mock surrender. "Whoa there, cowgirl! I'm just a humble painter, plying my craft! But I've seen enough of Vardinoy to know that, even by Faeroese standards, it's the loneliest and most desolate island I've ever visited. I'm an artist, for God's sake, and I pride myself on having an open mind. Besides, in my travels throughout the northern islands, I too have heard folk tales about strange things encountered at sea. Isn't that true of every seafaring nation? All I can say for sure, however, is that I've been exploring Vardinoy for more than a month, and the only extraordinary thing I've seen so far was the carcass of an enormous pilot whale that appeared to have committed suicide by hurling itself on to a formation of sharp *dranger.*

They do that, sometimes, you know—very social creatures, those whales. If one is expelled from his native herd, he might well choose self-destruction over exile. They're intelligent beasts, in a very alien deep-sea-mammal sort of way, and they probably have what we would define as 'emotions.' That notion fills me with wonder, so why would I laugh at the idea that there might be other wondrous things in those deep, dark, turbulent waters? I give you my word: if I see anything out of the ordinary, I'll report it to you at the earliest possible moment. You surely won't reject another pair of sharp, sympathetic eyes?"

"No, Mr. Dahl, we surely won't. Okay, then, I'm not going to 'whup out mah razuh' and change you into a soprano.' Here's my hand on it."

Eiden slowed the Land Rover as they reached the dock. "Can I take you closer to your lair, Andreas?"

"I can walk from here, thank you. It won't take me more than thirty or forty minutes to retrieve my paints. And I'm grateful for the offer to let me ride back with you. I would love to sketch the expedition members on their first day here, and they might enjoy keeping the drawings as souvenirs. . . . Besides, I've been all alone here for thirty-eight days, and it would be a pleasure to spend the evening with civilized companions."

"I have no objection," mused Karen. "And I don't think the others will, either. By all means, come join our little celebration. You can meet our other artist-in-residence, too."

"You brought an official artist? How intriguing!"

"Not 'official,' really, just a friend of mine and the wife of our photographer, a woman who's a very gifted amateur. Bring some of your work along, too, and I'm sure you two will have a good time comparing notes."

Dahl processed this information with a curious expression of inner intensity. "What's this woman's name?"

"Norma Davenport. She's a movie star—or at least, she used to be. Of a certain category of movies."

Dahl brightened with understanding. "You mean, what we used to call 'stag films'?"

"No, I mean hardcore porn. But be a good chap and don't bring up the subject unless she does first. She's definitely retired now, and her feelings about that part of her life are, um, ambiguous to say the least."

"My word, a real American porn star! That will add a certain *frisson* to the evening, for sure! Okay, then, I'll toddle off and get my paints and meet you back here in. . . ."

"Forty-five minutes," said Eiden.

Dahl bounded from the back seat and strode briskly eastward, his long legs covering the ground quickly.

"If I didn't know better," muttered Karen, "I'd say he's turned on by the idea."

"After five weeks of roaming around this Godforsaken place, even the Pope would get horny. And I'll wager that Norma would like nothing better than a chance to try out her charms on an appreciative stranger."

He and Karen walked toward the mounds of supplies, exchanging waves with the ever-energetic Birgir and his somewhat frazzled-looking crew.

"What a fantastic coincidence, running into Andreas Dahl out here of all places! I've admired his work for years—that's why my firm invested in those two paintings. Everyone in the Faeroes has heard of him; but until today, I'd never set eyes on the man himself. He's famously reclusive and almost never appears in public or grants an interview to the press."

"My, aren't we lucky?" snorted Karen, largely to disguise just how attractive she had found the shy painter. "I'm going to take a quick shower, retrieve what I came to get, and I'll meet you back here in, oh, a half hour."

When Karen returned, she was carrying over one shoulder a long, thin, protectively wrapped cylinder.

From the journal of Richard Sugarman:

We aren't exactly "roughing it" . . . I didn't realize how cozy and well-equipped this "campsite" was going to be until the heavy stuff arrived from the ship. A generator big enough to run networked computers, miniature street lamps, a compact but high-tech lab where Elsuba can run tests on anything curious we happen to find, a huge frozen-food locker, a wide-screen TV, a radio set that could make contact with Mars, a shower stall and a 200-gallon water heater. . . . No Army surplus pup tents and cold Beanie-Weenies for this bunch!

Our unexpected guest, Herr Dahl, ingratiated himself by pitching in and doing more than a guest's share of the hauling and stacking, so naturally we invited him to stay for the "Inaugural Ceremony" and the subsequent feast, which, Dewey told me, will consist of fifty pounds of prime T-bone, spare ribs, chicken breasts, and all the trimmings, cooked on a propane grill big enough to BBQ a yak! Since we all figured that such a gargantuan meal, consumed after a long day of manual labor and high excitement, would pretty much stupefy the lot of us, we planned to start eating at 9:00 and devote the 2–3 hours of twilight to some serious drinking.

Karen and Norma were assigned the job of organizing the "Opening Ceremony," and they did one hell of a job! And the Faeroes cooperated by providing a background that was as close to perfect as it gets, thanks to the long, slow Nordic-summer twilight.

When the Mistresses of Ceremonies decided the time was right—with the sunset pouring huge fan-shaped rays of scarlet and lavender through notches in the savage-looking westward escarpments—Norma went into her tent and came out carrying a 30-inch Burmese gong (which turned out to be a prop left over from one of Preston's porn epics) and started thwacking it rhythmically, as in "Bring on the dancing girls!"

Instead, Karen appeared behind her, marching in time to the gong-strokes and reverently carrying that mysterious cylinder she brought back from the ship. Birgir and a pair of crewmen, attired in their dress blues for this august occasion, began passing out iced-down champagne. Dewey and Preston then appeared, toting a lightweight flagpole, which they hammered into the ground on top of a grass-covered knoll that juts out into the lake. When they were done, Karen stepped up to the summit, placed her parcel on the ground, and spread her arms in the hieratic gesture of a high priestess, calling for silence.

"First of all, I would like to thank the Norse gods and goddesses for providing such a spectacular sunset!"

Applause, cheers, and rhythmic cries of "O-DIN! O-DIN!"

"I'm as ravenous as the rest of you, so I'll keep this opening ceremony short and sweet. But we all agreed that there must be *an opening ceremony, to mark the formal start of the Vardinoy Expedition. History tells us that many of the great explorers carried special flags with them on their journeys, designed to be emblematic of the enterprise on which they were embarked. Sir Edmund Hillary, I believe, carried a miniature Union Jack to the summit of Everest, and Scott carried a special flag on his epic trek to the South Pole. . . ."*

"And look what happened to him!" shouted Birgir.

Unflustered, Karen continued her oration: "Well, we're an international group, here, so instead of any national flags, Norma and I came up with a unique design that, we believe, aptly symbolizes the man who conned us—I mean, persuaded us all to come with him to this God-forsaken pile of rocks. So Allen, this flag's for you!"

She whipped the cover off, hooked one end of the flag to the lanyards, and damned if a sudden wind didn't spring up at just that instant to unfurl the banner—just as the sun bestowed one final glorious wink through a notch in the mountains, like a steamy, lurid spotlight. The design they'd chosen, and embroidered by hand, was a big heraldic variation on the drawing that Allen's son, Brian, had given his father at their last meeting: a stylized, rather heroic Allen Warrener, posing with drawn sword, above a weeping and subdued sea-serpent! Warrener was dumbfounded and so choked up that all he could say was: "Press, Dewey, I hope you bastards are getting pictures of this, so I can send 'em to the kid!"

After the cleanup, Dewey smashed up a mound of packing crates so they could have a bonfire. With the coming of full night, it was just chilly enough to warrant one. Allen and Karen had taken a jug of drinks to the top of a rocky spur that more or less marked the camp's southern boundary, and they capped off the evening by getting quietly zonked from sharing a doobie the size of a fat man's index finger. Drifting on the buzz, they reclined and grooved on the ever-changing spectacle of the Faeroese sky. A ceiling of heavy, curdled clouds had descended over Vardinoy, drifting smoothly overhead like the keels of spectral galleons, and the bonfire's flames rose high enough to paint them orange and saffron and liquid gold. When a breeze dipped low enough to ruffle the lake, the flames gave back little orange-slices of reflection, which only served to emphasize the lampblack void beyond the shore.

"That lake looks as though it were a hundred miles deep," murmured Karen, snug against Warrener's shoulder, cupping her hands around the joint she was struggling to light.

"Maybe it is—that would give our beastie plenty of room to hide," murmured Allen, reaching softly under her sweater, in search of a comforting nipple.

Karen had just lit the second, supplementary joint, and her voice had that thin reedy quality of someone who's just inhaled.

"Hey, sailor, want another hit?"

"Yes—tonight I do. Shotgun me, baby."

Blissed out, they burned this number down to a nasty little roach, then shifted positions so they could survey the whole campsite.

"It does look cozy, doesn't it?" said Allen.

"Very. But I was amazed at all the little luxuries you guys brought along. I mean, two hundred videotape movies? Admiral Scott must be rolling in his grave."

"Hey, we're soft, spoiled Americans—we have an image to maintain!"

"Do you really think you and Sugarman are going to collaborate on a book about this escapade? I mean, even if we *don't* find a monster?"

"Yeah, sure; why not? I was thinking of calling it *Ship of Fools Goes to Loch Ness!*"

"I like it, I like it a lot." Karen was quiet for a time, then she remembered something she'd meant to ask—before the second joint.

"Did Andreas do a sketch of you yet?" Karen asked.

"Nah, I wasn't in the mood and there were too many other folks lined up. I liked the one he did of you, though. Nice guy, I reckon."

"Yeah, he certainly comes on that way; but did you see the way Norma was making goo-goo eyes at him?"

"Oh, come on, you're imagining things. She was just pathetically glad when he took some time to look at her work, that's all."

"Oh, man, that had better be all. I mean, the last goddamned thing we need out here is for Preston to get on a jealousy trip."

"Never happen. Those two are bonded for life, Karen; and besides, from what Preston was telling me, they've started Doing It again. Seems like everybody's attached a lot of Significance to this Expedition! Except maybe for Richard, we're all here—how shall I say this?—in response to a spiritual crisis!"

"What about Eiden? I can't imagine the Mighty U-Boat Slayer *having* a spiritual crisis!"

Allen sighed and drew her closer. "Eiden's got his personal demons, too, although I didn't find out about them until that night we slept over in Tjornuvik. Some pretty heavy issues he's working through. . . ."

"Is that all you're going to tell me?"

" 'Fraid so, lady. He made me promise. You can ask him yourself, some time when the two of you are alone."

"By God, I will."

Allen cupped one breast and changed the subject. "Why don't we sneak back into our tent and do some serious tantalizing? Just to christen the place, so to speak."

Karen wobbled to her feet and held out a hand for him.

"Okay, let's go do some christening. Uh-oh, look what I see. . . ."

"I can't even focus on what you're pointing at."

"I see Norma and the dashing Mr. Dahl huddled close together over a sketch pad. And Preston studiously avoiding going over there to peek at their drawings."

"Don't make too much out of it, love. Everybody's drunk and stupefied with protein. He's just giving her some drawing lessons, that's all."

"You think? Well, Dahl had better hope she doesn't decide to give *him* some 'tips' in return. I get the feeling he's not too experienced with wild and wanton women. If Norma really decides to turn on the charm, he's a goner."

21.

THE AXE-CUTS

From the journal of Richard Sugarman:

    O, fortunate me! I've drawn the first watch at the newly activated Camera Position No. 3. Not supposed to take my eyes off the lake, etc., but the landscape is so fixed and unchanging—to my way of thinking, dull—that if a fish farted out in the water, it would register as a seismic disturbance. The setup is this: my position covers the middle and northern reaches of the lake; Position No. 2 is atop a promontory that juts out facing the southern portion, on the western shore about a quarter-mile from camp. Position No. 1 is located on that knoll where the Expedition Flag is flying. All three Camera Positions combined cover perhaps half of a very big body of water. The other parts, we'll have to inspect up close, using the inflatable boats. In addition to the heavy tripod-mounted cameras stationed around the lake, everybody's carrying a video cam or a motor-driven Nikon at all times.

    In sum, we have approximately 3.5 cameras for every member of the Expedition, which strikes me as overkill. But mark my words: if the monster decides to surface twenty feet from the camp—bet money on it!—it will do so at the exact moment when all of them are out of film or out of juice! Standing around waiting for the monster to grace us with an appearance is not the most brilliant strategy imaginable, but Allen's making this up as he goes along, I guess.

    Everyone slept late and woke up furry-tongued after the Inaugural Bash. When Birgir came on the PA system and announced: "Lunch is served, if anyone's capable of facing it!," we all managed to straggle into the prefab mess hall. Conversation was surly and sparse; but after the strong coffee had restored us somewhat, Allen banged a spoon on a cup and made his second Fearless Leader speech. Undeterred by groans and hisses—he just had to get it out of his system, I reckon— he announced that he'd drawn up a rotating schedule for the chores and camera watches . . . and then proceeded to drone on for forty-five minutes. I thought Preston was going to throw a plate at him.

Why didn't someone speak up and say: "Allen, this really isn't necessary now, so why don't you stick it up your ass until mid-afternoon, when we feel human again?" But nobody did! *For some reason, we all felt obligated to hear him out—me included. It was a very odd thing. Allen's gestures, his posture, his timing, the very* aura *radiating from him, turned him into a different man. His oration was a needless imposition, and maybe even rude, but for some reason we all felt compelled to pay attention, as though this were a matter of pressing importance!*

I was reminded of one of those squadron-leader briefing scenes from a World War II movie—Gregory Peck, say, in Twelve O'clock High. *I could just see War-rener tapping a swagger stick against a big acetate-covered map of the Third Reich and saying, in a gravelly but mesmerizing tone of voice: "The target for tonight, gentlemen, is the ball-bearing works at Schweinfurt." (Apprehensive groans from the aircrews—they've been to Schweinfurt before and they know it's a ball-buster!) "Weather conditions, I'm sorry to say, will be in the* Hun's favor, *and the charts at G-2 have informed me that our old nemesis the* Horst Wessel Flugzeug *is back in action, and they've been re-equipped with* Focke-Wulf A-4s, *the newest and best fighter Goering has in his inventory. So all you gunners, make every burst count. I want a good, tight bomb pattern, and woe betide the pilot who aborts without a damned good reason. Good luck to you all! Now,* synchronize watches!!"

I've noticed this quasi-military style before, a persona Allen slides into when he's really in Fearless Leader mode, as though he were slipping into an invisible uniform. I suppose there must be a deep inner tension inside a man who spent so much time studying and psyching himself up to be a professional warrior, and then got blown unconscious on his way to join his first firefight! What a dichotomy! Part of him deeply resents not having a chance to prove his valor, and another part is just as relieved that circumstances prevented him from getting his middle-class ass shot off.

I finally heard the story this afternoon, after Allen and Dewey had finished wrestling this big camera rig into position. With its oversized film magazine, it does *look something like a machine gun, so much so that Dewey got the notion of snuggling up to the hand-grips, panning the "barrel" across the campsite, and making "budda-budda-budda" noises.*

"Good shooting, squire," Warrener muttered; "I think you wiped out the entire expedition."

Dewey surveyed the panoramic view thoughtfully, a landscape utterly devoid of tree cover, and said something to the effect that "if the terrain in 'Nam had been as open as this, we'd've beaten their gook asses in six months."

Allen snapped back: "Yeah, and if New York didn't have so many buildings, it would make a great cow pasture. You still fightin' that war, Cycle-Man?"

Dewey mulled over that for a few seconds, then responded: "Yeah, sometimes. You know how it is: flashbacks, bad dreams and stuff. I guess it has something to do with two tours as a Huey door-gunner. Everybody I know who went over there has some moments. Hell, you were there, too—don't you sometimes refight it in your head?"

Allen's voice was cold as an ice cube. "No. As a matter of fact, I don't."

"You must've gotten lucky and caught a transfer to Europe or something. . . ."

"I didn't get transferred anywhere, Dewey."

This conversation, I thought, had taken a decidedly brittle turn.

"Well, what's the story, then? I mean, Preston said he met you in Pleiku, just before the Tet Offensive."

"Then get Preston to tell you about it. I've got other things to do."

And he was gone, just like that, leaving both me and Dewey with a what-the-fuck puzzle. So naturally, Dewey radioed for Preston to come over, and when he did, insisted on hearing the whole story.

Dewey cut to the chase: "How come you never told me what happened to Allen over in 'Nam?"

" 'Cause it wasn't any of your fucking business, Dewey."

"It is now, boss. Allen's in command of this operation, so as 'soldiers' under his authority, Little Dick and I want to know the whole scoop. Don't we, Little Dick?"

"We do, but I'd appreciate your maybe finding another nickname for me."

"I'll consider it, next time I see you nekkid in the shower. . . . Now come on, Press: tell us what happened!"

So Preston told us the whole bathetic story. What a saga. What an abortion.

Knowing all of this might not make me like Allen Warrener any better (and some days I like him a lot, even though it's more amusing to record his foibles in these pages!), but it does give me insights into why he is . . . the way he is. As Preston summarized, after he finished telling us the main story:

"You think he's moody and pretentious and contradictory, Richard? Well, you're fuckin-A right he is. Try to imagine the role he's had to play: First, he sustained serious combat wounds, but they're not even in places where you can see them!

Second, he's suffered on and off from post-traumatic symptoms for sixteen–seventeen years, but he can't—he won't—tell anybody why. Third, even though he paid the price for being in combat, he technically wasn't. Now, to you or me, that's just multiple ironies. Shit happens, you know? But for Allen, it's like being sentenced to a lifetime of doubt and frustration. To this day, he cannot look a another veteran in the eye and not feel every bit as ashamed as if he'd dodged the draft by running off to Canada!

"So that's the real story about Fearless Leader. You guys give him your support, he just might just turn into one. Now, if either of you so much as hints that I told you all of this crap, I will tie that hundred-pound camera around your balls and throw you into the deepest part of this lake. Capisce?"

Yes, sir, loud and clear. As Preston turned to go, Dewey surprised me with his comment.

"So I guess the main reason Allen's here is so he can get one more chance to slay the dragon. That right, boss?"

"That's one way of looking at it. And that's why I hope to Christ this whole nutty expedition doesn't come up dry. I mean, he doesn't need to harpoon the monster, if the fucking thing exists, he just needs to face it and know that, yep, it's real all right, and I've got the pictures to prove it and I didn't flinch when it growled at me. Whatever this thing is, it's killed people. And if it kills 'em so hideously that even a Nazi hero lost his marbles from seeing what did to his crew . . . well, if Allen can stare it down without fear, then he's won the right to a different future; he'll be free. All the bad luck and missed opportunities will be canceled out. So you guys cut him a little more slack, okay? He's earned the right to be a little flaky, and, if you ask me, it's a wonder he's not psychotic already, from having to live with that shit every day for twenty years or whatever. Will you do that for him?"

Dewey and I both swore fealty; how could we not?

"Good. Now that I've betrayed the confidence of my best friend, I'm going off somewhere and get stoned. Keep your eyes open and your traps shut."

And with that, he climbed back into the inflatable and sailed back to camp. After which, Dewey gave me an inscrutable shrug and ambled off to sail down to his camera position.

Boredom returns, along with writer's cramp. Everything—and I do mean everything—is quiet. I wonder: how many great shots of the Loch Ness monster were never taken because the cameramen just dozed off from sheer tedium?

(Ten minutes later)

Just took a look at Camera Position No. 2 through my binoculars and exchanged waves with Dewey, who was looking back at me with his binoculars. He was also, I think, huffing on a big fat doobie. Wonderful! There you have it in a nutshell, folks—the essence of the Vardinoy Expedition as I have seen it evolve: a boatful of quixotic, middle-aged crazies who've mortgaged their futures so they can make one last lunge for Glory, and yet are off-handed enough about it that when they actually get to the site of their quest, one of their first priorities is getting stoned. . . .

Allen Warrener had no intention of just planting people behind cameras and waiting for a lucky shot. In fact, with Preston's technical advice, he'd ordered the components of an automated, motion-sensor-driven control system: if anything larger than a cocker spaniel broke the surface, the burglar-alarm lens would switch on all three cameras and rotate them through overlapping arcs to obtain full photographic coverage of whatever caused the disturbance and the waters surrounding it. Unless and until that happened, the same system simply commanded the linked cameras to record three frames per second for 8.5 hours at a stretch—the length of time it took to run through a large film magazine at that speed. This method would at least give snapshots of any transient phenomena that might be worth further study: unexplained ripples or underwater currents too large or fast-moving to be generated by an ordinary breeze or an ordinary lake-fish. He'd assigned the camera watches on the first two days mainly just to give everybody something to do and to create the impression, at least, that Fearless Leader had his shit together and was operating according to a Master Plan. It had taken two days, in any case, for some of Eiden's electricians to uncrate, test, and weatherproof the sensors and their attendant electronics.

Great was the cheering when he announced to the Expedition, at the start of his now-customary after-breakfast agenda-setting, that the dull camera watches had been scrubbed.

"So what do we do for fun, instead of pulling camera watches?" asked Richard.

"Ah, that means it's time to do some serious exploring, Mr. Sugarman, and I don't mean just drawing a search grid over the map and meandering o'er hill and dale, either. We have to start somewhere in trying to figure this island out; so, in light of the confusion that exists over the location of the monster-sightings—does it come out of the lake, or out of the sea?—we ought to settle that one issue right away, if we can.

"Simply put: are there big tunnels running through the base of Vardinoy, connecting some part of the lake depths with the ocean? If there are, then we can plug in one big piece of the jigsaw puzzle right off the bat. Fortunately, I think there's a way we can settle the question, one way or the other, without hiring deep-sea divers and asking them to do something exceedingly dangerous, monster or no monster."

"I ain't goin into no fuckin' underwater cave," growled Dewey.

"Nor would I ask you to, savage-biker-lad! If we knew just where to look, maybe we could verify the existence of these big tunnels simply by seeing the entrance, which would be a cave mouth of unusual size that lets a lot of seawater in but doesn't spew any out. Fortunately, Eiden's friend, the curator of the local history archives at the Torshavn Library, recently discovered a newspaper clipping that tells us where to look.

"Back in 1883, when the mail boat stopped in that fjord north of us and discovered that, during the space of a single week, the entire village population had disappeared, his report triggered a lot of concern in the Danish bureaucracy. Had there been a plague? A natural disaster of some kind? A raid by some commercial or political foe? The public wanted answers and an organized search for survivors. So three days after the disappearance was reported, a Danish Coast Guard cutter anchored off the village and a platoon of Danish Navy sailors disembarked, along with an assortment of doctors, scientists, and a clergyman, just in case there were any bodies to be buried.

"As we already know, there were none. Except for pariah dogs and a few cats, the town looked as though a giant vacuum cleaner had sucked up all the inhabitants without touching anything else. Once the whole village had been searched meticulously, it was decided that the expedition should search the rest of the island too, on the theory that a freak tsunami or something similar might have caused some residents to seek high ground. Which begs the questions of why they hadn't come back and why there was no sign of a giant wave sweeping through the village, but there were a couple of newspaper reporters present and the authorities wanted everyone to know that they had done all the right and proper things.

"Apparently, this earlier expedition ran into one of the same problems that we've encountered now: there's no accurate map of Vardinoy anywhere to be found! So they'd brought a guide, a middle-aged fellow named Jensen who'd grown up on Vardinoy, but who had moved to Iceland as a young man, to find a job in the whaling trade. His factory ship just happened to be docked in Torshavn when the call went out for volunteers, and since he had still had relatives living on Vardinoy, he signed up. According to the newspaper account, he was willing enough, and no shirker, but alas, he was very fond of the aquavit, and customarily began taking a nip or two around ten in the morning.

"When the authorities asked Jensen if he knew of any place on Vardinoy where the inhabitants might be inclined to seek refuge if they thought a tsunami was coming, he said 'sure.' They'd head for a place known as 'The Axe-Cuts,' which was the highest cliff-top on the western coast, and which derives its name from a series of very narrow and very sheer crevasses that kind of slice up the summit and extend all the way down to sea level. But there's a fairly large plateau at the very top, with room enough for a couple of hundred folks. 'Okay, let's start there,' said whoever was in charge, so off they went.

"The newspaper account gives a detailed enough description so that we won't be able to miss this place when we see it, but I'll cut to the good part of the story. Good Mr. Jensen led them to the top, all right, but he developed a powerful thirst from his exertions, so when they got to the summit, he reached for his bottle—at the exact moment he was pointing over the edge of one of the Axe-Cuts, to show the others how deep and fearsome it was—and his sweaty hand couldn't quite get a grip. When he felt the bottle slipping, he instinctively lunged for it . . . and I guess you can figure out what happened. According to the newspaper account, 'his scream of dismay seemed to go on for many long anguished minutes.'

"Poor Jensen's comrade returned to the village and used the cutter's launch to search for his body. From the seaward side, however, the Axe-Cuts were simply inaccessible—the base of them was shielded by so many sharp rocks that even a small boat, at high tide, couldn't get within a hundred yards of the crevasses. The fellow commanding the expedition steamed over to Vesturoy and telegraphed Torshavn for an experienced climber—the only way to bring out the body was by tying a loop around it and hauling it up the same route by which it had fallen in. A professional bird-hunter from Vagar Island offered to try, for a fee of five hundred kroner, I might add, but his services proved to be unnecessary. When the retrieval party set forth the morning after the bird-hunter's arrival, the first thing they saw when they emerged from the mountain pass was the battered and bloated body of Herr Jensen—*floating in the middle of the lake.*"

Allen had timed the punch-line beautifully; the others were all leaning forward in their chairs. "You see where I'm going with this, people. We have to start somewhere, and verifying the existence of one or more big tunnels, connecting the lake and the ocean, would be no small discovery in and of itself. So, I propose we hike up there to the Axe-Cuts and take a look. Low tide is at twelve thirty-six P.M., so if we leave within the next hour, we should have optimum viewing conditions. At the very least, the scenery'll be smashing."

Dewey was still waving his hand, like a kid who urgently needed a bathroom pass. "Okay, F.L., so what happens if we get up there and we do see a gigantic cave mouth *and* we find a way to climb down to it?"

"Well, I plan to take some pictures and pat myself on the back, Dewey, but if you'd like to explore the dark underbelly of Vardinoy be my guest. Otherwise, I suggest we wait until Eiden can arrange for a qualified diving team to come up here."

Everyone seemed up for it in a big way. While they were filling canteens and wrapping sandwiches to stuff into their backpacks, Birgir showed up, towing behind the Land Rover a trailer full of electronic gear and carrying inside it the two technicians Eiden had engaged to install, calibrate, and test the sensor-controlled camera system. Also emerging from the passenger seats was Andreas Dahl, who hailed Allen heartily.

"I was lucky enough to hitch a ride with young Mr. Jakobsen, and when he told me what you folks were up to this morning, I thought it sounded fascinating. Would you mind awfully if I tagged along? If the location lives up to its fearsome name, it ought to be worth a sketch or two."

"Yeah, sure, why not? Haven't you explored that part of the coastline already, though?"

"Actually, no; I started on the eastern side and was working my way clockwise around the lake. Everything in the opposite direction will be as new to me as it is to you."

Allen was not surprised, although he was somewhat dismayed, when Preston took him aside and announced that he'd changed his mind about going on the hike. One of the new sensors needed recalibrating.

What needed recalibrating, Allen thought, was Preston's relationship with his wife. He and Norma had gotten into it, hammer-and-tongs, about two in the morning. The cause of the fight wasn't apparent, but the muted venom—audible to anyone who was still awake at that hour—indicated something more than a routine marital spat. Evidently, the argument hadn't been settled, whatever it was, because at breakfast the couple pointedly sat as far from each other as possible.

"You want to tell me what triggered World War Three in your tent last night, ol' buddy? Or did you just wake up and decide: *Nah, fuck it, I don't feel like photographing the most spectacular piece of scenery on the island*"?

"Dewey can shoot it as well as I can, Allen. Just let me stay here and sulk for a while, until I get a few things straight in my head."

At that moment, Allen spotted Norma, whose bright-eyed good cheer was transparently phony, stuffing snacks into her L.L. Bean backpack and pointedly making small talk with a very poker-faced Andreas Dahl.

"I think I get the picture, Press. What brought this on? I thought you and Norma were getting it on pretty hot these days. . . ."

"Yeah, so did I. But, you know, our dour Faeroese guest pretended he was interested in her artwork, and suddenly she's flopping on her back and spreading her legs."

"You're exaggerating; they've scarcely been alone together for five minutes. And I will risk pissing you off by suggesting that, if you'd shown a little more interest in her artwork, she wouldn't have been so quick to throw herself at Dahl—and, Jesus, look at the guy! He's embarrassed, she's being so blatant about it."

"He's also staring at her boobs like they were the first pair of tits he'd ever seen, too! I'm outta here, pal. Have an absolutely breathtaking day!"

Karen had walked up just in time to catch the end of this exchange, and one glance told her the story.

"Well, I'll be shipped in dit. I thought it would take her another two or three days to make her move. . . ."

"You saw this coming before I did, by God."

"From the moment Norma shook hands with him. I hate to break the news to you, Allen, but that woman's not glued together nearly as tight as you seem to think she is. I'll do what I can to defuse this; but if Norma's in the mood to stage a rebellion, nothing I say is going to stop her."

Allen rolled his eyes and groaned. "I don't fucking *need* this. . . ."

"Well, you got it anyhow, so you'd better start thinking about how you're going to handle it. Ah, here comes the rest of the gang! Good morning, Richard. All ready to get your feet blistered?"

"Hey, I was an Eagle Scout, lady—I used to climb three mountains every day before breakfast."

"And *I* was never more ready for an adventure in all my born days!" chirped Norma, so aggressively bright and vivacious that she seemed to be playing to an invisible camera. Just to make her attitude unmistakably clear to everyone, she turned to Dahl and tugged on his sleeve.

"Andreas, would you mind adjusting the straps on my pack? I like 'em good and tight."

"Christ on a pogo stick," muttered Allen, turning away in disgust and plunging ahead to take the lead.

If Vardinoy's geology was extreme, so on this morning was its weather, for in the six or seven minutes it took them to hike to the base of the nearest ridgeline, the sky changed from a springtime blue to a pall of utter gloom as thick, muscular rolls of cloud swept across their route from the north, glazing their faces with moisture and making the rocks dangerously slick. Without sunlight, the landscape became depressingly somber.

Then, within a hundred yards of the first serrated line of summits, things changed once more: a huge oval of sunlight dropped on them as abruptly as a spotlight being switched on, snapping the dun-colored stones into sharp focus, wiping away the muddy monochrome colors and replacing them with ochers and crisp cordovan browns, veined here and there with streaks of fool's-gold yellow, where the steely edge of naked rib-rock sparkled as though dusted with mica.

Beyond the first row of crests was a lunar plateau strewn with chaotic and sometimes huge blocks of stone—cubist tumuli, as though some ancient race had quarried its temples here and walked away before the job was finished. The hikers stopped chattering, for the climb up that first slope had been more tiring than it looked from below, and for a time the only sound, aside from the intermittent sigh of wind and the faint chilly sluice of unseen rivulets spilling from the higher peaks, was the occasional *"Ah, shit!"* of someone landing ankle-deep in a cold shallow tarn.

Twenty minutes of fairly rough slogging brought them to the first sharp thrust of the coastal peaks, where the vertical pleats of basalt were dotted with flinty knobs fluted by millennia of erosion, drooling long strands of water that the wind unspooled by caprice. All around them was evidence of ancient upheavals and seismic violence: huge slabs of igneous stone, like toppled menhirs, had calved off from the landward side of the cliffs. Allen was about to call for a break anyway, before they began the final ascent, when Richard Sugarman happened to glance over his shoulder and then call out:

"Hey, you guys, check out the view!"

The plateau they'd earlier crossed now appeared fantastically different from their impression of it while they were striving to cross it:

Like great white pie wedges, the clouds slid apart and through them poured sunlight like a river of gold. Now it was apparent that the path they'd chosen meandered through the starkest and wettest portion of that terrain, and to the south of its puddles and basins lay a broad expanse of gentler, heather-softened slopes. Shimmering a brilliant emerald, the grass rippled in trembling fans, lush as suede and spangled with clumps of scarlet juniper buttons, or flashing bright with outbursts of marigolds that danced in the wind like clouds of butterflies. Allen thought this panorama demanded contemplation while they could still see it.

"Take ten, everybody—let's enjoy this before we get socked in again!"

Karen pulled a sheet of plastic from her pack and spread it over a convenient ledge, then gratefully sat, knees swinging, and lit a cigarette. Allen dug into his pack and retrieved a still-cold can of Tuborg, then savored the single most delicious beer he'd ever swigged.

"Hey, Andreas," he called, "I see why you specialize in landscapes!"

Dahl nodded in vigorous agreement, delineating the scene with bold strokes of fine-tipped charcoals, labeling certain places for later working-in the colors.

"In a dozen lifetimes, I could not see it all! If, just once, I could really capture the essence of all this *light* in paint, I would feel that I had truly *done something!*"

By the time they resumed their climb, the sky was mostly clear, and it did not take them long to discern a definite *edge,* a sharp dark serration, and beyond it, a silver-gray suggestion of enormous open space. As they climbed higher and closer, they began to hear the sea-wind, pouring over the cliff tops like a river, and when that measureless sigh suddenly acquired a discordant, almost alien undertone, it had the effect of a warning.

"That's the wind being funneled through a gorge, I think," said Dahl. "We'd best proceed very carefully from here on. Some of these cliffs might not be as solid as they look. . . ."

But it was Karen who spotted the Axe-Cuts first, and her "Holy shit!" exclamation was enough to put caution into everyone's steps.

"Good navigating, boss!" called Dewey, shifting Preston's big Bolex to his shoulder and rotating its trio of lenses to get the optimum depth of field.

The fissures had been aptly named: between the stupendous sweep of the North Atlantic and the broad ledge where they stood were four thin crevasses, astonishingly narrow and sharp—their length could not have been less than two hundred feet, but their width was no more than twenty feet on the seaward side, tapering to a sharp convergent V just in front of them. And each one of them looked exactly as though a titanic axe blade had bitten four strokes into the mountaintop.

"If you want a closer look," said Dahl, "I would suggest approaching them on your hands and knees—there's bound to be one hell of an updraft roaring through them."

Very strange indeed were the ritualistic movements of each hiker, as each decided just how close he or she wanted to get. Dewey was determined to shoot some footage straight down into the nearest abyss, but even he inched forward like a scout probing a minefield. Allen didn't know if he was prepared to deal with the vertigo—the strangeness and scale of these mysterious fissures were somehow unsettling; they made the mountain beneath his feet feel irrationally fragile. And when he got within three feet of the nearest edge, he could indeed feel the power of the updraft.

When he did, after some hesitation, crawl to the narrow apex of the closest gorge and venture a glance at its depths, he beheld an amazing phenomenon: all the way down, as far as he could see—swirling, diving, squabbling viciously, was an uncountable multitude of gulls, a boiling white-gray froth. Amplified and grotesquely distorted by the reverberant funneling mass of the walls, their commingled cries seemed more bestial than avian—part squeal, part scream, partly a vast and angry sigh, the sound suggested the feeding frenzy of a huge and many-tongued beast far down in the surf-scoured bottom of the crevasse. One flock of seagulls gliding through an azure sky was a scenic cliché, but thousands of them seething inside a confined wedge of gloom was a near-abomination. Allen was surprised to feel Karen's hand groping for his. So rigid was her grasp that he was not surprised to turn his head and see how reluctant she was to wiggle one inch closer to the edge.

"Hey, c'mon, this is really worth seeing! Just poke the top of your head over, so you can see it! I'll hold on to you, if you like."

"What I think I would *like*," she muttered, "is to be a long way from here."

He put his right arm around her shoulder and secured a fist on one strap of her backpack. "Does that help?"

"Yes, it does. Christ, I don't know what creeps me out about this place, but now that I'm looking over the edge, I wish those damned birds weren't in the way, so we could see the bottom of it."

Then Dewey had the bright idea of tossing a handful of Cheezits over the edge.

In response to the sudden appearance of mid-air snacks, the seagulls surged after them in a deranged, shrieking tempest of wings and claws. Peering intently through that strobing vortex of scavengers, they were now briefly able to discern a tiny thread of white far below, a long white ivory needle stabbing into the root of the coastline.

"I'm getting dizzy, Allen—it's like looking through the wrong end of a telescope. And I don't want to be anywhere near the edge if those fucking birds decide they want some more junk food. Don't be long, okay? This mountain isn't as solid as it feels."

Why the hell would she say that?

Once the seagulls realized there were no more snacks descending from heaven, they clogged the sides of the shaft once more, grumpily fighting each other for space on the available ledges and outcroppings. Nothing but airborne rats, Allen thought, and then he turned to repeat the description to Karen. He was surprised to see how slowly, how delicately, she retreated from the abyss—as though her body were made of cooling glass. Not until she'd reached a spot well below his boots did she seem to feel secure enough to sit up and gaze around to locate the others, each of whom had scuttled up to the edge of one or another of the intimidating fissures and was now peering, with mixed emotions, into a similar maelstrom of birds and shadows. Observing Allen's expression, which she interpreted as one of concern, Karen reached out and patted his foot, forcing a smile on the clenched muscles of her face. That smile was intended to let him know she was all right. His blank response to it indicated that he had not yet considered the possibility that she might not be.

Now that he realized there was no way to get a clear look at the bottom of the Axe-Cuts, Allen's sense of wonder cooled rapidly. If there were tunnel mouths down there, they were just as invisible from this angle as they were from the open sea. He brushed the damp grit from his knees and explored their viewing plateau until he hit the scenic jackpot at an overlook reassuringly rimmed with a waist-high spur. He called for Dewey to come get an epic pan shot of the view.

"Oh, fuck, yeah!" said Dewey when he saw the vista.

There was just enough moist, particulate *stuff* in the air to oreate wondrous prismatic nuances of light and tint, from dusty gold to a delicate vaporous rose. And below, sweeping off to either side of their promontory, the Wagnerian flanks of Vardinoy Island reared majestic and stern from the North Atlantic. And as perfectly placed as the final inspiration of a gifted set designer, from the tumultuous surf several *dranger* of prodigious size towered in defiant solitude. Each was densely populated not only with gulls, but with gannets and fat, comical puffins; each species, disdaining the others, had staked out its own colony on the narrow ledges, and beneath the nests, hundreds of years of accumulated droppings had formed long, intricately shaped stalagmites of chalk-white petrified guano. Richard Sugarman, who had been made instantly queasy by his first look down the Axe-Cut he'd wandered up to, now joined them, and the primal vastness of the scene seemed to have rendered him speechless.

"What do you think, Richard?" Allen almost had to shout, so loud was the combined sound of wind and surf. Sugarman just spread his arms to encompass the whole panorama. Allen nodded his approval of this emphatic but ambiguous response.

"Right there, Richard, is the essence of Norse mythology. No wonder they believed in Ragnarok—the sea gave them so many previews of Doomsday, they must have always known how vulnerable the very Earth was beneath their feet."

"Yeah, I think we got a little preview of the Last Days ourselves. . . ."

"Huh?"

"That little summer thunderstorm we sailed through on our way up here from Copenhagen."

Allen just nodded, which was fine with Richard, for the professor was clearly in one of those moods when he was incapable of simply *enjoying* the view without also obsessively *commenting* on it.

No, that wasn't it. *Something's wrong.*

Allen turned his back on the spectacle and began to walk, very deliberately, back toward the Axe-Cuts, his eyes fixed on something. Richard turned and was surprised to see that Karen had not only gone back to take a second look into the nearest chasm, but she was standing, rigid as an iron rod, only inches from the edge. Even at a distance, he could see the trembling in her shoulders, feel the chill of paralyzed dread emanating from her. Her face was pale and her knuckles white, as though she were straining, without success, to pull back from a magnetic current. Her gaze into the pit was unnatural, fixed, helpless—as though sight itself had been sucked away into that emptiness. Everyone who saw her was certain of one thing: Karen was in real danger of falling over the edge.

Norma, who was closest to her, started to move toward Karen, but she halted, unable to reach out and touch her for fear that the shock would sever her last brittle strand of self-control and cause her to slide into that roaring void. Norma made a supplicating gesture to Allen and slowly backed away. He stopped at a respectful distance, afraid of what might happen if he moved too suddenly and startled her.

This close to her body, he could actually feel the sinister equilibrium, like a charged field building inexorably, draining her will, forcing her to stare down into the depths that she had retreated from only moments before. When he was as close as he dared to go, he began to intone her name, softly, rhythmically, over and over, until the familiar sound of his voice could penetrate the cold incantation of wind and muted waves, gradually raising the volume until it made an audible counterpoint to the deranged screeching of the gulls. Unquestionably she heard him—on some level of perception—and reacted by uncurling her right fist and forcing her hand to reach in his direction: a silent cry for help. While continuing to speak her name, he raised his own right hand until there was the gentlest possible contact between their fingers. He began to tighten them, by surgically fine increments of pressure, until he had enough purchase simply to yank her back from the edge. Then, with the sort of shriek a damned man's soul might make as it tried to flee from Hell, an unusually huge marbled seagull, clawing savagely in a sudden powerful updraft, slashed its wings like white sword-blades only inches from her face.

Karen screamed, and as she did, Allen seized her hand with all his strength and pulled her back from the abyss. For one howling instant, he felt his own balance shift, felt the hideous pull of nothingness, thought they were both going over; and perhaps they would have, except for the quick iron-hard grasp of Andreas Dahl's hands, encircling both Allen and Karen and hurling them backward. Allen was grateful for the painful impact of solid rock, and when he opened his eyes, Karen lay beside him, her breathing harsh and ragged but her eyes slowly filling with comprehension and relief.

"Jesus," she breathed, smiling wanly and shaking her head in astonishment. "I guess that's what you might call rapture of the pit! Thank you, gentlemen —I don't know what came over me, but I simply couldn't move."

Norma enfolded her with a crushing hug. "You okay now, honey?"

"Fine, fine—just a little shaky, that's all. I guess I just discovered a phobia I never knew I had."

Karen forced a plastic smile, but Warrener could tell she was faking it. Half an hour later, when the hikers began recrossing the plateau, Karen was seized by a malarial trembling. Allen waved the others forward, then hung back with her and held her until the shaking subsided. But her eyes were still dilated, like the eyes of someone coming off a bad drug trip, and she was trying to control her voice so hard that it cracked on some of the harsher consonants.

"Allen, it's entirely possible you saved my life back there. Something happened when I first looked over that cliff—that chasm seemed to *expand* until I felt like I was looking over the edge of the whole world! Or at least *our world,* if that makes any sense—and I was certain that if I looked long and hard enough, I could see into the mysteries that lie beyond. I felt that I was absolutely on the verge of either a stupendous mystical vision or a blackout, and for once in my practical hard-headed redneck life, I went for the vision instead of the here-and-now. I realize it damn near got me killed, but even so . . . I don't believe it was malign."

" 'Malign'? Do you mean the vision or the—hey, Karen, you're talking about this *spell* you had as though it were somehow directed it at you *on purpose*. Not to sound skeptical, but even the collective consciousness of a couple thousand pissed-off seagulls couldn't generate enough psychic energy to light a ten-watt bulb. And seagulls were the only things down in that crevasse."

She turned upon him a cool and glassy look. "How do you know that for sure?"

Observing him rendered speechless, she laughed a little, and the trembling subsided. "I gotcha with that one, didn't I?"

"Yep, you sure did. . . ." He took her hand and they resumed their descent.

"Promise me something, Allen. . . ."

"Anything, if it means growing closer to you."

"That's very sweet, love, even though you don't really mean it. But I still want you to promise me that you will never, ever, let anybody go up to the Axe-Cuts alone."

"Not even me?"

"Especially not you. Please!"

"I promise to consult with you first, how's that?"

That was not exactly what she'd asked for, but she understood that was all she would get from him, so she let it go. If and when she could figure out what had made her experience up there so entrancing, she would try to discuss it again; until then, as they often did when further conversation would have vectored them into areas of irresolvable conflict, they chose mutual silence and resumed their trek, each wrapped in solitary thoughts.

Despite being asked a multitude of questions, Karen refused to say any more about what she had experienced up at the Axe-Cuts. The dinner-table conversation might well have been strained, but for the gargantuan appetites everyone had worked up. After taking their turn at dishwashing, Allen and Karen went out on the Flag Knoll and shared a bottle of wine while contemplating the cloud-galleons streaming south through a succession of lurid sunset hues. When they bedded down in their tent, Allen lay down beside her and stroked her hair and shoulders with slow gentle motions, dismayed to feel how tight and deep was the core of tension still within her. And it didn't yield to his caresses; nothing soft and welcoming came up to meet him halfway. Indeed, and quite surprisingly in view of his innocent intentions, she chose to interpret his ministrations as an invitation to have sex. Having reached that conclusion, she moved warily apart, sadly but firmly putting a small physical—but a large psychic—barrier between herself and what she perceived as the inappropriateness of his timing. "I'm really beat, Allen—if you don't mind, I just want to crash."

"Well, sure, no problem," he replied evenly, sad that there were still such dead zones within their intimacy. Sex was nowhere in his mind—like her, he too could not think of a clumsier, more insensitive gesture, not at the end of this particular day. When he permitted her to withdraw without further comment or complaint, she favored him with a grateful little smile. "Thanks for being so understanding."

Jesus, do I always come on like such a goon?

Karen turned her back and removed her grungy climbing clothes, rising into the Coleman lantern's glow. As she bent over and pulled her arms from the sleeves, the lantern's glow gave a tawny flush to the upward-rising crescents forming her chest and hips. Her breasts, when she bent to turn down the flap on her sleeping bag, dipped from shadow into light—exquisite inverted bells, hard-tipped in the cool air, he could not avoid staring at the taut hard nipples as they reacted to the temperature. Seeing her thus, he *did* feel a sudden raw lick of lust for her, incongruous and unwelcome and far too late in showing up to justify the recent parting that had occurred in its name. He mumbled a rather truculent "Good night," then rolled away from her and resolutely closed his eyes. *See? I'm just as tired and uninterested as you are!*

Karen put a cup of wine on the crate between their cots, then reached under her covers and drew out her vanity case. From within, she extracted an amber bottle, opened it, shook out two large red lozenges, and gulped them down. Allen peeked through tight lids—she seemed oblivious now even to his proximity—and recognized the prescription: it was for Serax, 100 mg.—a potent, fast-acting sleep med she occasionally resorted to. Which meant that she'd be completely *out* in ten minutes or less. As she settled into a drowse, she reached across the space separating their cots and clumsily probed for his hand, showing that she'd been aware of his observation all along.

"I'm sorry, Allen. Maybe you should have left me home after all."

He made no reply in words, but quietly knelt beside her and just stroked her hair until she sank into a deep, quiet slumber. Observing that she had left the pills accessible, in case he wanted to use one, he helped himself to a capsule. Since he was not used to this medication, it dragged him under quickly.

But Karen was only feigning sleep—on a full stomach, the Serax wouldn't kick in for a quarter-hour or more. She did some yoga breathing while her mind replayed a silent movie of what had happened to her up there by the Axe-Cuts. Almost the instant she'd stretched out on her cot, she definitely felt a strong echo of the sensations she'd experienced on the edge of the fissure. It was like a *straining* toward some other place—it caused her to feel like an athlete pursuing a finish line that keeps receding before him, no matter how hard he sprints. She was puzzling over this metaphor when her partly self-induced trance suddenly deepened.

Now she had become a dowsing rod, a witching-wand, quivering toward a state of perception that was vivid but elusive, imperfectly focused but compelling. The amplitude of that yearning oscillated rapidly, like a fluctuating pulse. At first it was a sensation as faint and delicate as the beating of moth wings behind a membrane, but seconds later it seemed as close, as strong, as the hum of a giant turbine in a nearby room. As intensely as she wanted to identify the source of this energy, she couldn't find a portal that gave access.

But as her state of mind deepened, she did become cognizant of the larger *directions*, of cooler or warmer azimuths, and when she was "getting warmer," she felt/heard/tasted a vague crescendo of vibrations, as though a gong were being struck inside a great dark space and she was supposed to follow its tones, however elusive the sound might be from moment to moment.

She didn't know if she could ever explain to Allen, or to anyone, exactly what she'd experienced up there. Although everyone who saw her agreed that she had had a stunned, deer-in-the-headlights expression, she had been far from paralyzed. She'd been in a wholly different mode, for which she had no name or definition. She had not been like some LSD-crazed schizoid leaping from a rooftop because she just knew she had suddenly grown a pair of gossamer wings. No! She was at that place because *that* was as close as she had ever gotten, during any of her "spells," to the molecule-thin membrane separating the state of *being in a place* from the state of merely perceiving that the other place existed—the way some of her snake-handling Baptist cousins thought about Heaven. Karen, by contrast, had been drawn to the Axe-Cut's edge by an emanation grown suddenly too palpable to deny—some short distance away, perhaps in another quantum-physics continuum, was a *real* demarcation, and not only could she touch it, she might, under certain evidently rare conditions, *pass through it* and behold alien wonders. All she had to do was become more open to . . . whatever those vibrations were, and marshal her need, her courage, her desire to make that journey.

Up there on the windy verge of Oblivion, she had known, for a certainty, that the only thing preventing her from making that transition was gravity, the certain and shattering death that yawned a single step away. But the Source, as she now thought of it, had seemed *close*—down there, down in the roots of Vardinoy Island, so close that, in the deepest phase of her enchantment, she had picked up a kind of psychic spoor—biting and acrid as dry-ice vapor, and had it not been for the constraints of height and human frailty, she could have followed that spoor as surely as any predator ever sniffed its quarry on the veldt.

Down there, beneath the Axe-Cuts, in abyssal depths where no sentient life supposedly existed, something did, which was impinging—almost surely not for the first time—upon her consciousness . . . something that gave off a signature mental "scent" both intoxicating and horrid, of commingled age-old rot and fierce, unbounded vitality.

And now, drifting from the cot in her cozy Coleman tent, she was vectoring toward it once again . . . close enough to get the whiff again—

And to follow it >>> there are scenes it wants her to see, apparently.

Beneath its vitality and magnitude (it was big—she was certain of that) simmered a dark undercurrent of *fear*. She had not been afraid, as such, until she suffered the passing touch of that other entity's fear . . .

misery and loneliness immeasurable

>>>>>>**O, the sea was *boiling***

And >>>>

There was a pall of sulfurous steam that covered half the burning sky, like a black dome, thick, heavy with falling ashes and sparkling with meteorites of molten rock

Red-hot needles raining on a skin that covered mile after square mile of seething primordial ocean >>> her? Skin? Its? Skin?

And

That toxic dome of roiling cloud reflected the scorch of a stupendous holocaust just beyond the horizon

A large part of the planet was dying out there, and each new detonation spawned a sinister yellow corona of shock

And:

There were mountains, newly upthrust from the deeps, their sides as gleaming and keen as fresh-cut crystal. They were marching toward her/it and she wants to flee from their path (but she can't! why not?)—Eruptions so numerous they formed an orchard of fire—or was it all one huge many-branched eruption? (*Whatever! Just get on with it!* thinks the Karen-in-the-cot) She "saw" a blistering surge of magma shoot out its tongue across the horizon: a wound in the demarcation between Earth and sky

And

One of those newborn mountains exploded in an orchid of blue-white ferrous light—the sea spurted pillars of water and liquefied metals—she heard/felt the Earth howl in pain from the titanic and brutal processes that were shaping it

And at the very last instant of *communion* she glimpsed the North Atlantic sunder apart, like the Red Sea under Moses' wrath, and between the explosions of steam and magma, she glimpsed, rising from the tortured depths, the tsunami of volcanic core-stuff that would cool, ten thousand or ten million years hence, into the fanged peaks and gaunt harbors of the Faeroe Islands.

She died when these islands were born, or should have
or wished she had—

Nothing could survive the impact of that wall of magma. Until that moment, she had been no more conscious of "death" than she had been of "birth." Eons ago, she had achieved awareness, the first inchoate urge-to-sentience . . . and now that avalanche of raw semi-solid magma would snuff out her consciousness as quickly as a hurricane blows out a candle

She had only recently—ten thousand years ago?—defined the condition of being "alive," and now that she felt the growing heat of that rushing mass of planet-sculpting destruction, she was about to discover the antithesis of being alive—and so discovered the third concept, the one that bridges "Life" and "Not-Life" and it was a foul-tasting chemical change named "Fear"

Fear?

Quite simply, like all living things, she did not want to die!
Had she evolved a sense of irony, had she possessed the organs with

which to verbalize emotions, her demented laughter would have shaken up waves from a hundred square miles of the North Atlantic. . . . But the volcanic cataclysm killed it/her too fast for sensation

Or so it/she thought until

It/she regained consciousness and discovered

There are states of being much worse than oblivion.

Darkness and cold. No light anywhere she could extend her sensory probing.

All of her great mass—mile after mile of cellular matter—was imprisoned far beneath the bottom of the sea

Forever.

". . . and ever, amen!"

Wrenched back into her own time and space, Karen Hambly sat up in her cot, clammy with cold sweat, her body wracked by malarial tremors, the very marrow of her bones vibrating with terror.

Stay cool, girl—just pretend it was a bad drug trip and never, ever eat any of those mushrooms again!

Three feet to her right, Allen Warrener snored monotonously. She clung to the reassuring ordinariness of that sound. She was safe and sound inside a Coleman tent, that's where she *was*, and if, in the depths of her nightmare —already mercifully fading into fragments too jumbled to make sense—she had briefly imagined herself in communication with a consciousness too alien, too ancient, too downright impossible, to exist (at least on *this* planet), she was now right back where she was supposed to be.

But for whatever reasons, her senses remained preternaturally acute, and in order to tamp down their hyperkinesthesia, she swung off the cot and quietly rummaged in the crate where Allen kept his private stock of bourbon. There it was, and Wild Turkey, too. By God, nothing but the best for the Vardinoy Expedition! Not even bothering with a cup, she chugged a couple of ounces straight from the bottle, and rejoiced as the liquid napalm did its usual Rebel Yell inside her tummy. Appropriately in the mood now, she donned a warm robe and thick hiking socks, aligned her reading lamp so that she could see well enough to write in her journal but not so bright as to wake up ol' what's-his-name in the other bunk.

There now! Snug as a bug—pen in hand, good whiskey in the bottle, just the right amount of light to scribble by.

She began to write, knowing she would not magically find explanations, answers, or significant *patterns* in her jangled account, but certain that it was important to keep a record of these "episodes," in hopes that a pattern would emerge.

Let me put it this way: I am afraid to sit here in the night, on this end-of-the-world island, and listen to the wind outside our tent. I am afraid of what that wind might bring to my ears, amplified by those terrible howling chasms we found today. Not wanting to hear the booming waves as they continuously gnaw on the roots of Vardinoy. Not wanting to hear the savage squawks of those demented seagulls. Not wanting to imagine that, if I had fallen into that crevasse, they would have stripped the flesh from my still-warm bones just as mindlessly and ravenously as they tore apart the cheese doodles Dewey threw to them. Most of all, I don't want to replay the intimations I've been getting, from somewhere, *that Vardinoy Island was born of some ancient and stupendous cataclysm, some fracturing of the Earth's very crust, and that some kind of sentient being was around to see it . . . and either passed that memory along to its descendants or is somehow still around a zillion years later! Crazy, huh?*

If I thought Allen would believe me, I would, however, tell him that I'm now utterly convinced that there IS a monster here, or at least a monstrous force *or* presence—*what's the Latin phrase Allen likes to use? Oh, yes: the* genius loci— the indwelling spirit of the place itself.

I don't care how irrational it sounds, but I saw purpose *in the eyes of that giant gull who attacked me, not just instinctive savagery—Richard was right: up close and in a swarm of such numbers, seagulls are no more romantic than airborne rats. In the eyes of that bird, I saw not just malevolence, but malevolent* intent. *It came* after *me, with those dagger-sharp talons raised to cut out my eyes, and then to seize my clothing or my hair and drag me into the abyss.*

In my fugue-state, when I fancied myself in contact with an ancient and inexplicable consciousness, perhaps I had gotten too close *to something I was never supposed to see, and that murderous rogue bird—how often do you find a seagull the size of a condor, for Chrissake?—that bird was the seneschal, the agent, the gatekeeper, who was dispatched to stop me. Which makes it not just an aggressive scavenger, but a goddamned* assassin! *And what if that were literally true? What,* too, if just for an instant—no, make that two instances in one day—I really was in some kind of garbled telepathic contact with—whatever? Just for the sake of argument, we would then be in a very interesting situation. One "force" or "faction" or "spirit" seeks actively to get in touch, while another spirit or force or whatever wants me to go away or to die, because, for God knows what reason, I seem to "get in touch" more often and more deeply than anyone else.

I don't mean just "anyone else" in this expedition, either. I mean anyone else, maybe in a long, long time. . . .

So there's my lover and sometimes-friend Allen, snoring away, happy as a pig in shit because he thinks we might take pictures of a sea serpent . . . and I'm sitting here thinking we might have stumbled on to something much stranger, and potentially much more dangerous, than any sea serpent ever described.

The next few weeks could prove to be a lot more interesting than Allen ever bargained for. I admit it; somewhere deep inside my bones, I am more scared than curious. But it's like I've been hinting to Allen—there are reasons why I'm on Vardinoy too, and mine may well go back farther than his.

22.

ART LESSONS

From the journal of Richard Sugarman:

Camera Watch again. Only, this time it's voluntary. I like the combination of view and privacy. Every now and then a fish flicks the surface of the lake, but I stopped jumping for the camera two days ago. Aside from the fish and the wind, nothing disturbs that surface. I have a feeling that nothing is going to, either. Frankly, I'm bored shitless, and I suspect everyone else who is, too—most of the time.

A sudden flurry of movement over at the camp! Through my binoculars, it resolves itself into Norma D, her pack stuffed with easel and art supplies, making a big production out of preparing to accept another "art lesson" from our polite but slightly dour Faeroese guest, Herr Dahl, with whom she's been conspicuously spending more time than with her putative husband.

Preston's pretending to be very cool about the situation, which is a dead give-away that he's seething about it inside. Warrener tells me that strict sexual fidelity was not one of the rocks on which their marriage was founded—how could it be, given the business they were in?—so I think Valentine's distemper is not primarily caused by ordinary sexual jealousy. I think it's because Norma's getting something from Dahl that Preston never gave her, something he was too preoccupied to notice she even needed. Dahl is a respected, successful artist—a class act, as it were—yet he's taken the time and made the effort to tutor Norma, apparently out of a sincere regard for her potential talent! He displayed zero erotic interest in her; he hasn't even made any flirtatious jokes in her presence, so all the more reason why his attention is like psychic manna from heaven. He's considerate, soft-spoken, always courteous, and apparently sincere when he tells Norma she is capable of taking her artwork to "a whole new level."

If Andreas does secretly want to get into her pants, he's found the magic button to push. But, like Warrener, I too don't get any erotic vibes off the guy. He's civil enough, certainly, but there's something a little off-putting about that wintry smile of his. But still, here's this tall handsome Max von Sydow clone whom she meets in the middle of fucking nowhere, and who spends more time studying her pastels than he does ogling her boobs—all of these things must make him unique in her experience!

This messy, unexpected triangle has Fearless Leader mighty pissed off, that's for sure. He can barely manage to say "Good morning" to Norma any more. After all, Preston Valentine has been his closest friend since the Late Jurassic. A. W. may be a veritable Petri dish of paradoxes and ambiguities, but when it comes to simple old-fashioned loyalty, *he cleaves to that with the fealty of a Bedouin prince.*

After lunch, the two partners-in-art walked north on the old wagon trace. Dahl set a brisk, unflagging pace, and Norma was glad when he halted at a spot halfway between the lake and the pass. He pointed with his pipe stem at a steep meadow interestingly patterned with wildflowers and glacier-borne rocks and announced: "I think we'll set up here. Does this suit you, Norma?"

"What . . . whatever," panted Norma, surreptitiously inspecting her shirt to see if the sweat she'd worked up trying to match his stride had somehow broken through the shield of body powder she'd applied before leaving

Dahl strode purposefully into the gorse, dew streaking his trousers, hefting his massive paint box and heavy easel as though they were made of balsa wood. After a moment of determined aerobic breathing, Norma shouldered her own gear and followed. At a suitably level spot, Dahl halted and set up his rig. Norma chose a flat mossy boulder, close enough for her to lean forward and peek over his shoulder. Humming a Faeroese ballad, he positioned his canvas, laid out his kit, scooped up a blob of heather-green paint on the tip of a brush, and "laid claim" to the canvas with a bold slash of pigment. Then he glanced over his shoulder to make sure that Norma, too, had made that all-important first stroke. Synchronicity, for some reason, was an important starting point in these dual-artist rituals.

For ritualistic was the word for it now, even after only three previous painting excursions. The first half hour or so, Norma thought of as their "quiet period," when Andreas was utterly absorbed in his work and, by his body language and lack of chitchat, seemed to assume that she was equally absorbed in hers. After that time, depending on his mood, he would begin to talk. She'd come to understand the significance of that moment: it marked the stage in any given painting when he passed a certain threshold of confidence. Until that signal, however, Norma was expected to work quietly and intently on her own composition; she had learned quickly not to interrupt him until he sent her the proper signal. The first time they'd gone out together, she had kept on chattering after he began to paint, and had soon learned that he was displeased when she did so. It was not as though he'd suddenly turned and barked a command for silence, but his manner had grown curt and his responses monosyllabic. Norma wasn't slow about picking up social cues—in her former line of work, that kind of sensitivity was almost a necessity; so she had quickly divined his wishes and after that, the harmony of their shared mood improved greatly.

Norma took inspiration from watching Dahl's hands as he worked with the implements of his art. Each of his paintings strongly delineated a specific mood, and each was significantly different from the others, even though the ingredients were the same: water and stone, light and space, the hardness of the Earth and the mutability of the sky. Andreas cherished the limited but elemental ingredients that comprised the Faeroese landscape; he excelled in replicating the nuances of light and mass and space; he found them not simplistic or confining, but infinitely malleable and subtle, vital, even stirring. Those were the qualities that made his paintings command high prices from both museums and private collectors. One canvas might be somber, made heavy by a palpable weight of gloom, while the next work he finished, differing only in the shape and density of the stones or the volume and granularity of the light Dahl created to frame them, would blaze forth in pagan exultation.

In his most famous works, Andreas had conjured what one Copenhagen art critic described as "sun-ecstasies." Some of his landscapes, by contrast, were lit in a manner that was sly, almost coy, inviting the viewer's eye to "turn up the volume," to coax more radiance from those seductive surfaces than the artist had actually put there; at the other extreme, Dahl had sometimes managed to create the impression of light as a brute, bronze *oppression,* a tyrannical element that suppressed the solid waves and peaks with all the heaviness and inertia of a golden anvil. Taken as a whole, the corpus of his works conveyed the essence of his native land: the tense stasis of elemental forces that evoked a whispered legend of the music made by the molten dervish who dwelt in the planet's seething and violent core.

Look around you, murmured the darkest of his paintings, *at those basaltic crags. They have withstood a hundred million years of wind and surf, yet I say*

*unto you: take them not for granted, for the immutability of what you see is an
illusion, and there are forces in flux beneath your feet that could wash this all away
as though it were a child's sand castle!*

Awed by the power of Andreas's work, Norma at first felt her own talent
almost crushed beneath the disparity in their achievements. She had always
tried, without being very conscious of it, to make her pastels and watercolors
"pretty." Pretty to look at, pretty to hang on your wall. Her artistic goals were
modest, almost self-effacing, and over the years her technique had become
equal to the results she wanted to achieve.

But now, in the space of four vivid and surprising days, Andreas had half-
convinced her that there might be untapped possibilities within her talent.
Was "pretty" all she was capable of? Andreas, gently but insistently, had
admonished her to *let go*. "Look around you, Norma! This island may not be
'pretty,' but it embodies the basic recipe of Creation! Let the subject matter
dictate the technique. The harder you try to make this landscape 'pretty,' the
more wretchedly amateurish the results are going to be. Open your senses,
open them wider than you've ever done before, and you'll suddenly realize that
you can tune your aesthetic receptors, just like a radio, to the wave-lengths of
that which surrounds you! When you learn to do *that*," Andreas had promised,
"the mechanics of rendering a scene will take care of themselves."

Norma Davenport was not trailer-trash; she'd read a lot of books; she
knew perfectly well what "Existentialism" was and with whom it was safe to
use that word in a conversation. She understood that the process Andreas
had described was a kind of Zen Archery approach to painting: the ego does
not wield the brush so much as surrender wholly to the "It" emanating from
the painter's surroundings. Okay, that much was clear to her. But the process
of achieving such grace . . . that part of it remained elusive; she could only
study the Master's works as they evolved before her eyes, and soak up his
words when he deigned to utter them, fervently hoping that the Ineffable
would descend one day and guide her hand so that she might take her art to
The Next Level.

On this warm and sun-drenched afternoon, she could feel *something* shift
within her. She had been gazing intently at the landscape, hardly bothering
to glance down at her work, for almost an hour, but she suddenly became
aware of a new muscularity in her hands, a surge of vigor that shaped her
fingers in a new and awkward grip upon the brush. Something had seized

her hand and stayed it in mid-stroke, as if to say: either use that brush more deftly or throw it away! She had been trying to capture the hard-edged crystalline quality of one particular flinty outcropping, but her line was too timid, her delineation of *edges* almost effete! Angrily, she picked up a fresh stick of sketching charcoal and tried again. But this time, surfing on the crest of impulse, she bore down so hard that the stick shattered in her hand, covering her fingers with coal-miner's grime. Disgusted with her craft, her chosen medium, the obdurate resistance of the-thing-to-be-painted, she threw her brushes and paints to the ground, spat on her fingertips, and assaulted the paper with bare hands. Oh my God, she was ruining the original sketch, violating it, coloring *outside-the-lines!* And the rush of liberation was near-to-explosive. No longer was she just "sketching" those shadowy monoliths, she was reaching *into them*, manipulating and kneading them like dough, turning hard unyielding basalt into some new form of gritty igneous matter that she, Norma-the-amateur, had suddenly seized control of! So fixated was she on this new discovery that she didn't even notice when Andreas Dahl's shadow briefly interrupted her light. Only when the black smudgy paste had begun to dry, and she felt the paper start to fray under the force of her rubbing, did she emerge from her trance and realize how far and deep she'd just gone into a new and exciting place. Only then could she stop, lean back, reach for a cigarette, and register surprise when Dahl's hand suddenly crossed her vision, extending a lighter.

After a couple of deep drags, she found her voice: "Don't bother telling me, Andreas. I really ruined this one, didn't I?"

The gentle diffidence of his chuckle was completely unexpected.

"*Ruin* it? Good God, woman, you mutilated a mediocre little sketch and reset the bones so it came back to life as Frankenstein! The only 'ruin' I see are the shards of a broken mould! It's a goddamned mess, all right; it's sloppy and dirty and downright ugly, but it's also repugnantly, wonderfully alive, and that also makes it beautiful. Be careful, Norma, because you're now sailing into uncharted waters—and doesn't it feel good?"

Oh, yes, it did! She turned away, realizing that, for the first time in more years than she could tally, she was blushing. To hide her self-consciousness, she turned away from her own composition and walked over to study his, hoping that a little time and distance would help her make sense out of what had just happened.

The past ninety minutes had been so intense that by mutual agreement they decided to take a long break, retire up the hillside to put some distance between themselves and their work, and share the liter of cool Spanish wine Andreas had stuffed into the bottom of his backpack.

Norma didn't know where the question came from or why she blurted it without preamble; but once spoken, it could not be retracted.

"Andreas, do you have a family?"

He moved his pipe stem slowly across the curve of his jaw, regarding her almost warily. Then his mood changed again and although Norma could read nothing in his long chiseled face that suggested joy, his thin elegant mouth formed a hesitant smile.

"My father still is captain of a fishing boat, and he holds the office of, well, what you might call 'the mayor' of Norduroy. You must meet him someday—a man like an oak! My mother died when I was quite young, and I have no siblings. I am the classic only child, and very shy—my closest friends were pencils and crayons!"

"What's life like in your part of Norduroy?"

"Well, actually, there is no other part—there's just the one town, plus a few sheep and dairy farms scattered around the countryside. All told, I think the population numbers around twelve hundred—a real metropolis!"

"Weren't you lonely, growing up in a place so cut off from the rest of the world?"

Andreas answered very carefully: "Probably not as lonely as your life must have been during a certain period in your history."

Norma felt her cheeks grow hot. "So . . . you knew about that . . . stuff . . . all along?"

"Your husband's films were very popular in Copenhagen; and so were you, I might add. My word, Norma, what are you blushing for? Good Lord, we are all adults on this island, you know! Besides, I dare you to look me in the eye and tell me you didn't enjoy being . . . what's the Americanism for it? Ah, yes, a Pop Culture icon?"

No, for a few dazzling drugged-out years she *hadn't* minded it. But now, on the anxious cusp of middle age, under the steady gaze of this strong, solitary stranger, Norma's private calculus of morality was spinning like a loose compass. Although she hadn't really *thought* of herself as "lonely," she was so touched by Dahl's solicitation that, just seconds after he said it, her mind began a process of memory revision. She'd never had much truck with the militant feminists' rant about pornography *(Jesus, if I looked like Andrea Dworkin, I'd probably hate men, too!)*. What she and Preston had made was too high-class. It was "Erotica"! Nor had she ever considered herself a "victim" (unless the script called for it, or course!); but as soon as Dahl uttered the word, that description of her life suddenly became at least arguable.

Here was a man intimate with mountains and in tune with the shifting moods of the sea; an Artist, quite possibly a great one, whose evidently sincere interest had caused her to stop thinking in terms of "my hobby" and to start referring to her paintings, at least in the whispers of her heart, as "my art." So she thought things over carefully before replying to his question.

"I never thought of myself as being unhappy. . . ."

"I didn't say that. And I assure you, no criticism of you or Preston was intended. For some people, 'loneliness' is just a lifestyle choice, and not necessarily a sad one. It's only a state of mind, anyhow, not one's 'Destiny'! It can be chosen, you know, as well as inflicted. I am perfectly happy in my solitude. I suppose I was well prepared for it by my youthful environment: one small town, where half the male population is away all day and occasionally a boat goes out in the morning and simply doesn't come back. Ever. That's where your monster stories come from, Norma—it's hard, even for seafaring folk, to accept the notion that their loved ones and friends can simply disappear without any trace, or any hope of ever learning their fate. At the height of a gale, it's easy to demonize the North Atlantic as a howling, evil beast."

He drained the last of his wine, then went over to his easel and began cleaning his brushes; obviously, today's painting lesson was over.

"I have a theory about your 'expedition. . . .' "

"Oh, let's hear it!"

"And so you shall, my dear, otherwise I wouldn't have mentioned it! I think, possibly, that all of you came here because you all, each in his or her own way, fear the loneliness that comes not just with old age, but with the knowledge that all you did and thought—ostensibly revolutionary, even millennial—has already been consigned to irrelevance."

"Not all of us leaped at the chance to come here, Andreas. I came because it's my duty, or my job, to tag along with Preston, and Dewey came because it's his job to go where Preston wants him to go."

"Oh, Dewey's motives are deeper than that! Sometimes a foreigner who visits the Faeroes simply 'goes native,' and Dewey's heading that way, full steam ahead. Besides, didn't you tell me he once rode with a motorcycle gang? Viewed against society as a whole, that's a lifestyle that implies, at the very least, a willingness to embrace alienation." Then, abruptly shifting gears, he turned and stared right into her eyes. "And why did *you* come to Vardinoy, Norma?"

At the invitation, one last barricade of hesitation surrendered to his forthright charm and her version of events came pouring out, a stream-of-consciousness ramble whose emotional, confessional heat made her realize why and how strongly this man was getting through to her:

Preston used to talk to me the way Andreas does now, his line wiry intelligence and his untamed spirit always leaping, soaring, beckoning me onward in its wake, encouraging me to be free and take risks; yet all the time, that freedom was conditional on following Preston's *agenda . So many projects he was going to finish, after we made our pile in the porn biz, and after the flop of* Movie Man *he never started another. That joyful vitality that so beguiled me just seemed to shrivel up, and the only time I saw it rekindled was right after he got the phone call from Allen about going to Vardinoy and making an epic documentary about this nutty quixotic monster-hunt, but it didn't cause my motor to rev up again, because by that time the only thing I still shared with Preston was his cynicism, his brittle wit, his periodic flickers of domesticated lust. But when Preston got the chance to make another film, here on Vardinoy, the prospect set him on fire again, in the old ways; and for an incredible month or so, he was like he used to be: a man intoxicated by old dreams that had mellowed like a good wine, and how he wanted me to get drunk on it with him! I wanted to, I really tried to, and so I came here with him, but as always with Preston, the* prospect of fulfilling a dream was more *exciting than the work of actually doing it, and when I saw this desolate fucking island and realized I was going to be* stuck here *for the entire summer, I quickly felt myself drifting apart from him and just not giving a shit any more, whether he filmed this monster or whether the whole thing turned into a farce, it was all the same drab miserable prospect to me. . . .*

Increasingly, ever since the actual landing on Vardinoy, Norma had begun to think that Preston's sole motive for bringing her along was so that he might have his favorite five-star poke close at hand whenever the urge came upon him. Otherwise, Norma felt no more special than any other piece of camping equipment. Even Warrener's sometimes-nutty girlfriend, Karen, had paid far more attention to Norma *as a person* than had her own husband. And then she'd met this wandering painter, and suddenly her life had a focal point again. Or was she merely entranced by his novelty, titillated by the risk she was taking? God, her mind was a tangle!

Even while she was talking nonstop, there suddenly came upon her, all in a fevered rush, the notion that she very much wanted to make love to the Faeroese artist. And so confused were the emotions that charged through her head when she acknowledged her desire, that she averted her face lest Andreas read her like a cheap paperback.

". . . and so when Allen called Preston last spring and told him about Vardinoy, Preston got all fired up and agreed to underwrite the cost of all the photographic equipment in return for the rights to any good footage he might bring back."

"One moment!" Andreas held up an admonitory finger. "Did Allen Warrener actually finance a major part of all this? On a teacher's salary? I find that hard to believe!"

Norma was glad Andreas seemed so interested in these mundane details; she could speak of them at this moment much more easily than she could speak about "loneliness" or the techniques of landscape painting.

"Oh, I don't think his financial stake is very large—I've seen his house, remember, and it fucking well *looks* like a history teacher's house! No, the really big money came from his old friend Eiden Poulsen, who agreed to furnish the ship, the crew, and most of the supplies. Really, I never paid much attention when they were going over the plans—it just sounded like they were reading from a giant grocery list."

"The thing I don't understand, Norma, is why a man like Eiden Poulsen, who is probably the richest and most successful businessman in Faeroese history, would be willing to invest so much of his money in, well, *a crack-pot adventure like this!* Don't get me wrong, I'm just paraphrasing what the rest of the world would say about it, not necessarily what I think. What could possibly be in it for him? Has he always been interested in sea-serpents and such?"

Norma giggled as the impulsive reply burst from her lips: "He's doing it because he's a *Faeroese,* Andreas! Simple as that!"

Now it was Dahl's turn to laugh, as merrily as he seemed able.

"Bravo, Norma! I see you have a quick wit, too! I like that in a woman."

Still chuckling, he turned to pack his brushes. As he rose to fold his easel, Norma pressed another stroke forward on the tide that was now engulfing her.

"Andreas, tell me the truth. Don't you think we're just a pack of middle-aged idiots, running around here like bloody Boy Scouts, looking for a monster when we don't even know what it's supposed to *look like?*"

"Your motives must be . . . as varied as your personalities. Your friends comprise a very colorful bunch. Some would describe them as 'eccentric,' I suppose, but as a vagabond artist, who am I to call another man eccentric? I don't know where the line is drawn between mere eccentricity and sheer obsession, so I'll say no more. I shall be very curious to see how this all turns out. And I wonder just how long this 'expedition' will hang together when day after day after day passes, and nothing happens. . . ."

"So you grew up in this very neighborhood, and yet you've never even heard of the Vardinoy Monster?"

"I never said I hadn't 'heard of it,' Norma. Every society that lives on the edge of a vast and dangerous realm has its share of monster legends. We need them, perhaps, to explain the pointless random malignity of the ocean's wrath. One morning, a bold and lucky fisherman goes out to ply his trade exactly as he's done a thousand other mornings, only he's never seen again. We've had boats that disappeared like that only twenty miles from home. It happens. Not often, but it does happen. What Nature makes a mystery, men must always try to explain, no? So I keep an open mind. It I had seen all that these islands could show me, I would not still be roaming around out here in wet shoes, painting their portraits, trying to give form and meaning to their mute inscrutable souls."

Is there some way I can take his hand and still convey that if friendship is all he wants, then I'll force nothing more upon him?

Is his mouth as beautiful in passion as it is in laughter?

23.

ECHOGRAMS AND RUINS

For three days running, Allen and Preston took out the *Laertes'* motor launch, with Birgir, the First Mate, serving as navigator and helmsman. Birgir found their sonar-mapping activity somewhat dotty, but he also found Preston's fund of dirty-movie anecdotes endlessly diverting, dryly commenting at one point: "You know, cod fishermen talk about pussy, too, but they start repeating themselves a lot sooner than you do." It had been Birgir's suggestion to outfit the launch with a medium-priced Simrad unit. You could spend five times more on bells and whistles, if your purpose was to locate pieces of fallen satellites, but if you just wanted a clean, fine-grained cross-section of the ocean floor—down to 500 meters—and a recognizable profile of any critter larger than a minnow that swam into the sonar beams, then there was no point in spending money on a machine built to NASA specifications. The Simrad 2000, Birgir averred, was hard to break, easy to fix, and reliable in rough seas—which was the main reason so many Faeroese boats carried them.

And on their first two days of experimental bottom-mapping, the unit had performed flawlessly, except for one small problem—it didn't show any monsters. Or anything larger than a trio of adult seals, for that matter. Nor could it—or any other sonar yet invented—penetrate the abyssal rift whose actual depth had never been recorded. In Preston's view, this somewhat compromised the usefulness of what they were doing. "If there is a big slimy critter down there, that's exactly where it would hide, don't you think? The Vardinoy Beastie—preferred habitat 'Abyssal Depths.' "

"Are you *that* fucking bored?" countered Allen.

"No, man, I love these scroll-pictures of the bottom. And I love cruising around in this little whaler sipping Tuborgs with you two sad sacks. It's just, well, when you've seen one school of halibut, you've seen 'em all."

After the fifth or sixth time the Simrad's bobbin-like pen sketched a big mass of fish, the two landlubbers stopped jumping for their cameras and binoculars. Just before noon on the third day, looming storm clouds, plus a Mariners' Advisory on the radio, prompted them to call an early halt. They had mapped a third of Vardinoy's western coast and seen nothing of great interest. Even though the storm looked like it was veering away from them, Allen decided to pack it in at about twelve-thirty.

Ordinarily, Preston would have shut down the Simrad, but they were all lapsing into an off-duty mode, so the sonar continued to sweep and the recording drum continued to unwind its halftone profiles of uninteresting seabottom. They'd already mapped this section of the coast three times, anyhow. Conditions were calm as they turned into the sheltered bay leading to the empty village, and Allen was starting to doze. He was jolted awake when Preston saw something on the Simrad printout that made him leap out of his seat and bend over the takeup drum.

"Allen!"

"Yeah?"

"Come take a look at *this!*"

Preston held out the most recent bottom profiles traced by the recording pen, a strip of paper about four feet long. Allen saw nothing remarkable about the echograms, other than the fact that for some reason, probably thermal layers playing games with the sonar pings, the seabed profile was less distinct-looking than usual. "Sorry, but all I see is the same bottom-crud I saw the first time we surveyed the fjord . . . and the second time. What am I supposed to get excited about?"

"Here—compare the return we just got with the returns the Simrad sketched on the morning and afternoon of our first day out." Preston opened a bulging file case and retrieved the earlier echograms. The coordinates were the same, as were their course and speed and the general weather conditions. On all three strips of recording paper, the ocean floor displayed the same random assortment of dips and humps—except for the second half of the strip Preston had just ripped from the recording drum, where the smoothly undulating sine-waves suddenly bulked up into a curving ridge at least four times the height of any other elevation on the strip, and then, as though reacting to the sudden noise or vibrations of their boat, the big pillow-shaped bulge turned into a formless smudge, inescapably suggestive of some large creature suddenly making a lunge either for prey or to escape the sound of the sonar pulse. If it were alive, that enormous bulge, whatever it was, might have been reacting in pain, or in panic.

Warrener was trying to sound very blasé, but the excitement in his voice couldn't be suppressed.

"Press, this doesn't tell me shit. Maybe the Simrad's fucked up, or it ponged instead of pinged, or whatever the hell Simrads do when they malfunction."

Birgir's response was somewhat huffy. "I told you, Allen: Simrads do *not* just 'fuck up.' Besides, I ran through the diagnostics checklist this morning, when I was loading the recording paper and the ink wells."

"Thank you for your diligence, Eric the Snide. Preston, he's probably right, you know. All you're showing me is just a big, amorphous *bump.* . . ."

"What if that bump was just a tantalizing glimpse of *one part* of the creature? It's for damn sure not a seal, we know what they look like. I mean, we're doing this, in your own words, 'to search for anomalies' . . . and here *is* one, Allen. A pretty big one, too. Two days ago, the ocean floor looked like *this,* and for some reason this afternoon, it suddenly grew a humongous hump! Now in my book, that qualifies as a fucking 'anomaly.' "

Their eyes held for a moment, and then an old but long-dormant arc of excitement flashed between them.

"It's worth another pass, at least. Hey, Birgir, would you mind coming about and re-entering the fjord exactly where you did last time? I mean, down to the inch!"

"You're the skipper, Skipper." Birgir dutifully turned the launch and executed the requested maneuver. When they reached more or less the proper location, Allen knelt in the wheelhouse and scrutinized every inch of the graph paper as it unrolled.

"The bottom looks the same as it does in the first two passes. And since we have Birgir's word on it that the Simrad isn't fucked up, that means we definitely have an anomaly. But what kind?"

Preston waved the anomalous rendering, his voice growing testy. "What the hell difference does it make? We came here looking for something mysterious and by God, there it is!"

As soon as Birgir had secured the launch to the stone dock, Allen began to whoop and pound Preston on the back. It wasn't much, just the flimsiest hint of confirmation, but excitement blazed within them like a bonfire. Preston smacked the bulkhead and did a little stork-legged jig.

"We had a *contact*, ol' buddy! Damned if I know what it was, but something strange was going on down there and we got a snapshot of it."

While Preston broke open the ice chest and groped for two beaded Tuborgs, Allen studied the echograms once more, this time in silence. "Hey, Press, what did you say was the scale of this graph paper?"

"Each millimeter square equals three feet, why?"

Allen measured roughly with the tip of his finger. Whistled.

"Maybe we better hope the Simrad was fucked up after all, Preston."

"Why's that?"

"Because if we did pick up an image of something alive, or part of something, down there on the bottom, it measured approximately two hundred feet long."

Back at the campsite, no one shared Allen's enthusiasm over the Simrad graphs, which he waved in everyone's faces as though they were treasure maps.

"Allen," cautioned Karen, taking him aside, "it's just a big *smudge*. I know why you're excited, but until you record something that looks like a giant squid or Jaws or Moby Dick, it's just a *smudge*."

"But it's a two-hundred-foot-long smudge, goddamnit!"

The next day had been set aside for the first of the planned weekly mail runs over to Birgir's home island, Vesturoy. Warrener's original "Master Plan" had called for "shore leave" to be apportioned on a rotating basis to half the expedition, while the other half remained at the campsite to . . . well, in the absence of any lowlife neighbors who might steal the Tupperware, there clearly was no point in *anybody* staying behind. The automatic camera rig would capture anything large enough to be newsworthy—or, as Karen tartly put it, "Any life-form that doesn't set off at least one of those sensors, Allen, is probably extraterrestrial—you should be so bloody lucky!"

Eiden volunteered to remain behind and keep an eye on the camp; he had business affairs to catch up on, via radiophone and fax. Much to Allen's annoyance, another stay-behind was Norma, who announced, rather disingenuously, that she needed to stay and finish touching up some sketches— "I feel so energized by the new directions my work's taking, I just have to keep going with the flow!" At the sound of that hoary sixties cliché, Preston, standing behind Norma but in full view of the others, mimed poking his finger down his throat and upchucking. Andreas Dahl, probably forewarned of a potentially awkward confrontation, had not appeared until long after breakfast, fully burdened with easel, pack, and walking stick, giving a very good imitation of a painter–vagabond who was simply passing through on his search for the next dynamite landscape. Aside from banal and perfunctory greetings, he said nothing. Preston also held his tongue, but had donned, for this thoroughly provincial outing, his best Armani blouse and sunglasses, along with his "Movie Director's Bush Jacket," his most expensive-looking still camera draped casually over one shoulder; as a final, near-parodistic touch, he'd topped the ensemble with a snappy maroon beret decorated with the regimental crest of the New South Wales Borderers, whose enlisted men had made him an honorary messmate in gratitude to the "countless hours of solitary joy your videotapes have brought to Her Majesty's soldiers, in desolate outposts throughout the world."

Karen sauntered by and climbed into the Land Rover, rolling her eyes at the sight of Preston's getup. "Preston, you look like a cross between Maurice Chevalier and Pee Wee Herman. Let's get this show on the road, my pair of aging roués."

An hour later, as the *Laertes* chugged into the choppy straits between Vardinoy and Vesturoy, Warrener slid on to a leeward bench next to Preston. No one was close, and the wind erased their words instantly.

"Want to talk about it, man?"

Valentine shrugged and fiddled with his camera. "She's got a crush on that Faeroese painter, isn't it obvious?"

"Well, duh, sure it is. What is not obvious, however, is why you should be so torqued out of shape by a situation which is not exactly unique in the annals of your marriage. You two have never made a fuss about either person having an occasional extracurricular fling—in fact, I remember the days when you both used to brag about which celebrities you'd fucked and where."

"That was the seventies, Allen. All the chicks were on the Pill and hot to prove how liberated they were, all the guys were into 'pleasure without commitment,' and AIDS was still just some bacillus living inside a baboon's rectum in the Congo. Jesus, what a shallow, narcissistic crock of shit all that was!"

"Granted, but I wish I could go back in time for a little R-and-R. It would be nice to get laid without having to tell your date where you stand on gay marriages and global warming. Face it, man, we're both getting old, and nobody's jaw drops open any more when you tell 'em you once fucked Twiggy."

"Terrible Cockney halitosis, man! Knock a buzzard off a shit-wagon."

"And Nico. . . ."

"Like making it with the Angel of Death, especially when she'd shot up just before taking off her clothes. You want to know what's on the far side of the Moon? All of her bizarro orgasms . . ."

"Not to mention Julie Christie. . . ."

"Hey, motherfucker," Preston was laughing now, "there are *some memories* that are too sacred for mockery!"

"That good, huh?"

"It took ten billion years of evolution to create a mouth like that . . . and, Jesus, she was *funny* and tender, too." Warrener thought he had almost succeeded in shifting Preston's mood for the better, but after the fleeting Nights-in-White-Satin recollection of Julie Christie, the director turned morose again. "All those little romps, they were freebies. Some kind of crazy pollen in the air that put everybody under a spell for a few years—without that context, the memories are just mental Polaroids in an old wanker's scrapbook."

"Stop. Cut! Get a new dialogue writer, please. *Mental Polaroids in an old wanker's scrapbook?* Preston, I've seen you fire writers for lines like that! Just give me the bottom line here, will you? What's so different about Norma's infatuation with this painter and his Max von Sydow jawline from all those other little escapades?"

"This time it's a threat, Allen. Yeah, sure, she's had crushes before, so have I, and it was all temporary fun and games, no hard feelings, no recriminations —we actually *did* have it all in balance, for a long damn time."

"Permit me to take a stab at this: you are afraid that, dare I say it, Norma might actually be falling into serious love with our surprise guest?"

"I would never have thought it possible, but she has all the symptoms."

"Okay, then, let me ask you this one straight out: are you still in love with Norma?"

"We used to use that word a lot; on the good days, it sure felt like love to *me.* I hadn't realized until a few days ago, though, how long it's been since we talked to each other like two people who were *being in love,* the way you and Karen sometimes talk. . . ."

"You'd likely get a very different interpretation from Karen about the semantics."

"I *know you,* Allen Warrener. You're as in love with that fine young woman as you are ever going to be capable of! Elsuba fucked up your sense of reality-versus-fantasy, and Sylvia pussywhipped you until you couldn't piss a hole in the snow, but you, my friend, are still, and always will be, a god-damned Romantic and Karen fulfils that at the same time she serves up your daily requirement of Reality Checks. Lose her, and you'll never find another even close—and you know it."

"Eloquently said and duly noted. Now answer my original question: do you still love Norma?"

"I guess I must, otherwise I wouldn't be this hurt or this worried."

"Are we talking about a bruised heart, or a lacerated ego here? Oh, never mind, with you there's no clear-cut boundary. You asked for my opinion. . . ."

"As I recall, you broached the subject, not me. . . ."

"Well, whether you want it or not, here it is: Norma's not getting any younger, either, you know. Dahl's giving her something, by way of respect, and a certain kind of attention that doesn't come from either you or me without sounding like a constipated bowel movement. Dahl's got a kind of, well, 'Danish Modern' *cool* that's absolutely the opposite of your intensity. When you say, 'That's a nice painting, dear,' it sounds like you're calling back over your shoulder, 'by the way, dear, it's time for the dog to get his shots again—could you call the vet tomorrow?' But when tall, somber Andreas says it, organ music starts to play. He may not *mean it* any more or less sincerely than you, but something about the timbre of his voice and the way he choreographs that fucking pipe to make his points, it just gets Norma wet—I mean inside her head. How many times have you said to me, 'There is no more unfathomable mystery than sexual chemistry'? Well, bingo: your theorem is once again proved. Does Dahl feel the same way about her as she does about him? Who the fuck knows? Emotionally, he strikes me as a cold halibut. What matters is that inside Norma's head, Andreas Dahl's vibes or pheromones or telepathic tickle-feathers, they're feeding her something she's desperately hungry for. I think he's a great artist, okay? I also think he's a bit of a nut case—I mean, man, nobody you ever met loves the Faeroe Islands more than I do, but even I would go barking mad if I spent six months roaming around one of these islands by myself! For what it's worth, I don't get a single vibe of genuine passion coming off his skin, except for his own work. Yeah, okay, he might very well fuck her if she lays siege hard enough—unless the man's a eunuch, he will succumb. But what happens when she hops into the sack and finds out that beneath that cool, dour exterior there is just a cool, dour heart? Poof! Enchantment broken, prince turns to frog, wham-bam, thanks for the painting lessons, and home she will come to Poppa's tent."

"But there's more to it, Allen—there's all this bullshit about her paintings and 'nurturing her latent genius—' "

"Wait; stop right there. Did he actually say that to Norma? In mean, in those exact words?"

"She swears he did. She was giddy as a Girl Scout who just found her own clit for the first time, too."

"Well, okay, then, that's the key to it. He's this famous art-world superstar who also happens to be a self-proclaimed mystical hermit, and he's using psychology to help an amateur surpass herself and maybe develop her work to a whole new level. You and Norma were too busy getting rich to tap into that whole Guru Thing in the late sixties—now she's catching up to it. What's unhealthy about that? At least she's not studying how to play the sitar and walking around with a pimiento on her forehead."

"But the way she said it, it was like she was drugged or something. . . ."

"Preston, don't be so thick! You didn't have to pretend she was the female successor to Picasso, but if you'd taken her art a little more seriously, maybe hired some tutors, showed you understood how important it was to her, she would have gotten this out of her system years ago. Besides, who knows how talented she *might* be? How many years have you and I been aching to show the world what brilliant novelists and filmmakers we could be, if 'somebody' just gave us a chance?"

"I always thought her stuff was pretty! I told her so a thousand times!"

"She needed to hear something other than *pretty*,' Preston! 'Pretty' is Hallmark cards, or matadors-on-black-velvet. She might have been trying, really hard, to go way beyond 'pretty,' but she didn't have the vocabulary, the technique. Dahl's not just blindly praising her—I've heard them together!

He's really critiquing her work, and not always gently, but he's also teaching her new ways of seeing, new techniques, provided her with—"

"So help me God, if you say 'a new set of tools,' I will chuck you overboard!"

"I caught myself just in time. The way I see it, this is major therapy for her, and if you suddenly tried to compete on Dahl's turf, by going out of your way to discuss painting, she'd laugh in your face. Wait it out, man. Dahl's obviously not hot for her—or at least, he's mighty damn slow to warm up— and if Norma's got romantic fantasies, well, she's the only one in that relationship who does. It's like a fever. It'll run its course. What is it about this flirtation that has you so spooked? You afraid they'll elope one night? To *where?* Some abandoned shepherd's hut with a leaky roof and a stone toilet? How long you think Norma's going to put up with living conditions like that, especially living with a man whose teeth would break to pieces if he ever succumbed to one good belly laugh! With that guy, there is no small talk. And for damn sure, no pillow talk either. Endure, my brother, this passing distress, and meanwhile, find some ditzy Faeroese teenager to warm King Lear's bones tonight. Swear to God, if Karen wasn't along. . . ."

Valentine gave a seal's bark of a laugh.

"Old sod, your days of carefree casual fornicatin' are over! Karen might forgive one or two indiscretions, long as they happen at a teachers' convention in Minneapolis, but if you ever really and deeply humiliate that girl, she *will* leave you. An out-of-town quickie is one thing, but if you gave away one little piece of your heart as a souvenir afterwards, I don't care if you shower for a week and roast your skin in ultraviolet rays, she will take one look at you and just *know.*"

"I won't find anyone better, will I?"

"Do you have to say that in such funereal tones? Rejoice in your good fortune! If that young woman doesn't love you to the bone, I'm a codfish. Just treat her righteously, man, and she'll mate for life. Or, to put it more crudely, when you turn sixty-five, she'll just be hitting her prime. You are not a famous old goat like Henry Miller, Allen: this is your one shot at emotional and sexual comfort for your old age! Whatever you have to do to keep her, you *do it.*"

But Allen Warrener could find nothing more rousing to say than: "I aim to try . . . ," which was such a lame response that it throttled further conversation for a good five minutes. Both men filled that lacuna by guzzling

Tuborgs. No one else on the ship was paying any attention to them, so Allen was surprised when Preston sidled closer and bent his head like a man reluctantly entering a confessional booth.

"Look, Allen, I've spent the past few days toting up all my sins, and dealing with the shock of realizing how much I really care for my wife. See, I can admit it! But leaving aside the painting lessons and all that, there's something else that bugs me, and I don't get the feeling that you're tuned in to it yet."

"So tune me."

"Okay, by God, I will. For starters, do you actually *like* Andreas Dahl?"

"Well, I like his *work,* and at first I thought it was kind of a cool, funky coincidence when we found him on the same island—at least, I thought it was cool until it started causing trouble. But as for the man himself, he hasn't done or said anything to make me *dislike* him. He's not exactly the life of the party, but then most hermits are like that, aren't they?"

Valentine lowered his voice still more. "Look, I made my fortune in a business that has more than its share of sleazy operators. One reason I was able to steer an independent course during the early years was because I developed a sixth sense about which distributors were just ordinary sleazeballs out to make a quick buck, and which ones were in bed with the Mob. And one reason I stayed clean with the law is that when a girl came in to audition for a part, I could tell, sixty seconds after she walked into the room, whether she was hire-able or whether she was an undercover cop, a teenage runaway with a sixty-dollar-a-day habit, or just a hooker with delusions of stardom. Most of the deals I made were done with a handshake—I mean, I could listen to someone's voice, or look into his eyes, and just *know* whether or not he could be trusted. Do you see where I'm going with this?"

"You don't trust Dahl. And you wouldn't trust him even if Norma wasn't in the equation."

"I heard alarm bells ringing in my head the minute I laid eyes on the motherfucker. I don't believe for one minute that he likes us, or wishes us well, or wants us mucking around on his island. And as for Norma, I know damned well that he's *using her* just as hard as I've ever seen anybody get used, which in my business is saying a lot. What I can't figure out is *why* he's got it in for all of us and why in particular he's working this head-game on Norma."

"Aren't you being just a tad theatrical, Preston? You're acting as though

Dahl were some kind of threat! And now you're saying he's a threat to all of us, not just your besotted wife? Tell you what: one day when they're out painting together, let's go down to the old village and see if we can locate the coffin he sleeps in."

"Stop being facetious, damn it, and *think* for a minute! Aren't you at least theoretically concerned about the possibility that, if we suddenly find ourselves in a shitpot full of real trouble, we are stuck out here on the ass end of the North Atlantic and even if we sent an S.O.S. to Torshavn, it would take a patrol boat hours to get here? I mean, what if Dahl's a maniac and he's got a cult of deranged ghouls hiding in a cave somewhere, just waiting to fall on the camp one night? Or for that matter, what if we *do* run into a creature as big as that smudge on the Simrad graph and it turns out to be every bit as dangerous as that Nazi pilot claimed?"

Warrener turned his head; Preston was surprised at the glint in his old friend's eyes.

"This information is not for public consumption, Preston, but we have the means to defend ourselves if we need to."

" 'Means to defend ourselves?' Jesus H. Christ, Allen, what does *that* mean? If a two-hundred-foot-tall man-eating jellyfish suddenly surfaces off the side of the trawler, are you suddenly going to whip a tarpaulin off that deckhouse and reveal a depth-charge launcher?"

"Keep your voice down, God damn it! We've got enough firepower stashed at the camp to take on a Viet Cong platoon, and as a matter of fact, there *is* a deck gun stowed below. Eiden's drilled Birgir and the crew—they can haul it up and mount it in that old gun tub in five minutes or less. And to answer your next question, I haven't said anything about this because I don't want to hear any more shit about me being 'melodramatic.' We're talking about a very, very remote contingency here, Preston. And what does that have to do with Dahl, anyway? He's just one man, for God's sake. Dewey could snap him in two without breaking a sweat."

"I guess that's what does bother me, Allen. He is just one guy, so why do I feel like we might be in real danger all of a sudden? As for why that feeling is connected to Dahl . . . well, it starts with me wondering just why the son of a bitch happens to show up on the day we set up camp, and why he's taken such an interest in what we're doing here. At the very least, you've got to admit that his popping up out of nowhere like that was just a bit too much of a coincidence."

"Coincidence, yes. 'Too much' of one, hardly. I think it's just what he said it was—he spends his time roaming around different islands. That's how he does his work. Why shouldn't he end up on Vardinoy, sooner or later?"

"Granted, but why is he here *now?* If he's so keen on solitude and Nature-communing, I would have thought Vardinoy would have been one of his *first* stops."

"Not necessarily. I mean, he was born on Suduroy, so he just started there, at the southern end of the chain, and then he went to the next island on the horizon, and then the next one after that, and so on. He spends months on each island, remember? It would naturally take him a while to work his way up here—a decade, maybe."

Preston raised an interrupting hand. "Whoa, hoss! Where'd you say he was born?"

"Suduroy—the last big island to the south. Lovely place. On my second trip to the Faeroes, I spent three or four days there. There's this one place on the eastern coast you just gotta see, man. It's got—"

The verbal postcard would have to wait, for suddenly both Karen and Richard Sugarman, who were sitting near the bow, started shouting. Warrener looked up and saw both of them pointing excitedly to starboard. Heart pounding, he rose to a tense lookout's posture, hands clutching the wheelhouse roof, and beheld a big black dorsal fin slicing through a swell like the blade of a plow. Birgir shouted something in Faeroese; Elsuba answered him.

"What the hell is that?" cried Dewey.

"You tell him, Allen," said Elsuba, sending him the most unguarded smile she had yet bestowed in his direction. "I want to see if you remember the word!"

"*Grind!*" Triumphantly, he shouted the word into the wind, then explicated for the benefit of those not so well-versed in local customs. "A whale. Pilot whale, to be precise. Harmless to us, but no friend to the natives. Why don't *you* tell them, Elsuba."

"A single pilot whale, or one family of them, they're just part of the scenery. But if a big herd of them comes through and decides to stay a while, they can wipe out a fishing ground that's fed people for generations. Don't romanticize them—to us, they're nothing more than giant locusts with flippers. The Faeroese fisherman and the pilot whale have been traditional enemies for centuries. Have you ever seen one of the *grindedrabet,* Allen?"

"Never for real; only in movies."

"And what does grin-the-rabbit mean in English, please?" asked Sug-arman, gesturing to indicate that he was willing to accept the answer from either Allen or Elsuba, whichever of the two felt inclined to give it. The pilot whale, meanwhile, seemed to have taken offense at the topic under discussion, for he puffed an impudent spout and sounded with a "fuck you, too" flip of his tail. Elsuba nodded at Allen: *Go ahead and show off a little; after all, this man has never seen pilot whales before.*

"Okay, well, as I understand the custom, when a pilot whale herd is spotted, the fishing boat whose lookout made the I.D. has an obligation to spread the word, either by radioing himself or, if he doesn't have a radio, by pulling up to the nearest boat or island that has one. Once the herd's been tracked, all the available boats in the neighborhood go out and form a semi-circle around it, driving it into the shallows, where the whales can't maneuver. Once man and beast get within harpoon range, it becomes a slaughter 'grim and great' as the Vikings would say. The Faeroese drive the whales into shallow water and just . . . *kill them*, any way they can, using any weapon they've got. Both men and whales go berserk. The ostensible motive may be economic—I mean, a big enough herd of pilot whales can ruin the fishing for years—but the instincts behind the ritualized way it's done, those are straight out of Viking days, Richard. Have *you* ever seen a hunt, Elsuba?"

"Once, in Klaksvik, when I was visiting some friends. It was very bloody, of course, and I suppose I should have found it revolting and primitive, but somehow I did not. I was too swept up in the excitement to feel smug and superior to it. Allen's explanation is as good as any: we see a herd of whales, and we revert to being our ninth-century ancestors."

Dewey couldn't take his eyes off the streak of foam left on the surface by the sounding whale. "You mean to tell me that people actually go out and pick fights with those sum-bitches? That one there must have been twenty foot long if he was an inch!" It was clear from every straining line in his body that Dewey was fantasizing the greatest street brawl of his life, mano-a-mano against a three-ton cetacean!

Their conversations drifted; the whale's great solitary appearance had altered their mood. When it had leaped out of the sea—immense and glittering and totally unafraid of them—that had been The Real Thing, and it had caused a sudden jolt of excitement to reignite, concerning where they were and their purpose, after all, for being here. Sturdy and faithful, the aging trawler beat steadily closer to Vesturoy. From this leeward angle, the island's aspect was mostly pastoral, with its eponymous village, consisting of a hundred and fifty dwellings and stores, nested around a wide deep indentation of harbor. Already visible in the center of town was a large warehouse emblazoned with the Poulsen corporate logo. A swarm of small fishing boats crowded the harbor on the far side of a long stone breakwater. Near the quay itself, several trawlers were moored, each bearing the heraldic crest of the islanders' fishing cooperative.

A representative from Eiden's firm was waiting on the dock for them. After introductions, he announced that lunch was ready for them in the island's one café; after the meal, they could pick up their mail and whatever supplies they needed. As the expedition members assembled on the town's one stretch of paved road, a rumbling explosion rattled nearby windows. Heads turned toward the distant ridges high above the town, where a thin cloud of dust smeared one arc of the sky.

"Still depth-charging old U-boats, I reckon," Allen muttered.

The Poulsen representative fumbled through his English, then switched to Faeroese when he saw Birgir standing nearby and ready to translate. "They are making . . . um . . . explosions, to . . . to. . . ." Birgir finished the explanation: "He says they're blasting up in the mountains to build a new hydroelectric plant. Right now, the town's dependent on generators, and during the winter storms it's not always possible to get the regular supply of diesel fuel. It's the biggest sign of progress on Vesturoy since someone brought the first portable radio from Copenhagen."

The tiny restaurant was typical of what a trawlerman might find in any comparable Faeroese port: simple trestle tables draped with bright checkerboard covers, each table decorated with a small vase of plastic flowers. Lunch consisted of chowder, sausage, and several varieties of fish, complemented by hard but toothsome rolls.

As they left the café, they were greeted by another blast from the direction of the construction site in the hills. Allen went with the Poulsen agent to collect the mail; the others scattered around the small waterfront district, cameras at the ready. When Allen returned, pushing a wheelbarrow full of envelopes and packages, he spotted Dewey sitting beneath a rack of drying nets, earnestly haggling with a young Vesturoy man. The object under debate was a splendid, rather barbaric-looking sheepskin jacket, which the young fisherman was proudly wearing but which he was obviously growing less fond of as more and more American cash kept piling up in Dewey's proffered hand. Just as Warrener and his wheelbarrow rolled, squeaky-wheeled, past the two, a bargain was struck. The Faeroese sauntered off to display his newfound wealth, and Dewey luxuriated in the feel and heft of his new and ever-so-manly garment.

He roared with pleasure as he slid arms and shoulders into the burly sleeves, then shook his shoulder-length blond locks as the sheepskin molded itself to his powerful shoulders and massive torso. Allen stopped to watch the transformation: Dewey and that coat had been meant for each other and were now mated for life. Dewey looked both lovable and ferocious, like he had just leaped ashore from the deck of a marauding longship. After spinning around a few times, Dewey undertook a swaggering promenade along the quayside, bowing and making florid propositions in pseudo-Elizabethan to the numerous girls who'd gathered to watch the foreigners' antics—on this island, the arrival of so many outsiders constituted headline news. Allen also caught a glimpse of Preston, almost ludicrously elegant in his Movie Director's costume, trying to make some time with a couple of the older teenaged girls, although the dialogue, from what Warrener could hear of it, comprised more slapstick than seduction. Birgir spotted Allen and his wheelbarrow, and sent a sailor over to help distribute the mail, while the last of the camp supplies were being winched aboard the trawler.

The sea in the straits between Vesturoy and Vardinoy was choppier on the return voyage. Birgir steered in and out of random patches of sunlight, as though the old trawler were seeking warmth amidst the gathering gray. On the horizon to the northwest, tiny distant Norduroy faded in and out of sight, as insubstantial as a speck of lint. About halfway back to Vardinoy, close enough for the observers to discern human forms on the deck, the passengers spotted a solitary Gray Boat, long and thin, Orm-posts rising from bow and stern. As the *Laertes* overhauled the Norduroy craft, its passengers were able to make out four somber fishermen, heavily sweatered against the chill, struggling hard against the current with their oars. Mischievously, Birgir tooted the ship's horn, which startled the fishermen and visibly upset them, so that two of the dour crewmen looked up from their oars long enough to shake a fist at the larger ship. Richard Sugarman glared at Birgir—why startle those hardworking men?—his expression said, and then he stepped to the rail and gave an exaggeratedly hearty wave. The fisherman glared back sullenly and spat into the water before turning away.

"Friendly bastards, aren't they?"

"Damn Gray-Boats," muttered Birgir.

Karen asked: "Is that a family name, a political party, or some kind of insult?"

Birgir leaned over the bridge rail and tried to explain. "I suppose that blast on the horn was rude, but I've got no use for those fellows. 'Gray-Boat' is just our term for anyone who comes from little Norduroy, over there . . . when you can see it. They have this tradition of painting all their boats gray, though I don't know why. They're very clannish on that island; never had much to do with outsiders, not even my people on Vesturoy, and we're their only neighbors. Their only contact with the outside world is the twice-a-week mail boat. We never see them unless they come to our island to conduct some business, buy a piece of gear, or order a spare part from Torshavn. No intermarriages, no socializing, no friendly get-togethers between their community and ours. Bunch of codfish disguised as humans, my father used to call 'em. Everybody in these northern reaches lives a pretty isolated life, Miss Hambly, but those people, by God they're like monks or hermits! Makes you wonder why. . . ." Birgir's voice trailed off.

"Why what?" Karen goaded.

"Well, it's a very strange thing, but for some reason or other, the inhabitants of Norduroy always seem to be exceedingly prosperous. They always find the richest new fishing grounds, the new migration patterns, before anybody else—then they go fill the holds of their boats and only after they've taken all they can carry do they report locations, as required by our laws. Most people chalk it up to good luck; me, I am not so sure. But whatever the cause, the fishermen of Norduroy feed their families well, even if the rest of us suffer empty plates. You can't help but resent 'em for it, especially when they're so unfriendly too."

As if to underscore Birgir's sentiments, the crew of the Gray Boat stopped their manual labor, shipped oars, and switched on a surprisingly powerful auxiliary engine. Before long, the craft was all but invisible.

"Why were they using oars when they had a motor?" asked Karen.

"Good question. This isn't a place where you can fish with anything smaller than a purse seine, and I didn't see them towing one. . . ."

Without warning, the *Laertes* shuddered, bow to fantail, and lost all forward momentum. Then, like a bird with one shattered wing, she began turning, unbidden, to port, the wheel whipping out of the helmsman's grasp. Birgir recovered his balance and shouted "All engines stop!" By the time the power plant grew silent, the ship had turned almost a complete circle, her bow facing the northwest promontory of Vardinoy.

But she did not sit idle on the ocean. With such preternatural strength that the people on the fo'c'sle could sense the tug through the soles of their shoes, an invisible current was shoving the vessel, beam-to, straight for the towering *dranger* on the island's sheer west face.

"Birgir, what the fuck's happening?"

"Some kind of riptide, I guess," gasped the young first mate, joining the helmsman, a brawny fellow who appeared stunned by losing control, in trying to regain steerageway.

"Riptide, my ass!," snorted Allen. "Something down there is pushing us . . . pulling us, I can't tell which, and we've already gained three or four knots!"

"Six," corrected the helmsman, teeth clenched and corded arms bulging as he and Birgir strove with all their might to right the wheel.

"You men down there, lower the port anchor! Fast!"

Seven knots . . . eight . . . the big trawler was helpless in the power of whatever force had stopped her and was now shoving or towing her straight toward a cluster of freestanding monoliths, each one of which could rend her hull like a can opener. With a clanking roar, the anchor chain ran out and then . . . stopped. Through the intercom, an alarmed voice reported: "Birgir, the anchor won't play out more than twenty fathoms! It's caught on something, or blocked by something! Damned if I know what!"

"Drop the starboard anchor then!"

Nine knots . . . ten; the only thing retarding momentum was the ship's own broadside bulk, and the starboard side was tilting, tilting, until it actually dipped into the sea and a hundred tons of gray-green water rolled over the stanchions and davits and ventilator funnels, cataracts sluicing through every open hatch and porthole.

Allen Warrener thought the ship was going to founder, turn turtle right there, within a mile of the fanged cliffs of Vardinoy. Struggling to maintain his footing, he unlashed the nearest life ring and tossed it down to Karen, while Preston, Dewey, and Richard lurched like drunks on the ever-steeper deck, pulling life jackets out of creaky old lockers.

"Engine room, can you give me power now?"

"Starboard propeller's completely jammed, Birgir! Caught on something, maybe a submarine cable! And we weren't buttoned up down here, so that water we're shipping just put out the fires in Number One boiler! What the hell kind of current can do this?"

Birgir didn't bother to speculate. Inch by inch, literally turning the one free prop shaft by the power of pulleys and muscle, he and the helmsman were gaining control of the wheel, moving the rudder angle back to zero-zero degrees, and as they did so, Allen could feel the underwater grip, whatever it was, losing some of its tenacity.

"Engine room to bridge! I think we can move now."

"Port engine, all ahead one-third!" shouted Birgir, when the bow finally reached a right angle to the looming shore.

Seconds later, as mysteriously as it began, the undertow relinquished its hold over the *Laertes*. Birgir conned the ship to within three hundred feet of the nearest *dranger*, close enough now for his anchors to get a good purchase on the bottom. Both anchors rattled down without hindrance and held fast. Except for the pulsating fluctuations of normal currents, the ship was at rest.

Radar reported nothing unusual on the screen during the whole frantic interlude. But a diver inspected the starboard prop and reported that a gigantic wad of purse-seine net had somehow become entangled around the shaft and blades; working in relays, the two crewmen qualified for underwater work might be able to free the ship in an hour, but given how rapidly even a tag-team of divers would become exhausted down there, it would more likely take twice as long.

"Well, nothing for it but to start drinking heavily," mumbled Dewey, heading down to the galley refrigerator and its serried ranks of cold Tuborgs. The others relaxed as best they could. Preston, Karen, and Richard gathered on the starboard wing of the bridge, sweeping the cliff face with their binoculars and with the ship's antique rangefinder, still in working order. For a while, the teeming colonies of puffins were entertaining, and when the surf rolled back, they saw, and marked on the chart, the mouths of several caves that looked big enough to swallow a yacht.

Allen retired to a private spot on the fantail, where a big coil of hawser rope offered a comfortable seat and the cargo winch served as a windbreak, and opened his letter—the first he had received from his son, Brian. How hard the boy had labored to fill up two pages of notebook paper!

Summer vacation is fun. Have you seen any val-canoes yet? Dad, have you captured the Vardinoy Monster and can you send me a picture?

Then came a wrenching emotional gearshift. Something very bad happened last week. A speedboat had run over Gigantus, the manatee, and killed him. But Mom had assured him that Gigantus was now in Heaven, where manatees swim all day long in a clear warm lagoon, and there aren't any speedboats or developers bulldozing tons of crap into the canals where the gentle giants liked to drift. What a great sadness came from the boy's hardworking pencil strokes!

Warrener flashed back to that moment when his son—so proud, so secretive, and for a few precious moments so *close*—had revealed to him that dim, peaceful shape floating serenely in its turquoise grotto. Christ, he could see the dreadful moment: that arrow-shaped boat full of coked-up Miamians, tearing ass down the canal, throwing up a roostertail of shredded water lilies, and then a jarring thump and a sluggish upchuck of red in the prop wash *("Hey, dude, what'd you just hit?"),* and the manatee, its head carved open and its back lacerated, sinking, sinking, dying mute and bewildered, reduced to another mound of trash—and something wonderful and rare had been extinguished in his son's life, along with innocence. Allen could not help it: tears welled in his eyes, shed equally for boy and beast.

Wind and sudden chop sloshed over the railing, and he yanked the letter back, afraid the sea would snatch it from his hands. He dried the paper with his handkerchief, carefully folded it, and replaced it in the waterproof mail bag. Without meaning to, his son had passed an iron weight of grief into his father's heart. By the next time he saw Brian . . . too much time would have passed; he could express in a letter the pain he, too, felt about the manatee's pointless, infuriating death, but by the time Brian received it, the boy's grieving would be over and done. Children recover so much faster than we do, Allen thought—why even bring it up? While they had watched the creature together, he'd been able to share his son's sense of wonder, and thereby regain some fleeting contact with his own.

Did I say enough, reveal enough, for you to comprehend how much I love you?

Of course not. A chasm of circumstance and distance separates us now, so wide that no words, none of my pathetic symbolic gestures, can ever fling a bridge across that distance! In a couple of years, when the concerns of adolescence hit with all their force, you and I will be utter strangers to one another.

Ah, fuck it.

Brian had a good life now. Allen had vowed never to say or do anything to taint his son's perceptions of his surroundings or his mother's character; now all he could do was write another awkward but affectionate letter and hope for the best. By the time he saw his son again, the manatee's life and death would be a fading bittersweet childhood memory, like the rainy-day ache of an old bone fracture.

But Allen did fervently hope that the piece-of-shit boat-jockey who'd rammed the helpless animal would be drowned in the next hurricane or fall into the Everglades on a fishing trip and end up as an alligator's lunch.

"Allen . . . ?"

He recoiled in surprise at Karen's touch.

"Easy, big fella! I didn't mean to spook you."

"Sorry, love; I was a thousand miles away."

"Let me guess: some bad news from Brian?"

"You really are psychic. How'd you guess that?"

"My supernatural powers allowed me to notice that you're holding a letter from him. . . ."

"Remember me telling you about the manatee he'd befriended? Some drunken moron ran over the animal with a cigarette boat. They lose one or two of them a week down in Dade County. So what's up with you, kiddo? You're eyes are sparkling."

She held out her hand for him. "Come on up to the bridge. It's a shower, not a tell-er."

The trawler was anchored somewhere north of the Axe-Cuts, about four hundred yards out from the booming flare of surf against a jagged grove of *dranger,* some of them low enough to be real ship-killers in a storm tide, and the cliff face beyond was wilder, craggier, and more cave-pitted than the other parts of the western shoreline Allen had inspected. The big binoculars on the bridge had been maintained well, but flaking crosshairs and azimuth lines showed they had once been used to direct the fire of the trawler's four-inch gun. Had Eiden Poulsen once walked his shots onto a U-boat's conning tower through these very eyecups? The thought pleased Allen as he snuggled into the viewfinder. When he adjusted the focus, the cliffs leaped toward his face, their textures sharp and bitter, masses of wind- and storm-carved basalt, almost too complex for his eye to make sense of. But one particular feature kept drawing his attention: perpendicular to the trawler's starboard side was a gap that looked very much like a gateway, a portal, its mouth clearly marked by seething eruptions of foam. He judged the passage beyond to be perhaps a hundred feet long, and at the far end he saw portions of broad, calm water, indicative of a bay or lagoon, whose full extent was hidden from view by the towering walls framing its narrow entrance. On the inlet's far side stretched a broad, gently rising meadow vibrant with splotches of violet and crimson wildflowers, extending eastward until it was cut off starkly by the steep escarpments whose opposite side they had climbed to reach the Axe-Cuts. That concealed body of water, so tranquil in comparison to the turbulent surf that guarded its only apparent entrance, seized his imagination.

"Lovely," he muttered; "great place for a picnic."

"Great place for *something*," said Karen. "You still haven't spotted it, have you?"

"Spotted what?"

Sugarman, claiming pride of discovery, gently nudged Warrener's shoulder to the left.

"Focus on the very edge of the view through that channel. Not on the inlet, but slightly above it. Takes a few seconds for your eyes to adjust, but it's there."

It was, at first, nothing more than a slight disturbance of texture, not much different in color from the raw stones that framed it and sliced his view of it into a thin, straight edge-of-something. He adjusted the focus and squinted hard. Comprehension jolted him like a mild electric shock—just enough was visible for him to realize that he was seeing dressed, mortared stones, a *man-made* structure—and, from the look of it, no minor edifice.

"Karen," he breathed. "The map. . . ."

"I checked it carefully," she said, just a touch smugly. "There are no, repeat no, man-made objects shown anywhere on Vardinoy except for that deserted village."

Allen's mind raced. "Now, *if* that bay or lagoon is big enough, and the channel leading into it is navigable, it would be an ideal spot for sailors to take shelter from a storm."

"There might be other buildings, too," suggested Richard, "that we can't see from here—it might be the ruins of an ancient settlement!"

"Viking Age," whispered Allen. "It could really be Viking Age. . . . Richard, remind me to buy you a steak dinner when we get back to someplace where they have steak dinners." Leaning over the bridge rail, he shouted: "Hey, Birgir! Do we have enough time for a little sightseeing?"

Birgir's reply was uncharacteristically grumpy as he came stomping up the ladder from below. "Yes, you've got bloody time! The divers found more than one net tangled in our propellers, so God knows how long before we're rid of that junk. That means this was no accident, Allen! Remember how the Gray Boat crew was bustling around on deck when we were steering directly behind them? God knows why they did it, but I think they deliberately dropped every net they had, tied into one big mass, directly in our path— like planting a minefield. If I ever see those bastards again   "

"But why on earth would they do something so hostile and dangerous?"

"You tell me, Mr. Warrener. Were they trying to sabotage our ship, leave us helpless so we might drift into the rocks? Or was that just a warning shot across our bow? Maybe there's something in that hidden cove you spotted that they don't want us to see. Go find out, will you? Take the rubber boat with the electric motor—I don't want to risk the motor launch in that channel."

No submerged traps thwarted their slow passage through the channel, and as the vista beyond spread wider and wider, they were rendered mute by both its pastoral beauty and by their first full view of the mysterious man-made structure.

"My God," said Karen, as the boat glided into almost a square mile of utterly calm water, framed by towering heights and fed by a hundred silvery streams—and dominated, frowned over, by the massive, gaunt, roofless shell of what once had been a stone cathedral. Half-buried patterns of foundation stones adjacent to the chapel marked the location of long-vanished ancillary buildings. Isolated from the rumble of surf and the keening of high winds, the Edenic hidden valley and its calm, sheltered lake were suffused in a soft, ageless, mournful silence.

Landing the battery-powered runabout proved to be unexpectedly tricky: the overburdened keel scraped on submerged rocks several times before crunching ashore on a beach of glossy black pebbles, just south of the

flat-topped hillock where the ruined cathedral loomed. They approached it
in silence. Over centuries, the building's foundation seemed to have sunk its
roots into the rocky heart of Vardinoy. From a distance, the ruined church
had seemed squat and crude, almost primitive. But with every step closer, the
edifice gained in stature, aspiring to the monumental.

Allen judged the walls to be at least a meter thick, more where the larger
stones bulged outward. Raw stone was certainly abundant in this place, but
many of the lower, load-bearing rocks must have weighed half a ton! Straggly
draperies of sea grass trailed down from the roofless top, like the tonsure of a
giant monk, and from a multitude of chinks, ancient stains formed a glassy
skin in dreary shades of rusted brown and tarry black; darkened, too, was the
coarse mortar used to join the stones—streaks of black ran through it like distended veins. Aside from the crumbling chancel door, the only openings were
three high, arched windows on each side wall, looking more like arrow slits in
a castle than sources of illumination. When Allen mentioned this detail to
Richard Sugarman, the younger man nodded solemnly.

"Given how isolated this place is, and what the world was like back then,
whoever built this place wanted it to be as much a fortress as a house of worship; it was probably provisioned to withstand a month-long siege, and those
windows probably had wooden scaffoldings where archers could shoot down
in relative safety. You didn't need elaborate fortifications to withstand a
Viking raid—just good thick walls. If the Norsemen couldn't sack a place in
a week or less, they usually said to hell with it and sailed on to find some
easier target."

"So this really is Viking Age?"

Sugarman led him around to the front entrance again, pointing out some
decorative motifs carved in the overhead archway. "Definitely Gothic style.
Maybe as early as the ninth century, probably no later than the eleventh—
by that time, Christians and pagans were all mixed together in this part of
the world. My guess, though, would be the mid-tenth century."

Elsuba, Warrener now saw, was kneeling close to the foundation, laboriously trying to extract a chunk of mortar without causing it to crumble into
powder. Finally she succeeded and came over to show it off as though it were
a hidden jewel.

"I've seen some of this stuff before, guys, in a few of the oldest buildings
in Torshavn. It's made out of crushed sea shells and pulverized fish bones—

they used smushed-up innards for the binding agent. When it dried, it was as good as cement. Ingenious notion, really."

"So that would make this place . . . how old?"

"I concur with Richard's estimate. The first recorded settlers came in the late ninth century, and by 1200 A.D., they would have been using imported lime. So, yes, tenth century is about right. Which makes this as old as any building still preserved on these islands—maybe older. This may, in fact, have been the *first* permanent structure ever build on Faeroese soil. I'm amazed that nobody's discovered it until now."

"Well, if you didn't know it was here and you weren't staring straight through that one aperture in the rocks, you'd never see it. We just got lucky."

Karen seemed spellbound by the ruined cathedral. Almost reverently, she stroked the ancient stones, even pressed her cheek against them. "This place could be a thousand years old . . . and we could be the first people to touch these walls since . . . whoever built it. I don't see any No Trespassing signs, so let's go inside."

Spreading out in the dim, cool interior, each explorer followed his or her fancy. There wasn't much to see, really: stone floors, some nondescript patches of debris that might once have been wooden pews, a plain stone altar at the western end, cracked and badly decayed. Warrener walked a circuit of all the sides, peering closely at every irregular patch of wall, turning frequently to gaze at the open rectangle of cloud-flocked sky high above. "I wonder what happened to the roof. . . ."

Sugarman remarked that he, too, was puzzled, for he had seen no trace of beams and no debris that looked as though it had ever served to support a ceiling.

"Two theories: one, they never finished it, or maybe never even started it, and two, there was a fire that consumed it utterly. Take your pick."

"Fire" was the more dramatic option, but the interior walls had been open to the elements and a thousand years of rain had left such a dark patina on the stones that only some very sophisticated laboratory tests could have determined whether or not fire had ever touched them.

Preston had been snapping his Nikon almost nonstop, and when he paused to change film, he said: "I think I'll scramble up the side of the valley and get some wide-angle shots. That's the only way you can capture the sheer scale of this thing. Say, Allen, you want to come along?"

"Yeah, sure—the view ought to be something else." He started to issue a general invitation to the others, but a sharp glance from Preston caused him to hesitate. On their way around the northern rim of the lagoon, they paused to observe Dewey, whose mind had clearly been blown by the setting and the ruins. He had detached himself from the others, and was joyously leaping from hillside to rock outcropping, scattering flocks of seabirds in his path. As he splashed through a mountain creek, sunlight caught the corona of spray, and for an instant he was surrounded by a penumbra of radiant mist. He had loosed his long bronze hair, and his sheepskin jacket flapped around his shoulders like a chieftain's cloak.

"Jesus, would you look at him? Your boy has gone native, Preston, and the spirit of Odin clearly has him in thrall."

"Yeah, he's into it, all right. One morning he's going to show up wearing a horned helmet, carrying a spear, and singing 'Wotan's Farewell' in flawless German."

Twenty minutes of puffing and scrabbling brought them to an excellent vantage point. Allen, once he got his wind back and could focus on the scene below, was surprised at how high they'd climbed. The figures crawling around by the cathedral looked like ants. From this height, too, it was more readily apparent that the afternoon was waning. "I'd better burn up some Agfachrome while the light's still good. Hand me the tripod, would you?" Warrener settled on a sun-warmed rocky ledge and soaked up every detail of the panorama, concluding that he was not likely to see anything more wildly yet serenely beautiful if he lived another hundred years. Preston was all business, switching lenses, jabbing light meters, muttering about *f*-stops and focal lengths. The Nikon clicked and whirred incessantly.

"Allen?" Click. Whrrr, whirr. Click!

"Yeah, Press?"

Click-clack! Whrrr. . . .

"I've been waiting for a chance to speak to you alone ever since that whale jumped out of the ocean this morning and almost made me shit my drawers."

"Umm-hmmm. So now's your chance. Wanna go on a whale-hunt?"

"Do you see one going on at this moment? God damn it, stop rubber-necking for a minute and pay attention to me."

"I am, Press. I'm just not very interested in a Serious Discussion right this minute."

"Well, you got one coming, like it or not. Remember something you said this morning? You told me that Andreas Dahl was born on Suduroy, right?"

"I guess so—don't really remember, nor do I much care where he was born."

"Well, maybe you ought to. Because yesterday, I was pumping Norma for more information about him—you know, trying to find out what his angle was, what was really going on between the two of them. Oh, nothing much, she said; just . . . talk. About what, I said. Oh, about painting, about our earlier lives, about what it was like to grow up in a place as isolated and inbred as Norduroy. *'Nor-du-roy,'* Allen. That's his home town, home island, whatever." Preston pointed to the northwest.

"Okay, so what? Who gives a shit where he was born, Preston?"

"Like I said, maybe you and me and everybody else *should* give a shit, because last week he told Eiden Poulsen he was born on Suduroy, which is all the way at the other end of the chain. And that was a bald-faced lie, Allen! He's from *Norduroy! Over there! Where the Gray Boats come from!*"

Karen, Elsuba, and Richard watched, with some amusement at their awkward descent, as Allen and Preston returned from their picture-taking tête-à-tête. Twice in the last ten minutes, Birgir had tooted the steam whistle on the trawler—repairs, evidently, had been completed. In any case, it was time to go: the sun was dipping under the rim of the seaward cliffs, and cold shadows were filling the old cathedral.

"I've seen my share of ancient churches," Richard was saying. "Notre Dame, Westminster Abbey, Coventry . . . and in its own way, this place is just as magnificent. What a setting! It's like a cathedral inside a cathedral— the sea on one side and those bloody great cliffs on the other! I'll bet this is where the people from the deserted village used to worship. That explains the wagon track around the lake—at some time in the past, there must have been a way over those ridges into this valley. Look at all those tumbled rocks. The only thing that could have scattered them like that would have been one hell of a landslide."

Karen turned to Elsuba. "Are you sure you've never heard of this place before?"

"Positive. Maybe there's an antiquarian in Torshavn who could tell us something about it, but I doubt it. Anything this old would have attracted some archaeologists, but we haven't seen any sign of a dig. As far as I can see, no one has disturbed this silence for about nine hundred years."

Karen smiled broadly.

"I know what you're thinking," Sugarman grinned back at her.

"Do you indeed?"

"You're thinking that, whatever else happens, whatever else we do or do not find, we *have* made a real discovery. We may not learn the truth about the Vardinoy Monster, but we *did* find this magnificent ruin."

In a tone of quiet triumph, Karen said: "You bet your ass we did."

The *Laertes* tooted its whistle again. The sun vanished. It grew chilly inside the church, and a strong, fitful wind ruffled the lagoon. Unnoticed in the gloom, Dewey had slipped back inside, drawn to an oddly shaped patch of moss he had noticed earlier on the wall in the nave. For ten minutes, racing the fading light, he had been gently scraping the moss clear with his knife. Now, his eyes glittering, he ran his roughened fingertips over the dim outlines of a Celtic cross—obviously part of the original construction—and the bulkier, less-faded outlines of the shape that had been superimposed on it. An undulating, bestial shape, part serpent, part . . . Dewey didn't know. Octopus? Giant squid? An omnivorous all-devouring blob? In the deepening dusk, the thing's outline seemed almost fluid, and he was glad it was only stone, for its shape awakened an atavistic tickle of dread in even his tough heart. The creature, or the Great Orm, had obviously been incised over the cross at a later date, a pagan motif subjugating the sickly sacrificial Christ, and whoever had defaced the cross had gouged the stone roughly, as though with sword-point. When he had uncovered the whole of this disturbing palimpsest, he brushed off the dust of centuries, dug into his backpack for a flashlight, and beamed a flashing signal to the people grouped around the entrance, who had just been joined by Warrener and Valentine. In unison, they turned to Dewey's beacon, shading their eyes and shouting questions at him.

"I think you'll want to see this, guys and gals."

"See what?" grumped Allen. "C'mon, Cycle-Trash, it's time to get back to the ship."

"Fuck the ship. Birgir ain't gonna strand us here. While the rest of you been jawboning, I found it for you."

"Found what?"

"The Great Orm, Professor Warrener. The giant sea serpent, maybe the real Vardinoy Monster. Somebody carved his picture down here . . . about a thousand years ago."

24.

A Reconnaissance in Niflheim

Karen Hambly had a lot to think about on the night after the discovery of the ruined cathedral, and the threads she wanted to grasp were elusive, faint, and unlikely to be there when she woke up in the morning. But Allen kept chattering excitedly about the day's adventure, to the point where Karen found his very enthusiasm almost unbearably irritating. But instead of snapping, *Allen, will you kindly shut the fuck up so I can try to initiate a mystical communion with whatever-it-is that keeps following me around?* she decided to lull him with an erotic surprise. While he babbled on, she slid into his cot and began touching him in ways that seldom failed to have their intended effect. When she felt the stirrings of a first-class erection, she licked his ear and whispered, "This one's just for you, baby! To celebrate the best damn day we've spent on this island." His eyes rolled happily, for she had just uttered a code phrase that absolved him of any responsibility for delivering reciprocal pleasure. He had official permission to lie back and savor the treat.

As Karen had anticipated, the rapid cycle of tension and release acted on him like a sledgehammer on a slaughterhouse steer. Five minutes after her final draining swallow, he was so far gone that nothing short of a gunshot could have brought him back. Karen smiled ruefully: it never failed—not with any guy she'd ever slept with. How quickly and gratefully they fell asleep once you'd made it clear that post-orgasmic cuddling and pillow talk were not expected. They all claimed they enjoyed the afterglow rituals, but none of them really did. Allen at least made an effort, but twenty minutes was his limit—beyond that, he turned surly and ostentatiously drowsy. You could set your watch by it.

But tonight, that was fine with her. She had planned a controlled experiment, and her preparations were ritualistic. Although she'd given up using the stuff after her experiences as a groupie, she still had a couple of hits of blotter acid sealed in an airtight container (one simply didn't throw away fifty bucks' worth of good LSD!). She carefully divided one of the tabs in half and washed it down with a swallow of lukewarm Diet Pepsi. Next, she packed her favorite pipe to the brim from one of the dime bags of Appalachian Brown Lung she'd scored on campus the week before departing for the Faeroes—ten generations of moonshine-brewing had taught North Carolina's mountaineers a thing or two about raising and nurturing contraband substances! She'd been chilling a bottle of not-too-shabby Chablis in the tent's ice chest, and this would be both her refreshment and her communion cup, if it came to that. Lastly, as a precaution against having to cope with a sudden Bad Trip, she stuffed a bottle of Xanax into the breast pocket of her flannel shirt. She was as ready as she could be, given her ignorance of what had really happened during these . . . dreams? visions? seizures? Whatever the episodes were, she wanted to learn if she could enter that state at will—and bail out if she wanted to. She needed to learn more, but hallucinatory trances were tricky things, sometimes involving risks that were not commensurate with the potential for enlightenment. She auto-suggested herself into a meditative state and sipped wine for ten minutes, before the acid transmitted that first no-turning-back-now-old-girl signal to her nerve ends. She knew she was on the verge when the dim flame of the Coleman lantern suddenly became one of the more fascinating phenomena she'd ever observed. Yep, it was kicking in and time for her to go to the spot she'd picked out, before she got too high to walk straight.

Outside the tent, the campsite was peaceful and homey, its main pathways softly illuminated by Eiden's clever grid of garden-path lamps. No one was stirring, but snores could be heard on all sides, a remarkably varied diapason of volumes and timbres. Karen walked on, feeling reassured by the good nocturnal vibes. She had chosen the flat-topped promontory where she had hoisted the flag on their first night beside the lake. It was remote enough for privacy, yet close enough for somebody to hear a cry for help. She unfolded a lightweight camp chair and covered her legs with a terry-cloth comforter. Just in time, too, because that old blotter acid was coming on like a Van Halen encore and she needed immobility to ride out the first wave of shakes and muscle twitches. Both to deepen her receptivity and to smooth out the "learning curve," she now consumed that brimming bowlful of primo grass, methodically burning the entire load down to the tarry dregs.

"Oh, wow," she whispered. *Houston, we have lift-off!*

Her sense of time dilated like a slow-motion shot of rosebuds ripening in the spring. The acuity of her night vision took a quantum leap, and when she focused on a bright yellow-orange glow seeping over the eastern peaks far across the lake, she rather hoped it heralded the approach of a UFO. By God, if she were ever going to have a Close Encounter, this was the moment! But, no, it was only the moon; but what a moonrise she beheld! It turned the eastward ridges into glowing wedges of ebonite, conjuring upon the lake a vast swarm of eel-shaped reflections, and bathing her in sacerdotal light. Good thing I'm so relaxed, she thought; one burned molecule on just the wrong synapse and this whole luscious panorama could transform into a seriously creepy Bad-Trip-Ugly-Thing.

Time was hers to command, and so she willed it to become slow and gelid, a substance she could reach out and manipulate. *Hey, Allen, did you know that the space–time continuum feels exactly like a new pair of rayon panties?* Now she could feel the changing texture of her own brainmeat, becoming more porous and spongelike. Lighting a cigarette took about twenty minutes of Trip Time, or seemed to, but when she took the first drag, it was the best smoke she'd ever had. *"Ain't we the Stuff?"* piped a passing carcinogen. *"Don't worry, sister, tonight's a freebie! Me an' the guys ditched our Cancer components on the way into your lungs, so you can enjoy that cigarette without the usual Guilt Tax."*

Karen whispered to the flagpole: "I have just had an imaginary conversation with a cancer molecule. Does that mean I'm on the . . ." she would have said "verge" or "cusp" or "edge," but before the chosen word came out she was suddenly There; having melted into a liquid, a nice red wine apparently, she poured herself out of the camp chair and enjoyed a roller-coaster cascade down a long, gentle slope, the burnt-ocher walls of a canyon rising on either hand and a pale, woolly sun bathing everything in a sickly orange radiance, and then she slid off the chute and landed in a tidal pool that was surprisingly warm. . . .

Well, of course it would be, *now wouldn't it, this* IS *the mid–Tertiary period after all.*

No, it's actually the Year of Our Lord Ten Fifty-Six A.D.
Who are you and why can't I see you?
Because I'm imaginary, Karen—a product of that kick-ass communion

wafer you ate about forty minutes ago. . . . However, you may think of me as Brother Bartholomew, same era . . . belonged to an obscure and short-lived band of heretical Irish monks and naturally got hounded out of Europe by the Church. Why else would we have willingly settled on this God-forsaken rock?

So you ended up here and you built that cathedral?

Not single-handedly, my dear girl, I assure you! It took years and years, and mind you, one of the reasons we got booted out of the Church was our refusal to obey that nonsense about celibacy . . . wives and children enough to keep us from degenerating into drooling imbeciles after a few generations . . . we could have made a thriving little town here in time . . . but you saw what we had to use for mortar, and making a big batch of that shit was time-consuming . . . slowed us down a lot . . . that plus having to maintain a small standing army in case the Gray-Boats' attitude changed from sullen tolerance to hostility.

You mean the Norduroy people—clannish and unfriendly even then?

Let's just say 'indifferent,' which really pissed off the Abbot, I can tell you! He thought that when our cathedral was far enough along, the sheer size and majesty of it would lure the yokels into the tent, as it were, and awe them into signing up for Jesus.

Didn't happen.

We did have contact with them occasionally, of course. We had a ter-rific blacksmith, fella nicknamed John the Wall-Eyed Welshman, and when the Gray-Boats needed some metalwork done, they'd sail across the straits and trade us a whopping load of fish for his services.

So they DID have great luck as fishermen?

Damnedest luck you ever saw, any time of the year, good weather or foul, their boats went out empty and came back full, almost like some-body gave 'em directions to the right spot! Some of the boys thought they had to be in league with Satan to have such persistent good fortune, and they did have a pipeline to *something*, because, pagans or not, they never had much to say about Odin or Thor or any of those guys . . . we discussed the matter endlessly, as clerics love to do, and of course, as you already sur-mised, our cathedral was designed to be a fortress, if the need ever arose.

They showed no interest whatever in you, except for needful trading?

Only one time, when a big, skinny old man, who was obviously their chieftain or the High Priest of their faith, surprised us by asking for a tour of the church . . . wasn't much to see at that point, just some pews made from driftwood and the big altarpiece crucifix in the nave. The old chieftain and his entourage weren't too impressed . . . showed no emotion whatever until they saw the cross, and for some reason that symbol seemed to infuriate them . . . they glared at us ferociously and stormed back to their boat, and at that moment I at least understood that the uneasy truce was now over, that they meant to attack and exterminate us, down to the last suckling babe. . . .

How long was it before they. . . .

Attacked? Only a week or so after the chieftain's visit, and they caught us unprepared because there was such a gale blowing that night that Christ Himself couldn't have crossed those straits . . . or so we thought.

But the Gray-Boats got across the straits, didn't they?

Aye, girl. Methinks they were aided by the same demon or Elemental who showed them where to drop their nets . . . they crossed the straits as though the water were dead calm, and by the time our lookouts spotted their boats massing in the lagoon, it was too late to make a proper defense. . . . We made a brave fight of it, though, and my arrows took down four at least before their grappling hooks started landing faster than we could throw them down

So my last moments of earthly life were spent burying my diary under a massive stone near the baptismal font, so that all record of our achievements, beliefs, and tribulations should not be erased utterly from History's scroll. And if you find and read it, you may learn a thing or two that will help you to escape

THIS!

And Karen is sucked through a howling vortex—Instant Bad Trip U-Turn, break out the Xanax, girl, can't move my hand, can't control it, landing on some new and awful plane and the portal I entered is gone, hidden, locked, and

She's staring at an endless ash-gray plane, scoured by a chill pitiless wind that rakes the gray sand into tiny knives, scraping the meat of her brain, the membranes of her sight, a wind that rattles the shriveled gourd-like fruits hanging from the twisted black limbs of a stupendous and solitary Tree

They might resemble human skulls, those petrified rinds, but for the fact that they bear no eye sockets, no flayed slits of mouths, and from what might have been the neck, they trail long knotted filaments of matter, like mile-long braids and now she hears another voice, a clotted and hideous parody of Brother Bartholomew's cultured tones, malice and despair and fathomless rage that has no outlet, saying

Welcome, Karen-Child, to the anteroom of Niflheim, where the souls of the newly slain are hung out to dry, until the minions of Ig-Dra-Cell come forth from their deep domain and harvest the living, wind-cured integuments which your mind describes as 'braids' and in a sense they are, for it is their fate to be woven for eternity into the warp and woof of those mile-long carpets that line the cold hard floors of Valhalla

Time to wake up now, Karen, before this gets any weirder!

You are wise beyond your years and you are clever and brave, to find your way to this place

That's a different voice! A chorus of voices! The gourd-like things are speaking from the tree, and their soul-braids writhe wildly as though trying to spell out words to me, show me symbols and patterns of vast significance

But why?

He waits for you to contact Him, as once you did so long ago, when the terror of confinement unlocked the ancient power latent in your, what-do-you-call-it? Hypothalamus, perhaps? All these new-fangled words! Anyhow, from four thousand miles away, He felt your terror and because it was so much akin to His own, He loaned you preternatural strength, sending it through the planet's crust by means of an Extrusion and thereby are the two of you bonded. Better believe it, sweet buns! And now He waits for your touch. . . . He has been alone for so long, and of all those who have chanced to learn of Him, only you are wholly sane and who knows for how long, eh? He hopes:

Perhaps *your* touch will be gentle. Karen-Child

For He would like to know what gentleness feels like, before the coming of Ragnarok. . . .

What you ask of me is not possible! How can I befriend a god?

Good question, but one of the rules is that you have to find the answer on your own

I can't do this! I won't! This isn't real! This is Alice down the rabbit-hole!

**Does this plain look real? This tree? The friendship of a god
is not lightly to be spurned, nor gained without a mortal risk! But if you
do not accept the charge laid upon you, Karen-Child, then very soon the
soul-gourds of your friends will hang from this tree, just as ours have hung
for millions of years! You cannot conceive of how bitter the sap of the
World Tree truly is!**

*I'm not listening . . . not listening . . . this is a Bad Trip and I just
popped six Xanax so I think I'll be leaving soon and all of this will be nothing but
the fragments of a bad dream because*   all this shit is impossible and
there are no Norse gods and there are no talking-soul-gourds with the
WORST-LOOKING dreadlocks I ever saw. . . .

**Consider what you have learned. Weigh what we have told you! And
Karen-Child, if you want a little taste of just how fucking REAL this is,
we're going to unshield your itty bitty brain for just one second, so you
can feel what It has endured since Vardinoy rose blistered from the sea!
Get a grip, kiddo, 'cause this is gonna hurt. . . .**

The neuron pathways in her brain and the silver conduits in her spine
all screamed at once, and Karen Hambly learned in the passage of a single
second that absolute pain and absolute madness, melded into one, create
a sensation that is far worse than either thing alone. It is, literally,
unendurable

And yet there is something alive that has endured it for eons.

Karen jerked wildly when Allen tried to embrace her, disoriented to find
herself back inside the tent, in his bed with him, with no memory of having
made the journey.

"You must have had one hell of a nightmare, love," he said, genuinely concerned and quite taken aback when she responded with hysterical laughter.
Before she could do or say something that would irreparably damage their
relationship, she forced herself to swallow a few more Xanax, promised she
would try to tell him later, and fled into her own bed after giving him a perfunctory kiss. He meant well, of course, but in her present state, even the
brush of his body hair prickled her skin like a hideous rash. He was still
making solicitous noises when the tranks kicked in and zonked her out
beyond the maddening mosquito-buzz of Allen's voice.

25.

Vardinoy, End of the Sixteenth Day

From the journal of Richard Sugarman:

We found the document right where Karen said we would: under a big stone in the nave of the ruined church. Her pointing it out that way spooked me. Allen too, I think. Must have spooked her as well, although she tried hard to be nonchalant. She doesn't look well: pallid skin, shadows under her eyes, and her nerves are right under the skin—you can almost see them twitching.

When we got the document back to camp, we found that the outer wrappings of sealskin had preserved the contents remarkably well. And the writing, though faint, was legible. Of course the sheepskin papers were tightly stuck together, but after Elsuba carefully steamed them for a half hour, they became pliant again. I guess I'd hoped to find it written in runes or Old Elf dialect—something Tolkienian! But it was all in Latin. They all looked at me: he's a law major, he's taken Latin! Well, sure, but it was LEGAL Latin, not the everyday patois of the streets!

When I expressed doubts about being able to do the job, Allen naïvely asked: "What's the problem, Richard? Is this some kind of old dialect?" To which I superciliously snapped: "Allen, Latin is Latin. 'Old' is the only flavor it comes in! Look, I'll give it my best shot, but I can't promise you a graceful, nuanced translation."

I'm sorry I bit his nose off—he was practically salivating at the prospect of the Expedition actually unearthing a document of genuine historical significance.

So anyway, I'm about 300 words into the first scroll now, and I'm at least translating the gist of it. Fascinating stuff! The author recorded the annals of a very early settlement, perhaps the first *settlement, by an excommunicated band of heretical Irish monks. Married Irish monks! No wonder Rome kicked them out. So far, I've not found any references to "monsters," and that's just fine with me.*

Other business: after lunch I took a long solitary walk—the weather was balmy and my need for privacy urgent. I settled down on a mossy hummock north of camp, nice smooth mossy slab for a backrest, lapboard, journal, and a book to read.

Thoreau overlooking Walden's Evil Twin, the Vardinoy lake! After a while, I saw movement out of the corner of my left eye and turned in that direction to see what was making those strange rhythmic gyrations. Damned if it wasn't Dewey, who had climbed 150 feet up a ridge so he could practice his Tai Chi routines. His long yellow hair was unbound, rising and falling in slow waves as he practiced the gavotte-of-the-constipated-cranes or whatever it was, his sheepskin jacket flapping around his barrel chest, knife at his hip. Perched 150 feet up a mountain in the middle of this Wagnerian landscape, he looked like something out of a Conan story—a barbarian warrior dancing to invoke his uncouth gods.

I watched him for a long time; then, as he finished his ballet, he bowed in my direction and waved. The son of a bitch knew I was watching all along and had been staging a performance. He climbed down and settled on the hummock next to mine, luxuriating in a post-workout smoke.

"I couldn't help but watch," I told him. "You're the only interesting thing I've seen all day."

"I know. That's why I gave you the 'tourist' version, not the hardcore version. Hey, Little Dick, I was watching you, too. . . . What's that you're writing so industriously?"

"I'm keeping a journal of what happens. Or doesn't. Maybe I'll write a book about us some day."

He pulled out a canteen and offered me a drink. Pure aquavit! After I could breathe again, I liked the sensations spreading through my head. By the time the canteen was half empty, Ol' Dewey and me were the warmest of friends.

"Here's a good quote for you: 'Dewey Tucker confessed that he really really got off on the Faeroese scene and wouldn't mind living the rest of his days in those islands.' "

I took it down verbatim, then said "You would fit right in, Dewey."

"I would, and that's a goddamn fact! Why just yesterday, I was talkin' to Birgir about signing on with a fishing boat and learning the trade. Whaddaya think?"

"Why the hell not? It's a man's job. Find yourself a big blonde goddess to share your bed, and spend your declining years mending nets in the sun. You could do worse."

I noticed that he was staring with great interest at the book I was reading—a compilation of verses from the Faeroese and Orkney sagas. The cover showed wild-haired guys with spears standing on the prow of a dragon ship.

"Can I see your book for a minute?"

He flipped through the pages, reading a few at random, lips moving, mumbling, then slowly nodded his head in a gesture that combined recognition,

413

pleasure, and longing. "Aw, Jesus, listen to this!" Then, in a voice that suddenly lost
its shit-kicking twang and assumed a bardic baritone, he read aloud the following
lines:

> *Leaped we on the black-keeled boat.*
> *My prince, unyielding Thorfinn*
> *Ravaged in the blade-storm. O*
> *Will ravens feast this night!*
> *Odin gave our sword arms strength,*
> *Our foemen's iron-clad bodies piled*
> *Black as carrion on our streaming decks.*
> *Our blades are reeling, drunk from blood!*
> *We trod the backs of slaughtered foemen,*
> *Spear-weary stand we o'er their corpses*
> *Grim and silent are our thoughts;*
> *Grim and silent—falcons resting*
> *on a great black oak.*

"Holy shit," Dewey sighed. "That's my kind of poetry! How much of this stuff
is there?"

"Tons of it. Not to mention operas. Take the book along if you like, 'cause I'm
about to O.D. on that stuff."

After thanking me profusely, he scampered back to his perch, opened the book,
and was still sitting there, motionless and rapt, when I left two hours later.

Norma was trying to become proficient with oils, but it was not easy. Used
to the fragile tactility of pastels, she found the thicker medium slow and
obdurate. Nevertheless, she persisted, for she now believed that these very
difficulties were strengthening her talent. "Building new eyeballs," was how
Andreas described the process.

She had chosen to paint a pastoral meadow that lay about a kilometer
from camp. It was pleasing to her eye and full of interesting shapes. Having
first painted a literal representation of the view, she was now over-painting
it, seeking through a willful distortion of perception to discover the
scenery's "inner character," as Andreas called it. She was working on the
wildflowers, painstakingly subverting the colors of reality with arbitrary

hues chosen by whim. The doubloon-yellow marigolds were now a bilious olive green; the scarlet jumper buttons she had mutated with thick brittle caps of purple. She knew, not far into the exercise, that the result was a hideous muddle, but she now believed that even her failures were valuable steps in the metamorphosis of her painting, from what it had been to what it might ultimately become. She was eager to hear Andreas's comments about this piece; he would be able to see qualities she could not, and, with a few words or gestures, reveal to her new possibilities, alternative techniques more suited to her hands, her eyes, her mind.

Her flesh.

Andreas was away that morning, she did not know where. He had merely stated in his firm, uninflected way that he needed to work alone that morning. He would see her this evening, if she could get away from the camp.

Could she ever! Not just tonight, either. What remained for her now was to figure out a way to leave Preston without provoking undue rancor. She no longer resented him, exactly—the powerful rush of her feelings for Dahl had swept her beyond that. Old affections, suppressed resentments, even the unexpected cache of residual guilt, which surprised her, all were settled in her mind. She recognized her debt to Preston, acknowledged the once-considerable depth of her feelings for him, and accepted her obligation to make this move—a permanent one, she believed—from his tent into Andreas's hut, as painless as possible.

At the memory of what had transpired yesterday in Dahl's room, a tropical butterfly began to beat its wings in her abdomen. Norma dabbed at one last marigold, rested her brush, and sank into the luxury of remembering.

Two days ago, after a briefer-than-usual sketching session, Dahl had turned to her with one of his rare and precious smiles and asked if she would like to see the house where he resided. The invitation had taken Norma completely by surprise.

"Oh, you mean in the village?"

"Not exactly in the village, but a little farther down the coast. There are some paintings there that might interest you."

"Anything you do would interest me," she had responded.

He met her in the mountain pass, a steep forty-minute hike from camp, and led her down to and through the village, across the eastern arm of the fjord, and finally into a sheltered cove fed by a surging creek. He'd built a plank bridge to reach the abandoned hut: stone walls, sod roof, a large kitchen/dining room, a bedroom, and a small windowless alcove where he stored his easels, canvases, and supplies. The air was cool and redolent of linseed oil, turpentine, and the humid aroma of thick-squeezed pigment. Underlying all of that was the comforting fragrance of his pipe tobacco.

Norma felt a dizzying anticipation unlike anything she had associated with sex for more years than she cared, at that moment, to count. She spotted a stack of finished paintings leaning against the dining table, a big shaggy thing constructed from slabs of driftwood.

"May I look at them?"

"*Of course. In a way, it's* essential *that you look at them.*"

Dahl poured each of them a tumbler of aquavit and left her standing at the table. He took a seat, filled his pipe, and smoked, coolly watching her. Through an archway, she saw his bed. It was in the corner of her sight as she looked at the paintings, and even after they absorbed her full attention, she was aware of its closeness.

These pictures were certainly different from any of his other work, although they were instantly recognizable as his. Their power was not casual; instead, they commanded the observer's attention, like scenes from some ancient, barbaric ceremony. His manipulation of texture and mass was transcendent; the power of night and dread were here adumbrated with a master's touch. He had painted into these harsh land- and seascapes the elements of an apocalyptic Norse legend. She beheld enormous sea serpents with malachite eyes, rising in fearful majesty from storm-lashed fjords; the Earth itself was embraced by the arabesques of a vast root system whose shape suggested, faintly but irrefutably, both sentience and purpose. And finally, she viewed abstractions that distilled these concrete images into crushing blocks of darkness that conveyed horrific weight and density.

"Andreas, these are . . . they almost make me afraid."

"*Almost?*"

"Yes, because it's more a feeling of awe than fear. What I'd feel if someone showed me a picture and said, in all seriousness, 'Here, look upon the true image of God.' "

He seemed quite pleased with her choice of words. He put down his pipe and, for the first time since they'd met, his eyes burned into hers with unequivocal fierce desire.

"Norma, I want you," he said simply. And she walked to him, her skin so alive it felt electric, as though it would give off sparks at his touch. He led her into the bedroom and began slowly to undress her.

Oh, Preston, if you could have captured that afternoon on film, you'd have made the masterpiece you always dreamed of making!

She had wanted to impress Dahl with her virtuosity. And at the first contact between her straining opulence and his lean strength, she unleashed a veritable detonation of flesh. ("Lights—camera—ACTION!!") She was resolved to rend him apart with delights he had never dreamed of, to gorge him with sensations he could not name; to dazzle him with inspired improvisations of movement and manipulation. She was in her element now. She was air and water, oil and fire; she was candy, lava, a goddess, and a slut. She dashed herself against him like a wave; she flowed tantalizingly over his flesh, leaving small tidal pools of bruises, nettle-red nail-furrows, and even the marks of her teeth. At the apex of her film career, world-famous statesmen had volunteered to commit treason in exchange for less than she was giving Dahl now. She was pulp and silk and pearls and mink and the steaming juice of nectarines.

He responded to every nuance, but he did not lose himself in it as every other man in her experience would have done. Instead, he took it all while surrendering nothing, giving back nothing, save the hardness of his presence within the storm she had unleashed. She beat against a core of him that remained impervious. He took and took all that she offered until she was gasping and slick with giving, raw with openness, and then he slowly began to impose his own rhythm on her; inexorable, accelerating only by the slightest, nearly imperceptible degrees, driving calculatedly through the luxuriance of her offering, reaching singlemindedly for a deep and secret place inside her that all her giving had left undefended, and slowly filling it with his own power: a measured, sacramental antistrophe to her ferocious abandon. This was, for Norma, an unprecedented domination—one that absorbed all her powers to excite, digested them, and grew stronger from their nourishment; then when he drove his concentrated force deep into the grottos of her raw and humbled flesh, she could but yield, give up the goods as no man had ever compelled her to do before.

She lost herself, finally; moved and breathed as he commanded, helpless before the looming shadow of a tremendous blood-black convulsion, far distant at first, but unstoppable. He was summoning it, drawing it out of her at a pace of his own choosing. She began to cry softly, a frightened little-girl wail that became as constant as the rush of the creek outside their bedroom window. Her first orgasm was like none she'd experienced before, so convulsive as to carry a hint of extinction; and with every subsequent climax the velocity of erotic release was faster, harder-edged, eradicating every cofferdam of reserve she'd ever built inside her psyche, until she was anchored to consciousness only by the hardness of his presence inside her. Each cymbal-crash of pleasure segued instantly into the next until she reached a condition of blind, thrashing delirium. And none of it was faked, as had sometimes been the case in Preston's movies, but devastatingly real. Finally, Andreas found his own moment, flipped an internal switch, and allowed himself to erupt, growling a harsh, almost resentful cry, and she felt thick needles of fire pierce her spine and the image in her mind was that of a seabird being torn asunder by an arctic gale.

Afterward, he lay quietly, breathing-down with calculated regularity, like an athlete coming off the last lap of a marathon. There was no banal small talk about how great it had been, for which Norma was grateful. When Dahl did speak to her, it was with a new, yet measured, level of intimacy. He maintained a certain reserve—volunteering just enough information to feed the combustion of Norma's near-monologue, drawing from her all manner of strangely quotidian information about her life at the campsite. That was agreeable to Norma—if that was what he wanted. Throughout her adult life, on screen and off, she had tried to be what a million faceless men lusted after. Now she was focused, body and soul, on becoming what this one man wanted. In time, she would discover what that might be, and mold herself accordingly.

Norma relaxed in the cocoon of warm but solitary afterplay, nattering on, guided by an encouraging grunt here and a restrained chuckle there, while daydreams of future happiness cavorted like Olympic gymnasts in the arenas of her imagination. This first sexual encounter with Andreas was Norma's Ground Zero: everything else in her life would radiate out from this glowing point. Her next act would have to consist of distancing herself psychologically, and literally, from Preston. Why wait? Tomorrow, if feasible, she would leave a letter—tender but firm, one whose contents, she knew, would not come as a total surprise. Perhaps she did owe him an in-person explanation, but the letter would suffice, and mark the formal break, while sparing both of them the ordeal of a pointless face-to-face apocalypse.

"In a way, it'll be a relief for him," she rationalized to her mostly silent bed-partner, *"I know it will. God, the tension of having to bed down in that tent every night, it's been sickening for both of us."*

"I'm sure it has. You'll move in here with me, of course, until I make some arrangements. Then we can go away together. You *will* come with me, won't you, Norma? I've never lost myself in any woman as I did with you today."

In reply, she sugar-coated his brow and cheeks with hot tender kisses, permitting him to feel the slow hot tears of joy escaping from her eyes. "Yes, Andreas, I *will go anywhere on Earth with you."*

Later, when they'd gotten dressed and were sharing a pot of coffee around the trestle table, Norma rehearsed her strategies aloud. "I don't want to hurt Preston any more than necessary. Better to do it quickly, right now while he's got so many things to distract him. He and Allen will get drunk together and bitch about women. When their hangovers subside, they can get in their little boat and cruise the lake, listening to that damned Nimrod device or whatever it is—"

"Have they heard any new tunes on it lately?"

"Huh? Oh, you mean through the hydrophone-thingies? Nothing worth talking about. Nothing much has happened anywhere on this damned island, except maybe for finding that old church."

"What church?"

"An old ruin they discovered when the trawler broke down and almost drifted into the rocks, some place just above the Axe-Cuts, I think. They were all excited about it, of course, and then when Karen had one of her visions and told them about an ancient scroll or something buried under the altarpiece, everybody flipped when they actually found it, right where she'd told them to look! I'm beginning to think that girl's got real, you know, *powers!* Anyway, Dick Sugarman's trying to translate it, since he's the only person here who knows Latin."

"An ancient document . . . in Latin? How fascinating. Tell me more, Norma, please."

"That's about all I can tell you. I guess it must have some historical value, since Allen keeps it locked in a steel box in-between translation attempts. And I really do hope it turns out to be something important so Allen can call a press conference in Torshavn and unveil this great contribution to archaeology . . . and then they can all get patted on the back and go home, forget all that crazy stuff about monsters. . . ."

"Norma, could you find out some more about the translation?"

"Not if I keep spending time having cosmic sex-romps with you, my Viking dreamboat!"

She leered at him and made as if to nip his shoulder. He drew back and his expression turned sober so suddenly that Norma winced as though avoiding a blow.

"Why the hell are you so interested? Aren't I more fun than a bunch of moldy old church records?"

"Of course you are, my darling, but I have always been interested in the history and lore of these northern islands. If there's been a discovery of any significance, I'm naturally curious to learn more about it."

To mask her irritation, she became playful. She leaned over and did a number of things with her tongue. "And *I'm* curious to learn more about what turns you on, you cold-blooded Viking."

He moved away from her. "Don't tease me, Norma!"

She glanced down and verified that, despite his prim objection, he was responding sexually. "Oh, I'll tease you, mister. I'll tease you until you can't stand it another minute." She giggled, wrapped a blanket around herself, and danced away from the bed. He glared at her, cheeks red, mouth taut, unable to deny the effect she was having.

"Come and get it, my man, come and get it!" She lowered the blanket slowly, pulled it so that her breasts spilled out in a wave of hot flesh. He rose and came toward her. She laughed and danced away, whirling around the kitchen table, then sashaying through the portal that led to the adjacent boathouse. Narrow ribbons of light poured through cracks in the roof, tiger-striping the gloom. She looked around to get her bearings and noticed a small motorboat pulled up into the shadows.

Then Dahl's strong hands clamped wide around her shoulders, and his mouth ravaged the downiest curves of her neck greedily, bruising, near to drawing blood, as though by trying to tease her way through his veneer of detachment she'd somehow wakened a priapic madman. Growling with commingled lust and anger, he tore the blanket from around her body and flung it into the sea, then he scooped up her whole body and bore her down onto the thwarts and seats of the boat, knocking the breath from her lungs. Brutally clamping her wrists together and wedging open her legs, he took her savagely, contemptuous of her protests, crushing her against the hard cold wood, forcing her orgasm to surface from beneath a tide of pain.

And even that second time was better than anything in my movies. Even the hurting he laid upon me.

"Earth calling Norma! Are you still on this planet, over?"

Karen was smiling at her, a bottle of wine and two cups extended in Norma's direction.

"Oh, Jesus, Karen, I don't know how you found me, but that wine looks like it was sent from Heaven, so I'm glad you did!"

"I was out walking, saw you hard at work on your painting, and figured even Michelangelo needed a wine break now and then. How's the work coming along?"

"Well, there it is. Like it?"

Karen thought it was dreadful. The pale charm of Norma's former style had been abandoned and replaced by a muddy imitation of Andreas Dahl's.

"This is quite a new direction for you, isn't it?"

"Yes! Andreas has been helping me see things in new ways."

"And those bruises on your shoulder . . . Andreas helped with those too, I suppose."

"For heaven's sake Karen, please don't be judgmental. I can't help it if I'm crazy for the guy. I mean, it's been over between Preston and me for a long time. Up until now we've stayed together because it was more convenient than the alternatives. The marriage had just become an old habit, you know? Not something that still had a pulse. . . ."

"I'd already figured that out." Karen patted her hand. Norma sighed.

"Thanks, honey. I'd hate it if you started putting me down for not 'standing by my man' or some such crap. I know, breaking away out here in the middle of nowhere is more than a little weird. But then, whoever would have thought that I'd find a man like Andreas in a place like this?"

"Who indeed? Well, as you say, everything on Vardinoy is a little strange. Preston's going to be upset, of course, but at least he has plenty of activity to distract him and he has Allen's beer to cry in. . . . He'll bounce back, probably quicker than you think."

"I hope so because I really don't want to hurt him. And I don't want the rest of you to think I'm deserting the cause. It's just that, with Andreas, I feel a whole new dimension opening inside me. And I *like it!*"

"How does Andreas feel?"

Norma, now mildly tipsy, began to giggle. She put a sisterly hand on Karen's arm. "Pretty damned sore, I imagine."

"It was really that hot, huh?"

"It was! Oh, Jesus, it was. You'll never believe this, but the second time we made it, we actually did it in a boat. That's where the bruises came from—humping our brains out on a goddamn boat."

"You're kidding—"

"No, so help me, right there in a boat. Rub-a-dub-dub!"

"Sounds like kind of a turn-on! Tell me everything! How'd you, um, arrange yourselves? How big was it? I even want to know what color it was!"

"Color?" Norma began to giggle. "Well, you know: flesh-colored! But as to how big it was—"

"I was referring to the boat, you silly goose, not to Mr. Dahl's equipment!"

Now they were both tittering inanely, although Karen was pretending and Norma wasn't.

"Well . . . I don't know . . . I wasn't paying much attention to that kind of stuff. No color at all, I guess, just a sort of dull gray. But as to how well-endowed Andreas is, you know what they say about tall lanky men, and in this case it's true! I. . . ."

Norma nattered on, dredging up all the raunchy particulars; but she was too intoxicated by love, or too drunk, to notice how hard Karen's eyes had become, nor, as she continued to gush superlatives, did she realize that Karen had stopped paying the slightest attention to her right after she'd uttered the word "gray."

26.

A Visit to the Doctor

Allen Warrener stepped through the curtain that separated Elsuba's tiny lab cubicle from the communal dining hall. She looked up from a microscope and gave him one of those Doctor's Smiles that could be switched on and off like a minor appliance.

"Birgir said you wanted to see me."

She nodded and handed him a file folder half an inch thick.

"Here's something that might prove useful to you, Allen. It's a rough ecological analysis of the lake and its environs. I don't have either the training or the equipment to do a really sophisticated workup, but at least I could study the food chain, the water, and the species we've seen, and extrapolate from those things. It's really elementary science, but it might prove useful."

"Yeah, it could. Thanks." He flipped through pages at random: tables and graphs and a dense sprinkling of words like "zooplankton." Unwilling to admit his ignorance, he nodded appreciatively at two or three pages, then closed the folder with the air of someone who had no intention of ever opening it again.

"I'll study it more carefully tonight, but for now, what's your conclusion?"

"There's no reason why this lake couldn't support a large life form. Mind you, I said 'could.' If there is some extraordinary creature lurking down there, my best guess is that it could be a previously unknown species of eel—very, very *big* eels, to be sure. Interesting creatures, eels—no one knows the upper limits of their size, but they're kind of like squid—there's no inherent physiological reason why there should even *be* an upper limit. But if there are such creatures around Vardinoy, they would be extremely elusive and you would only see them by chance—eels are very territorial and they don't like it much when their habitat's disturbed. That's one plausible explanation for why many of the sightings happened during or right after a major storm."

"How would we ever prove they exist, then?"

Elsuba shrugged, as if to say *That's* your *problem, buddy, not mine!* "By deduction and by keeping a sharp eye out for indirect evidence. No scientist has ever seen a giant squid before, either, but we know they exist because we've found half-digested pieces of them inside the bellies of sperm whales. Just because no one's ever documented this hypothetical species of eels doesn't mean they don't exist, either."

"*Eels*, Elsuba? Can't you give me something more exciting than eels?"

"Look, Allen! I'm a doctor, not a zoologist; all I'm saying is that based on the environmental data I've collected, eels seem the most plausible candidate. And what's so disappointing about eels, anyway? If you discovered a colony of thirty-foot-long eels, they would qualify as 'monsters' by anyone's definition! I invested a lot of time and effort preparing that data for you— the least you can do is to keep an open mind."

"I appreciate all the work you did, Elsuba, but I didn't ask you to do it."

"No, but you bloody well should have, because without basic science to support the myths, all you and Poppa have in your 'archives' is the world's largest collection of 'blob' stories!"

"Oh, yes, now the truth comes out. You've never believed in this expedition from the first, have you?"

Elsuba returned his scowl with interest. "Since you brought it up, Allen, no—I don't believe in it. I think you'll be damned lucky to find a giant eel. We've been here almost a month, and there's been no sign of anything more exotic."

"God damn it, Elsuba, your own father's as committed to this project as I am!"

"Yes, he is, and I don't understand *why*. He's a realist who's never had much patience with fantasies. He and I can have a great conversation about any topic under the sun—*except this expedition!* The minute I bring up the subject, he just shakes his head and goes completely silent. Look, I agreed to come along because my father said he wanted a really good doctor close at hand in case of an emergency—when he used the words 'really good doctor,' he put the hook into me, knew all the right buttons to push. Okay, so I agreed to be the medic, out of loyalty to Poppa. But also because I really wanted to see an old friend again—his name was Warrener and you might have met him long ago."

"Your father has very good reasons for being here, but if he hasn't revealed them to you, I won't violate his trust by explaining. Trust me, Elsuba: this is not an old man's idle whim or some kind of weird tax writeoff for the

Poulsen Corporation. He may be ready to tell you now—the next time you two are talking privately, just come right out and ask him."

"You're right, Allen. I'll try to do that before I leave."

"Before you *what?*"

"Leave. Depart. Vamoose. Bye-bye. I'm going to Vesturoy on the next supply run and from there back to Torshavn. If I'm going to set up my own practice before winter, I have a great deal of work to do. Surely you can understand."

"Elsuba . . . don't go. Not now! Or at least not until I've atoned for being such an asshole."

"From what I've seen and heard, Allen, you would need four or five reincarnations to balance the books in that department. Let me try putting it another way. I was *born* a Faeroese, Allen. I grew up looking at stuff like this every day. The sea, the mountains, the puffins, the clouds—because the islands are my homeland, I do love them; but for God's sake, Allen, I can't get excited about how 'exotic' and 'spectacular' it is. To me, it's just 'home'—and I've been stuck on this barren rock for almost a month now, with virtually nothing to do. Except for the day we found that ruined church, I've been bored out of my mind. That's the main reason why I undertook this research project—just to give myself something to do! I'm sorry, Allen, but I've made up my mind—there's absolutely no reason for me to stay here any longer."

"What if we *do* find something really amazing on Vardinoy?"

"For your sake, I truly hope you do, but that's got nothing to do with *me.* If you and your companions do find the 'monster,' and it holds still long enough for you to take its picture, then you'll become famous and probably rich, too. You can buy Vardinoy and turn it into Elsuba World, if that's what will satisfy you. But Elsuba herself, in the flesh, has had all of Vardinoy she can take. If there's a genuine emergency, there's a very capable doctor at the Vesturoy clinic. Oh, for God's sake, Allen, stop looking at me like that! I'm not deserting your expedition—I'm just not *needed* here!"

"Yes, you are. *I* need you to be here. . . ."

"Define your terms, please."

He did not know this adult woman well enough to read her nuances of expression, but at that moment she wore a mask of indifference.

"All right, fine, let me lay it all out in the daylight. Coming to the Faeroes when I did, at that particular point in my life, and then meeting and falling in love with you . . . and then having to sail away only ten days after discovering you—Elsuba, it warped the whole structure of my life! I'm not delusional; I know how I've allowed that one experience to distort my perceptions of people and events—I know all that! But the obsession took over when I was too young and too romantic to defend myself. It's too deep, it's been inside me too many years for me to uproot it now. But at least I have the real flesh-and-blood Elsuba close at hand, and she's gradually replacing the mythical girl I put on a pedestal long ago. If you leave Vardinoy now, the fantasy Elsuba will reclaim her throne—I know it sounds crazy, but I can't control the mythical woman I made up in the first place."

"Hold it, Allen! I will not be blackmailed! You're telling me that unless I hang around as some kind of ambulatory therapy-fetish, you're going to turn into a full-blown schizophrenic or something? That's about the vilest kind of threat you can make to a physician, don't you realize? Well, that settles it—I'm out of here in the morning, and for all I care you can create a dozen new psychoses nobody's ever heard of—just don't do it until I'm gone, okay?"

His voice was rising. "There is *more to it than that,* lady! It was from your lips that I first heard the name 'Vardinoy'; you planted that seed, you made the Faeroe Islands the most magical place in the world for me, and I think that gives you a stake in what happens here! There's a direct line running back through time, from this moment on Vardinoy back to the moment you and I shared that first kiss." Allen held out his hand and Elsuba was surprised to see that it was rock-steady and his eyes held no unshed tears; for that reason alone, her impulse was to take his hand. She even moved to do so, but then pulled back her hand as though she'd seen a viper waiting to strike at first contact.

"Allen, what happens between two young people during the space of ten days is not 'love' so much as a kind of benign infection—a very high fever. Love takes much, much longer to. . . ."

"I know what I felt, Elsuba, and it was not just a fever-dream."

"Damn it, Allen I know what you felt, too! You were the most enchanting guy I'd ever made it with! You were so fucking *intense* that it made me a little afraid of you.

"You showed up in Tjornuvik, for God's sake, this tiny dismal fishing village on the arse-end of nowhere, the dark-eyed swashbuckling foreigner who actually was *writing a book!* The instant you crossed my threshold and shook my hand, you 'snowed' me like an avalanche. Honest to God, I couldn't wait

to crawl into bed and masturbate with your face in the center of my fantasy
. . . what the fuck are you laughing about?"

"Oh, just the fact that I jerked off twice that night thinking about *you!*"

These mutual confessions might have defused the situation, and the laugh
they shared was reviving, but Elsuba had rehearsed her resignation speech
too many times for the emotions behind it to simply wilt away under the
warmth of a little camaraderie. With a sigh, she doggedly pressed on:

"Since the day we parted, when I was too chickenshit to face you and left
that farewell letter instead, I have often—*often,* Allen—thanked God that
we shared those days and nights. It *was* a lovely time, Allen; I honor it and
cherish its memory. But it was not the only lovely time in my life, and I
daresay not in yours either. I am glad, I'll always be glad, that we were lovers,
but I refuse to build a shrine to your memory, and you should never have
built one to mine! Why is it that a part of you just keeps holding on and
holding on? Don't you want to shed that burden and start living a real, committed life again, without always having to compare every new person you
meet to an impossible, consecrated ideal?"

"Elsuba, I—"

"No, Allen, hear me out, please! There's another reason for my leaving.
You see, before we actually met again, that rainy night in Poppa's townhouse,
I'd sort of gotten it into my head that it might be really great to sleep
together again, just for *auld lang syne,* you know? But then I realized you
were spoken for, and I thought: well, of course he would be, wouldn't he?
And that was cool too, because I liked Karen immediately, and the two of us
might have become good friends, if we could only exorcise *your* bloody interfering ghosts! She's a good, strong woman, and you make her put up with so
much horseshit that I don't know how she stands it!"

"Elsuba, I—"

"Don't even *try* to interrupt me now, Allen—don't you dare! There's one
more point I want to make: ever since I joined this crazy tea party, you've
either ignored me or treated me as though I were made out of glass. My God,
Allen, you haven't even asked a single question about my life since we went
our separate ways! How do you think that makes me feel? I've led rather a full
and interesting life, by God. My existence didn't just *freeze* in one place on the
day you sailed away. I've become a doctor, I've been honored by my peers, I've
published some damn fine research papers, and I really wanted to tell you

about those things. I wanted you to be proud of me. But you never showed the slightest concern for Elsuba-the-grown-up-woman. You could hardly stand the thought of her, because her very presence was tarnishing the golden statue of Elsuba-the-Goddess. *What gave you the right to seal me in amber?*

"And now, everybody else in your entourage can't decide how to relate to me because they're waiting for a cue from you and *you haven't given them one!* They start a friendly conversation, and suddenly they withdraw as though I were radioactive! I don't enjoy being treated like some kind of living legend, Allen. So there's the lot, all the reasons why I'm getting out of here as soon as I can. Are you any happier for knowing them?"

Allen didn't have a name for the emotion raging through him. He was surprised to hear the coldness in his voice: "Before you go, I'd be grateful if you examined Karen thoroughly. She seems utterly exhausted, and she isn't sleeping well. I'm afraid she might be coming down with something. . . ."

Sarcasm oozed from her tone: "You mean one of the many tropical diseases that thrive in these latitudes?"

"Very cute."

"As a matter of fact, I already have examined her—she came to me yesterday. Yes, she is exhausted, and she's not sleeping well, so I gave her some industrial-strength tranquilizers and a bottle of vitamins. What's really undermining her is some vague but very deep sense of malaise, and frankly I'm not sure where that's coming from. Now, she would rather submit to torture than tell you this, but you ought to know: when you didn't immediately start following me around with your tongue hanging out or frantically trying to get me into your bed any time Karen was out of range for five minutes, she really felt enormously relieved. You scored some major points, even though you didn't earn them. Do not misjudge her, Allen. If you treat her with respect, she will be the comfort of your old age. If you don't, she is perfectly capable of walking out of your life forever."

"Spare me the lecture, Doc—don't you think I know that?"

Now Elsuba did take his hand.

"I'm sorry it worked out like this, Allen. Truly I am."

"Do what you have to do, Elsuba."

He turned and left the room without another word, a man cut loose from the mooring posts of old dreams, his heart in freefall and his mind as tight as a cramped muscle.

Eiden Poulsen spent that night in the captain's cabin of the *Laertes*, ostensibly because he needed to preside, by radiophone hookup, over a board-of-directors meeting in the morning. That was true, but his real reason for spending the night aboard was not corporate business, but his ongoing private investigation into the origins and affairs of Andreas Dahl. After a rowdy dinner with the crew, Eiden locked himself in the communications room and began methodically contacting the employees he had put on the case. By midnight, he had collected enough new information to justify a conference with Warrener. And one of the things they must decide, Eiden reluctantly concluded, was just how much information they needed to share with the others. When Eiden came out of the cramped communications room, he felt starved for cool fresh air. He opened a bottle of cold aquavit from the refrigerator in his cabin and climbed up to the starboard bridge wing, where there was just room enough to open a folding chair and stretch his legs. The night was clear, and they were far enough north for the "Midnight Sun" effect to display an attenuated twilight glow all night long. Eiden knew that as a consequence of tonight's fresh intelligence, he would be forced to replay the mind-movie of his son's death; better to face it wide awake and defiant, sitting in the captain's chair of a man-o-war, here beneath God's honest and clear Nordic sky, than to grapple with it in the vortex of a nightmare. This way, he had *some* control; and he was going to need all the control he could muster if he were going to unravel a skein of events so hopelessly beyond his ken. He gagged briefly from too big a swallow, and while he struggled to regain control over his breathing, his gaze came to rest on the tiny horizon-smudge of lights that represented Norduroy. He briefly considered a closer peek, using the big range-finding glasses, but rejected the idea—if he actually saw a Gray Boat moving in the straits, his gaze upon it would be so venomous that its crew might sense his emotions and suddenly *know* there was a mortal enemy close by. They must not let Dahl suspect that they were on to him, for Dahl's schemes—whatever they were—seemed pretty far advanced. As Eiden saw it, the Expedition's main advantage was that Dahl regarded them as a pack of naïve eccentrics. Let him continue to think that. Eiden needed time to devise a counterplan, and for that he would need to call on Allen Warrener's rusty but once-impressive grasp of strategy.

Is it once again time to go to war?

The Gray Boat fishermen had brought his son to the tiny clinic on Vesturoy; four lean and stone-faced men who were uncommunicative but who were bound to obey the unwritten code of mariners: if you find a survivor from a sunken vessel, you must render him aid. To the Vesturoy constable and the doctor who ran the local clinic, a spokesman for the Gray Boat crew recounted the barest facts: there had been a sudden savage squall out in the straits last night, and this morning, on their way to their usual fishing grounds, the Gray Boat's crew had spotted the overturned keel of a capsized vessel, and this single survivor clinging, half dead, to the rudder. They had rescued him and brought him to the nearest medical facility—their duty was discharged—now they were going back to their normal day's activity.

Better if the boy had gone down with his ship! Drowning is a terrible death, but the human brain shuts down at the same instant the sense of panic becomes all-consuming . . . and at that point, a drowning man no longer knows *he is drowning; Merciful Oblivion shrouds his final spasms. Eiden had no idea just how much of his son's brain was still functioning during the final hours of his life, but he prayed for Oblivion to come swiftly and for consciousness not to return. In addition to a skull fracture that should have killed him outright, Kristofur's jaw was broken, his tongue bitten in half, his right lung pierced by splintered ribs, and God alone knew what his other internal injuries were.*

The worst of it, though, were the ghastly necrotic blue swellings that continued to creep over more and more of his skin as Eiden kept vigil, producing a foul-smelling seepage through cracks in his skin. By late afternoon, the stench was so unbearable that Eiden was about to ask the doctor for a pair of autopsy noseplugs . . . and at just that moment, his son's eyes fluttered open, full of nightmarish awareness.

One look and Eiden knew his son wasn't seeing a hospital room; he was almost certainly hallucinating the presence of whatever-it-was that had last filled his sight before he passed out, clinging to the upturned keel of a capsized ship. During the U-boat war, escort captains perforce became connoisseurs of fear, but Eiden had never seen greater terror on any man's face than what he saw on the ravaged face of his son. It could only have been the look of a man confronting a form of death so shockingly unexpected that the sight of it had burned out the connection between optic nerve and mind. Eiden began to move toward the bed, his hand extended, his son's name gently forming on his lips, but halfway there he saw a terrible change— Kristofur's eyes began to bulge, the cords on his neck became swollen, engorged, as though inexorable pressures were inflating every cavity in his body. And at the instant his hand made contact, his son's face . . . erupted. Kristofur screamed open the bandages holding his jaw together. Eiden heard the rustle of splintering bones and rending sinews. Flakes of indigo-crusted skin fell away as the boy struggled to rise; and when the scream finally emerged, it rose on a geyser of bloody fluids and liquefied bone, a scarlet fountain as thick and rich as clotted cream, accompanied by the hiss and fart of vile gases, so that even as his son finally and mercifully died, Eiden Poulsen's only possible response was to hurl a projectile of vomit into the corpse's face.

Now, on the bridge of his ship, he shuddered at the memory. He glanced at the chronometer and was astonished to see that it was almost 4:00 A.M.; in the northern sky, a shooting star winked mockingly at him.

Go to bed, old man. Tonight, you grasped one end of a long slippery thread, and who knows what you will find at the other end?

If I know one thing for certain, it is this: the sea did not kill my son. It may have sunk his ship, but it did not slay him. The sea doesn't do that to a man.

Once Eiden had accepted the awful reality of his son's death, the hardest thing to reconcile was the certainty that he would *never know* what the boy had seen, or imagined he was seeing, in his final seconds of awareness. Eiden's rage had no target, no focus, not even a name. It was as though something had risen from the depths of the Atlantic solely to inflict a terrible doom on Kristofur, and then drawn back into the eternal frigid dark, leaving only an enigma so impossible to resolve that it would be a lingering torment for the rest of Eiden's days.

Or so he had believed, until he saw the corrupted flesh on that old fisherman's arm in Tjornuvik; until he saw the Gray Boats of Norduroy, where men lived who had pulled his son from the sea and who knew more than they had said to the constable on Vesturoy.

In his seafaring days, he had entrusted his ship to intuitions less certain than the one that gripped him now: there *was a connection* linking these circumstances; there were hard-eyed men on Norduroy who could tell him what had killed his son; and Andreas Dahl might well know their names.

Eiden slept, finally, for a few hours, never leaving the captain's chair. A quick raid on the ship's medical kit quashed the hangover, and by the time he radioed the campsite he felt both rested and energized. He requested Allen and Elsuba—no one else—to join him in his cabin at their earliest convenience.

431

When the three were gathered and the door shut, Eiden plunged right in: "As you both know, I have tasked a number of my employees to do a little snooping in regard to our friend Mr. Dahl. Last night I got some interesting information. According to the official records, there was no one named Andreas Dahl born on Suduroy—not in all the years since the Danish bureaucracy started keeping such data. In fact, there is no record of anyone named Andreas Dahl being born on *any* of the islands, not during the applicable range of dates. The only island for which such records do not exist is Norduroy. The people there have always refused to send that kind of information to the government in Torshavn, and nobody's ever called them on it. If a birth certificate exists for that man, you'd only find it on Norduroy."

"Can't something like that be subpoenaed?" asked Elsuba.

"Surely. But by doing that, we would alert them—whoever 'they' are—to the fact that we're suspicious. You can be certain that all documents pertaining to Mr. Dahl will vanish long before a magistrate arrives to search for them. The point is not documentation, but proof positive that the bastard's lied to us, which in my book means that we cannot take any of his statements at face value."

"Agreed," said Allen. "But lying about your birthplace isn't a major crime. What else did you find out?"

Eiden cleared his throat and nervously clenched his hands. "Allen, I think I'd prefer to share that information with my daughter in private . . . if you don't mind. It's time Elsuba learned the full truth about how her brother died."

"Oh, my God," whispered Elsuba.

"And after she hears what I'm about to tell her, I don't think she'll be in such a hurry to leave Vardinoy."

Allen nodded and opened the cabin door. On impulse, he leaned over and kissed Elsuba's forehead before exiting. "I'll be in the galley, wolfing down a huge breakfast. Just buzz the intercom when you want me to rejoin you."

Forty minutes later he reentered the cabin. Elsuba glanced at him fiercely, her face pale, her hands balled into fists. For an instant, she looked to be on the verge of throwing a punch at him.

"All right, Allen, you'll get your wish: I'm staying. How could I leave Poppa to deal with this alone? But right this minute, I wish I'd never met you or ever heard about this goddamned island!"

"Elsuba!" Eiden's voice was sharp and very patriarchal. "Allen is not responsible for what happened to your brother, nor is he to blame for my current state of mind—my 'obsession,' as you persist in calling it. Like it or not, we're all caught up in this thing together."

Just then, the intercom buzzed, and they heard excitement in the voice that emerged from the speaker: "Cap'n Poulsen! Cap'n Poulsen, sir!!"

Eiden's expression of alarm changed to one of relief when the breathless radioman explained the reason for his excitement: "Whale hunt sir! Damn big one!"

"How far away and in which direction?"

"West of Norduroy, heading into the straits. The Gray-Boats are tracking the herd, and they plan to drive it into the harbor at Vesturoy, in about two hours, they estimate. They've asked for the *Laertes* to broadcast the traditional signal, as they haven't a powerful enough radio."

"By God, signalman Holmboe, take down this message and broadcast it far and wide, giving the coordinates of Vesturoy harbor: '*Haul in your nets, all true and brave Faeroese, and join us in a whale-slaying!*'"

Eiden put Birgir in temporary command of the ship; he declared that he'd seen enough whale hunts and would prefer to stay in the camp, using the computer uplink to do some more "snooping" with regard to Andreas Dahl and his community. Allen drove the Land Rover back with all the zeal of a stock-car racer at Darlington, and found, as he'd expected, a beehive of activity. Birgir re-hitched the trailer to the Rover, and Preston immediately began cramming it full of camera gear, aided, to a certain degree, by Dewey, who was so excited by the prospect that he kept jumping from one foot to the other, like a kid with a full bladder trying to get his teacher's attention. When Allen emerged from the driver's seat, Dewey ran over and hugged him effusively.

"You da man, Fearless Leader, you da man!"

Brother, these guys are pumped! Even Norma and Andreas Dahl were there, sketchbooks in hand, the very picture of innocent curiosity.

"Anybody seen Karen?"

Elsuba sidled closer and said quietly: "I don't think she plans to go, and don't you make a big fuss about it."

Determined to do exactly that, Allen strode to their tent. There he found Karen, dull-eyed, sitting apathetically on the edge of her cot, dejectedly smoking a cigarette.

"Hey, better get ready, girl! This is the chance of a lifetime!"

"I'm sorry, Allen, but I just don't feel like going."

He fought to control his temper. "Are you nuts? I showed you pictures of the whale hunts! You said you'd love to see one 'before Greenpeace has them outlawed.' Your exact words!"

"Yes, and I meant them at the time; but this morning, I'm just not in the mood to watch a bunch of big helpless mammals get butchered."

"Oh, spare me the sermon. This isn't a baby-seal bop, Karen, this is the real thing! Man against brute! Berserker Vikings with blubber knives! Primitive blood-lust! The chance of a lifetime to see this ritual!" He was imploring her now, completely knocked off-balance by this particular mood-swing and feeling almost betrayed.

"Just go on without me, Allen. I'll be fine here with Eiden." When she lifted her face, he couldn't tell whether she was sorry to compromise his fun or merely impatient for him to leave. Pissed off at her attitude, Allen made it easier by petulantly throwing a few items into an overnight bag and stomping out of the tent.

Elsuba opened the Land Rover's rear door and gave him an I-told-you-so look when he slid on to the seat beside her. "She's not coming, I take it."

"No, Madame Karen is not coming; Madame Karen has the vapors!" He slammed the door. Everyone but Dewey was already jammed into the vehicle. The ex-biker was trying to cram a few more items into the trailer. Preston impishly leaned out of a side window and baited Dewey with one of their hoariest two-liners:

"Hey, Dewey, you comin'?"

"Nah, boss, jus' breathin' hard! Hwah-hah-ha!" Still chortling from that sledgehammer witticism, Preston and Dewey high-fived each other and whooped. Warrener relaxed—this trip was going to be okay as long those two could still laugh.

Just before Birgir turned the ignition, Dewey stood up on the trailer, untied his pony tail, threw out both arms, and bellowed a grizzly bear's war cry that filled the echoing hills.

27.

THE WHALE-KILLING

Preston Valentine snuggled into the shoulder stock that braced his camera against the trawler's vibration and squinted into the viewfinder. He panned experimentally from left to right, from Vesturoy to the open water of the straits between there and Vardinoy, covering the arc smoothly, with a fluid steadiness born of much practice. The motion only bobbled once, when the heads of Norma and Andreas Dahl crossed the invisible crosshairs. Preston smiled grimly. How like a telescopic rifle sight one of these zooms could be! The notion did not trigger a vision of high-powered bullets shattering their skulls—such fantasies of revenge were alien to him, even as he savored one in passing. Today was not a fantasy-time; he wanted to be fully alert to the realities that would soon be passing before this same lens. He'd felt pain earlier, when he saw that Norma and her new mate were brazenly attaching themselves to the occasion, and he had seen a tremor of displeasure cross Warrener's face as well. But Norma was still technically a member of the expedition, and Dahl had not been dis-invited; indeed, he continued to behave with his customary chill courtesy.

Preston did expose a few feet of Norma and her consort sketching—it might make a good cutaway shot when he edited this footage later.

He felt better for doing that. He had learned, during his long career in a volatile industry, to temper his innate romanticism with stoic pragmatism. Given a situation which was professionally enjoyable, and given, simultaneously, a personal hangup that could suck the juice right out of that experience, he had learned to put all personal problems into a mental safe-deposit box for the duration; with practice, it became no harder than pushing a bit of gristle to one side of an otherwise appetizing meal. And today, he damned well didn't feel like brooding over his heartache; later, he would have painful issues to deal with, but for today he had banished them. The truth of the moment was that Preston Valentine, camera poised to record a bloody ritual few outsiders had ever witnessed, was in his element—and he loved it. This was not one of those daydreaming projects he and Warrener used to bullshit each other about; this was *happening* and his camera was *there!* He would film the whale-kill with the same imagistic brilliance Hemingway had deployed to write about bullfights. Why settle for less? He *was* an artist, what? Norma or no Norma, monster or no monster, he and his oldest friend had committed to this adventure; they were *here;* it was really going down; and on that level, Preston Valentine was happier than he had been in years.

Dewey Tucker was burning up film magazines already, strafing everything in sight with his zoom lens. Even though the whales were not yet visible, there was plenty to see: the flotilla from Vesturoy had finally jockeyed into position, like a waterborne chorus waiting for a principal to come on stage. After changing film, Dewey bent back to the eyepiece and began shooting once more. At the start of the pan, his view was filled with the bobbing, brightly colored boats from Vesturoy, oars shipped and outboard motors idling, slickered crewmen tense and expectant. Dewey zoomed in for vignette closeups of their faces: their eyes squinting against the glare, their hands gripping the shafts of their myriad weapons. Muted-copper sunlight struck from the blades of flensing implements, sword-like blubber knives, and long javelin-thin harpoons. As tradition dictated, this was a wholly masculine task force, comprising grandfathers, men in their prime, and adolescent boys, their eyes goggling with excitement. The armada also carried numerous erstwhile whaleslayers whose dress and awkward postures proclaimed them to be shopkeepers, school teachers, or postal clerks, not hardened fishermen. Yet in their eyes was the same straining ferocity that burned in the gaze of the true sea dogs.

Most of the horizon in front of the boat line was filled with the dark green bulk of Vesturoy Island. The shore was peppered with onlookers, gathered most thickly on the two arms of high ground that curved out from the breakwater. It was into that cul-de-sac that the whales would be driven. The boat line extended in a shallow curve out from the southern end of the bay to an open flank in the straits, perhaps six hundred yards from end to end. Birgir had stopped the *Laertes* slightly behind the northern end of the boat line, both to keep the big ship out of the boats' way and to give the onboard cameras an optimal position from which to film the action.

Preston traversed his camera past the last boat on the open flank and extended his zoom to its limit. Like a row of game beaters thrashing the veldt, the driving contingent of Norduroy boats steered the whales into the mouth of the waiting trap. In front of them, a great expanse of blurred water demonstrated both the size and the agitation of the whale pod. Ghostly puffs of water erupted, as though machine-gun bullets were raking the sea. Through the telephoto lens, Preston fancied he could almost smell the creatures' raw wet funk.

He cut away from the approaching whales and got some closeups of Birgir standing picturesquely at the trawler's helm. Lowering the camera, he asked: "How long before they get here?"

Birgir's eyes swung from the end of the boat line to the approaching patch of froth, now broken by quick winks of glistening black. "No more than ten minutes, I should say."

"Can you tell me what's going to happen—what to expect? So I'll know where to keep the camera pointed."

Birgir gestured with his hands: "Well, the Norduroy boats will just keep driving the whales straight into the open end of the boat line. Once that's done, they will put their boats in line next to ours, sealing off the mouth of the bay, and then the whole line will start moving in toward shallow water, driving the whales before it."

"Why don't the whales just put on some speed right now and head back into deep water? I thought they were supposed to be so fucking smart."

"They are: compared to a herring, they're bloody Einsteins. But when they panic, they revert to pure herd instinct. There are no leaders, no individual whales to show them a way out of the trap. It's always struck me as very strange, how they will allow themselves to be driven to their doom. Up until the very moment when they bump their bellies on the shallow bottom, they could easily escape just by sounding and going under the keels. But they never do."

"Sounds like a one-sided fight to me."

"Well, the whales don't just lie there waiting passively to be butchered. Just like any species of cornered animal, they'll fight back—and some of them weigh three tons, you know. A berserk three-ton mammal is not 'helpless. . . .' "

Preston moved from the bridge wing to the forecastle deck, so intent on the approaching whales that he stepped right between Norma and Dahl in order to get the best shot, and was hardly aware of their proximity. He was, however, mildly surprised to see Warrener and Elsuba standing together at the bow, pointing at the whales, taking pictures, and talking with an ease and volubility far different from the strained, formal conversations he had witnessed before. He had time to think: *this place is putting us all through some heavy-duty changes*—and then there was no more time for thinking, only for filming.

The whales rushed into the open neck of the boat formation, hitting the water, and each other, like a hundred freight cars careering into a pond. Preston could hear their mewling chirps of fear and grunts of exertion as they crowded into a dense mass, pouring into the wide end of a funnel from which there could be no escape. Heaving black bodies slashed the sea into lather. Serried ranks of dorsal fins ripped the foam like medieval flails. Preston could feel the nearness of the animals as palpably as a change in air pressure. The air he breathed turned raw and rubbery, almost as though the beasts were sweating.

Then the pod was past. The Gray Boats, nearly twenty of them, filled with grim-faced men, moved to close the northern segment of the line. While this maneuver was being accomplished, the whales kept plowing forward until a sense of the impending shallows passed through their ranks. Their forward motion slowed, shudders of confusion and hesitation passed through them, and clusters of the animals began to move in circles, their sinuous bodies sliding over one another, flukes lashing the water, blowholes puckering, venting angry spray with popping-beer-can sounds that were startlingly loud.

Now the boat line began to move forward slowly. Crewmen began to whack the water with oars and blades, shouting and cursing and banging harpoon shafts against the thwarts of their boats.

A ritualistic excitement tingled along Allen Warrener's spine, needling into the caves of his heart like some thick, hot drug. His face was flecked with drying spray where the wind had caught the plume of a passing whale and bent it into a feather of fetid vapor whose last falling droplets seemed to baptize him. His muscles ached with an almost-forgotten longing for violent movement—the whales, it seemed, were not the only creatures who could communicate herd emotions. As they sensed the shallows and began to recoil upon themselves, a shiver of expectancy went through the whole line of sea-flogging boatmen. He felt it; Elsuba, who had of her own volition stationed herself at his side, also felt and responded to it. He registered—oddly without surprise—the sensation of her hand grasping his arm.

Passing into waist-deep water now, tightening like a noose, the boat line compressed into a warlike formation—harpoons extended like the spear points of a marching phalanx. The whales, boiling in a slick dense mass between the boats and the shoreline, burst the sea with their panic, their instinct of pending doom. An impatient young sailor, balancing precariously at the front of a skiff that was moving recklessly fast, arched back like a javelin thrower and loosed a thin bright harpoon trailing a retrieval rope. It hissed into the fringes of the herd, striking the dorsal fin root of a straggler. A current of fear jolted through the herd, a communal spasm, as the spent weapon nicked rubbery hide, flicked a small arrowhead of blood into the air, then fell free, its thrower feverishly hauling it back. A cheer sang from the boats: first blood!

Crazed now, the whales hammered into the shallows. As they roweled the bottom, the sea bloomed velvet clouds of mud. The touch of solid earth against their bellies triggered madness. As more and more of the beasts sought to occupy an ever-shrinking volume of water, their density became insupportable, and from a herd, they degenerated into a mob. They pounded the sea into a gleaming black froth as four animals fought desperately to fill a space sufficient to hold two.

Then the boatmen were on them: harpoon volleys rose and fell on the outer edge of the whale-mass. Geysers of dirty foam crashed back over the crowding boats. Terrified whale spouts blew clear, then—as blades sank deep—explosively jetted crimson. Cringing from the ring of pain, the whale-mass grounded into the shallows, wallowing and wild. Men in the nearest boats looked at the beasts eye to eye.

Allen's attention was diverted by some commotion on the deck behind him. The trawler's crew was hotly beseeching Birgir for permission to lower the boats and join the kill. Laughing, he waved assent. As the sailors put the two lifeboats over the side, Allen saw that they had already, from God knew where, produced an arsenal of implements for cutting, slashing, and stabbing.

He also noticed Dewey, deep in an altercation with Preston. Preston was gesturing at the cameras, Dewey at the whales. Shrugging angrily, Preston waved away his rebellious assistant and resumed his filming.

By the time Dewey had secured permission, the lifeboat nearest him was already winching down. Dewey yelled at the crew to wait, then disappeared into the galley and emerged a few seconds later brandishing a fire axe. The trawlermen applauded the sight. Dewey peeled off his sheepskin jacket, then reached around with both hands and unbound his hair. The wind pulled it into coppery billows. Then he leaped into the boat and clapped his new comrades on their backs.

"Elsuba, I *am* going in that other boat!," Allen shouted, a sudden contagion bubbling in his blood.

"Allen, for God's sake just stay here and watch! If you don't know what you're doing, you can get very badly hurt in one of these things!"

"Of course I could!" Impulsively, he planted a kiss on her scowling lips. He spun free of her restraining hands, yelled at the occupants of the other boat, then ran over and stood beneath Preston's camera tripod on the bridge wing.

"Hand me down the video camera, Press! I am off to duel with Leviathan!"

"Am I surrounded by assholes today, or what?" muttered Preston, delivering the requested item. "Don't forget to keep wiping the spray off the lens."

Warrener tumbled awkwardly into the waiting boat. Davit lines hummed briefly, and they hit the water hard. Unbalanced by the camera weight, he sloshed into a pool of oily scupper water, filling his shoes with the stuff. The trawler men bent to their oars, and the boat jerked past the big ship's bow. As they cleared that high cleaver of gray steel, Allen saw Dewey's boat suddenly leap out from behind the port side, as though shoved forward by some giant Neptunian hand against the stern.

Dewey, wild with the knowledge that he was heading into the greatest rumble of his career, had simply taken command. He crouched in the bow, braced at a heroic, outthrust angle, knuckles white on the axe haft, teeth bared, hair streaming, shouting: "Row, you motherfuckers, row! Row till your goddamn lungs burst! Put your balls into it and ROW!" The crew might not have understood the words, but the blood lust behind them was unmistakable, and they wore the look of men who were willing to follow their impromptu captain not only into the midst of the whales, but, if he asked them to, straight into their open jaws.

Allen panned his camera as Dewey's boat rocketed past. Then he glanced quickly back at the trawler, saw Elsuba's anxious face, felt something open inside him at the recognition of her concern. He waved with tentative bravado, then turned back around before he could see her response. Then his boat entered the storm, and all his attention went toward keeping the camera steady as the boat began to lurch, pounded on all sides.

It was like lunging headfirst into a wet, clammy avalanche. The sea boiled, spewing up living black torpedoes. All around him, men cried out in excitement, fear, and consuming rage. The whale-mass had become a blood-streaked cauldron: beasts as long as twenty-five feet twisted and convulsed. Up close, the smell of their madness was heavy, dank, scorched by a ponderous electricity, a growing reek of blasted salt turned into iodine by waves of blood. Dead whales clogged the outer fringe of the mass, rolling heavily, leaking blood, stippled with shafts, split like vast soft pea-pods.

Some sailors chose their targets carefully, tracking a single beast with the concentration of gunners, then jabbing out with their harpoons in precise, economical motions. Others ganged up on the closest whale, closed with it and mauled it gracelessly, stabbing like alley fighters until it stopped moving, then hastening on to another, until their blades broke or sank and their arms grew too weary for more.

To Dewey, it seemed that the action was taking place in a state of slow-motion purity, a perfect feedback loop between the violence within the slayer and the terror of the slain, each emotion intensifying the other.

He dragged deeply on the mood, belted it down, opened his veins and mainlined it; went, in fact, berserk—not in the clichéd sense of the word but in the precise Viking-age historical meaning of it, so that his condition was recognized and understood instantly by those around him. Cheered on by his crew, their own weapons now drooling red, he led them like a demented coxswain through the logjam of bellied corpses, through the lashing fringes of the dwindling herd, straight into the heart of the tempest, where an impossible tangle of whales were digging themselves into the bottom mud in water no deeper than a man's thighs. Flukes lashed down—great dripping guillotine blades driven by mountains of hysterical muscle.

Dewey felt the wind and spray of their passing as his boat rammed head-on into the thickest formation. While the crew dipped blades on either side, Dewey knelt in the bow, knees dug into the keel, striking huge two-handed blows with his axe. He was slick with blood: his hair was matted with it, his beard knotted into soggy clumps with it. Blood and foam made a mottled river down his chest, and he spat bloody oysters of sea water back at the whales.

Finally, a violent lunge from one stricken beast tore the slippery axe from his hands and bore it under. Undeterred, Dewey took up an oar and simply began beating the whale with it. On the fourth blow, the oar snapped. Howling, Dewey drew his Bowie knife, and before anyone could restrain him, leaped from the boat on to the back of a wallowing fourteen-footer that was grinding its belly against the bottom, curling its fluke like a scorpion trying to sting. As Dewey landed and dug his knees into the creature's flanks, it spouted violently into his face. Dewey plunged the knife into its blowhole. A massive shudder humped him up and down like a bronco rider. Two more strikes of the knife brought up sluggish blood. The sight of it threw Dewey into a renewed frenzy: he clawed at the wound with his knife, ripping, digging, until, each time he struck, his hands vanished to the elbows in a thick weltering dome of gore.

Eventually, the beast lay still beneath him. Dewey sheathed his weapon, leaned down on the dead whale like a man kissing a spent lover, then slid off, dazed, into the surf. Narrowly dodging both whales and flying missiles, he waded ashore, found a spot, and hunkered down to watch the last of the slaughter, his eyes burning above rust-colored cheeks.

Allen had been absorbed in capturing the incident on videotape, and he was surprised to see, when he turned his attention back to the wider view, that more than half the pod was already dead. A fair number of boats, out of weapons, had withdrawn to the outer circumference of the killing circle, their exhausted occupants struggling to light cigarettes with wet red hands.

As Allen adjusted the focus, he centered on a small boat, one that had been pressed back until now, sliding forward as larger craft withdrew. In it were two youngsters and a fierce old man, grandfatherly, gripping a heavy harpoon with an old-fashioned curved tip, a relic from another era. The old man urged his young rowers on, toward a heaving fifteen-footer that had broken free close by their boat. In his excitement, or his diminished strength, the old man misjudged his throw and struck the whale a glancing, slicing blow that opened a superficial gash near the tail fin. The lance fell out and the old man struggled to haul in the line attached to its shaft. He did not see the tail fin, spitting blood in a scarlet pinwheel, rise towering above him. When it fell, like a dynamited building, it struck the boat inches from his feet, flipping him like a giant spatula. His mouth open in a soundless cry, he collided in midair with the upswing of the fin, then fell, his back bent at a crazy angle, astonished eyes open to the sky. He was dead before he hit the water.

Allen's boat had closed in too, and the crewmen were snapping out their own blades. The man next to him, a stubble-faced trawler veteran whose eyes nested in a web of adobe creases, was momentarily distracted by the spectacle of the old man's death. While his attention was diverted, a dying whale rolled suddenly on to his extended harpoon. The shaft whipped up, cracking the man's forearm with a sound like a small-caliber gunshot. Groaning and clutching his wound, the sailor rolled back into the boat.

Instinctively, Allen grabbed the harpoon with one hand. At the touch of its rough wet shaft, his whole purpose changed. He carefully replaced the camera in its waterproof case. He hefted the weapon—which was considerably heavier than it looked—and took aim at the nearest whaleback. After glancing quickly at the *Laertes* to make sure Elsuba *was* watching, he made his throw.

There was not much muscle, and less skill, behind the toss. The blade penetrated a few inches, barely piercing the blubber, but still, he was enormously pleased with himself. The whale—not bothered one bit by Allen's shaft but simultaneously, and mortally, wounded by several others—corkscrewed wildly. Allen never had time to realize that it was not his harpoon that had caused this reaction, for the whale's movements flung the shaft right back at the thrower, striking him smartly on the side of his head.

Strong men chanted in a slow red dance as he dropped, senseless, on top of the sailor with the broken arm.

28.

CHAIN DANCE

Allen Warrener's face felt as fragile as an eggshell. He raised his eyelids very slowly and was puzzled by what he saw: a smoky rose-gray light seeping through a double-glazed window, which told him nothing. He cringed as an arc of sudden white cut through the comforting dusk, then retreated, elusive as a UFO. He heard someone moan; the voice was familiar, but the sound came from far away. Then the bright light returned, causing his pupils to dilate painfully. The bright light maneuvered in and out of fuzziness, like a comet passing through wool, and finally clicked off.

Brusque long-fingered hands applied pressure at several very tender points on his skull, and when he winced and tried to pull away, a voice he eventually recognized as Elsuba's commanded him to "Hold still, damn it! I'm almost done here, and you wouldn't like it if I had to start all over again. I don't want my handiwork ruined by an unruly patient." Her face came into view, a shadowy oblong blocking out the twilight, and Allen's surroundings finally jerked into focus. He was lying in a dormitory-like room, the only occupant of six beds.

"Where am I, and why do I feel so Godawful?"

Her hands fluttered, deftly snapping steel implements back into their cases.

"Be glad you can still feel *anything*—why you didn't break your neck is beyond me. We're in the Poulsen Corporation's sailors' dormitory behind my father's warehouse on Vesturoy, and the reason you feel so bad is that a two-thousand-pound whale tried to knock your head off. While you were out, I put sixteen stitches in your scalp. And a neat job I did of it, too. Here, take two of these before you try to do anything more strenuous than breathing."

Guidelines of Life from the sixties, No. 293: *When somebody offers you a free pill, take it.*

But these two capsules felt as large as plover's eggs, so he slopped a lot of water over his shirt trying to choke them down.

444

"That better be something good, and how long before it kicks in?"

"Ten minutes and, yes, I think in the sense that you mean the question, it's something 'good': the strongest Demerol in my medical bag-o-tricks. Here's a dozen more for later. Do not exceed two every five to six hours and—"

"I know," he interrupted. "Do not drive or attempt to operate heavy machinery! *Ouch!* What now?"

"Just covering the sutures with a bandage. Don't be such a baby." After she patted the corners into place, she leaned back and regarded him like a mother lecturing a naughty child. "You were a damned fool out there, Allen. And I'm afraid you have no future career as a harpooner."

"Yeah, I guess it was a pretty lame performance. But, Elsuba, I *did try.* I didn't do very well, but I did try."

"Yes, Allen, you did. And I realize how . . . important that was for you. I shouldn't tell you this, but as they were carrying your body back to the quay-side, one of the Vesturoy sailors turned to me and said, 'Your boyfriend may not know which end of the harpoon goes into the whale, but he's got balls the size of grapefruit!'"

"Well, that's something, anyhow. You're right, it was important to get in that boat and go for it. It was worth this crack in the head just to look up and see that you were watching. And watching like a woman who cared."

"Of course I care, Allen! Didn't you understand a single word I said the other day, when you and I were talking in the lab?"

"I heard you, yes, but I'm still working on the 'understand' part. Anyway, it was great that we saw a whale hunt together—before you leave, I mean."

"I'm not leaving, Allen; or don't you remember my telling you that either?" She smiled gravely down at him and touched his cheek with two cool fingers. "Not after this morning, when my father told me *everything* about my brother's death. How could I leave him to deal with this alone? It would be like desertion. I'm not sure I buy the theory that some sinister outside agent poisoned my brother and made his skin turn blue, but obviously Poppa does, so I'm going to stay close to him until he gets this obsession out of his system."

"I'm glad you're staying. And not just for the old reasons."

"Maybe that knock on the head did you some good!"

He began to draw up his knees, hesitated. "Okay for me to walk?"

"Sure; I think I would have noticed if you'd broken your leg too. But if anything suddenly starts to hurt, stop doing it."

He swung into a sitting position. There was already some distance between his consciousness and the pain—maybe he could go to the chain dance after all. Maybe Elsuba would go with him. Gingerly he touched the bandages, trying to ascertain their boundaries, and discovered that the patch covered half the left side of his skull.

"I'll be damned—the million-dollar wound," he laughed.

"The what?"

"A corny reference to old American war movies—pay no attention if I start babbling. We're not too late for the party, are we?"

"What party?"

"Isn't it a Faeroese tradition to hold a marathon chain dance after one of these whale slaughters?"

"God, you really *do* know a lot about our customs, just like Poppa said. I suppose it is a tradition; anything that happens more than three times in a decade *becomes* one. And to judge from their exuberance, I would say the good people of Vesturoy are as ready to party as any bunch I've ever seen. But they haven't started yet; I guess they're still dividing up the spoils among the boat crews who took part."

"Good, then we haven't missed anything. Would you like a date for the Dead-Whales Party, lady?"

"I'd better say 'yes' so I can keep you from harming yourself again!" She extended her hand and helped him rise to a standing position, a move that triggered a wave of dizziness and almost sent him crashing to the bed again.

"Take it easy, sailor! I only accept dates from men who can walk without my having to hold them up." Laughing easily now, arm in arm, they left the spartan dormitory and descended a cobbled side street, working their way to the edge of a large and boisterous crowd. Now Allen could see the source of that rose-gray tint that had puzzled him earlier: a sharp ridge of charcoal cloud squatted massively on the westward heights, muting the summer twilight into an eerie, artificial-looking dusk that seemed to well up from the sea itself. In front of them rose a mountainous pyramid of flensed and gutted whale meat, hauled up from the bay with block and tackle. The useful parts of each corpse had been already been cut out and divided amongst the participating crews according to an ancient formula, with the choicest bits awarded to the lucky sailors who first spotted the herd. The mound of tripe and what Elsuba called the "garbage parts"—what was left after the meat had been distributed—had been erected to serve as fuel for the giant bonfire. Tired but exhilarated men, draped in plastic aprons coated with blood, wandered about, kicking overlooked chunks of offal into the bay, where a blizzard of seagulls eagerly devoured this unprecedented bounty. Pointing to the mountain of guts, Elsuba clarified their significance: "Those are the combustible parts, and from the size of the pile, I would say we're in for a long night of partying. They must have brought out every bottle of booze on the island."

My, but that Demerol was starting to kick in nicely! He'd forgotten what a mellow high you could get from that particular medication; rediscovering it now was a most felicitous happenstance. He and Elsuba moved away from the crowd, tiptoeing over the larger leftovers, dodging streams of sanguine water where men with hoses were sluicing away the residual gore. She directed his gaze at the Gray Boats, now riding low in the water from the weight of their share of spoils. "Yet another example of Norduroy's legendary good luck on the sea."

"Yes, they beat everyone to the draw again. I swear, it's uncanny."

"You would think the crewmen would hang around the party. . . ."

Elsuba shivered. "I'll never be able to wave at one of those boats again, not after what Father told me this morning. The Vesturoy people have a saying: 'You look as cheerful as a Norduroy man at his mother's wake' . . . I wonder if they *ever* smile."

Someone called Allen's name and he swung around to the sight of Dewey Tucker, barely recognizable beneath a palimpsest of grue, cigarette clamped in his slitted mouth, the flensing blade in his right hand plunged deep into a slab of whale ribs, both feet hidden under coils of bluish guts. Preternaturally bright, his eyes still held a trace of the berserker's glow. "Ever see a rack-o-ribs this fuckin' big, Mr. Warrener?"

"Not in the hands of a Georgia cracker, I haven't. Just curious, but do you plan on taking a shower before the chain dance starts?"

Befuddled for a moment, Dewey looked down at the butcher's apron and the strew of whale guts piled around his feet.

"Yeah, I plan to, but I'm havin' too much fun to stop right this minute."

Elsuba leaned as close as she dared. "Would you like to spend the night with a lovely Faeroese girl, Dewey?"

"Does a bear shit in the woods, Miss Elsuba?"

"Then take my advice and put down your toys and go to the sailors' dorm and clean that muck off of yourself. When you start dancing around the bonfire, you're going to smell like a whale's fart. Help yourself to the spare clothes in one of the lockers, man! Haven't you noticed that cute little dark-eyed girl who keeps sneaking looks at you?"

Allen looked, but could not see anyone fitting that description. Still, because he wanted to, Dewey imagined this chimerical female fan and immediately dropped his carving tools. He was a man who fought whales! What female onlooker could resist his virile power tonight?

"Thanks for gettin' my priorities straight, Miss Elsuba," Dewey called over his shoulder as he trotted uphill toward the dormitory.

"A wild man with a heart of gold," muttered Elsuba. "After setting him up like that, I hope he does find a date for the evening."

Two old friends now, they strolled along the quay, pausing beside the tarpaulin-covered body of the fisherman who had died in the thick of the melee. Already, garlands of flowers covered his shroud. "They won't bury him until morning," said Elsuba, "probably at dawn, when the dances are finished. That way, his soul can still attend the celebration."

"You know, I sometimes wonder just how much of a dent Christianity made in these islands. . . ."

She smiled and looped her arm through his again. "Well, for nine hundred years or so, my Norse ancestors managed to mix up all the rites of Jesus *and* of Odin, and the contradictions never seemed to bother them. I figure it works just as well for their descendants too."

Pedestrian traffic thinned out at the far end of the breakwater. In order to gain a panoramic view of the scene as a whole, they climbed to a vantage point overlooking the harbor. Allen could scarcely take it all in—this was a sight that he would never see again, and that few outsiders had ever seen at all: held inland by the tide, a huge oil-slick of blood covered the sea from the beacon on the outermost breakwater to the mooring cleats on the water-front, a thick red gumbo laced with thousands of strips of sliced-off blubber. Incongruously, the shredded bits of blubber reminded him of nothing so much as those black curlicues of retread tire shed by eighteen-wheelers along the medians of any American freeway.

Out on the sea of blood, a few boats still moved, their passage marked by glutinous whorls; indeed, the smell of so much blood had charred the air, making it ride heavy and feral in the lungs, sour as iodine. "If the smell makes you nauseous, Allen, I have some nose plugs in my medical kit."

"Doesn't bother me all that much," he said, waving away her offer. Rather surprisingly, he found the fleshy charnel bouquet wholly appropriate.

A flock of small children chirred past, heading for a sequestered cove near land's end, where one young explorer had obviously discovered something wonderfully gross. "Some day, those kids will tell their kids about this day, and the Great Whale-Killing of Vesturoy will become a local legend. . . ." said Elsuba. Whatever the kids had found, it was exciting them greatly. This piqued the two adults' curiosity, so they strolled over to have a look. Eagerly the kids led them to an overhang and pointed down to the surf line. There, inflated like a surrealistic balloon by the gases of decomposition, floated the enormous intact all-in-one-piece gut of a very large pilot whale: a shiny lavender orchid, five feet across, both fascinating and repugnant. One of the older children, evidently responding to a dare, dropped a sharp, heavy rock on the center of the taut mass, puncturing the membrane, and releasing, like a jet of mustard gas, a fetid reminder of the beast's last meal. Warrener gagged and lurched for fresh air. That had been *too* intimate, and the children, shrieking, dispersed to tell their chums about the monumental gross-out they had perpetrated. The two adults watched the twilight's attenuating glow turn the sea a sullen purple, while the shift in tides brought a welcome land breeze that gently purified the waterfront air. They sat quietly on the headland, undisturbed by anyone, and talked as they watched the sea darken to a plum-colored glaze.

Somehow, the whale-kill had broken down the barrier between them, and the waxen warmth coating Allen's nerve ends—the fuzzy benediction of opiates—made him feel tranquil yet quietly, not aggressively, sexy; everything felt good; even the envelope of Elsuba's proximity was sexier than some hurried copulations he'd known; he was perfectly content simply to enjoy her company. There seemed no boundaries that their words couldn't cross, no topics that were off limits. Allen learned all about the difficulties encountered by a Faeroese "hick" girl trying to distinguish herself in the snooty ambience of Copenhagen Medical School; about her struggle to achieve such excellence that she simply could not be ignored; about her grueling internship; and about her affair with a famous—and married—heart surgeon, the devastating breakup of which had contributed to her decision to return to Tjornuvik and open her own modest practice. As he listened, Allen felt a growing admiration for her: she had defined her goals early and pursued them tirelessly. She had grit and resilience of spirit, and he did not doubt that, even if she never became a rich doctor, she would be a damned good one.

By the time the picnic tables were set up and all signs of the earlier butchery scrubbed away, their dialogue had become so easy and unconstrained that it seemed the most natural thing in the world to hold hands when they walked back to the site of the night's festivities.

Between two and three hundred revelers thronged the waterfront, cheering lustily as a color guard of torchbearers marched solemnly toward the waiting pyre. Elsuba explained that being designated a fire-kindler was an honor bestowed on the men who had distinguished themselves by bravery that day. After working their way through the crowd, each of the four men stationed himself at one corner of the pile—representing, Elsuba whispered, the four cardinal directions of the wind—and after a brief invocation, applied their brands to the base of the combustibles. When the four jets of flame conjoined as one, that was the signal for a parade of handcarts to appear from the shadows, each one groaning under its cargo of kegs. "Looks like they plan on some serious drinking," Allen commented. "Don't you?" Elsuba teased, pulling back the hem of her sweater to reveal a two-pint flask.

Mugs and bottles spread out from tapped kegs into many waiting hands. "The Entrance of the Tuns into Valhalla," Allen quipped, as a ruddy-cheeked jovial stranger handed him a mug the size of a spittoon and clinked a toast. As the bonfire rose to its maximum height, its flames sparkled from hundreds of bottles and steins.

"Once they get rolling," Elsuba briefed him, "don't be surprised if a total stranger comes up and hugs you and tries to drag you into the dancers' circle—there are no strangers at one of these fiestas, so please don't be shy. Not with anyone."

Now, that *was an interesting little verbal cue. . . .*

"I don't intend to be. I fought a whale too, remember?"

A burly Faeroese sailor loomed out of the crowd and slapped Warrener on the shoulder, crying, "Don't feel bad, my friend—there was courage in your throw, if not much skill! To be a good harpooner takes years of practice—I'll sign you on as an apprentice . . . if I remember this conversation tomorrow!" and having assuaged Allen's pride, which didn't really need it, thanks to

Elsuba's Demerol, the friendly giant donated a pint of aquavit, tousled Allen's hair, and vanished into the crowd.

"My God, what would they do if I had *killed* that whale?"

Elsuba chuckled. "Oh, tie you up and throw you in the local volcano as an offering to Odin! Once these ceremonies get going, it's share and share alike, and that fellow saw you didn't have a bottle, so he passed his on to you. And you didn't even recognize him?"

"That was Dewey?"

"Yes, it was, in full Viking persona! All cleaned up and obviously making friends left and right. . . . Go easy on that stuff, Fearless Leader, it's one hundred proof and it doesn't mix too well with Demerol."

"On the contrary," he mumbled, downing a fiery gulp the instant her back was turned. *Sixties Maxim No. 138: If one pill works, two pills will work twice as well.* While Elsuba was still scanning the crowd, he dug out another capsule and chased it with a third gulp. *Mellow City, here I come!* Aloud to Elsuba: "Spot any other members of the Expedition?" Before she could reply, someone smacked him on the shoulder and spun him around. It was Birgir, natty in his dress blues, and carrying a Tuborg bottle in each hand. "It's almost time for the dancing to start! Tonight, Allen, we'll make you an honorary Faeroese—but you have to join the dance!" Warrener, who could now most definitely feel the alcohol and the Demerol high-fiving in his nervous system, was giving it some serious thought. Some official-looking gent ran up to Birgir and handed him a ceremonial hat that made him look more like the Elf King than a trawlerman. With the headgear came a gold-painted wooden replica of a harpoon, and when Birgir mounted a nearby crate and waved it aloft, the crowd grew silent at the sight of him. Arms wide, Birgir began to intone a chant in Faeroese, the sound of which reminded Allen of a Lovecraft character invoking Chthulhu and the Elder Gods. Elsuba explained:

"He's blessing the dancers and the Caller of the Dance, the one man on Vesturoy who's memorized all five thousand verses of the *Slain Whales' Ballad.* Shhh—listen!"

In priestly orotund tones, Birgir thundered the refrain:

> *"Raske drenge,*
> *grind at draebe,*
> *der for lyst!!"*

"Which means?"

" *'Strong men are we, and killing whales is our delight!'* If they're going to dance to *that* one, we've got a long party ahead."

"Suits me!" Without quite knowing how it happened, Allen and Elsuba were being moved into the circle of dancers. Ordinarily the clumsiest pair of shoes on the ballroom floor, Allen at that moment felt like Nureyev. The crowd separated into three concentric rings, each dancer grasping the hand of whoever was on either side. Elsuba kept a tight grip on his right hand, and when he turned to see who his other "partner" was, he discovered he had linked up with the town postman, the same slightly florid, pot-bellied gentleman who looked after the Expedition's mail. They nodded affably and the man's hand was hot in his. The postman made the universal mime for I-sure-am-thirsty, so Allen handed him Dewey's bottle and down the hatch went an impressive belt. The clerk's cheeks turned bright red and, as he handed the bottle back to Allen, he suddenly threw back his head and howled like a wolf. From various points in the circle, a dozen others sounded an echoing refrain—fishermen, grocers, accountants, or school teachers, the Rite of the Slain Whales made everyone equal. Perspiring in rivulets now, the postal clerk thanked Allen, and insisted that Allen drink the remainder. Allen smiled, shrugged, and tossed it back. He gagged on fire; then, when he had successfully held it down by vigorous swallowing, he nodded at the postman and gave out with a timid, experimental whoop of his own. "More, Yank, more!" encouraged someone farther to his left. Allen realized that, like a locomotive gathering speed, the chain dancers were shuffling to the left, pausing for a syncopated lurch backwards, then chugging left again—a fundamental pulse was being communally established, and once it got up to full speed, three hundred drunken Faeroese would manifest a juggernaut of momentum. Elsuba reached over and took the empty bottle from his hand. "Better pace yourself, Olaf-the-Inebriated! You're full of Demerol too, remember?"

Oh, yes, he remembered. Fought down the urge to shout: "Best fucking high I've had in ages!" and contented her with: "Don't worry, I gave Dewey the keys to the Rolls Royce—he'll drive us back to Vardinoy!" Playfully, he stuck out his tongue, and was astonished when she learned forward and made as if to bite the tip. That's when he realized that the reserved Dr. Poulsen was herself working up a snootful.

Circles complete now—inner and outer moving left, center moving right—the dancers took their cue from the bonfire, which blazed a column of spitting, popping, blowtorch-flame twenty feet into the air. As he lurched around the circle, more towed by the postman and pushed by Elsuba than propelled by his own skills, Allen managed to catch sight of the others: Norma and Dahl were sketching earnestly from atop a cargo container; Preston was burning up film and putting his slickest moves on a waitress named Astrid whom he'd already flirted with in the café; Dewey was all but besieged by the local nobility; and there was even ol' uptight Dick Sugarman tongue-wrestling behind the beer kegs with one of Astrid's friends . . . or cousins, whatever.

"YEEEE-HAW!" bellowed Allen Warrener. *Looks like everybody gets laid tonight!*

Everybody?

Karen isn't here tonight, and it would be dastardly to take advantage of that, said Jiminy Cricket.

Eat my shorts, frog-bait; it was HER choice, HER decision. She could not have been unmindful of the possible outcomes.

Now the Caller-of-the-Dance, a sixty-ish gentleman decked out in the national folk costume and spry as the leprechaun he resembled, swung into the center of the circle, microphone in hand, and began establishing the "ground bass" with hand claps and exhortations. The crowd picked up the beat, which gradually spread to all three rings of dancers. The Caller nodded his approval—Everybody together now!—and dropped the metaphorical starting flag by removing his Snow-White-and-the-Seven-Dwarves cap and tossing it into the bonfire. He chanted the first verse, then three hundred lusty throats roared the chorus. *The Ballad of the Slain Whales* was well and truly under way, and three hundred hands raised bottles and cups and roared a salute, maybe to the Caller, or maybe to Odin and the thundering rhythm of His ancient powers.

Whale fat sizzled and banged; upturned bottles winked in the firelight; and everyone over ten years old, the whole population of Norduroy, became a single vibrant organism, dancing, drinking, shouting, stomping, and grinning like maniacs.

When an unexpected fermata broke Allen's rhythm, Elsuba wagged a stern finger at him.

"Naughty, naughty! I saw you sneak another pill! You're a wicked little boy and Momma's going to punish you for disobedience when we get back to Stalag Poulsen!"

"Oh, yeah?" he leered back at her. "Is that a threat or a promise?"

She sidestepped the question by suddenly steering out of line and plopping him down on a shipping container. "You look a little peaked, Allen. Let's take a short break."

"Unlike the first time, Elsuba, I am up for more dancing!"

She patted his hand. "I know. This is a far cry from the first time—God, you were such a wallflower that night!"

On their fourth night together, she had taken him to the Tjornuvik town hall to watch an itinerant troupe of expert folk dancers from Torshavn, and given him a capsule history of the Faeroese chain dance while they were waiting for the performance to begin.

The *a capella* Faeroese ballads could be traced back to the days when the Vikings settled the archipelago—fragments of them were written down in the Middle Ages—then crossbred by the influence of European traders steeped in the troubadour tradition, and further enriched by contributions from the fleet of Spanish pirates who'd looted and briefly occupied little Torshavn in 1510; the troubadour influence had melded seamlessly with the original Viking-age material, and the hybrid art form had been codified, and written down, starting in the late 1700s, by which time the pure medieval chain dance forms—once common throughout all of Europe—had largely died out. Only here, in the isolated Faeroes, did this vibrant form of folk art continue to flourish.

Each village had a Caller-of-the-Dance, a respected and often hereditary office; his lifelong task it was to memorize the basic canon of ballads, many of them comprising thousands of verses. The Caller, like a good conductor, was not bound to follow a scripted narrative; he was free to interpolate local events and characters, thus transforming the ballads into oral histories of his community, while still adhering to the basic narrative, so that even the most elaborate cadenzas must eventually return to the "key signature" of the original story.

As the Caller narrated, the dancers circled around him, belting out the chorus; there was constant interaction between the Caller and his flock.

Primary tempo and inflection were dictated by the Caller's style, and were then elaborated upon by the dancers' pace, stride, and vehemence. Tempos accelerated and the general clamor of stomping feet, clapping hands, and verbal punctuation grew much louder when the verses described a dramatic incident; tempos broadened and lyric expansiveness soothed the overheated participants when the Caller decided everyone needed to recharge their batteries. The range of gestures and footwork could be very elaborate, modulating from lusty floor-shaking Cossack leaps to gliding, almost waltzlike swoops that brushed the dancing floor lightly as a sigh.

Variations of the melodic line, set forth in six-beat measures, were ornamented by quicksilver changes of stress and accent, and each successive measure was tied to the next by pronounced, often quite extreme, syncopations. The net effect was that each segment of the ballad became a spacious, single-breathed paragraph, while simultaneously sustaining a structural arc that might rise and fall over the course of six hours, yet was always propelled by an insistent, hypnotic rhythmic tension. *A medieval "Bolero,"* Allen had described it after his first exposure to the genre. When the dancers really got worked up, the mood verged on that of a bacchanal—flirting was encouraged, but there were limits to any public display of lewdness. These people were, after all, at least putative Danish Lutherans; but that didn't stop the communal mood from getting pretty steamy as the level of inebriation increased.

Allen and Elsuba caught their breaths, switched to beer instead of the stronger stuff, and Allen was astonished to see from his watch that he'd been dancing for eighty-five minutes. Perhaps a third of the original participants had dropped out by now, too exhausted or too drunk to continue. But the celebration remained a spectacle. The dancers were suspended in Time, somewhere between the ninth century and the twentieth! If viewed from overhead, the rings of dancers would appear to expand and contract like the valves of a giant heart—toward the fire, then back, teasing the flames, the expanding/contracting motions always subordinated to the circular momentum. Bottles rose and fell, glinting in the firelight; every face glazed with sweat and flushed with exertion, ripening the features of the young and melting years from the elderly; many an unlikely coupling would take place on this night, of that he was certain. By the time they'd gotten back their wind, a series of deep fatty pockets inside the still blazing pyre of whale meat suddenly exploded like a string of cherry bombs, jolting everyone into a new spurt of communal energy. Elsuba leaned closer and inquired in a seductively throaty tone: "Are you ready for the grand finale?" Her cheeks were flushed, her incomparable eyes flashing, her feet and shoulders keeping time with the music; flames danced in her gaze and her hair flowed out like two golden wings.

"It would help if you had a few hits of speed in your medical cornucopia. . . ."

She spun into his awkward embrace and turned their faces into the cool bracing benediction of a sea breeze.

My God, she's stewed! The Ice-Princess is gettin' down!

"I have something just as good," she murmured on the portal of his ear, and before he could even draw breath she framed his face with both hot slick hands, pulled him close, and imperiously stabbed his mouth with a feverish, gloriously sloppy drill-bit of a spiral-tongued kiss.

When he came up for air, he panted: "Now, that was a blast from the past! Can I have a prescription for those?"

She appraised him very intently and switched into her Doctor's Voice. "Speaking as your as your Primary Care Giver for the evening, and as a friend who knows you well—"

"*Knew* me well," he corrected, a trapped sparrow of panic beginning to flutter in his stomach.

"Be quiet, damn you, and stop *editorializing* everything! My professional judgment is that it's high time you stopped observing the Dance of Life and threw yourself into it with all your heart. Rejoin the dance with me, that's my prescription, and this time Allen, this time just *let go!* I've studied you for weeks now, and I ask myself: why has this decent, passionate man been so miserable for so much of his life, and my diagnosis is: you stopped dancing! The music changed, so Allen Warrener decided to stop taking part. You've been waiting twenty years for someone to play an old favorite on the jukebox . . . and tonight you've got your wish. Those people are singing a song that's been calling to men like you for a thousand years. This is your chance, mister—join me in the climax of the dance now, or you'll never get another invitation."

"I . . . I don't really know if I can keep up. I mean, I'm having a good time just *watching*."

"Only a pervert is someone who 'just watches'!" She favored him with a smile that was both generous and calculated, verging on lewd suggestion. He was knocked off balance by this turn of events. Not sure what was coming. Not sure what he wanted to happen next. Not sure of too fucking much at this point. Elsuba shook her head stubbornly and a swath of her hair brushed across his face, a blaze of scents, not the least arousing of which was the light, hot musk of her woman-sweat. She was offering both enticement and a dare. Her whole body was energized, and when she extended her hand, he was mesmerized by the rhythmic sway of her breasts and hips, and by the dark smoldering violet of her taunting eyes. *If you do not take her hand now and join her on the journey she has planned for the two of you, then a doorway closes forever. Time to put up or shut up, macho-man.* He grasped her challenging hand, felt twenty years of bottled-up passion focus in his gaze, and finally crossed the line: "Okay, baby, I'm in."

The original three rings of dancers had contracted to one big sloppy circle as drunks were led away, children put to bed, and the elderly called it quits. With Elsuba on his right and Dewey mysteriously appearing on his left— by chance or design, Allen wondered—Allen *linked* with the ceremony. The circle's power surged through him like electric current as soon as he took his place within it. Feeling recklessly free, he let himself be carried into the music's glowing heart, surrendering utterly to the pagan gestalt, no part of him, this time, holding back and finding fussy imperfections.

The Caller somehow signaled his small rubato fluctuations, just a fraction of a second ahead of the dancers, and they responded as one soul, in exactly the way their "conductor" intended. Was this telepathy? Herd instinct? Magic? Allen didn't care and did not question a phenomenon that was palpably real. He'd let go, and it had come into him. Dewey felt it too— probably more powerfully than he did. During one slow tempo modification, Dewey tossed his wild man's mane of hair, and the bonfire bestowed around his transfigured features the halo of saints on a Byzantine icon. Obviously drunk as a skunk, Dewey nevertheless danced with the svelte power of a Nijinsky, and at one point, during a diminuendo, he turned a rapt and utterly tranquil gaze on Allen, spread his arms to encompass everyone, and fairly shouted: "Hey, man, we was *born to do this!*"

Like a slap from a Zen master, Dewey's cryptic pronouncement, combined with his Rasputin-like stare, conveyed perfectly to Allen that Dewey meant, by "this," not just tonight's celebration but the whole Vardinoy adventure; Dewey's conviction that tonight's fête was a curtain-raiser, not a finale; and that he, Dewey Tucker, was now attuned to primal frequencies in the very air around him, that he really had come to inhabit a Viking twilight woven from equal parts of his new environment and his own imagination. Dewey was also letting Allen know that, like Karen, he too had begun to *pick up something*.

"There's more weird shit coming, isn't there?" Allen shouted back.

Dewey nodded with absolute conviction. "You're starting to get it too, aren't you, brother? Don't ask me what 'it' is yet, because the Norns haven't finished weaving our rug yet, but it's going to be somethin' awesome—I saw that in the blood of the whale I killed. He let me see it as a way of honoring my courage, he breathed some of his power into me, one warrior to another, y'know, with that final bloody spout."

At that moment, Allen was prepared to believe it. Further conversation was drowned in upbeat music, however, as the Caller cued a dramatic transition, picking up the tempo and shifting metrical gears into a span of six-beat measures—in effect, launching a cadenza, which forced the dancers to improvise in order to reach the cadential *STOMP!* in unison; and by opening himself to the circle's arcing current, he did it perfectly. Time swirled away in the dance. Barely tethered to his own flesh, Allen felt some deeply inward part of him mingle with the spiraling whale fires, soaring skyward. Twenty minutes, thirty, he didn't know or care; he wasn't tired, his mind was clear of all confusions; and nothing hurt. He rejoiced when his former partner, the laughing postman, slithered up and crushed him in a steamy hug, greeting him effusively in pidgin English and thrusting at his chest yet another pint of aquavit. After tilting his head back for a lusty swig, he tried to hand it back to the mail clerk, but the portly red-faced fellow only pressed it back into Allen's hand, pulled another bottle from the many pockets of his folk costume, and shrieked joyously as he poured half the contents over his own head. At that point, a stout indignant woman, presumably Mrs. Postman, encircled him with a pair of huge florid arms and dragged him away.

The fresh infusion of alcohol lifted Allen like a booster rocket. He began hearing the music with his own anatomy—a complex phenomenon of blood pressure, pulse rate, and firing synapses that he absorbed not only with his ears but also, by osmosis, every nerve-synapse in his body. He'd become wired in to the dancers and there was no need to hold anything back now.

How foolish his earlier reluctance seemed! He was weightless, transparent, anchored to the Earth only by his connection to all these other good people and with all his senses burning down to a single point: Elsuba's hand, spot-welded to his, flesh melting into flesh, hot and throbbing. It occurred to him that he'd experienced entire afternoons of sexual congress less rewarding than this contact with her hand! He reveled in her nearness, in the fire-warmed woman-musk that radiated from her every time her hair brushed his feverish cheeks. They were incandescent, and all who danced around them could see it, for he could read that in their eyes. Not missing a beat, he turned and really *looked at her* for the first time since she had come out of the rain into Eiden's house, and once again, her eyes just drove nails into his heart as the shimmer of fire-blaze and shadow shifted their color almost too fast for him to follow, from dark haunting violet to a mysterious smoky hyacinth. Her hair drank in the firelight and revealed, like Salome's teasing veils, one of his favorite regions on the memorized map of her body: the shadowy secret curve that started behind her ears and traced a delicate hollow down the long white slope of her neck: a sacred region where once his tongue had summoned music from her throat.

She felt the frank, appraising quality of his stare and returned it after letting him see one sharp tuck of indecision at the corners of her mouth. Then some internal debate was settled, and she abruptly steered him out of the circle, through the tipsy, boisterous onlookers and under the shadows of a warehouse roof where the air was cool and the darkness private.

"No more dancing! Doctor's orders—you must have the pulse rate of a hummingbird! Have you any idea how long we've been dancing? This second time, I mean."

"Not a clue."

"Just over an hour and a half, which is quite enough for a man who narrowly escaped a skull fracture today."

Allen knew the moment had come when one or the other would simply have to say the words that would send the rest of their evening careening in one of two very different directions. He was prepared for either finale; he had burned alive there in the heart of the dance, and on this night at least, he'd come as close to being adopted by the Faeroese as any outsider could be.

"All right, Dr. Poulsen, no more dancing. Do you have anything else in mind?"

"Yes, I have. Are you game, Allen? Really and truly?"

He'd been expecting it, but now that Elsuba had opened the door for him he felt apprehension well up through the murk of his intoxication: an ice cube plopped into a warm drink.

"I fought a whale today and danced like a berserk Viking tonight, so I guess I'm ready for anything."

"We shall see," she muttered, taking his hand and leading him back through deserted lanes to the sailors' dormitory, where she locked the door, drew the window curtains, cut on a small reading light beside the bed, and proceeded, in a very businesslike manner, to remove her clothes, until she stood before him in nothing but a pair of very unsexy knee socks and a rather frumpy, utilitarian pair of panties.

Allen reached to turn off the light. An imperious smack of her hand stopped him. Anonymous darkness was not an option, then. Deliberately and calculatedly, she had stripped for him in the most unflattering light available. He sank back on the bed, staring at her, knowing that if he averted his eyes for so much as one second, she would take this evening's fund of beautiful memories and crush them in front of his eyes. He felt absurdly like a patient on an examining table, frightened by the slow drugged beat of his heart and feeling as clumsy as a surgeon wearing boxing gloves. On their walk uphill to this antiseptic room, he'd entertained vague hopes that they might finish this reunion by steering a comfortable middle course: some snuggling, a lot of reminiscing, maybe some lush but ultimately restrained making out, and for him that probably would have been enough. But Elsuba wasn't letting him off the hook so easily. She had upped the ante, and by slapping his hand, denied him the solace—or was it the crutch?—of darkness. She had stripped for him in a mode shorn of romance, under a cone of light both harsh and calculatedly unflattering, revealing pitilessly every imperfection Time had wrought upon her flesh. The challenge she posed was brutally clear and obviously a one-time offer.

Okay, soldier, either take a stand or sound retreat; this is where you either liberate yourself from the past or drag it behind you like an anchor for the rest of your days. I will not stand naked before you again.

But her disrobing, so calculated and intentionally bereft of any hint of the erotic, had flung down a gauntlet he wasn't ready to pick up. She intended nothing less than the ritual murder of all illusion, yet she could not understand the enormity of what she was asking of him. His senses trembled with fever and confusion.

For more than twenty years, he had lived with a very specific and very elaborate construct of the past. Even at this cruel moment he knew that he had once—it *was* a fact; it *had* happened—made long sweet languorous love to an early version of this same woman; and after that affair ended, he had spent uncountable hours reconstructing every detail of the experience, seeking to immortalize and save from Time's corrosion the finest memories he would ever own. On a very small scale, he had wanted to become Proust. But the only way to keep Elsuba-the-memory safe and inviolable had been to entomb something of himself within that reliquary too; perhaps he'd succeeded too well, had authored a personal Talmudic commentary rather than a viable work of epic fiction, and, by so doing, had unwittingly stunted his own emotional maturation.

He understood that he'd lived through—indeed, lived close to the heart of—a great deal of very interesting history, and he'd wasted the chance to use those decades as material for new work, new perceptions—so many of those events had registered on his consciousness as *inconvenient*. Like steamer trunks filled with heavy stones, he had dragged the memory-myths behind him, through every change in his life, down the corridor of years, just so he could preserve one sacred space in the continuum where he could retreat and find solace after each successive frustration and compromise. The Elsuba he had constructed eventually replaced utterly any real, reliable memories of the actual young woman, imperceptibly altering the very chemistry of recollection. She had been remade from a warm and complex, sometimes irritating and immature, but always beautiful, eighteen-year-old girl into a coldly perfect three-dimensional mosaic, a *museum collection* of perfected metaphors, shards of imagery, enameled icons which he depended on, like magical amulets and thrice-blessed fetishes, to stanch his wounds, subdue the harshest moments of doubt, mute the impact of despair, refute the implications of failure. She had been consecrated and remade into Our Lady of Tjornuvik.

Staring slack-mouthed at her naked body and wanting to shrivel before the challenge in her eyes, he flung pathetic handfuls of recollected metaphors at her: Elsuba's hair had looked . . . *thus.* Elsuba's eyes were *these colors* . . . Elsuba's breasts suggested *"this" inventory of marvelous natural forms and "that" menu of succulent viands* . . . he had rendered her anatomy in jeweled atomistic detail (or, as Preston had chuckled drunkenly over an early draft, when Allen was still capable of laughing at his own stylistic excesses: "I never knew there were so many ways you could describe one wet pussy . . ."), and the goddess he had conjured eventually became the standard of cruel, unfair comparisons, the yardstick by which he measured the worth of all subsequent women.

Now, lying supine and stoned and staring up at this strange, strong, grown-up, uncompromising woman, a doctor no less who looked for all the world like she was preparing to snap on a pair of latex gloves and administer the Prostate Exam from Hell, the realization crashed over Allen Warrener like an icy wave:

He no longer had the slightest idea how the real eighteen-year-old Elsuba Poulsen had looked, or tasted, or smelled; nor any reliable memory of how they had made love or in what favored configurations, or of what they had learned from each other that would be of value with other lovers in later times. And those were the memories he should have honored and preserved, and carried forward through his years.

Pawing feebly at the air between his numb loins and this cool, imperfect, too-fleshy, too-saggy, too-flawed, too-veined, and much too self-confident woman, he went down a drain, his mind reaching frantically for some life-preserver correlation between the woman standing here and the lover he'd enshrined in memory; but his mind touched nothing but dust, stale upon the floor of an empty vault. He *wanted* what she apparently was trying to draw from him now: to leap free of the past and live bravely in the present, but all he felt was the panic of a man about to use up the last oxygen in his coffin.

She must have seen the confusion in his eyes, and she certainly heard the shallow panic-attack rasp of his breathing, because her expression softened and her voice became very gentle, and she permitted him to see a hint of the pain that aging brings to every woman who's been told by far too many men how stunningly beautiful she is.

"Please, Allen, don't turn away from me. Am I so changed from what I was that you find me repulsive?"

His tongue would not function, and his eyes betrayed the cruelty of the inventory his mind was taking: whence came this ripened heaviness to her calves (although the shape was certainly pleasing enough), that slight thick-ness to her ankles (were they always like that? Had he just not noticed? Not cared?), that surprising little rosette of veins on one thigh—such an imperfection would never have made it into the Canon, yet it might well have been there all along, a simple birthmark rather than a stigma. Her knees . . . no longer glossy, no longer pink smooth domes, but wrinkled gargoyle faces that mocked him as she bent them, to step out of her remaining undergarments. Her breasts were losing their war with gravity now, although they were womanly and full, and her nipples were not the lustrous pink pearls he remembered, or had rhapsodized into memory; they were modest ocher nubs in sand-dollar aureoles. His mouth, however, might transform them.

"... *her belly curved down to a golden pool of shadows. ...*" (Christ, had he ever written such stuff?) Her belly was that of a woman in early middle age who had given birth to at least one child (the white striations of old stretch marks, the long-healed scar of a C-Section), and her pubic mound was much rounder, thicker, darker than he remembered . . . her thighs heavier and fuller, but of course they would be, and he'd never cared for women with tight streamlined marathon-runner thighs anyhow—there were places where a woman should feel like *meat*, not like plastic. . . .

She kicked her underwear aside and took one challenging step closer to him, within range of his touch. "Well, here I am. Do you like *anything* you see?"

His tongue was a wooden stump. "I . . . didn't . . . know you'd had a child. . . ."

"You never bothered to ask. Just like you never bothered to ask about anything else that has happened in my life since we parted. Yes, I have a son. He is nine, and his name is Carl, and he's living with my ex-husband in Copenhagen, until I can establish my practice here. Then he will come live with me."

Tides of silence sluiced in the air between them. The dust of Time drifted as motes in the light.

"Maybe he and Brian can be friends. . . ." he said, almost gagging on his own tongue-tied banality.

"Maybe. But only if you and I become friends first, Allen." She gripped his shoulders fiercely. "Would you like for me to hold a mirror in front of you, while you stand in front of me as naked and unashamed as I'm standing before you?"

He grasped her wrists and returned her glare, conscious of how sweaty he was and how foul his breath might be. He turned his face away, not in revulsion for her but from anxiety about his own bodily funk; but her womanly smells were starting to intrigue his senses, so what was all the fuss? *If I need a shower, she'll fucking tell me!*

"Toothbrush, right?" she relaxed her grip and smiled. He nodded. "Yes, I was just thinking the same. For both of us, I mean. So many of my patients have aquavit on their breaths that I don't notice it any more. Here—I have an extra one in my handbag. And this glass of water."

Two adults . . . two parents . . . no spontaneity for us, old girl. Got to take care of basic hygiene first! Hard to believe there was a time when we didn't think twice. So she sat on the edge of the bed, and like a recuperating patient, he struggled to a sitting position and they both gave their teeth a perfunctory but confidence-restoring scrub. Elsuba plucked his toothbrush away and resumed pretending to pin him down. The gravid but startlingly hard tips of her breasts brushed his chest as she bent over him. His physical reaction was prompt and natural—nothing like a sudden hard-on to diminish spiritual confusion. . . .

"Don't make me work too hard at this Allen. And don't hide behind guilt, either. Karen knew bloody well this might happen and she let me know, unequivocally, that she wasn't bothered by it, and would not hold it against either of us. This is a night apart from Time—you were thinking that earlier, weren't you?"

"I was, shit I *am*, pretty stoned, Elsuba. . . ."

"Well, you see? You can always blame it on alcohol and opiates if you feel guilty in the morning. God damn it, look at me when I'm sticking my tits in your face! I may not be the goddess you wrote about, but there aren't many guys who'd walk away from me."

"I'm not walking away. Just getting my bearings, that's all."

"Here: this is due north!" She grabbed his left hand and cupped it around her right breast. "Feels okay, doesn't it? Look, Allen, I am not the girl you made love to on that hillside overlooking Tjornuvik. I don't honestly know if I ever *was* such a person, especially after you finished turning me into . . . Brunnhilde or Isolde or somebody like that. But I know it was real, and our passion for each other was real, and it was grand while it lasted. Are we any less desirable to each other now? I'm every bit as real as your dream woman ever was, and I'm here and she's not—she never will be. As I remember, though, I was pretty damned good."

Bending down with almost frightening force, she stabbed a kiss into his mouth, hard and deep as a spike. He softened under it. And when she performed that old trick that he'd loved so much, corkscrewing her long lush tongue, he responded to it as he always used to do, with a shudder of lust.

"You always seemed to enjoy that little trick; am I still good at it?" she said, coming up for air and breathing hard.

"By God, you're the only girl I ever slept with who could do that! You can't imagine how I've missed it."

"And you still have those wonderfully soulful brown eyes. I used to think you could see the magic beneath the world more clearly than anyone I'd ever met. There's not as much magic, I suppose, as we thought there was when we were young, but there's still so much that's beautiful. Open your eyes to it again, Allen." He was moving his hands over both breasts now, and found their heaviness silky and comforting and the nipples not nearly as mundane as they had first appeared.

"We were pretty damned good together, weren't we? I mean, I didn't just imagine that. . . ."

"No, you didn't just imagine that, my dearest, first, and sweetest love. We were so damned good, it's hard to believe how inexperienced we were. Can I show you what I've learned since then?"

"Just show me who you are now. That will be more than enough."

"Yes, but it all comes in the same package, doesn't it?"

He moved his hands into her hair, rejoicing in its fullness and heat, pulling her mouth close again. "Maybe I've learned a few things too," he said. "It might be fun to compare notes."

And so a strange but very desirable woman was in his arms, and she was proving to be a wise and skilled and tender lover. A ripening heat came from her, and a scent of arousal as keen as woodsmoke. They explored each other solely with kisses for an avid half hour before he panted: "Let me get out of these clothes, damn it!"

She assisted the process vigorously and with a lot of mutual giggling. When he moved to cut off the bedside lamp this time, she didn't stop him. The Dance-Caller and the hardcore partygoers were still at it, creating a perfect rhythm for their two bodies as they began to take the measure of each other's changed but still arousing flesh, and the attenuated glow of the bonfire was just bright enough, just warm enough, to conjure a fine and subtle radiance. For the rest of the night, they were ageless.

29.

EIDEN AND KAREN

After the Land Rover had departed, Eiden Poulsen breathed in the silence as if it were a rare fragrance; he needed some silence, needed to measure the boundaries of his own feelings within the field it created. The brief message from Torshavn, affirming that Andreas Dahl had lied about his place of birth, was folded in his hip pocket. He knew, rationally, that one lie did not a conspiracy prove and one falsehood did not make Dahl an enemy. Men told lies for many reasons, not always bad ones. Eiden Poulsen had no more lived a spotless life in that regard than any other successful businessman.

He went into the mess hall and made coffee, but after a single cup he went to a storage cabinet and brought out a bottle of aquavit. He had grown fonder of the bottle recently, to be sure. On nights when the memory of his son was too vivid, when the sense of loss came back too strongly, he had sought its company. But never before at so early an hour. Defying his own self-discipline, he cracked the seal. Today he was willing to violate his own strictures; there might be something to gain from breaking old patterns, flaunting the order of things, rearranging his senses a little. Eiden had a feeling that, just out of sight, just beyond comprehension, a jungle of suggestion was growing around him. He needed to slash new trails in order to find his way through it. Perhaps the alcohol would help; prayer certainly hadn't.

He went outside and paced the meadow near the camp. Eiden was certain that, given time and opportunity, he could get out of Dahl all that Dahl had hidden about himself. This island was a wasteland perched on the edge of nowhere. If necessary he, Eiden Poulsen, could be its law, its conscience, the enforcer of its justice. Who was there to stop him? Who was there even to see him? He stared up at the mottled sky until his eyes ached. There was no more a god in that sky than there was in the sea. Poulsen respected

Nature, acknowledged its grandeur, but he had seen too much of its mind-less rage, too much of its gratuitous cruelty, to believe that it was governed by anything more purposeful than the blind balancing act of chaos.

The landscape's emptiness vibrated around him as he suddenly spotted another human figure, walking toward the edge of the lake—a slender brown-haired woman climbing the knoll where the expeditionary flag hung limply in the stillness. He felt no surprise at Karen's appearance; he hadn't seen her getting into the Land Rover with the others, so it was entirely nat-ural that she should appear, sooner or later.

Nor was she startled when his reflection joined hers on the surface of the lake. Smoking a cigarette, she pitched a handful of pebbles on to that inky mirror and as the concentric targets of their fall marked silent chords along the surface, she said: "You can tell it's deep, even though you can't see it—its breath is always cold, even in the sunlight."

"So you too decided to stay behind. . . ."

"I had to." Shrug.

"Didn't you want to see the whale hunt?"

"That's part of Allen's Faeroes; I don't think it's part of mine."

"I thought you came here to share those dreams with him."

"I did. I expected to. What I didn't bargain for is that my own dreams would take over once we got here. I'm not on his trip any longer, and I'm not sure I can explain what my own trip is. Not yet. It's as though we were moving through the same space, but at some point the tracks diverged, and now they run through very different terrain. I hadn't expected that. I had expected to walk together hand in hand into the sunset, all of that shit."

"Have you and Allen had a fight?"

"No, that would be too easy. It's almost as though my feelings for him can only be of any use, any value, if I follow my own path and don't even try to stay tied to him."

"And what is that path, my dear?"

"I believe that I'm experiencing Vardinoy for what it *is*, but Allen still fil-ters everything through his idea of what it *ought to be*. These islands are like pages he wants to write a story on."

"What are they to you?"

"Rocks. Water. Darkness under everything. The horror of the ultimate deep. . . . Life shouldn't exist down there, any more than life could exist in the space between the stars, but life is down there all right. And it's as alien as anything from another galaxy could be."

"You speak as though you have seen it," Eiden said, gently.

"Maybe I have."

He waited for her to continue. She smoked in silence, then stared back and forth between the smoldering butt and the surface of the lake. "Oh, fuck the ecology," she finally said, flipping the butt into the water. "Have you got another glass of that stuff that I could have?"

Back in the mess hall, she shuddered down a long swallow before blurting: "I saw that rogue wave coming before it hit our ship, during the gale. I couldn't warn anybody because I didn't really understand what was happening to me and no one would have believed me anyhow, but I *did* know it was coming, and, God, I didn't want the burden of prophecy!"

After she was silent for a few minutes, Eiden gently prompted: "There's more, isn't there?"

"It happened again up by the Axe-Cuts, only that time it was more personal. It was something that came straight for me, that I was tuned in to, and that didn't really affect the others who were there with me. It was as though I had stumbled upon an actual spoor—a literal trace of something on those rocks. I smelled it with my mind, and it was raw and cold and wet, and as dark as the deepest sea. What I felt, though, wasn't just terror—it was mixed with awe, as though I had caught the faintest glimpse of something that would knock the breath out of me if I could see the whole of it. And when Allen found me frozen on the edge of that dropoff, it was not just fear that held me there, but a kind of rapture. As though something was calling out to me from down there in the crevasse, and if I stayed there on the edge long enough, I might hear an answer."

"Allen was shaken. He was afraid for you."

"And he was right to be, Eiden. Looking back on it, I know I was in very real danger of toppling over the edge."

"And the ruined church? The document we found there after you told us where to look. . . ."

She seemed to study the table intently, playing a quick shell game with the salt and pepper shakers before responding. Finally, she sighed: "Okay, then, here is where it gets *really* weird. I dreamed about that place, and in my dream, I saw it while it was still under construction, when there were people living on the site. At the end of that vision, I saw them attacked, over-whelmed, by marauders in Gray Boats, and I saw that document being hidden in the very place we found it. Jesus Christ, am I crazy or what?"

"Have you mentioned any of this to Allen?"

"No. If I told him about this vision stuff, he'd worry at it like a dog gnawing a bone. And after a few days of being solicitous of me, he would start to resent it as a complication."

"But sooner or later, he must come to terms with what's happening to you."

"Soon, I must tell him. Things will intersect again, and it won't be too long before they do."

Just thinking about it made her head throb.

"Shit, I'd better not drink any more of that stuff on an empty stomach. Why don't I fix us some sandwiches?"

While she prepared the food, Elden switched on the radio and followed the progress of the whale-killing. To Karen, the broadcasts might as well have been the squawking of foreign astronauts. Detached from the blood lust of those on the scene, Karen could only derive from the rising tempo of voices the same sort of emotion she might have felt sitting in a movie the ater whose projector lamp had gone out, listening to the soundtrack noises of people making love; it was so remote as to be faintly ludicrous.

Well, she had accomplished one necessary thing today, just by not going: she had given Allen and Elsuba a chance to get together without her being present or even in range of their concern. Had she offered to disappear for a while, gone back to live on the trawler for a day or two perhaps, he would have refused, protested as though it were a matter of his personal innocence. Several times, she had been on the verge of suggesting ways in which he might bridge the chasm between himself and Eiden's daughter, but she had kept silent, certain that Allen would have insisted that everything was "all right." Plainly, it was not; it was so out of joint that the tension it created had communicated itself not only to Karen, forced as she was to live with it for part of each day, but to the others as well.

After they had eaten the sandwiches, she made coffee and drank two cups, while the radio transmissions crescendoed to a peak, then died away. The killing had been accomplished. After a time, Eiden, who had sipped half a cup of coffee and then abandoned it for more liquor, cut off the radio and excused himself from the dining cubicle, saying: "I'll be right back. Wait, please."

Alone, the radio now silent, she heard the wind grow stronger as the afternoon deepened. When she had examined Karen for exhaustion, Elsuba had indicated a desire to leave the island, the expedition, and—tacitly and finally—Allen Warrener's life, with much more finality than if she had never reentered it at all. That information had opened a sadness in Karen, and a premonition that the lack of resolution it implied would eat at Allen like acid. She had hoped that some occasion would arise that would at least throw Allen and Elsuba together long enough to put a period at the end of things, one way or another, rather than leave them in a state of raw ellipsis.

Well, be careful, lady—you might get what you wish for. She smiled ruefully at her reflection on the surface of a rinsed plate. What surprised her was the certainty that, whatever happened between those two, she could handle it, would not be hurt nearly as much as she would have been by the distance and coldness that had been growing between the two former lovers. Karen herself was caught in a rising tide of personal feelings and experiences, too powerful and too demanding of her attention to admit peripheral pain. Whether Allen came back chastened and subdued, or whether he ran off with Elsuba into the sunset, now was the time for that relationship to find a new equilibrium, or to end for good. Karen had too much else to think about to waste any more feeling on it; and the things she had to consider were important not only to her, but—how did she know this with such certainty?—to Allen as well. And if he brought back any guilt from his overnight stay on Vesturoy, if he and Elsuba had used the occasion to spend the night together, he could bloody well keep it in his pocket like an old dried-out Trojan; she did not want it waved at her like some trampled battle flag.

She was drying her hands when Eiden returned, a pair of framed photos in one hand and another half-full bottle in the other. He smiled at her shyly, his weather-carved face suddenly touched with a tipsy sweetness.

"Sit, Karen, please sit. I'd like to show you something."

The face that smiled back at her from the matched leather frames was surmounted by a shock of wild yellow hair; gray eyes laughed, staring unafraid at the future's promise. Only, to judge from the apparent age of the right-hand photograph—the same lad dressed for work, pullover and slicker hat, standing on a slop-strewn deck with an out-of-focus sea gumming in

470

the background—there would not have been much future left at the time the shutter was snapped.

"Your son?"

"Kristofur, my only boy," said Eiden. And much else, as the afternoon wore away and the level in the bottle slowly fell. The room cobwebbed softly into shadows; once, for a brief time, there was a soft hissing of rain on the corrugated roof. Eiden had decided to tell her everything about the way his son had died; the horror of it, the nagging unresolvable mystery, the first faint connections between Vardinoy and those long-ago circumstances; trying to make her understand why he was here and what he was seeking. By the time his words began to run down, the bottle was empty. She did nothing to slow his drinking, even when she realized that he was accelerating toward unconsciousness. He threw down each slug like a man driving nails, a race between passing out and passing over into tears, and he a man too proud to cry.

Just before he went too far under to talk, she told him about the hidden Gray Boat of Andreas Dahl. At that news, Eiden rose from the table, knocking over his chair, and clumsily hugged her, saying: "You spotted the bastard too? Good girl! Wasn't born on Suduroy at all, y'know. Bugger's from Norduroy all right! And I'll rub his nose in his own lies!"

"Eiden, I'm going to take you to your tent and tuck you in now. Can you make it that far?"

"Let me get outside, get some air, get my sea legs back. I'll make it, girl."

Once in the tent, he fell out of her arms on to the cot, sinking quickly into a besotted doze. She pulled a light blanket over him and as she did so, he reached out and squeezed her hand, perhaps not even aware he was doing so. When his snoring deepened into regularity, she went outside and sucked in great lungfuls of air, her throat raw from too much smoking.

It was the deepest, slowest part of the long summer dusk: the mountains flat sheets of matte black, the lake, motionless, giving back the chill lavender of the sky, its waters seemingly as thin as the silvering on a mirror.

Karen soon turned from the scenery, which wearied her now, and walked to her own tent. The soft crunch of her feet on the gravel only emphasized the stillness. Once inside her tent, she lit the lantern and tried to read, but it was no good—she was listening too hard. If she listened too long, she would become afraid. Gathering her book, a flashlight, and a couple of sleeping pills, she retraced her steps to Eiden's tent.

She turned the gas lantern low, just enough of a glow to read by. Eiden's presence comforted her. He looked peaceful now, like an old sleeping lion, and drunk though he had been, she nevertheless felt certain that if anything came against her in the night, he would waken, full of strength and resolution. She reached over to his face and gently brushed back a stray curve of ash-colored hair. As she did so, she experienced a curious desire simply to crawl into the cot and lie beside him. Did old Solomon's concubines feel such a chaste and loyal need for propinquity? She smiled at the notion, returned to her paperback. Fifty numb pages later, she took one of her sleeping pills. Closed her eyes. Made transit

across a soft and insubstantial sea

to the cove where the unroofed cathedral squatted like a forgotten cenotaph

and the cove was wreathed in fog, and all sounds were muted, even the sound of stealthy oars as the Gray Boats crunched softly ashore disgorging grim and silent men, who drew their blades, with a soft hissing-snake sound, and set about the slaughter. . . .

(NO!)

NO!! She was shaking Eiden and calling his name over and over: "Eiden, oh my God, Eiden, wake up please! There's someone out there, please wake up!" and he firmly but gently put fingertips to her mouth and grabbed her hand, whispering hoarsely: "Hush, girl! I'm awake. Hush now, and let me listen!"

The sound was as faint as two pebbles rolling together, and it came from the direction of the mess hall. Eiden's feet came quietly from under the blanket, and he knelt beside his cot. His hand groped under folded clothing and touched the wooden grip of his old wartime Webley revolver and the heavy inert box of cartridges beneath it. Tiny, incisive clicks seemed to sparkle in the darkness as he loaded six blunt .303 rounds into the cylinder.

"Wait here, Karen."

"No fucking way."

"All right, then, stay behind me and keep your eyes peeled to the sides."

Flashlight in left hand, revolver in right, Eiden pushed through the tent flaps. A half moon, low over cut-glass mountains, showed the outline of the mess hall and beyond it, the lake—an immense blot of ink. In between, shadows of a different texture, mere flickers of darkness. Beam of light, dazzling, revealing two, perhaps three furtive winks of movement near the shoulder of the road. At light's touch, the apparitions twitched into rapid motion, scraping stones, loudly now, panicky perhaps. Twice, the night was shattered by the blinding cone of light from the muzzle of Eiden's pistol, the detonations obscenely loud and followed by thunderous rattling echoes flinging wildly through the valleys and gorges. Long range, hopelessly long range for a hand-cannon like the Webley, but sparks erupted only inches from the last running fugitive. Karen's ears rang like tam-tams as the shots' reverberations died away.

They found the mess hall door ajar, overturned folding chairs, a spilled bottle of ketchup. The laboratory had not been vandalized, for care had been taken to ensure silence, but it had been thoroughly rearranged and it took them a while to discover that the manuscript from beneath the ruined church, still protected in its airtight container, was gone.

30.

COUNCILS

From the journal of Richard Sugarman:

The theft of the manuscript has changed everything; put us all on edge. We got back from Vesturoy happy but whacked out from the all-night party, and everybody—including Allen, whose shit-eating grin told us all we needed to know about his evening—was smiling and refreshed. But when we drove up to the campsite, we were greeted by a very different-looking Eiden Poulsen, red-eyed and disheveled, with a great murderous pistol strapped around his waist, looking like some wild old Balkan partisan. As he told his story, I got a sick feeling in my gut: the last thing we expected, the last thing any of us was psyched up for, was an intrusion on OUR island by human enemies.

Fortunately, we had taken the precaution of having Valentine photograph the entire document. It is from enlargements of those images that I have made my rough translation, which I finished late last night. The document is a chronicle, apparently set down in bits and pieces over several years by the abbot of the settlement, an Irish cleric named Lamor Mac-Othna, who'd adopted the nom-du-Jesus of "Brother Bartholomew."

His sect—which, alas, he never actually names—was expelled from Ireland for unspecified heresies, one of which was surely his belief that it was okay with Jesus if he and his followers got married and had families! He organized a convoy and sailed for the west, convinced he would discover a new land, verdant and peaceful, where he and his flock could found a "New Holy City." But one week into their odyssey, they ran smack into a gale, and when things calmed down again, they found themselves right where we were when we spotted the opening to that hidden cove—the only place in sight where they could disembark. Must be God's will, right? So they set to work eagerly. Using stone and wood from cannibalizing their boats, they built a rude but fairly comfortable little settlement, and by the time their first winter arrived, they were ready for it, having brought a lot of livestock with them, and supplementing that with fish and bird products—pretty monotonous diet but certainly enough to keep them going. Mac-Othna was an enlightened man—he notes the need for a broader gene pool if this New Jerusalem were to survive. Life was harsh, but by the standards of the late eighth century, they were doing okay.

His narrative takes an interesting turn early in their first spring, when Mac-Othna learned that he and his flock were not the area's first and only settlers. Boats were seen coming to and from a distant island which, from its description, could only be Norduroy. All attempts to establish any kind of close rapport with these people were coldly rebuffed. Nevertheless some trade between the two communities did take place, because Mac-Othna had brought along a blacksmith whose skills evidently surpassed anything available in the other settlement. Interestingly, he several times makes note that the motive for trading with "the Gray-Boats" was hunger. It seems that when the fishing periodically went bad around Vardinoy, food could always be obtained by barter from the Norduroy folks   for some reason, their catch was always greater than their needs. Mac-Othna mentions this several times, as though it really bothered him not to be able to figure out how they did it.

He also had a problem with the fact that the other community didn't worship Christ; had never heard the name, in fact, until Mac-Othna sought to introduce them to the Gospels. His passionate attempts at conversion were met with scorn and derision. "What real man would worship a god who went so meekly to his own murder?" was the main objection.

As to the matter of who or what the Norduroy people did worship, it was evidently not the common pantheon of Norse deities, which Mac-Othna, as a medieval Irishman, would certainly have been familiar with. Let me quote him: "Their god, they assured me, was a living thing, not a transcendent invisible spirit; this deity had dwelt upon the Earth before the mountains rose, at which time it migrated far below, into the center of the Earth. The chief tenet of their faith, however, is also a 'resurrection,' for they believe that at a fore-ordained time, their deity will come forth into sunlight and reveal himself fully to Man, becoming the emperor of all nations. And where is this living god, I asked. And they replied: 'Your house stands above it, as do our houses, and our boats, and all the islands thou canst see!' "

Mac-Othna makes no editorial comment about size, etc.

Relations between the two communities remained peaceful, if frigid, for a year or two. A few pages later in the manuscript, however, Mac-Othna describes the origin of friction: "They have tolerated us, it seems, and little more. For as the walls of the church grow taller, the Norduroy men become more threatening."

Evidently, if you didn't worship their god, you weren't allowed to build a competing temple on his property . . . or something like that. There goes the neighborhood!

Mac-Othna was no fool as a tactician, either—his search parties had discovered an active tarpit which discharged very flammable goo. So their carpenters build a pair of half-scale catapults, invited the Norduroy leaders over for a demonstration, and with one salvo, at a range of a hundred yards, set fire to a wooden target. What he didn't show the hostile neighbors was how friggin' long it took to reload the weapons. But they did the job, acting as a deterrent— only one longboat at a time could navigate the entrance, which was covered night and day by the launchers.

The Gray-Boats simply waited until there was a conjunction of no moon, heavy rains, pea-soup fog, and surf conditions that landlubbers would probably consider "impassable." Of course, it wasn't, not for mariners as experienced as the invaders. Here's Mac-Othna's final entry, written just as his small band of militia went forth to fight the raiders at the water's edge:

"God grant that this chronicle should survive, to tell at least how we put our trust in God and good Irish steel, and died as braver men than we had lived."

Here the manuscript breaks off, in mid-passage; that's it. Nothing in it about monsters or Great Orms, but it does suggest that the Norduroy people have a longer history of being anti-social than anybody realized!

(Much Later:)

We all gathered in the mess hall, two days after the robbery, and I read the translation aloud. Much discussion followed, particularly about the break-in. Suspicion naturally falls on Andreas Dahl, who could have engineered the theft even though he has an ironclad alibi because he was on Vesturoy that night, partying with everybody else. Of course, an ancient manuscript—even a grocery list—has intrinsic value, but how did the thieves know we had something like that? And how did they know where we'd stashed it?

It was finally decided that, for the time being, the only thing we can do is locate that house Andreas lives in (and Norma too, now, I guess) and search the place, with or without his permission.

I hope to God we're just dealing with a common burglary; but on Vardinoy, that would be asking too much. . . .

Eiden went with Allen to the village. Dahl's hut, when they found it, was smaller and meaner than they'd expected. The smell of over-fried fish curdled the air above the entrance. Allen knocked. Dahl's expression was peevish when he opened the door and grudgingly bade them enter. He didn't look like a conspirator so much as a newlywed whose supper had been interrupted by a salesman.

Norma nodded curtly when they entered, eyes going wide at the sight of Eiden's holstered pistol. She rescued the fish, which was popping loudly on a two-burner camp stove, and mechanically stirred the contents of an iron pot simmering over the fireplace. The meal smelled heavy, greasy, and poorly prepared.

"A drink, gentlemen?" said Dahl, already pouring aquavit into his own glass.

"I'm afraid this isn't a social call, Andreas," said Allen. Dahl's eyebrows made inquiry, then he shrugged and tossed the entire glassful into his mouth, signifying his indifference. Norma glared at the interlopers. She was spectacularly incongruous in this peasant's-hut setting: a dirty rag wrapped around the handle of the frying pan, a cigarette spilling ashes on one of the charred cutlets, her hair dull and clumped as though it hadn't felt a brush in weeks. She had the slightly ridiculous, slatternly look of a rich girl who'd gone slumming for weekend party only to find out, Monday morning, that the masquerade had somehow turned into a new career.

"Norma, would you mind if we spoke to Andreas in private for a few minutes?"

"As a matter of fact, I would mind, Allen. I'm trying to fix dinner, as you can see, and I have no intention of leaving the room. Anything you have to say to Andreas, you can say just as plainly with me standing here."

"Okay then, I'll cut to the chase. Our camp was broken into on the night we were partying on Vesturoy, and that manuscript we found in the old church—which turned out to be pretty valuable, incidentally—was stolen from the laboratory."

Dahl refilled his glass and looked over it at his accusers, a sardonic smirk edging his lips. "Let me see if I get the picture, Allen: you've been robbed, and so you come here to . . . to tell me about it? Or to accuse me of doing it? I'm not such a remarkable man that I can be in two places at once, and you saw me on Vesturoy at the time this alleged crime occurred."

"I also know that aside from Birgir and Norma there, you're the only person who could have known about the document."

Eiden lost his composure at that point, roughly slamming a wooden bench against the table and seating himself with both fists clenched, eyes drilling into Dahl's. He growled something guttural, and obviously insulting, in Faeroese. Anger flared briefly in Dahl's eyes, but he suppressed it just as quickly. Ignoring Eiden's insult, Dahl continued to speak calmly in English. "If you care to search the place, go right ahead. I assure you, I do not have your precious manuscript, nor did I hire some thugs to break into your camp. I was on Vesturoy all night, with Norma, sketching the festivities. I continued to sketch long after you, Mr. Warrener, had departed with Poulsen's daughter for a cheery discussion of theoretical physics or a brisk debate about the contemporary relevance of Marxism. Am I close?"

"A friendly word of advice, Andreas: you don't do sarcasm very well. Stick with cold, aloof, and snooty—they suit you much better. And now, thank you, we *will* have a look around."

Norma clanged the frying pan down on a stone ledge over the blackened fireplace, snarling: "You two have got some kind of fucking nerve!" Eiden moved to each corner of the room, peering into cupboards and behind furniture. There were few hiding places. Allen sniffed around the bedroom, where he found that the juxtaposition of the new lovers' styles was almost funny: Dahl's clothing was neatly folded, and his personal effects were arranged with anal precision; Norma's duds were strewn all over the room, and on the bedside table—an upturned shipping crate—sat an ashtray overflowing with lipstick-smeared butts. The tiny window was evidently inoperable, for the air was close, stale, verging on foul. As he poked around in this decidedly unromantic chamber, Allen slowly became aware of another pervasive but much more secretive odor. It took him a moment to identify it as the unique effluvium of stale sex. The room was steeped in it. Only a marathon amount of heavy-duty humping could have generated such an afterglow of pussy in the air. He would omit this detail when reporting the visit to Preston. . . .

"Nothing in there but a cloud of old skank," he said, raking Norma with a glare that colored her cheeks.

"It wouldn't actually *be* here, of course!" snapped Eiden. "But I'll bet he knows where it is."

Dahl was standing now, hands on hips, his posture defiant. "I must say I'm surprised, Allen. I didn't realize I had behaved in such a manner as to make you think I would violate your hospitality."

"No, all you did was manage to steal my best friend's wife in record time."

"Allen, nobody 'stole' me! I'm here of my own accord, and quite prepared to take responsibility for the fallout. I didn't want this to happen, it just did."

"Ambushed by Cupid—and at your age, too."

"Fuck you, Warrener."

"Both of you calm down," said Dahl, suddenly the very voice of conciliation. "Norma's here because she wants to be. She's far too intelligent and sensitive a woman to give in to mere impulse."

Allen was incredulous. "That's the biggest crock of bullshit I've heard in years, Andreas. I'm amazed you could say it with a straight face."

Norma saw an opening and lunged for it with her claws out: "God gave him a fantastic tongue, Allen, and the talent to use it where it counts."

"Reverting to a previous incarnation, are you Norma? Too bad the cameras aren't rolling."

She was about to trade another volley, but Eiden's cold, acerbic tone cut off the argument.

"Just tell me one thing, Dahl: why did you lie about your birthplace?"

"I don't know what the hell you're talking about, Poulsen."

"You claimed you were born on Suduroy, but there is no record of it. I think you were instead born on Norduroy, and I'm wondering why you might want to hide that fact."

Dahl's voice was assured, but his eyes stabbed a quick blade of irritation at Norma, who was the only possible source from whom Eiden could have gotten this information. "You're confusing things, Poulsen. The two places have similar-sounding names, that's all. As for why my parents didn't fill out the birth records, I really don't know. I don't remember the occasion very clearly myself, and I've always assumed I was legal and accounted for. It's crushing to learn otherwise."

Stalemate. Accusations had been hurled and denied, and nothing was in the hut that in any way implicated Andreas Dahl. Even Allen, who had led the charge to the front door, was starting to feel embarrassed—if Dahl was up to something, he was now aware of their suspicion; if he wasn't, they had done nothing more than ruin his supper.

Norma tried the Woman Scorned gambit. "Look, Allen, you see how it is. I'm with Andreas now and I intend to stay with him. I know it's sudden, but I'm absolutely sure of my feelings. I don't want to hurt Preston, but surely you could see how far apart we'd grown. He just wasn't ready to face the truth."

"He knows he's made some mistakes."

Norma snorted. "Yeah? Who hasn't? But this is not his fault, and it's *not* something I went looking for. It just happened. You know, like falling in love used to be? It happened, and I'm glad it did."

"But you didn't have to just leave him like that, pinning a note to his pillow. That's low-rent, Norma; not your style at all. I'd never have figured you for being so chickenshit."

"I know. I owe Preston a long, serious, and probably unbearable conversation; can you blame me for putting it off? All right, then, I'll hitch a ride back with you and pack the rest of my things and he can say whatever he wants to say while I'm doing that. I warn you, after fifteen minutes, it's going to sound like World War Three in that tent."

"Probably. But it'll clear the air. I'll drive you back here when the confrontation's over, if that's still what you want."

"Oh, yes, Allen, that *will* be what I want. Andreas, you get two helpings of fish tonight. I'll be back around midnight."

Dahl rose, made concerned, protective gestures. "Norma, I think perhaps I should go with you. At least be close. He may get violent."

Norma laughed. "Preston? Violent? Oh, man, that would be so out of character, it's funny to think about."

Preston was, in fact, quite reasonable and subdued—for the first fifteen minutes of their confrontation. He admitted his negligence, and pledged contrition, self-abnegation, ten thousand Hail Marys, whatever it took to make her happy. He was, in fact, so sweetly reasonable and cloyingly sincere that she felt the first real pang of guilt she'd known since the start of her affair with Dahl. But when she turned to say something consoling, and took a final close look at her soon-to-be-ex-husband, all of her resentment rose to the surface again. God, he looked pathetic! Hunched on the edge of his cot, his wrinkled clothing hanging in hobo clumps, a thin drooping pierrot, advertising his misery by the sour crescents forming under his arms. He practically stank of remorse.

"I swear, baby, from now on, you'll have all the time and space you need to develop your artistic side! Just don't depend on *this man!* You *don't know him!*"

"I know he's not a thief, Preston; and I know he's a great artist and a beautiful, sensitive man."

"He's a slick, lying manipulator creep, Norma, and he is *using you!* I just don't know what for, yet."

Norma stood up and glared at him through the smoke from her cigarette. "And what were *you* doing with me, Press, in all those movies where I spread my legs for your cameras?"

"I was 'using' you so you could earn more in a month under my cameras than you'd have made in a lifetime waiting tables in that redneck roadhouse where I found you!"

"Okay, man, point taken. I went along with it so I would never have to talk to another bill collector as long as I lived, and for that I thank you. And I hung in there with you when the Mob ran you out of the porn business, didn't I? Did I ever say one cautionary work while I watched you blow two million dollars on the worst art-house turkey of the decade? Whose beer did you cry in when the critics turned on you after *Movie Man* opened, and closed, in the same week? And who defended you when the lynch mobs came after those God-awful Hammerhead atrocities? I did, Preston, right up until the night when my son ran away. That was when I felt my love for you start to crumble."

"But Norma, I'm on a roll now, honest to God! Even if there is no Vardinoy Monster, I've got the most spectacular footage I've ever shot—I can make a great documentary about *not* finding a monster, if that's how it goes down."

He tried to embrace her contritely, but encountered only rigidity. Out of desperation, he played his last card.

"Norma, baby, I can't finish this movie if I don't have you beside me."

She pulled away from him and picked up her overnight bag.

"You almost had me going there, man, until you tried that 'stand-by-your-man' line. Christ, be honest with yourself, even if you can't be honest with me! You don't 'need me beside you' to finish this movie—if you did, you'd have paid more attention to me before I ran off with Andreas. Just what is it that makes me essential? Do I change the film magazines? Do I call out the light-meter readings? Or is it just the fact that I'm the only piece of ass available on this entire shit-heap of an island? I'm sorry, Preston, but anything you say now is going to be too out of character and way too late in the game.

For what it's worth, I really do hope you win an Oscar for this film, but there's nothing I can contribute that'll help you do that. I'll have Allen come pick up the rest of my stuff."

Before ducking under the tent flap, she turned back and gave him a chaste little kiss on the forehead. "As far as the legalities are concerned, I'm sure there are divorce lawyers in Torshavn; I'll make it as cheap and painless as possible."

As she stooped to exit the tent, he made one final appeal. "It isn't even about me or the movie! Just don't give yourself completely to this one man. He doesn't love you. He's cold and dangerous, and if you go with him, I'm afraid he'll do something worse than just break your heart!"

"Really, Preston, he's just a reclusive guy who paints landscapes, that's all."

"No, no, he isn't!"

But she was already gone. Numbly, he picked up her suitcases and carried them outside, where Allen, avoiding eye contact, took them from his hands. He was surprised by how dark it was, until he saw the solid rack of cloud that had settled over the island. All he saw of Norma's departure was the twin red dots of the Land Rover's taillights, tracing a pair of ruby sine waves up the mountainside. When the vehicle entered the pass, they winked out. And Preston Valentine began quietly to weep.

31.

Litmus Test

The ride back with Warrener was mostly silent and tense. Norma ventured a few remarks in her own defense, but Allen was in too prickly a mood to discuss the matter. Well, fuck him, Norma thought. She was feeling rather spunky. Back there in the tent, she had not wavered in the face of Preston's wretchedness. Her resolve had been tested, she was more certain of her course than before, and now she felt so seized by righteousness that she wasn't in the least bothered by Warrener's scorn.

Allen had to park the Rover at a considerable distance from the hut, due to the terrain. Vapor swirling up from the furiously rushing creek hid the lights of the hut—the Land Rover's powerful beams vanished in a dark, misty void. Allen didn't volunteer to carry Norma's luggage over the spindly improvised bridge; instead he batted the horn five times, just enough, she suspected, to irritate Andreas, who was probably moving as fast as he could. Still, it seemed a very long time before Dahl appeared, trudging dutifully toward them. Indeed, Andreas's face was an expressionless mask; he did not seem especially happy to see Norma again, nor was he visibly discomfited by Warrener's sulky glare—he merely gave off a hard, gray presence. His welcoming kiss was perfunctory; he seemed annoyed by the heaviness of her luggage; and he muttered a low "Bloody hell!" when one of his feet slipped into icy water. Norma turned to give Allen a brittle hug, but he'd already put the Rover into reverse and did not return her feeble wave.

Moreover, when she entered her new "palace" this time, she was acutely aware of how mean, even squalid, it was—and how poorly ventilated. Well, damn it, the windows hadn't been opened for a hundred years, so it was no wonder half of them remained stuck. She noticed that Andreas had barely pecked at the fish she'd cooked. Well, she'd never pretended to be Susie Home-Maker! She was on the edge of sniping at him for not appreciating all her domestic labors when he thrust a glass of chilled aquavit into her hand and clinked glasses, smiling now—thank God!—proposing a toast to "the wedding night." As her tension subsided, Norma downed the first drink in record time, and was working on her third when she realized Andreas was just reaching the bottom of his first.

"You're falling way behind me, Andreas! Drink up! We're celebrating, remember?"

"Yes, I know we are." His smile was a bit tentative. "I just don't want to have so much to drink that I cannot take full advantage of you!"

"Don't you worry about that, sweetheart. Drunk or sober, you're the best! You take me places nobody's ever taken me before."

Mockingly, he toasted the interior of the cottage. "Oh yes! Welcome to the Honeymoon Suite of the Vardinoy Plaza, the island's premier resort!"

"Hey, I like that word 'honeymoon.' I can't recall too clearly, but I don't think Preston and I even *had* a honeymoon. And I really do feel like this is our wedding night. Or does that seem silly to you?"

"Not at all. You seem like a nervous bride to me, a little uneasy about your new abode, a trifle shy and even a little bit fearful. But very beautiful for it."

She nodded slowly. "It's so strange, but you know, I do feel like a teenager again, inexperienced and not too sure about what's coming next—so to speak!" She giggled and tilted her face coyly, but Dahl continued to regard her with the same controlled, impassive smile as before. "Oh shit, I can see I'm going to have to stop talking in American idioms."

"Don't worry—in Danish we use the term 'coming' too! Maybe we'll both do some of that, eh?"

" 'Some'? Mister, I'm ready to go off like a string of firecrackers. Let's pretend that I'm your virgin bride and you're a prince from . . . oh, how about the Kingdom of Atlantis? That's appropriate, I think."

"I'm awfully dry to have come from beneath the sea. . . ."

"Well, that's my fantasy for tonight—and after all, it's almost as if you had come from the sea! I met you in the middle of nowhere, on this uninhabited mountainous island on the edge of the world, and suddenly you've changed my life forever. It *is* like you rose up out of the sea to claim me."

She came over to his side of the table and sat in his lap, pressing his proud mouth with a hot liquory kiss.

"All right then, I claim you!" He returned her kiss with a harsh amount of interest. The force of it excited her, bruised the softness of her emotions, and caused a lascivious pulpy sensation to blossom deep inside her. Five minutes later they were ripping each other's clothes off.

The roller-coaster ride of her emotions, the length and tension of the day, and the amount of alcohol she had consumed all combined to put her timing off, render her reflexes less fine than she wanted. Her "wedding night" was therefore not as memorable as she had programmed it to be, for she had earlier resolved to do a number on him that would leave him awed by a sense of good fortune, show him what a virtuoso he had hooked up with. Instead, he assumed the dominant role; he bent her to his own methodical will, leaving her rubbery and raw, exhausted from climaxing, yet not satisfied in that warm, blanket-cuddled way she had hoped to find at the conclusion of the session. Skyrockets in flight, oh yes, but afterwards, thorns scratched lightly at the skin of her exhaustion. She sought to distract herself, put it aside, by fixing another drink to go with her usual post-coital cigarette. They had left a lantern on in the other room, and by its faintly romantic glow she traced idly the planes of his breast.

"I know who you are," she giggled softly. "You're the man from Atlantis."

"If you like. If that's how it pleases you to regard me."

"It does. My man from Atlantis—so strong, so full of hidden powers, just like the sea itself."

"If that's what you want me to be, Norma. . . ."

"They say the people of Atlantis had great mystical wisdom, but it's now gone forever, lost beneath the sea. Tell me, Andreas, do you have mystical powers? Do you know the secrets of Atlantis?"

He was silent for a long time, deeply contemplative; and then he lifted her face so that she could look into his eyes when he answered: "Yes. Yes, Norma, I do."

Silence between them—prickly and alive with current. A thrill of anticipation curled up her spine, a silver vine climbing purposefully toward a pale sun.

Jesus, he means it. *He's serious!*

"Let me get something to drink, too," he said, rising. "Before we talk about . . . things. Care for a refill?"

"Please." Her voice came out in a kind of expectant croak. As he fussed about in the other room, Norma drew herself up on folded knees beneath the bedsheet, suddenly tense as a bowstring.

"Here you are, " he said pleasantly, like a waiter in a sidewalk bistro. He sat down opposite her and clinked glasses. No merriment in his eyes, though. What would the phrase be? *Dead sober?* He took a deep breath before starting.

"First of all, I have a confession to make."

A fearful uncertainty stabbed through her. She'd heard that preamble before, and nothing good ever followed those words. *Here it comes: he doesn't really love me; or he's already got some other woman on another island; or he's really gay and this was just an experiment that didn't work out; or maybe he has a gorgeous mermaid waiting for him down beneath the kelp.* On the cusp of his "confession," he seemed to hesitate.

"Go on, Andreas; we're all adults here." With great effort, she kept her voice level, lubricated her throat with a swallow of aquavit that went down like hot oil.

"Well, you see, I *am* responsible for the theft of that manuscript from the camp. Not me personally, for, as you know, I was by your side on Vesturoy all night. Some of my kinsmen took the document. When you told me about it, I had a suspicion that it might be of great importance, and so it has proven to be. What I want you to understand, to believe, is that it rightfully belongs to us. It means more to the people of Norduroy than it possibly could to your friends. We took it because it is rightfully ours."

"My ex-friends," she corrected. "But, Andreas, who is 'we'?"

"My family and my people. Call them my 'clan,' if you wish—all the inhabitants of Norduroy share a connection, something more than mere genetics."

"But then, you *did* lie, just as Eiden said. And if you could lie about that, then you could be lying about—"

His kiss silenced her. "No," he said harshly. "I do not lie about my feelings for you, Norma! You must trust me, as much as you love me. Will you give me that trust?"

"Yes. . . ." What else, now, at this stage of things, could she say?

"Then listen carefully to me: your friends, the people you came here with, they don't know what they've become involved in. They have stumbled onto something like blind men blundering around in a dark room. By causing that document to be stolen, I was simply trying to forestall them from meddling in affairs they cannot understand, from finding out things they have no right to learn. This is *dangerous* knowledge, Norma."

"You and your people would harm my friends? For a grungy old manuscript? You've got some tall explaining to do, mister."

"I *am* explaining! Let's start with this: your friends all think that the first settlers in the Faeroes were those crazy Irish monks, back in the ninth century. The history books claim it was a band of Vikings, at about the same time. That's what everyone should keep on believing. But the truth is that my ancestors came ashore on Norduroy almost three centuries earlier. That was a time of religious wars in the Northland; Rome was in decline, Christianity just starting to flex its dogmatic muscles. My ancestors were proudly and passionately pagan, believers in the Old Norse Gods; and during one of the many internecine wars of the time, they found themselves on the losing side. Their leader—a great and powerful warlord, from whom I am descended—had taken as his bride a prophetess, a seeress, from the faroff lands of Finnmark, a woman as dark as the others were fair, and she imparted certain visions to him, about a land to the west, a forlorn and lonely place, but a place where they would find refuge and peace. Having lost the war and suffered banishment on pain of death, the chieftain organized his people into a small fleet of longboats; and, trusting to the visions of his mysterious consort, he led his followers to Norduroy. There were several hundred people—enough to populate the island and to defend it if necessary.

"Their quest was successful, Norma. They found an island large enough for their new colony; they found abundant food in the sea and among the great flocks of birds. Their sheep and cattle multiplied. They felt . . . how shall I put this? *Protected.* Because once they were settled on Norduroy, the prophetess told them that they were now the chosen guardians of, well, a god. Was it really an elemental spirit that had taken corporeal form? Was it a creature of this Earth, but unlike any creature still in existence elsewhere? Some ancient, primal, *experimental* life form? It seemed to be all those things. We have our 'theologians,' of course, men who argue endlessly about its origins and essence, and the nature of our relationship to it, but I think such speculation is idle. What was—what is—essential is that this entity was real; it *existed,* even though by all logic and by the theories of modern science it *should not exist.* During the years of the first settlers, it revealed itself—something of itself, anyway, and the seeress interpreted something of its nature, because she was sometimes *in contact* with it. Indeed, it had sent her visions since she was a small girl, visions that ultimately drew her to Norduroy. It was a living thing; it dwelt incredibly deep beneath the land *and* the sea, in fact; it seemed rooted in eternity, for it was older than humanity, older than the dinosaurs! It may well have been Nature's first prototype of sentient life on this planet, and that means it is older than some of these mountains. It is almost as old as Time itself.

"We not only worshipped it, we shaped our culture and our daily lives around it, shielded it from the meddling of outside eyes, from those who would be so terrified by its alien-ness as to loathe it. It repaid us by enabling us to prosper, in a place where life itself was marginal and 'prosperity' only an idle fancy. Communicating through the chieftain's woman, in some manner she could not describe, it gave us knowledge that allowed our settlement to survive many a harsh winter. My people have always known where to cast their nets, even when other fishermen struggled merely to exist; our warriors went a-raiding and always fell upon settlements that were too weak to repel them, yet were excellent sources of grain and iron and livestock—"

"Wait, don't tell me: slave women, too?"

He smiled; again that sardonic twist to his thin but expressive mouth, that look of power under control. No doubt in Norma's mind: that part of Andreas Dahl was a turn-on. "Yes, to be sure. Our menfolk were not monks! And the original settlement contained only one woman for every four men. Had we not imported more females, there would have been strife among the men, and genetic degeneration among the populace as a whole. Norduroy would now be populated by drooling imbeciles. But instead, we prospered. Even in the eighth century, when what the geologists call a 'little Ice Age' caused widespread starvation, even then, our bellies were full, and our women bore strong children.

"In time, of course, the first chieftain and his consort grew old; among the slave women, there was one who seemed to possess the same visionary turn of mind, and she was trained to develop her powers, to become the second most powerful member of the community, the intermediary who could sometimes bridge the unimaginable gap between the human inhabitants and the mysterious entity that had become their deity. Thus was a tradition born, and as generations passed and our knowledge increased, tests and criteria were codified—"

"How to Spot the Priestess?" Norma said the words with a growing excitement; her intuition and Dahl's behavior were hinting at the ultimate purpose of his history lesson.

"Just so! Each generation needed to find, and indoctrinate, a woman to be . . . well, we call her simply 'The Voice.' Sometimes she was found among the descendants of the original settlers; more often she had to be sought, often in lands far away from Norduroy. We had an elaborate network of traders and scouts, 'secret agents' if you like, who conducted their normal business, engaged in trade or diplomacy, but whose primary purpose was to *keep their eyes open* for women who might qualify, one day, to fill the solemn office of The Voice. Such women were found in Ireland, in modern-day Spain, in Muscovite Russia, and once in the very sea itself: a Norwegian woman, rescued after a ship smashed into the cliffs of Vardinoy. This woman became one of the greatest Voices of all. She communicated with the deity as no other woman had yet been able to. Her 'ordination,' if you will, marked the coming of a new era for Norduroy.

"She was also my grandmother. Shortly before she gave birth to my father, seven years after she had been proclaimed The Voice, she contracted a mysterious and dreadful sickness. Her flesh turned blue, gradually turned necrotic, until she was as foul to look upon as any leper. She had fits, spells, during which she shouted blasphemous curses at the god-thing, and afterwards she would rave incomprehensibly for hours. The illness that ravaged her body caused her great pain, and eventually it drove her mad. Yet even at the end, she had occasional periods of lucidity.

"Just before she died, in one last period of calm and rationality, she made an urgent prophecy to my father. What she said was this: After the passing of a generation, a very special woman would come 'near unto Norduroy.' Not *to it*, mind you, not *on it*, but *near it*. This woman would be from far across the sea, and the people must be on guard to locate her, for her sojourn in these waters would be brief; but if they found her, she would be the greatest Voice of all time—a priestess of incredible sensitivity and power. After my grandmother died, a heavy silence fell upon our land, and the spirits of my people grew heavy, for there was no Voice to replace her.

"But now, a generation *has* passed, and my father is an old man. But he sensed, when word about your expedition reached us via our agents in Torshavn, that the time was at hand for the prophecy to be fulfilled! And when he saw the *Laertes* drop anchor in this village, he announced that the woman my grandmother had spoken of was close at hand, 'near unto Norduroy.' "

"Oh, sweet Jesus," whispered Norma.

"You *do* understand where all this is leading, don't you? You do realize why I am telling you these things?"

Dazed, she fumbled for a cigarette. "I don't believe this is *happening!* Andreas, you crazy beautiful man, are you seriously telling me that I might be that woman? That I might become a . . . priestess?"

"You'd be treated more like a queen. You would be honored, cherished, adored by a whole population! And you would gain access to both great power and great wisdom. Not everyone is convinced of this, but I am! You *are* the woman whose coming was foretold!"

"My head's spinning. . . ." Norma took another, very long, drink. "So what you're doing now, right this minute, amounts to a kind of *job interview?*"

"That's a somewhat cold and vulgar way of putting it, but yes, if you want to think of it as such. In order to persuade others of your candidacy, it will be necessary for your to undergo certain tests, rituals—nothing painful, I assure you! And it's important that you undergo these tests of your own free will. Do you understand?"

Euphoria spread a sunrise glow through Norma's mind and body.

"Where do I sign?"

"I beg your pardon?"

"Another idiom! It means: yes, I'm your girl!"

"Good. I knew you would feel that way! Now, tonight, we must proceed to the next step. Think of it as . . . a kind of *audition.* . . ."

"I'm ready. Right now! I've never felt more ready for anything! When and where does this happen?"

"In a cavern on the coast, not too far from here. Get dressed warmly—it will be chilly on the open sea."

It was, but the slow rolling fire inside her—was that from the booze? The sheer outrageous strangeness of it? No matter the source, this inner glow kept her from shivering in the night air, kept her from turning away from the cold chop and the buffeting wind. Dahl steered his gray motorboat in a wide detour around the *Laertes*, so that no lookout might spot their passage, and then turned south, following a course parallel to the island's western flank, just outside of the phosphorescent turmoil of the surf. The sheer black mass of Vardinoy loomed hugely above them.

Norma shivered getting into the boat, but Andreas had wrapped his knees around her and handed her a rough blanket, so by the time they left the trawler's lights behind, she was feeling not just warm, but a touch feverish. From the impress of the wind, she knew they must be moving briskly, but it seemed to her that they barely crawled upon the water. Dahl said nothing, intent on his navigation. How did he know with such certainty where they were going? Oh well, he knew, that was all, that was enough. He was her man from Atlantis, was he not?

As the boat changed course, angling in toward the bulk of the cliffs, closer to the dim churn of the surf, the temperature seemed to change. Or was it her own temperature? Heat pressed in two converging waves through her; startling, not necessarily unpleasant, as though she'd been given an injection of some kind. Her weight seemed less beneath her; even the boat itself felt absurdly light and insubstantial, a cockleshell of dry leaves, bobbing like a cork on a sea of rolling oil. Norma licked salt from her lips, raw as tears, with a tongue that seemed thick and unreliable. That aquavit stuff was potent, and she was not used to it. She knew she had had a great deal to drink, but by now, after all that vigorous fornicating in the hut, the booze should be wearing off. That must be it—she was sobering up. Have to do something about that.

"Wush—shad—rink," she said loudly, throwing her voice upward.

"What? Can't understand you," Andreas called back, not taking his eyes from the sea.

Oh, shit, that did not come out right at all. Try again, carefully: "I said: I wish I had something to drink"—the last word came out as a bawdy roar: "dah-rrINK!!," while the rest of the sentence had an exaggerated primness that made her giggle. Then, wordlessly, Dahl pushed an inert object into her hands, warm from its closeness to his body: a flask. She rubbed it wonderingly, astonished at its strange texture, at the way the warm aluminum seemed to rub itself back against her fingertips. The elementary mechanism of the screw-cap defied her efforts to unfasten it. She finally plunged the end of it into her mouth and used her teeth to open it, thinking: is this what it's like giving head to a robot? The first swallow went off in her system like napalm, and she trembled as it surged through her.

She felt herself solidify on the harsh planking of the boat, Dahl's knees still cupping her ribs, and she was newly conscious of the smell of spray, the increased violence of the boat's motions, the nearness of white water, and—suddenly looming in front of her—the proximity of the portal through which they were attempting to pass: a gap, not more than six meters wide, framed by a blunt stump of rock on one side and a jagged row of lesser rocks, surf-washed, like saliva bubbling over broken teeth, on the other side. Dahl was steering between them, through a channel no wider than the boat was long, into a treacherous flume where curdled water hissed and spat like angry snakes. Not that this spectacle made her afraid, only exhilarated by her confidence that Dahl would get them through it. How strong and fine he was! And yet, for all that she loved him, there were times when she could have done without the savage depressing monotony of the landscape in which he chose to dwell. *It will be better when we get to his village, when we have a real house and a bed that does not smell, beneath the sweet accumulations of our own funk, of mildew.*

Agitated waves slapped the boat as they shot through the flume, then got sucked into a big wave, thrown high on top of it, then shot into calmer waters with a hard flat smack that rattled her teeth. Vardinoy towered over them, a featureless wall that blotted out the stars. At one point ahead of them, the dim glow of surf seemed not to break against the cliffs, but to rush wildly into their heart, penetrating deeply before vanishing. Norma used that faint visibility as a point of reference with which to measure the rest of their surroundings. She saw, opening before them, a stygian arch, beyond which, with hollow and distorted noises, the surf vanished into a profound darkness.

"It's a cave! Jesus, Andreas, how did you find this place?"

"You can't find it, unless the tide is out. At high tide, no boat would survive the passage we just made."

The architrave of night loomed over them now, a great stone portal sliding over the stars. She had a quick image of a vast shadowy cloud, a sentient dark nebula drifting through millennia of light-years of space, devouring suns like grains of corn—*Jesus, what was in that drink?*—and then the darkness was total around them. Inside the cave, the air's texture changed and all sounds came into her ears distorted, as though the laws of acoustics were different in this place.

Andreas's flashlight blinded her as its light cut across a swirling pool of ebony water and spilled chaotically over wet black rocks. The light finally came to rest on a sloping shelf of basalt. A few feet closer and she could discern a rusted iron ring driven into the stone. Dahl cut the motor, stumbled awkwardly to the bow, threw a line through the ring, cinched it tight, then held out his hand for her to grasp.

"I have to hand it to you," she said when she was once again standing, dizzily, on cramped unsure legs, "this is the creepiest place I've ever seen for an initiation ceremony."

He waved the flashlight, and she glimpsed arching walls streaked by moisture and the dull ferrous stains of bleeding minerals. In brackets along the wall, she saw what appeared to be torches, their tops waterproofed by layers of plastic. But Dahl did not opt for their theatrical lighting. Instead, he reached into a hidden niche in the wall and brought forth an ordinary white-gas lantern. It sputtered to life, bright as a welder's arc. Norma felt her pupils flash-dilate, and the sudden brightness exploded on her optic nerves with painful intensity.

While Dahl busied himself with the lantern, Norma sat down on a damp outcropping and tried to stifle a fit of the giggles. This, really, was *too much!* And if Andreas were not being so damned solemn, she would have let him in on the joke. What a flash of *déjà vu!* Except for the boat, the whole place looked ridiculously like the set Preston had designed for the second feature they had made together, a specimen of occult porn titled *Cult of the Ram,* in which she had played the sadistic consort of a Satan-worshipping orgy master, a Charles Manson clone, complete with drugged-out Rasputin eyes and a Van Dyck beard. After ingesting massive dollops of drugs, they had lured innocent girls with big tits (wide-eyed backpackers, biker bitches, and an entire Girl Scout patrol, if she remembered correctly) into their cavern headquarters and there turned them all into howling, insatiable sluts, programming them with drugs, with torture and bondage, with orgasms too great to be endured (or *believed),* but it all looked terrific on the screen and the porn-circuit ate it up and yelled for more—more, particularly, of Norma, who had looked quite spectacular in her custom-fitted black latex merry widow, its ribbon-thin garter straps causing the opulent whiteness of her long, ripe thighs to swell into glossy mounds; rouged nipples, too, of course—*we tweaked them before the start of each shot, so they would inflate*—bobbling like raspberries. She had ended up, of course, a victim herself, chained provocatively to a cave wall just like the one she was looking at now, long tapering legs spread wide, tinted pubic hair like a fist of auburn fire, while a chorus of cult members in crimson robes chanted and danced around and copulated in baroque permutations on tables of varnished styrofoam rock.

There was a splash far back in the cave, and her reverie shattered.

"Oh, shit! What was that?"

She clutched at Andreas's muscular arm. He was now holding in one hand a box of plain, undecorated wood, and was holding something else in his other hand, wrapped in cloth.

"Don't worry; it was only a seal—we must have disturbed his rest."

Slowly, he draped over her head a necklace of cool stones. She took its pendant in her palm and stared at the image engraved on it: sort of octopus-like, or maybe a hydra's head of stylized snakes, or an equally stylized representation of an upside-down tree with many long snaky branches. The ornament tingled on her skin; it was heavy—the wearer would always be conscious of its presence. More and more, she felt disoriented, flashing from fever to chill as she had on the boat. Only Dahl's touch gave her direction and certainty. He led her toward a grotto that opened in the shadows. His lantern did not throw light into the gloom, beyond illuminating an arch of tar-colored rock.

She sensed that the ritual, whatever it might be, was starting, and a delicate filament of anticipation wriggled inside her, oddly sexual. She was still, in a part of her mind, rooted in flashback—as though this moment were a retake, an additional shot Preston had conceived after the main production was wrapped. The two experiences, past and present, seemed to converge on both sides of her, with herself, wafer-thin, sandwiched between them: two scenes painted on mattes of glass, vivid and shining, but without thickness or mass. Dahl was leading her now with commanding force, as though sensing that she was blurred, unsure of where she was in time, wanting to give herself to the ritual, wanting not to disappoint him, but also wanting to break free from the cocoon she felt wrapped inside, wanting to tell him how strange and funny it all felt, and why. He would understand. The little twitch of irritation she felt in his hands, guiding her through an open portal and into its pitchy interior, as though he were expecting her to say or do something specific . . . something *else* . . . as though he sought to damp down a mounting impatience with her.

Well, excuse fucking me, but I'm doing the best I can and when I tell you what I flashed back on, you'll see why it's so hard for me to take this seriously!

"Norma, just go forward into that little cave in front of you. Inside, you will find some stones to sit on."

"Ooooh-*kaay!*" She fought the urge to giggle crazily.

She stepped into the vestibule of the inner cave, standing in front of pure darkness. Dahl stepped back, and as he did so, a thin simulacrum of light licked at the darkness before her eyes, so that a patch of it just in front of her seemed to move slightly. Then all was still again. *Just shadows playing tricks on your head, girl. That or another damned seal!*

Why did she now feel so drunk, much drunker than she should have felt, knowing her capacity and the amount she'd consumed? If only she could get over this feeling of flippancy. But she really wanted, half-expected now, to behold a horror-movie coven in druidic robes come chanting into the cavern, making arcane signs with their hands, the torches sputtering melodramatically and a robed priestess at the fore, her long hair flattered by the torchlight, carrying some massive ancient book of evil lore, bound in human skin of course, and fastened with big bronze clasps; all chanting; all singing; all dancing!

"Andreas?"

"What?" A scissors-nip of irritation in the reply.

"What do I do now?" Her words no longer rattling on the unseen stones, but seemingly soaked into the blackness in front of her, where she had imagined a ripple of movement.

"Just sit there. Extend your hands forward."

"Okay, sure. Whatever."

She raised her hands, as dim and insubstantial as moths, and gingerly extended them. She encountered only a moist darkness in which air currents whispered, delicate as a single hair against her skin, as though something far distant were displacing a large volume of air whose faintest trace had floated back, tenebrous as smoke, cool, smelling faintly of minerals. Yet there was nothing more tangible. She might as well have been holding her hands out over the edge of a cliff. She let several long minutes pass before speaking.

"There's nothing there, Andreas. Just empty space."

He did not reply for a long time, while she strained to hear him, dutifully keeping her arms outstretched until the effort began to cramp her muscles, until the silence began to crackle in her ears and rosettes of retinal light began to choreograph the darkness.

"Andreas? What next?" Did she imagine that she heard him sigh?

"Nothing. Nothing more."

"That's all there is to it?"

"Yes, that's all. You can come back now." A stiffness in his voice, masking something. He stepped close, light flared, his extended hand white and close. Grasping it, she staggered, rubber-boned, back into the cavern.

He was smiling, albeit tightly, and the sight of that smile flooded her with relief and renewed adoration.

"Did I get the part?"

"What?"

"Did I pass the test?"

"Yes, of course. Let's go back now and get some sleep."

She tried, as he was putting her to bed with the motions one might use to stuff a pillow, to interest him again in sex. He gently but firmly rebuffed her, brought her a last, very strong, drink—after rinsing away all powdery traces of the drug he had been emptying into her aquavit all evening long— then sat on the edge of the bed and absently, mechanically, stroked her while she drank and grew drowsy.

"Andreas . . . promise me one thing: don't go back to the camp at night. They have some guns, I think. Preston told me about 'em one night after he and Allen had been up late drinking."

"Guns? I never saw any weapons when I was there. I wonder where they keep them."

"I think they're locked up in one of the crates in the laboratory."

"Thank you for telling me," he whispered. The glass dropped from her fingers, and she began to snore. The sour, boozy smell of her breath repelled him. When he was certain she was deeply asleep, he tugged on his sweater and went outside.

Inside the boathouse, his father's boat, two silent crewmen in the stern, bobbed slowly. The old man glared demandingly at him.

"Well, is she the one?"

"No, father, I'm sorry, but she's not. It must be the other woman, the quiet one. This one failed utterly to make contact. Even the drugs did not increase her sensitivity—it only made her clumsy and disoriented."

"How could you make such a mistake, Andreas?"

Dahl turned away from his father's anger. "I made a hasty judgment, because I wanted this woman. I enjoyed her body as I have never enjoyed another, and so I wanted her to be the one. I wanted her so badly, it clouded my thinking. Forgive me."

"She knows too much now; she has learned things about which she must not speak!"

"I know. I understand. It's my fault, and I'll correct it."

"Go back inside that hut and take care of it now!"

"No, father, not yet. We need her, for the moment. They have guns hidden in their camp; she knows where they are, and she may be able to get the keys."

"Are you sure she will do this for you? Betray the trust of her friends?"

"I don't know how many of them consider her a friend any more, not after she moved in with me. But give me a day or two to prepare her, and she will do whatever I ask her to do."

32.

NIGHT OF THE STORM

From the journal of Richard Sugarman:

July 10, 10:20 A.M.—A glum, sultry day. Nobody's following any kind of agenda. Why bother? We've drifted into some kind of a Situation, one that's barely started to define itself. Whether or not you believe literally in the "monster," there's now an unspoken conviction that we've gotten ourselves involved in something vaguely but pervasively ominous. And there's not a goddamned thing we can do to learn more about it, either, so we're sort of sitting around waiting to see or hear something else.

Each of us has his or her own personal take on what's happened and personal guesses/preferences as to what might happen next. We feel more united, I suppose, because we all share the sensation of being inside a psychological bull's-eye, but whoever or whatever is affecting us, it's still so conjectural that instead of getting our shit together—organizing patrols, or something; I don't know—we're all lying around in the unusual eighty-five-degree heat, each of us killing time in our own way, hoping that someone will come up with a plan (other than simply packing up our stuff and going home . . .). A plan, that's what the Vardinoy Expedition needs; a strategy; but without more knowledge, how can we formulate one? Even though we've all accepted the fact that something decidedly weird is going on, we continue to drift off in separate directions, succumbing to personal moods, indulging in old habits, tracing the same old grooves again and again. I wonder: what would another, more ordinary bunch of people do in our situation? I haven't a fucking clue, because it may well be that nobody ever has been in a "similar situation."

Dewey Tucker is stretched out, armed with the Webley, on one of the now-abandoned camera positions, bare-chested in the heat, clutching that anthology of Old Norse literature. Every time he finds a verse or a saga-passage that strikes him as being relevant to his new Viking persona, he becomes animated, whirling around and landing mighty imaginary blows with his "air axe." The man's gone native with a vengeance; given the chance, I think he'd trade his Harley-Davidson for a longboat and a helmet with two horns sticking out of it.

And—mirabile dictu!!—Allen Warrener is actually writing! Karen/ Cassandra is sitting comfortably close but not hand-holding close. Despite what almost surely happened between Warrener and Elsuba on the night after the whale hunt, things seem easy between those two now; sitting together in the sun like that, they remind me of nothing so much as a retired couple rocking back and forth on the porch of their getaway cabin, each one doing a favorite crossword puzzle that doesn't hold the slightest interest for the other one.

3:12 P.M., same day: *A weather alert relayed to us by the trawler: there's a low-pressure system the size of Texas careering toward Vardinoy from the direction of Greenland. All sorts of potentially nasty things might happen when it rams into the northern extremity of the Gulf Stream, which Vardinoy happens to squat in the middle of. Eiden suggested that we all plan to sleep in the mess hall tonight, and sent Birgir and his sailors to rig additional lines to all the tents. Gale-force winds, he predicted; and a monsoon-like downpour.*

10:45 P.M.: *It's a whopper, this storm front! And if Preston still needs any dramatic cutaway shots, he surely got them this afternoon. By supper time, the sky was a solid vault of charcoal-colored cloud; gusts of gale-force wind were making the reinforced tent ropes moan and the taut sides crack like flat-handed slaps. For the last half hour before the rain started falling, the entire valley was bathed in an eerie silver-green hue; thermometer plunged 12 degrees in 15 minutes; everything had that waxen kind of edge, like you were peering at it through one of those glass-bottomed boats.*

The storm hit while we were eating supper, heralded by a fearsome freight-train roar and deafening timpani rolls of thunder. For a while, the racket of driven rain against the corrugated roof of the mess hall was too loud to talk over, and the dinner-table conversation, none too sparkling to begin with, expired. After the dishes were washed and the eating area tidied up, we all sat down for a jolly evening of enforced intimacy. Nobody fancied a run to the tents through that deluge, assuming all the tents were still where we'd left them and not flying toward Norway.

The bar did a brisk help-yourself business, and most of us were at least a little tight by the time the rain slacked off enough to resume conversation. Preston played one of his favorite inclement-weather games (Find the Weirdest Shortwave Broadcast), but the reception was so lousy that he popped a cassette tape into the boom box instead. It was one of those "Best of the Sixties" compilations. Young Yuppie that I am, I recognized The Stones, The Who, Crosby-Stills-and-so-forth (the only rock group I can think of that's named like a corporate law firm), and the Jefferson Airplane. (Never cared much for anything except "White Rabbit," but under the rain's relentless drumming Gracie Slick's laser-beam vibrato actually sounded rather stirring.)

Eiden and Elsuba tolerated it; Dewey zoned out playing air guitar and periodically requested a Charley Daniels tape, which earned him glares and "fucking redneck!" insults from Preston. He and Allen, who'd both been packing away an awful lot of booze, were diddy-bopping around the room until they started panting and wheezing, at which point they slid into Mawkish Nostalgia mode, swapping lots of "Do you remember_____" anecdotes that would have been terminally obnoxious if they hadn't had the sense to keep their voices down.

It was all very groovy, no doubt. But to someone my age, it also seems a little pathetic. All over the world, millions of ex-hippies were starting to feel angst about the fact that they didn't "die before I get old"; and now that more of their existence is behind them than ahead of them, they very much didn't want to die at all. Warrener knows the truth; he was on both sides of the sixties upheaval, and now he just thinks everybody was full of shit. And Karen used to cry because it was all happening when she was too young to run away and by the time she turned sixteen, it was all over but the posturing. Allen's tried to tell her it wasn't all that great, in one breath, and now there he is with Preston, all but teary-eyed thinking back on how great the music was, how benign the drugs were, and don't forget those oceans of guilt-free sex!

Karen alternately laughs and fights down her sadness. If you were a twelve-year-old girl with a drunken lint-head for a dad, the fantasy of being able to run away to San Francisco "and meet some groovy people there" must have seemed like buying a Greyhound ticket to Heaven. . . .

Sorry, sweet thing; for the consolation prize, you get to spend one whole summer on beautiful unspoiled Vardinoy, facilitating a one-night stand between your burned-out lover and his one-time muse. Maybe the worst thing that could happen to us here is that we all get what we want. Except for me, of course; one way or another, success or failure when it comes to the Vardinoy Monster, I'm getting a book *out of this!*

From time to time, the storm abated and caught its breath, subsiding into an ordinary heavy downpour, then rolling out its heavy artillery again. After the impromptu sixties' Revival had run its course, the Expedition members paired off or retreated to their favorite seats and a mood of almost-domesticity settled over the room. At 9:24, Preston announced that Inspiration had seized him and asked if anyone would mind if he commandeered the stereo and a set of headphones, so that he might commune with Vitaphone, the Muse of Independent Cinema. Now he was in full creative spate: fresh pack of Marlboros, fresh pint of booze, virgin legal pad, and a handful of his favorite tapes.

The thought had been tickling his subconscious for several days: he needed a Reserve Plan, in case the "monster" concept didn't pan out (*undependable things, monsters—never one around when your cameras were loaded and ready—can't live with 'em, can't . . .*). His fine-tipped marker had been stuttering over the pad ever since. Allen kept tabs on him and nudged Karen when Preston abruptly popped on a tape that was part of his personal sacred Canon: Barbirolli's incomparable 1960 Vaughan Williams Fifth: English as gin, and when you were in the right mood, every bit as intoxicating; wet green hillsides and summer gardens. "I think he's going into overdrive," Allen observed. "Sometimes," Karen said, "a good old-fashioned shafting is just the thing to get the creative juices flowing. Not in your case, I hasten to add." She leaned over her open book and gave him a gentle, reassuring kiss on the cheek. "I haven't gone anywhere, Allen. Except in my head. There is no place I'd rather be, and no one else I'd rather be with." Touched and a little surprised, he reached into his briefcase and pulled out his own scribbled-on legal pad. "In that case, I think I'll work on my own new project. Gotcha, didn't I? I wasn't going to show it to you until it was rolling a little better— an essay. Haven't tried one of those for years. It's about the very concept of 'monsters' and why late-twentieth-century man needs them every bit as much as the ancient Greeks or the medieval mystics. Preston's got the right idea: we should have something to work on in addition to this film. At first, the words didn't come very easily, but now . . . it's starting to flow."

In Preston's case, the ideas were not just flowing, they were tumbling like acrobats and it was all he could do to keep up with them. The basic idea was so simple, so classic, that it seemed a stroke of genius. However the Expedition turned out, he and Dewey would stay on for a while, setting up shop in

Torshavn, taking passage on one or more of Eiden's ships. They would film an elemental story, as simple as Flaherty's *Nanook:* men against the sea, ordinary fishermen doing ordinary things, but raised to the level of heroes by virtue of an environment both dangerous and photogenic.

Of course, the film didn't *have* to be a documentary! Even more respect would come his way if he grafted on to all the documentary footage a suitably simple, pared-to-the-bone narrative. So exotic was the setting that even the simplest tale of love and courage would seem to be set in a fabulous realm—these islands! Change it into a narrative and open the doors for Allen to write a screenplay! Why the hell not? Even Warrener's sternest critics admitted he had a gift for two things: landscape descriptions and dialogue. Preston's magical camera work would remove the burden of the former, and Allen could charge full-speed at the latter. Yes!

Money was no problem, at least for one feature; call it (as his critics certainly had) blood money or come money, he had enough resources for this one feature, and if it was good enough and won a few film-festival prizes, he would have no problem finding investors for the films that came after it. There was a certain type of venture capitalist who liked shoveling cash into the hands of repentant sinners. And speaking of that, Norma would surely be back by that time. It wouldn't take her long to get over her infatuation with that clodhopper painter! Hell, Dahl couldn't be *that* great in the sack, could he? How long could such a woman put up with playing the princess of fishermen, the peasant bride?

My God, look at how many pages of notes I've got! And look at how empty that bottle's gotten. . . . Time to get another out of the fridge. . . .

Ooops!

He had knocked over his glass, eliciting a snicker from Dewey. "Up yours, cycle-trash." Elsuba raised a cautioning hand, and he could no more ignore her than Warrener could. "Preston, you'd better go easy on that aquavit. If you're not conditioned to a life-time of drinking it, like Poppa, it can kick you in the head like a mule. That is its nature."

Preston lurched for the refrigerator and withdrew a fresh pint. "Its nature," he repeated dreamily. "Aqua-bloody-vit has its own 'nature'? What a splendid way of putting it. Indeed it does, dear lady! It's the lubricant for the entire Scandinavian film industry. Bergman suckled this stuff from his mother's tit." To prove, perhaps, his potential to beat Ingmar Bergman at his own game, Preston took a big manly swig and waved his hieroglyphic notes at Allen and Karen.

"Whatcha got there, buddy?"

"*Ideas,* my man! Best bunch of ideas I've had since, um, since we first discussed making a film about the Vardinoy Monster, in fact."

"You don't say?" said Karen, turning a wry gaze at him. "Well, we can all see how wonderful *that* turned out to be. Goosed by the muse, huh?"

"Positively *reamed,* sweet-buns! Hey, Allen—you ever tried your hand at writing a film script?"

Karen reached over and squeezed Allen's hand. A look passed between them that muted the storm's roar. Allen raised her hand to his lips and kissed the knuckles very gently.

"Even my sternest critics say I have a good ear for dialogue. . . . Why don't you re-read those notes in the morning, and if they still seem like the greatest thing since oral sex, I'll sit down and talk it over with you. We need a backup plan in case our beastie's too camera-shy to show up."

Suddenly Preston's eyes were filled with tears, and he leaned forward to embrace his friend. At which tender moment, naturally, Elsuba's prophecy came true, and that last big guzzle of unadulterated aquavit turned his stomach like a flapjack. He stood there, red-faced, waiting for the room to stop spinning and his breath to resume its normal course. The urge to be sick passed slowly.

"Guess I can't put the hard stuff away like I used to. . . . We're gettin' old, aren't we, Allen?"

"Yeah, I reckon we are, Press, but it beats the alternative. Sounds like the rain's slacked off for a while—why don't you hit the sack?"

Preston nodded, very carefully placed his bottle on the dining table, gathered up his notes, and draped a poncho over his head and shoulders. After making courtly bows to Karen and Elsuba, he left the mess hall on the run.

Taking advantage of a lull in the downpour, Preston paused and sucked in great hyper-oxygenated lungfuls, washing the sourness of a suppressed puke out of his throat. All things considered, he felt pretty good. He'd really given the old brain cells a workout tonight, and he felt sure that the notes he had taken would indeed make sense tomorrow. And the next day. And would keep on making sense as the concept jelled. That was an important little breakthrough for Allen, even mentioning "what next?" in case the fucking monster turned out to be a byproduct of the locals' fondness for aquavit. They'd both been good boys tonight.

Twenty feet from his tent, the bottom dropped out of the sky again. He put his head down and ran the rest of the way, exclaiming "Yesss!" when he finally slid under the tent flap and discovered that in his wisdom, he'd remembered to light the Coleman lantern, leaving the faintest cheery glow inside. Wait a minute . . . he hadn't *been* inside, not since breakfast. There was cigarette smoke in the air, but not his brand; and a whiff of scent that was all too familiar, only now it was fresh and vernal, not stale and mocking and fading like funeral flowers, the way it had been ever since. . . .

"Hello, baby. I'm back."

Successive waves crested over him: amazement, joy, bewilderment, the instinctive caution that comes when wishes are too easily granted. Norma was back. Just like that. He accepted it, let the reality of it settle over him like a warm dry towel. After all, this was not their first reconciliation. He did not ask how she had gotten here from the uninhabited village—Birgir and a few of the sailors had scooters they tooled around on when boredom got the better of them. Or maybe she got on her broomstick and flew over the mountains, while an invisible orchestra played *Night on Bald Mountain*. . . .

"Sit. Dry yourself off, for God's sake. I laid a towel out on your cot."

"If you're a hallucination, you can save us both a lot of time by disappearing now, because I'm pretty drunk."

"I didn't expect to find you and Warrener holding a twelve-step meeting in the mess hall. Don't worry—I'll catch up with you."

"At the risk of learning more than I probably want to, can I ask what brings you back into my life on a night like this?"

She shrugged and smiled sheepishly—*well, like, you know, man, shit happens and then shit un–happens, right?*

"The short version? A bolt of fucking lightning hit the creek outside of that hovel Andreas calls 'home' and I woke up into a cold, dank stone bedroom that smelled of burned fish and dirty clothes, and I rolled over and there was Mr. Wonderful with his mouth open, snoring, and I thought: that's the wrong guy. Thanks for the painting lessons, Siegfried, but if two weeks of sharing a bed with me won't motivate you to rent a warm hotel suite in Copenhagen, where they have this marvelous new invention called 'Room Service,' then how much could he really want me?"

Still befuddled by this good fortune, Preston nodded and thickly muttered: "He doesn't sound like your dream date, sugar."

Preston took out a cigarette. Norma leaned over the gap between their cots and the butane flare of his lighter brought out the golden highlights in her hair. She still didn't need to color it very often—good Confederate genes. Very glossy, that hair—she'd been brushing it patiently while she waited for him.

"You and me, we've been down a long road together, Preston. I couldn't pull the plug on our marriage just like that. I'm never going to be a great artist—but I will get better at it because of what Andreas taught me. Maybe that's all I really needed, just a pat on the back and a few more moments of your time. You know, when you finish this great documentary and launch your second career? Let me have one too."

"You got it, baby. I know where it all went wrong, and I can change. I am changing! In fact, there's a lot of that going around these days. Maybe *that's* the Vardinoy Monster: everybody who even looks at the place instantly experiences a mid-life crisis. Even week-old babies. That's why there's nobody still living in that shithole of a village. They all got a massive panic attack and leaped into the sea."

They shared a small laugh, and she seemed at ease. Just as casually as changing shirts, they'd fallen into a warm shared mood. Looking back over the years, Preston thought they'd had more good days together than bad, and what more could you ask from a marriage?

Norma stretched languidly. Rain pounded heavily on the tent roof. Thunder rumbled to the north—the village was taking a drubbing. Preston hoped the next big lightning bolt would hit Andreas Dahl's ever-so-distinguished aquiline nose.

"It's really coming down, isn't it? We made love in a summer rain once, not long after I met you, Preston. We did it every which way you can think of."

He nodded, then realized she probably couldn't see him, so he leaned forward and offered his hand. She took it. "I remember," he said, trying not to get choked up. "In spite of every shitty thing I ever did and said, I do remember the sweet times."

She disengaged her hand in a manner that was also beckoning. She rearranged herself on the cot, feet pushing covers, making a place for him.

"We've never done it on Vardinoy. Maybe if we had. . . ."

He wondered if that were true. Maybe this place did cast a spell on you, and on your partner. The aquavit felt like a big wad of cotton filling his gut. She was clearly inviting him to make up for that particular oversight. He marshaled his resolve and spoke one of the many phrases that were jostling for a place in line at the base of his tongue.

"I took you too much for granted, and I'm sorry for that."

Silence for a few beats, while she digested that apology, automatically rubbing herself on the belly, which was still youthful and silky. He visualized those exquisite, almost transparent wisps of red-gold down that started precisely two inches below her deeply scooped navel. And suddenly, his desire for her came to life, insistent as a shaken fist, hard-wired to his spinal cord. She sensed the transition, reached forth and encouraged it. "Is that a harpoon, or are you just glad to see me?"

Then her hand began to massage his growing hardness, and she sent a whispered invitation out to lick him, a lascivious curl inflecting her words: "Come into bed, baby, and I'll make sure you never, ever take me for granted again."

It was really easy for Norma now, this cold-blooded virtuosity. It was so easy to make a man feel *special*, if that was your goal. Norma served up to him all his favorite delicacies from their private erotic smorgasbord, all the items on the menu that she thought he would have missed the most, knowing they would all seem subtly fresh and more exciting because she was now so changed. Poor sap—all her days and nights with Andreas had recharged her sexual batteries, and their memory was on her tongue like candied fruit. Preston was rampant but slowed by alcohol, an ideal state for her to run-the-fuck, as her dyke friends liked to say, and she played his nerve endings like Heifetz playing a Strad; with every touch, every murmured endearment, she lavished on him the longest, most sustained buildup he'd experienced in a very long time.

And Preston reclined into the sensations like a potentate sprawling on silk pillows, happy to let her shape him, to reawaken in him the certainty that she was the best, the most inexhaustibly stimulating woman he had ever encountered. He was so taut now that if his dick had been a snake, it would have molted on the spot. She knew exactly what he wanted and she was going to give it to him, not as an offering of love, but as a means of gaining leverage.

"Hey, Press?"

"Umph . . . yeah, what? Don't stop!"

"Before it slips my mind—I left something in the mess hall. Is anybody sleeping in there now? You know, like a sentry?"

"Nah, baby, there're people inside drinking and shit. Somebody'll be there to let you in, but don't go there now!"

"Don't worry. First things first."

Norma thought that, all things considered, she was giving the best performance of her career. She was working very hard at becoming the woman Andreas would want for his mate, the woman he would be proud to have selected above all others. *I am the Priestess*—and if that meant learning how to cook fish the way he liked it, she would learn. *I am the Priestess,* she thought again, in a regal chamber of her mind, the word striking her consciousness like a seneschal's staff ringing on a marble floor. Of course she was giving an inspired performance! A calm, self-assured glory filled her at the thought of the fabulous, though still undefined, future that would be hers after Andreas and his people had *invested her!*

It was stirring to realize that she, alone of all the members of the Vardinoy Expedition, knew that the object of their quest was not a monster at all, but a kind of god.

She had been in its presence, and if she did as Andreas had bade her do, she would be initiated into deeper and holier mysteries—that much, he had promised her.

But first she had a job to do, another test of her worthiness had to be met, and she was inspired by the prospects. But for the aquavit in his system, Preston would have popped his rocks long ago. She kept him quivering on the verge until—yes!—he actually begged. And then, of course, she kept him on edge for another few minutes before pulling his cork with one final almost brutal scoop of her mouth and a downright mean, but really quite inspired, twisting of his balls, already so engorged that they felt like ostrich eggs, and he bellowed like a bull, painting her tonsils with liquefied spinal cord and subsiding, after three or four secondary spurts, with the predictable imprecation: "Oh, Jeeesus. . . ."

Norma stroked him into sleep; it didn't take long. He was snoring by the time she finished her post-coital cigarette.

Just to make sure, she sat quietly, listening hard, for another fifteen minutes. Her timing had been even better than she'd realized, for not long after Preston started snoring, there was quite a flurry of traffic outside. The folks who'd taken shelter in the mess hall were taking advantage of a lull to head for their tents. Norma heard Karen and Allen, splashing through ankle-deep puddles, sing out in unison: "Nighty-night, Preston!" as they sprinted past. For a while after that, from their tent, came a faint waft of music—incongruously, Brahms—and then even the Vienna Philharmonic was drowned out by the renewed downpour. Now was the time for her to complete her mission.

She spoke Preston's name, like an incantation, half a dozen times, each time slightly louder than the last. His snores never broke cadence. Satisfied that he was too far gone to hear her movements, she fumbled in the nest of his discarded trousers until she found a set of keys, including a shiny new one which must be the mate to the new lock on the mess hall. She dressed quickly and warmly. Before venturing out, she carefully surveyed the campsite through the tent flap. The entire enclave was dark and silent under the rain. Time to go.

Norma splashed through tarns of rainwater, avoiding the wet heavy crunch of the gravel paths. She followed the wagon track's northern verge until she reached the ravine where Andreas waited underneath the shelter of a big outcropping, a curtain of rain falling inches from his face.

"Did anyone hear you?"

"Are you kidding? You couldn't hear the Mormon Tabernacle Choir in this mess."

"And you're quite certain Valentine doesn't know you stole his keys?"

"Yes, quite sure," she insisted. "And here they are, baby." She held out the key ring as though offering him a scepter.

"You did well, Norma; very well indeed." Yes, she had, actually—in some respects, she had surprised herself. Expecting an embrace, she tilted her face toward his, but had to be content with a quick, tight-lipped peck. "That'll do for a down payment," she teased. "That shiny new key's probably the one to the mess hall."

And so it proved to be. Dahl opened the door easily with his first try, pulled her inside, and closed it upon total darkness. He cut on a small flashlight. The place had been left in some disarray, forcing them to step carefully through the clutter, following the flashlight beam toward the laboratory nook. One corner of the space was packed with crates, some empty, most not; each one stenciled "Scientific instruments! Handle with care!"

"That one, I think," whispered Norma, pointing. "I've never seen that one opened before."

Dahl knelt and read the label: "PHOTOGRAHPIC FILM—DO NOT X-RAY!" Nodding, he pulled out a small iron prybar and levered the crate open while Norma tensely held the flashlight like a nurse assisting surgery. Inside was a wooden tray neatly filled with bright yellow boxes of film. Dahl lifted that and grunted with satisfaction when he discovered three field-stripped Hechler and Koch assault rifles. He was reaching for one of the weapons, his fingers closing around the trigger guard, when a much brighter light pinned him in place and Birgir's menacing voice stabbed the darkness, coming from the far corner behind them, where the young trawlerman had set his ambush and waited patiently for the past hour.

"Stand up slowly, Dahl, and don't try any funny business with the light or the prybar." Birgir switched on the overhead lights and Norma could now see the big Webley in his right hand, the barrel unwavering.

"Norma, you go stand next to Mr. Dahl. I had a feeling you might come back, looking for the guns, that Norma would tell you where they were—we baited a trap, you see, and for the past several nights one of us has slept in here, waiting for the rat to come back. You have some questions to answer, mister."

Birgir had a walkie-talkie on his belt and he was reaching for it. Right now, it was two against one, but in a few minutes Norma and her lover would be surrounded by the others. Her mind raced furiously—the future she had mortgaged was in jeopardy and she had to act quickly or lose it. *I am the Priestess! I can stop this from happening! I can save us if I can only distract Birgir for an instant, because Andreas is ready to pounce on him if his gaze flickers for one instant. One instant's distraction . . . well, gentlemen had always been distracted by* these!

Norma's raincoat was already open, and Birgir could see she wasn't armed. So he hesitated, for one fatal second, when she suddenly ripped open her shirt, baring her breasts to the light. The sheer incongruity of the act was sufficient to seduce Birgir's concentration; he stared at her with his mouth agape. He couldn't help it, no man ever had; his eyes simply had to lick her body. Birgir realized what she was doing, but that realization came a second too late. Andreas picked up a brown quart bottle of developing fluid and hurled in straight into Birgir's face. The Faeroese uttered a short, bubbling cry and clawed at his eyes. Blood and chemicals, rancid on the air, streaked his face and ruined his vision. He stumbled, waving the revolver and wiping at his eyes, trying to refocus on Dahl through a painful blur. But Dahl was already on him, chopping his neck with a double-handed blow and kicking him in the stomach, so that Birgir's shout for help was masked by a quick rattle of thunder. Following through, Dahl smashed Birgir's wrist against a table-edge and the Webley skittered across the linoleum floor. Norma saw Dahl take deliberate aim now and repeatedly kick Birgir in the head and face, and she knew something was going horribly wrong. The kicks produced a series of brittle breaking-bone sounds, followed by a sodden grinding, and she realized that Dahl was not simply disarming Birgir—he was going to kill him. She froze into a numb, wooden thing, mere spectator to the brutal end of it. Dahl took Birgir's big flashlight and methodically rained blows on his already fractured skull. When he was satisfied there was no pulse, he dragged the body into the shower stall, closed the curtain, then coolly stepped to the sink and washed the gore from his hands.

"Help me finish this," he barked, his eyes searing into Norma's limp resolve. She could only stand there, trembling and making tiny mewing sounds. Dahl stepped forward and lashed out with his palm, laying a streak of fire across her cheeks, flooding her mouth with the taste of salt.

"Hold the fucking flashlight, you bitch!"

She automatically opened her hand and received the slippery object, then pointed it where Andreas indicated. He knelt and swiftly gathered up the receiver assemblies from the rifle crate, stuffing them in his coat pockets.

Then he yanked the light from her, his hand stabbing like a claw, and rapped her hard across the temple. She fell to her knees, groggy, and he circled her like a spider, slipping a noose of fishing line over her wrists and pulling it tight, yanking back her hair and stuffing a wadded dishcloth into her bruised and bleeding lips. She could only whimper now, and when he tugged, hard, she staggered in the direction he wanted, like an animal on a leash. No point in trying to yell for help; the time for that was long past, and she was in such a state of shock that none of this seemed real. He dragged her outside, into the rain, down to the edge of the lake, and there he hurled the assault rifle mechanisms as far as he could throw them. Thunder drowned their splash. Then he pulled her around the side of the camp, up the bank of a stream, through a wild tumble of slippery boulders, jerking her upright when she fell, until they came to a path hidden deep within the rocks, a trail she'd never seen before. He pushed her before him and jabbed her back with the flashlight, and by its wild and rain-streaked beam she staggered upward. Unable to accept the reality of what was happening, her mind blanked into a mantra of denial: *He's going to stop soon and turn me loose, and there will be an explanation—he will tell me when we get to where we're going, and then it will be all right. I am the Priestess, and he wouldn't dare harm me!* Part of her wanted simply to bolt and run, but she was off balance and she would fall, and he would bring that awful flashlight down on her head as he had done on Birgir's and she would die here, rot here, where no one in the world would know to look for her remains.

Ahead of them, the rocks opened upon a steeply canted plateau. Overhead, the storm was a seething cauldron, as though parts of the ocean had leaped wildly into the sky. A ferocious wind roiled over the cliff-tops, driving icy needles into her eyes, and for the first time, she heard a sound . . . like nothing she had ever heard. Something about it prickled her spine with pure atavistic terror.

Dewey awakened with an old but unforgettable feeling, one he had first experienced during a long-range patrol in the Central Highlands. His instinct had been right then, and he knew it was right now. It was not just that "they" were in the vicinity, but that "they" were *close*. He came fully awake instantly, a surge of adrenaline kicking in to give him that combat edge, that extra second of reaction time, that sharpening of the senses that sometimes means the difference between life and death.

He hadn't discussed it with anyone, but ever since the theft of the manuscript, he had known "they" would be back. He didn't know who "they" were, but he had already made the transition to thinking of them as "the enemy." After the gathering broke up in the mess hall and he'd passed the Webley to Birgir, he'd gone to his tent, slipped into his rain gear, smudged his face with lamp soot, and armed himself with the long sharp flensing blade he'd kept as a souvenir of the whale-killing. Then he went out into the night, into the darkest heart of the night. If they were out there, he was going to stalk them and find them. He was ready. The storm, after all, gave them perfect cover; Hannibal and five hundred elephants could have sneaked up on such a night and not been heard.

During the last hour of daylight, Dewey had reconnoitered the sheltered places in the rocks north of the camp, and for the past hour he'd moved stealthily from one spot to the next. He was about to give it up, though. The weather was as bad as a monsoon, but there wasn't any triple-canopy jungle to protect him from the worst of it. No matter which direction he faced, the tempest wind shoved buckets of water into his face and drove spear-points of water through every chink in his clothing. His feet were getting numb and he was dying for a smoke. Darkness was absolute except for when the lightning flashed—a plentiful but hallucinatory source of fitful illumination. Fatigue and common sense were starting to weaken his earlier bellicose resolve. Whoever "they" were, they were amateurs, not Viet Cong sappers. Finally, after ninety miserable minutes, he decided to call it off and head down to the mess hall for a cup of coffee with his pal Birgir.

Dewey ducked his head as he left his partial shelter, and the rain slashed harder into his eyes; he picked his way carefully toward the camp. As he drew nearer and the angle changed, he thought he saw a faint smear of light inside the mess hall. The distance was too great for him to be sure, but for some reason the sight triggered off a whole set of half-forgotten jungle reflexes—all of his rain-lulled synapses fired at once and he became as alert as a wire with current surging through it. He increased his scuttling pace until he found a point overlooking the building; his knife came readily to hand, in a combat grip.

A brief lull in the downpour allowed him to see two figures emerge, struggling, slipping in the mud, and then a fresh gust of rain wiped away the sight. When his vision cleared again, the figures were barely discernible, and were for some reason heading uphill between two outcroppings of stone. From the way they moved, Dewey knew there had to be a path; he could find it again, with any luck, and if they did not realize he was behind them, he could overtake them. But for the moment, the focus of his alarm was not the two mysterious figures, but the mess hall itself. Something was wrong in there.

Inside, he saw signs of a struggle: overturned chairs, a salt shaker streaming over the lip of the dining table—beyond, the dark portal of the lab and the shower cubicle beckoned and he went in that direction, calling Birgir's name, heart pounding. Near the shower stall he flipped on the lights. The fresh bloodstains led him on, his gut tightening with every step. The blood trail thickened near the shower stall, whose green plastic curtain was smeared with what looked like drying streaks of red tempera paint. Behind the curtain he found Birgir—as broken and violated-looking as any corpse he'd ever seen, dead from so savage and methodical a beating that Dewey almost gagged at the sight.

Enraged, kicking chairs out of his way, Dewey emerged into the rain, and was astonished to see a third figure, a hundred yards ahead, following the path of the first two, moving steadily up into the middle distance through a forest of rain whorls that flailed the rocks like small tornadoes. Cursing in a strangled, vicious litany—he had liked Birgir immensely, had thought him a man's man, honorable and strong—Dewey fought to impose a veneer of caution over his rage. He took some deep breaths, steadied himself, then struggled deeper into his sheepskin jacket and set off after the strange nocturnal procession.

Karen had waited until Allen was asleep. It had been pleasant sitting with him while he drifted off, no strain in their closeness now, especially under such an oppressive storm. If the attraction between them was less demonstrative, there was a wary kind of respect growing in its place, tentative but surprisingly undemanding. Of course, she had known, without a word being said or a Significant Glance being exchanged, that he had spent the night with Elsuba after the whale-kill. Yet it pleased her that he had not broken down in an excess of guilt and confessed all to her—as the pre-Vardinoy Warrener would surely have done. Whatever had happened, he seemed to have come back freed from some of the paralyzing cobwebs of his past. He'd treated her with tender diffidence, accepting the fact that their relationship was changing, but seemingly knowing that any preconceptions of what sort of intimacy might grow between them would be unwise. Like Karen, he would have to go with the flow for a while. Had he accepted, as she had—at first in misery and then with a cool resignation that surprised her—that on this voyage they were now seeking separate but kindred dreams? If he could remain patient and follow his newly recalibrated inner compass, she would soon bring him into the growing ambit of her private knowledge about this place. But first, she had to be sure; she had to seek more knowledge, raise the bets with her subconscious, take a risk or two, go more deeply into . . . that other place. She needed a better view of the psychic terrain through which she was starting to travel.

It was time for her to Go In again. The marijuana had previously helped her to go deep. Now, desirous of going deeper still, she dug up from the depths of her suitcase, wrapped in a tampon package, the two remaining lightweight hits of LSD she had scored just before packing. Using a cup of bottled water, she downed the first tab; hesitated for a few moments, listening to the feedback of her brain-waves, then—what the hell?—popped the second one. Beside the water bottle, she laid out enough sleeping pills to knock out a camel, again wanting the option of being able to bail out if things got too heavy.

Then she turned the Coleman lantern down to a whisper and lay down. And listened hard to the rain.

Going deeply into the sound of the rain, hearing Philip-Glass rhythmic patterns in it that were quite amazing.

(Softly it begins. . . .)

*It's very gradual, this taking-of-form. It's the form of whatever entity is out there, or under or covering, for all she knows, the whole floor of the North Sea. Its vastness is unmeasured, yet she is sure: it is the biggest thing in the sea. And, somehow she knows, the oldest. Her consciousness melts with its formless, alien, inarticulate Awareness. All around her is that now-familiar silky primordial sea, thick as soup, skin-or-membrane temperature, it is beautiful just **to be** and to float along.*

(That small part of her that is still lying in a cot in a tent on Vardinoy understands that this is **memory**, but not her own or that of anything that should still be alive.)

But "memories" she has seen enough of, so she wills the fugue-state to become deeper, and the drugs in her system gladly wipe away the pastoral seascape and open a portal for her, and she's seized with vertigo at how much D
E
E
P
E
R
she's going.

She wills herself to decelerate, and the acid obliges. And so she arrives at "The Present," *its Present,* at any rate, and instead of the limitless freedom of floating on the surface, she senses dark confinement.

It/she tries to stretch, a simple exercise, any animal is capable of it, from an amoeba to a grizzly bear and desires it so much it/she aches for the simple relief of voluntary extension.

It cannot. Its confinement is everywhere and absolute.

Always it wants to move. Always. Yet it cannot. It is hermetically encysted.

(So: this is what acute claustrophobia feels like, raised to the power of madness.)

That's her last conscious thought for a while, for she's now totally at one with this creature. And her presence causes a surge of panic such as it has not felt since the last Ice Age.

OH GOD OH GOD OH NO, THIS CAN'T BE HAPPENING CAN'T BE HAPPENING CAN'T CAN'T CAN'T BE . . .

But it is. It is the same as always. The mountain imprisoning it doesn't move. Since it regained awareness in this miles-deep prison, it has never moved. Trembled faintly, yes, but never really moved, not so much as a millimeter. This is how it's been since the volcano exploded back in the days when the planet was young and raw, and the lava flowered into a tsunami, and the last thing it knew for thousands of years was the sudden coldness of that wave's shadow blocking the beloved sun, and then the abyss opened and took her/it down its cold endless black throat. Since that incalculably long-ago trauma, the core-of-its-being has not moved, for a mountain grew when the lava cooled and that mountain became weathered ancient Vardinoy. Now she knows something essential. And wishes to God she did not. There's a billion tons of basalt imprisoning its core, its nucleus, its essence, that huge aching part of her/it that longs to be mobile, to be free.

Time became meaningless, infinite, geological change a fleeting thing by comparison. But it/she still has some control over the huge outer mass, shapeless and protoplasmic, yet tough-fibered and impervious to age, because Evolution had chosen it for its first experiment in consciousness, its first fumbling blueprint for a higher nervous system, an organic brain, or at least a complex sensory organ.

Evolution did not abandon its first child. During countless millennia of pondering its situation, it changes from the dumb-but-happy sea-floater of infancy into a highly evolved organism. It experiments, and finds that its secretions, its pseudopods if you will, also have sensory powers, and it strives to develop them. In time, it discovers that with infinite patience, it can extend filaments through minute fissures and cracks, channels thin as threads, cold capillaries left over from the cooling-lava time. Over the centuries, it distracts itself by mapping those channels and exploring them, secreted-substances which slowly bored through the very rock, breaking it down into nutrient chemicals. It lacks the physical power to free its core, but at least it can, in time, send its extrusions crawling over the seabed. As Evolution's first Bright Idea, it has no natural enemies, and any creature who takes a bite out of those extensions quickly regrets it. Its touch burns like acid, and as for devouring a part of it—well, a myrmidon shark took a couple of feet one time and went quickly mad from the agony. It cannot evolve skeletal tissue, or muscle, but it becomes in time much more limber. Its extrusions sometimes probe hundreds of miles, and at the far ends, they can expand into bulbous nodules even though their connection to the core is wire-thin. The extrusions also supply nutrition, for there's not much, animal or mineral, that it cannot break down into sustenance. It feeds all the time, quite unconsciously, as a pre-programmed survival instinct. The core can intervene, but seldom chooses to any more. The extrusions are not conscious, not sentient, any more than a foot shares function with the brain that commands it to walk.

So its outer mass, its envelope, is not helpless; is in fact far-wandering, once visiting the Marianas Trench, but finding it too dark and oppressive for anything but a quick reconnaissance; and the giant squid, while no more immune to the dire effects of snacking on its flesh than the giant shark, were as pesky as mosquitoes.

(My God, nobody knows they can grow that big!)

The extrusions are **of it**, but they are not it. Its being—that-which-is-her/its essence—is the part that yearns to stretch, to move. And, always, cannot.

Suicide is an appealing concept that absorbs its attention for a few centuries during the Late Tertiary, but that's a dead end. Evolution did not think of it as useful.

(Karen, starting to come down, to come back, understands now. What she endured when she was trapped in that concrete pipe was but the merest taste of

what this being had endured for millions upon millions of years. Her raging, mindless claustrophobic attack was but the faintest reverberation of the anguish this being had known since the Earth was young and violent. That's when it became cognizant of her and dispatched a long extrusion to make contact with this small but somehow kindred being. It sensed her, then. Maybe one of the insects she felt tickling her sweat-rivering face was the tip of an extrusion. Whatever the method, they had, briefly, connected, *kin in terror and desperation. Perhaps the extrusions were crudely telepathic. Why not, after so long a time? And with nothing else to do but focus on developing the sensitivity of those elongations? But to stay in this close a proximity to it is to invite madness. It is simply too alien. But not so alien that it isn't aware of her and isn't, somehow, pleased to feel this renewed contact with her. It doesn't get visitors. The horror of lightless confinement is not to be endured. Yet it is endured. It is a fact. It must be borne. Yet it cannot be accepted as eternal. She senses that, just possibly, this vast yet pitiable entity might have constructed its own mythology.* **Don't go there, girl! Get out now!** This has been quite enough exploration for one session.

So without thinking, she murmurs "Good-bye, I'll be with you again soon," and feels its sorrow at her departure as she begins to spool back into her tent on Vardinoy, ashen and bathed in cold sweat.

There was no question in Dewey's mind now. This ghost of a trail was leading toward the Axe-Cuts. It was steep and narrow, and flushed with runoff that hissed and slopped over his boots, but it was cleverly, almost certainly intentionally, angled so that it could still be ascended during conditions this extreme. Perhaps it was most often ascended in these conditions, for certainly it had been used with some regularity or it would have vanished. The storm gusted powerfully again, and momentarily he lost sight of the third figure he was trailing. Cursing, he forced the pace, driven by a sense of urgency.

There: ahead and pausing. Dewey was close enough now, after one dangerous sprint over ankle-twisting ground, to see that it was Karen. That knowledge brought him up short. Gigantic clouds strobe-lit like Grand Canyons adrift in the night—the stones glowed slick yellow-white, a salvo of lightning, and it was followed by a sudden eerie calm, a pause while the wind changed directions again, and Dewey thought he heard, far ahead and faint, the sound of the sea in rage; but farther still, oh so much farther, a deep ululating moan, answered by another, similar cry many leagues distant. The hair on his neck stood erect. It was as though the substance of his every nightmare had been given tongue and turned loose on a storm-lashed ocean. That sound put the fear of God into Dewey Tucker the way nothing else had done except his first time under enemy fire.

Karen is walking, but she does not really feel her passage over earth, through rain. She has come part-way back from the bed of the sea, from the gut of the planet, but hasn't really awakened. The last thing she remembers is donning her raingear and sneaking out of the tent.

Now she's homing in on a distant unidentifiable sound and somehow knows that at the end of this journey, she will learn more about that phenomenon than she might care to learn. Growing more awake by the moment, she presses forward.

Norma saw the cliffs spread before her, riven by knife-thin chasms, and she knew where Andreas had taken her and she had an appalling idea of why. She tore herself free from his predatory grip and whirled like a dervish, her senses reeling. Between puffs of stinging rain, she blinked her eyes and shook her face, trying to regain control of at least her sense of sight. But she ended up facing the sea, and saw it for the first time, through a window of lightning-lit clarity between the fists of rain: a sea in torment, run through by blades of fire. Down on their ledges, those ghastly birds were squalling, too, a thin wild piping, and the driven waves struck Vardinoy like howitzer shells. It was as though Nature was trying to destroy this abomination of an island, pound it into mud. And out where the horizon reared up into angry teeth, she heard again those unknown but terrifying cries.

Andreas Dahl spun her around. In the lightning, his face was a fluorescent death's mask, his eyes deep caves. He gestured wildly toward the sea.

"Do you hear them? Those calls? Frightening, aren't they? It's the Great Orms, coming back, because they know the time of the Emergence is near! It's long been foretold that when the time was near, the Orms would return from their hidden waters, and now it's happening!" Brutally, he yanked the gag from her tortured mouth. "Say hello to your new companions, Norma! Call out to them for mercy!"

"Andreas. . . ." her voice, wind-whimpering, a child's bleat, a fluttered rag of protest and incomprehension, was torn to shreds by the storm. "Andreas, what's happened? You told me I was your Priestess! You told me I would be a princess among your people!"

"*You . . . are . . . nothing!*"

Rage gave her a voice now. There was no other response she could make and stay sane through what was apparently about to happen. "Goddamn your lying heart, you fucked me blind and told me I was your Priestess! You dragged me inside the stupid fucking cave and put me through some kind of idiotic initiation ceremony and told me I was the One, the Voice, the leading lady! You *promised!*"

She struck at him with her bound fists, like mallets of white rubber. He leaned his head away from the weakened blows, lazily, contemptuously.

"But, my dear, you turned out not to be that person! And so you are of no further use to me!"

She was, finally, weeping and pleading nakedly for her life. "Andreas, I would have gone with you, anywhere! I would have gladly worshipped your god!"

"Look down, then, you slut, and meet him face to face!"

He pushed her over the edge of the crevasse.

Even as he saw Andreas Dahl, backlit by lightning, disappear—not falling, but with measured descent as though on a hidden staircase—at that moment Dewey heard Karen's scream go silent in mid-cry, cut off as though her mouth, her entire throat, had suddenly filled with stones. His vision was sharp now, combat-charged with adrenaline, and he was certain that he saw a change in the texture of the darkness inside the Axe-Cut: the darkness had substance, and was *rising* to meet Norma's falling body, so that she did not plummet into the abyss so much as sink very slowly out of sight.

Karen woke on the edge of a cold emptiness, screaming—not because she was on the lip of the chasm, but because she had seen *over it*. Had seen the mottled thick darkness move like cold undulating tar, a descending wedge of living shadow, hundreds of feet deep. And just before Dewey's strong arms gripped her and hurled her back from the edge, she had seen—far down inside that living darkness, mouth opened in a silent rictus of agony, glowing blue-white with an unholy refulgence—the shape of Norma Davenport. Writhing. Still alive.

Book V:

RAGNAROK

. . . I swam

In the blackness of night, hunting monsters

Out of the depths, and killing them one

By one; Death was my errand and the fate

They had earned. Now Grendel and I are called

Together, and I must come. . . .

—*Beowulf* VI: 421–426

33.

BONES ON THE BOTTOM

From the journal of Richard Sugarman:

Everything is changed now. This landscape, which looked so heroic just a few days ago, whose moods and elemental colors so invigorated me—which even gave me, for the first time in my middle-class Jewish life, some empathy for the whole Nordic Thing—now looks as grim and oppressive as a dusty old set from Bayreuth.

Why didn't I sense it before, the overwhelming malevolence of these vistas? Vardinoy was spawned by cataclysms, sculpted by violence and tempest. It exists, frail and tiny despite its peaks, at the sufferance of an ocean whose capacity for mindless destruction we have already glimpsed. A landscape like this should feel solid, eternal! But I look upon Vardinoy now, and all it suggests to me is a reference point by which to comprehend the terrible immensity that surrounds it. There are titanic latent forces all around us, and just as those forces once gave birth to Vardinoy, so too could they obliterate it. Perhaps our coming has awakened them from centuries of dormancy . . . but centuries mean nothing to them, and human lives are as dust. Perhaps Allen and Preston (and that wacko, Dewey) still think of these things as "challenges" to be met with virile determination, but I have no desire to test my manhood against the immeasurable. No contest. The Gods take the wreath every time.

Yesterday I chanced to see the group portrait Preston took of us on the day we set up this camp, and compared it mentally to the way we look today. In the earlier picture, we look like teenagers who've just been given an unexpected holiday. This morning, when Dewey woke those of us who were sleeping and gave us the terrible news about last night's events, I could see how visibly we've aged since then.

All except for that bastard Warrener! His expression was ambiguous. I realize he came here for the very purpose of putting himself through some serious and maybe redemptive changes—but now it occurs to me that perhaps he came here hoping *to find something scary and dangerous—a second chance to be the hero. Somewhere deep in his psyche, he may be* glad *that the rules have changed, the gloves have come off, the middle-class restraints have been chucked overboard.*

It was dawn by the time Dewey half-led, half-carried poor Karen back down from the Axe-Cuts, and the rain had tapered off, leaving a chilly fog, like a mourning shroud, over our valley. After examining Karen, Elsuba gave her a sedative injection and tucked her under some blankets. Karen said nothing during all the time she was conscious—just stared into some awful private distance and then collapsed like a catatonic.

Then Dewey led us into the mess hall and showed us Birgir's body. The minute we walked through the door, we could smell the blood. I've never seen such damage inflicted on a human body from a hand-to-hand struggle: rib-points poked out through the front of his shirt, white as tubers growing out of red clay soil. His face was barely recognizable, for his head was just a ghastly compost of skull fragments and red-gray pulp. The drain in the shower stall was clogged with jellied chunks of "cranial matter." Preston, who was already in a state of shock from Dewey's very cautious description of what had happened to Norma, took one look at Birgir and became violently sick. Even Elsuba, hardened as she must be by tours of duty in trauma rooms, went pale and sagged into a chair. Eiden reacted with good, healthy rage, knotting his fists and cursing in several languages.

That's when I saw Warrener's eyes. His expression changed like a kaleidoscope. Revulsion, regret, anger—all those emotions went through him, yes—but as I watched, they were replaced by something wholly unexpected. Allen emerged from that grisly crime scene with the look and bearing of a man who has suddenly, in an unexpected place and time, found a possible answer to a lifelong question; had it thrust upon him in an obscenely perverse manner, yes; but, having accepted that, Allen seemed suddenly to have discovered within himself an unknown capacity to embrace "the Hor-rah, the Hor-rah!" His behavior during the next few minutes seemed to confirm that diagnosis.

While the rest of us just stood there, stunned and nauseated, Allen got to work. He knelt, slipped his arms under Birgir's body, and hoisted it up, like a combat medic evacuating a fallen comrade. Blisters of congealed blood swelled between his fingers and broke into slow, sticky rivulets. He was calm, but there were tears filling his eyes. When he turned, the body balanced over his shoulder, Birgir's blood was daubed on his face, like war paint. His voice was low and harsh and steady.

"There's a tarpaulin folded up beside the generator—would someone please spread it on the mess table?"

Elsuba and Eiden brought the heavy plastic tarp inside. Dewey stepped up and helped Allen lower the corpse into the center, then the two of them wrapped the tarp around Birgir's remains, their motions oddly tender, and sealed the makeshift body bag with half a roll of duct tape. Their eyes met once and held contact. Dewey nodded at Allen, as if to say: Well, Bro, now you seen the elephant too. I reluctantly helped Elsuba hose out the mess in the shower stall, first with water and then with disinfectant. The stench of blood and violated tissue faded.

As the gunk swirled down the drain, we uncovered Eiden's old Royal Navy revolver. Dewey fished it out, broke the cylinder, and held it out for Warrener to inspect.

"He didn't have time to fire it."

Suddenly, Warrener smacked his own forehead and looked around in a panic.

"The guns, Eiden! Did they find the guns?"

(GUNS?? WHAT FUCKING GUNS??)

Eiden rummaged through a disorderly stack of boxes and crates, then stood up with a defeated look on his face.

"They stripped the bolts, probably threw them into the lake. Except for the Webley, we're virtually defenseless."

"Maybe not. If he didn't throw them far enough, we might be able to find them with the Simrad and dry 'em out. Until then, however...." Allen turned to Dewey and scrutinized him with that new brothers-in-arms look. "I couldn't help but notice the smell of rifle lubricant coming from your tent the other day. You wouldn't happen to have brought along a souvenir from your days in balmy Southeast Asia...?"

"Very observant, mon capitain. I got an AK field-stripped in a camera case."

"How much ammo?"

"Four loaded mags and about two hundred loose rounds, ball and tracer."

Allen grunted approvingly, then bent down again beside the stack of supply crates and shifted them around until he came to an unmarked wooden box with heavy rope handles attached. He opened the padlock and started counting the contents. All I could see were tufts of excelsior padding the inside.

"At least Norma didn't know to tell him about the grenades—"

"Grenades?" I blurted. "What were you planning to do here, start an insurrection? How come you never mentioned all this firepower to the rest of us?"

Allen snarled right back at me: "Because I didn't want anybody to accuse me of being overly dramatic, Richard!"

From a shadowy part of the mess hall, Preston's voice rose in a grating wail: "Will you guys please stop arguing about hand grenades and help organize a search for my wife?" In the thin soak of morning light, Valentine looked like a wraith: his eyes were glassy with shock and his hands were shaking uncontrollably. Elsuba stepped close with her first-aid kit and offered him a couple of pills. At first he shook his head, then changed his mind and popped them into his mouth. She offered a cup of water, but as soon as he gagged them down he leaned his head on her breast and began to weep.

Eiden and Dewey are taking Birgir's body to the trawler now, to place it in the deep-freeze until they can arrange for a formal burial at sea, which is what Birgir would have wanted, I think. In their absence, Allen's trying to organize a search for Norma's body—as soon as the Land Rover returns, we'll haul the Simrad unit to the Laertes *and mount it on the motor launch. Nobody's come right out and said it yet, but there doesn't seem to be a snowball's chance in Hell of finding her alive. And if she did fall into one of the Axe-Cuts, her body could be halfway to Iceland now, depending on the currents. In the meantime, if only to keep Preston distracted, Allen's suggested that they mount the Simrad on one of our rubber boats and try to locate the missing bolt-and-receiver pieces from those assault rifles. Needle-in-a-haystack, probably, but I feel like I should help. More later.*

And here it is, "later." Much later. Working on my third cup of aquavit, need to finish this entry before I flake out. We enjoyed a partial success—the Simrad gave off a clear echo of something hard and metallic, just a few feet from the point where the lake shore shelves off steeply into unmeasured depths. The bolt/receiver piece was undamaged; as soon as it's dried off and re-lubricated, we will have another weapon to add to our little arsenal. That H and K is a light, simple-to-use weapon, and I intend to learn how to hit something with it. As Dewey remarked, we're now a frontier outpost in Indian country—anybody who can't handle a firearm is a liability. Even I must agree.

Let me end this journal entry by bringing the narrative full circle: last night's events have changed everything. Vardinoy now seems a dark and dangerous place. The ambience is charged with menace—but then it always was, potentially. It's just that when the monster was theoretical, that frisson of danger was stimulating, even fun. Now, in a manner very different from anything we might have expected, the monstrous, *at least, has entered our lives, stolen in on the night, and taken two friends from us, killing them each in a hideous and unnatural manner. Of course, there are human enemies behind those crimes, not sea serpents, but the obscurity of their motives and the extreme violence of their deeds frighten me more than any left-over plesiosaur possibly could.*

We all gathered in the mess hall as darkness fell. No one feels like being alone in an isolated tent. Not, at least, until Dewey and Eiden return and we can mount an armed guard over the camp. We are all agreed on one thing: perhaps there is some kind of monster out there, in human form and maybe in league with something that isn't human at all. We've all felt the cold breath of something vast and dangerous; with the coming of night, it seems to be suffused in the air all around us. We huddle together, and Karen just made the most perceptive comment of the day: "Now I know what cavemen felt on a dark night. Before they discovered fire."

The search for Norma's body began at noon. Karen was still unconscious, and Elsuba wanted to stay with her. Dewey had slapped together his North Vietnamese assault rifle and was mounting perimeter patrols, setting up noisemakers and tripwires across any dead-ground approach routes. Elsuba had strapped on her father's Webley, and two sailors from the *Laertes*, grimly mourning their murdered shipmate and eager to get a crack at the men responsible, augmented the security, one toting the H & K and the other a snub-nosed Enfield Mk. III from the ship's arms locker—a rifle even older than the trawler itself but just as reliable. Satisfied that the camp was well protected, Eiden and Preston prepared to mount the Simrad on the trawler's motor launch and conduct a grid search around the Axe-Cuts. But all this planning proved unnecessary. For at two o'clock in the afternoon, one of the seamen walking guard let out a yell that could have been heard in Torshavn.

Norma Davenport's corpse had just bobbed to the surface of the lake.

Dewey and one of the sailors went out in a rubber boat to bring it ashore. Although Allen tried to talk him out of it, Preston insisted on viewing the remains; after hauling the body into the boat, Dewey had seen all he ever wanted to. When Preston broke free of Allen's grip and tried to remove the plastic sheeting Dewey had used for a shroud, Dewey intercepted him with two martial-arts moves that knocked him out as effectively as ether; the trawlerman who'd helped fetch Norma—looking rather queasy himself—slung Preston over his shoulder like a sack of flour and lugged him into Elsuba's tent.

"Rest of you stay back, God damn it, except for Allen and Elsuba. None of you need to fuckin' see this! And if you try, I'll cold-cock you just like I did to Press!"

Norma had evidently struck the rocks on her way down, for there were compound fractures in one arm and one leg. But those were the least of her injuries. Her flesh was so bloated that it had split the seams of her clothing—ninety percent of her skin looked like a hard blue balloon on whose surface some child had scrawled hundreds of squiggly lines with a white laundry marker: hairline fissures where the blue encrustations had cracked and split. All the soft-tissue areas of her head and face had collapsed as though imploded; her empty eye sockets had shrunk to the size of wrinkled navels. The stench was abominable.

After giving the still-groggy Preston an injection—so he wouldn't suddenly interrupt the procedure—Elsuba had Allen clear off the dining table and then shooed him out so she could perform the best autopsy she could with her limited resources. She took copious tissue samples from the discolored flesh of the "burned" areas, but the most remarkable thing she found in her examination was the state of Norma's skeleton. The soft matter inside the bones—marrow, connective tissue, bundles of blood vessels, ligaments and nerves—was all just . . . gone. The words "hollowed out" appeared several times in Elsuba's notes. When she was done, Elsuba asked Dewey and Allen to fix up some kind of container, so the remains could be transported to the trawler's freezer, and then she asked her father to come inside and look at one of Norma's arms—only that; the rest of Norma's distorted body, Elsuba kept under cover.

"Poppa, I'll spare you the whole sight, but I do need you to take a look at this arm and tell me something: is this similar to what you saw on Kristofur's face and the body of that old sailor you interviewed in Tjornuvik?"

When Eiden went pale and staggered to the sink to throw up, her question was answered.

"I hate to ask you, Richard, but it's kind of important—I need somebody to go with me up to the Axe-Cuts again, while there's still plenty of daylight."

"I'd just as soon not, Allen—unless you make that an order. . . ."

"Oh, stop it with the Fearless Leader crap! I'm asking you because Eiden's too old, Elsuba's disinfecting the mess hall, Karen and Preston are funked-out on sedatives, Dewey's on guard duty, *and everybody else is fucking DEAD, okay?*"

"I'll be right with you, chief; let me get on my hiking boots. . . ."

. . .

"What do you expect to find up here?"

They'd taken the short route, and this time the hike hadn't seemed very long at all, even though they had to make numerous detours around spots that were still flooded from the storm.

"During one of her lucid moments, between sleeping pills, Karen insisted she'd seen Andreas Dahl going down one of the fissures after he pushed Norma over the edge of another one—she thinks he used a hidden path of some kind, or a rope ladder . . . something like that. If she's right, we need to know about it, because that gives Dahl's people a way to sneak up on the camp. If there is a rope ladder, we need to take it down so they can't do that. And I might need some help carrying it back. But first, if we do find a way down to the bottom of one of those damned things, I want to take a good look around."

But in the central of the three chasms, they found not a rope ladder but a carefully constructed permanent one, constructed out of solid iron pitons driven deep into the rocks and complete with guardrails, for which they were extremely grateful.

At the bottom, they learned that the tides had greatly enlarged the thin gorge, carving out a spoon-shaped inlet on both sides of a tidal channel that led to a cave entrance big enough to drive a small car into. At low tide, at least, it was possible to walk from the bottom of the ladder to the mouth of the chasm and, by turning north, walk dry-footed along a pebbled causeway that appeared to lead all the way to the hidden cove where the ruined church brooded in secrecy. For some reason, the usual horde of seafowl was absent, although the massive stalagmites of guano lining the sides of the cut testified to their frequent occupation of its ledges and knobs. Out of the wind, with ample sunlight streaming down from above, the bottom was not the grim, wet tomb Allen had been dreading. As long as the sunlight lasted, in fact, it was downright pleasant. Both men were tense from the long climb down, so they sought a ring of warm flat rocks and a few slugs of bourbon from Allen's second canteen.

"With a little décor and a proper marketing campaign, we could turn this place into a real tourist trap," observed Richard.

"Yeah—but would you want to ride a boat underneath Vardinoy?"

"Not for all the *Geld* in Switzerland. So you think there are tunnels in all of these things, leading to the lake?"

"In this one and the one Norma fell into, at least. And that's consistent with the stories we've collected . . . about sightings on the coast and in the lake. All connected. Great place for a monster to hide out, isn't it?"

"You know, I really wish you hadn't said that!" Richard glanced warily at the black mouth in the cliff. "And while we're alone and basking at the beach, why don't you tell me what the fuck is *really going on!* Two of our people are dead—one murdered and Norma might as well have been—and the one valuable thing this expedition's discovered has been stolen. It's obvious that we're not wanted here, but I haven't a clue as to why. And while we're talking on the level, how about explaining why you seemed almost *happy* when you were picking up poor Birgir's body?"

" 'Happy'? Far from it, Richard. I liked Birgir a lot—we all did. It was just a coincidence, that's all. Because the moment I lifted his body, I had this little private epiphany. Some of the puzzle pieces came together. For one thing, I realized that we're dealing with a tangible evil, not a mythical one. And the source of that evil? All the evidence points to Norduroy. Andreas Dahl *did* lie to us, you see. About where he came from and why he's on this island. He and his people want us off of Vardinoy badly enough to kill for it, so whatever 'it' is, it's not trivial. Do you see why I became a little manic?"

"Frankly, no. . . ."

"We came here in search of a mystery, and by God we found one! Exactly what's *here* that's important enough to murder people for? Intrinsically, there's not a goddamned thing! No buried treasure, no secret military installations, no oil deposits, no diamond mines—hell, there aren't even any inhabitants! So what is it the people of Norduroy are trying to hide? Or to prevent us from discovering?"

"Maybe Dahl's just a psychopath."

"Almost certainly, he is—just look at the way he butchered poor Birgir! But Dahl's just the front man for something much bigger. I was too busy gazing at my navel to figure it out, until Karen, God bless her, gave me some insights. Dahl hasn't behaved like a serial killer, and he's not the kind of sicko who tortures stray cats in his basement. Instead, he's a quiet, disciplined kind of madman. In other words, a *fanatic*. He doesn't kill in order to steal something valuable, or because some government is paying him to do it—but he is capable of killing for his *faith!* Now, take it one step further: what if all the inhabitants of Norduroy were True Believers too?"

"A cult of some kind? With Andreas playing the part of Charles Manson? That's pretty wiggy, Allen. But it is consistent with his style—those cold eyes, that inner rigidity, like he always had a broomstick up his ass."

"Then you buy the hypothesis?"

"So far. Keep going."

As they rotated slowly in the tilting sunbeam, Allen tried to connect the dots: the strange and somewhat sinister behavior of the Norduroy men during the rescue of that shot-down German pilot . . . the old sailor he and Eiden had interviewed in Tjornuvik . . . the nightmarish death of Eiden's son after his ship foundered in the waters near Vardinoy . . . the violent end of the Irish monks and the cryptic references the ancient Norduroy men made to their "deity." . . .

"Wait, wait a minute! That cancerous deterioration on Eiden's son and on the old sailor's arm, do you think that might be caused by some poison or concoction the Norduroy people inflict on . . . *non-believers* who fall into their hands?"

"No, Richard; they're not sophisticated enough to be dabbling in germ warfare. But suppose, for argument's sake, that there *is* some kind of exotic life form capable of manufacturing an organic compound that literally rots the flesh of anyone who comes in contact with it—and somehow the Norduroy people were immune, or protected, or had an antidote? The oceans are full of creatures that secrete or inject toxins! Everything from flowery little anemones to jellyfish. And what if this thing is *really big?* Norduroy was settled about two hundred years before Mac-Othna and his merry Irish heretics landed on Vardinoy. It was a violent age, but if Norduroy was home to an animal that could be turned loose against an invader, that could squirt acid on his troops, capsize his ships maybe, then the people on that island would be invulnerable. *Under protection.* Something that keeps you safe in a turbulent world, well, you would first of all be damned glad you were on good terms with it, but after a few generations of coexistence, people with a pagan mindset might very well start to worship it."

"Allen, those Irish monks died nine hundred years ago!"

"Right, but Norduroy hasn't *changed* that much in nine hundred years. They may have diesel engines and electric lights, but they're as isolated as it's possible to be in the late twentieth century, and they're isolated *by choice!*

Who knows what weird shit they believe in? Not to mention what twelve centuries of inbreeding will do to the hardiest gene pool!"

"Okay, for the sake of argument, let's say Norduroy *is* populated entirely by degenerate religious fanatics who worship a giant poisonous sea sponge—why haven't they gone out and proselytized? From what their neighbors say, the main thing they've always wanted is just to be *left alone.* Which isn't too hard for them to do, given where they live. They're not sending prophets abroad to evangelize for this . . . whatever-it-is. For that reason alone, they don't behave like a cult. We ran afoul of them because we just suddenly showed up and they perceived us as a threat to their way of life, or maybe as blasphemers, because we wanted to take movies of their . . . Protector, if you will. Even if I grant all of that, Allen, I still don't see where you're going with this."

"Ah, yes, well, that *is* the problem, isn't it? If we try to probe any deeper into this business, what's to prevent them from sneaking over and mas-sacring the lot of us one night, just like they did to the Irish settlers? I simply *have* to find out more! And even if I wasn't already in too deep to back out, there's still Eiden's oath of vengeance to consider. He *will* get to the bottom of this, even if he has to do it alone; but as brave as he is, he's an old man—he wouldn't stand a chance. If I pulled out now, it would be like desertion."

"And of course, you won't do that."

"Could you?"

"I might have given a different answer a few days ago, but no, I couldn't either. Not after what happened to Birgir and Norma."

"No question about it: Andreas Dahl is one evil son of a bitch, but I'd hate to see him die before I learn the reasons why he is like he is. We're not dealing with flying-saucer nuts, here. These people are *motivated,* and they're motivated by something real."

"Tell me honestly, Allen, if you do learn enough to satisfy everybody's curiosity, would you call the magistrate in Torshavn and have Dahl arrested, or would you bushwhack him yourself?"

Allen's face was unreadable, except for a flicker deep in his eyes, which Richard found disturbing.

"I guess I *could* do that, couldn't I?" he mused, shifting positions as the light shaft began to fade.

"Way up here, nobody would ever know. . . ."

"That's right, Richard."

"Except you."

"That's right too."

Richard thought he was beginning to figure something out. Vardinoy was no longer a dream-landscape for Allen Warrener. It had turned into an arena. Or, perhaps more accurately, a battlefield.

The light was almost gone—only their faces remained in it now. Their feet crunched on mounds of calcified bird crap. Allen was gesturing, winding up to make another point, but his foot landed badly on a glazed rock, and he fell, cursing, into the shadows. White dust rose from his impact.

Richard went over to help him up, but Allen waved him away and just pointed. In his fall, he had triggered a rock slide, and the largest boulder had taken a freak bounce and bashed into an apparently solid mound of petrified bird droppings. This geological anomaly cracked open like a giant eggshell and as the last slant of declining sunlight poured into the opening, it revealed a pit dug into the strip of beach at the Axe-Cut's narrow end. Inside lay a great heap of human bones, including dozens of broken skulls and leering portions of jaw. Threaded through rib cages were withered leather belts and empty sheaths—these were not Viking-age remains. Jutting out, as though it had been placed there for their eyes to discover, was a piece of slate on which words had been carefully inscribed with an awl or a nail. The language was Faeroese—a farewell message from someone who not died instantly when striking the bottom; perhaps his fall was cushioned by the bodies of those whose bones had shattered earlier. In the fading light floating through the shaft, they recognized *"Krist"* and *"Gud."*

"I think it's a prayer, Richard. 'Christ' and 'God' . . . here, and here, and here. I hope the Lord was listening to the poor bastard. Let's take it back to camp, have Eiden translate it. And let's climb back up while there's still some light in this pit—suddenly it's gotten too creepy for comfort down here."

Both men climbed in silence for a while, until Richard simply had to say it:

"Are you thinking what I'm thinking?"

"Human sacrifices? Could be; but if so, the Gray-Boats must've given up the practice several generations ago. Those bones have been here a long, long time. On the other hand, we might have been looking at the site of a one-time massacre."

"Oh, Jesus. . . . The abandoned village!"

34.

Disturbances in the Earth

On the morning after the discovery of the cairn at the bottom of the Axe-Cut, Allen thought it might be worthwhile—now that its previous occupant was long gone—to make another, more thorough, search of Andreas Dahl's dwelling. As they approached the hut, Eiden suddenly asked: "Are you going to go home now, Allen, or stay?"

"I'm staying. The others should be given a chance to leave, if they want to. This thing has turned into something very different from what they signed on for."

"And Karen, Allen; what about her?"

"I haven't talked to her, really talked to her, since the night Norma died. I'm not sure I *can*. She seems very far away from me, Eiden."

"Then tell me: are you unhappy that she's 'fallen under the spell' of the Faeroes in her own way, without your guidance, but just as deeply as you once did?"

"It isn't that, Eiden. It's a feeling that she *knows* something that could be important. I don't know how she came by the knowledge—she can't or won't tell me—but I am certain she knows something I don't, something that might help me to understand what the hell we've blundered into. That makes me a little bit annoyed with her."

Eiden's reply came slowly, but his words were firm: "You're right, of course—she confided that much to me. But I honestly don't believe that she knows how to describe what she's learned. When she figures things out, she'll tell you. When a person chooses to remain silent until the right words have formed, it's not secrecy so much as wisdom."

"Well, excuse me!" Allen grouched, kicking open the door of the old stone farmhouse. Even in daylight, the place was full of stale gloom; to Norma, it must have been like living in a cave. A complete search didn't take long, and at first they only turned up the usual debris of transient occupation: cigarette butts, empty food cans, some scraps of clothing. Then, under the bed, Eiden found a small stack of sketches, and Allen, searching the last cupboard in the main room, found a rolled-up map and a ledger-sized book, mildewed and water-stained.

The map was clearly based on the same wartime survey the expedition had consulted, only this copy had been updated, in meticulous detail. Their camp's location was marked, of course, and another set of hand-drawn changes indicated the Axe-Cuts. Running here and there along the entire island were faint sets of parallel dotted lines which seemed to delineate the approximate configuration of a network of subterranean passageways, most of them branching out from or contiguous to the Axe-Cuts. If the scale was even roughly accurate, there was no longer any mystery about how Norma's body had surfaced so far from where it had vanished.

They spread the stack of drawings on the table, one by one. All were of the same brooding genre as Dahl's public work, but their content seemed more sinister in tone: the arrangement of forms did not reflect nature, but went far beyond it, so that the shapes of mountains and waves and clouds became suggestive and anthropomorphic. One large drawing had been reworked so many times that at first it seemed an abstraction. But as Allen kept staring at it, he began to see a central shape underneath the smudges and furrows of many reworkings: a brown-black bulk surrounded by dozens of thick limbs or branches, which in turn divided into hundreds of spidery, hair-thin wisps, like capillaries blooming from major arteries. Viewed as a whole, there seemed to be a rigid, almost palpable tension binding the frantic elaborateness of the composition, and the whole sheet was blotted with smears and alterations, as though to mark successive creative encounters with a subject that the artist couldn't quite get down on paper to his satisfaction.

"What in the hell is that supposed to be?" said Eiden.

"Damned if I know, but I'll bet a good shrink could have a field day with it."

"We should take all of these back to camp. What's in that book you found?"

"Nothing exciting—a lot of old names and dates in Faeroese."

"Let me look at it."

Eiden began carefully turning the stained vellum pages. "It's a register from the village church. *This* village, actually. It lists births, weddings, and deaths, mostly, with a few notations about weather and fishing conditions. Nothing else here except the name of the place: *Fugla Fjordor*—'Fjord of the Birds.' "

"Pretty name. How old is the book?"

"The last entry is, let's see . . . August eleven, eighteen eighty-three. After that, blank pages."

"Still, Dahl must have hidden it here for a reason. Let's take it back too."

A half hour later, Allen entered his tent, Dahl's sketches and the ledger tucked under one arm. Karen smiled thinly at him, pale against the navy blue of her sleeping bag. "Hi, stranger," she said, both tenderness and regret mingled in her voice.

"Hello, lady. How're you feeling?"

"Better and better. Elsuba's a good doctor."

Karen's expression told him nothing—if there was any irony in that last remark, it was for him to find.

"I've been worried," he stammered, still standing, shifting to another foot, suddenly measuring the true extent of the gap between them and not liking it.

"So was I. So *am* I. I'm sorry for being so remote from you, Allen. I wish these mood swings would go away, but they're only getting stronger."

"Do you still love me?" he blurted, the ground shifting beneath him.

"Yes." Her voice was solemn. "But there's something overshadowing my personal feelings, and I'm afraid it's dominating everything else right now."

"I'm sorry, Karen, but I just don't understand."

Urgently now: "Allen, I want you to disband the Expedition. Now. Today."

"You're out of your fucking mind."

"I've never been more serious, or more certain, in my life. You don't know what you might be dealing with, and you can't conceive of how dangerous it might be."

"And you *do* know 'what we're dealing with'? Then for Christ's sake, how about telling me?"

She knotted her fists in frustration and beat them on the cot.

"I don't know enough to tell you what you want to hear! What I do know is that Andreas did not kill Norma—he pushed her off the edge, yes, but something else actually killed her. I saw something . . . enveloping her, absorbing her body, and all it looked like was a mass of shadows or a black cloud. That's all that registered before I blacked out again."

"Karen, it was dark and rainy and you were overwrought. . . ."

"Jesus, Allen, do you know what you sound like? Like Chadwick Merritt debunking your sea-serpent theories! I am telling you what I *saw,* and I'm telling you it was like nothing any of us has ever seen or even imagined! You wanted to be the big, brave monster-hunter—well, buster, whatever I saw, it was by God monstrous, it was monstrous as all hell, and it's already caused two of us to die, and if you don't get these people off this island, it may be the death of us all!"

"I'd already planned to call everybody together this afternoon and give them the option of going or staying. I can't *force* anybody to do either."

"Yes, you can! You're the *leader,* and you can just dissolve the Expedition and *send* them home! Allen, listen to me; it isn't only because of what I saw the night Norma died, it's more than that. I'm sure this thing exists because, in some crazy spaced-out way, I've been in contact with it. I've dreamed things, seen things in my mind that could never have come from my own imagination."

"Everybody's subconscious has a shit-load of weird stuff floating around in it, love. . ." He stopped when he saw that don't-patronize-me look on her face. He tried again, from a different angle: "Okay, let's suppose you have been picking up . . . what? vibes? Okay, vibes then, from some outside source. . . ."

He stopped at that point because her face had suddenly transformed, her eyes gone glassy and her fingers knotting the sleeping bag convulsively, as though a seizure were imminent. Allen ran outside and yelled for Elsuba.

As he turned around and moved to Karen's side, Dahl's sketch fell out of his grasp and drifted across her lap like a big, dirty leaf. At the sight of that convoluted, many-branched shape, Karen began to scream, legs flailing to kick the image away. Elsuba entered, doctor's bag flapping at her side, took a quick look, and deftly filled a syringe. Karen seemed not to notice as the injection went in; her screams quickly subsided to groans, then to dry, rattling whispers.

"Old," she breathed, "so old . . . older than anything."

Another minute and she was under.

"Allen, she needs to be in a hospital. Shock, hallucinations, fatigue . . . she needs bed rest and better medical resources than I can provide here on Vardinoy."

She closed her bag, suddenly very businesslike, looking at him levelly: "You'd better come with me to the lab."

While passing through the kitchen alcove, she poured mugs of coffee for both of them. "It's a bit rank in there just now," she said, sliding open the partition to the lab compartment. "The coffee will help, I think. I've run out of nose plugs. . . ."

Inside the cramped lab space were strong chemical smells, and, beneath their acridity, something more insidious, touched with a sickly sweetness.

He looked around the room. "Where did you put . . . er. . . ."

"Norma's body? In the freezer aboard the ship, of course. Where else could I put it? The smell is from tissue samples. I've done all I can do here, with this equipment and what little I remember about pathology, so I had some of the sailors put her in with Birgir's body, until a proper autopsy can be arranged. I can't wait to hear what the doctor who performs it will have to say. . . ."

She sat down and peered steadily at him over the rim of her coffee mug. "Allen—Dahl did not kill Norma. *Caused* her death, yes, but he did not literally kill her. Something else, something organic, did. I haven't a clue yet as to what it might be, but I think it's safe to say that, yes, we do have a monster out there somewhere. And I hope you've got a big crucifix, because whatever it was, it drained most of Norma's blood—took it right out through the pores of her skin. It did the same with the bone marrow—dissolved it and absorbed it. God knows what its diet may normally consist of, but as far as human beings are concerned, it doesn't mess around—it goes straight for the most nutritious and organically rich substances in the body. I don't know about the internal organs, but I suspect, just from handling the corpse, that part of the brain is gone too. I didn't feel up to checking.

"This thing secretes, probably even projects, a very potent substance that isolates, breaks down, and draws out the nutrient chemicals it wants; and in the process, it has the same general effect on human tissue as some kinds of strong acid. Some of the more venomous jellyfish do the same thing, on a much smaller scale; but if this stuff is similar, then my guess is that the main chemical agent is some kind of incredibly complex polysaccharide. I don't think this stuff is active all the time; it probably gets triggered off when something edible comes in range, or maybe when its owner gets angry or feels threatened. Make no mistake, Allen, this stuff is potent. Once it breaks down the constituent molecules of whatever it's after, then the nutrients, minerals, what-have-you, can be sucked out. 'Absorbed,' to use the German aviator's word for it, and presumably transported, through the protoplasm or whatever the thing's body consists of, to its vital organs. Chemically speaking, this substance is unbelievably complex, even elegant, and its corrosive effects can be turned on or off, or made stronger or weaker, as the central nervous system commands; it's an organic secretion that can be 'programmed,' and that tells me we're dealing with a life form so alien that it might as well have come from another galaxy.

"I'm thinking the acid compound may be so corrosive that, given enough time and patience, the controlling nucleus could bore a hole through the entire planet. There are limits to its strength, though, because it has no skeletal support, no muscle tissue as such, so those bore-holes would be pencil-thin . . . but on the other hand, they could be hundreds, even thousands of miles long. *Theoretically.*"

"Any theories as to why Norma's body was almost destroyed in a short period of time, but that old sailor I interviewed in Tjornuvik didn't show any ill effects until years after the war?"

"I suppose it was because he only came in contact with it second-hand, when he picked up the wreckage, which in turn had literally been in the clutches of the thing's extrusions."

"So Karen was right all along: there is something alive down there."

"Yes, and if its substance is as flexible, as protoplasmic, and as capable of tunneling through rock as I suppose it to be, then parts of it, extensions of it, could be anywhere around us. The lake, the sea, the tunnels—it could survive just as well in fresh water as salt. In a pinch, if it got hungry enough, it could survive by leaching the minerals it needs out of solid rock. And it's pretty damned big—no part of Norma's skin was untouched. It surrounded her, drew her inside of its mass, which means it's at least big enough to fill up one of the Axe-Cuts."

Allen stood, his shoulders slumped wearily. "This isn't what I wanted."

"Why should it be, Allen? Why should it ever be?"

Since he had no answer to that question, he turned from theory to pragmatism. "I've asked everybody to meet in the mess hall in about an hour. In light of what we've learned, I simply can't ask them to stay. What about you?"

"Frankly, I don't want to be within a hundred miles of this thing. And unlike Poppa, I cannot blame it for my brother's death as though it were a thinking, reasoning organism. It can no more distinguish right from wrong than a shark. If it gets hungry, it feeds. Omnivorously: birds, fish, plankton, iron and phosphorus for dessert, and human beings if they happen to get in the way. This creature has no morality, and why should it? It seems beautifully designed to do just one thing: survive. Everything else is just background noise. Unfortunately, my father doesn't see it that way. He's demonized it; to him, it's a personal enemy, something he must take revenge on. So for his sake, I'll stay. Maybe also for your sake."

He started to move toward her, but her cool smile did not invite further intimacy.

"There's something else, too, Allen. Something rather creepy. In spite of what I just said about it being driven by pure, primal instincts, I think it's possible that there's a connection between this thing's activities and the abandonment of the village. Those pieces of bone you found in at the bottom of the Axe-Cut? The bits of clothing, belt buckles, rusted watches, that sort of thing—they all date from the late nineteenth century. It could be that you and Richard discovered where all the missing villagers went. The disturbing question is why they all leaped into that chasm, or who pushed them.

"Anyway, you were right about the writing on that piece of slate: it was the last prayer of a dying man. I've translated it, but I almost wish I hadn't."

She handed him the shard he had found amid the bones. It read: "May Christ receive my soul before I am claimed by their god, for I have seen his face and it is the very visage of Night!"

Allen's eyebrows shot up, but at least he regained an expression of alertness and determination. "Thanks for all your work, Elsuba. I'd better go speak to the 'troops' and bring them up to date. Would you mind looking in on Karen again?" Elsuba nodded. He turned again at the door. "One more thing, Elsuba . . . what was the exact date of your brother's death?"

"April . . . the eighteenth, I think it was, nineteen-sixty-five. Why do you ask?"

"I'm not sure yet. I just want to check out some dates, to see if there's a correlation with monster sightings. It's probably just a wild hunch."

From the journal of Richard Sugarman:

In the end, of course, when Allen had finished speaking, we all agreed to stay.

The meeting was a close-to-absurd parody of those war-movie scenes where the captain asks for volunteers for a hazardous mission and everybody steps forward after uneasy glances at the other guys in the platoon. You know part of it is bull-shit peer-pressure and part of it is a very real desire to pit yourself against the haz-ards you've been warned against. The mixture differs in each of us, I guess, but it is there—although I wonder, as I write these words, at my own sanity for not hop-ping the next available boat off this dreadful island. But my male ego's running on high-octane right now. I just could not go forward with my life if I left here before at least some of the mysteries were solved, some of the questions answered.

Still, my God, at what cost do we gain this knowledge! Norma and Birgir dead! Dewey convinced he's a reincarnated Viking hero! Preston addled with guilt and grief! Karen slipping into what certainly looks to me like schizophrenia! And Warrener—still trying to balance out his whole fucked-up life by playing Captain Ahab. God damn him anyway!

Allen returned to his tent after the meeting broke up, intending to pick up the old village register and take it to the research nook in the mess hall. Karen appeared to be asleep, but when he knocked over a pill bottle, she opened her eyes and recognized him. She looked tired beyond simple exhaustion, and the gray shadows gathered under her eyes had acquired a look of permanence. She waved feebly at him and patted the edge of her cot. He put down the ledger, sat beside her.

"How are you feeling now?"

"Not crazy any more, at least."

"I didn't mean. . . ."

"Of course you did. Because for a minute there, I *was* crazy. Dahl's sketch—it was like the ultimate Rorschach blot. It made my subconscious start howling again. That's not literally what the creature looks like, I think, but the sketch was obviously Dahl's attempt to make a symbolic representa-tion of it, and he came too goddamn close for comfort."

He told her what Elsuba had learned in the lab, and of what they had tried to extrapolate from the meager facts. When he finished, Karen said: "I don't think there's much I can add to that. When I'm in contact with this thing, I'm always in a trance. Everything seems very vivid at the time, but it's like a dis-organized slide show, and when I come 'back,' my brain tries to impose coher-ence on it. I don't know if the images I'm processing are literal memories, or my interpolations; but if they are real, actual snapshots of times and events this being has witnessed, then its sentience began so far back in time that it can remember meteors gouging into the raw, red Moon! Its recollections, Allen—they start really close to the Beginning. As in 'Let there be light.' "

"Karen . . . nothing, *nothing* could be that old."

"I know." She smiled thinly and kissed his hand. "And nothing the size of the Loch Ness monster could possibly remain unidentified for so long, could it? And yet, it is so." Her tone changed, sharpened. "Allen, have you talked to the others about leaving?"

"We met just a little while ago. They all voted to stay."

"And when you asked them about that, was it *after* you'd told them that, yes, there really is a Vardinoy Monster?"

"Yes."

She shook her head sadly but without anger. "You bastard. Of course they'd stay, once you told them that. I mean, that's why they all came, isn't it?"

"Maybe. Partly. But if they wanted to join me in hunting for monsters, it was for their own private reasons, not mine. I mean, look at you—you're practically on speaking terms with it."

"Allen, believe me, there is more than enough of this thing to go around."

"Are you telling me everything you know, Karen?"

"All that I *know*, yes; maybe not all that I suspect. Don't ask for that, because I don't have any coherent words for it yet. When I do, I'll share them with you. Because if we're going to get through the next phase of this without dying or going mad, we're all going to have to work together, maybe fight together. You see? My prediction was right! You and I will come together again, when things begin to converge."

"You're certain that they will 'converge'?"

"Oh, yes. There's a tension building up beneath the mountains, beneath the sea. A quickening." Karen's eyes grew heavy again, and she seemed on the verge of drifting off. But before she surrendered to Elsuba's sedatives, she grasped his hand one more time.

"Just one more thing, Allen. This creature is dangerous, yes, but I don't believe it's evil. I'm not sure yet if its consciousness includes moral distinctions of any kind. But the people on Norduroy who serve it, they're a different matter altogether. Andreas Dahl may not be the only psychopath among them."

" 'People who serve it'? What does that mean?" He wanted to hear more, but she was under again, her breathing deep. He kissed her mouth gently and received a ghost of pressure in response. Then he picked up the mildewed ledger and returned to the mess hall.

Once inside, he pulled a chair up to the packing-crate desk in the "library" corner. Stacked in one crate were selected volumes from his own collection—the most useful, the most cared-for—works that he wanted close at hand in their original format. The greater part of his files, quite an extensive body of factual and speculative data, carefully cross-indexed, had been committed to microfiche. He poured coffee from the perpetually warm pot on the galley stove, switched on the fiche viewer, and began screening pattern after pattern of white letters against blue fields, his right hand occasionally flicking to a ballpoint and notepad.

An hour passed; the coffee pot was empty. Elsuba came, refilled it, and left with only a perfunctory greeting. Still he delved through the slick blue sheets, popping them into the viewer, one after another. When Eiden had read aloud the date of the last entry in the village register, something had nudged at Allen's memory; and in the hours since, that nudge had turned into an itch he simply had to scratch. A conviction was upon him now that an important piece of the Vardinoy Mysteries was within his grasp, hovering just out of sight, a moth beating in the darkness just beyond a windowpane. He followed his hunch through scientific articles and into the thickets of tabloid clippings, like a diviner with a forked stick looking for the place where the vibrations would come up from the Earth and mark the spot to start digging. The nudge in his brain became more insistent, until, after two hours of eyestrain, he had eliminated a hundred false leads and brought his intuition into sharp enough focus for him to realize that what he sought might not even be in his personal files.

He cut off the fiche viewer and reached into the crate that held the camp's general reading matter. His hand hovered—the dowsing rod zeroing in—then descended on a current edition of the world almanac. He found the topic heading "Significant Natural Events and Disasters of the 19th Century," and halfway down the column under that: "Eruption of Krakatoa, August 12, 1883."

He glanced at his notes: the last entry in the village ledger was dated one day earlier.

The dowsing rod shook urgently now, but the rational, academic part of his mind was not convinced. Coincidence, pure and simple, albeit a dramatic one. He knew himself well enough to be suspicious for that reason alone.

Then he flipped the almanac's page and read the comparable data for the twentieth century.

"Major eruption of Grimsvotn, Iceland, August 9, 1942. . . ."

He checked his notes again. Bauer's Condor had gone down over Vardinoy on August 10, 1942.

Half an inch farther down the page: "Major eruption, Surtsey, Iceland, April 15–April 19, 1965. . . ."

Eiden's son, fished from the stormy waters between Vardinoy and Norduroy during the night of April 16; died of injuries on April 18—terribly disfigured by whatever he'd come in contact with, in the waters near Vardinoy, while hundreds of miles to the west, the Earth shook and groaned and spewed mile-high clouds of steam to mark the violent birth of a new island.

Now he was certain there was more to this than coincidence. Allen stood and paced restlessly, trying to turn his whole being into an antenna. On his fourth lap around the room, some inner circuit became complete, and he moved unhesitatingly back to the work table. In a box of miscellaneous notes, he located a cassette and popped it into the boom box. He began to search, advancing the tape twenty feet at a time, by the counter, pausing to listen to a few seconds of speech, then fast-forwarding again. As he heard the old fisherman's growling two-packs-a-day voice, he felt his pulse quicken. Finally, he just let the tape play through, afraid to miss what he was looking for. The old man with the rotting arm droned on, telling of his grim encounter with the men in the Gray Boats, telling of the dying German airman: ". . . he was crazy with pain and with fear, too, if I'm any judge of men. Took three of us to get him into the boat and hold him down while the captain broke open the medical kit and shot him full of morphine. He was howling and yelling things and a couple of times, his eyes rolled in his head like he was having some kind of seizure. He kept pointing toward Vardinoy and yelling something about eggs."

"Eggs?"—Allen heard his own voice, rendered oddly nasal by the cheap microphone—"What do you mean, 'eggs'?"

"I mean that's what it sounded like to me, not knowing the language. He kept yelling something about 'eggs' and being in a drizzle. . . ."

He shut off the tape recorder and poured himself a drink from the liquor supply. After taking a couple of swallows as a buffer against the intensity of his feeling, he leaned toward the bookcase again and brought forth his much-thumbed concordance to the Norse myths. The part he was looking for was not marked, but his general familiarity with the material enabled him to locate it after only a brief search.

He replayed the tape; reread the page. More than twice:

YGGDRASILL:

"Terrible horse," or "The Horse of Ygg (the Ogre)"; Norse name for the World Ash Tree that became Odin's gallows tree—a gallows being poetically linked to a horse *[drasill]* on which men rode to Death. Like Christ's cross, Yggdrasill was regarded as the **axis mundi,** for its roots supported the Earth, its trunk passed through the world's hub, its branches stretched toward heaven and were hung with the stars. Under its roots by the Fount of Wisdom lived the three fate-goddesses or Norns. A mighty serpent constantly gnawed at the tree, and its eventual demise would cause Doomsday [Ragnarok], when the entire structure of the world and the heavens would topple: Earth, Midgard, Niflheim, Asgard, all the realms save Valhalla.

35.

FLARES

After dinner, Allen told the others about the volcanoes; only about the volcanoes.

"Got to be a coincidence," snorted Preston. "Krakatoa's on the other side of the world. Even an eruption in Iceland would be too far away to bother this thing. How could it possibly know?"

Elsuba, adopting the manner of the Objective Scientist, countered Preston's objection. "How do horses know when there's an earthquake coming? Or butterflies know how to cross a continent and return to the same garden for mating season, year after year? An explosion the size of Krakatoa would make a modern seismograph jump off the lab table in Stockholm. And many animals, and multitudes of insects, have senses even finer than a seismograph."

"That still doesn't explain why it becomes aggressive! Why would an upheaval in the South Pacific arouse the passions of a creature living in the North Atlantic?"

"Because it remembers," said Karen, softly.

She saw how the others were staring at her, and snapped: "Stop looking at me as if I were some kind of freak! I'm just thinking logically. Look, if your dog gets his leg broken from chasing cars, for the rest of his life he's going to cringe whenever he hears the squeal of brakes. That's probably what happened to our beastie—it had a massive volcano-trauma once and now, whenever it senses a big eruption, it gets spooked."

Elsuba continued her minilecture: "It's what science calls 'autotrophic': it synthesizes food from the raw chemicals in its environment, which it breaks down into nutrients by means of that acid-stuff it secretes, or shoots out, or however it works. Normally, you would only find this kind of feeding arrangement in single-celled creatures, which in our day happen to be very small. But there's no inherent reason *why* they're microscopic—or why evolution might not have experimented with a giant single-celled life form at one time. If the process worked on a micro-scale, why not on a macro-scale too, especially if this thing was one of Nature's early prototypes. On the molecular level, it probably feeds twenty-four hours a day, with no more thought about it than a plant gives to photosynthesis. If a human being or an animal happens to be around, well, that's just one more source of nutrition, but probably no more appetizing than a school of fish or a big clump of algae. And it's truly omnivorous—this thing could synthesize the nutrients it needs from the minerals in solid rock, if there was nothing better around. It might take longer than with organic material, but if it wasn't in a hurry, it could do that."

"Oh, it's in no hurry," Karen smiled at a private jest. "If there's one thing it's got plenty of, it's *time*."

Before she could elaborate, the ship-to-shore intercom made a squawk. "Poulsen here; go ahead!" Eiden called over his shoulder.

"Message for you from the Chief Magistrate in Torshavn, Cap'n. He says it's private . . . and urgent."

"Bloody hell, what's this about?" Eiden pulled a chair to the radio table and settled a headset over his ears and mouth. Conversation drained away, and the others leaned forward to get the gist of Elsuba's whispered translation of Eiden's replies. First the father, then the daughter, soon dropped their bantering tone, and their expressions became grave. Eiden remained seating, under the headphones, for a long minute after he signed off. He stood and tossed the headset on to the desk, then turned to the room at large.

"It would seem that the Devil lies not in the 'details,' my friends, but in the bloody coincidences. My old business associate, the Chief Magistrate, informs me that there's growing evidence of an impending, and rather large, volcanic eruption, about to take place in our very back yard. The preliminary shocks are too mild for us to feel, but there've been hundreds of them, and we'll soon be able to feel them quite distinctly, because the disturbance is centered in the straits between here and Vesturoy. When a helicopter flew over that area earlier this morning, the crew clearly saw discolored water and a plume of steam rising into the sky."

"My God," said Allen, "that's exactly how Surtsey got started!"

"Quite right, and if this baby volcano is even half as big as Surtsey, then we're in for quite a show. The pressure will build up for a while before it blows, of course, but any time after the next seventy-two hours, something nasty's going to come boiling out of the sea. The government has ordered the evacuation of Vesturoy; the first ships will arrive tonight."

"What about Norduroy?" asked Dewey.

"Yes, well, I did inquire about those people, but the scientists think they're far enough away to be safe. Torshavn asked them if there was anyone who wanted to get off, and, as you might predict, the answer was 'No, and mind your own business!'

"We ought to be relatively safe," Eiden went on. "This campsite is about five hundred feet above sea level, and we're shielded by that great rampart of cliffs to the west. The Torshavn authorities say we can leave or stay, 'at our discretion,' which means that if we do get into trouble and yell for their help, we'll be the absolute lowest priority. Anyone having second thoughts?"

Preston was now in full swing once more, and even though his bravado was mostly a façade, he managed a fairly stirring oration: "Well, I also say *screw 'discretion'!* Think about it, guys—you don't get the chance to film the birth of a volcano every week! Not only would it be a contribution to science, but it would be a fantastic climax for the documentary. If Karen's 'beastie' does show up, he'll probably come out at night, and he's already camouflaged by his coloring, so we're not likely to get a closeup of Godzilla and his fangs under the best circumstances. But, hell, man, have you ever been able *not* to watch the television when they're showing volcano footage?"

Dewey loyally seconded his boss. "I say we film that sucker with every camera we've got. Come on, troops, we can't leave here without some kind of spectacular footage, not after all we've been through. Hey, Eiden, is the ship anchored in a safe place?"

"Yesss," Eiden ruminated, obviously trying to remember the fjord's exact location on the map. "It's a bit farther away, and the arms of the fjord are a good four to five hundred feet high, so I don't think the vessel's in any real danger. Even a major tsunami would break up against the coast before it got to the village."

"In that case, what's to decide?" said Allen, smacking Preston on the arm. "We need a climax—we all do from time to time—and Odin has generously put a new volcano in exactly the right spot for us to film its birth pangs! Let's go for it!"

Richard was on his feet, registering the sole "Nay!" vote. "Are all of you crazy? I've seen films of Surtsey, too, but what if this thing isn't like Surtsey? What if it just raises a gigantic pressure dome and then fucking *blows up all at once* like Mount St. Helens? The tsunami from Krakatoa, if I remember correctly, was about two hundred feet high! Anybody thought about what we would do if lava bombs the size of Volkswagens start dropping on our tents?"

Allen raised both hands and whistled for silence.

"I think we're all tiptoeing around something else, so let's stop being coy and get it out into the open. If volcanoes are what turns our monster on, for whatever bizarre reason, then our *best chance* to film it, maybe even in daylight, is from now until whenever the primary eruption takes place. It's like setting out bait, people. If this creature got so agitated by Krakatoa blowing up on the opposite side of the planet, it ought to go bonkers when it feels the vibes from this new eruption. I for one am not going anywhere, from now until the dust settles, without a camera. Does two-spectacles-for-the-price-of-one get your motor running, Richard? An exploding volcano *and* a sea monster in the same frame? If that doesn't excite you, you don't have a pulse!"

Out-voted, Sugarman gave a massive Jewish shrug and declared that, yes, he *did* have a pulse and he'd be damned if he would spoil everybody else's fun. For his magnanimous courage, he was awarded a double shot of aquavit and applauded when he tossed it back like a seasoned trawlerman.

Dewey drained an entire quart of Tuborg without taking a breath, and when he'd gotten their attention with that trick, he offered another suggestion. "You know, it occurs to me that we ought to start hauling our photographic gear up there before it gets dark—you know, stake out the good angles and cache some film stock, filters, waterproof coverings, a portable sauna, that sort of thing."

The others voted on his proposal, and it was approved unanimously.

Karen was more energized by the news than Allen had seen her since before the advent of her "monster dreams." She helped Allen decide which personal items to backpack up the mountains, and then she helped him haul the flare guns and projectiles out from their storage area. Dewey whistled appreciatively when he saw Allen hefting a flare pistol.

"Hey, Fearless Leader, where'd you get that flare gun?"

"Eiden and I brought all sorts of toys. I figure, if the volcanoe's sending up flames already, it'll mess up our night vision. Going back down, we might need something bigger than flashlights."

"I see. And if the monster makes an appearance, me and Preston will need some more light to shoot by."

"Well, yes, there is that, too."

Allen and Karen took turns adjusting each other's packs and distributing the weight of their loads.

"You know, Allen, we could cut a good twenty minutes off the hike if we used that trail I followed on the night . . . you know. In the storm and all."

"Think you can find it again?"

"Yeah, I think so. It's kind of permanently grooved on my brain."

Shrugging elaborately to settle his load, he turned and looked at her appraisingly. "Are you certain you want to go back up there? I mean, the last time you did, you were traumatized by what you saw. . . ."

She nodded emphatically. "I think it's safe for us up there tonight. Maybe safer than it is here. I don't like the idea of leaving Eiden alone to guard the camp."

"I don't like the idea of a man his age trying to make that climb. How do you sense these things, love? Are you . . . *in contact* with that thing? Can you actually tell where it is?"

In a patient, lecturing tone, she reiterated the point she'd been trying to impress upon them ever since she had revealed what she'd learned about the entity.

"Remember: the reason this creature reached out to me is because it's *trapped* down there. I don't know if its core, its nucleus, the *conscious* part of it, is under Vardinoy or out there beneath the straits, but that part of it never moves. It can't. No one has ever seen it. All we can see are those extrusions it sends out, and those can be the size of a redwood or the size of a human hair. You may as well get used to the idea that whatever you manage to get on film, it isn't going to look like most peoples' idea of a 'monster.' Sorry I couldn't produce something more like Godzilla."

"Well, I'm not *too* disappointed by the lack of fangs and claws!" He wasn't disappointed about anything, not at this moment. A sense of impending adventure had stimulated everyone in the camp, washing off their feelings of impotent passivity.

Karen felt the changes too, and the mood in their tent, as they were strapping on their packs and accoutrements, had been refreshingly playful. After they'd inspected each other's packs, Allen ruffled her hair playfully; to his surprise, she responded by embracing him urgently and smearing a hot, gooey kiss on his mouth.

"If we're not too tired when we get back . . ." she murmured in a husky voice, "why don't we jump-start our sex life again?"

"I was hoping you felt that way, too. You look rather fetching in that hiking outfit. A little dykey, perhaps, but very hot . . . in an outdoorsy kind of way."

"You too, Fearless Leader, you too."

They went into another clinch, but were interrupted by three impatient blasts from the Land Rover's horn, followed by a scream of feedback on the camp P.A. speakers and an exaggerated summons from Preston: "Now hear this, now hear this! The volcano-watching party is assembled and ready for inspection, and if Mr. Warrener and Miss Hambly don't show up within the next two minutes, they'll be left behind!"

It didn't take long for Karen to locate the shorter path—now that she knew it existed, she was surprised no one had discovered it before the night of the storm. She took the point, with Allen at her side whenever there was enough space for two abreast, and the others straggled behind, single-file. They had timed their departure at the start of the slow subarctic twilight, so they would still have sufficient daylight to set up the cameras and stake out the best vantage points when they reached the top.

As they reached a certain altitude—like crossing an invisible border—they gradually became aware of the seismic activity out in the straits. Through the soles of their feet came the mutter and hum of unseen turbines. Overhead, the dome of sky expanded as they neared the cliffs: cloud-masses folded into dramatic towers, and the twilight's glow was darker but more urgent. Ahead rose the last, most formidable escarpment before the actual summit. At this point, they still could not see the straits, but they sensed that powerful transformations were taking place, and their collective mood became charged with expectancy.

As they crossed the shadow-massif leading to the Axe-Cuts, they experienced a profound sense of peripheral menace, as though something vast and implacable brooded just beyond their sight. Their silence grew strained as they scrambled up the final, and steepest, gradient below the summit. They had reached the literal end of the trail, and the final slope was open enough to accommodate everyone. By unspoken agreement, they stopped and formed a line, so that they all might encounter the view simultaneously.

No longer just a vibration, they heard for the first time the dim timpani roll of muted violence, and a sudden wind-shear brought the first hint of sulfuric vapor to their nostrils.

"Let's all step out together, what say ye?"

"Count the cadence, Allen!" Preston urged.

"Expedition, atten-HUT! On my count, ten steps forward. *Left . . . right . . . left, right, left!*"

In formation, all together, they arrived.

"Holy shit!" cried Dewey. Preston was right behind him, long legs pounding, top-heavy with the big Bolex, which seemed to grow out of his shoulder like an ungainly second head. He too was stopped in his tracks by the sight.

They stood on the edge of their island world. From this height, the full molten sphere of the sun was still visible, but swollen and distorted, by the clouds of an approaching weather front, into a blazing comet. It turned the oil-smooth sea a sulfur-yellow, varnished the water to a dull gloss; the straits were bisected by Vesturoy's shadow, an enormous black arm stretching out as if in supplication.

"I see it, boys and girls!" Preston waved vaguely at the straits, then began to unfold the legs of his tripod. "It's at about three o'clock, if you use Vesturoy's shadow as high noon."

With the sun almost snuffed out, Vesturoy's shadow melted into the sea; all contrasts dimmed; all perspectives lost definition. The quickening of night made it easy to spot the volcano: a splotch on the mysteriously calm water drew Preston's attention, and when he turned the focus knob he could see the turbulence at its center, where glassy water domes, pressed up by the massive pressures building far below, heaved up in slow motion and then disintegrated, sending out concentric humps, not quite large enough to form waves yet. Just visible was a slowly rising ribbon of vapor—it had started far below, as a violent convulsion on the sea floor, but emerged, filtered through a thousand meters of cold and darkness and steel-crumpling pressure, in the form of a belch.

A distant swarm of motion redirected his gaze: Vesturoy's waterfront was dusty with the running lights of ships, and a sparkle of flashlights and lanterns moved through the streets, converging on the docks. Wraith-like boats formed a queue along the breakwater. The evacuation had begun.

Darkness seemed to accelerate the geological crisis. They jumped at a sound like a bass drum struck with a ball of silk. A minute later, the sea swelled into a large blister, strained, then broke into a lazy curdle of foam, as runny as a raw egg dropped onto a lukewarm skillet. Karen flipped a cigarette —rather contemptuously, Allen thought—into the Axe-Cut and asked to borrow the binoculars. After a moment's observation, she said: "If it didn't sound like such a B Movie cliché, I would say there was something 'unnatural' about that weather front. Did you notice?"

"Yep. Sometimes Nature *is* a B Movie, I guess. The words 'fraught with portent' come to mind. , , ,"

As it steadily advanced, the wall of mist seemed to gather darkness and substance, moving over the sea like a blanket being steadily pulled by unseen hands. Norduroy, the merest dot even through binoculars, vanished as they watched. In its wake, the vanguard of mist towed a phalanx of heavy clouds. The air had grown perceptibly cooler. The rumble of submarine percussion grew louder and more insistent. But with the end of ambient light, there was little to see and nothing to film.

"If we're going to see some lava, it won't be for a while yet," Richard observed. "Why don't we get out of this wind and eat our picnic food while we can?" There was agreement from the rest of the Vardinoy Expedition, and after searching by flashlight they found a suitable bowl-shaped depression in the lee of the cliffs. All of them sensed that a crescendo was building out in the straits, but straining their eyesight and muttering impatiently wouldn't hurry the process. Nor would these pilgrims even think about retreating until they'd captured *something* spectacular on film. Since there was always a chance the other guy had forgotten to pack all the essentials, all four of the men had stuffed a bottle of aquavit or a fifth of bourbon into their packs, and as Dewey philosophically put it, "May as well drink up, laddy-bucks—I don't intend to carry any extra weight back."

During the meal, they could hear the rumbles and thuds growing louder. The night had an eerily incomplete feeling, like a powerful drug-trip hallucination that had hung fire before its complete realization. Gradually, conversation ebbed, as they contemplated what changes they might see when they rose from their snug enclave and trooped back to the windy edge of nowhere. Karen rested her head against Allen's shoulder, and he gratefully inhaled the scent of wind in her long hair. "I think we should all get in the proper frame of mind, don't you?" she whispered.

"We got enough to share with everybody?"

"Are you kidding? Dewey's got three or four 'fatties' in his film pouch, and I've got half a dozen pre-rolled . . . been saving 'em for a special occasion, and the birth of a new island is about as special a thing as we'll ever see—in a few hundred years, if it doesn't self-destruct, that baby volcano will become Vardinoy, Junior."

"We'd better pray it doesn't 'self-destruct,' lover—at least not while we're up here in our box seats. I guess it's time to break out the goods."

Dewey had beaten her to it, however, and was stoking up a joint the size of a wiener. He passed it ritualistically to his left, and after contemplating it with some skepticism, Elsuba took it and sucked in a big, walloping toke.

"Mmm. Good shit," she gasped, holding the smoke into her lungs.

"Nothing but the best for my comrades," Dewey exhaled. Karen lit one of hers and started it around in the opposite direction. The collective mellowing-out soon became palpable. As though announcing the start of the show, an insistent drum-roll reminded them of unfinished business.

"Curtain going up, I think," muttered Karen, snipping out her joint and tucking it into her breast pocket. "Everybody ready?"

Ready indeed! Up they climbed, leaning into the wind, spurred by the increasing tempo of seismic action. Allen returned to the spot he'd found earlier—a broad smooth slab that seemed designed as a bleacher seat for three or four spectators. Senses preternaturally keen but reassuringly relaxed, Warrener took his seat and polished his binocular lenses. He was jarred from his reverie by Elsuba's elbow—she'd taken the place on his left and was motioning for him to snuggle closer. Instinctively, he looked around for Karen and was mildly surprised to see her on Elsuba's left side, her arm thrown unselfconsciously around the older woman's shoulder. *Aren't we the cozy trio?*

"What the hell," he said aloud, shrugging and moving closer to the two women he had loved the deepest and longest.

. . .

They might as well have been the last six people in the world, calmly awaiting the arrival of ultimate entropic Night. A welcome and unexpected sense of comfort swaddled Allen. God, he adored these people! And if the world, or their world at any rate, did end tonight, what better company to be with? Time buzzed away in the wind.

All ambient light was gone now, and between the darkness and the massive encroachment of the strangely purposeful-looking weather front, it was no longer possible to discern the border between sea and sky. Both elements were drowned in the same vat: a contiguous gulf of black velvet. Was the actual sea level ten feet below him, or three thousand? He resisted the very silly impulse to dangle his feet over the edge and find out if he could touch water. The stoned absurdity of the notion made him giggle. An unidentifiable female elbow jabbed him in the side and Elsuba shushed him, and Karen muttered: "Have a little fucking respect, hippie swine!"

"Yes, yes, mistress. I am your obedient slave, in this as in all things!"

"Allen, you are so *full of shit!*" Elsuba got the giggles too, then got control of them and adopted a gravely attentive posture. A charged but contemplative silence settled over the watchers. Darkness pulsed below them. The boats evacuating Vesturoy sparkled at a remote distance. But the expectant stasis of the scene suddenly changed as the scattering of running lights began to wink out. That massive weather front, as though responding to an unheard signal, began to advance again. In the time since they'd last studied it, the nature of the formation had changed: the purple-and-pink mist rolling ahead of it was now gone, and in its place was a battleship's prow of clouds as hard and dense as cement, cleaving the night as it moved. It had gathered power and size during its pause, and it had drawn strength from the thermal currents rising from the straits. Warrener estimated it was moving at four or five miles per hour, basing his calculations on the length of time it took for Vesturoy's lights to vanish completely, snuffed out like cinders dropped into a well.

Continuous sounds rose from the volcano site, closer and sharper and oddly ringing in timbre, like a tam-tam struck by gravel. As the cloud-wall moved over it, the sea coughed a slow, gigantic oyster and all watching eyes focused on the point of origin.

"Look!" Karen called softly. "You can see the fire!"

Where she pointed, the water had begun to glow—a smudged yellow blot, the relative size of a cigarette tip. It oscillated in size, contracting to a point, then expanding briefly into a pulsing yellowish eye. Every time the light brightened, it produced a sound like funeral drums wrapped in crepe. Allen could visualize the process now: deep below the sea, fire sprouted through cold ink and minutes later its glow reached the surface, more distorted, more attenuated by its passage, than starlight that had traveled from a nova at the Milky Way's rim. Allen put the binoculars down, for it was easier now to focus on the disturbances with unaided vision. A pair of concentric dough-nuts surfaced, their color a grainy orange-lemon, and their pulsation, as they broadened and spread out from the epicenter, was hypnotic. "One . . . two . . . three. . . ." Karen was counting the seconds until the detonation. When it came, it had the grindstone edge of boulders tumbling in an avalanche. The diapason of grunts, rumbles, thuds, and protracted belches was now continuous.

"I think I'm going to move back from the edge just a little bit," Karen said. "Trying to keep that thing in focus is making me lightheaded."

Allen was instantly aware of the tension in her voice. But he was slow on the uptake, swimming in mood, snug in a womblike narcosis, lulled by the easy closeness of his two favorite women, and for an instant he flashed resentment at Karen for interrupting the amniotic coziness that was so refreshing, so blissfully uncomplicated. He had, in fact, been drifting into a sexual fantasy involving *both* women, and had started snickering at the sheer incongruity of being perched three thousand feet above the birth pangs of a volcano and suddenly sporting an erection fit to break a two-by-four.

But the mood sloughed away when Karen called his name. Grudgingly, he stuffed the fantasy back into its vault, disengaged from Elsuba's arm, and turned. Karen had retreated some six or seven feet, and even in the darkness, he could see how rigid she'd become and how wide were her eyes.

"Can anybody else hear that," she pleaded, "or am I losing my shit?"

"I do hear something," said Preston. "Out there, under the weather front. Damned if I know what it is, though."

The cloud wall towered above and in front of them, like a castle rampart inexorably rolling forward. It would soon obscure the pulsating rings of fire. Between its leading edge and the cliff-top on which they were seated was a pure inky void, a canyon carved in midair.

"There it is again!" cried Karen.

"I heard it that time," said Richard.

From the journal of Richard Sugarman:

How can you describe a sound that few living men have heard? A sound for which we have no point of reference?

Take a drumbeat—sampled from one of those giant jungle-movie hide-covered altarpiece drums the size of a car; record it at half speed, to drag it out and roughen its texture; overdub a pedal chord from the pipe organ in Westminster Abbey; overdub that with the hiss of a hundred cobras and the howl of a run-over tick hound; add the bellow of a bull seal in heat; take that tape loop and feed it through a couple of reverb circuits; play it back through a bank of rock-concert speakers; then play it back at full volume and stand half a mile back.

That's what those noises sounded like. Sort of.

It made your skin crawl. You didn't know what it was, not consciously, but somewhere deep inside, your DNA recognized it: it was the kind of sound that made cavemen throw more wood on the fire and clutch their spears tighter. Things were bellowing to each other, things from an unthinkably remote age! Only Karen did not seem astonished—merely terrified that a remote possibility had suddenly come into the picture.

"What are *they*?" We all directed the question at her, but at first she didn't answer it straight.

"They're really coming," she whispered. "They know the time is close, and they're gathering, just as the legends foretold! My God, it's really going to happen!"

"What's 'going to happen'?" snarled Warrener. He had been in a profound reverie, that much was obvious, and he was wallowing back into reality, and he didn't like it one bit. He came up in a simian crouch, with an irritated, put-up-your-dukes scowl, sour-tempered because he was having to deal with another Karen-crisis just as he was: off-balance, his fight-or-flight reflexes clogged by all the pot he'd smoked, unprepared and resentful. You could read his expression with almost comic clarity: Aw, shit, woman, what is it THIS TIME?

"The Great Orms," Karen said. "They've come out of their hidden places to bear witness to the Emergence!"

At the sound of that identification, Allen flashed back in time: the wall tapestry in Eiden's living room; the recurring motifs in Viking culture; the legends a thousand years old and tabloid headlines from last month, all spoke of them: the Long-Necks. Huge, inscrutable, they had been sighted not only in Loch Ness, but in a hundred bays, lakes, bogs, and tarns all over the world's northernmost inhabited latitudes. But never proven, never definitively photographed.

Until now, maybe.

A deep, slithering, close-to-sexual excitement uncoiled in the pit of his stomach. He was in the presence of a Mystery; he was on the verge of confirming a Legend. Only once before had he felt this sensation: out on the Lapland fells, surrounded by quicksand pits, under the cold emerald light of the *aurora borealis.*

Hardly had Allen processed the import of those distant antiphonal cries, when they were answered by a stupendous foghorn blast right below his feet. Dewey was so alarmed that he grabbed his Kalashnikov and slammed a round into the chamber. Allen reached out and pushed the barrel down, urgently telling Dewey to "Cool it, man! There's no evidence they've ever harmed humans, so for God's sake don't scare them away! Get your camera instead and start figuring out how to shoot under flare-light."

Fully alert now, he moved next to Karen and pulled her close.

"They're not here to hurt us, are they?"

"No," she said, her voice tiny against his chest. "They're here because of the volcano, and . . . I'm not sure what else is going to happen."

"All right, we'll deal with things one at a time. Right now, we've got a chance to film something that's eluded a million cameras. Are you all right with that? Are you getting a grip? Don't spoil this for me, Karen."

Her eyes revealed a mixture of misery, awe, and resentment. But she nodded and retreated behind some sheltering rocks.

Turning to the others, Allen groped for the flare gun and dropped a magnesium projectile into the breech.

"Dewey, Preston, get your lenses wide open and be ready to shoot down over the edge at the instant I pop this flare. It's got a parachute, so you'll have a few minutes of light—make the most of it, because this could be the shot of a lifetime!"

He crept as close to the edge as he dared, pointed the flare pistol with both hands, aiming almost straight up, and squeezed the trigger.

A meteor sizzled out from his fists, tracing a zipper of daylight behind it. He averted his eyes from the ascending missile, casting them down instead, toward whatever might be revealed by the flare.

When it burst, the clouds burned a bone-lime white. Thrown into stark relief, the cloud wall loomed gigantic a hundred feet away, as bright and hard-looking as a concrete wall.

Between the base of the cliff and the cloud wall's leading edge gleamed a narrow band of black water, stippled with chalky white boulders, the surf bashing against them in a vivid ivory spew. And there it was: an enormous glistening hump, directly below them, streaked with breaking waves that sluiced between the ridges of its spine.

"Dear God, it's *huge!*" cried Richard.

"Preston, are you getting this?"

"I'm shooting, Allen, I'm exposing film, but how do I know? The light's too weird, the angle's too steep—shit, I just don't *know!* We're getting something, but I don't know if you can tell what it is."

Sputtering like a pan full of bacon, the flare drifted down until it was level with their cliff-top. Before the Orm's hump vanished in a petulant blast of foam, they saw the serpentine shadow of its brontosaurus neck outlined against the pale cloud wall. As the creature moved away, before it slowly vanished, it turned its head and stared disdainfully right at them, permitting them a brief, chilling glimpse of its burning yellow eyes.

As the Long-Neck disappeared beneath the cloud mass, it seemed to bid them farewell, giving voice to one last honking cry; it was answered by a chorus of more distant answering calls.

"Jesus, there are dozens of those things out there!" Elsuba was gaping in raw amazement, like an incredulous physician who has just seen a witch doctor cure terminal cancer with a chant and a rattle of fetish sticks.

"The Horn of Heimdahl," said Allen, shaking his head. "Hey, Karen, did you see the size of that fucking thing?"

But Karen had turned her back on the sea and was instead pointing a quivering finger in the opposite direction, toward the distant campsite. "Oh, no," she groaned. "Oh, please, not that too!"

"What's the matter *now?*" demanded Allen, kneeling beside her, his face impatient. He was clearly getting tired of this Cassandra routine and was too exhilarated from seeing the Orms to disguise his impatience. "Hey, pat us on the back or something! We just shot the first unimpeachable movies of Nessie's first cousin! We did it, lady, we're all going to be famous!"

She didn't even turn her head, but groped blindly for his hand and when she found it, squeezed it in a vise.

"Allen . . . the Orms only show themselves when that other creature is active. I can sense it now, and it's *very* active. It's coming out of the lake, right this minute."

"How the hell do you . . . never mind. If you say so, we'd better check it out."

He broke the flare gun, slapped a fresh round into the breech, and tried to gauge the proper angle for lobbing it in the direction of the camp. "Hey, Preston, turn your camera around and aim for the lake. We might get a two-fer tonight. If Madame Karen's intuition is correct, the Vardinoy Monster's about to make his debut."

This time, Allen aimed for distance, not height. The projectile arced away like a tiny comet and burst at maximum range, but still considerably short of the lake. When the flare burst, it only provided a confusing sight: the ridges and outcroppings looked like a lunar landscape, ragged and chaotic, twitching in hard jittery shadows; and at the farthest edge of illumination, the lake gave off a muted, wrinkled reflection that somehow didn't look *right*.

"It looks flooded," Richard said.

"Have you felt any raindrops tonight? Something's happening, for sure, but it's not an ordinary flood. We need to get down there as fast as we can. Karen, can you show us. . . . Damn it, Karen, snap out of it! Are you going to guide us back on the short route, or just sit there in a funk?"

Resentfully, she glared at him and stood, angrily jamming her arms through the straps of her pack. For an instant, panic pinwheeled in her eyes. She seemed overwhelmed by the sudden escalation of things: behind her, the cloud wall rose in silent majesty; beneath it, huge inscrutable beasts from the caves of myth bayed their chilling cries across the sea; a volcano thundered in its birth pangs; and to the east, rising from the lake she had stared at for weeks, the Vardinoy Monster was sending forth its probes, perhaps to wreck their camp, perhaps to reconnoiter, how the hell could she figure out its motives?

"All right, Allen, *all right!* I'll lead you down there, but by God I am not getting close to that thing!"

Stumbling after the ovals cast by their flashlights, the group threaded its way behind Karen, moving with reckless haste. The first one to stumble was

Preston, who almost snapped an ankle trying to arrest the fall of his camera. While Dewey helped Preston back to his feet, Allen caught his breath and reloaded the flare pistol. They were, he estimated, halfway to the camp, and this round should give them a good look at what was happening.

Except that this round proved to be a dud. It sputtered and flung out sparks, and its parachute deployed properly, but the main payload didn't ignite. Still, by watching its descent, Allen did observe another puzzling phenomenon: instead of hitting the lake and hissing out instantly, the glowing cinder simply stopped falling, considerably higher than ground level, and then began to descend again very slowly, as though it were falling through molasses.

"There is something big down there," he affirmed.

"Let's hurry, Allen, I'm worried about Father!"

"He'll be fine—he had plenty of time to see what was happening and to get away from . . . whatever it is. You'll see, he'll be just—"

Bam! Bam-bam! Bam-bam-bam!

As if to mock Allen's assertion, they heard the report of six shots from Eiden's Webley. It was not aimed fire, but a panicky fusillade, as though he were emptying the piece at a horde of charging savages.

Ten minutes later, their track merged with the old wagon road along the shore, putting them a hundred yards north of the campsite. In the combined beams of their flashlights, they beheld not rising floodwaters, but an undulant mass of black tarry stuff, some portions of it quite far above the shoreline.

"Poppa!" shouted Elsuba.

"No need to yell, daughter. I've been close at hand, watching you people stagger down the hill and praying you wouldn't all break your necks." From inside a nest of boulders, Eiden Poulsen stood up and took a hesitant, off-balance step toward them. He almost toppled over, and they heard a loud clink of bottle-glass against rock. Reasserting his dignity, Eiden tried to affect a bluff, hearty tone. "Welcome, shipmates! Here, have a drink with me before you meet our new friend. Believe me, you're going to need it!"

Elsuba raced to his side, but he waved her away and continued to lurch forward with the exaggerated caution of a drunk who doesn't want to make things worse by falling on his ass. The half-empty bottle and the warm revolver seemed to balance him, and he managed to reach the road without incident. But when Allen turned a light on the old skipper, Eiden's face was contorted by emotion. His red-rimmed eyes rolled toward the campsite and he gestured in that direction with his still-warm revolver. His laugh was as harsh as a rusty nail. "Oh, you'll need something bigger than those pocket-torches, if you want to see it *all*. You'd need a searchlight from a cruiser to see all of it! Matter o' fact, you'd need a cruiser's main armament to even get its fucking attention! Six three-ought-three slugs I put into it—didn't even slow it down. Y'see, it's too bloody big for us. It's *just too bloody big!*"

Allen had reloaded the flare gun, and now he popped another one off, aiming almost vertically, for maximum illumination. When the projectile burst, they all cried out in astonishment, horror, or by sheer reflex. All except Karen, who had taken a seat near Eiden and had put a comforting arm around him. She was neither frightened nor surprised, and her remote I-told-you-so expression reminded the others that she had, in fact, told them so. While they reacted violently from the sight, she simply appraised it with curiosity, as though to confirm what she already knew.

Flare-light ran down the tarry masses in rivulets. Near the center of the lake, rising as high as the tallest lamp pole in camp, rose a dense mound of viscid black matter, unquestionably organic. Flowing out of the water and curling up the shoreline were massive extrusions of the same material, great ropes of ebony gelatin, some of them ten feet in diameter, groping across the road and into the camp like enormous eyeless slugs. The remains of someone's tent lay crushed beneath one of them, like a dead moth. Its texture seemed to change as the flare drifted; they could make out shifting layers of depth within the central bulk. Thick and heavy-looking, densely viscous, that central mound was internally mottled in a patternless, chaotic way that slowly changed before their eyes—like sacs of squid ink squirting through a granular matrix. They could not see any external features, nor anything that looked like a major organ. When the dying flare drifted shoreward, they were able to see how the thickest extrusions narrowed and divided into hydra-head clusters of thinner diameters—rubbery strands as thickly interwoven as a mat of seaweed. These closest protuberances were fanning out, methodically, as though under command of a central nervous system and a consciousness, seemingly for the purpose of exploring the maximum territory in the most efficient manner.

"Cameras are rolling, Allen! Give us however many flares you have left, and we'll get some dynamite footage."

While the extrusions continued their slow progress, utterly oblivious to the bright lights sputtering above, Preston and Dewey burned up all their remaining film supply. When his film ran out, Dewey carefully put down his camera, unslung his AK-47, and fired half a magazine from the hip, putting a good tight group right into the central mound in the lake. His tracers sizzled as they impacted, and once inside, they caromed slowly around in wild, decaying orbits. There was absolutely no reaction from the target.

"Godzilla mother-FUCK!" yelled Dewey. "The bastard didn't even flinch!"

From her perch on the rocks, Karen mockingly suggested: "Why don't you try pouring a thousand pounds of salt on top of it?"

"Very fucking funny," snapped Allen. "Hey, Dewey, I've got it! We need the grenades! Let's get the grenades!"

"Now you're talkin'!"

Leaping over the black cables and hoses and snakes littering the ground, the two men ran into the mess hall and emerged a few minutes later with a heavy crate slung between them. They chose the flagpole mound as the optimum position, and while the others gathered around, Dewey used his Bowie knife to pry open the lid.

"We brought two kinds, dude," said Allen: "concussion—to stun something —and white phosphorus, to burn anything too big to stun. Which would you suggest?"

"Definitely Willy-Peter, man! Them other things'll just get it pissed off."

"Can't have that, now, can we? But doesn't it occur to you that if this creature gets turned on by volcanoes, maybe it's not going be scared of fire. . . ."

"Not bein' *scared* of it is not the same thing as being *fireproof.* This shit can melt through an inch of aluminum—it *will* make an impression!"

They each pulled out an inert cylinder decorated with attention-getting stripes, pulled the pins, and threw a salvo at the count of three. The first pair of grenades landed high on the glistening central bulk and rolled halfway down to the water before exploding. The night was shattered by hundreds of feathery streamers, each white ribbon trailing a nodule of sticky, furiously burning phosphorus. There was too much smoke and visual confusion to observe what, if any, damage was being done to the mound, but once the two started chucking grenades, they were too hyped up to quit until the crate was empty. They invited Eiden to throw the last missile, and this one rolled deep into the lake before going off, its underwater flash revealing an immense taproot of matter, as big around as a subway tunnel, descending unbroken toward the bottom of the lake.

"I think it's moving back!" shouted Eiden. Slowly, without any sign of urgency, the farther extrusions began to telescope inward into thicker ones, and all of them began to contract into the lake, where the big central mound, streaming smoke and spattered with guttering chunks of burning chemical, now began to submerge: a mountain shrank to a hillock, the hillock to a hump, and then the whole stupendous mass of it vanished, leaving boiling smoke and phosphorus nuggets bubbling in the water, like demonic chunks of dry ice.

"We did it!" shouted Allen, clapping Eiden and Dewey on their backs.

"Indeed we did!" Eiden seconded. "How would you express it, Dewey?" Eiden gave an inspired Danish-accent imitation of Dewey's down-home Georgia drawl: "We burned that suck-ah's ass!"

While the trio was capering around the knoll in a spasm of self-congratulation, Karen trudged wearily up to them and bleakly surveyed the scene. She lit a cigarette and shook her head at the three men. When they ran out of steam and ceased their whooping and hollering, Karen sighed and in a chilly, sobering voice said: "I hate to spoil your fun, boys, but you didn't scare it off. It withdrew for its own reasons, either because it had found out what it wanted to know or because it sensed I was present and it wanted to protect me from accidental harm. But get one thing straight, so you won't have any dangerous illusions: you clowns did not *hurt* that thing. You didn't *burn* it. You didn't even *startle it. All you did was feed it some candy!*"

36.

CATECHISM

Karen sat on Flagpole Knoll, staring moodily at the now-calm, unruffled surface of the lake. Allen hunkered just behind her, slumped against the flagpole. He heard the scratch of her lighter, and the sudden acridity of Marlboro smoke triggered acute nostalgia for the quick fix of nicotine. As though reading his mind, Karen held the pack out. "Would you like a smoke, Allen?"

His emotions waffled. "Better not—it's been four years, after all, and a relapse at this stage would be. . . . Aw, fuck it, give me one."

He took a deep, savoring drag, exhaled reluctantly, and impulsively thumb-flipped the butt into the lake.

"Too strong for you after all that time?"

"Nope. Too good. If I finished one, I'd go right back to two packs a day." He sighed and stood up, surveying the campsite, where the other members of the Vardinoy Expedition were excitedly pacing off measurements of the extrusions and repairing the damaged tent.

Allen said: "Seeing it—or some part of it, anyway—changes everything. We *have* to go now. Even Eiden won't want to fuck around with that thing, now that he's seen what he's dealing with."

"Go where?"

"Back aboard the ship, for the time being, until we can reload all our shit from the campsite. Then back to Torshavn. Then home. We don't have any other choice, love. This wasn't an attack, I think, just a kind of probe to see what we were up to. But what if that creature does decide to attack us? We put enough firepower on that hump to kill a herd of rabid water buffalo, and it didn't even feel it."

Karen took his hand and gently said: "You see now, don't you, Allen? It is not what you thought it might be, not like anything any of us could have imagined.

"It's much more alien and incomprehensible than anything you could name. I suspected as much, but having a mental picture and actually seeing part of it . . . two very different things! I think you're doing the right thing, Allen, by pulling us out now."

"Will we be safe aboard the trawler?"

"Safer than here, I think."

"Okay, then, let's get this show on the road, just in case it comes back. Be close to me when I tell them the plan, will you, lady?"

"Am I still your lady?"

"More than ever, and for the rest of our days, if you'll have me."

They shared a comradely embrace, then walked hand-in-hand over to where the others were milling around.

"Listen up, folks! The way I see it, what happened here tonight, combined with what happened to Birgir and Norma, puts a whole new light on our situation. I'd like for everybody to pack whatever clothes and stuff you need immediately, and then we're going back to the ship and not coming back to this place except in the daylight, to break down the camp and haul the equipment off. After we've loaded our gear on board, I propose that we find a safe place on Vesturoy, where we can film the eruption . . . and after that, why don't we all just go home?"

His speech was greeted with half-relieved, half-ironic cheers, but no one protested the evacuation, including Eiden Poulsen, who had already radioed the trawler to stand by for their arrival, informing the radioman that the Expedition was "temporarily" packing it in, for reasons he would explain later.

Dewey Tucker glumly inspected his last clean T-shirt, then remembered that the ship had a laundry unit adjacent to the crew's quarters. He wondered whether to keep the AK-47 within reach, or to field-strip it and put it back in his luggage, as he would soon have to do anyway. He finally succumbed to the habits of old Army training and broke the weapon down, running a cleaning patch through the bore—he had fired it tonight, after all, and if he forgot to clean the powder residue from the bore, he would have a Dirty Weapon, and that was both unforgivable and dangerous. He couldn't envision any further need for the AK. If Dahl and his accomplices had been sneaking around last night, they too would have seen that enormous thing rising out of the lake and if they had, they wouldn't be anywhere near Vardinoy by now. Dewey admitted it: that thing had freaked him right out, and even he would have hesitated to get into an altercation with a being that could eat half a banana-clip of 7.62-mm slugs and not even become visibly annoyed.

"When faced with an enemy of overwhelming strength," he muttered, snapping shut his suitcase, "the wise commander knows he must retreat in order to wait for another opportunity."

"What the hell are you mumbling about?" grouched Preston, from his side of the tent.

"Sun Tzu wrote that," huffed Dewey indignantly, "or something very similar to that, anyhow."

"Jesus, Dewey, you really were gung-ho tonight, weren't you? Rumble in the jungle! *Mano-a-Beast-o!* You probably came *this close* to buying yourself a Viking funeral!"

"That thing has to have a vulnerable spot, man! Doesn't it? I mean, doesn't *everything?*"

"That motherfucker doesn't fit into the category of 'everything.' "

Dewey shoved toothbrush and soap container into his shoulder bag, then very reverently placed his dogeared copy of *The Norse Sagas: A Modern Rendering* into the side pocket. "Them good ol' boys would have known how to deal with it!"

"Which 'good ol' boys'?"

"The Vikings, you idjit! See, what people don't understand is how *practical* they were! They didn't say 'Such-and-such-a-thing is impossible,' they just took the world as they saw it and didn't question what their eyes showed them. If they didn't have enough force to beat a foe in battle, well, their reputation alone was so intimidating that nobody wanted to fight 'em, because even if you won, you'd still lose a lot of valuable warriors; so they would parley with the superior enemy and make him think they were doin' him a favor by arranging a very shrewd peace treaty. That way, they could get *part* of what they wanted without having to fight for it, and the enemy commander would go away boasting about how smart *he* was, because he'd just negotiated his way out of a battle with a boatload of them crazy Norsemen! If you couldn't kill an enemy, the next best thing was to seduce him into becoming your ally. Whatever the problem, they figured out a way to come to terms with it, know what I'm sayin'?"

"And what if they couldn't even *understand* it? What if they ran into something like that critter we saw earlier?"

"Well, then, God damn it, they did *another* smart thing! They backed off and said, 'Hey, we can't beat that monster, and we don't want to piss it off, so maybe we should just *worship it!* "

There was little conversation as they took their seats in the Land Rover. No one could avoid noticing that whereas it had previously been a tight squeeze fitting the whole Expedition into the vehicle, now there was room for everyone. Eiden looked so tired that Allen offered to drive, and he did so very cautiously, not wanting to outrun the headlights, warily searching for an ambush around each blind hairpin curve. He was relieved when he came through the north side of the gap at the summit and beheld in the distance the faithful *Laertes*, warmly illuminated and snug in its mooring lines, the gangway already extended and a sailor waiting at the top to assist them.

Bedraggled and dispirited, they lined up single file and let Eiden lead them up the gangplank. As his foot hit the deck, Eiden impulsively shook the hand of the sailor on watch and blurted: "We have an incredible tale to tell, my friend!"

"And on any other occasion, we would be very interested to hear it," said Andreas Dahl, stepping from the shadows under the bridge; the old German Luger in his hand was pointed straight at Eiden's heart. Another man emerged behind Dahl, preceded by the figure-eight snout of a double-barreled shotgun. The sailor beside the gangway drew a revolver. From the abandoned village behind them, three more armed men stepped into view.

Dewey's suitcase suddenly felt very heavy. He set it down carefully, so that no metal parts would clink within, then he raised his hands.

"What happened to my crew?" demanded Eiden.

"They're safe, for the moment. And their continued safety depends mainly on your cooperation."

Dahl swung his rifle toward Preston. "Mr. Valentine, if I remember your professional habits correctly, it is your custom to keep your most recently exposed film in that pack you have slung over your shoulder." Preston just glared at him. "If you'll be so good as to step over here, one of my men will relieve you of that burden. And you, Dewey, please abandon any thoughts of doing something bold and Viking-like. Not even *my* ancestors could deflect a bullet fired at this range."

A burly Norduroy man, carrying a very old but well-oiled Springfield, stepped up to Preston and wrenched the satchel from his grasp. He tore it open and held up for Dahl's inspection three film canisters sealed with yellow light-proof tape. He translated the labels into Faeroese and Dahl nodded. The sailor carried the film cans over to the portside railing, opened them, and unspooled their contents into the water below. Then, with a mocking bow, he returned the empty canisters to Preston.

"Dahl, you scumbag!" snarled Dewey, bristling and tense.

"Cool your jets, Olaf!" said Preston, his fists knotted and his hands trembling.

"I regret that that was necessary," said Dahl, "for I have some idea of how hard you worked to obtain the unique images on that emulsion. Nevertheless, the taking of those pictures was an act of blasphemy, and unless I ordered those images destroyed in full sight, it would be hard for me to control the emotions of my less sophisticated kinsmen. My cousin, for instance, Halfdan—he's the man with the shotgun—doesn't even think we should waste time conversing with you; he simply wants to cut your throats and throw your bodies overboard. But the veneer of civilization clings to me, and I believe we can find an accommodation far short of such extreme actions. Besides, I have accepted your hospitality, however grudgingly some of you may have given it, and by the old traditions I am obliged not to harm you, unless you make it necessary."

"What about Birgir, you son of a bitch?" said Allen.

"He made it necessary."

"What are you going to do with us, Dahl?" said Eiden.

"Most of you, I'm going to confine securely for a day or two, down in the cargo hold. After a certain point in the coming chain of events, you'll be of no further use to me and no further threat to my people, so you will be released. But from one of you, I want something considerably more . . . involved. Allen, will you and Karen please come into the captain's quarters with me? The rest of you, make yourselves comfortable on the fo'c'sle deck. If you're hungry or thirsty, one of my men will bring you food and drink, including alcohol in moderation. You'll be guarded closely, however, so please—no silly heroics. The rest of these men would really have very little compunction about killing you."

Holding the Luger close to Allen's back, Dahl separated him and Karen from the rest and directed them up the stairs and into the captain's cabin, pausing to dog the hatch as he closed it. He switched on the lamp over the zinc basin, sat down at the fold-up desk, and indicated with motions of the pistol that the other two should be seated on the bunk. Dahl took a bottle of aquavit from a drawer under the writing desk and offered drinks, while pouring one for himself. Karen shook her head emphatically, and when she did, Allen, who had already been reaching for a glass, also declined.

"No drink, Allen? Well, suit yourself, although it's hardly like you to turn down a free tipple. I think I'll have one, if you don't mind—this business of ambushing people is disagreeably stressful . . . not my kind of thing at all, really, but rank has its duties."

"Stop socializing, Dahl, and tell us what you're going to do with us."

"With you and your companions? Just what I said I would do: keep you detained for a couple of days so you won't get into any more mischief, and then send you back to your campsite—minus any radio equipment, of course. We will sail the trawler out into the straits and scuttle her. No evidence, you see, including those two frozen bodies below. We'll sail back home in our own boats and you people can fend for yourselves. You won't starve, and you can amuse yourselves by making smoke signals, or spelling out 'Help!' on the ground with your underwear—assuming, of course, that you survive the eruption that's about to take place.

"So much for the rest of you. As for Karen, my plans are a bit more complex and will require some explanation. If I am to be successful, it depends to a great extent on her willingness to participate. So, my dear, I shall now speak mainly to you. I ask you to hear me out before judging me, and to weigh carefully what I'm about to tell you, regardless of any personal animosity toward me."

"Karen is staying with me, you bastard."

"Really, Allen, you're in no position to object. You would do well to listen too, because what I have to say will surely be of interest to you as well as Karen. I'm trying to be courteous, you see, but I could just have you thrown into the brig."

"Take the drink, Allen, and let's hear what the deal is."

Allen glanced at her uneasily, disturbed rather than reassured by her composure. Nevertheless, when Dahl held the glass out for him, he took it.

"Good! So, then, from the beginning. . . . Tell me, do you know when these islands were actually settled for the first time?"

"Of course we do," snapped Allen, purposely inaccurate, not wanting Dahl to know how much of the purloined manuscript Sugarman had translated. "Ninth century, probably by the Irish, who quickly either were overcome by, or intermarried with, some Vikings."

"Wrong, on two counts. The first settlement took place about two centuries earlier than the history books tell you. And it was not accomplished by a boatload of seasick Irish clergymen, but by a great Norse chieftain, a man from whom I am descended."

"Should I applaud, or bow?"

"What you should do is remember how uncomfortably tiny the brig is on this ship!"

"Keep quiet, Allen, please!"

"Thank you, my dear. You always were the sensible one. Anyhow, my ancestor had the misfortune to be on the wrong side of a civil war, and so was banished, along with several dozen of his family and retainers. Whether he *intended* to colonize one of the Faeroes, or his tiny armada was blown here by a storm, is a matter of contention amongst those of my people whom you would call 'theologians'—all that matters, really, is that when the sun came out and the waves grew calm, his ships were out there in the straits and directly ahead was the island we know as Norduroy. It was larger than Vesturoy and contained much more grazing land than Vardinoy, and there was plenty of fresh water, abundant fish, and edible birds. So this is where the leader chose to set up his new realm.

"The gene pool was too limited for them to have lasted very long without their offspring turning into drooling imbeciles, but fortunately my ancestor was not just another live-for-the-moment barbarian. He envisioned a secure and prosperous little kingdom, one that was perfectly in harmony with the needs and resources of its inhabitants and easily fortified against any hostile trespassers. So when spring came, the king led his finest warriors on a long raiding expedition, and when they returned in the autumn, three ships instead of one, they brought useful plunder, a band of newly recruited warriors—who had been persuaded either by his oratory or the sharpness of his sword—and, most importantly, a boatful of females, thereby ensuring the future of the bloodlines. This cycle was repeated every year for several generations, until there was a strong and vibrant community on Norduroy, with sturdy houses, an ample food supply, and a flotilla of very successful fishing craft. Our chronicles also state that, at some point in the mid-eighth century, all of the Norduroy ships began to decorate their prows with representations of the Great Orms—which my ancestors adopted as their emblem, a symbol of their proud, free way of life.

"Their numbers are few now, alas, and no man knows their secret hiding places, but in those days the Great Orms were a common sight; but until last night, no one had seen a Long-Neck in the Faeroes for two hundred years! Don't you see, Allen? The widespread use of the Orm motifs began here— on Norduroy, that is; and in a very short time, all of Europe identified that dragon-prow design with Viking savages! So feared were their annual raiding expeditions, and so respected was their military prowess, that the symbol spread as far east as the Urals, as far south as Constantinople!

"By the time those insipid, whey-faced Irish monks, burdened with their concubines and their broods of snot-nosed little bastards, set about building their pretentious church in that hidden cove here on Vardinoy, they were interlopers inside the borders of a strong and prosperous kingdom. As the old western-movie cliché has it, the town wasn't big enough for both of them. Any questions?"

Allen had been waiting for the moment to throw this rhetorical hand grenade: "Just one, Andreas: was it your people or the Irish monks who discovered Yggdrasill?"

Dahl's eyebrows rose in surprise, but his voice was calm: "No. We did. Or, more accurately, my ancestors did." He smiled thinly and lifted his glass in salute. "Bravo, Allen! You certainly have done your homework. By making that connection, you've greatly surprised me, I admit."

"Excuse me," said Karen, "but what the hell are you two talking about?"

"A recent deduction I made that I'd planned to tell you about last night, before things got so hectic. It turns out our ancient beastie has a name, doesn't he, Andreas?"

"That it does. But whether that name was in use when the first settlers arrived, and they just transferred it when they discovered the Being's presence, or whether my ancestors spread the Yggdrasill myths as an interpretation of something quite beyond their ken, I cannot say. Our theologians wrangle about that detail endlessly. Well, since you've studied the Sagas diligently, you also know that the Vikings packed a lot of rather ambiguous symbolism into the Yggdrasill figure. Were they writing about a literal giant tree that supported the world in its branches, or were they lavishly flinging metaphors about, as they so enjoyed doing? But to my people there was nothing ambiguous about Yggdrasill. It was, it is, a god-like Being—note that I refrained from flatly declaring 'It is a god.' No one knows exactly *what* it is, only that it exists and that our fates have been intertwined with it for centuries.

"In the first few decades after they discovered it, my ancestors became insufferable zealots. While other cultures just invented their gods and goddesses and then defined them by means of charming, fanciful stories, *my people* had the real thing living in their basement, so to speak. And they were very cocky about that, every bit as militant about spreading their faith as were the early Christians. But their numbers were few, and for every community that heard the tales from their lips and became instantly 'converted'—usually as the alternative to being hacked apart—there were many other communities who heard only fragmentary, embellished, and wildly distorted accounts. That's how 'myths' *get started*, isn't it? By the time the sagas came to be codified and written down, the Yggdrasill tales were many generations removed from their source.

"Now, I yield to no one in my admiration for the poetic eddas, but their treatments are florid embellishments of a single basic fact: there *exists* a God-like entity, a Being that has survived from measureless antiquity, and whose face no man has ever beheld, except perhaps in dreams . . . and nightmares. All we've seen are those dark extensions it projects on to the surface. Where, exactly, is the central nervous system entombed? Again, no one can do more than speculate. Perhaps it lies beneath the straits. Perhaps we're standing over it right now. It sends forth those extrusions according to its own inscrutable whims and necessities. When it's calm, 'just browsing' so to speak, the extrusions are harmless. But when it's feeding, or agitated, down in the nucleus, and you can see those shimmering blue patterns inside, then you'd better not come in contact with it. Everyone who experiences prolonged contact . . . inevitably dies. Some quite rapidly, some very slowly, but all horribly.

"The inhabitants of Norduroy discovered its existence during the third or fourth decade of their settlement. And for several generations, all they could do was fear and respect this mysterious neighbor. They knew it was very, very dangerous at certain times; they knew that the extrusions were strong enough to bore through mountains. Indeed, some of their homes and barns were rent asunder if they happened to be in the way. Now, how else could the people of that milieu relate to such an entity, other than nominate it for godhood? It has all the qualifications, doesn't it? It is vast, inscrutable, essentially unknowable; and although it must be immensely powerful, it was not always wrathful or rampant. Same traits as Yahweh, when you think about it, only without the nasty vindictiveness. Rituals of worship and placation swiftly evolved, and of course certain men came forward and claimed to have special insights into the Being's nature and purposes—self-anointed 'priests,' of course, and ninety percent of them quite bogus. But you can't empirically verify such claims, so you tend to give your priests the benefit of the doubt. You might resent them for putting on airs, but you never knew for sure; maybe they were *on to something!*

"All of that changed during the reign of the first king's great-great-grandson. When he returned from one of his annual raiding expeditions, he brought with him a wildly beautiful Irish woman, the former concubine of a defeated chieftain, who was regionally famous for being gifted with second sight, for going into trances and coming out of them with prophecies that turned out to be more or less accurate. She was haughty and sure of herself, and legend has it that the king was madly in love with her. So she was made welcome and told to make full use of her powers: to divine something of the Being's intentions, and to be the intermediary between it and the people who worshipped it.

"She was the real thing. Her methods and abilities were mysterious, of course, but it soon became apparent that she did indeed have the power to . . . if not exactly *converse* with the Yggdrasill-creature, at least to interpret its moods and wishes, insofar as those could be rendered in human speech, and to make it, in turn, aware of the community's respect, awe, and veneration. A tradition was born with that woman, the first of many women whom we designated The Voice. Just before she passed away, at a remarkably old age, she handed down instructions for how to locate a successor, what traits to look for in another woman, and sure enough, even though it might take years of searching, my people always found a younger replacement.

"Our destiny became intertwined with our worship. Thanks to divinations received from The Voice, the people of Norduroy were never in want. We are not much for socializing with the other islanders, of course, but we

are known for being the luckiest fishermen in the Faeroes. Now you understand why: we always know in advance where to drop our nets!

"At other times, we've been given warnings about storms, our shipwrecked mariners have been kept afloat by quiescent extrusions until we
could rescue them—that sort of thing. It is an ongoing relationship, and one
that is crucial to my peoples' well-being. That's the reason we are so protective of this knowledge, so uninterested in trafficking with people who are not
aware of our reality. But what protects the relationship most is the outsider's
sheer inability to take the legends of the 'Vardinoy Monster' *seriously*."

"Tell me, Andreas," said Karen, "how big is it, really? And where does
it live?"

"Another hair-splitting issue for the theologians! No one knows, because
no one has ever seen it whole, nor can anyone mark upon a map the exact
spot where its central mass lies imprisoned. We only know that it's very, very
deep, and that the core of it never moves—cannot move! It uses the extrusions to find nourishment, yes, but also to explore the places it cannot physically inhabit. They have been sighted a thousand miles away. When reduced
to the thickness of a human hair, they can pass through the pores of mountains, and theoretically there is no place on Earth where they could not go.
But even if one appeared in China, for instance, even though it is thousands
of miles long, it is still part of one enormous, continuous entity, and each
particle, no matter how microscopic in size, is always directly in touch with
the core that controls it."

"This 'core,' is it like the nucleus in a cell?"

"Again, there has been endless speculation, but to me that's as futile a
question as 'what color are God's eyes?' Take away all the religious trappings,
and our relationship with the Yggdrasill-entity is a rather mundane kind of
symbiosis: we provide it with devotion and, for lack of a better word, 'companionship'; and in return, it helps us out from time to time. We observe ceremonies, which it might or might not find pleasurable; we protect it from
the potentially harmful scrutiny of the outside world; we bide our time; and
we accumulate knowledge. Things have been balanced in this manner for
centuries. But that is about to change, and that's where you come in, Karen.

"The most important aspect of our theology derives from a prophecy
which was the final—and therefore regarded as the most vital—utterance of
the original Voice: after more than ten centuries, she said, a great cataclysm

would liberate the Being, and it would rise in majesty from the sea, revealing itself wholly for the first time.

"Well, now is that time, and ours will be the first human eyes ever to gaze upon the wholeness of this being! When that volcano growing out in the straits finally explodes—that will be the symmetrical instrumentality of the Entity's liberation! The volcano's detonation? That will be the sign heralding Ragnarok—for real, Allen, for real! There will be enormous devastation when that pressure dome blows up, but the force of it will be directed *away* from Norduroy. And when the lava cools, after many years, there will be a twin island conjoined with Norduroy, and it will be the new dwelling place of Yggdrasill!"

"That sure sounds impressive, Andreas. Will we get to see it on the nightly news, or is it only showing on pay-per-view?" Allen managed a quick exchange of glances with Karen, and each signaled to the other: *This guy is barking mad!*

"I'm not sure I understand."

"I was merely asking: when will this amazing event take place?"

"Some time in the next forty-eight hours."

Allen sucked in his breath. If the volcano was going to erupt with *that* kind of power, the chances of its "force" being directed away from Norduroy by divine intervention were slim to none. This close to the epicenter, the tsunami would be a hundred feet high.

"The Being will rise amid the fires! Its strength will be magnified a thousand-fold! It will be revealed at last, and all men will know its majesty and its power! And we, who have served it for so long, will be its intercessors with the human race. We will all become its priests, and we will be rewarded with unimaginable riches and blessings!"

"Coming back to Earth for a minute," said Karen, in the patient tone of a paramedic trying to coax a jumper off a bridge, "is there a historical pattern between volcanic eruptions and the behavior of this thing?"

"Oh yes, a direct connection. Unreckoned millennia ago, a titanic prehistoric eruption caused to become entombed far below the ocean floor, and ever since then it has explored the planet's mantle with the probes it sends out. It has an incredibly complex system of remote sensors, always alert, always receptive. It has waited, many thousands of years, perhaps many thousands of centuries, for a second, almost identical near-by eruption, one that will undo what was done to it so long ago. That's why it becomes agitated and more dangerous whenever it senses a major eruption, anywhere on the planet. Imagine the loneliness it has known, imagine the longing it has endured! No human mind could bear its circumstances for one second. But I think you already understand that, Karen. I think you've had intimations of these things."

"You've heard us tell the story of the German Condor pilot Bauer. How does that fit in with what you've told us tonight?"

"At about that time, there was a very strong eruption off the coast of Iceland. The Being was extremely agitated, shooting out extrusions left and right. One big mass broke the surface off the Vardinoy coast, and another, smaller mass emerged in the lake—that is why there's a certain ambiguity in Bauer's account, because from the air, he could see those manifestations in both places. It was just bad luck that caused them to bail out when and where they did. Mind you, we can do nothing about accidental sightings of the extrusions—as transient phenomena go, they're relatively unspectacular. But this time, there were massive portions of it above the surface, and believable witnesses, professional airmen, who might be credible enough to motivate an investigation. Until the time of its Emergence, the existence of the Being must remain only the vaporous, maddeningly unspecific legend that you are so familiar with. My father was among the men on Norduroy who saw that plane go down, saw the crews' parachutes open. Perhaps their observer had even taken photographs to back up their tale. That's why the Gray Boats went out to find the Germans, so that their story would not become known.

"It was largely a wasted effort on our part. Several of the crewmen descended right into the mass of extrusions and were absorbed by them, just as any source of nutrition is absorbed. There were only two survivors. One, the pilot, was rescued; but, as you know, he went mad and killed himself. The other man, we found inside a cave. He had severe injuries, and unfortunately died in our care."

"You mean your daddy and his henchmen murdered the poor bastard."

"No, I do *not* mean that at all, Allen! We are seamen, sir, and we do not butcher survivors whom we pluck out of the ocean. The man sustained fatal injuries when he landed hard against the cliff and bounced off the rocks below. He had zero chance of recovery—if there had been any hope, we would have nursed him back to health on Norduroy and kept him there in comfortable isolation. In time, he would have become a convert and a normal member of our community. But half the major bones in his body were broken, and his skull was cracked so badly that my father could see his brain! All that could be done was to terminate his suffering quickly. Call it murder if you like, but the men who performed the deed regarded it as an act of mercy."

"All right, we have a stalemate in this instance. But tell me what you know about one more event."

"You're starting to try my patience with these questions."

"If you want my cooperation, Andreas, please answer them," said Karen frostily.

"I'll do my best. . . ."

"On the night of April sixteenth, nineteen-sixty-four, during an eruption of Surtsey, there was a shipwreck out in the straits. It may have involved one of these 'extrusions.' Did your people have anything to do with rescuing the survivors?"

"I was only a boy then. I'll ask my father."

Dahl exchanged words with the sentry outside the cabin door, and after a few minutes, an old man entered the room. His face was as sharp and cold as an axe blade, his eyes half-buried in a wattle of weather lines. He looked past his son at the two Americans, his expression oscillating between hatred and a desperate expectancy. He continued to stare at them while he spoke at some length about the incident. Allen realized that he had seen this old man before, through binoculars, at the thwarts of a Gray Boat.

After his father left, Dahl resumed speaking in English. "I'm not sure why this event interests you, but here's what I've learned: there was a storm that night, a very bad one, and a ship did founder. My father took a boat out the next morning, to look for survivors, just as any self-respecting seaman would do. Only one man was found, a young fellow, terribly injured. Since there was no doctor on Norduroy, my father took the castaway to the clinic on Vesturoy and left him there. As for the Being, we know that it *was* agitated during that period, yes, but there were no sightings of extrusions in these waters, and so far as we know, no connection between a Partial Emergence, as we call those sightings, and what happened to that ship. Conditions were extremely hazardous, so it was probably just an ordinary shipwreck."

"No, it wasn't. That young sailor your father rescued . . . he soon developed a hideous degenerative condition, in addition to his other injuries. He might have survived the broken bones, but not that gangrenous rot that ate his flesh. I'm told, by a witness, that he died an excruciating and loathsome death. And his symptoms were identical to those suffered by people who have had massive contact with this god of yours."

Dahl shrugged. "Most unfortunate for him, of course, but if that was what killed him, we certainly had nothing to do with it. My father could not have learned about it from the victim, because the young man was unconscious, and evidently his symptoms didn't show until hours later. That sometimes is the case, if the extrusions are not actively feeding when the contact occurs. Now that I've answered your question, you answer mine. Why are you so concerned about this incident? If his exposure was so massive, he was surely quite insane before he expired—he couldn't have known where he was or what was happening to him."

"Oh, I think he knew. He tried to tell about it, but his jaw started dropping to pieces before he could say anything."

"How do you know these things? You were only a college student at the time."

"A friend of mine was present when the boy died."

"What a coincidence! I assume from your tone of voice that this friend is a mutual acquaintance."

"Yes. It was his father, Eiden Poulsen."

"Ah, now his hostility toward me becomes more understandable! He thinks the Norduroy men are to blame for his son's death, and that they are in league with the so-called monster. And being an old Viking, he wants the satisfaction of revenge, I suppose."

"That's about the size of it."

"Then he'd better pick a fight with the deity, not with us. We only serve it; we don't control what it does."

"What about the people who used to live in that village out there? What happened to *them* when your deity got so upset by the eruption of Krakatoa?"

"We don't much like to talk about that, but if you must know, there was a huge Emergence right here in this fjord. Extruded matter flowed over the docks and into the streets, an unprecedented thing! Many of the inhabitants were simply absorbed—those things appear sluggish, but when the consciousness controlling them is upset, they can lash out like scorpion tails!

"But there were survivors, some dozens of them, and that presented us with a dilemma. Never before had so many outsiders seen an Emergence—so many people, all telling a consistent story, might cause official inquiries, unwanted public attention to a matter that was, frankly, none of the outside world's business. So we sent a considerable force to the village, rounded up the inhabitants, explained the situation, and gave them a chance to come to Norduroy and join our community, or be silenced. Only a few of the more easily intimidated accepted our proposition. As for the rest, they were in fact 'silenced.' I'm sure that seems barbaric to you, the action of bloodthirsty fanatics, but the men who carried it out were not savages and took no pleasure in performing their duty."

" 'Duty?' You sound like an apologist for the SS! 'You can't imagine how tough it was, having to shove all those Jews into the showers day after day!' I can bloody well tell you how that 'duty' was performed! Those innocent people were lined up at the top of the Axe-Cuts and pushed over the edge. That's not religious zeal, Andreas, it's fucking mass murder! How can you call yourself a civilized man and condone that?"

"My people did what was necessary to preserve their way of life! The occasional wild story by a solitary fisherman—nobody takes those seriously. They're just another sea-serpent yarn. But a hundred eyewitnesses, all backing up each other's accounts? No, that couldn't be allowed to happen."

Mouth agape, Allen turned to Karen. "Do you hear this man? He's absolutely in denial! I'm sure the Inquisitors felt the same, just before they lit a fire under a heretic!"

"Shut up, Allen." Andreas Dahl seemed to come out of a momentary reverie, and the mask of affability fell away long enough for him to reach over and crack his pistol across Allen's face, not hard enough to tear the skin, but hard enough to send Allen to the floor with an angry red welt rising on his cheek. Karen knelt and cradled his head in her arms.

"Touch him again, Dahl, and I'll walk away from you and your jellyfish-god forever. You won't have a Voice. Yes, that's right—I can see where this history lecture is leading, and I think you'd better control your temper if you want my cooperation. Am I getting warm?"

Dahl nodded and poured another drink for Allen.

"All right, there was no call for my outburst," he conceded. "And I was lying—I did learn more from my father than I admitted. The villagers weren't pushed. They were lowered gently on ropes, which were then cut, so that it was up to Yggdrasill what their fate would be . . . so that our hands wouldn't be covered in innocent blood. There was reason to believe that the Being had been active there, that part of it still was down at the bottom of those crevasses. . . ."

"Just why did they think the creature was still down there?"

"Because the fissures that you call the Axe-Cuts were opened by the convulsions it went into when it sensed the Krakatoa eruption."

"Jesus Christ, is it *that* big?"

"No one will know for sure until the Emergence, how many times do I have to tell you? But already it's more restless than anyone can remember, sending out extrusions left and right. The problem for us. . . ." Dahl fidgeted and looked as though he would have started pacing the room, had there been enough space to allow it. "The problem for us," he began again, "is that we've been without a proper Voice for too long. We have no clue as to its intentions or wishes. We interpret some of its erratic behavior to ill temper. The last woman who held the office had an unusually close rapport with it— contact between them seemed to . . . bring it comfort. The maidens who watch over the Chamber of the Voice used to report seeing extrusions waving about, as though it were searching for her. By now, we've been out of touch with it for so long, it may think we have abandoned it at the time when it needs us the most. Therefore, it's critical that contact be reestablished, for everyone's sake, before the volcanic explosion."

"And you think that I am the one to replace The Voice?" Karen had suspected Dahl was leading up to that, but to see it confirmed on his face was flabbergasting. Seeing how flustered she'd become, he held up his hands almost pleadingly.

"I know you are more sensitive to its emanations than most who actually served as The Voice! But that is not enough—the woman so honored must have courage and conviction, she must be *attuned* to that act of communication. If she loses that willingness, the actual contact can go badly wrong— instead of allowing her consciousness in, the Being might respond defensively, throw a jolt of secretion right into her forehead."

"So it senses fear, like any other animal?"

"Most assuredly! We believe that it senses the soul and heart of each woman who aspires to become The Voice. If a new applicant for the post flinches at the very first contact, she seldom gets a second chance! I . . . *we* cannot afford a mistake. Contact must be reestablished, before the Being grows angrier or more distraught—the damage it could do if its full wrath were awakened and it was free to move about, one cannot imagine."

Karen had recovered from the first shock. Now she modulated her voice so that a touch of self-interest colored her words. "The woman who is chosen to be The Voice—does she acquire power and prestige if she performs her duties well?"

"No one among us is more honored, or enjoys more comfort, if that is her desire. Most of them lead rather austere lives, however, because the solemnity of what they do changes their personalities. Refines them, you might say."

"Well, I could use a little refining, but what happens if Yggdrasill rejects a newly appointed Voice?"

"That would seem to depend on how . . . offended it is by what it reads of her heart. It may simply withdraw from contact permanently, or in extreme cases, it does something to her that either drives her insane or kills her. But in your case, Karen, I have no doubts whatever—you will be accepted! You must believe I am sincere when I say that!"

Allen shook off his dizziness and the pain of Dahl's pistol-lash and protested at this turn of conversation. "Now wait a goddamned minute, this is. . . ."

"Allen: *shut up* and let him finish! *Please!*"

"You may not believe this part, but I swear it is true. Your coming here was foretold in a prophecy by my grandmother, in fact, for she was that last and most exceptional Voice. In the days before the Full Emergence, she said, a very special woman would appear, a woman from across the sea. We were told to 'seek her on Vardinoy,' and were given an approximate date. When we did find that special woman on Vardinoy, it would be a sign that the day of Emergence was close at hand. Such was the prophecy, and such was my appointed task: I headed the 'research committee,' the network of Norduroy agents who kept watch for this woman's arrival. Either I myself or one of my most trusted colleagues has been encamped on Vardinoy for the past eight months. It just happened to be my turn, when this ship came gliding up to the quay. The rest, you know: how I made contact with your party, how I misidentified the woman I was sent here to find. I know you hold that against me, but so does my father and many other people. I am trying to do the right thing now, and it is costing me a lot to speak with such honesty, but time grows short and our need for The Voice has become overwhelming.

"Make no mistake, Karen, this volcanic eruption will be extraordinarily powerful—we *must* learn the exact time and place. Perhaps we are meant to evacuate Norduroy, temporarily, sail around to the east of Vardinoy and put the whole island between ourselves and the eruption, like a big shield. *We don't know* what we're expected to do! Without a suitable replacement to act as The Voice, we *cannot* know! And think, too, how much that knowledge could do to save the lives of your friends! We won't harm them because after the Emergence, there will be no reason to keep the Being's existence a secret! All mankind will know and be astonished! The greatest minds of civilization will flock here for a chance to communicate with it! After all, it's been a witness to all the ages of Earth since the Creation! Think of what we could learn from it!"

Karen gestured, with an easy imperiousness that Allen had never seen her manifest before. He observed her with renewed interest, for either Dahl's implicit flattery really had gotten under her skin, or she was doing the greatest job of Method Acting he had ever seen.

"You're forgetting one thing, Andreas. I'm not reassured by the fact that I'm only your second choice. And I'm even less reassured by what happened to the lady who was your *first*."

"Try to understand, Karen. In every generation, some few of us are chosen to go abroad and serve as windows upon the outside world, as gatherers of intelligence, let us say. My cover story, and also my regular occupation, was that of a wandering landscape artist. It was always understood that I must return to my community whenever I was summoned, and my father sent for me soon after rumors began circulating in Torshavn about some kind of expedition that was being financed by the millionaire Eiden Poulsen.

"Word had it that a group of foreigners was coming to join him. Exactly as the prophecy foretold! To be the man on watch, the one who persuaded this woman to join her destiny with ours, this was the greatest honor, and the gravest responsibility, I had ever known. But . . . I was captivated by Norma the first time I met her! I wanted *her* to be the one. And anybody with half a brain could see she was fed up with her marriage, that she was emotionally susceptible. I confess it: I wanted her, intensely. And she does, as you Americans say, 'come on strong.' "

"*Did.* She *did* come on strong."

"Yes. Quite. I can explain my actions, but I cannot ask you to excuse them. I was so blinded by my desire for her, I wanted so much for her to be the one, that I became savagely angry when I realized my mistake, realized I had betrayed my people's trust, out of dumb, animal lust. When Norma and I had our final confrontation, I lost control; I took out all my shame and anger on her. In a moment of madness, I thought I was also striking at my own weakness."

"Then why didn't you push *yourself* off the cliff, asshole?" Allen sneered.

"Oh, don't play the moralist with me, Allen! You've already labeled me a madman, a murderer, and a religious fanatic, but I don't give a damn about your judgment. I happen to believe that the fate of Norduroy, the heritage and history we have preserved, the faith we have nurtured—and which has given us a stable, prosperous life in the middle of a barren wasteland—all hang in the balance. *For twelve centuries* we have guarded one of Life's greatest enigmas, and the culmination of those centuries is fast approaching. This is no trifling matter of doctrine, this is life or death for my people. I will fight to preserve our way of life, and kill for it, too, if I must!"

Dahl checked his anger and turned his scowl into a lazy, contemptuous smile. "And besides, who the hell are *you* to lecture me about right and wrong, you ineffectual, self-pitying *little* man? You were play-acting as a great explorer of the Unknown, a Seeker after hidden Truth, only you wanted to find some safe, folksy kind of mystery—a picturesque sea serpent gliding through the fog, just close enough to photograph, mind you, but not so close you could smell its breath! Then, having proven your courage, you could sail away and make a lot of money selling a few seconds' worth of blurred movie footage to the television networks. A low-risk, cozy little triumph! But when you realized there was something up here truly beyond human experience, something that could kill you just as soon as fart in your direction, all you could do was blunder along from one day to the next, while your friends started dying, one by one! I saw through you in five minutes, you phony! You are ever-so-sensitive to nature, so cruelly treated by Life, and such a sad, thwarted poet. Monster-hunter? Shit, Allen, you're just another macho-man showing off his muscles on the beach."

Karen intervened, like a teacher breaking up a playground tussle. "Andreas, if you want anything from me besides contempt, you'd better back off right now!" Allen, flushed, gnawed his lower lip and put his empty glass on the floor, hoping the other two would not see how his hands were shaking.

"I beg your pardon, Karen. It's just that Allen and I have no further reason to hide our true feelings about one another, and the urgency of my situation doesn't leave room for me to be a hypocrite."

"That's better . . . nice and calm. Now, just so I have everything straight in my head, I want you to summarize your proposition."

"Very well, here's the bottom line, as you Americans say: you are unquestionably blessed with a rare and marvelous power—of empathy, of communication, of nascent telepathy, call it what you will, it is a genuine gift. My people need the guidance that can only come from someone using that kind of power on their behalf. This part of the Faeroese archipelago is about to be turned inside out by an event that has no parallel in human history. You're being given a chance to play a pivotal role in that drama; in return, you will be given privileges and honors beyond your dreams . . . and you'll be instrumental in setting your friends free—because if the Emergence is successful, they and their stories will become irrelevant. A god will then bestride the Earth, and you will already enjoy its favor."

"What about Allen? Can he join me?"

Dahl was irritated by the question but continued to play a smooth hand. "Yes, of course, if his heart is open and his motives are sincere."

"And how will you be able to determine that?"

"I won't. But after you become The Voice, you will."

Allen jumped up, eyes wild, hands imploring. "Karen, this is the craziest load of shit I've ever heard! I can't believe you're seriously considering what this lunatic's proposing to you! Come live in our cool, New Age utopia—no worries, as long as you keep the giant squid happy and read it bedtime stories when it has the colic! Christ, listen to yourself!"

"I don't know if he's crazy or not, Allen, but everything he's said is consistent with the visions I've experienced and the weird changes that have affected all of us ever since we landed on dear old Vardinoy. I've been on this journey longer than I realized, and this is where it was taking me, all along. Whether or not Dahl's interpretation is on the money, there's a pretty good chance of that volcano tearing a big hole in the North Atlantic, so I think it might be important for everyone's survival . . . if I at least audition for this part and see what I can learn." She turned to face Dahl, who was sitting tensely on the edge of his chair. "Andreas, do you swear by the deity you believe in, that neither you nor any of your people will harm Allen and the others? And furthermore, that you'll release them from the ship and let them go unmolested back to the campsite, where they will at least have some cover from the eruption?"

"I won't harm them, but I cannot vouch for . . . the Being."

"Let me worry about that. Okay, then, I guess this is the place where I sign the parchment in blood."

"No, this is the place where you pack your toothbrush and some clean underwear. We'll leave for Norduroy in thirty minutes."

"I'll be ready. Now, if you don't mind, I'd like to be alone with Allen for a while."

Dahl's composure wavered; obviously, his first inclination was to refuse. But Karen had not phrased her request as a question—she had issued her first command.

With a curt nod, Dahl left the room. They could hear the sentry outside chamber a bullet in his weapon. Karen knelt and took Allen's trembling hands in her own. She saw on his face a tumbling chaos of emotions: helpless anger, tender concern, regrets for every needful thing he'd neglected to say or do. . . . He stared at her as though she were already drifting beyond reach. Since the first night they'd slept together, she had tolerated the contrary swing of his moods, out of her deep conviction that he was not yet all he could be; and in recent days, she had seen new strength growing in his heart. He might yet prove worthy of her investment.

But the responsibility had devolved upon her to be the fulcrum of their survival, and if Allen broke down now, she didn't think she could go through with it. She put her palms lightly against his temples and raised his face toward hers. Her voice became almost rough:

"Do you remember when I told you that I would discover my own reasons for coming to these islands? Well, now I have; so please, my love, don't do or say anything to blur my resolve. If any of us are to have a future that lasts longer than tomorrow, we must have more knowledge! And whether I like it or want it or not, it seems I'm the only one who can obtain that knowledge. Do you understand?"

"I think so. . . ."

"Then you'll understand why I can't let this parting drag on for one minute longer than is absolutely necessary! So kiss me and let's both get on with it." As they embraced, she whispered in his ear: "You and the others wait for me at the campsite. I think you'll be safe there, and I'll get back to you as soon as I possibly can."

One more kiss to his forehead, like a formal benediction; and then she squared her shoulders resolutely before knocking on the door. Dahl opened it and led her away, while the sentry came in to take charge of Allen.

She glanced back for one more look at him and saw that his eyes were filled with tears. She only hoped he was strong enough not to shed them.

37.

KAREN IN NIFLHEIM

When the Gray Boat pulled alongside the *Laertes* at dawn, Andreas Dahl's father was at the tiller. His previously hostile manner had changed dramatically. Like an equerry assigned to escort a princess, he'd changed into a clean, formal suit, slicked back his hair, and scrubbed the fisherman's grime from beneath his nails. When Karen appeared on the port side, he smiled and gestured for her to descend the rope ladder Andreas had unrolled moments earlier. Smiles, she decided, did not come naturally to the old man's weather-carved face; he had the idea of it, but his facial muscles had to work at the task—so while his sincerity could not be questioned, his smile had the look of a pasted-on accessory. Yet when the old man reached to assist her descent, his touch was gentle and diffident, almost courtly. He hovered solicitously until she was securely seated in the gently rocking boat.

Only Dahl and his father attended her on this voyage, the latter seated at the bow, teeth set against the breeze, eyes slitted against the cold chop that slapped over the Orm-carved prow, while Andreas settled in the aft seat and snuggled the tiller under one elbow. Karen occupied the center seat, the only one with back- and arm-rests; the seat of honor, apparently. There was no small talk. Even Andreas kept his gaze downcast, as though a glowing nimbus surrounded her; homage was her due, now that she had accepted the proposition he'd made to her.

As the Gray Boat angled across the straits, north by northwest, the humpbacked shape of Vesturoy faded in the mingled murk of morning fog and volcano steam. A mottled haze, smarmy and polluted-looking, hung over the sea in that direction, and every now and again she heard the muffled timpani roll of submarine eruptions. Above the site, at a wary altitude, two TV news helicopters hovered like gnats. Watching for volcanic activity made Karen think too hard about the friends she'd left behind, so she turned

to the east and searched the dawn, looking for an omen. A light, creamy
overcast dulled the glare of the new sun and colored it pewter; the clear sky
above was a vault of sooty pearl that spread the morning's light evenly, like
a vast wash of watercolor.

Now that she had acted, taken up this challenge, Karen felt that she had
finally zeroed in upon the locus of those undertows that had drawn her
thousands of miles from home; the point of origin for those visions that had
alternately frightened and exalted her since she first set foot on Vardinoy.
And, as she had intimated to Allen just before they parted, she was beginning to draw strength from the act of embracing Destiny—what else could
she call it, since everyone else apparently did too? Yet by accepting the role
that Dahl had proposed to her, she had surrendered the comfort of all prece-
dent. Uncharted waters, indeed! Her solitariness was as palpable as stone.
Andreas seemed to feel that, too, and acknowledge it; the very way he looked
at her, when he had the temerity to look at all, had changed profoundly.
Moreover, Dahl's respect was untainted by the subjective desire he had felt
for Norma. She, Karen—"the sensible one" he had called her, as though she
were a pair of shoes—could be honored as his priestess, to be sure, but he
would never think of her as a possible consort. In honoring Karen, he simultaneously belittled her as a woman! Clearly, he had never before been
so addled by lust as dear Norma had made him. It was almost—*almost*—
possible for Karen to understand how his anger had burgeoned into murder
when she realized how mistaken his choice of women had been. The man's
primary mission in life—so vital to the well-being of his people—had been
to locate the special woman whose coming had been prophesied. Dahl's
years of wandering had not been the odyssey of an aesthete—he'd been *on
duty*. As well regarded as his paintings were, the man's true purpose in life
had remained secretive and always confined by the strictures of a pagan creed
that had passed into mythology, hundreds of years ago, in every other part
of the Northland save this one insignificant island. What loneliness, not to
ever share his beliefs with anyone; how steadfast he had been in serving his
people! If he had not brutally murdered two of her friends, Karen would
have found much to admire in Andreas Dahl. What a sense of outrage he
must have felt when he realized he had squandered his honor on a woman
who, all unknowingly, had subverted a lifetime of ascetic discipline simply
by being her own voluptuous self! Poor Norma! In all her career as a sex

goddess, she'd never had a more profound effect on any man—and she wasn't even acting.

Yes, poor Norma! My God, what had it been like to die inside this thing?

Karen had blocked all speculation about that out of her mind; but now that she had greater knowledge, she could fill in the blanks.

Starting with her last clear sight of Norma, falling in slow motion, writhing inside a mound of living black matter, her body outlined in ghastly blue-white chalk as the creature's internal secretions began *processing* her while yet she lived, filling her silently screaming mouth with organic napalm . . . she would have felt not just unbearable pain, but the corrosive dissolving of her own flesh, starting with the softest, most frangible parts, so that her tongue would have started to liquefy, even as she sought to voice her agony; her eyes went next, and the spongy fibers of her lungs, the skin of her breasts and the petals of her fabled vagina, all would have begun to granulate long before she lost consciousness. Hers was a death that combined all the nastier properties of drowning and being burned alive, one molecule at a time—in short, of being *digested.*

And Karen was actually going to let that thing touch her? Even as the sun made a golden mask of her aquiline features, terror flooded her bowels like an ice-cold enema. She fought desperately to remain as composed as the Orm-shaped figurehead in front of her; if she moved now, so much as an inch, she would lose it. She would shit herself with fear, quake and howl like a mad woman! She would have prayed to the Christian God, there were still some remnants of Southern Baptist buried within her, but she had long ago shed her faith in *that* deity; so, instinctively, she beamed her silent imprecations not toward Heaven, but downward, toward that immense alien consciousness beneath the sea, whose reality she *did* believe in, begging it to lend her strength so that she might continue to play out the one scenario that might result in freedom for her lover and his companions, so totally at the mercy of those zealots who had captured Eiden's vessel. No visions came to her this time, but perhaps the Vardinoy Monster did respond to the frantic plea of its acolyte: like a spreading blanket, calmness began to rise within her. She slipped back into character, regaining her poise and outward dignity; resolve smoothed out the jagged edges of panic, and she felt her heartbeat slow to a measured, even rhythm. Indeed, all of her metabolic processes were downshifting, by the combined effects of her will and those amorphous overlapping—almost conjugal—manifestations that had become so familiar, yet remained so inscrutable.

O Yggdrasill, do not forsake thy servant Karen in this, her hour of testing and trial!

Now! Full-force, she made Contact, and primitive brute instinct caused her to throw back her head and moan, as the possession she had prayed for suffused itself throughout her sinews and jolted the circuit breakers of her nervous system. Both Dahl and his father gaped in surprise at the seizure, but their expressions were signs of awe rather than alarm, as they saw her transfigured and interpreted her spasms as an affirmation of their own faith. Not since the moment that she'd broken free of that old drainpipe had she felt so preternaturally *alive!* Her brain distended and reeled from the staggering sensory input: colors became textures, sights roared in her ears, impossible combinations of hyperkinetic sensation that dazzled, licked, bathed, and sighed like the wind in a forest. She opened wide her eyes and mouth, and *drank* the sunrise, inhaled it like a drug, gulped greedily the salts and savories of the dawn: a raw, protean, wet-iron taste/smell/synapse-frying full-throttle *orgasm* of renewed vitality! The force of her will, boosted by infusions from the Other, became huge and tumescent—whatever its origin, this was POWER! She exulted in the reality of it, and the return of self-control that channeled it to her purpose. So the good people of Norduroy needed a vatic spokeswoman, did they? Okay, they were about to get the Voice to end all Voices!

All traces of fear vanished. A volcano was giving birth to a new molten island! Eons of myth were about to become reality! And she, Karen Hambly, lint-head child from a rundown bungalow in the Project, was the fulcrum that held stupendous forces in fevered equilibrium. The total mass of Earth had condensed to this one small point—in the vast empty reaches of the North Atlantic, she was in the *one place that mattered.* She vibrated like the oscillating crystal at the heart of God's wristwatch. On this day, it was she who gave this desolate place its meaning; she who would become the focusing lens, the key turning in the lock of Time; the gyroscope that kept Tomorrow on course, the critical referent of Earth, sea, and sky! Karen knew, at that moment, that she was indeed the woman Andreas Dahl had sought; she knew that somewhere far below, the Vardinoy Monster and the Deity of Norduroy, the World-Tree of the Vikings, was with her in this boat.

Whatever the true nature of that entity, she was about to enter into its presence as no human being had ever done before. Soon she would learn what it was, beneath those palimpsests of metaphors and symbols; she would be the conduit—no, the living interface!—between the raw red chaos of Creation and the world of twentieth-century Humankind. Whatever it was, she would soon know more about its nature and intent than any priestess had ever divined; she was *where she belonged*.

She was back inside the known and comforting dimensions of her own body, a slender young woman with long wind-combed hair and fierce dark eyes, sitting as though carved from basalt, in a small, perfectly ordinary motorboat, positioned between a father who dominated his people and a dutiful son who had murdered two of her friends, and yet she felt no awe toward the old man, no hatred for his son, no fear of the subterranean Being they both worshipped. She had a vital rendezvous to keep, a mission to perform, and from the size of the crowd assembled on the waterfront, she was about to make her debut as a priestess in front of the entire population of Norduroy.

Until this morning, Norduroy had been nothing but a tiny indistinct silhouette jiggling in the lens of Allen's binoculars. Now it assumed definition and detail as the boat drew closer. She had hitherto envisioned the eponymous capital of Norduroy as being a drab, primitive sprawl of rude huts, like some impoverished hamlet in the foothills of the Andes; and its inhabitants, she had always assumed, would tend to resemble her two companions: dour, cheerless, preoccupied zealots.

The reality was very different; the long tradition of prosperity Dahl had adumbrated was clearly in evidence. Not for these folks were the defiantly brash primary colors so favored by the citizens of other Faeroese towns, but their preferred shades of off-whites and variegated grays were soothing, not grim in the least, and the buildings were sturdy, modern-looking, and often framed by tiny cared-for gardens. There weren't any cars, of course, because there was only one town, but Karen saw plenty of mini-vans and scooters. A marching line of steel pylons testified to ample hydroelectric power, generated up in the mountains. Between the commercial waterfront and the residential blocks curved a handsome municipal park, complete with spouting-whale fountain, a gazebo big enough to hold a brass band, and a children's playground full of swings and climbable/slide-down-able structures, and next to that, a balloon vendor and a jolly ice-cream stand! She also noted a clinic, a school, a library, a bookstore, and a tall radio mast, which would have brought in news and music from stations all over northern Europe. The private homes were well built, with expensive slate roofs instead of sod, and a simple, unpretentious architectural style that reminded her of the clean functionality of the Shakers.

What Karen knew to be the most common daily business of Norduroy— the catching, processing, and exporting of fish—seemed on this day to have been suspended. The quay and the long boardwalk-topped breakwater were thronged with people of all ages, as though anticipating the arrival of a major celebrity.

With a slow, deep shock, Karen realized who that celebrity was.

When the boat made contact with the old tires lining the quay, Andreas jumped out and secured it with a few expert twists of mooring line. His father, after actually *bowing* to Karen, climbed up first, and was immediately engrossed in a conversation with several other elderly men—the village council, perhaps? After securing the boat, Andreas extended his hand to her, with all the casual grace of a trained courtier. The sheer unfeigned courtesy of the gesture almost made her laugh, but there was nothing frivolous about his expression: his eyes were bright with excitement, and his mouth was grave and handsome. For a reeling instant, Karen understood why Norma had found him so sexy—this insight lapped swiftly through her loins, a furtive but sisterly serpent's tongue of speculation, quickly suppressed. Conscious of the many spectators, Karen was grateful for his support—she hadn't expected to be put on public display, and the heavy sense of Occasion was making her rubber-legged.

But once she stood on the quayside, she squared her shoulders, threw her head back with just a touch of queenly hauteur, and was hit by a druglike rush as the crowd's attention, very close to adulation, struck her with a physical impact. She half-expected someone to bring forth a crown and scepter, and to her surprise, she enjoyed the sensation.

Dahl and his father ritualistically took escorting positions to one side and respectfully behind her. Both the setup and Andreas's gestures made it clear that she was now expected to pass in review before the entire population of Norduroy.

So they wanted to inspect the goods, huh? Very well, then, she would give them a promenade to remember! Striving to look like Elizabeth the Great, but feeling rather more like Joan of Arc, she proceeded to review her new subjects. The villagers examined her with hopeful, expectant eyes. Karen tried to maintain a demeanor that was both confident and a bit aloof—one does not look for gladhanding familiarity in one's High Priestess. But her composure nearly broke when, halfway down the line, a small boy ran out from the bystanders and pressed into her hand a froth of marigolds, still damp and smelling of windblown heather. No more than six, he trembled in awe when she knelt down to accept his token. Here was an aspect of things she hadn't counted on: a small boy with red cheeks, tousled hair, and a chapped rosebud mouth, who seemed transformed with joy when she ruffled his hair and accepted his gift. Ambiguity softened her heart. She had agreed to come here, accepted this outlandish role, primarily as a duty to the companions who were still in jeopardy on Vardinoy. But instead of finding a cult-like group of puritanical fanatics, ready to slaughter and pillage on behalf of their grim, ancient creed, she had been welcomed with reverence and trust by people who were not discernibly different from those she'd found elsewhere on the Faeroes.

Guided by Dahl's touch on her elbow, Karen turned right at the end of the waterfront and began to walk up a gradual incline, up toward the foothills. Lord, but she wished Preston could be filming this! Waving, tossing flowers, murmuring encouragement, the reclusive people of Norduroy were wishing her well as she marched into the hills to do what they could not: confront, on their behalf, a strange, ancient, and possibly malign being unlike any other known to science or theology. Children held up their toys for her touch; a pregnant woman ran behind her and kissed the hem of her cloak. She was starring in a low-budget, feminist version of Palm Sunday, and on the face of it, the whole business was a ludicrous farce. Except for one thing: the Deity happened to be real. She had seen it, or at least those snaky extrusions that served as its sensory organs. She'd communicated with it, but she had so many unanswered questions to ask: was it telepathic or just broadcasting on some prehistoric wavelengths which her brain interpreted mystically? Did it have a brain as such, or just a mass of undifferentiated ganglia? Did it have emotions? Cognitive reasoning? A soul?

Since when was it necessary for a god to have any of these things? All a deity has to do is simply BE! Be so inscrutable and powerful and potentially dangerous as to compel awe. End of job description.

That paralyzing spasm of fear she had felt out in the straits was gone now. Replacing it was a far subtler consideration: she'd undertaken this High Priestess gig in order to retain her personal liberty while she figured out how to help her friends back on Vardinoy. Knowledge would help; knowledge of this entity and knowledge of how its worshippers thought about certain matters. How to treat the nonbeliever, for instance. But now she was starting to wonder—what if she had her first one-on-one session with it, and she came away from the experience so mind-blown by what she'd learned that she no longer *cared* what happened to Allen Warrener and Co.?

The last scattered farm buildings vanished behind a curve in the track, and there was no way forward except by means of a narrow footpath, scrupulously clean and drained, paved with thousands of pearl-like sea-polished stones, set down in a swirling, yin–yang pattern of alternating blacks, whites, and grays. The motif, she guessed, was intertwined branches, but the execution was so stylized she couldn't be sure. The footpath wound through a series of narrow shaded gorges for about a quarter mile, until it terminated in an oval clearing backed by a sheer basaltic cliff. Ahead was a half-moon bridge over a wide sparkling creek, and on the far side was a large stone-walled cottage, complete with Seven Dwarves wainscoting and round adorable windows. "Your quarters," said Dahl simply. "I'm told it's much more comfortable inside than it would appear."

Dahl and his father halted on the far side of the creek, and the elder Dahl ceremoniously rang a bell attached to a stone pillar beside the footbridge. The cottage door opened slowly, revealing a backdrop of warm yellow light and the outlines of two young women. As they stepped out into better light, Karen observed that they wore no makeup but each was comely enough, in a chaste, self-effacing way.

"My handmaidens, I presume?"

"If you like," said Dahl quietly. "Their duty is to assist you in any needful way. Right now, they're going to prepare you . . . for. . . ."

"My audition?"

"No, Karen—you've already passed that stage. This is where we must leave you."

There was no mistaking the reverence in Dahl's voice. To him, this was a holy place. Both men solemnly shook her hand.

"But . . . what do I do? What's going to happen?"

"The two attendants will bathe and dress you appropriately. Then they will escort you into the Chamber of The Voice. There's a comfortable chair near an opening in one of the walls, and a smooth place for you to rest your forehead. Make yourself comfortable and clear your mind of superfluous thoughts. What happens after that, I don't know—my grandmother could not or would not describe the experience."

"How long will it take?"

"Time? It takes as long as it takes, that's all. When your mind clears again, just pull the bell-rope hanging next to the opening, and the attendants will come and assist you."

Karen didn't care for the implications of that word "assist," but her misgivings had grown more abstract as her eagerness for knowledge had grown sharper-edged. It was high time to get on with this thing!

As the two attendants led her inside, she smiled at her mind's choice of words: indeed, in more ways than one, it *was* time to "get on with this thing. . . ."

She'd half-expected the hut's interior to be like the set for a B movie: heavy furniture, arcane symbols decorating the walls, the ambience dark and sepulchral. It was neither. Her companions lived in two cubicles, simply furnished but not harshly monastic; the rest of the rooms were for Karen. They were clean and spare, except for the living room, which had a fireplace, a radio, and a surprisingly big library, although most of the volumes were in Danish. Wall rugs lent color, oil lamps provided warm illumination, and there was a luxurious wading-pool–sized bath. One of the attendants, after showing her around, pointed to the pool and said: "Excise my poor English, but you should come to bath now, okay?" The girl was no older than twenty, Karen figured; a straw-blonde with milky skin, naturally pink lips, and a dusting of freckles. What a loss if virginity was a requirement for the job!

Karen followed the girls into the bathing area, where they shyly disrobed her and pointed to the pool.

"Bring on the mare's milk!" she said, sinking into the pool.

"I'm sorry?"

"Nothing, my dear. This water feels like heaven; thank you for preparing it."

Gently but insistently, the other, non-talkative, attendant took the washcloth from Karen's hand and began soaping her until she was covered with rich lather. Karen felt like true royalty now—the water's temperature was exquisitely balanced to that of her body; as long as she lay quietly, she basked in the sensation of floating on air. The silent girl soaped Karen's back and arms, and as her hand began to lather the puckered slope of Karen's right breast, the girl allowed her attention to wander and sneaked a look at her new mistress. Her caresses had an innocent, androgynous sensuality that Karen enjoyed very much. When the other attendant, the straw-blonde, poured a jar of herbs into the water, Karen relaxed almost to the point of falling asleep, but when the silent girl had finished rinsing her back, she began vigorously to massage it with a woolly-feeling loofah. The changeover from languid sensuality to astringent vigor woke her up and stimulated her whole body. *Exactly what it's meant to do.* And when the talkative girl brought her a bowl full of warm, muttony broth, Karen suddenly remembered how long she had gone without food and gulped it down. *Chock full of drugs, probably, but who am I to complain about* that?

Sure enough, while the girls were toweling her dry, a wave of itchy-tingly pleasure swept through her capillaries; remarkably like a good-quality codeine high. So far, every aspect of this preparatory ritual had been enjoyable; these people manifestly meant her no harm. Apprehension and curiosity were now balanced evenly in her mind—perhaps the ideal mood from which to approach this sort of thing. Not that she knew exactly what "this sort of thing" was going to be.

The English-speaking servant brought out a wide homespun towel and indicated through signs and motions that Karen should stand still and permit herself to be dried. After the drying, the maids dressed Karen in a long, soft flannel robe, light-gray with runic symbols embroidered on the bodice in contrasting white. As a final touch, the blonde handmaid tied Karen's hair with a length of satin ribbon. Then they both stood back to inspect their handiwork, and, after a touch here and a brush there, they were satisfied. In unison, they bowed.

The preliminary rituals were over. Karen took a couple of very deep breaths and squared her shoulders: Queen of the May or Bride of Frankenstein, she was ready.

The two girls led her to a door in the wall opposite her sleeping quarters. The one-who-never-talks opened that portal silently, disclosing another, smaller, triangular-shaped chamber at the bottom of seven stairsteps. Karen paused on the threshold, because the expressions on the two girls' faces were so expectant, so full of tremulous emotion, that she simply had to hug them both. Then she went to the threshold and took one step down and one step forward.

Down . . .

    Forward . . .

        Down. . . .

And the door was closed behind her, a sound whose finality she did not care for.

Aside from its peculiar three-sided shape, the room was very plain. She'd expected, perhaps anticipated, something more baroque: guttering torches, wispy incense-holders, that sort of thing. But aside from a single oil lamp and the deeply cushioned chair Dahl had described, the only decoration was a symbolic representation of the great World Tree painted on one wall. Dahl's people, she knew, had connected the World Tree myth with their mysterious Being, not the other way around, and there was logic to it, because both the creature and the great tree were rooted underground, in Niflheim, that curious Viking version of Hell, where the chief form of punishment appeared to be boredom. The Great Tree's taproot penetrated the several crusts of the Earth and drew nourishment from its molten core, and its multitudinous branches soared high enough to pierce the floor of Heaven.

At the base of the triangular chamber, directly in front of the sturdy, padded chair, was a small opening, now covered by a sliding gray curtain. There was nothing else for her to do but have a seat, pull open the curtain, and lean forward until her forehead rested in the cup-shaped depression above the opening. She limbered her body with deep breaths. Wondering how many other women had performed this ritual during the past thousand years, she closed her eyes and tried to relax. The stone was cool and worn so smooth that it felt almost pillow-soft. Karen cleared her mind and waited.

But not long; not long at all. Something enormous stirred far below, something big enough to displace a large volume of air and propel an unnatural breeze into Karen's face, and after one experimental breath, she sucked down that air greedily, for it was moist and refreshing, as though each molecule was hypersaturated with oxygen.

This time, she knew, it was going to be a very different experience from those jumbled, badly edited collages she'd assembled back in the tent. As intense as those communications had been, they were always disjointed, and they had always raised more questions than they had proffered answers. As the rising breeze blew harder and she began to hear the sounds of organic matter rubbing against rock, she opened her eyes long enough to see a thickening of shadows in the opening, and just as quickly closed them again when she felt that sensation of warm oil touching her forehead, just as it had done long ago, when she was dying inside the concrete pipe. But what came next was as different from that childhood experience as the difference between sniffing heroin and spiking it straight into a vein.

Thus did Karen and the Vardinoy Monster introduce themselves to each other. She learned that it was genderless and had always been solitary; if Father Evolution had created its mate, the two had never met. Its incomparably strange consciousness gradually superimposed over hers, and eventually Karen gave it "permission" to explore her mind as deeply as it wanted to go, and for fifteen minutes, she sat still as a stone while feather-light, wire-thin extrusions probed her and penetrated the pores of her skin. Such was the ensuing state of intimacy that Karen's consciousness melded with that other, terribly alien, awareness. She saw through its "eyes," which were packets of specialized nerves designed to collect information from a spectrum far exceeding human comprehension, from light waves now unseen but which were common when the planet was young and newly cooled. It/she had no facial features and no massive organ corresponding to the brain; instead, encased in a thick, tough oval membrane, its sentience was housed in a vast tangle of waving ribbons, nourished and activated by a distillate of that corrosive blue acid it secreted—a garden of exotic ganglia, organized in a hierarchy that had made sense only at the dawn of Time. She learned that it had "found" her because it had sensed a wildcard gene, an evolutionary throwback that made her a powerful receptor, and it had learned how to organize the visuals it wanted to share with her. After all, it had been completely alone for untold eons, and the urge to communicate was overwhelming, but until it modified the amount and speed of its input, Karen could not keep up, felt as though her head were about to explode. But it was sensitive to the feedback of her distress and modified its sendings closer to the spectrum of human senses and that initial warm spot on her forehead is expanding, and from that point, projects a skull-cap of extrusions, enclosing her head like a living helmet

Which makes her feel

INVINCIBLE!

(Oh, yeah!! That's more like it, m'lord!)

It has pondered THE
UNIVERSE, and concluded that Time, not Space

**Is the primary element for EVERYTHING, and that its per-
sonal supply of Time was virtually infinite. In fact,**

Time is what it understands most intimately—

Karen is being infil-
trated gradually, even tenderly, with an almost loving attention to courtesy, so she does not experience the sense of demarcation that might be
expected when she permits her consciousness to be subsumed within its
dreams, its recollected emotions, if that is the word for them:

It had no parents, just
simply

Evolved from a micro-
scopic dot

Into a creature of sub-
stantial size

It owns the Earth, a living singularity, Evolution's first garage project
(the later models will be much more practical!), but after it reaches a certain size, perhaps, Karen's dimmed brain calculates, a mile square, with its
Core rising in the center, bulbous and tough!—after it reaches this age
and size, which for lack of a better term could be called "adolescence," it
discovers the bliss of . . .

FLOATING!

in the warm, shallow, sparsely populated sea. It has no natural enemies,
and it absorbs nutrition automatically, unthinkingly, so FLOATING is
pretty much all that it/she does, but it is far from monotonous, for there's
always something pretty exciting going on at this early stage of Time:
meteors exploding on the Moon, volcanoes thrusting up from what had

been tranquil lagoons, continents forming and eroding, the occasional giant storm which blows and howls for years at a time until, eventually the sun comes out and the floating resumes, as peaceful and sensual as it ever was; it "sees" without eyes; it "feeds" without a mouth,

    And it doesn't MISS those things,

    For its sleek, simple, tough-as-leather design is

    Perfectly adapted to the conditions of its world.

                Father Evolution

                                    You see, had not yet

                                    Come up with the

                                    whole Death

                                    Thing; it just seemed simpler to engineer this prototype life form to live forever, barring a freak natural accident (Father E. isn't allowed to interfere with those!). It is wholly self-sufficient, doesn't even have any reproductive drives; perhaps one day it will have to subdivide, but Father Evolution is still pondering the efficacy of that.

    Meanwhile . . .

                                    It/she just drifts and absorbs food; it is very

                                    Pleasant: If one has no concept of passing

                                    Time, then one has no sense of boredom.

    Together, they see flinty young mountains rising and crumbling; they idly watch the Moon change from meteor-pocked boil into a white-gold eye of frigid tranquility.

                    (Good Lord, how much Time
                    would have to pass in order to
                    see such things, track changes
                    on a geological scale?)

It grows; it floats around; it figures things out. But this Edenic period cannot, does not, last, for Evolution has work to do shaping the Earth too; now that the seas are primed, they can take care of themselves.

> *Despite the centuries that have*
> *Passed, the planet is still young*
> *And unstable, and periodically*
> *Bombarded from outer space.*

It remembers many meteor strikes, but this one stands out, because when the shock wave subsides, the air becomes opaque and there is nothing but shadows and darkness and distant burning mountains.

One day
   It drifts close to a volcanic range—strictly out of curiosity—and discovers that when it floats in their vicinity, it "tastes" certain minerals in the water which have an invigorating effect on its consciousness and metabolism. The hot spicy mineral-thick waters near volcanoes are its favorite floating grounds.

> *(This shit probably is highly*
> *toxic for us; for the Floater*
> *it's candy, crack, and nicotine*
> *all rolled into one. It loves the tang of*
> *hot sulfur!)*

Its/their favorite place is a steaming newborn plateau, miles wide and still dripping lava at some points of its circumference. Oh, the waters here are *good!* But uncomfortably hot.

(Funny how its senses increase in range and sophistication as it slowly grows—it is now more sensitive to climatic change than it used to be; and it has periods of impatience, something like irritation; what is my purpose, Father E? ((Oh, nothing much, my "son," you're just an experiment whose end result is still a question mark. Don't call me, I'm busy sculpting the Himalayas for the next, oh, ten million years. Give or take. . . .))

In other words, it's become an adolescent. *(If Karen could laugh, she would.)*

The idyll they've shared ends suddenly. Their volcanic island starts shaking one day, when they're drifting very close, gorging/absorbing those corrosive minerals that it finds so necessary, not realizing how powerful and toxic—to *other beings*, that is—its internal secretions are becoming.

Something's *wrong*.

The sea is vibrating and vents far below are screaming. We can hear them! Louder, louder, more violent. Time to float away, perhaps. *(What is this new and dreadful sensation? Karen of course recognizes "fear," but her host has never felt it before and simply becomes confused. Instinct tells it to drift away from the steaming, rumbling plateau, and finally it does that and Evolution takes another step, because it's found out that one valid response to Fear is to get away from the source of it!*

Unfortunately, it's too late. In an explosion so vast it could have been spotted by an observer on the Moon, what was water becomes fire.

In the violence of their birth, the liquefied new mountains scoop out a titanic cavern in the seabed; and they expel mountain-stuff in such vast quantities that half of the Faeroese archipelago is formed by this one seismic catastrophe. When the smoke finally clears and the red-hot magma cools at last, the very shape of the Earth has been changed:

There are mountainous islands now where before there was only cool oozy sea bottom, and in their aggregate mass, those mountains weigh a measurable fraction of the planet's total gross weight.

Stunned into a coma by the force of the detonation, it/she is unconscious for some thousands of years and when it wakes, the return of awareness is total, sudden, and chaotic.

Where is the light? There is no **light**!

Why can't I/we move? I/we **want to move**!

But we cannot.

(Oh no! Sweet Jesus, this cannot be happening? But it is. There are fucking mountains on top of us and I'm like a spinal patient who can wiggle only one toe and can never rise from his bed no matter how much willpower he exerts. I/we cannot stand this imprisonment another second! I want to float free! Please, Father Evolution, just let me move one inch! ((Sorry, kiddo; the rules of the experiment have changed. I'll check back with you in, oh, a hundred million years or so.))

Come back! Have mercy on your earliest sentient child!

There is no answer. There is no light. There is no movement. The enormity of its situation sinks into its core awareness and

It screams for a hundred years. . . .

It heaves and writhes, or tries to, with all its considerable strength, in mind-clawing panic, but even its strength is not sufficient to budge the mountains that have buried it alive.

It wills death, but all that happens is the shutdown of its core, which becomes a huge sphere of arrested consciousness, flash-frozen in self-willed oblivion. Unwittingly, it's now turned its fate over to the blind survival mechanisms with which Evolution has so lavishly—and, as it happens, cruelly—equipped it.

Millennia pass. While its core remains in stasis, its outer substance and micro-level chemistry undergo profound changes on an accelerated time scale. Its food-gathering process changes: it finds edible minerals; its extrusions, needle-thin and often hundreds of miles long, brush against aquatic life-forms and zap them with the blue venom, paralyzing them in frozen agony while the acid breaks down their flesh into its constituent compounds and dispatches them, in distilled liquid form, toward the core.

Which continues to become more sophisticated even though it has shut down its own perceptions. Suicide is not an option; Evolution designed it for the long haul, and so it evolves toward pure survival—the fact that it does not want to survive in its present circumstances is totally irrelevant.

What wakes it again is the tantalizing vibrations from a nearby Icelandic eruption. By now, it's not without a primitive sense of logic: it was imprisoned by a violent cataclysm of the Earth's crust, and it stands to reason that someday, another cataclysm will set it free. Longing and dreaming for that day is its only hope, its faith, its theology, so to speak. It concentrates on developing the extrusions, exploring the Earth through tiny fissures, which it can extend (but not widen; that can only be done when the tip emerges into open air again!) with concentrated bursts of the blue venom. It exercises its sensory collectors, specialized conduit cells that travel in the middle of the extrusions; it learns how to "see" with them.

These activities lessen its sense of helplessness; they are diverting; they are making it stronger and more complex, for the time of its Emergence.

And then one day, it hears a faint but growing sound of something vast and implacable coming closer. The water its extrusions sample grows colder.

(Karen realizes what is coming: the first and most massive of the Ice Ages. And the prospect of cold darkness and crushing weight causes its Core to quake with terror: it can only "watch" as the pitiless white wall inches closer and finally begins to cover the mountainous islands above its prison.

It's like drowning. But drowning by the slowest incremental degrees.

It shuts down all metabolic systems to minimal survival-only levels. After several thousand years, the ice retreats and it reawakens. (*Well, that wasn't so bad, really, as long as we can shut down into semiconsciousness like that!*) But during this warm thawing period, it develops into an organism too complex to do that any more.

Therefore, when the glacier wall returns, it cannot escape again into suspended vitality.

(NO! please, not AGAIN! I CANNOT ENDURE IT AGAIN!)

But it must endure; there is no way it can do anything else. If the first time was like drowning, this time is like being buried alive. In slow motion. The intervals between Ice Ages and thaws become shorter. The glaciers advance and retreat, advance and retreat, and each time they advance, its ordeal starts all over again.

It remains and endures: fixed in place for millennia. It continues to develop on a cellular level, however. It can now read and interpret the finest, subtlest signals of change in the sea and in the planet's crust. It has felt and catalogued every volcanic eruption since the last glaciers retreated, trying to find a pattern, a predictable time of liberation. No good: these things are random.

Without really meaning to, in strange, brooding, incomprehensible ways, it becomes stupendously wise.

And at some point during the middle of the ice-age cycles

It goes completely insane.

Since the Late Pleistocene, it has existed only for the fulfillment of its own private demented mythology: one day, in a titanic explosion, it will be liberated, resurrected; that the same Evolutionary forces that imprisoned it will turn full circle and break it free again, smarter, more powerful, more willful, than any other creature that has ever lived on this planet.

With the possible exception of Man.

The Earth whispers to it: *Patience. Patience. In the fullness of time, the crust will fracture, and your prison will dissolve in fire, and in the wake of the volcanic explosion, it will rise, transcendent!*

(Which more or less brings Karen/us up to the present. *Already, it can feel the shiftings of tectonic plates, the gathering of pressure. Its extrusions are every-where, testing, sampling, updating the situational data.*)

The being's excitement is itself volcanic. It strains against the imprisoning mountains, knowing that soon they WILL move! Riding the wake of the lava, it will burst free, gigantic and ecstatic, never again to know darkness, cold, or immobility!

It wanted Karen to know these things. *(It cannot, of course, speak to her, but her mind gives it a voice: low, beguiling, and enticingly wise.)*

It's been aware of Karen almost since her birth. Now and then, a human is born who has a wild gene, an evolutionary quirk, that enables him or her to pick up the creature's vibrations. Most of those humans have ended up in asylums, or committing suicide, but Karen is different,

It **likes** Karen.

She knows not to read too much into this astonishing communication; it probably "liked" all the other Voices, too, as a dog might like a fleeting, anonymous pat on the head—that gesture is appreciated, of course, and it has repaid the Norduroy people, through the Voice, by showing them where the best fishing grounds are, no matter what the stupid old Gulf Stream does.

Look! There goes a school of fish big enough to feed this island's people for years! Should you wish to learn where this bounty is, you need only superimpose your specific longing, visualize it, and you'll get feedback from your proximity; you'll learn the exact location and course of the fish. GOOD fish, too!

Karen spurns the offer: *This Voice doesn't give a damn about fish; you insult me. No stinking fish for THIS Priestess! Why dream small if you have my powers?*

Yes, why indeed! Here you go; take your pick; Happy Trails!

She reels, mentally, from the tsunami of data, tremendous packets of inchoate information the extrusions have gathered over Time; from this Noah's

Flood of information, with leisure and practice, Karen would be able to cull an
awareness of many fabulous things:
> *Enormous undiscovered pockets of petroleum and natural gas;*
> *The cyclic migrations of all edible fish; whole nations can be fed,*
wasted ecologies restored!!
> *A sunken U-boat bulging with the gold bullion of the Reich*
> *And the REAL location of Atlantis!*

Did she want still more? *No, thank you; that will do for the moment.*

(Truly, the Voice had powers beyond anything known to these clodhopper fish-
ermen. With knowledge such as she had just been given, even a tiny community
like Norduroy could dominate the Common Market, put Saudi Arabia out of
business; and **she** *would be the instrument that makes such things happen—*
there would be no human being more powerful! Visions of that power lapped at
her like tongues of silk. She visualized the jewels and designer outfits she would
wear, the expensive cars she would drive, the awesome fees she would command for
her brokerage services:)

Why, she needed only to point to a map and say to the peti-
tioning diplomats: "Here's where you'll find oil, and there your natural gas.
My cut is the customary twenty per cent of the gross, just leave the gold with
my two Sapphic acolytes in the other room and next time you come, take off
your fucking shoes before entering my Presence!"

Let Dahl and his fellow bumpkins take their fish; all the cod
and halibut they can eat for a thousand years. Whoop-tee-doo! She's
incredulous: for nine hundred years they've had access to this kind of
information and nobody ever thought to ask for anything more than
seafood??

Well, SHE had thought to ask, and now she could take this barren
turd of an island and turn it into her private estate; live in a palace of gold;
import bronzed young muscular lovers with great swinging clubs of phal-
luses at her command. . . . And if We are in a charitable mood, perhaps we'll
allow a conjugal visit from our current consort, that going-bald-on-top,
slightly pot-bellied, well-intentioned but almost totally ineffectual man

who's made a train wreck out of his life. On second thought, fuck Allen Warrener. What a human zero!

(*Wait! What's going on?*)

Why remain loyal to HIM? He brought you here to search for a monster and instead you found a god, or the closest thing to it you'll ever meet, and by becoming its confidante you've been handed the Keys to the Kingdom. All you have to do is . . . whatever it wills you to do, in its whimsical alien way.

(*Hold it right there! I'm hanging up the phone now, so take your stinking tentacles out of my head!*)

She has to struggle to free herself from the extrusions, which causes it to feed back anger and hurt and bewilderment. The Earth's crust WOULD split, and on a tide of molten fire this thing would be loosed into a world simply not ready to comprehend it. Rising out of the sea would come a living mountain, immensely powerful, conscienceless, deadly to the touch when he wants to be, and utterly, pathetically deranged.

She finally tears her head free and in pique the Entity shoots a dart of blue stuff into her brain, not lethal, but disturbing enough to hint at what it COULD do to her if it chose; the impact of that jolt turns Karen's metabolism inside out: she writhes in pain and moves her hips in ecstasy at the same time, and she feels a change in the very meat of her cortex.

You don't spurn the friendship of a god without paying a price. How many myths have warned us about that? Whatever that price was, whatever damage the pissed-off being had spiked into her, its effects were not immediate; perhaps, at the last instant, it pulled its punch; which means that Karen still had some time to act.

She tugged hard on the bell rope and drew the curtain over that black orifice, from which now rose a wet, noxious, smothering odor like that of rotting mushrooms. The contact spot on her forehead felt like someone had placed a hot coin there. Just before the blonde attendant entered, Karen fainted.

She came to on a soft woolen sleeping pad, her burning head soothed with some kind of salve. The shy blonde attendant was bent over her, washing her tenderly with a warm cloth and murmuring to her in a Norse dialect that was surely the oldest language she had ever heard.

She waved the girl aside and tried to reassert control of her body. She couldn't even raise her left arm until the fourth try, and when she brought it close enough to read the time and date on her watch, she gasped.

She had been in the communicants' chamber for sixteen and a half hours.

38.

Flight

At the moment Karen looked at her watch, disjointed memories of the communicant-experience flooded her mind. She went limp and just let the tide of images wash over her, barely aware of her attendants' solicitude. There was nothing else for it; it would take her a long time to digest the experience. All she could do for the moment was replay it in loops until she fixed the pattern and hierarchy of impressions "Yggdrasill" had shared with her. She also wondered if all the women who'd served as The Voice had gone quietly mad sooner or later, for dementia must be the consequence of prolonged contact to that *thing*. Not foaming-at-the-mouth crazy, but incrementally, cunningly deranged, playing off their contact with the Being in exchange for greater wealth, power, and status. That was what it had promised *her*, and insofar as it could feel human emotions, it *liked her!* It was reasonable to suppose that it had showed her images it had not vouchsafed to her predecessors. . . . Generosity, or seduction? And what kind of a god would so nakedly reveal its own suffering? A hundred million years of darkness, cold, loneliness, and insanity, culminating in the form of a death wish wedded to a reincarnation fantasy.

But there at the end, when she'd rejected its invidious attempt to bind her loyalty to its service, it had "spat" a drop of blue venom onto that sensitized spot on her forehead. Was that a spontaneous gesture of pique, or a mechanism it had used before against women who'd balked at serving it? Time would tell; it *could* have killed her. But now there was in her bloodstream at least a trace of a toxic compound of a kind that might no longer exist on Earth except in that mad thing's bloodstream.

Well, that could not be undone; there was no antidote; she would deal with the effects when and if they showed up. Meanwhile, she *had* gained useful knowledge: the approximate mass and strength of the Being (immense, in both cases, but far from invulnerable); and the nature of its pitiful motives—she'd learned as much as any human being could absorb. Most importantly, she now knew the date, the probable magnitude, and almost the precise hour of the volcano's eruption. She had to act quickly. In fact, *now* would not be too soon!

She visualized the volcano's site once more, as it had been "shown" to her: a great dome rising toward the surface . . . enormous and irresistible pressures confined within it, swelling like a boil; its eruption would be shatteringly powerful, and, yes, it *would* liberate the Being from its subterranean prison, so that it could fulfill its lust for oblivion, by ponderously heaving its Core into the great red ulcer of spurting lava. But so great was its mass that the effect would be like jamming a cork into the outlet. Eventually, the thing *would* be consumed, of course, but for some minutes at least, it would deny the swelling lava and accumulated gases any outlet, multiplying their explosive power exponentially, turning what would have been an impressive but not catastrophic eruption into a blast whose destructive potential would equal that of a hydrogen bomb.

Her first impulse was to summon Dahl and convince him of the true danger to the people of Norduroy: yes sir, this was going to be Ragnarok, all right, but contrary to your belief, you're *not* going to be spared. Your God barely thinks of you at all, in fact. You must evacuate Noduroy immediately or it will be hit, first with a devastating barrage of lava bombs, and secondly by a tsunami seventy feet high.

It was not concern for Andreas Dahl's safety that motivated her. She didn't give a damn about Andreas and his flinty, humorless father; Andreas was a murderer and a cold-blooded fanatic and he bloody well deserved to die. No; Karen's warning would be for that rosy-cheeked little boy who had given her flowers; for all those innocent Norduroy people who had welcomed her with such trust and hope, and, of course, for these two Vestal Virgins who waited on her hand and foot—they all deserved a chance to live.

But she couldn't simply call a town meeting and speak her prophecy to the population en masse; Dahl and his fellow extremists wouldn't allow that. The hierarchy around here was clear: Karen speaks to the Being, Karen conveys the Being's wishes to Dahl; Dahl informs his cultist henchmen, and they decide together how much the general population needs to know. Would Dahl believe her? Would he act on her information even if he did? It

was not, after all, the news he wanted to hear. His faction had staked everything on the notion that, after being spared in the cataclysm, the island of
Norduroy would enter a Golden Age. Now here came Karen, who had
ample motive for being deceitful, after just one session in the Voice's
Chamber, telling them bluntly that their Deity didn't give a flying fuck and
that they had only two choices: flee the island while they still could, or stay
here and be roasted and/or drowned. That would not be an easy sell.

Like so many zealots, Dahl's people would fall back on *faith;* they might
interpret Karen's warning as a test of their loyalty. And her sudden appearance
with such a dire message would cause him to have her watched even more
closely. No; the Cassandra bit wasn't going to work. Perhaps there were enough
sensible skeptics who would move to high ground and thus save a portion of the
population. Ultimately, their survival was not her responsibility.

*It's time to make the hard choices, girl. You must think only about Allen and the
others on Vardinoy.*

If the creature missed its aim, or went completely nuts and changed its mind
at the last minute, the western cliffs of Vardinoy were so high and massive that
none of the people encamped by the lake would be harmed. But if the beast
did manage to clog the pressure vents with its enormous bulk and the super-
eruption occurred, then Vardinoy was in grave peril. Not from the tsunami, or
from the barrage of lava bombs—few of those would make it all the way to the
interior; the worst danger, she was certain, would be the effect of that intensi-
fied blast when its shock wave smote the porous maze of tunnels and caverns
honeycombing the foundations of Vardinoy. Large portions of the island
would fall into the sea, and the lake would surely flood in a violent surge.
Between one danger and another, her friends didn't stand much of a chance.

Another reason, then, why she could not approach Dahl. He already
despised Allen Warrener. As the self-appointed spokesman for The Voice,
the conduit who got the straight dope from the Deity, Andreas and his followers wanted to preserve everyone who was willing to accept their post-
apocalypse leadership. Of course, the Deity would probably die—its
death-wish had been communicated to Karen with searing clarity—but
Dahl's revised theology would emphasize its transformation into a spirit.
Perhaps he would claim to be the only one whom that spirit communicated
with, thus eliminating the office of The Voice, which had always been a
potential threat to secular power.

Well, damn it, I AM The Voice, and I will speak my warning only to those I cherish!

Karen's mind raced; she would have to make her move soon. It seemed likely that Andreas would come tomorrow to check on how she was getting along. She wasn't a good enough actress to fool him; he would sense that she was holding something back. And, while he would never dare lay hands upon The Voice, he might well order his goons to kill one member of the Expedition, solely to convince Karen that he wasn't just jerking off about wanting *all* the information from her.

The harshest fact now came into focus: Karen could not fulfill her responsibility to her friends on Vardinoy without staining her conscience with the thing that she *had* to do on Norduroy, in order to escape undetected. Dahl knew she'd agreed to become The Voice under duress; almost certainly he would have posted sentinels to keep watch on this building. It was dark now, though, and would be dark for another two and a half hours. The house was secluded; if the interior lights were off, no one would see her leave, and the path down to the village was twisty and often walled off by rock formations. If she could just reach the harbor, find a boat, and be out in the straits before sunrise, she would steer for Vardinoy by dead reckoning. She could not, of course, come ashore in the harbor, not with armed fanatics in control of the *Laertes.* She would steer for the hidden cove next to the ruined cathedral and land there. She thought she had enough strength to climb the precarious ladder inside the central Axe-Cut, and then hike the two kilometers to the encampment. An exhausting trek, to be sure, but the urgency of her mission would provide the necessary stamina.

Very well: she'd made a good plan. But she needed time and privacy to execute it. Time to find a suitable boat. Time to cross the straits without being pursued. If the alarm was raised immediately after she fled the hut, she'd never make it to the harbor, let alone to Vardinoy. *What next? Let's see. . . .*

She suddenly couldn't think; mind-scramble! Half the muscles in her face cramped and burned, and her vision blurred as she felt the blue venom rearranging certain nerves inside her skull. The spasm passed in seconds, but it left her gasping and beset by a throbbing headache.

What the hell is that stuff doing to my brain?

The girl with coral lips sponged Karen's shoulder tenderly.

But as convincing as the two servants were, Karen suspected they were also her minders. She had seen a telephone cable running into this dwelling, but had not seen a phone in her quarters. If she suddenly bolted, the attendants could call the village, and Karen would never elude recapture.

Ineluctably, she was being deprived of all options but one. She forced her conscience into a corner and tried to seal it off from her rational thinking. It did not yield peacefully; the act she now contemplated was abhorrent in the extreme. She couldn't remain here while Allen and company were in such danger; and single-handedly, she could not subdue two strong young women to the extent that she could bind and gag them securely enough to immobilize them for at least an hour. They had to be taken out of the equation; that was the only remaining option.

Slam! She was hard up against it now. While the straw-blonde girl bathed her, Karen distanced herself from any feelings of compassion, even as another part of her mind twisted and dodged the inevitable. Perhaps she could just knock them unconscious! She'd seen it done enough times in the movies, so how hard could it be? How hard *did* you hit someone if you wanted to put them out for six hours instead of six minutes? She had no idea; not the slightest. Probably, she would have to crack them on the head almost hard enough to kill them. Why not exert a few more foot-pounds of force and make certain they stayed down?

I am not a killer!

Nobody is, until the moment comes when killing is the only alternative to disaster. One bleat over the phone from these servants, and not only would Karen's escape be thwarted, but Andreas might order the re-imprisonment of the people on Vardinoy. Or their execution.

Do it now, *before you start thinking too hard about the enormity of it!*

Karen pointed to the antechamber outside the bath area. "I'm too exhausted to move, my dear, but I just remembered that I left a piece of jewelry in there, on the floor probably. A . . . a ring, yes. Would you mind looking for me?"

The girl patted her arm and stood up, smiling, happy to be of service. "Of course I don't mind. My happiness is to do your bidding."

Come home with me and wash all my dishes, then.

Karen crouched on one knee as the girl turned away, and wrapped her hands around one leg of the stout wooden stool the attendant had been sitting on.

"Right down there, you ninnie! By the lamp! On the floor!"

Puzzled, the girl got down on her hands and knees, as vulnerable a position as Karen could hope for. The sound of running bare feet made the girl turn her head with an expression of innocent curiosity. With all her might, Karen swung the stool against the side of the girl's head. The sound of the blow was astonishingly loud: the hollow *snak!* of a skull being fractured, and the girl sank down like a sledgehammered cow, the vitality draining from her wide-open eyes even before she hit the floor and blood gushing from her nose and mouth.

An inquiring voice called out in Faeroese. Karen heard the rustle of the other attendant's robe and sandals and hid behind the door to the bathing room, the stool cocked above her head. But her hands were greasy with sweat and blood and the stool shook so hard she almost dropped it. When the quiet servant swished into the room and saw the gore puddle at her feet, and saw that Karen was no longer in the pool, she opened her mouth for a scream.

Hit her NOW!

But Karen was so revolted by her earlier violence that she pulled this punch, hesitated just enough to miss the servant's head and land instead on her shoulder, a clumsy glancing blow that inflicted lots of hurt but no serious damage. Grunting with pain and surprise, the attendant turned around and faced her assailant. The stunned expression on her face was piercing: *I have treated you kindly! Why do you hurt me so?*

"Because I must!" Karen snarled aloud as she swung another blow. But her victim was alert now, and agile—she ducked her head, so that instead of crushing her skull, the stool merely opened a flap of skin on her scalp. Blinded by the sudden flow of cranial blood, the servant lurched blindly backwards . . . and fell into the pool. She rose up screaming to wake the dead, so Karen struck a third blow, but she was tired and disgusted by now, and this time all she did was mash the poor girl's nose.

Can't I do this over again, without such crude butchery?

Even while her mind was begging for that impossible mercy, her hands clamped around the servant's throat and she held her head under until she stopped thrashing and went limp. Karen waited, making sure the woman wasn't playing possum. After four minutes underwater, that possibility could be ruled out.

I drowned this woman! With my own hands, I drowned her!

Karen vomited into the pool. After the spasms subsided, she methodically washed the blood and puke from her clothes as best she could. And before she fled the house, she stepped once more into the Chamber of the Voice and shouted down the sacred hole in the wall: "Die, you obscene mother-fucker! You're way overdue for extinction, so just go ahead and DIE! And I hope it *hurts!*"

In a closet near the front door, Karen found a gray woolen cloak, good camouflage if there was any fog tonight. She extinguished all lights inside the hut before opening the front door. She walked on the verge of the path, so her steps wouldn't crunch on the gravel. She spotted the watchman easily when the man lit a cigarette, and she detoured through a jumble of boulders to avoid being seen by him. She saw no one else and made good time, leaving the path when she came to the first stone-walled pastures and creeping into town from an unexpected direction. The harbor was shrouded in mist, and some of the houses glowed from within as early risers puttered around.

Down at the waterfront, she crouched in deep shadow and surveyed the scene carefully. The boats nearest her were ocean-going vessels, much too large for a stealthy exit, even if she could handle one alone. She had to find a suitable craft, and she had to find it fast—dawn wasn't far away now. She studied the problem methodically, absent-mindedly rubbing the contact spot on her forehead. As she did so, however, she felt it grow warm again, and her thinking became more focused, her will more powerful. Perhaps the Being hadn't launched its chemical dart out of anger, but as a way of *changing her attitude,* by demonstrating how much strength and lucidity she could gain by becoming its acolyte. How confident she felt! Of *course* she could do this! There had to be other, smaller boats, and she would soon find one, just exactly the right one! She took a step to the right, and the contact spot on her forehead grew cold; a step to the left, and it grew warm again.

Getting warmer, getting colder—this is fucking ridiculous!

But it worked, because the warmer/colder sensations led her straight to a suitable craft: well maintained, large enough for the other Vardinoy people to crowd in; simpler to drive than a stick-shift car, loaded with fuel; and, best of all—God bless the Faeroese and their nonexistent crime rate—the key was in the ignition! She untied the mooring line and let the boat drift away from the dock.

But she still wasn't home free. There were people abroad now, not many—

but if even one of Dahl's people should recognize her, pursuit would follow swiftly, recapture would be almost certain. The distance to open water and freedom now seemed hopelessly far.

No, it wasn't! Her forehead tingled again and she closed her eyes and concentrated very hard, until she regained that hotter/colder mindset. Guided as though by the whispers of an expert pilot, she suddenly knew where a swift, subsurface current bisected this harbor—all she had to do was take one of the emergency oars and row until she felt that current grasping the keel. It would bear her as far as the end of the breakwater, far enough for her to risk cranking up the motor.

A dozen careful strokes of the oars and she felt the current seize her boat, exerting a firm but gentle push eastward. Satisfied, she stowed the oar and watched the harbor recede behind her.

And so, rigid as a figure carved from slate, a study in gray—cloak, boat, water, and drifts of fog—Karen swung the rudder in the general direction of Vardinoy, turned on the engine, and surged ahead at fifteen knots, into the brisk chop of the open straits.

Far to the south, she saw crisp flickers of what she identified as lightning, until she heard the precisely matched thunder a few seconds behind each illumination; now she identified the source as the quickening of seismic action down at the volcano. She pushed the throttle to wide-open, not wanting to waste another minute.

This renewed urgency distracted her, so that she was surprised by, and dangerously slow to react to, the sight of another Gray Boat nosing slowly through the dense pre-dawn fog, on a collision course, and moving much too fast for her to evade or run away from. One of the crew spotted her, and the larger craft put on more speed, closing to investigate this solitary seaman. Karen felt naked, pinned in place by the stares of four young crewmen and one skinny old tar who was obviously in command. When he turned to bark an order, she recognized the hawk-nosed profile of Andreas Dahl's father.

What was the old bugger doing out here? Patrolling, possibly, in case refugees from Vesturoy tried to land, or a government boat tried to convey an order for mandatory evacuation of Norduroy; it didn't matter why that other boat was out here—what mattered was that Dahl's father had recognized her and almost certainly had guessed what she was trying to do.

The elder Dahl gestured wildly at her and spat curses at her in Faeroese.

For lack of a better response, Karen shot him the finger. Even if their reverence for her new title prevented them from harming her, four strong men could simply overpower her and truss her like a turkey. Back to Norduroy they would take her, where her violent—and no doubt blasphemous—deeds would be discovered, and presumably punished. If they didn't kill her first, she would drown with the rest when the tidal wave struck. *What a shitty way to die!*

Now the old man was close enough for her to count the spiky bristles tufted from his ears. He gestured at her furiously, eyes bulging with malicious indignation: *stop your engine or we will ram you!* Although she really had no choice but to comply, the thought of surrendering to that old goat made her blaze with anger. Had she submitted to the obscene touch of the Being, had she steeled herself to commit double homicide, only to be intercepted by a crazy old man, to be hauled back in disgrace and impotence, and to suffer the inquisitorial retribution of the madmen who followed Andreas?

But when her forehead suddenly began to burn, she realized that she wasn't nearly as helpless as that boatload of pirates thought she was. Not now, not here! She had achieved a hard-won unity with the sky, the sea, and the mountains above it, the dark canyons below; she was the sole remaining agent of balance and reason in a maelstrom of insanity; she had become *essential* to the working-out-of-things. Who the hell were these oafish, smelly fishermen to get between her and the cause to which she had bound herself by the act of murder? The thought of Dahl's father laying his gnarled hands on her body filled her with loathing . . . and at once, the mark upon her forehead flared in harmony with her rage, as hot as a branding iron.

When the pursuing boat drew within grappling range of hers, she threw back her head and screamed: *"I'm warning you, you putrid old fucker: if you touch me or my boat, by the god you believe in, I will have you struck dead where you stand!"*

A crewman who evidently understood English whispered into the patriarch's ear, and he scowled ferociously at her for an instant before his macho posture crumbled and Karen saw the fear seeping into his eyes. He was cowed by the power radiating from her in burning currents. The spot on her forehead was as hot as a blowtorch, and she was somehow radiating that straight into the old man's eyes. She felt a tremendous upwelling of force within her, a sensation so violent that its recoil tilted her boat near unto capsizing. As gray-green water sloshed over the gunwales, Karen roared a terrible cry straight into the old man's face, and he fell before it, groveled, understood just how truly Karen had become The Voice, because she was pulverizing his eardrums with sounds no human throat could have reproduced, with an agonized shriek from far beneath the sea, an implacable oath hurled at the men of Norduroy, by proxy, from an entity that had no mouth.

Across the straits, now tinctured lilac and strawberry by the gathering sunrise, there appeared a single high dark wave. Just before it reached the Norduroy boat, it surged into a twelve-foot comber, all viscid and ebony, exuding a bleak and mineral stench. It poised over the boat for one instant, blotting out the dawn and forcing the sailors to look up. All of them began to scream as the extrusion-wave dropped down on their boat like a living guillotine, tearing it in half. They were still screaming soundlessly *inside* the wave, writhing in slow motion just as Norma had done, scourged by whips of mottled blue fire that was already liquefying all of their softer parts even before it smashed the surface with a sound like a cannon shot. No more did Karen see of the Norduroy men. They would live, she thought, for some seconds yet as they plunged into the icy darkness far below. Cold rags of salt water splattered her face and rivered down her skin. She paid no attention; she merely stared fixedly at the bubbles seething on the surface, until, like a madwoman, she began to laugh hysterically.

When reason returned, about ninety seconds later, she wiped the spray from her face, started the motor again, and resumed her course toward Vardinoy.

39.

Ringside Seats

After transporting the Vardinoy survivors back to their campsite, the Norduroy men had methodically destroyed their radios, the inflatable boats, and anything else that might have facilitated an escape. But, almost contemptuously, they didn't touch the provisions or anyone's personal effects. Isolated and trapped they might be, but they had ample food and drink.

After the Norduroy men drove away in Eiden's Land Rover, it was already two in the morning. Nobody got more than two or three hours of ragged sleep anyhow, so when the volcano's rumbling became audible at the campsite, they decided to make the best of it, pack some provisions, and hike up the shorter route to the Axe-Cuts, where they would have the world's best seats for the show. Elsuba made sandwiches; Eiden grumpily filled his thermos bottle with coffee and two canteens with liquor; Preston and Dewey debated which kinds of film stock to take along; Allen stomped clumsily from one activity to another, trying to keep everyone's spirits up, especially his own.

And Richard Sugarman, of course, scribbled away in a corner of the mess hall, trying to convey the sureality of their situation: "The possibility that Dahl's henchmen might return and murder us seems excessive; but they have marooned us in a dangerous time and place—unless Karen somehow returns with orders to the contrary (*A writ of* habeas corpus *signed by God?).*"

By the time they started out, the distant rumblings had become continuous, oscillating in a rhythm that suggested respiration. By the time they reached the summit, dawn was only an hour away. They chose to put some distance between themselves and the Axe-Cuts, selecting instead a broad and sturdy-looking plateau a hundred yards north of those sinister fissures. The spectacle was everything they had hoped it would be.

Ringed by its own wrinkled reflections, a bubbling claret eye had sprouted from the sea. Part of that fiery bull's-eye was forming into a still-submerged but clearly visible cone. As though an unseen giant was pounding an anvil, fans of sparks sprayed up a hundred feet or more; by their strobe-light glow, the observers could see the underside of the immense roll of smoke now pouring skyward from multiple fissures. Vesturoy harbor, to everyone's relief, was empty; evidently, the evacuation had been completed earlier that night.

The drama playing out below them had the effect of distancing them from the previous day's miseries; a defiant ebullience raised their spirits.

"I wonder if the lava will bury Vesturoy," said Preston, adjusting the *f*-stop on his Bolex. There was no reply, because they were all thinking the same thing: how big would the eruption be and how wide was the radius of danger? Dewey prompted some information:

"Hey, Allen, what was the name of that big mother-volcano you told us about? The one in the Pacific, you know, 'cracker' something."

"Krakatoa; biggest eruption in recorded history."

"No shit? Well, what if this thing we're looking at turns out to be that big? Worst-case scenario, what would happen?"

"It *wouldn't* happen, Dewey. There hasn't ever been a volcanic eruption of that magnitude in this hemisphere."

"So maybe one's overdue. Just suppose it *did* happen here. What could we expect?"

"You really don't want to know, man; take my word for it."

"Yeah, I do!"

"Okay, then." Allen sighed and recited the facts in a dry, lecturing tone: "The Krakatoa eruption was clearly heard three thousand miles away; ashes from the explosion were deposited over an area of one-point-five million square miles; the smoke from the crater was fifty miles high; and the tsunamis—there were several of them—ranged from eighty feet to a hundred and forty feet high. Anything else you wanna know?"

Dewey gulped and shook his head.

Out in the straits, fire sprouted, bathing their faces in a lurid glow; a few seconds later, they heard a growling, grinding sound, as the pressures shifted masses of rock. They were all trying to visualize what would happen if a wave a hundred feet tall smashed into porous, honeycombed Vardinoy. One thing for sure: this cliff they were sitting on would be the first thing to go....

As they watched, the preliminary eruptions thickened in the central disturbance, and deeper, more puissant convulsions spewed aloft the first actual lava they had seen—red wriggling eels of it. The stronger pulses of illumination gave them a clearer look at the fantastic tower of knurled smoke rising miles into the sky, whose upper reaches now glowed with a hint of the coming sunrise.

The spectacle discouraged conversation. Allen nursed a cup of coffee in one hand and a cup of Wild Turkey in the other, alternating sips. His gaze kept boring through the remaining darkness in the direction of Norduroy. He was grateful when Elsuba slid over beside him and took his hand, after carefully lifting the bourbon cup and putting it aside.

"Karen will be all right; you'll see. She's a very strong and capable young woman."

"And braver than I could have imagined."

"Yes, she is that. You know, Allen, if a woman like that loves you, then you're not the colossal failure you took such masochistic pride in believing yourself to be."

"I'm not sure how much to resent that remark, but I'm sure I will after I untangle the syntax. . . ."

"Oh, Allen, what I mean is that you were overdramatizing your life even back when we were lovers! But at that age it was kind of cute. . . . In a middle-aged man, it's just a turn-off. I'm glad you're shedding some of that. So what if you made some promises to yourself that couldn't be kept, and life made some promises to you that it didn't keep? Those are not great tragic failures, they're just ordinary disappointments. If you'd just accepted that, maybe you could have gotten on with your life and scored some ordinary victories, instead of thinking you needed to do something heroic, historic, bigger-than-life, to atone for your shortcomings."

"My life isn't over yet, Elsuba."

"No, but it has reached a climax of a rather unusual kind. From now on, for all of us, everything will be reckoned as 'pre-Vardinoy' and 'post-Vardinoy,' assuming we survive the eruption. Everything that happens to us from now on will be colored by what we've experienced here. So tell me, Allen: what will *you* take from Vardinoy?"

"The knowledge that we did find the Vardinoy Monster."

"Anything else?"

"Give me a hint. You're trying to cue me. . . ."

She squeezed his hand. "I'm not a fortune-teller, just an old girlfriend."

"Okay, then, I take away the honor and pleasure of your friendship." He bent low so that only she could hear. "I do still love you, Elsuba, but now I realize that I love that other lady, the one who went to Norduroy because she wanted to save my life by risking her own, more than I have ever loved anyone else. And if Karen will still have me, then she is what I want to take from Vardinoy."

"Good answer! There's hope for you yet."

Their reverie was interrupted by Eiden Poulsen's growl. He'd been slugging down the aquavit pretty hard, and now he was grimacing with rage.

"I want my ship back!"

"I'm sorry, Father, but there's nothing we can do about that, and you know it."

Eiden paid no attention to his daughter's counsel. "Not only do those bastards worship the thing that killed my son, but now they've stolen my ship too! By God, it's intolerable! If only we still had our weapons. . . ."

"We do have some, man," said Dewey quietly. Eiden perked up instantly and scuttled over to Dewey's side. Elsuba shot Dewey a warning look, but he didn't see it.

"Do you still have possession of that fearsome Viet Cong weapon?"

"Sure do; neatly packed inside my suitcase, which Dahl's people, being amateurs, neglected to search."

"Yes," said Eiden, "but that's not enough. There are seven or eight armed men aboard the ship. Unless they're stupid enough to line up where you can mow them down, we're hopelessly outgunned. We'll never regain control of the ship with just one weapon."

"What about two?" said Allen. "The day after the manuscript was stolen, I unpacked one of the assault rifles and a handful of clips and hid it under my mattress. I didn't tell anybody because . . . well, because Karen's behavior was so unsettling, I didn't want her to know it was there. You know. . . ."

Allen licked his dry lips.

"And I'll bet Dahl's goons overlooked that case of concussion grenades, too, since they were labeled as 'canned goods' or 'farming tools for the Indians' or something like that."

"If you're right," said Dewey, "those could give us the edge. Them fishermen ain't likely to recognize a stun-grenade, or have enough sense to close their eyes when the flash goes off. That'll blind a vulture for half a minute."

"Well, then," said Eiden, "we might have a shot at a boarding attack after all!"

An especially loud detonation caused them to turn back toward the straits. They could see more of the growing cone now, for it had finally broached the surface, and the vibrations were strong enough to shiver the cliffs beneath their bodies. Richard was focusing binoculars on the explosions, trying to read the import of their timing and force. But some instinct kept pulling his eyes back to a point just east of the shrouded cone.

"Hey, folks, there's something you need to look at. Just on our side of that cone! It wasn't there ten minutes ago, I swear."

Awash like an upturned boat, there had appeared an enormous seething dome. Wavelets rolled over it and were burned into vapor by its heat. It resembled the back of a giant tortoise, a quarter mile wide. And growing. In terms of latent menace, that dome seemed to radiate a much greater threat than the spectacular but so far harmless fireworks going off nearby. It bespoke a planet-cracking accumulation of gaseous and tectonic pressures, straining to get out.

While the others studied this new and sinister feature, Richard swept his glasses to the right, just to make sure Nature didn't have any more surprises, or that the Monster hadn't come up ahead of schedule. There was just enough ambient light now for him to spot a small Gray Boat beating toward the coast of Vardinoy with its single occupant as still as a wooden figurehead at the wheel. He turned the focus knob and gasped when the image grew sharper.

"Hey! Everybody! Look down there—at about four o'clock from the volcano. In a boat, heading this way. It's Karen!"

40.

THE STORMING OF H.M.S. *Laertes*

Karen managed to steer her boat into the hidden cove beside the ruined church, but the last of her self-control slipped away as she passed between the headlands that had kept the old cathedral hidden for a thousand years. Her hands, clutching the wheel like talons, began to cramp so badly that she had to steer the final distance by shifting the weight of her body. By the time the boat's keel grounded on the black-glass beach, it was all she could do to splash ashore. When her feet touched dry land, she sank to her knees, shrieking wordlessly at the sky, clawing blood from her arms, and shuddering in disgust when every orifice in her body voided simultaneously.

It took Allen, Richard and Preston almost an hour to find a navigable route down the cliffs, and another twenty minutes to backtrack toward Karen's presumed landing beach. Meanwhile, Eiden, Elsuba, and Dewey had fashioned a climbing harness out of thousand-pound nylon rope, so that if necessary Karen could be hauled up by brute strength.

It was well they had the rope, because by the time Allen reached her, Karen was feebly trying to clean herself with wet sand and shivering on the edge of hypothermia. Working in tandem, he and Richard managed to jam her into a sweater and improvised some protective leggings out of duct tape and a swatch of sailcloth they found stowed in her boat. Getting her to the top was a stop-and-go ordeal; sometimes she was conscious and able to help, sometimes she fought against them. By eleven o'clock, however, they finally had her back in her sleeping bag, and Elsuba's examination disclosed nothing more serious than total exhaustion, assorted cuts and bruises, and a curious burned-looking spot on her forehead. After hydrating her and administering a sedative, Elsuba dabbed the burn with ointment and declared it was "nothing to worry about." She and Allen remained in the tent, and eventually they joined Karen in slumber.

When Karen started calling their names very impatiently, they awoke to find her sitting upright, fully alert, and feisty as hell.

"Elsuba, hand me some clothes, please. Allen, I want you to assemble everyone in the mess hall as quickly as you can. Tell them I've got the real lowdown on the Vardinoy Monster and some other important stuff."

"You shouldn't leap out of bed, Karen," cautioned Elsuba. "You're still in shock."

"Shock? Oh yes, sweetie, I surely am! But I have to keep going—we all do. There's no time to spare, and when I explain some things, you'll understand why. Damn it, I said hand me some clothes!"

When they were all gathered together, she summarized what had happened to her in the last twenty-four hours, trying as best she could to answer their questions.

"What finally drove it insane, I think, were the Ice Ages. The extrusions couldn't handle extreme cold; they shorted out, they became brittle, they sent back only static and sensory garbage. When it beheld the ice wall inching toward its location, it endured the second-worst trauma of its existence. And because the glaciers advanced and retreated in cyclical rhythms, it was forced to endure that trauma over and over and over. Imagine being in a cold, lightless tomb, sustained only by the sights of sun and open vistas you perceived through a million small windows . . . and then watching those windows grow dark, one by one, until you were alone in the freezing, absolute blackness beneath a range of mountains! The glaciers crushed it into a straitjacket, multiplied the horror of its confinement, deprived it of all stimuli. It longed for extinction every time it heard the inexorable grinding advance of the newest ice wall, but of course it could not *will* itself to death. Evolution hadn't put suicide in the blueprints; quite the opposite—this thing was designed simply to exist and survive, nothing more. It longed for 'death,' but the very concept of death hadn't been programmed into its consciousness! Blindly, automatically, its metabolism evolved according to its prime directive: just keep on living. So it got through the ice ages in a kind of deranged coma. . . . The closest analogy would be suspended animation, or a fainting spell that lasted hundreds of centuries, until the planet warmed up and the ice retreated.

"Eventually, it learned how to dream; but the cost of that ability was delusion, derangement, a systemic form of insanity. It couldn't even starve itself to death, because it automatically absorbed at least minimal nourishment whether it wanted to or not.

"And so it has remained, exactly where that first volcanic cataclysm entombed it, back in the dawn of Creation, trapped beneath a mountain at the bottom of the sea . . . screaming without a mouth; kicking without feet; clawing without hands; utterly forgotten by whatever force or process designed it; alive and aware and hopelessly insane. The centuries before the volcano were the Garden of Eden, and simple oblivion is its concept of Paradise. It kept projecting variations of the same basic image: a volcanic eruption of titanic scale. Its last memory of freedom and happiness was cut off by an eruption; so, by simple logic, if such an event could entrap it, another such event would have the power to liberate! That's why it's spent millions of years mapping and recording geological events. It senses volcanic activity even on the other side of the world. No seismograph built by man has a greater sensitivity. It listens to the shifts inside the Earth's crust with the same intensity as a prisoner who hears another inmate trying to tunnel his way out of the dungeon.

"It has sustained hope, staved off despair, by engendering something that's all too human: *faith!* And the primary tenet of that faith is simple: sooner or later, there will be another eruption in this part of the world, and that eruption would be powerful enough to break the very mountain that holds it captive. Then, it would once more experience the unspeakable bliss of *movement!*

"But if and when it does become mobile again, its intent is to haul its own enormous bulk across the sea—that sea to the west of us, the straits between here and Vesturoy—and flow into the fire, become one with it, and achieve . . . well, I suppose the word is 'transcendence.' Unencumbered by its gross burden of matter, it will awaken, on the far side of its immolation, in a new place, a new state of existence, which you and I would call 'Paradise.'

"So now you understand why so many sightings coincide with volcanic eruptions, even ones that happen on the other side of the world. I don't think those above-water appearances have any purpose—they're just blind, knee-jerk reactions. If a ship or an airplane or a fisherman happens to get in its way, that's just tough noogies, because its chemical processes are in overdrive when it's upset, and the extrusions can be lethal, as we've learned. . . . Mostly it kills by reflex, not even conscious of doing so, but I know it *can* kill intentionally, even though 'malice' is too social a concept to it to understand; but really, all it wants to do is cease existing—that's how it thinks of 'death.' It just wants to slide into that nice new volcano and find out what's on the other side.

"Right now, it's extremely agitated—and who wouldn't be? For our monster, this is the Big One, folks, the event it's dreamed about and mythologized since before the dinosaurs. It is absolutely certain of what's going to happen, because it's got the biggest database in history: first, a huge submarine earthquake will set it free—it'll very quickly learn how to propel itself again; and secondly, it will rise to the surface, something that has unimaginable symbolic importance to it; and finally, it will float or roll or swim, whatever the fuck it *does,* right into the heart of the eruption.

"But not the eruption you can see right now, not into that piddling little cone out there. It's figured out exactly the optimum moment to off itself, and that will be just a few seconds before a gigantic pressure dome explodes—maybe it's visible now. . . ."

"It is," said Elsuba quietly. "Sort of like a giant bread loaf steaming under the surface."

"Oh, God, I'd hoped maybe this part of it was a fantasy, but I guess not. Okay, when it lands on that pressure dome, it'll be just a couple of seconds before the thing blows sky-high. And because the creature's bulk is so enormous—shit, the core alone must be a cubic mile—it's going to put a huge organic plug into the only outlet there is for all that built-up pressure. Even if it dies instantaneously from the shock, there will be so much inert matter left that the fire can't consume it fast enough. The net effect will be to compress the explosion, multiply its original force exponentially. Without it interfering, we'd get to see a medium-sized, very picturesque volcanic event, sort of like Surtsey when it first rose out of the sea. But if that same amount of force is compressed and held back for the time it will take for the lava to burn away its bulk, then we're looking at an explosion roughly on a par with one-point-five hydrogen bombs. At the *very* least, it will annihilate all life in the northern half of the Faeroese archipelago."

Karen's voice was hoarse; Allen handed her a cup of coffee and lit her cigarette. Karen sipped and smoked and fixed each person in turn with a demanding gaze, making certain she had eye contact before continuing.

"That's the gist of it, campers, straight from the . . . well, you know what I was going to say. Nothing short of a tactical nuke will stop this being from carrying out its plan. And if it does, thousands will die. We'll be luckier than most: we'll just be vaporized, instead of drowned by the tsunami. In order to keep the worst from happening, we need to do two things. One, get the hell off of Vardinoy. Two, broadcast a warning, while there's still time. That part of it we should do right now."

Eiden shook his head ruefully. "I'm afraid we can't. Dahl's people wrecked or confiscated all our communications gear, precisely so we couldn't contact the outside world."

"Well, shit, then the only thing we can do is recapture the ship. Guys, is that doable?"

Dewey looked at the other men, and when they somberly nodded, said: "It's doable, but only if we get real lucky and catch 'em by surprise. Me an' the guys were discussing it earlier. Dahl put seven or eight men on the ship, and probably only one or two will be on guard at any given time. If we can surprise the guards, I think we can handle the rest. Those fuckers are just fishermen."

"Wait a minute!" Elsuba came to her feet. "They may be fishermen, but they're armed to the teeth and there's twice as many of them and my father is too goddamned old to be playing Blackbeard games!"

Eiden smiled sadly. "Thanks for the vote of confidence, daughter. I was thinking more along the lines of Lord Nelson. . . ."

"Retaking the *Laertes* means fighting! You're not Viking warriors, damn it!"

"Neither are they, and four of us have at least seen combat."

"Very briefly," chuckled Allen, shaking his head.

"Listen to yourself, Allen! You guys think this is some kind of macho game, don't you?"

Karen stepped close to Elsuba and placed a calming hand on her shoulder. "Not this time, honey. If the guys don't take the ship, we all die. It's that simple."

During the silence that followed, Dewey sidled over to Allen and threw a burly arm over his shoulder. "How much do you remember of your S.F. training, ho'se?"

"More and more of it's coming back with every passing moment."

"By God, I will fight to get my ship back!" growled Eiden.

"You'll get yourselves killed!," Elsuba whispered. Karen hugged her close and nodded.

"I don't like it, either, Elsuba, but don't even *think* I might be wrong about this scenario. I have been inside that fucking thing's *head*, and it has the great-granddaddy of all death wishes. And I know, because it knows, that just before ten tonight, the pressure building up under the straits will trigger a submarine earthquake powerful enough to set this creature free. Once it is loose, there's nothing to stop it from doing what it wants to do, which is die. I wish there were some safe alternative, Elsuba, but there isn't. Not for us. Either we get as far away from Vardinoy as we can in the time remaining, or we will surely die here. All of us."

Richard tried logic and moderation: "But this changes everything. Everybody's in the same boat now, so why couldn't we persuade Dahl's people to join forces with us, in the name of mutual survival? We trade information for a fast boat, and everybody lives through the night!"

"Nice thought, Richard, but it won't work. Dahl and his followers have been getting psyched up for this event for years. They think their Golden Age is at hand. Not even The Voice could persuade them otherwise. Not this Voice, anyhow. Not now, not after. . . ."

Karen shook her head tiredly, as though trying to expunge a bad memory.

"What do you mean?" countered Elsuba. "From the way Dahl tried to sell you on being the high priestess, those people seemed ready to bow down and worship you."

"Not now, they wouldn't. I'm their mortal enemy now. Just by fleeing Norduroy and coming here, I've betrayed their god."

"Isn't there some way we could just slow it down, divert it, so it doesn't land on the pressure dome at such a critical moment?" Elsuba was still groping for an alternative, but Karen shook her head.

"I wish there was, but I repeat: this thing is as big as the island of Vardinoy, maybe bigger. Nothing will slow it down, short of blowing up part of its core. Unless you've got a piece of heavy artillery stashed in your suitcase, there's nothing we can do to prevent it from going where it plans to go."

"Well, then," said Richard, gamely but carefully, "we'd better work out a plan for seizing the ship."

"I think I already have," said Karen. "I'll go back to my boat and sail north, then turn into the fjord where the ship's tied up. That will distract the guards. You guys will have to be in position as close as you can get, watching for me. I'm hoping that when they spot me, the Norduroy men will run over to the port side to see what's going on. At that moment, you hit them from behind. Use those concussion grenades; use Dewey's AK, and Allen, you use that Hechler and Koch thing, the one under your cot that you think I don't know about."

"But what if they take a shot at *you?* What if they've already been told about your escape?"

"I don't think they've found out yet. . . ."

"Found out what?"

"I'll tell you later, Allen. I just think we still have a while before the guards aboard the ship will be alerted, so let's get started now, okay? It'll take me an hour and a half to two hours, to return to my boat and sail up the coast. You can walk to the village in about that same amount of time if you start right away." She stopped, grimaced slightly, rubbing her forehead. "Elsuba, I need to hit you up for some speed, if you've got any."

"I've got some Ritalins; they ought to do the trick."

"Let me walk with you part of the way back to your boat," Allen pleaded.

Karen shook her head. "No, Allen. I don't know how much strength I have left, but I simply can't afford any distractions until this thing is done. We'll have time enough for each other later. I promise. Remember when I predicted our two journeys would become one again? Well, as of tonight, they have. And they will be from now on."

Nobody was looking, and nobody gave a damn anyway, so the Norduroy sailor at the top of the gangplank shifted the weight of his bolt-action Enfield to his left shoulder, stepped up to the rail, and pissed over the side.

"I could blow his pecker off right now," whispered Dewey.

The approach march to the village had been easy enough, and they'd been able to deploy close to the ship without being spotted. Preston was going to film the action—of course—and had set up inside a partly collapsed hut facing the trawler. Despite his pleas to join the action, Richard had been ordered to stay behind and work the backup camera. Only Allen, Dewey, and Eiden would storm the vessel.

Allen had expected to feel jittery, troubled by the possibility that he might be shot by a fisherman whose status as a warrior was even more negligible than his own, or that he would freeze instead of pulling the trigger if the time came for *him* to kill. But instead, he felt curiously detached, as though he were not, in fact, Allen Warrener, but some fictional character about to face his baptism of fire. This sensation of nonreality, and therefore of invulnerability, had come over him when he was slapping the barrel and receiver together, and thumbing 7.62-mm bullets into a trio of long black magazines. At one time, he had sought such a test as the one he was about to confront, but twenty-odd years had dulled the killer reflexes the Army had honed inside him.

At the outer edge of the deserted village, they had halted and diagramed various tactical plans in the dirt. In the end, they all agreed that the simplest plan was usually the best, and that Dewey was the man to lay it out.

"Allen, Eiden, you run straight up the gangplank while they're distracted by Karen, and roll your grenades under their feet. I'll cover you with the AK in case somebody pokes his head out and wants to take a shot at you, but more'n likely the only one who'll be armed is that doofus on guard duty. Even if he calls the others topside when Karen appears, they're not likely to bring their weapons along. Eiden, what did the Royal Navy teach you about hand grenades?"

Eiden smiled grimly. "Always pull the pin with your finger, not with your teeth like they do in the movies!"

" 's all you need to know, basically, except these are stun grenades, not frags, so remember to close your eyes before they go off or you'll be as blind as they are. And put some of Elsuba's cotton in your ears, 'cause these suckers are *loud*."

As they threaded their way toward the waterfront, Allen carefully folded into his backpack the bedraggled flag he had taken from the knoll beside the lake. He wanted his son's banner with him when he went into battle for the first time. The boy need never know anything more than that, but that was something important.

"Taking your kid's flag with you," whispered Dewey. "That's good, man, that's good mojo. It's got to be lucky for you—you fought your first battle under it."

"What the fuck're you talking about? This *is* my first battle."

"Wrong, very wrong. The other night, when them ex-tru-shuns were coming out of the lake, you showed no fear, my man. You were sharp, standing upright and chuckin' those willy-peter grenades just as cool as John Wayne. So, you see, you ain't a complete cherry after all."

"Yeah, but those things weren't shooting back."

"If we get a little bit lucky, them Norduroy turkeys won't either."

Now Allen was crouched alongside Dewey and Eiden in the shadows of a crumbling old storefront. They were still an uncomfortably long distance from the gangplank—thirty yards or so—but this was as close as they could get without being spotted. Somewhere off to their right, Preston and Richard were in place with their cameras, ready to record the skirmish for posterity. Elsuba was hiding in the middle, with the medical kit and already laying out morphine syrettes and bandages.

At present, there were four Norduroy men visible, in addition to the bored-looking sentry with the Mark III Enfield, who was the only armed man in sight. "That's very good," whispered Dewey, "because with that old rifle, he'll only have time to get off a couple of wild shots before we are *on his ass!*"

Their plan, they hoped, was idiot-proof. At the moment of maximum distraction, Allen and Eiden would rush the gangplank, each carrying two concussion grenades, while Dewey picked off the sentry and anyone else who offered resistance. If the stun grenades did their job properly, they should knock the spirit out of the Norduroy men. Eiden would pick up the dead sentry's rifle and Allen would cover the other stunned sailors with his. Dewey would continue to hang back with the AK in case anyone emerged from belowdecks or attacked them from the bridge above.

It was time for Karen to make her appearance. One of the sailors paced the bridge, smoking a pipe. Three more were playing cards and drinking, sitting on the base of the bandstand gun tub. The sentry finished urinating and zipped his fly. Allen could hear the patter of droplets on the quiet water. Dewey passed his binoculars to Eiden, saying: "Where would the others be if they ain't on deck?"

"In the galley, fixing a snack; in their bunks, having a wank; and one man standing watch in the radio room. That's where we have to go first, after we secure the deck—we don't want them raising the alarm on Norduroy."

"If this works out, do we have enough people to handle the ship? In case there's no other choice, I mean. . . ."

"That won't be necessary, Allen. The first thing I intend to do is to free my own crew . . . oh, yes, I see what you mean. Yes, if necessary we can handle her with only two or three people." Eiden's voice was tight and his fingers knotted around the grenade in his hand.

Dewey motioned for the glasses. Squinting hard, he strained to see the distant object that had just moved into his field of vision. "It's Karen—she's just coming into the fjord. They'll see her in a minute."

Allen raised his own field glasses and focused: there she was, a robed young woman, still and stately, surrounded by a hieratic nimbus that could be sensed even at this distance. If those men on the ship really believed she was The Voice, then her grave and mysterious appearance would certainly rivet their attention.

One of the sailors beneath the old gun-tub happened to look up. "Hey!" he shouted, pointing toward the approaching boat. The sentry at the gangplank, however, did not follow the other Norduroy men over to the portside railing. He only craned his neck in that direction and slipped the rifle from his shoulder.

"That motherfucker's no fool, " said Dewey. "We've got to do it now, so run as fast as you can up that gangplank. Don't get spooked when I start shooting—the rounds will go over your heads, I promise!"

The sailor on the bridge batted out his pipe and descended the portside ladder, wondering what the commotion was about.

"Okay, you guys—now!"

Dewey moved out first, covering half the distance to the gangplank in a silent lope, his feet barely chuffing on the rubble. He reached his chosen vantage point and knelt behind a cluster of decayed pilings, aiming the AK over the top and looping the sling around his forearm.

Allen and Eiden sprinted forward now, rather less stealthily and a great deal less quietly, over the same general route as Dewey, only they swept past him, heading straight for the gangplank. And as it loomed before their pounding feet, Allen could feel a change in the air—like wet ozone taking a big charge of electricity. He could predict the exact instant the sentry was going to turn in their direction and raise his muscular tattooed arms to bring up his old rifle for a shot.

Now the sentry brought up his weapon, but the muzzle swept right past Allen's head—the fool was aiming at some crazy irrelevant tangent far over

Allen's shoulder. The sailor squeezed off a single shot. Allen didn't really hear the report but he saw the flame from the bore—and then a precise three-round burst from Dewey's AK scissored the man at his midsection, audibly snapping his spine like a wishbone. Already dead, he slid face-first over the railing, the Enfield clattering to the deck, where Eiden could easily scoop it up.

The gangplank slapped under Allen's feet and as soon as he reached the deck, he lobbed his first grenade at the knot of gaping men under the gun tub, just six or seven feet away. The sputtering missile bounced when it landed and the sailors instinctively flung themselves away from it, arms upraised, only to be boxed in by Eiden's grenade, rolling toward them from another angle. Allen dove behind the gun tub's pedestal and covered his ears just as the grenades went off.

Even with closed eyes and protected ears, the blast was stunning, and the flash bright enough to outline the veins in his eyelids. Shock waves hit his face like an open-handed slap, cracking his head back. Then it was up-and-at-'em time: Eiden lunged forward, working the bolt on the Enfield, and Allen raised the H-and-K, his fingers suddenly buttery and unreliable.

But no additional shots were needed. The flash-bang grenades had thoroughly cowed the Norduroy men. One young man kept pawing at his weepy eyes, shouting that he'd gone blind, and the backs of his hands were seared pink by the flash. An older sailor, standing beside the temporarily blinded one, was in shock, his glassy eyes staring vacantly, two thin rivulets of blood trickling from his ruptured eardrums. All the others raised their hands quickly, thoroughly cowed—a pathetic foe after all. Allen waved his weapon threateningly, enjoying a tough-guy rush when they flinched from its muzzle. Dewey joined them on deck, the AK held tensely at his hip, covering the prisoners.

Then Eiden pounded Allen on the arm, snapping him out of euphoria. "The radio room! Quickly!" Allen realized it was not over yet, maybe not the hardest part, but he dutifully followed Eiden up the starboard ladder to the bridge, into the cool dim space of the wheelhouse, and then up against a closed door, from behind which came the sounds of electronic equipment being smashed.

"He's destroying the radio!" Allen shouted, kicking the bulkhead in frustration.

"Blast the door open!" Eiden gestured wildly, unable to swing the big Enfield inside this cramped companionway.

Allen pointed the assault rifle and fired twice. The reports were unbelievably loud. A ricochet zinged off the bulkhead, leaving a hot dangerous smell in the air, but the door still held. Cursing, Allen thrust the barrel inches from the lock and fired a burst of four. This time, the NATO surplus slugs punched clean through the mechanism.

The Norduroy man behind the door was pale with fear, but even as his body tensed from the anticipated bullets, he kept smashing his hammer into the radio set, each blow throwing up a cloud of sparks and shattered components.

"For Christ's sake, Allen, shoot the bastard!"

But Allen's arms had lead weights hanging from them; it was taking him an absurdly long time to lift the weapon into aiming position. But he was, he really was, going to do it—when Eiden pushed him aside, drew his antique Webley from its Royal Navy holster, and shot the cringing man in the heart.

Allen stammered defensively: "I was . . . I was. . . ."

"It doesn't matter. We're too late anyway. The radio's ruined, and he certainly had enough time to get a signal off to Norduroy."

That should have been the end of it. Allen was certainly ready for it to be over. But two more things happened in quick succession.

The first was a throttled underwater explosion that shook the *Laertes* like a torpedo strike. The one unaccounted-for Norduroy man, after hearing the commotion on deck, had raced down into the ship's bowels and lit the fuses on two homemade dynamite bombs that had been planted, on Dahl's instructions, just in case it became necessary to scuttle the ship quickly. The fugitive sailor then ran up a ladder, leaped off the fantail, and managed to swim halfway to the dock before Dewey stitched five holes across his back.

One of the fuses had been carelessly wrapped, and an oil drip from one of the fuel lines had soaked it through, rendering it useless. But the one successful explosion was crippling. It blew out a flap of steel plate on the port side, just above the waterline. Half the contents of one fuel bunker spewed into the harbor and salt water contaminated the rest.

After helping to lock down the five remaining Norduroy men in the cargo hold, Allen learned about the other thing that had happened, the worst thing. He learned about it just as he was leaning over to inspect the oil slick oozing out through the ruptured hull. He learned about it when he heard Dewey calling his name, in a strange choking voice, and he knew something very bad must have happened when he saw tears streaking down the big biker's face. Dewey took his arm and led him gently to the starboard side and pointed toward the spot where Elsuba knelt, sobbing, her medical kit open and a garland of futile bandages strewn around her feet. Her hands continued to clutch the stiff, unresponsive leg of the man sprawled before her.

Allen felt as though someone had clubbed him in the kidneys. Crying Preston's name aloud, he lurched down the gangplank and staggered across the quayside. As he drew near, Elsuba turned on him, teeth bared, eyes swollen, and shouted: "God damn you and your monster! And God damn my father's crazy need for vengeance! I'm glad you won your little battle, Allen, because this was the price you paid for victory!"

She broke off, sobbing convulsively—the sort of tears that come from people who do not weep easily or often, after they've been ambushed by a massive sorrow.

It had been that single, weird, seemingly pointless shot from the sentry's rifle, a round which otherwise would almost certainly have smashed into Allen. The guard, not accustomed to the sight of certain modern artifacts, had spotted Preston standing up and exposing film through his big shoulder-cradled Bolex. Thinking the big black film magazines on top signified some kind of machine gun, the sentry had elected to fire his snap shot at Preston, rather than at the two armed men pounding up the gangplank. His bullet struck the camera lens head-on, shattering it, drilling through the eyepiece, and penetrating Preston's right eyeball before passing into his brain, carrying glass shards and bits of torn metal with it. Preston's eyes were closed, and the only sign of damage was a swollen purple ring around the punctured eye, like a bruise he'd taken in a barroom brawl. The expression on his face was familiar, a blend of excitement and professional concentration. Allen knew what Preston's last thought must have been: *Man, this is going to be good stuff!*

Dewey held Allen, muffling his grief like a big, friendly, pig-tailed bear, while Allen howled desolately into the deep pile of Dewey's sheepskin jacket. Dewey let him cry for a couple of minutes, then grabbed his shoulders and whispered: "That's enough for now, buddy. When this here mission's over, you and me can go out to a bar somewhere and get shit-faced and let it all hang out. Right now, though, everybody needs for you to keep your shit together, 'cause we still got a long march ahead of us. So get a grip, my man, and do it now. You know that's what Preston would want. You're still our Fearless Leader, and nobody ever said it was gonna be easy."

41.

In Hazard

No trace was found of the *Laertes'* original crew. After some none-too-gentle interrogation by Dewey, one of the captives admitted that Eiden's sailors had been taken over to Norduroy, shortly after Karen's departure. Once there, presumably, they had been given a chance of serving the local Deity or facing the consequences of apostasy. There was nothing to be done for them, so Eiden hardened his heart to their fate and grew more determined to have vengeance.

The Norduroy men were herded back into the hold and locked down tight. Then, under Eiden's careful guidance, Allen and Dewey turned valves and called out the numbers on gauges until Eiden had isolated the flooding in the portside fuel bunker and corrected the ship's list with a delicate bit of counterflooding on the starboard side.

After this much had been accomplished—a task requiring two sweat-soaked, muscle-straining hours—Eiden assembled what was left of the Vardinoy Expedition in the wardroom and spread a big chart of the Faeroes across the green baize tabletop. He consulted some figures he'd jotted down on a notepad.

"Here's how things stand. We've sustained some fairly heavy damage but we can still make normal speed in calm water. However, there is no chance— I repeat, *no chance whatever*—of riding out a tidal wave. Those damaged plates in the hull would peel back and this ship would go down like a brick.

"Furthermore, the explosion dumped half the contents of one fuel bunker into the fjord and contaminated the rest. I estimate we have enough fuel left for three hours' steaming at the highest speed allowed by our present condition. On top of that, our radio's been pranged.

"If that pressure dome blows up with as much power as Karen thinks it will, then our only hope is to sail down the eastern side of the archipelago, keeping as much land between us and the tidal wave was possible. Even assuming we can maintain a moderate speed, the nearest village in that direction is about three hours away, right at the limit of our fuel. Even if everything goes in our favor, by the time we get to a radio, it will be almost too late for our warning to do any good. It galls me that, after all we went through to get this ship back, we have no better alternative, but the facts are the facts."

"Wouldn't there be working radios over on Vesturoy?" asked Richard.

"Who knows? The lava flow's already started burning some of the water-front buildings. If we had ample time, of course we could do a house-to-house search and probably find a radio, but we *don't* have time—and I refuse to risk anyone else's life when there's a chance of escaping in the trawler."

"That sounds pretty damn close to hopeless," muttered Dewey.

"Maybe not," said Allen quietly. The others turned to look at him: grease stained, gauntly unshaven, eyes burning deep in their sockets—something fierce had been loosed inside him by Preston's death, and the others, even Karen, had shied away from him, stifling even their expressions of sympathy.

Now his voice grew more confident. "If I understand things correctly, Karen, the real danger comes from the timing of this creature's escape, and from its determination to throw itself onto the pressure dome at the worst possible moment—from our point of view, that is. If that *doesn't* happen, we'd be facing a large but hardly apocalyptic eruption—a bit dicey, but certainly nothing that's going to generate a monster wave. Am I correct so far?"

"Yes . . . but—"

"Let me finish, Karen please. Now, if this creature *could* be delayed, diverted, thrown off schedule, just for a few minutes, just until that pressure dome blows its top, then it wouldn't matter what the thing does—it can go right ahead and swim into the fire, and burn itself up without causing any disastrous side effects.

"Karen, you also said something back in the mess hall that gave me an idea. You said there was no way of stopping this thing short of *blowing it up*. If—and it's a big 'if,' I know—but *if* we managed to set off a big enough explosion *inside* its protoplasm, as close to the nucleus as possible, would that slow it down enough to make the difference?"

"I suppose so, Allen, but I doubt you could do any significant damage with anything less than a truckload of dynamite."

"That's sort of what I have in mind. Remember the day we went over to Vesturoy to get the mail? Remember those explosions we heard? They were blasting out the site for a new hydroelectric plant, way up in the mountains—which means they probably had a big supply of dynamite."

"But Vesturoy's been evacuated; everybody's gone."

"Right, but why would the construction crew go to the risk and trouble of carrying off a lot of high explosives, when the whole island's going to be covered with twenty feet of hot volcanic ash by tomorrow morning? Vesturoy's been written off, even without a super-explosion from that pressure dome. Whatever explosives they had up at that construction site are probably still there. Who'd be fool enough to load a bunch of dynamite in a ship that might be hit by a lava bomb? Christ, you all saw that place through your binoculars—it looked like the evacuation at Dunkirk over there!"

Eiden moved his previous notes aside and began to sketch an outline of the *Laertes*. "I think I see where you're going with this, Allen. Pray continue."

"Okay, here's the idea: we sail into Vesturoy harbor, commandeer a vehicle, drive to the construction site, load up all the explosives and fuses we can find, and then, anchored at a safe distance from the action, we pack the bow with dynamite, in effect turning the ship into a giant torpedo. Karen's given us the approximate coordinates of where the monster will actually emerge, so we just lie in wait for it. Given its humongous size, plus the fact that it hasn't had any physical exercise in about a trillion years, it should be a big, slow target. We simply aim the ship at it, light the fuse, lash the wheel, then hop into the motor launch and haul ass in the opposite direction. The ship's momentum ought to drive it into the protoplasm too deep for the thing to dislodge it before the 'warhead' blows up. Moreover, if the entire bow disintegrates, that adds several tons of shrapnel to the payload—that will almost certainly stun it, if not kill it; confuse it, throw its timing off, at least long enough to prevent it from tamping down the eruption and amplifying its power."

Elsuba leaned forward, her face showing a mixture of hope and skepticism. "How do you know the people in the motor launch will be able to get far enough away to be safe? It won't take much of a tsunami to capsize a small boat like that."

"That would be true if we stayed in open waters; but I plan to steer for the cove where we found the old cathedral—it's the closest sheltered place.

I don't know if the launch will fit through the entrance channel, but we can ram it most of the way through and either let the wave carry it in or climb the rest of the way on foot. We should have a couple of minutes, and if the pressure dome isn't blocked, the tsunami won't be a hundred-foot horror, just a very large wave, which I understand are fairly common on that coastline."

"You'll need at least two people aboard with you to pull this off," said Eiden. "I of course will be one of them—she's my ship."

"Count me in, too, chief," said Dewey.

"Let me go, too," said Richard. "You can use a fourth hand."

"No, Richard, and that's an order. You find a good vantage point and write down everything you see. It should make one hell of a climax for your book." Allen held out his hand. "I know this trip's turned into something much different from what you bargained for, but you've done your share and more, and I appreciate that. And I'm sorry for all the bad parts."

Richard spurned the handshake. "Oh, yeah? Are you really? It's also been a lot more than *you* bargained for too, *professor*, and I don't think you're sorry about it one damn bit!"

"No," said Allen flatly, returning the younger man's stare. "Right this minute, I'm not one bit sorry."

Twenty minutes later, the *Laertes* was ready to weigh anchor. The hum of diesels gradually made itself felt through the deck at their feet—the trawler was coming to life again, and she seemed eager to cooperate in her own kamikaze demise. When Allen went to the wardroom to tell Karen and Elsuba that everything was ready, he found Karen slumped over the wardroom table; when she raised her head, he saw the desperate weariness in her eyes, and notice too that the quarter-sized burn mark on her forehead had turned an angry red.

"How did you get that, love? You never told me." He gently touched her cheek.

"A close encounter of the bulkhead kind, during all the confusion. Elsuba gave me something warm-n-fuzzy for the headache."

"Lucky you."

"I'll just step outside and leave you two alone for a while. . . ."

"No need, Elsuba. I'm not going to make a long farewell speech, just cop a nice kiss. Now, both of you ladies promise me you'll watch the fireworks from up on the cliffs. I wouldn't want either of you to miss the last charge of the *Laertes*."

"Don't worry, sailor, I came halfway around the world not to miss it." Karen rose on wobbly legs and hugged him with thin, trembling arms, murmuring: "I'm proud of you, and afraid for you, too."

"It'll be a piece of cake, darlin'." Then Allen moved rather more awkwardly to embrace Elsuba and to whisper in her ear: "We'll always have Paris, kid."

"That's pretty lame, Allen," she said, "but it's sweet too."

"Just like I used to be?"

Elsuba grinned, somewhat ambiguously, and swatted him on the butt as he opened the wardroom door. Just before he closed it, Karen called out:

"Tear him a new one, Fearless Leader!"

What surprised Allen the most was the cacophony of bizarre *sounds* associated with volcano birth, which added a whole new dimension to the spectacle. Small detonations were going off continuously now, below the surface, a perpetual rumbling and belching; and when a spray of anvil-sparks shot up, or a geyser of steam vented, they were accompanied by weirdly suitable noises. When the trawler passed as close to the rising cone as it dared, he discovered a whole new diapason of bizarre sound effects, both gross and subtle.

From somewhere deep beneath a cloud of mud-colored steam came an immense, drawn-out grinding, exactly as though a big rusty nail were being pried slowly from a board. Far below, fire-tortured bowels of rock broke wind in a long chain of intestinal complaint, which coincided, fittingly enough, with Allen's first whiff of vile sulfuric gases. From cavernous creaking growls to the falsetto roar of lions-sucking-helium to the shrilling of demented piccolos, the sounds grew more exotic, more outlandish, as the *Laertes* sailed past the lava mound and altered course for Vesturoy's harbor.

Most of their view of the harbor had been blocked, until that moment, by the much-enlarged dome, which was now some fifteen feet high and two hundred feet across; up close, it resembled a great lead-colored blister, its surface lined with tiny cracks, through which seeped yellow vapor into a dense miasmic cloud. Where the sea lapped around its circumference, the hump-backed islet seethed and bubbled as new accretions of heated matter, forced upward by the growing pressure below, attacked the cooling surf with serpentine hisses. Although none were active when they sailed past, lava flows had broken through already, and where they had cooled, their surface looked as wrinkled and pleated as the rump of an old bull elephant.

As the dome passed out of sight, the size of the active cone's outflow could be estimated. The cone had been spewing tons of ash for the past eighteen hours and was now connected to Vesturoy harbor by a wide plateau of smoldering cinders and sputtering gray mud. The cone's mouth was expelling a dazzling continuous fountain, comprising wiggling fillets of lava that roiled the air above it like gobs of translucent red meat; the crater below resembled a deep rock-rimmed navel whose circumference was scored by hundreds of thin neon-red veins. From the depths came wet, ponderous sounds, the labored groan of escaping gases, like a tuba with a crushed bell. The largest flow formation was on the cone's west side, where three thick streams of lava had conjoined atop the ash-plateau connected to Vesturoy and had formed a foot-high rolling tide of semisoft basalt, which was inching slowly, by fits and starts, into the deserted harbor itself. It was actually quite beautiful, that jellied carpet-roll: the cooling crusts turned a rich stained-glass purple, then cracked open, from the implacable pressure of backed-up lava, into raw, day-glow orange lesions. On the flanks of the new isthmus, where red-hot creepers had been fused by spraying surf, the molten flow had cooled into shaggy-glass tree stumps, folded and refolded until they resembled the fantastic root system of a banyan tree.

Most dramatic of all was the effect of raw lava striking the sea. The strife between white-hot magma and ice-cold Atlantic surf generated a continuous boiling spray whose droplets, when cooled by the air, quickly turned into thousands of glassy marbles, lashing the ocean like broadsides of grapeshot. At the very cusp of fire and water, where two primal elements tried to destroy each other, tortured spurts of lava danced and writhed like scarlet spiders.

Behind a yellow-brown scrim of smoke, the setting sun glowed a rich sepia brown. The time was 7:09 P.M. Even if everything went smoothly from here on, Allen's plan left scant margins for delay.

Eiden took a sighting on the umbilical plateau connecting the harbor with the cone and proclaimed it to be six hundred feet long, but still two hundred feet from the shoreline. Already, sporadic lava-orbs were bombarding the northernmost flank of Vesturoy town. Eiden set the engines for dead slow and began looking for a safe place to dock. Even as the ship lost headway, a blob of molten rock the size of a basketball scored a direct hit on a warehouse roof two blocks away, punching a hole through the top and igniting some kind of very feisty material stored within—the walls collapsed in just under two minutes. Eiden kept the ship in motion, putting as much distance between its stern and the bombarded areas as the harbor's size allowed. Near the southernmost end of the quayside, he cut the engines and used the rubber-tired flank as a brake, letting the trawler grind massively along until it was slow enough for Allen and Dewey to risk leaping over the side and throwing some clumsy but functional knots around a pair of big bronze bollards. The *Laertes* came to rest very cooperatively, her new coat of warpaint barely scratched.

After joining them ashore, Eiden pointed north, a worried expression on his face. "Bad bloody luck, mates, but the road to that construction site begins just where those fireballs are landing. It looks passable now, but it won't be for much longer. We'd better hijack a suitable vehicle as fast as possible, or we could find ourselves trapped."

Inside the third garage they blasted into, they found a Toyota truck with all-terrain tires and plenty of gas; just the ticket! Vesturoy town was larger and more sprawling than it had seemed on their earlier visit, and they took a number of wrong turns before they located the road leading north. By that time, the advancing lava tide was only four blocks away, and such was its radiant heat that Dewey and Allen felt obliged to cover the right side of their faces. Viewed from head-on, the flow looked much more destructive, powerful, and dynamic than it had seemed from the side. A rich charcoal black, the leading edge was rough and knobby with wads of coke and streaming lumpy cinders. The leading edge of the flow was creeping forward irregularly, an inch here, a foot there, in jerky, lurching increments; but it was a juggernaut, unstoppable and combining the destructive powers of an avalanche, a prairie fire, and a giant bulldozer. Just before the Toyota pulled away and started uphill, Allen saw a pleasant white bungalow, three blocks from the waterfront, suddenly poof into a fireball. Within seconds, its windows popped like pistol shots and the last thing Allen saw was a pane of glass riding on a tongue of fire, like a riderless surfboard.

A journey of two miles, hairpin curves most of the way, past eerily deserted pastureland, brought them finally to the construction site. Concrete mixers and earth-moving machines had been abandoned aimlessly inside a graded oval of cleared terrain. There were only two buildings in sight: one was a trailer filled with blueprints, hard hats, and time books; the other was a shed crammed with hand tools and pneumatic compressors.

"No dynamite in there!" Dewey threw a brickbat into the tool shed, creating a dreadful clatter.

"Of course not. Too close to the site itself. Spread out and look for a bunker or a magazine dug into a hillside, something well protected."

Dewey spotted the magazine, two hundred feet from their truck, a concrete semicircle firmly rooted in a mountainside, with blast walls designed to funnel any accidental explosion into empty space. The metal door was secured by a padlock and since they deemed it too risky to break through with firepower, Dewey jogged back down to the equipment shed and returned with a Paul Bunyan sledgehammer. Four mighty, clanking blows sufficed to shatter the lock. There *was* dynamite inside, crates and crates of it, enough to vaporize the trawler; there was also a big roll of primer cord, two detonator boxes, and some hundred-foot spools of old-fashioned waterproof fuse cord. No one could think of any practical way to use the detonators, so they loaded the fuse coils into the truck, along with all the dynamite they had room for. As an extra precaution, Allen and Dewey dragged out a heavy-duty tarp, spread it over the cargo bed, and watered it down with the hose that had been used to sluice concrete residues from the pouring buckets.

The sun was almost gone when they started back down, and the sky so murky that Eiden had to turn on the headlights. Each outward bend in the road offered an elevated view of the northern end of town, where conditions now verged on the apocalyptic, entire blocks swirling into firestorms powerful enough to generate their own thermal updrafts. Every now and again, exploding propane tanks spun crazily through the air like runaway V-2s.

The lava wall had been mightily reinforced since their first passage; it was now four to six feet high, ugly and savage-looking, and its myriad thrusts of steaming slag looked ominously like bared fangs. As they tried to find a way around these flaming roadblocks, a sudden shift in the wind sent the volcano's breath in their direction, bearing the char and stench of the Earth's distempered bowels. This close to the firestorms, they began to suffer the effects of their cyclonic winds—hot, putrid gusts that blew clouds of ash into their windshield, coating it with a layer of loathsome black dandruff. Eiden cut on the wipers to maximum power, and their scraping blades opened brief windows of clear vision. Satisfied, Eiden sped up again, only to suddenly rise up in his seat and tromp down on the brake pedal.

"Oh, shit," said Dewey.

A river of molten rock had burst through a brick retaining wall and spurted across the street only twenty feet from where they had stopped. For a hypnotized moment, they just stared at it, fascinated by its sinister dynamics, its pseudo-vitality. It sizzled like frying meat and humped forward in jerky stabbing motions that mimicked a host of angry boa constrictors. It seemed an evil thing, like some form of crypto-life come bubbling up from the cauldrons of Hell; but it was also terribly, majestically beautiful—this river of crimson and gold had equal power to obliterate a city and to create a new island where empty waves had rolled before. Allen became dangerously mesmerized until Dewey shouted in his ear: "Warrener, Goddammit, close the door so we can get out of here before one of those the pretty fireworks drops one on top of that half ton of dynamite we're carrying!"

It was full dark by the time they finished converting the trawler into a crude guided missile. They packed the dynamite crates into the bow and covered them with sheet metal, to shape the blast forward as much as possible. After some experimentation and debate, they chose a seven-minute fuse, threading it through ventilation shafts up to the shelter of the navigator's tiny radar shack, the most sheltered spot above deck level. Seven minutes, counting from ignition; ignition commencing as soon as the creature's nucleus rose above water; time enough, God willing, to sight the target, set a collision course, lash the wheel in place, move aft to the fantail, drop the motor launch—already attached to fifty feet of stout Manila hemp—over the side, shimmy down the rope, cut themselves loose, start the engine, and put at least a mile between themselves and the unpredictable results of their scheme. They all knew they were cutting it thin, but luck had been with them so far.

Before shoving off from Vesturoy, they released the captive Norduroy sailors, whose zeal was much diminished after spending a whole afternoon listening to large explosions all around them. Two of them men offered to serve on the trawler's crew, but in view of the circumstances, Eiden declined.

"Climb over to the western side, put as much land as possible between yourselves and the eruption, and remember that the louder the blast, the higher the wave. I would say 'good luck,' but frankly I hope all of you die. Now get the hell off my ship, you bilge rats!"

None of the three men on board wasted another thought for the Norduroy castaways. Their fate, ultimately, would be decided by the fate of their strange and alien god.

"Life jackets on, gentlemen, and prepare to man your battle stations," said Eiden, cranking the throttle to "ahead one-third" and executing a wide turn to port, intending to circle around the less-active eastern side of the volcano.

"Permission to make a suggestion, sir?"

"Granted, of course."

"Well, if the old girl's going in harm's way, she ought to have a fitting battle flag, don't you think?" Allen delved into his backpack and unfolded the now-tattered ensign his son had designed for Dad's Expedition.

"Very appropriate! Run it up the halyards, Lieutenant Warrener!"

Dewey was about to burst with excitement. When the strong breeze unfurled the homemade banner, he pounded Allen on the back and jumped up and down, yelling: "Oh, man, this is fuckin' great, isn't it! Just great!"

When neither Allen nor Eiden reciprocated his enthusiasm, Dewey subsided. A businesslike silence descended on the bridge while Eiden carefully conned the ship out into the straits, giving a wide berth to all discernible volcanic activity. Off their port side, magma met water and great fountains of spray erupted into the night, lit by lurid flames from beneath. The volcano seemed to be resting for a moment; the prevailing sound was the gasp of seawater meeting superheated magma. Inside the beveled cone, furnaces glowed behind lavender veils, and the reflection of leaping sparks cast golden crescents on the purple-black water.

When Dewey casually thrust an open pack of cigarettes under his nose, Allen automatically plucked one out, lit it, and sighed contentedly as the nicotine rush percolated through his tight-strung nerves.

"Damn, that's good!"

"Ain't no point in bein' abstinent tonight, Fearless El!" After patting him on the back, Dewey began to recite some verses from the Norse sagas. He no longer stumbled over the vocabulary or fractured the rhythms; his renditions had become truly bardic, and the words stirred Allen's blood, as they had always done.

"You've gotten real good at reciting that stuff, Dewey."

"Well, I have you and Little Dick to thank for introducing me to the glories of Norse lit-a-choor. And you know something else, Allen? You were absolutely right about this place. The Faeroes, I mean. Not many places left where a man can feel like a man without violatin' somebody's sensitivities! I've never felt so much at home. Like you did, right, back when you had your fling with Elsuba?"

"I guess so, Dewey. That all seems two or three lifetimes ago now. I used to think I wanted to come back here and live . . . for good. I mean, settle down, raise kids, the whole nine yards."

"Then why didn't you?"

"Why didn't I live here, or why didn't I marry Elsuba?"

"Yeah—either, both, whatever. I know she was gorgeous when she was eighteen, but so are ninety-eight percent of the girls I've seen here. I mean, they're all goddesses! So you could have married one who was almost as gorgeous as Elsuba, had some beautiful Nordic children, become the national poet or something. What happened?"

"I don't know, Dewey, but for some reason, people like me never do settle down in the place we love best in the world. That would somehow spoil the 'specialness,' you know? If I had emigrated here, pretty soon I would have stopped feeling the magic of it. I'd have done the same dreary day-to-day shit as any middle-class father: hustling for money to pay the gas bill, worrying about how the kids'll get through the winter without catching the flu, wondering if I'm still good enough in bed to keep my Nordic goddess happy while she washes dishes and changes the stinky diapers . . . I'd end up subscribing to the Sunday *New York Times* and daydreaming about being back in a big city, where I could go to concerts and first-run movies and hang out in bars with witty, sophisticated people. But the funny thing is, I think I could live here now, and be mighty damn happy—long as Miss Karen was living with me. And unless I had made this trip, I'm not sure I could have been happy living with her anywhere."

"You're a lucky s.o.b., you know that? Those are two fine ladies who love you."

"Yes, they are."

"If I can interrupt you two philosophers for a moment, would one of you check the radar screen? We're not far from the coordinates Karen gave me, and I want to make sure that creature's not sneaking to the surface ahead of schedule."

"I got it, skipper." Allen bent under the radar hood and followed the green sweep as it spun around. It showed empty sea except for a puzzling arc of arrowhead blips curved across their course, about a mile ahead.

"Eiden, you'd better take a look at this."

They counted eight small blips and one rather large one. "Damn it!" snarled Eiden.

"What's going on?" asked Dewey.

"I completely forgot, but the man I shot in the radio room had plenty of time to get a message off to Norduroy. So now they've assembled a bloody *fleet* across our path, to stop us from interfering with the resurrection, or whatever they call it."

"The 'Emergence,' I think," muttered Allen. "How could they know what we were planning to do?"

"I don't think they *do* know what we're up to—they just want to make sure we don't get in the way, that nobody interferes with their private apocalypse."

"We need to think this through, chaps." Eiden cut speed and turned the *Laertes* ship around. When they reached a point only one mile from the picket line across her path, Eiden went to the big spotting glasses and strained to get a better look at the "enemy fleet."

"I count eight wooden fishing boats backed up by one large steel trawler, probably Dahl's 'flagship.'"

"Can we break through their line?" said Dewey.

"Probably, if we all keep our heads down when they start shooting. They don't know we're damaged, so if we come steaming full-speed right at the trawler, she *will* get out of the way to avoid being rammed. I recommend we just bluff our way straight through the center."

"I don't," said Allen. "With all respect, Eiden, there's something a little too convenient about their formation—it's as though they *wanted* us to try doing that."

"Now that you mention it . . . shall we go take a closer look? It might be helpful to draw some fire and get an idea of what kind of weapons they're carrying." Eiden spun the wheel and increased speed; all three men donned gray Danish Navy helmets and fastened their chinstraps. The *Laertes* shuddered and pushed through a bank of noxious haze, emerging in full view of the Norduroy ships. Allen put his face into the eyecups of the big spotting glasses and studied the opposing line carefully. The glasses were powerful enough to let him see the faces and clothing of the "enemy" crews. They were uniformly grim and determined-looking, and some were cursing and shaking fists at the *Laertes*, while others were frantically sending messages with blinker-lights.

Blinker-lights?

"Everybody get down! Eiden, come right full rudder, and steer one-eight-zero! The bastards are firing at us!"

"Christ-on-a-tricycle!" yelled Dewey, as the starboard running light exploded not far from his head, followed by a ragged, spattering fusillade that spiderwebbed the windows and zinged and whanged off the hull and chipped paint from the bulkheads and gouged up fans of splintered wood from the decks. The firecracker pop-pop-pop reports grew in volume until the entire line of Norduroy boats rippled with muzzle flashes. Eiden threw the wheel into a hard turn, rang on speed, and headed into the nearest patch of smoke.

"I saw something stretched between those boats, Eiden. I think that's why they're trying to lure us into a straight-on attack—might be more of those purse seines that stopped us dead once before. If they can immobilize us, we'd be dead meat for a boarding attack."

"Purse seines," grated Eiden. "I saw a glimpse of something odd, too, but it took me a minute. . . . I think you're right, Allen. Damned clever trap!"

"How many sailors they got on that many boats?" Dewey grimly laid out a row of AK-47 magazines on the chart table, whose raised edge would keep them from falling off during a hard turn.

"At least sixty or seventy—hell, probably every True Believer on Norduroy who owns a firearm." Eiden nodded encouragingly at his younger friend. "Any ideas as to tactics, Allen?"

"I'm thinking. . . ."

Allen took a pencil from the chart table and looked again at the green images on the radar sweep.

"Look, if all these boats are hooked together by nets, then they're not very maneuverable, so why don't we just turn their flank? We start our run here, at the southwest end of their line, as close to the volcano as we dare to sail—the flashes and smoke will make us harder to see—and we come out here, at a forty-five-degree angle to the opposite end of their line. From that point, we would be under fire from all their boats only for a short period of time; once we get *here,* the guys on this half of the line will have to stop shooting for fear of hitting their own boats. We make a sharp turn to port here, which throws their aim off again, and we run parallel to the last two boats, then just plow around their right flank and head for open water. We'll get the bejesus shot out of us, but only for a couple of minutes. Even that big steel trawler wouldn't be able to chase us until it works up speed and turns completely around, and by that time, well, that's about the time the Vardinoy Monster's supposed to make his debut. What do you think, Eiden?"

Eiden studied Allen's zigzag sketch and made a couple of measurements on the chart with calipers.

"It might work; the water's deep enough on that side; but we run the risk of getting pounded by rocks and lava bombs from the damned eruption."

"It's quiet enough now," said Dewey.

"Yes, but if Karen's intuition is correct—and I tend to think it is—then things are going to escalate very quickly."

"All the more reason to use a flank attack. They're expecting us to try breaking through their center, from the direction of Vesturoy harbor—which they probably saw us steaming into. But their ships are just as vulnerable to volcano debris as ours, some of them more so—that's why they haven't pushed their flank any closer to Vesturoy. Whatever we do, there's a risk involved—but at least this way, we can avoid getting fouled in those damn nets and having sixty pissed-off guys with harpoons swarming over our railing."

"Okay, we'll do it that way," said Eiden, snapping the calipers shut decisively and stabbing their points into the chart like darts. "We'll turn their flank and just take our chances with flying lava. But before we go charging back into the fray, I'd like to even the odds somewhat. Come with me, chaps."

While the sea anchor held the trawler a half mile off Vesturoy harbor, Eiden led them down into the engine room, where puddles of fuel oil, bilge water, and a dead codfish that had somehow washed aboard made the air smell very nautical indeed. Eiden yanked a tarp off the top of a long narrow crate, the sort of workaday object no casual visitor to the engine room would likely pay much attention to.

"As I told Allen, Dewey, the *Laertes* was briefly recommissioned as a naval auxiliary during the Cuban Missile Crisis, and after we stood down, I just didn't bother returning our emergency armament to the Danish government. Meet our friend-in-need, Mister Oerlikon!" Eiden levered the crate open with a prybar, and the smell of cosmoline poured out, keen as a blade, unmistakably martial.

"Holy shit," breathed Allen. "You really did bring it."

"Yes, of course. I've always thought that, for a piece of machinery designed to blow airplanes out of the sky, the Oerlikon was remarkably graceful. Very nearly a piece of sculpture. But that's just me, I guess."

Not even the three of them could possibly have manhandled such a heavy weapon up to its mount, but by jury-rigging a hoist and harnessing the power of the aft cargo winch, they were able to walk the piece up ladders and through hatches until they could fit it onto an electric forklift and more or less drive it forward to the empty gun tub on the fo'c'sle. The combination of a block and tackle and brute strength enabled them to fine-tune the positioning and drop the gun securely into its mounting brackets. While Eiden tested the elevation gears and shot some lubricant into the rough spots, Allen and Dewey went below to the forward hold and used the antique power hoist, once intended to deliver four-inch shells to the trawler's main gun, to bring up fourteen drum-shaped magazines, each one containing sixty rounds—alternating tracer, explosive, and armor-piercing. Each shell weighed half a pound and was as long as Dewey's outstretched hand.

"Show us how to load, Eiden."

"Very simple. Here, flip this latch straight up—like so—insert the grooved bottom of the magazine so that it lines up with those metal flanges. . . ." Allen and Dewey ran through the drill several times. Aside from the heaviness of the loaded magazine, it was child's play.

"Were you expected to fight a Russian sub with a single Oerlikon?"

"Well, I doubt the Faeroese fishing grounds were high on the Warsaw Pact's list of strategic targets, but our official designation was 'Fisheries Protection Vessel.' No one ever told me what we were protecting the fisheries *from*. Hostile enemy fishing boats, I suppose—that's about all we could have taken on with a single twenty-millimeter. . . ."

"Which is exactly what's waiting for us out there," mused Allen.

"Here, Allen, get into firing position—that's right, slip your arms through those padded shoulder-rests—those will minimize the recoil. The sight is a simple ring-and-post affair; center your target inside the rings, and you can't miss."

Allen snuggled into the U-shaped shoulder rests and experimented with traversing and elevating the sights. The cannon was well balanced, with its center of gravity precisely at the pivot on the pedestal mount. He felt quite at home behind this weapon.

"I like it."

"That's good, because you are the one who's sodding-well going to shoot it," said Eiden. "I'll be too busy conning the ship, and Dewey will need to move around so he can maximize his sniping. . . ."

"Yeah, but when you need to reload, holler and I'll pop into the gun tub to help."

"So, by default, Mister Warrener, you are hereby named Senior Gunnery Officer of the armed escort trawler H.M.S. *Laertes*."

Allen cracked a parade-ground salute. "Cap'n Poulsen, sir, I wouldn't have it any other way!"

42.

The Emergence

Well, here it came after all: his long-postponed date with Mars! Too bad he couldn't think of any internal monologue that wouldn't sound like a bad Hemingway parody. Allen Warrener finally goes into battle—and a more incongruous opponent would be hard to imagine. Better weird than never, right? He would soon find out.

From the bridge, Eiden called some advice: "When you engage the steel trawler, just hose down the bridge—I'm not sure how thick her hull is, and those A-P rounds are at least forty years old!"

Allen nodded; Dewey winched in the sea anchor; Eiden sent more power to the engines; the ship gained speed slowly—all of this as the volcanic cone vomited a great clot of lava and the hot wind from the expulsion gusted over the bridge like the plume of a passing comet. The cone was growing visibly now, quaking with heavy detonations, lashing the sky with quirts of fire. Just as the trawler reached seven knots, a single long-range lava bomb, glowing cherry red and about the size of a toaster oven, struck the bow, emitting a sound like a cheap brass gong. When the impact-splash cooled, it left a glassy sunburst on the deck, vaguely Aztec-looking.

Looking skyward, Allen saw countless streaks of red and orange arching over the straits, a lightshow comparable to those World War II photos of nocturnal flak barrages over London and Berlin: skies so bewoven with lethal tartans that it seemed impossible for any aircraft to slide through their interstices. But the real fascination, for him, had always lain in the fact that, however dense those tracer-arcs looked in a photo, for each line there was only a single point, at any given moment, which was dangerous; the rest was illusion and slow emulsion speeds. This struck Allen as a nice, modest, philosophical conceit: *the fire-lashed skies were never as dangerous as they looked!* Such speculations, he knew, would not distract Sartre from buttering a croissant;

but the pleasure given to his intellect by this one, appearing at just this moment, seemed to hold real significance. His mind had not enjoyed dancing through abstractions in many years; it felt good, this awakening of areas in his consciousness that had lain fallow for so long! *Lots of acres to plow, there, boy!* Perhaps this sparky little mental *click!* heralded the opening of a refurbished wing of Warrener's Psycho-Cultural Museum. . . . Now that would be a fine thing to take away from Vardinoy! If fallow areas of his intellect might be coming online again, he asked of them, humbly, only the rewards and comforts of their own processes—no great achievements, no heroic projects, just solid creative thoughts, maybe carrying with them a few particles of grace as they passed through his consciousness. On the threshold of mortal danger, he actually felt a small sweet bud of promise open deep within him—everything that happened from that moment until the outcome of tonight's dire enterprise would be preternaturally vivid and memorable; best of all, he was not afraid. Here on the haunted sea around Vardinoy, he really had done what he needed most to do: walk away from the comforting but barren inertia of old habit and, with a shrug, turn his back on what had once seemed crippling failures, vain delusions, betrayals by Time.

What the hell? To have lived for a bit over forty years, even poorly, was to learn *something!* The dualities of Allen Warrener's past and future were finally embracing Present, where all was balanced out. He felt his soul come into focus, wondered what the hidden price for this enlightenment might be, and didn't much care. Whatever the fare for Charon's service, he had the exact change in his pocket.

Coming into focus as well was the looming primary eruption. The submarine disturbances were rattling the sea's bones; the pressure dome had become immense, the size of two football fields; still it only seethed and vented steam, but the vapors around its base had acquired a slimy, feverish look, and spreading gradually across the straits was a reeking miasmic fog that smelled like the armpits of Satan.

"Man, Dewey, if there was ever a time and place where you would expect to see a monster. . . ."

"Won't you be disappointed if we don't, *hombre?*"

"Now that you mention it, yeah, I would indeed."

Dewey had prepared for battle. He'd stripped off his shirt and was now clad only in his Harley jeans, boots, and the scruffy sheepskin jacket that had become, for all practical purposes, his Colors. His unbound shoulder-length hair rippled in the poured-steel glow of jetting flames, like a hydra's head of gilded serpents. His arms bulged with muscle; a palimpsest of old tattoos jitterbugged along his skin like red-blue imps; and for ten minutes he'd been rubbing a whetstone on the blade of his Bowie knife, the weapon he had used to wrest the life from and to imbibe from, or so he claimed, the defiant fighting spirit of a two-ton whale. Allen had never seen him quite this . . . dare he call it "philosophical"? Dewey was outwardly calm, but when he turned to look at Allen, the bale-fire glow of the berserker was gathering in his eyes.

Eiden's voice over the bullhorn: "Get ready, lads—we'll be coming out of this cloud cover in just a few seconds!"

Dewey's nostrils flared, and his mouth curled in a feral grimace, yet his voice, when it issued from those grim lips, was soft and almost courtly. He clasped Allen's hand and said: "I want to thank you, brother, for bringing me here."

"I can see their line," called Eiden. "You were right, Allen—if we take out the last two boats on the right flank, we can get around the rest."

Allen and Dewey had just enough time to high-five each other before Eiden hit the ship's siren and the H.M.S. *Laertes* sliced into clear night air, with the lines of a tubby old trawler but the attitude of a PT boat. Less than a mile away stretched the Norduroy boat line, and Eiden steered straight for the center of it, pegging the throttle into the red until the *Laertes* began to shimmer at the threshold of stability.

She clove through the last scarves of gritty smoke and came out in full view of her adversaries, who must have perceived her backlit by the flares and thunders of Ragnarok. Eiden knew that, for Allen's maneuver to work, he had to hold to this straight course for another quarter mile, enduring a concentrated cone of fire from the enemy line in order to disguise his true intent.

Allen was mesmerized by the sight of the Norduroy flotilla, by how quickly the range was closing, and at first he seemed to pay no attention to the humming noises passing around his ears . . . until Dewey tackled him and pushed him under the gun tub's quarter inch of encircling armor. "Keep your damn-fool head down, F.L.! Don't you know incoming when you hear it?"

Allen grinned mischievously. "Sure I do—I just wasn't gonna duck until you did!"

Dewey wagged a finger in mock severity. "Let them fishermen burn up lots of ammo; and when Eiden says 'open fire,' try to put out bursts of three—I know it sounds dumb, but your brain keeps track of your ammo supply better that way. And remember, you got a half inch of steel on that gunshield, so you're better protected than anybody you're shooting at! When you need to change drums, just yell 'Change me' or somethin'."

"Too late, dude—I'm already changed! Yeee-HAA!"

Shotguns, varmint rifles, fowling pieces, and war-surplus relics from a half dozen armies—Andreas Dahl's undisciplined militia blazed away furiously and the *Laertes* jangled as from a hailstorm.

"Get ready, lads!" Eiden commanded. "But hold your fire until I give the order!" Allen unfolded his knees behind the Oerlikon's armrests, then stood up and slid smoothly into firing position, peering intently through the narrow notch in the splinter shield. The boat line sparkled and flickered, but because of the continuous thunder behind, Allen heard no individual shots, only the xylophone clatter of rounds hitting the trawler, and he could see the wicked little flashes of ricochets and the inward dimpling of gun-tub steel as bullets were directed at him personally. He estimated they were now only three hundred yards from the Nord'uroy line, but Eiden gave no order to fire, so Allen made himself as small as possible and continued to track his target—a big sturdy-looking sloop that anchored the right of Dahl's battle line—until it filled the Oerlikon's ring-and-post sight.

Eiden began to slide into his turn, keeping it shallow and incremental so as to mask his intentions as long as possible, which was sound tactics but which also meant that the *Laertes* was exposing more and more of her starboard beam at the same time she was converging on the defenders. Even the worst shot on those boats could hardly fail to hit the trawler now, and the clangor of slugs on steel doubled in volume. Portholes shattered, railings and stanchions were shot away, the sides of the wheelhouse grew stippled as though worked over with a punch awl; the cacophony suggested a dulcimer being fed into a buzzsaw.

Finally, Eiden's voice crackled through the bullhorn mounted under the bridge: "Gentlemen, if you please, you may commence firing any time it's convenient!"

"Payback time, Allen!" yelled Dewey, popping up and ripping a long intimidating burst.

"Yeeesss!"

Allen lined up his sights on the sloop's wheelhouse and mashed the firing lever on the Oerlikon's right handlebar. The padded armrests punched his shoulders, a jarring athletic impact that shook his teeth and snapped his head back in a sharp but oddly reassuring rhythm, like slightly pulled jabs thrown by an old sparring partner. Golfballs of yellow light sailed from the Oerlikon's long thin barrel, tearing off a radio aerial, shattering a small searchlight, and shredding an old-fashioned kapok life ring. He adjusted for recoil and the relative angles of the two vessels, this time aiming for maximum damage, and pegged the sight on the fishing boat's waterline. In careful three-round spurts, he walked his shots from bow to stern, punching ragged plate-sized holes in the wooden hull, causing the target to shudder violently with every impact, hammering it until its very shape grew blurred by swirling clouds of splinters and vicious water-spikes, and blowing in half the fishermen's small lifeboat. When the hammer clicked on air, he shouted "Change me!" and Dewey scuttled quickly to his side, flipping a fresh 41-pound magazine into place as though it weighed no more than a whiskey bottle and chucking the empty drum over the side.

"Good to go!" He smacked Allen on the shoulder and resumed his methodical sniping, which had already put three Norduroy sailors on the deck, one of them virtually without a face. This time, Allen leaned his weight differently, tilting the barrel a few degrees higher, and was thereby able to inflict significant damage on the target ship, gouging out portions of the engine cowl, deckhouse, and smokestack, and pumping the last eleven rounds into the enclosed bridge, which simply collapsed under the hammering, one side of the roof dropping at a slant and, to judge from the outcries beneath, probably braining the helmsman. Dewey was already hefting a fresh drum when Allen heard the second run dry.

There wasn't much return fire coming from the target now, and the wild fusillades from the other boats weren't really aimed at anything in particular, so Allen decided to ignore it and to continue his efforts to sink this one particular ship; if he could do that, he would enlarge the space available for Eiden's flanking maneuver. As the range closed to fifty yards, he impulsively slung all of his remaining rounds into the damaged wheelhouse and adjacent superstructure. He hoped to slay the captain and any other leaders sheltering there, but because he'd already collapsed a portion of that structure, he also thought it reasonable that a second going-over might so enlarge the existing holes as to penetrate all the way through the keel. Given a choice between bailing for their lives and taking the time to line up accurate shots at him, Allen thought he could predict which activity the surviving crewmen would make their first priority.

In four- and five-round bursts, he squirted shells into the already-damaged superstructure; the results were gratifying. The wheelhouse roof disintegrated, burying the injured helmsman and anyone near him; the circular foreground in his sight picture was filled with bits of splintered planking, shards of the instrument panel, puffs of broken crockery, glittering twisters of glass, angry spikes of flame, a fluttering dog-eared copy of *Playboy,* and a pair of bent binoculars with somebody's hand still wrapped around them—a cauldron boiling over, sparkling with yellow sunbursts from the strikes of his H-E rounds, and strobe-lit by ricocheting comet-tailed tracers, one of which set off a dandy secondary explosion when it struck lantern oil, petrol, or the vessel's paint locker. Unseen Norduroy hands struggled to dump overboard a ratty old mattress furiously smoldering—and almost succeeded until Dewey blew three fingers off someone's hand and the greasy mattress-torch fell back into the welter of general wreckage. A rising wind flushed most of the smoke to starboard, permitting Allen to see two spurting jets of water, indicating he'd drilled at least two inch-wide holes in her bottom, and amid the gnarled clutter of what had been the crew's sleeping compartment, he glimpsed torn-off limbs and a sticky red gumbo made from pulverized anatomies. Already listing fifteen degrees, the target boat was afire in six places that he could see and several more he couldn't; pouring a river of oily smoke right into the eyes of the gunmen on the second and third boats in line, this anchor-of-the-right-flank vessel was clearly going down.

One furiously angry-looking Norduroy sailor did pop around the starboard bridge wing and futilely discharged both barrels of a twelve-gauge in Allen's general direction, only to catch an AK round in his windpipe in return. Clutching his punctured throat, the man staggered in a mindless circle, spraying blood like a broken water pump until Dewey's next Kalashnikov shot turned his skull into an exploding watermelon, and he dropped out of sight for good.

While Allen was systematically devastating the right-most vessel in Dahl's battle line, the sailors aboard the others were still able to bring their firepower to bear on the *Laertes'* starboard side; even though two thirds of them couldn't shoot without hitting a friendly vessel and the gunmen who did have a decent firing arc were partly blinded by smoke and fumes, they evidently weren't hurting for ammunition, for they were firing wildly, nonstop; and at this range, a half-blind imbecile could hit *something* on the *Laertes!*

"Hey, Allen, some of the rifles they're usin' belong in a fuckin' museum!"

Dewey's observation was confirmed by the spongy reports of numerous black-powder weapons intermingled with the sharp ear-jabbing cracks of Mausers, Enfields, and Krag-Jorgensens. *Snap-POOM!* Was that . . . ? Yes, by God, it was! Someone was banging away from the steel trawler's crow's nest with a flintlock! Well, why not?, thought Allen. A big slow dumb highly toxic ping-pong ball from a Brown Bess could kill you every bit as dead as a steel-jacketed round from the up-to-date NATO assault rifle lying next to him in the gun tub.

It must have been obvious to Dahl, or whoever was in tactical command, that Eiden's course change and Allen's concentrated effort to sink one par-ticular vessel had as their ultimate purpose a wide end run around Dahl's flank; a signal lamp on the big steel trawler's bridge urgently clack-clacked his new orders: *Cut free of other ships, act independently, stop them at all cost!*

The boat Allen had systematically mauled was now a wallowing ruin, burning furiously, its starboard side chopped to shreds, seawater sucking in and torrents of sodden debris gushing out. But the sum-bitch was still afloat and still blocking their path, so he traced the exhaust pipe from its tiny galley and poured another ten rounds into the presumed location of the cook's big propane tank. *("Tear 'em a new one, Fearless Leader!")* Tracer strikes drilled deep, and a geyser of kitchen utensils sprayed aloft in response, until the final tracer round struck the propane tank and the sagging, gnawed-on superstruc-ture abaft of the bridge disappeared in a sudden boiling scallop-shell of fire. From the center of the conflagration, a flame-engulfed sailor high-jumped over two sets of railings and launched himself into the Atlantic, landing with the sound of a quenched poker. Hairless, earless, lipless, the burned man's head burst from the water, a charcoal briquette with an open screaming mouth. Allen's stomach flipped at the notion of salt water sloshing over third-degree burns, and he was glad when Dewey put the human torch out of his misery and then signaled his respect by shouting: "May Odin bid thee wel-come in the Great Hall, O Son of Yggdrasill!"

The exploding propane tank had ripped the bottom open, and the much-abused sloop sank like a cinderblock, carrying all but three struggling crewmen with her. Neither Allen nor Dewey fired at the trio—they were out of the fight for good, and the sudden quenching of fire and dissipation of smoke revealed that the second boat in line, now cut free of the entangling nets that had bound it to the third, was churning up a furious wake and making a perpendicular turn to intercept the *Laertes*. Allen spotted something large and black mounted on the third ship's bow and shouted a warning.

"Hey, Dewey, take cover! I think that sum-bitch is packing a deck gun of some kind!" Dewey risked a quick peek, almost laughed, then yelled back: "Nah, man, what that is, is a—"

CHNG-BLAM! The "deck gun" fired, Dewey saw what appeared to be an aerial torpedo hurtling in their direction, and he swiftly pulled Allen down from behind the Oerlikon just as the gun tub's steel wall shook with a violent impact and a big explosion shook their teeth. When the smoke cleared, Allen beheld what appeared to be a giant black arrowhead jutting through the gun tub's protecting rim.

"As I was about to say," Dewey resumed, "that was an explosive harpoon, dude! That bastard just tried to Moby-Dick you! Ain't that against the Geneva convention?"

"The spirit, if not the letter. You all right, man?"

"Just some scratches. Help me wrap this bandana around my head, keep the blood outta my eyes. I am now going to kill that harpooner!"

"There're other guys shooting at us who need killing a lot sooner than he does—we'll be long gone before he can reload that blunderbuss!"

"Well, anyway, congratulations on sinking a ship!"

"Holy shit, I did, didn't I?"

"Yeah, that only leaves seven more to go. . . ."

But not for long. With the right flank now open, Eiden was pouring on the knots, and the trawler was steadily churning through the gap in the enemy's boat line.

The entire engagement had taken perhaps two minutes—some detached, transcribing part of Allen's brain was taking notes—but this wasn't the occasion to speculate on Time's dilation process, for the big modern trawler, the "flagship" of Andreas Dahl's ragtag flotilla, had put on full speed, surged out of line, and was now executing a sharp turn to port, heading into the *Laertes'* fading wake. It was coming up fast and straight, and making three or four knots more than the structurally damaged older ship could handle.

"If he overtakes us before the creature comes up, aim for the bridge and try to slow him down!"

But both ships were moving rapidly over increasingly choppy seas, and Allen had trouble bringing his sights to bear as the trawler was bow-on, presenting him with a small, steeply raked target. His first shots barely nicked the angled bow, doing no damage and caroming wildly off, incongruously graceful blobs of light that finally melted into the backdrop of the geological drama unfolding near Vesturoy. Allen raised his sights until the strip of steel across the bridge railing filled the first two sight-rings, and hammered a long freight-train burst, sawing back and forth. Jittering shell-strikes danced over the bigger ship's upper decks, picturesque to be sure, but apparently doing no significant damage. Dahl's ship didn't veer away; if anything, it picked up more speed and bore down unflinchingly. Five hundred yards now separated the two vessels.

Eiden swung his helm to take evasive action and to give Allen a better shot at the other trawler's bridge, but the wounded *Laertes* responded sluggishly, without her former spunky alacrity—a tired old ship. Allen had time to secure another Oerlikon drum on to the steaming breech before Dewey shouted: "Grab on to something—I think the motherfucker's gonna ram us!" They both dropped behind the bullet-chipped gun tub and clutched the tripod mount, braced for collision as the big steel bow plowed closer and closer. *Christ, it looks like the fucking* Bismarck!

But Dahl had something more personal in mind than a crude ramming. At the last moment, he ordered a sharp turn and cut his engines. Glancing blow or not, the impact felt and sounded like two freight trains colliding; after the initial crunch there came a long, grinding shriek as the two ships' hulls scraped together and cancelled out each other's momentum. Whoever was in tactical command of Dahl's flagship, he was no amateur: there were sharpshooter positions built in a host of suitable locations, all fortified with sandbags or dirt-filled crates, and from behind them well-protected riflemen opened a brisk suppressive fire on the *Laertes*. A blast on the ship's whistle initiated the throw of a dozen ropes and cables attached to grappling hooks, which the three defenders could not dislodge without exposing themselves to the heavy fusillade. As an added measure, teams of strong-armed men, stationed behind the radar mast and high up in the crows' nest, began to hurl gasoline bombs on to the smaller vessel. The barrage of Molotov cocktails didn't pose a critical threat—there wasn't much they could set fire to—but as a distraction they were definitely effective. Pinned down and vastly out-gunned, the three defenders could only cringe and gape at the sight of the large, well-armed boarding party that came boiling out of hatchways bran-dishing harpoons, blubber knives, clubs, and a motley assortment of pistols.

Dewey managed to shoot off two of the grapples with AK fire, and Eiden darted out with a fire axe to chop off a third that had become entangled in a ventilator pipe, but there were too many lines and too much covering fire to mount an effective defense against so many. Eiden killed one assailant with the last shot in his Enfield, then he unholstered the old Royal Navy Webley. Just as the first wave of boarders surged across the gap between the ships, Eiden strode fearlessly out to the bridge-wing, brandishing the big revolver and shouting defiance: "Get off my ship, you murdering bastards, or by Christ I'll shoot you down like dogs!" The attackers didn't even pause. Eiden emptied the pistol, hitting two or three men before he was driven back by a hail of answering fire.

Allen watched the boarders swarm over the rail as though it was a scene from an Errol Flynn movie. That was nearly *all* he could do, because the Oer-likon's barrel wouldn't depress far enough to engage any target closer than twenty feet—and the 20-mm was the only weapon they had that might have evened the odds. So he picked up the Heckler and Koch, chambered a round, and decided that the first man he killed would have to be that big burly s.o.b. who'd just leaped on to the *Laertes'* fo'c'sle from the other trawler's lifeboat davits—because he was close, because he was determined-looking, and also because he was preceded by six and a half feet of harpoon point. If he wasn't stopped, Allen would be within thrusting range in about three seconds.

As soon as the first boarders landed, all the sharpshooters save the one in the crow's nest were forced to cease fire, otherwise they'd be more likely to hit their own people than any of the defenders. Trying not to let the attackers' bloodthirsty battle cries spook him any more than their physical proximity already had, Allen braced the H & K on the rim of the gun tub and drew a can't-miss bead on the big harpooner's heart. But just as he started to pull the trigger, the men of the boarding party fell silent, stopped in their tracks, hesitation, doubt, and even fear showing in their eyes. Some of Dahl's warriors actually recoiled a few steps.

They had just come face to face with a specter from their own legends.

Naked to the waist, bayonet affixed to the old AK-47, Dewey Tucker rose from behind the gun tub, transfigured into Full Berserker mode. Even Allen felt his power and could do nothing but lower his weapon and bear witness.

"Who will be the first of you to die?" Dewey roared.

And somehow, even though, as far as Allen knew, the ex-biker had never studied a foreign language in his life, he was challenging the attackers, not merely in Faeroese, but in Old Norse. When not one of the Norduroy men replied, Dewey began to laugh; he kept on laughing as he walked forward very slowly and deliberately, firing precise and deadly three-round bursts, his unbound hair streaming in the wind, his barbaric sheepskin quickly covered with powder residue, sweat, gun oil, and blood; his tattoos *dancing* independently of his control; imbued with the unholy vitality of imps, they capered like mad tiny fauns across the hillocks of his corded weight-lifter's muscles; he seemed ten feet tall and the copper wires of his beard flung sparks before him as he advanced: terrible, implacable, and clearly touched by the Old Gods as no man had been since the triumph of Christ over paganism; and all, including Allen Warrener his closest living friend, cringed before the weird and baleful radiance that encased him. Odin had come back for one brief resurgence via the medium of Dewey Tucker's flesh, and the fishermen of Norduroy felt their courage turn to water, for who among them wanted to draw first blood from a man so favored by the ancient creeds of the Northland?

Who slays this man will have his eyes torn out by ravens!

Seven men died from his bullets before the hammer clicked on empty;

Two more he slew, and three he slashed quite nigh unto death before his bayonet came off;

A charge of bird-shot wrapped a scarlet garland 'round his head;

But still he howled berserkers' laughter

Until they tore out his tongue;

He did not feel it.

When the AK's stock broke, it was matted with the blood and brains of three;

Or more than three—no one could have counted;
A fire-axe seized he from a bracket under the bridge.
And like a giant woodsman felling oaks
He chopped a scarlet highway through the foe. Despite a dozen wounds
and more—he laughed
And up until the very last, when Odin's bale-fire flickered low,
His mighty footsteps barely faltered.

Allen did what he could to support Dewey's one-man banzai charge. Every time he had a clear shot, he popped a 7.62-mm round into the mass of retreating Norduroy men and almost always put one down—it was hardly necessary to aim. Dewey was so drenched with gore, his own and that of his victims, that he seemed clad in a cloak of vibrant scarlet fur. Strong men looked into his eyes and fled back to their ship rather than confront the wrath of his axe, the supernatural strength of his thews. He kept attacking even after the slippery axe-haft flew from his fingers. He kept attacking even when one eye was torn out and his left arm dangled from nothing but a rope of sinew. He kept attacking even as his guts uncoiled behind him like an endless purple snake. His last victim was a man he pinned against the railing and leaned against until the sailor's spine cracked like a wishbone.

Those who had survived and fled back to the Norduroy ship watched in awe as Dewey rose from this final killing, wanting to bear witness to a hero's end—had Andreas Dahl himself stepped forth to bushwhack Dewey, his own men would have torn him limb from limb.

Dewey was slashed and torn and pierced by steel as well as lead, and nothing of him still lived—could possibly have still lived—except his eyes and his indomitable heart. He held up a bloody middle finger toward the stunned and silent watchers on the other ship, spat from his gashed and mutilated mouth a mostly intact human ear, and, with his final breath, won passage to Valhalla by throwing back his half-scalped head and summoning the strength to loudly implore: *"ODIN! BEAR WITNESS TO MY DEEDS AND JUDGE ME WORTHY!"*

Dewey's onslaught had cleared most of the boarding party from the *Laertes*. But now that Dewey was dead, some of the Norduroy survivors were rallying. Allen wasn't surprised to see Andreas Dahl climb down from the bridge and start haranguing his followers, pointing contemptuously toward Allen, who thought the gist of Dahl's commands were perfectly clear even in Faeroese: the two trawlers were still webbed together, the Oerlikon couldn't depress low enough to hit anyone who made it to the *Laertes*, so shake off that pagan melodrama and finish the job—one good rush and victory is ours!

But the Oerlikon *would* depress low enough to hit the railing of Dahl's vessel, so just to discourage the boarders more, Allen swung the cannon from left to right and methodically blew off all the rat-lines and grapples, so that the two ships began slowly to drift apart. He paused to reload before blasting the last connecting line, but it snapped without any help, unable to withstand the tension caused by the weight of two ships, and to Allen's amazement, the line whipped back and wrapped itself around the arms and torso of Andreas Dahl, who was still gesticulating wildly in a vain attempt to rally his remaining followers for another assault.

Ensnared, unable to raise his pistol, furious at the way his own men hesitated to help untangle him—the Oerlikon's muzzle was still pointing in their general direction, after all—Dahl became apoplectic, calling down the wrath of Yggdrasill upon the blasphemers of the Vardinoy Expedition.

"He *will* rise, Warrener! Your friend there died in vain! All of your pathetic attempts to thwart His purpose will avail nothing!"

"Don't think so, Andreas. We're going to stop your giant blob. Oh, by the way, Karen had a very intimate conversation with it, during her brief tenure as The Voice. Contrary to what you believe, Yggdrasill actually doesn't give a rat's ass what happens to you and your people. But all of you men from Norduroy who speak English, hear me well and translate my words to anyone who wants to learn the truth! And the truth is this: if you don't evacuate Norduroy before that pressure dome blows up in a half hour or so, you're all going to die. Your deity won't lift a tentacle to save you. Matter of fact, it doesn't even like you very much. It never has. You were useful to it in minor ways, and mildly diverting sometimes, but that's all. If you get on the ship's radio right now and tell your families to flee the island, some of them might survive what's coming. If you put your trust in that lying sack of shit Andreas Dahl, then Norduroy's going to be an underwater theme park by sunrise. That's the vision given to The Voice, straight from the God's own mind!"

"Liar! Blasphemer!" Dahl's very desperation lent credence to what Allen had said. Men began to back away from him and turn their weapons away from Allen Warrener. Allen called up to the bridge.

"Hey, Eiden—now's your chance, while he's all trussed up in his own grappling line!"

Poulsen stepped out of cover on to the port bridge-wing and waved mockingly at Dahl. "Unfortunately, I seem to be out of ammunition. However, by virtue of the powers granted to a sea captain in a time of war, I hereby deputize you as the executive officer of H.M.S. *Laertes,* and that gives you the authority to execute Mr. Dahl for numerous capital crimes!"

"Thanks, skipper!"

Allen climbed back into the gun tub and snuggled into the Oerlikon's armrests. Dahl struggled fiercely to untangle himself.

"Stop play-acting, Warrener! You haven't the guts!"

Allen cocked the cannon.

"For the deaths of Kristofur Poulsen, Norma Davenport, Preston Valentine, and Dewey Tucker, I hereby sentence you to death by, well, by a firing squad of one."

The half-pound 20-mm rounds passed completely through Andreas Dahl without detonating, obliterating with their high velocity such massive chunks of his anatomy that he was literally torn in half. The part from the waist down actually took a couple of mincing steps, while the top half, its owner's eyes bulging in disbelief, toppled over the rail and into the sea.

Didn't think I'd really do it, did you, you murdering scumbag?

The steel trawler picked up speed and steamed off in the direction of Norduroy, blinker lights relaying new orders to the smaller craft, most of which hadn't caught up yet with the two dueling trawlers. They, too, turned around and beat for home. Allen hoped that some of them, at least, might make it.

The *Laertes* drifted on a sea that belonged to her alone.

But the old warship had been rammed, shot full of holes, and sabotaged from within, and was almost out of fuel. She had taken all she could take. After securing the Oerlikon, Allen wearily climbed to the bridge and reported for duty.

"Until today, I never took pleasure in watching any man die," said Eiden, grasping his hand. "Now, Acting Lieutenant Warrener, kindly station

yourself by the master fuse and be prepared to light it in about three minutes." Allen glanced at his watch in amazement; during the excitement of the
battle, he had almost forgotten their reason for waging it. If Karen's prediction was right, that was all the time remaining before the Being's emergence.
He swung binoculars toward the flaring volcanic cone and the adjacent but
infinitely more menacing dome, and their appearance now had an unmistakable aura of climax: the dome had risen five feet since the last time he had
scanned it. The steam pouring from its enlarged circumference had an angry,
scalded look. It was unmistakably a thing about to go violently out of
control.

A pressure wave lifted the trawler, and large, fat, leprous-looking bubbles
rose all around. Karen had been right on the money—the great submarine
earthquake, overture to the main eruption, had begun. In canyons miles
below, mountain ranges of antediluvian rock were sliding, breaking; the
seabed was reshaping itself on a scale that had not occurred in eons. No
sooner had the ship stopped quaking than the sea around Vesturoy roared
and boiled and the eastern third of that doomed island broke asunder
and slid into the turbulence surrounding it. The first, and lesser, eruption
had finally begun—a destructive overture to the main drama still to come.
The familiar broken-tooth shape of the cone flared outward on all sides, an
exploding carnation, its reds and oranges so bright they hurt his eyes, and its
yellows so violent they all but screamed as they stabbed into the cold North
Atlantic; lava bombs the size of ashcans, trailing banners of rippling fire,
soared like punctuation marks above the roaring crescendo. Nearer at hand,
the sea heaved as though nuclear depth charges were shaking the bones of
Vardinoy. Glassy mounds of silty water heaved to the surface, murky with
bottom mud that had lain undisturbed since the Moon was mostly smooth,
settled in those abyssal canyons a billion years before the dinosaurs. Unimaginable, the scale of convulsions that could push such mountainous swells to
the surface! Unimaginable, too, was the now-liberated being that was big
enough to displace so huge a volume of sea water! Allen tried to visualize the
vastness of the changes racking the seabed below, but always his mind drew
back; there was no human scale of reference; perhaps there was none in all
of recorded history. These rich organic thunderheads rising to the surface?
These were the ashes from the cooking Fires of Creation! Miles beneath this
vessel's keel, cyclones were raging in the far, eternal dark because something

was in motion that had never stirred before, displacing such an enormous mass that it must be the size of half a dozen Vardinoys!

The Being was free; and it was rising.

And it had a reception committee. . . .

Allen had just lit the master fuse inside the tiny radar shack when he heard a sound that froze him in place. Once again, there came antiphonal blasts of unearthly sound, chorales and responses from both sides of the battered old trawler. He knew instantly what it was: the Great Orms were back, and just as it had on the first occasion he'd heard it, the timbre of their cries made his skin crawl. But tonight, fittingly, the Orm-calls were closer, and the beasts themselves seemed lined up in formation, almost like a fleet of escorts shielding the *Laertes* . . . or monitoring its progress, for what inscrutable reasons he could not begin to guess. But the Orms knew an epochal event was pending—had they come out of their hidden grottos to bear witness, to participate, to fulfill some unimaginably ancient ceremonial function—or perhaps to make certain that the sacrifice of this old ship was conducted according to protocols only they, the Orms, still comprehended? This time, Allen had to see them close, so as soon as he ascertained that the fuse was burning properly and according to the timetable he'd worked out, he ran to the main deck, knowing he had only the briefest splinter of time in which to indulge his curiosity.

The first long-neck broke the surface only a hundred yards from the starboard side.

Great God, they were huge! Apostles, seneschals, heralds, some kind of prehistoric Greek chorus—whatever their role in this event, they were assembling with grave and massive dignity. Allen gaped at Legend: the long, muscular, phallic sweep of its neck, the expressionless but somehow wise arrangement of features on its blunt horse's head, surmounted by a tarry mane of organic kelp, which framed, in turn, its reflective yellow beaded eyes, which showed no recognizable human emotion yet radiated unmistakable . . . awareness? intelligence? even wisdom? He would never know. Warm mist jetted from its flaring nostrils. It paced the trawler, on the same course, the gigantic featureless hump of its body elbowing the sea into a V-shaped swell, more stately and far more elegant than the erratic club-footed wake of the faltering *Laertes*.

Allen groped for a camera, but there wasn't one. He brayed laughter at the absurdity of his situation: for thousands of years, men had debated the existence of these gigantic and somehow noble beasts, and the first time they reveal themselves to a dedicated monster-hunter, he hasn't so much as an Instamatic on hand to take the definitive picture.

Again, the Orm opened its polyp-fringed mouth and gave vent to its cry, and the sound evoked in Allen a bone-deep wave of atavistic response—part religious awe, part stark, cave-dweller's terror. And this time, the cry was taken up and echoed by a dozen more. He ran to a ladder and climbed to the searchlight platform in order to get a better view. He beheld, backlit by the rolling oily eruptions of the primary cone, majestic on a sea of orange glass— a dozen, no, *more!* Many dozens! The immensity of the sight was comparable only to the strangeness of his certainty: they were *all* here tonight. Every surviving member of their species had gathered to bear witness, or perhaps to allow Allen Warrener to bear witness to *them.* A trio of the great beasts sailed by as though attracted by his speculations—or flaunting them! Here was all the "proof" Science could possibly want, and here was a credible witness *without a camera!* "Well, of course, numb-nuts, what did you expect?" As if in mocking reply, one of the Long-Necks snorted in his direction, giving him a superb view of his lacquered-bead eyes, the huge wet cave of its mouth, and the bizarre but somehow wondrously expressive sine-wave motions it made with its neck.

Well, here they were, and in great abundance: a veritable army of beings out of myth, a confirmation of every loch-lake-river-tarn-and-sea monster legend he'd collected in his files, all drawn here! And for what reason? To worship? To wait in attendance? Or to serve that Entity which was rising even now from the rubble of its sundered prison?

How he wanted time to savor the sight—not to mention a good camera to record it! A lifetime's frustration and bitterness were here refuted and swept away by the simple fact of *proof;* by bringing back that proof, he would wipe the record clean of every failure and compromise whose portion he had eaten. What novel could he have written equal to the triumph of altering forever Man's understanding of what was "real"? His name up there with Darwin's— a heady prospect indeed! Allen Warrener, whose discovery in the realm of zoological science was no less than that of Columbus, or Newton, or Leibniz, in their fields of expertise.

But of course, he'd left his camera behind, for he'd come on this occasion to fight, not to take snapshots. He wagged a remonstrative finger at the nearest Long-Neck. "You know something, you guys would be comic if you weren't so inscrutable! Well, I'll see you later, if there is any 'later,' but right now I've got the world's oldest life form to blow up, and the clock's really ticking!" He waved jauntily at them—as the thought occurred to him for the first but not last time that he might have become a little bit deranged by this point in the evening's program—and then he ran up the ladder to the bridge, shouting to Eiden:

"It's lit, Skipper! Time to tie the wheel and get the hell off of this floating bomb!"

Eiden Poulsen stood at the helm of his ship, steadfast and proud, a man carved from oak and weaned on the cold salt milk of the North Atlantic.

"She brought us through, Allen. A trawler with the soul of a battleship! I knew we could do it . . . one last battle, one last mission, and then a sailor's grave "

"Well, say good-bye to her, Eiden, because we're really running out of time awfully fast and . . . Eiden? For God's sake, man, let's go!"

"Am I still in command of H.M.S. *Laertes?*"

"Of course you are."

"Then, Mr. Warrener, I am giving you a direct order: get into the motor launch, cut loose from the trawler, and go back to that good woman who loves you. I'm staying here."

"Don't be melodramatic, Eiden! The fuse is lit, the ship's on course, and you're—"

"Finished, is what I am, Allen."

Eiden turned, and Allen saw the gaping purple hole below his left shoulderblade, and the cofferdam of wadded towels Eiden had stuffed into the wound and bound in place with a girdle of duct tape. Movement brought a grimace of pain and a thick, clotted cough.

"Most of the lung's gone, I'm afraid. While you and Dewey were repelling the boarders—and my God, I'm glad I lived to see *that*—one of the buggers sneaked into the wheelhouse and laid me open with a blubber-knife. I killed him, of course, and kicked him off my bridge, but the damage was done. Internal bleeding, lad, and it couldn't be fixed if we were right outside the hospital door. Hurts a lot less than you might think, for what it's worth. . . ."

"There's got to be something I can do!"

"Yes, there is. You can hop into the motor launch, get the hell away from this floating bomb, and go live a long, happy life with Karen, who's waiting for you back on Vardinoy! And if you have a son, you might consider naming him Christopher. That would please me."

Allen wanted to embrace Eiden Poulsen, but there was nowhere he could put his arms without reopening the old man's wounds.

"It's better this way, Allen. This way, I can aim the ship right for the heart of that abomination, and know—as I breathe my last—that my son has been avenged." Eiden raised his hand to stop the words Allen would otherwise have felt compelled to speak.

"I know: you feel love for me, and I for you. Honor me as a father figure, you're more than welcome; and know that I am proud of you: always, you were a weaver of dreams, and today you proved yourself a warrior as well. I know how long you've wanted to hear those words, and now you have heard them from your captain. You have my blessing, Allen, but now you have no more time—so get the hell off my bridge!"

Allen hurried aft, marveling at the power of a blessing to hold back grief. His mood was close to the hard-shell Baptists' vision of the Rapture; so much had been granted him on this day of convergences! He had been in battle, and he had been victorious; he had faced the blood and chaos and terror and emerged from it sane and cleansed of many interest-bearing sins; when the moment came, he had not hesitated to kill, and he felt neither joy nor revulsion, but the soldier's quiet pride in having survived by the strength of his will and his skill at arms; he had traveled half the world in search of a monster, and he had found it; he had set in motion the plan that would destroy it; and he had been given Eiden Poulsen's blessing: to live, to transcend his past, to seek happiness with the woman who had risked her soul and sanity out of love for him; and he had put to rest his faded obsession with another woman; a strong, good, beautiful woman who had weighed him carefully and found him worthy of being her friend. His happiness could not have been greater had he stood before the gates of Heaven and felt them open at his touch.

He resolved to be worthy of all these blessings, and of the friends who had died as a consequence of his transformation. This state of grace—so sweet, so luminous, so empowering to his future—lasted precisely sixty-two seconds.

And then it began to crumble. The motor launch, carefully rigged for a quick escape from the fantail, was a blazing ruin—a gasoline bomb had gutted it and the Norduroy marksmen had turned the hull into a Swiss cheese, just to make sure no one could possibly use it. Aware of just how close madness now lurked, he chose to laugh instead of cry.

"Well, fuck me three ways from Sunday!"

He had no idea what to do next.

One step at a time—you can still get through this.

Well, there was always one of the ship's four old-fashioned life rafts, and a chance, at least, that he could paddle or drift or ride the waves beyond the radius of danger. Using his powder-stained hands and the spiky end of a fire axe, he wrestled with the stiff, tarry knots holding the raft in place—not much time left, but with any luck—yes, the ropes were starting to move! He'd drop the raft overboard and jump for it.

But a sudden change in the ship's status told him that time had run out. And that something had gone terribly wrong.

Instead of accelerating and steaming straight at the dome, the *Laertes* was slowing, and her bow was swinging off course. The angle between the packed explosives and their intended target was growing wider by the second. He abandoned the life raft and ran to the nearest intercom station. He rang the bridge and waited to hear Eiden's voice on the other end.

"Eiden? Eiden, you're veering away from the target! What's the matter with you? God damn it, bring this ship around, or a lot of people are going to die!"

Finally, the bridge responded and he heard, above the growing crescendo of seismic chaos, a hoarse, blood-gurgling reply: "A-a-llennn. . . ." And then a loud bang as the intercom handset fell and smacked against a bulkhead.

He ran forward and up the ladder to the bridge, already knowing what he would see: Eiden was dead, the wadded bandage torn from his side by the pressure of dammed-up blood, and the weight of his body was turning the helm in the wrong direction, and his lifeless hand had cut the throttle to half-speed as it fell.

For one deranged instant, Allen Warrener refused to accept what was happening. Frantic to live, terrified at losing the halcyon future he thought he had earned and been given permission to seek, he cursed and howled and raged, kicking at the compass binnacle, rejecting the evidence that closed off, one by one, every alternative future, but there was none. He could accept the stark, merciless, ever-so-unfair course of action still within his power, or he could put a firearm in his mouth and declare himself out of the game. All that prevented him from doing so, from pulling the plug out of sheer resentment, was the realization, ludicrous though it was, that no one could hear his curses, no one could witness his 7.62-mm vote of abstention, except the inscrutable giant Orms, and the inexplicable mountain of living matter now rising to reveal itself in the fire-drenched night. Karen, of course, could not see inside the wheelhouse, and so she would never know that his final act of will was not a noble act of sacrifice, but a petulant middle finger raised at God and signifying: "This sucks, and I won't do it!"

But somewhere up there on the cliffs of Vardinoy, Karen *was* watching, and his decision, in that attenuated sliver of time, would create the image by which she would remember him, and the legacy she would pass on about him to his son.

It came down to this: he did not choose to be brave; he did not want to be; he did not know if he could endure the next few minutes without howling like a craven dog—but he could not dishonor the courage Karen had already shown by refusing, as his final act of choice, to confront the Being as she had done.

And the knowledge that she was watching, and that the actions he chose to take would be the final testament of his love, brought clarity, certainty, and the final tilt from denial to acceptance.

He eased the body of Eiden Poulsen away from the helm, stood at attention and saluted the fallen hero, and then took his place as the last captain of H.M.S. *Laertes.*

May your blood be the glue that holds my feet at their post—may my hands not falter at the helm—may I steer this brave old ship to an end worthy of her and of my friend and mentor . . . and the father of my greatest love . . . and may I . . .
OH MY CHRIST!

The Emergence of the Vardinoy Monster was slow and stately, as befit a god; it did not rupture or do violence to the sea, but displaced a tremendous volume of water that spread out in a smooth, glossy, symmetrical circle, which lifted the trawler to a height equal to its own and set it back upon the water without imposing any strain upon its frame. It was a living mountain, filling more and more of the straits until it was almost the twin to Vardinoy,

only its surface was smooth, glistening; and as it continued to rise, it was surrounded by a corona of flowering mud and varnished with streaks of algae,
plankton, and organic soup that had sunk to the ocean's floor uncounted ages
ago. It seemed capable of flexing and altering its density, for it was soft and
yielding when it first broke the surface, but as it grew it acquired a fibrous
strength that gave stability to its visible mass: three hundred feet high and
half a mile across . . . and that was just the part of it Allen could see. Vast
portions flowed outward rather than upward, and the deliberation of its slow
and shifting mass seemed to indicate a cautious exploration of its new
freedom.

Allen sensed the delirious joy it must have felt—its emanations were so
powerful that they vibrated in the air and could be sensed with human
organs. How glorious it might be to share its exaltation, as Karen must surely
be doing! Allen sampled it, briefly, and it put to shame every great drug trip
he'd ever experienced. Although he felt certain he could have opened his
mind more widely to those emanations, he rejected the temptation. Out of
pity both for the creature and for himself, he could not permit that alien
ecstasy to infiltrate his heart, or else his will might not withstand the horror
of its destruction.

It was moving now, at a shallow angle to the trawler, in the direction of
that great tense vapor-streaming dome out in the straits. Its purpose was
fixed; it sought in the imminent fire a transcendence commensurate with its
uniqueness—perhaps its private version of Heaven; or perhaps Father Evolution, like a more familiar God, was hurriedly stoking it with the illusion of
free will, so that it might square the circle, cancel out a long-ago mistake,
delete as swiftly as possible History's greatest organic Singularity, by compelling it willingly to terminate the dark and dreadful cycle of its unintended
existence.

As Allen aimed the bow at the center of its towering bulk, he glimpsed
more intimate details, for the change of environment and the wave of . . .
emotion? metamorphosis? excitement? hope, even? The *changes* it was experiencing had triggered intense chemical activity, and the inky demarcation of
its Core was simmering with fibrous webs of bluish light; coruscating
shadows formed like ink blots, dispersed like dust clouds in a distant nebula.
Really, it was close to beautiful, in its incomprehensibly alien way, and terrible too, by virtue of its potential to destroy, absorb, obliterate. It did not

belong in this continuum; it had been slated for simple extinction billions of years ago. All of Earth's other life forms were the products of alternate evolutionary paths. This organism had been tried out and rejected; it had vague suspicions along those lines, and now that it was mobile again, stimulated directly instead of through the proxy system of extrusions, it might very well come to resent the notion that all its eons of loneliness and imprisonment had been without purpose, a kind of cosmic "Ooops!" And instead of immolation, it might choose to force a reckoning.

But so far, it was following the scenario Karen had "read" from its consciousness. With immense and palpable urgency, it gathered momentum—muscular planes thickened inside its outer mass. Already, it had learned self-propulsion!

Allen glanced at his watch and then at the distance between the being's outermost projection and the tense, steaming dome that was its destination. It was moving now so rapidly that the ship would hit it too late! The trawler and those aboard it—living and dead—would vaporize in the dynamite blast and the Being would continue, unperturbed, to block the primary eruption's only outlet long enough to cause the cataclysm that Karen and her friends had sought, at the cost of their lives, to prevent.

At the last moment, however, the entity halted, indecisive; it seemed almost to be listening to an unheard command. Allen swung the helm accordingly, realigned the ship with its target, and poured on the speed. If the thing remained in place for just a few more seconds, he could not possibly miss. There would be no second chance, and the fuse was burning down to its last few inches.

The thing's outer membrane, infinitely malleable and filling his sight like the wall of a skyscraper, shuddered and undulated; he had the uncanny sensation of watching the organism conduct some kind of internal debate. To follow its original plan, or to hang around for a while and see what this new world might have to offer? A new and mighty expulsion from the cone generated a hot buffeting wind that swept across the Being's hesitant mass, and Allen drew close enough to inhale its scent, gigantic yet disturbingly intimate: no man had ever breathed that odor, for it was the smell of the primordial deeps, cold and redolent of eternal darkness, of the bottom-ooze that had accumulated, eon after eon, from the decay of life forms that had been extinct for millennia, that had never been touched by sunlight, never swept by wind or rinsed by rain. It was the smell of decay on a geological scale, and yet it was also suggestive of Life in all its latent variegated richness and infinite potential. When Yggdrasill expired, that scent would vanish forever.

And the molecules of Allen Warrener, what spice would they add to this bouquet?

No more did the Being hesitate. Whatever had interrupted its desire for self-destruction, the argument had evidently not been persuasive. It folded in upon itself, its texture becoming more grainy, its nucleus surging up from the depths that had obscured just how vast and seething with vitality it was.

Allen's moment had come, and his course was true. He was, by now, almost as insane as the entity he sought to destroy. "I have a ship, and a star to steer her by!"

It was easier if he kept chattering, anything to divert his mind from what was about to happen, and it occurred to him that if he were about to destroy, or cause the destruction of, the oldest form of life on the planet, the least he could do was have a friendly chat.

"Hey, you! Yeah, buddy, you with the big freakin' nucleus and the Blue Meanic Juice! My name is Allen Warrener, and I've been a fan of yours for years! So how've ya been, all this time? What's your real name, by the way, because the guys in Marketing think Yggdrasill is a bit of a mouthful, and...."

How desperately he wanted it suddenly to manifest some awareness of him! He was ready and wide open to receive some kind of telepathic greeting, something that would muffle his appalling terror during his final seconds; some sign that the Being recognized their destined connection, some respectful word that would make him feel exalted and noble instead of scared shitless of the agony those blue flickers would bring with their touch, something like: "Welcome, my brother, my executioner, my liberator! My last and most intimate companion! Thank you for coming unto me, and into me, at last!"

But it remained as silent and enigmatic as it had always been, as remote from the concerns and perceptions of Allen Warrener as a creature might be that had drifted eternally in the cold between the stars. So Allen made it up as he went along—anything to get through the agony of the next few seconds! He forced himself to stare fixedly at the cold blue razor-knives that waited to peel away his flesh, one particle at a time, but it showed not the slightest concern for his existence . . . or the end of it.

"Hey, Preston? I hope you're getting all of this on film!"

The bow of H.M.S. *Laertes* penetrated the outer membrane with just a slight hesitation, and then Allen was free-falling into a thick, lukewarm, sticky-slick-oily-sandpapery opalescent pool where lightning flashes bathed his hands in mottled electric blue excruciations and just before it got to his eyes, he was able to see his fingers liquefy and then his eyeballs were two enormous blue screams and his mind, in simple self-defense, disconnected itself from the all-enveloping agony of his flesh so that he knew an instant's mercy when the stump of his dissolving brain sang along with Preston Valentine's spirit a bawdy little limerick they'd devised one drunken night in New York City, and the oldest living thing on Earth made what it could out of the final mantra of a minor flowing source of nutrition that had once been a man named Allen Warrener:

> *Oh, the last time I dined with the king*
> *He did a most curious thing!*
> > *He pulled out his tool*
> > *And called for his fool,*
> *And he said "If I play, will you sing?"*

Karen was able to follow most of the battle between the trawler and the Norduroy boats, but she became fretful and restless during the bloody, savage fight against the boarding party. Too much time had elapsed, the Emergence was almost at hand, and her eyes hurt so dreadfully that she was afraid she might not see the climactic event. Every time she turned the focus knob on her binoculars, it felt as though someone were squeezing her optic nerves in a vise.

Both Richard and Elsuba gasped in amazement when Yggdrasill manifested itself on the surface—but Karen was more concerned about the fact that the creature's intended path and the course of the trawler were diverging. The Being moved more quickly than she had anticipated, leaving a huge and clumsy wake as it surged toward the churning witch's brew of lava, steam, and explosive gases, and the gigantic, wildly unstable dome that was now larger and more dangerous-looking than all the other volcanism combined.

Ring on more speed, Allen! Hard a-port! It's getting away from you!

But the being registered the *Laertes* as a surface-thing inert and bereft of interest. Karen had seen Dewey go down in a welter of struggling, firing, slashing men—but even through her strong binoculars she could not tell if his body lay amid the broken gory corpses strewn around the gun tub. She had not seen Eiden, during or after the skirmish, and assumed he was still at the wheel.

Then she saw a microscopic Allen, surveying in despair the burning hulk of the motor launch—and seen him running forward, up the bridge ladder and out of sight, while the ship lost speed and veered off course.

Eiden is dead or badly hurt. Take the wheel, Allen! Find your course, or the Monster will blow our world apart!

Under control again, the *Laertes* picked up speed anew, and her bow began to turn, but slowly, much too slowly, and the living mountain was only seconds away from rolling its immense tide of matter over the straining dome, and its weight would be enough.

Karen stood and turned first to Elsuba, then to Richard.

"Both of you do as I say and get back from the edge. *Now!* I have to try and slow it down for just a few seconds. . . ." *And I just might explode in your faces. . . .*

She draped the glasses around her neck and walked to the last sharp boundary of land. Before her, the sea was on fire, the Monster was undeterred, and Allen had only one chance to succeed in the task for which he had just mortgaged the rest of his life. Karen knew the Being's frequency, and knew that no human consciousness, not even hers, had ever fully attained it without paying the price of madness or worse. The spot upon her forehead began to blister from within; the meat of her brain began to swell; the blood in her veins seared the chambers of her heart. Either she would get that damned thing's *attention* or the effort would tear her apart, and if she did not die, she would surely spend the rest of her days staring blankly through a barred window and mechanically drinking her meals through a straw.

Her muscles were trying to turn inside out; her fists were white; and the bones in her hands were curling, gnarling, crippling her forever if she did not bring that frequency into a state of coherence and power that might well be intolerable to human flesh. Either she would make contact, or her skull would burst and her eyes flow down her cheeks like molten glass.

Hear me!

Hear my Voice!

And the answering blast that almost set her brain on fire:

Leave me alone, now.

She was inside its Core, where madness and pain and its stored recollections of all the planet's Time were poised on critical mass; its inchoate emotions were equal in their power to the tectonic forces straining under the dome, and she had the effrontery to demand of it the one thing it simply could not do:

WAIT!

When it felt—absorbed? swallowed? tasted?—the command, the stupendous incongruity of her request was enough to halt its progress.

For two, three precious seconds, it considered her demand, distracted perhaps by the clarity of her connection to its roiling billions of electrochemical processes—for it had always been diverted by learning about new phenomena; and it had not contemplated anything really interesting since the first atomic bombs. This communication was even more novel, but so transient and nonsensical that it was assessed, recorded, and dismissed, all within the span of 3.2 seconds. But because Evolution had infused it with the notion of symmetry, it felt obliged to respond before Karen—and Humanity, and all the history of the Earth—ceased to exist.

It laughed. And dismissed her, not unkindly, forever.

Good-bye, Karen-child.

And then expelled her utterly from its consciousness.

The living mountain, impatient at the brief delay, resumed its vast, implacable movement.

Directly in the path of the churning, unwavering *Laertes.*

You're right on target, Allen. There is no need to endure the agony that Norma felt! Don't wait for the dynamite! Use a gun! Pull your plug!

The ship was dimly visible; a tiny pinpoint of light burning its way through the nuclear membrane and into the core-stuff—the last cinder of a dying star. A tremendous shudder went through the creature when it registered this penetration, a violation so intimate and so alien that it must have been startled to the depths of its mad eternal consciousness. Did it feel astonishment in that last conjugal instant before the metal star nuzzling its heart went nova?

The *Laertes* vaporized in a dull silent spasm of light. Blue waves—pain? shock? ecstasy?—rippled like sheet lightning through the creature's bulk.

At that moment, right on cue, the huge straining pressure dome blew up. The last thing Karen saw was a sunburst on the sea, and the outlines of Elsuba and Richard, flash-frozen on her dying retinas in tones of chalk-white and black-light purple.

Below their feet, the planet shuddered; the shockwave blew them flat; the ground-zero flash seared their skins and blew a scorching breath across their bodies. First, among a series of spectacular events, the wounded creature lurched wildly across the straits, no longer in a coherent towering mass, but in a chunky, vomitous surge of discontinuous matter; it went into the eruptive fires not in one tremendous self-willed motion, but in an agonized tidal encroachment, so that its dying was slow and vile, choking the air with an unspeakable stench. The damaged nucleus, when it finally heaved itself into the roaring cauldron, was still massive, and it throttled back the kinetic pressure long enough to cause a second and even more puissant blast—violent enough to unleash a sixty-foot tsunami that inundated the remains of Vesturoy and wiped out the entire population of Norduroy, whose inhabitants, for reasons the authorities never understood, and in defiance of all common sense, had remained gathered en masse along the waterfront. The only survivors from that island were half a dozen sailors from the *Laertes'* original crew, who stated they had been locked up inside a farm building at a slightly higher elevation than that reached by the tsunami.

On Vardinoy, one of the Axe-Cuts fell into the sea, with a crash that flung the three spectators far enough back from the edge to save them from going over. Great pieces of the island, including the ancient ruined cathedral, vanished forever beneath the waves. When the church disintegrated, its collapse opened an enormous cavern, whose existence no one had ever suspected, and from it there flooded forth a veritable necropolis of human bones, white as grains of rice against the gray-green after-shock-waves. Vardinoy's labyrinth of caves channeled the primary tsunami's force so that numerous pits and subterranean channels emerged, while others collapsed, altering forever the island's shape and reducing its landmass by about a third. The section of cliff-tops just south of the Axe-Cuts, however, remained largely intact, and the three survivors of the Vardinoy Expedition were spotted there the next morning by an orbiting helicopter carrying a news team from Copenhagen.

A government launch from Torshavn rescued them later in the day, together with a small quantity of personal effects and two knapsacks stuffed with rolls of film and video tapes.

In assessing the Vardinoy Eruptions, as the event came to be known, scientists later expressed gratitude for the fact that the two eruptions of the pressure dome had taken place separately, not in one combined super-blast. It was calculated that the explosive force of those two detonations, if it had been concentrated into a single event, would have caused severe loss of life and property throughout the entire Faeroese archipelago.

Epilogue in the Form of a Letter

Mr. & Mrs. Richard A. Sugarman
2007 Park Road East
Charlotte, N.C.
Dear Brian—

By now, you should have had time to read the typescript of my journal, and to realize that it differs, in much detail, from the book I wrote about the Vardinoy Expedition. As you requested, I am enclosing the DVD transfers made from the films and tapes shot during that unforgettable adventure. I've superimposed the dates, so the footage is in chronological order, but otherwise I've done nothing to edit it.

Don't expect too much from the footage of the eruption, the emergence of the mysterious life form we called a "monster," although its behavior was more pathetic than "monstrous" . . . for the most part. We were shooting against bad, irregular light, from a long distance, and under conditions—to put it mildly—of stress. My techie acquaintances tell me that some of the new digital enhancement techniques might significantly improve the images, but so far I haven't decided whether to do that or not. So what you'll see is raw footage in every sense of the word; in some of the shots, if you didn't already know what was happening, you might find it all but impossible to make sense of what you're seeing. That's the main reason I've never tried to edit the material into a coherent documentary—none of the media production companies have been impressed enough to help finance a digital makeover. (A final irony that your Dad would have appreciated!)

As you noted, there are places in my journal where I'm a little rough on your father. I could have edited those out before sending it to you, but you're mature enough now to understand that everyone worth knowing is a mixture of admirable virtues and all-too-human weaknesses; it would not serve any purpose for me to portray Allen dishonestly. He was not an easy man to understand; his motives and courses of action were not always clear even to him, and that made him, some of the time, exasperating to work with.

685

It was only during the last week or so of my acquaintance with Allen Warrener that I felt as though I were truly getting to know him. The primary thing you should understand about him is that he hungered desperately for your respect (he knew that he already had your love); that he was driven, to a great extent, by his desire to accomplish something splendid by which you could remember him.

I know you respect his memory, but I also understand how you could still be puzzled as to an appropriate way to remember him as a man, *rather than the institution of the Dead Father, which is how you were raised to regard him.*

Well, there was nothing he wanted more than for you to be proud of him, and I think you have every right to be. Whatever your Dad's failures and shortcomings, it was his destiny to achieve in death the uniqueness *that eluded him so painfully during his life.*

For Allen Warrener did something that no man—literally none—had done since the Heroic Age of mythology: he went forth bravely and did battle with a god; and because of his sacrifice, many thousands of good people are alive today, and many of the beautiful islands he loved so passionately still exist *today, that would have been wiped from the Earth otherwise. Few men have achieved more than that.*

Well, that's about all I have to say, in this letter anyhow, except that we hope you can come visit us during your Christmas vacation. Aunt Karen is very excited these days, because there's a new digital technology that "translates" the images she can detect with her damaged optic nerves and organizes it into coherent pictures on miniaturized screens contained in a pair of "projection goggles" not much bigger or heavier than ordinary eyeglasses. If it works, and the technicians are very hopeful, she'll once again be able to "see" well enough to read large-print books.

Not that her handicap has ever slowed her down! We learned just a few days ago that the Association of High School English Teachers had voted her "Teacher of the Year" at their annual convention! I'm very proud of her, and the recognition is richly deserved.

Anyway, we both send our love, and we look forward to seeing you again soon!
All the best,
Uncle Dick